Critical acclaim for Gloria Vitanza Basile:

THE HOUSE OF LIONS

''Passionate . . . panoramic . . . brilliant.''
　　　　　　—*Best Seller* Magazine
''A rousing saga of violence.''
　　　　　　—*Los Angeles Times*

APPASIONATO

''A dynamic read. Compelling from first to last page.''
　　　　　　—John Jakes
''This could well be—and deservedly so—the best selling paperback fiction of the year.''
　　　　　　—*Publisher's Weekly*

THE MANIPULATORS TRILOGY

''Powerful and exciting.''
　　　　　　—*Publishers Weekly*
''It takes quite a writer to write a trilogy and Gloria Vitanza Basile is up to the task.''
　　　　　　—*Critique*

And now—Gloria Vitanza Basile's explosive new novel . . .

EYE OF THE EAGLE

EYE OF
THE
EAGLE
GLORIA
VITANZA
BASILE

PINNACLE BOOKS **NEW YORK**

This is a work of fiction. All the characters and events portrayed in this book are fictional, and any resemblance to real people or incidents is purely coincidental.

GLOBAL 2000: EYE OF THE EAGLE

Copyright © 1983, HOUSE OF LIONS, INC.

An original Pinnacle Books edition, published for the first time anywhere.

First printing, November 1983

ISBN: 0-523-41960-0

Can. ISBN: 0-523-43081-7

Cover illustration by Paul Stinson

Printed in the United States of America

PINNACLE BOOKS, INC.
1430 Broadway
New York, New York 10018

9 8 7 6 5 4 3 2 1

Author's Note

To acknowledge the countless people who contributed to the massive research done to bring about *Global 2000* would promote an endless task. Special thanks must go the S.C.A.N. program of the Los Angeles Library, to Mrs. Gilpien and her staff who searched interminably for facts I insisted existed someplace in the world, and which were finally located through the marvels of computer science.

Special thanks are due to dedicated UCLA librarians whose patience and cooperation exceeded all others. To the consulting professors—nuclear physicists who asked to remain anonymous—I shall be eternally grateful for their concise, honest evaluations in describing the incalculable and frightening prospects of nuclear war. They insisted: *there is no such thing as limited nuclear war!* (After studying, analyzing and organizing my research, I became a devout believer.)

I also thank T.P. for his clear, incisive reports on up-to-the-minute political global upheavals during the past three years of research, especially for the clarification of highly complex conspiracies behind each scenario.

Although *Global 2000* is a story of fiction, the story is based on historical fact. For that portion projected into the future I admit to a highly active imagination, aided by third-eye perceptions and sheer audacity. And I pray nothing contained in this story comes to pass.

Lastly, I thank posthumously Ben Hecht, an admirable American who, when all phony earthly facades and religious dogmas were stripped away, became what he was in the beginning and ultimately at the end:
A HUMAN BEING
above all else!

Gloria Vitanza Basile

Dedicated to

FRANCIS ALBERT SINATRA

"There is a power in the world we seldom mention in the House of Commons . . . I mean the secret societies . . . It is useless to deny because it is impossible to conceal, that a great part of Europe—the whole of Italy and France and a great portion of Germany, to say nothing of other countries—is covered with a network of these secret societies, just as the superfices of the earth is now covered with railroads. And what are their objects? They do not attempt to conceal them. They do not want constitutional government; they do not want ameliorated institutions . . . they want to change the tenure of the land, to drive out the present owners of the soil and put to an end ecclesiastical establishments. Some of them may go even further . . ."

Disraeli in the House of Commons
July 14, 1856

PROLOGUE

Prologue

WASHINGTON, D.C.
4 July 1984

A MOLTEN SUN BROKE OVER THE HORIZON at dawn. The air was stifling, unbearably hot. A pall of silence descending on the concrete seat of government thickened. Rising temperatures threatened to make this the heat wave of the century. Intelligent city dwellers had left D.C. to celebrate the holiday sanely in cooler temperatures.

In the White House Rose Garden not an insect moved in the appalling heat. Even the sweet-smelling scent seemed atrophied, the fragrance of blooms absent. From somewhere inside the West Wing the dull ringing of a telephone assaulted the silence. Security guards at the exits and entrances barely moved. Soon they'd go off night shift, reporting no incidents.

Inside the deserted communications center near the Press Room, lights on computer counters and communication centers blinked indiscriminately. Needles on countless gauges went berserk; needles that should have remained stationary at zero indicated incredible overloads, others dropped to zero and whirled randomly.

Now dozens of warning lights flashed crazily in the muted room.

And then, a staccato of accompanying sounds escalated into shrieks. Electronic devices, whipped to a frenzy as computers began the clickety-clacking sounds of printing readouts on computer screens.

Chief technician and Communications Officer Glen Harlan entered the room stunned by the strange goings-on. The expression on his sharp, angular face was one of disbelief. Overwhelmed by what greeted him, uncertain where to begin, he strode to the main terminal and scanned the readout from the

Maryland Space Agency, his face draining of color. His fingers groped frantically for the panic button summoning his skeletal crew of aides manning holiday communications traffic.

Six sleepy-eyed technicians staggered into the room, immobilized at once by the uncoordinated insanity of unmanned machinery in action. Reading Harlan's hand signals, moved by the stark panic registered upon his features, they went to their stations.

Radar screens were activated. Headsets in place, the men turned on video monitors, radio and parabolics, direct communications devices. The lines were jammed. Voices hummed in amazement, as readouts and digitals conveyed the reality of the impending crisis. Once their initial shock was over, the men demonstrated cool efficient teamwork.

Harlan ran fingers through his brown hair nervously. He approached a glass cubicle containing a panel of *Code Red* emergency buttons at room center. Heads turned, one after another, eyes riveted to observe their chief.

Was this the dreaded moment? Ground: Zero? The moment Harlan pressed those buttons . . .

Mallet in hand, poised to strike the glass, Harlan hesitated.

One blow crushed the glass . . . Emergency alarms would trigger warning systems and other alarms . . .

Harlan sweated copiously. One error and the fail-safe system would necessitate time-consuming reprograming, one they could ill afford if the Space Agency's initial communique proved in error. Before he penetrated the sensitive systems he must be absolutely certain of the maximum dangers involved.

He glanced at the clock. Six A.M. Thirty minutes! He had *thirty minutes* in which to evacuate the White House, signal the Chief Executive in the West Wing, the NSC (National Security Council), Joint Chiefs of Staff and other governmental VIPs high in priority.

Harlan lowered his arm, replaced the mallet in its niche alongside the pedestal base. Daubing at the pouring sweat with his elbow, he moved to his desk, picked up the blue phone, and contacted Maryland Space Agency direct.

NEW YORK CITY
9:00 A.M.
Newspaper extras hit the street.

2

THE NEW YORK TIMES
JULY 4, 1984
HEADLINE: FRONT PAGE
NUCLEAR EXPLOSIONS DEVASTATE MIDDLE EAST!

NEW YORK (AP) Before dawn today satellites orbiting the earth at speeds of 50,000 MPH began relaying photos of incredible devastation in the Middle East. Maryland and NASA Agency officials maintained a grim silence pending verification of facts. Sources report that strategically placed nuclear warheads exploded energy in excess of 150,000 megatons of TNT. Unanswered questions pose frightening prospects to the world.

High government officials in the United States and the Soviet Union say they are shocked by today's event. Russia's proximity to the devastated areas creates immeasurable peril to that nation. The extent of ravagement, fallout, radiation and toxic fumes intensify the dangers.

The complications created by the presumed multi-megaton airburst cannot be calculated at this time. Communications with European capitals are jammed. Defense authorities conclude the high-altitude blasts sent out a shock wave or EMP (electro-magnetic pulse) which may have burned out computerized communications for thousands of miles.

CHICAGO TRIBUNE
July 5, 1984

HEADLINE:
NUCLEAR ATROCITY!
WHO IS RESPONSIBLE?

WASHINGTON, D.C. THE WHITE HOUSE IS OUTRAGED. PRESIDENT MACGREGOR categorically denies charges from sources alleging that both the United States and the Soviet Union knew in advance but did nothing to prevent the catastrophic nuclear eruptions in the Middle East. The President labeled the multi-megaton blast as immoral, irresponsible and insane.

THE WASHINGTON POST
July 5, 1984

WASHINGTON, D.C. (AP) President John Macgregor

will address the nation and the world this evening to express America's outrage and shock at the unconscionable destruction of the Middle East. As soon as *safe* areas are determined by authorized agencies, medical supplies, food, and clothing will be deployed via air. Teams of voluntary doctors and nurses are being organized to assist survivors.

Meanwhile, a debate between proponents and opponents of the anti-nuclear issue has generated hostility once again.

THE WHITE HOUSE
9:00 P.M.

It was madness! Bedlam was the order of the day, as if a state of siege existed. Security screws tightened, the grounds were impenetrable. Army helicopters hovered and dipped overhead patrolling the grounds, relaying information to communication terminals and officers carrying air-to-ground transmitters.

Floodlights at strategic locations, normally rotating in brash illumination, were dark. Fully armed servicemen from all branches of the military formed phalanxes at each entrance to the Pennsylvania Avenue residence. Secret Service men huddled in teams, gazing outside the White House gates at the gathered throngs. Thousands of silent people carrying lighted candles took the brunt of their wrath. Why didn't they all go home? Crowds compounded the complexities of their jobs.

Secret Service men working in anterooms inside the White House reviewed tactical emergency strategy devised to protect the President and all government VIPs included in the Strategic Command Force's itinerary. Could any of them duplicate Glen Harlan's cool? Son of a bitch had restrained himself from pushing panic buttons and miraculously saved their asses. He deserved a medal for that piece of fast thinking.

The Oval Office, galvanized by the very power generated by the men gathered inside it, vibrated the rafters with tension, shock, urgency and stupefaction brought on by the unexpected chronology of events.

President John Macgregor paced the floor in deep thought. An hour ago he had faced the nation on television, revealing a tougher side to his nature than previously demonstrated. He ignored the formidable gathering of aides and advisors seated in

4

a semicircle around the impressive burnished oak desk, and these were not men easily ignored.

Present were White House aides Bill Miller and Tom Kagan; General Brad Lincoln, briefing officer; the Secretaries of State Anthony Harding and of Defense, Charles Norton; and members of the National Security Council. Each had contributed to the pervasive fractious and increasing global discord, especially the political disaster created by the limited nulcear foray in the Middle East.

Harding, scowled fiercely, like a glaring, unadaptive eagle lost in the confines of captivity. In his late fifties, the impressive, handsome, seldom ruffled man spoke in a low-keyed, gravel-voiced whisper. ''All attempts to uncover responsible parties who triggered off those nuclear warheads, impossible presently—''

The President cut him off sharply, his attention riveted to his briefing officer. ''We *know who*, don't we, General?'' President John Macgregor, a man of colossal self-confidence, pivoted on one foot, blue eyes sparking flints at the former CIA-NSA veteran. His scathing glance contained no condemnation of General Brad Lincoln personally. Inherent in his sarcasm was condemnation of the Joint Chiefs of Staff and other advisors seated nervously, red-faced before him, shifting uncomfortably in their chairs. The President's stinging venom and outrage was not lost on them.

''This mucked-up business in the Middle East would not have happened if I had stuck to my guns! Never will I permit you *experts* to dissuade me from my instincts!''

''Mr. President,'' Bill Miller, senior presidential aide interrupted, ''Moufflon addressed seventy-eight WPCC [World Powers Central Committee] delegates last February. We all received the same data—''

''He risked his life to provide us with the true facts!'' Macgregor retorted. ''No one listened. Not the Soviets, not the U.K., not America! He outlined step by step what would happen and no self-respecting nation lifted a hand to avert this holocaust conceived by insane minds!''

''The burden of responsibility doesn't rest solely on America's shoulders.''

Turning from Miller, the President's eyes fixed on General Lincoln. ''Doesn't it? Where do we look to mend the rupture—now, after the fact? It was *your* baby, General. You gave it

5

birth, nutured it against impossible odds. Our government provided Moufflon a platform to address the WPCC and we pulled the rug out from under him. We let him down. ME!'' He thumped his chest. "I let him down. I let America down!'' The outburst ventilated, he sat down heavily at his desk, a burdened man. "I knew the enormous risks involved. Executive privilege was mine to employ. I resisted, being worn down, influenced wrongly by my advisors—and I use the term loosely! I, who should have known better, permitted the adroit propaganda hurled against Moufflon to cloud the issue. Moufflon's PROJECT: MOONSCAPE described the apparatus, meticulously detailed its strategy to the final countdown. Yet none of you believed him. I did and failed to demonstrate that belief!''

Collectively the Oval Office occupants squirmed uneasily; some drummed nervous fingers on their thighs; a few bit lower lips; feet tapped agitatedly on the thick carpet. Each doing personal penance for contributing to the aborted PROJECT: MOONSCAPE.

Glen Harlan, Senior Comm Officer knocked on the Oval Office door. He entered, glanced at the President. "The Russian Premier in on the hot line.'' The President nodded. Harlan closed the door behind him.

Macgregor stared at the fire-engine-red phone, loath to pick it up. "What do I tell the Premier?'' His voice, laced with sarcasm, was aimed at the sleek hawks seated around him. "Do I hardline it? Insist the Soviet Union's increasing build-up of military capability is beyond justifiable and legitimate needs to defend itself? That Soviet disruptive projection of power into Third World Nations is exploitive? That Soviet encroachments in Africa, the Pacific sea lanes and oil-rich nations threatened the vital economic interests of western democracies? Shall I impart the usual rhetoric prescribed by my *advisors?* Or do we set aside all of the foregoing and level with him, admit to the Premier that we permitted ourselves to play for time we did not have?'' His hand moved to the phone. "Moufflon's brief, his summation, is now relegated to past history. If only half of it had provided inaccurate—''

"Monday morning quarterbacking, Mr. President—'' Miller's intended balm fell short of its target.

The President glared. He picked up a thick manila file, slammed it hard on the desk. "It's all here in this goddamned folder, and

6

we failed to heed it. The lives of millions senselessly wasted because some son of a bitch leaked portions of Moufflon's speech. All nations deny culpability. Now, *ex post facto*, the President of the United States must make like a goddamned superman to salvage what remains of the world!''

Glowering darkly at the inequities of public office, then like a man coming awake in his own nightmare to find he was merely a mortal from whom colossal achievements were expected, he fixed a new mask into place and glanced at Miller. ''Are the interpreters ready?'' On signal he inhaled deeply, expelled the air, picked up the ominous red phone, and bracing himself adjusted swiftly to a voice that was most likely to disarm the formidable man in Moscow.

''This is the President . . . Mr. Premier?''

Premier Nikolai Andreevich Vladechenko cleared his hoarse throat, a voice seared by the preference for vodka. ''Yes, yes, Mr. President. So, it appears we are to become referees of destiny?''

Satellite transmission enabled the superpower adversaries to view each other on screens as interpreters and electronics experts worked diligently behind the scenes to ensure proper transmission.

''With that assumption, Mr. Premier, comes profound responsibility. May I suggest, in the interest of both our great nations, that we unite, recommit ourselves to peaceful coexistence?''

The Premier grunted low in his throat. ''Peaceful coexistence implies ambiguities, Mr. President.''

''In my nation, the issue at stake presently is: Does Russia believe in world domination or peaceful coexistence?''

The Russian Premier glanced nonchalantly at a circle of politburo members and advisors fanned out before him, earphones in place, listening to the conversation, their eyes on the screen.

''Forgive me, Mr. President, I assumed the issue at stake to be the nuclear ravagement in the Middle East—the premeditated atrocity of horrendous proportions.''

''Of course, you are perfectly correct.''

''Mr. President,'' said Vladechenko, seldom looking at the screen, ''the Camp David Accords were invalidated long before July, 1984. Errors and miscalculations were contributed by all sides. Remember, please, that our country was excluded from any decision-making policies in the Middle East.''

There was silence, punctuated by deep stentorian breathing, as interpreters conveyed the Premier's words.

"In what remains of our unsettled world, where shifting policies and realignments occur, even now, in the wake of so appalling an atrocity, Mr. Premier, we must both increase restraints."

"Power, Mr. President," sighed the Russian, "is a precious commodity. It takes centuries to refine and respect its capabilities. Power in the hands of crazed fanatics who attempt to control the world is as volatile and dangerous as exploding megaton bombs. If your nation had not adopted so arrogant a step-child, and desisted in arming those militant, violence-oriented peoples who cannot be trusted with power—" Vladenchenko broke off in mid-sentence, a sigh of futility escaping his lips. He anticipated the President's rebuttal and was not disappointed.

"Forgive me, Mr. Premier. It does us both a great disservice to belabor an irreconcilable past. Agreed? The insanity of the past twenty-four hours proves that the hope for mankind's survival lies only in solidifying relations in a peace we should have enjoyed long before catastrophe blighted our world. We are beyond mutual recriminations for alleged wrongdoings. Sir, we cannot, must not, permit military confrontations to escalate until only ashes remain on our planet. World preservation, not destruction, must be our foremost consideration. Together we must stop the present dangers that plague our very existence."

"Mr. President, I rejoice in hearing those words. Our priorities, as difficult to wrestle with as your domestic and economic travails, force us to endure equal hardships. You do understand that our proximity to the nuclear wasteland and our inability to penetrate the Caucasus for fuel places a profound burden on all Russians."

President Macgregor hesitated. Briefly he glanced at his Secretary of State. In diplomacy it was considered a blunder to pin down an opponent. He hedged. "I have studied the satellite photos in depth. I sympathize with Russia's dilemma. America, too, faces crises—perhaps not as immediate as yours. May I speak with candor, sir? Are you certain you possess no knowledge beyond that delivered by Moufflon to the WPCC Delegates in February?"

"You must believe, if I did, my communication would have

8

been instantaneous. Am I to assume that you stand at the center of an island of doubt?''

''One of immense proportions, Mr. Premier.''

A full six seconds of silence hung heavily, during which interval glances were exchanged. Then the rhetoric turned vague. Only the two leaders seemed to understand the discussion.

''We face catastrophe unless we locate the common denominator.'' The Premier shuffled through paper on his desk as he spoke. ''Russia has vocalized discontent in recent months and is desirous of arms limitations. Now, at the top of the heap—nuclear war. Extinction!''

''Catastrophe, indeed! A forecast neither your nation or mine seek,'' Macgregor admitted in the same baleful tone employed by the Soviet Premier.

''You are fortunate your burdens last only eight years. Mine . . . ?''

''Yes, Mr. Premier?''

The marked hesitation by the Russian allowed for a slick transition.

''This man, Moufflon. You agree we share joint responsibility?''

''Clarify, sir. What responsibility?''

''I fail to understand you, John Macgregor.''

In the Oval Office heads tilted obliquely at the unexpected magnanimity, the silent observers interpreting the importance of the Premier's casual gesture.

''Seventy-two hours following the WPCC conference, the First Directorate of the KGB received word of an international contract. It is unimaginatively labeled, TARGET: MOUFFLON. All global assassins received the news. The contractor is unknown. Russia is prepared to offer Moufflon sanctuary.''

''Ah, yes. He refuses sanctuary.''

''You *did* know?''

''No doubt when you received word. America's burden is ponderous, obligatory. We placed him in dire jeopardy, and will not abandon our friend. However, he clearly indicates he needs no sanctuary from either the United States or the U.S.S.R. He refuses to communicate with us. Are your people more successful?''

''I shall send you by diplomatic bag a resume of our findings. Meanwhile, Mr. President, following reports submitted by our nuclear experts, we must meet. You pick the site. Nothing must take priority over this. Agreed? Are, uh, you, uh . . .'' The

Premier glanced up into the camera, his eyes seemingly riveted on the President as they bounced off the screen. "We shall discuss the matter in depth when we meet. *Do svidanya*."

"Yes, *do svidanya*, Mr. Premier. Until we meet again."

The conversation ended. Transmission faded as the screen turned black. John Macgregor sensed the Premier wanted to impart something of consequence, but didn't—for the same reason he himself had abstained from specifics—listening ears.

In the past year since this Moufflon business began he had learned more from General Brad Lincoln concerning clandestine operations than in his entire political career. He glanced at his advisors. Which among them were anacondas? Which were mongooses? All were presidental advisors, experts in the art of persuasion. He turned to them, waiting to hear these *experts* perform the post mortem on the Premier's speech.

President Macgregor ushered the last of his entourage out the Oval Office door. Introverted, he declined to involve himself in the dissection. Sensing his alienation, they left him.

At his desk, the President unlocked a safe that deceptively formed part of the office furniture. He removed five manila files marked: HIGHLY CLASSIFIED. *FOR THE EYES OF THE PRESIDENT ONLY*.

The first file was labeled: ZELLER FOUNDATION, Zurich, Switzerland. The second: BANQUE SUISSE NATIONAL, Zurich. The third: AMADEO REDAK ZELLER, Zurich. The fourth: *ATHENA*, code name for Valentina Miles Varga Lansing. The fifth: TARGET: MOUFFLON.

John Macgregor poured hot coffee from a silver service carafe at a nearby serving cart. He spooned honey into the bone china, berating himself for not having reviewed the files more critically. *How long had he had them?* Too damn long to have ignored them.

He picked up a phone, called the West Wing to ascertain his wife Geralee's safety. "I'll be in the Oval Office, in case you need me," he said. "You sound in excellent spirits, despite what's happened. You're all right? Well, if you need me. . . ." He hung up.

Moufflon! . . . Moufflón . . . ! Why hadn't he listened to the warnings? Moufflon had spelled it out before the WPCC Conference in Maui last February. My God, *five months ago!* And he had done nothing to circumvent the tragedy! God forgive him!

John Macgregor sipped his coffee in silence. He had never permitted himself the luxury of self-preservation except during a political campaign. He had a nation to preserve now, a solemn oath to keep. And, if at times he felt inadequate, he must never show it; frightened, he must never flinch; confused, he must master that confusion; hemmed in by phantoms, he must always dominate. At times he felt naked in adversity. Still, he persevered as he did at this point in what remained of time for the human race. Time . . . time . . . time permitted him no luxury to reflect.

He'd put it off too long. This night's agenda demanded full perusal of the files, a determined effort to fit the contents into sane, orderly fashion and bring into clearer focus an understanding of this man, *Moufflon,* the most wanted, hunted man on the globe.

The President sank down on the sofa, the files on the table before him. He turned on a high-intensity lamp, settled back, feet up on a pillow, the first file in hand, as he adjusted his glasses. He stared into space reflecting.

Was it a year ago? Or longer? Major Brad Lincoln had approached him with a crazy, harebrained scheme that had evolved into something neither crazy nor harebrained, but had succeeded in turning the world inside out.

BOOK ONE

"... We form an association of brothers in all points of the globe. We have desires, interests in common and aim at the emancipation of humanity. We wish to break every kind of yoke, yet there is one unseen that can hardly be felt, yet that weighs heavily upon us. From whence comes it? Where is it? No one knows. No one tells. The association is most secret, even for us, the veterans of secret societies."

                                ... Carbonaro Malegaro
                                Naples, 1835

Chapter One

ARLINGTON, VIRGINIA
THE PENTAGON
10 January, 1983

MAJOR BRAD LINCOLN SAT STONY-FACED AND MUTE in a back room at the Pentagon in committee hearings, listening to rumors of global conspiracies floating in and out of foreign embassies in D.C. A six-month sentence of tedium! Flimsy conjecture, routine summations and an occasional insight into provocative games of international Monopoly played for incredibly high stakes had as much effect upon committee members as petard. Witness after witness parading through the chambers had added little substance to the massive trivia fattening the files.

The entire scenario was grating on Brad's nerves.

Was he tired? Fucking tired of the incessant doubletalk? The battle of semantics—a waste of taxpayers' dollars and loss of precious personal time was maddening! He was rapidly losing objectivity.

It had occurred to him a month ago he no longer listened to the witnesses; actually, he barely noticed them. He desperately needed a change, else he'd soon be fitted for a straitjacket.

He awakened that morning mercurial, at odds with himself, racking his brain for any reason to submit a green absence slip. Each excuse created was instantly rejected. What inner compulsion forced him to sit here in time-consuming, repetitive, crowing sessions. *What?* So far into the morning he hadn't figured an answer; nothing exceptional had happened.

Still, that morning a curious anticipation rummaged through him, a feeling that something earthshaking was about to happen.

No, he wasn't a seer, but his past had contributed to these feelings; he rarely ignored them.

15

Major Lincoln, a hard-bitten, spit-and-polish veteran of three wars, major global conflicts, and a long, varied career in intelligence and counterinsurgency, stood slightly under six feet. Solid brawn and muscle, a well-preserved fifty-eight-year old, he looked and acted at least fifteen years younger. His deeply tanned, unlined features, rugged good looks, the clear, azure penetrating eyes, reflected none of the perilous life-and-death adventures which had shaped his life. What appeared as ennui, today was apathy, sheer disgust for his role at these Pentagon hearings.

Lincoln had working for him a blocking-out process, an acquired occupational trait he likened to the capabilities of a bird's nictitating eyelid: a device permitting him to zero in and weed out unessential data input to his brain. Brad's brilliant expertise was in cryptology, taught him by the *backroom boys* at Bletchley Park, England in 1940, under the skilled leadership of Commander John York in the *Enigma Operation* and that spectacular code-breaking machine, *ULTRA*. Brad had helped to decimate the German code, enabling the Allies to win crucial battles, and this led to continued promotion in Office of Strategic Services activities.

At war's end, counterinsurgency was lauded in the omnipotent corridors of the CIA. Later, thrust into an influential coterie of top-echelon politics, Brad Lincoln played an effective, behind-the-scenes role at the autonomous National Security Agency, a secretive high technology-oriented agency, unaccountable neither to Congress or any federal agency. Brad felt at home in NSA, since it had evolved from the telecommunications and coding operations developed during World War II.

Six months ago Brad's world changed dramatically when a mysterious executive order demanded his presence at these inane, utterly ridiculous Pentagon hearings. Moved by the stupidity and exorbitant spending of taxpayers' money, he protested. Refusal, he learned, meant instant dismissal, or being farmed out to some fucking pasture in the lower regions of Afars and Issas. This after a lifetime of dedication to his country, was anathema! That a man of his background, talents, and experience to be subjected to these incredibly stupid shenanigans stunned him.

Worse . . . his covert committee assignment demanded interminable processing, evaluation, analysis and utilization of countless categories of intelligence, a sifting and weeding-out of useless data, a mental warehousing and microscopic scrutiny of any pertinent information related by the speakers. It was boring . . .

16

boring . . . boring! Certainly not what he deserved. He sipped his coffee, grimacing distastefully. Inexplicably his attention shifted sharply to the video screen on his console. A distinctive Cambridge accent triggered a reaction from him. Brows knitting together, he flipped several switches on the console activating a videotape recorder, voice and ocular prints. Zooming in for a close-up, he studied the Nigerian's features critically while listening through earphones.

". . . We are victims of the Triple D-G syndrome. Dope for diamonds, dollars and gold! The panic and chaos of combined financial disorder, assassinations, attempts at destablizing nations, represents a malignancy ready to trigger thermonuclear war. That a cabal exists, comprised of criminal elements and the most esteemed figures in society, is not new to us. That they hide under masks of respectability while conspiring the most vicious crimes against humanity is no longer tolerable. Dope for dollars, diamonds and gold, laundered through prominent international banks in exchange for nuclear arms in so rapid a buildup deserves instant investigation. Four decades have passed since Hiroshima and Nagasaki. Four decades have not produced peace, but cold wars, social revolutions, political and economic disasters, soaring inflationary spirals, oil shortages, oil gluts, race riots, immense poverty, and daily threats of global genocide. Daily the threats grow more agonizing. Nuclear arsenals in the hands of fanatics aimed at the annihilation of mankind—''

Lincoln momentarily tuned out the Nigerian. *So what else was new? The neutron bomb? What a crowning achievement for mankind! The ne plus ultra in the field of nuclear physics! Another device to rid the world of excess people!*

Repetition . . . it was nothing but repetition. Neutron bombs in the hands of Middle East fanatics; the proliferation and escalation of global nuclear arsenals; impending nuclear war; specters of terrorism, international hit-squads running herd in nations generating incredible amounts of monetary power threatening world leaders . . . these had authored enough paranoia to catapult the world into a dizzying spinout. Few knew of the behind-the-scenes propaganda created to exaggerate world tensions.

17

Triple D-G! Dope for diamonds, dollars and gold! The Nigerian failed to mention oil!

Brad scanned the printed speech. Although the Nigerian's contribution to the dull, repetitious hearing was articulate, it was as vague as all those that preceding him.

The James Bond mystique, long gone from his work, was not the reason for Brad's boredom. It was the long trail of never-ending *rumors*. Not *flash-intelligence*, not *manufactured* rumors, but *real* rumors leaked from these high-level sources which confounded the intelligence community, creating *uncontrolled* turmoil, a viable enemy in any intelligence operation. Lack of control meant rumors . . . rumors . . . rumors . . . and each one had to be investigated in this boring tedium.

Rumors:

The Israelis were gearing up to annihilate the Arabs!

The Arabs, bent on destroying Israel, had seduced aid from Russia!

The United States, erecting statues to itself as the global guardian, was often touted as the promoter of global genocide!

Zionist Jews had promised to stay out of Israel's politics in the sixties, were back again orchestrating falsehoods, causing splits within Israel and pushing the Arabs into building up their defenses!

Rumors!

Brad grimaced at the list of speakers on the agenda. Men of letters, diplomats, statesmen, paid informers dumping fertilizer on the investigaory committee.

It was all bullshit!

Major Lincoln sat back in his chair building temples with his fingertips, blocking the dated material from mind. For years it was facts which substantiated the proliferation of nuclear arsenals in the Middle East. *Christ! It was the stockpiling of these arsenals that was steamrolling the world toward doomsday! That's what this fucking three-ring circus was all about! To learn facts!*

The Soviet emissary approached the lectern. A hush fell upon the room. Brad glanced down on the floor at the slight commotion, then fell into apathy without glancing at the agenda. Uri Mikhail Gregorevich spoke out in a loud, clear voice.

". . . Members of this distinguished committee, vicious rumors aimed at deteriorating USA-USSR relations escalate uncontrollaby. Of mutual interest to both nations and the world is the need for a determined effort to bring a halt to these grossly exaggerated lies. The Soviet Union believes the USA to be a key conspirator—the secret supplier of strategic weapons to impassioned Middle East zealots. That it has in the past secretly supplied other revolutionaries with arms to overthrow the governments of various nations is a matter of historical record. The United States refutes this and counters with like allegations blaming Russia. If the United States *has* armed these nations, Russia understands. At stake are the world's largest oil reserves. If false, the rumors must be stopped, the air cleared between us. Russia is not so naive to believe this can happen unless both nations meet in an honest effort to preserve the peace, and take to task those nations that willfully subvert these efforts for personal aggrandizement.

My visibility here, today before this honored fact-finding comisssion, is neither to confirm—or deny the foregoing remarks, but to share with the United States knowledge compiled recently by our intelligence forces. A unique covenant of master propagandists is at work, employing clever anti-Soviet, anti-American materials in ways irreparably catastrophic to both our nations and ultimately threatens the existence of mankind. There is evidence that there exists a calculated strategy designed to escalate the presently strained USA-USSR relationship. Attempts to rewrite the world according to the gospel they preach is unacceptable to my nation . . ."

The mid-morning American pick-me-up of caffeine and carbohydrates arrived to stimulate the committee members. Brad sipped the hot brew, lowered the volume on his earphones, studied the printed speech, thinking what a *fucking* never-ending battle. He read:

". . . Iraquis fight Iranians. Afghanis fight Pakistanis. Even the British were forced into confrontation with the Argentines. Brothers fight brothers in Central America and in Africa. In 1982 the Palestinians continued to erupt Israel's forceful legerdemain and in turn we all saw the shameful destruction of Israeli forces—using American-made weapons—upon Lebanon and especially Beirut. They violate the peace with impunity, seize lands illegally, while United Nations dele-

19

gates debate the semantics of illegal seizure. When the underdog views how heavily the scales of justice tip pro-Israel, why is it such a surprise when Arabs appeal to the Soviets for aid?

The United States sold AWACS to the Saudis. Israel's failure to block this action through its powerful Zionist lobby brought swift retaliation—annexation of the Golan Heights! And a three hundred million dollar payment of appeasement in American taxpayer dollars to Israel! Did the stinging, verbal denunciation of Israel for its unjustified, flagrant breach of international law by the United States and United Nations affect Israel? No! The aggressor, Israel, arrogantly flouts them. It repudiates all criticism.

Brad's troubled eyes darted to the video screen, jolted by the apprehension shuddering through him. He studied the Russian. Handsome, tall, well-dressed, debonair. His eyes returned to the speech, to the name of the speaker. Uri Mikhail Gregorevich! *Jeesus!* Gregorevich was the junior member of the Soviet Politburo! Dynamite stood before the lectern. He sat forward, his senses coming alive. Here before the committee stood perhaps the second most powerful man in the Kremlin. Premier Vladechenko's *protege*! *Christ!* Was this to be his American debut or political suicide? An epitaph? To make so dramatic a statement, denunciating Israel in times when it was unpopular to do so, took nerve!

Brad watched the Russian move away from the lectern. He glanced below him out of camera range, and observed four KGB agents flanking the outspoken diplomat, escorting him from the chambers.

Well, Uri Mikhail Gregorevich—you've got guts!
. . . And in this corner, ladies and gentlemen . . .

Judging from the murmurs from the committee, the Russian had provided the first stimulation in months.

Brad glanced at his watch. Damn! An hour before lunch. He tapped his boot impatiently against the side of his desk, scanned the next speaker, listening through his headphones! *Christ!* All the committee needed now was a French philosopher. He tuned out the Frenchman, placed the Russian's speech in his briefcase.

The world was turning into a cesspool of hatred and madness and the Frenchman spoke of love for the human soul. Man had learned nothing in his time on earth—*nothing!* The Middle East was ascending to an arena of psychosis. Other nations, observing Israel's arrogant behavior were mimicking that nation, boldly demonstrating the same acquisitive tactics. The danger being the *apers* possessed neither equal clout or the bankrolling capabilities of Israel. Their only solution to the current world destabilization— nuclear war! The stench of it clung to the atmosphere, spreading its sickening, infectious paranoia.

And the Frenchman philosophized!

All of those fanatics in that festering hotbed of Middle Eastern hatred needed keepers. Words could become lethal weapons, which threatened to blast off a confrontation without countdown at the first insult!

Brad glanced at his watch: fifty minutes before lunch. He began his own countdown as his patience thinned. Nonsensical words flavored by spicy rumors, provoked turbulence in him. For Brad to lose control, give way to anger, *visible* anger, was rare. Hot spots erupted globally and these assholes offered appeasement via kindergarten tactics.

London Bridge was falling down. No one put Humpty Dumpty together again in a way that made sense. These men of the Pentagon, believed—actually believed—they could play Little Jack Horner forever!

He'd had enough! He wasn't about to sit around like a clucking mother hen listening to backyard gossip and let his mind atrophy! Six unproductive months tore at him. He was wasted in this role. Yanking at his briefcase, Brad opened it, began packing it, oulining, as he did, a mental resignation to his superiors at NSA. They could take their job and shove it! In moments he'd escape this insanity and embark on a lost weekend! He'd get stinking drunk.

He was determined to make his exit before the next speaker made it to the lectern.

He didn't. *Damn it to hell!*

Tall, powerfully built, a black man in a burnoose filled Brad's video screen. The *voice!* An Oxford-accented voice struck a familiar chord in Brad Lincoln. His eyes narrowed, trying to focus clearly on the speaker. He ran his finger down the agenda to the blue insert—a last-minute witness. No advance speeches had been doled to the committee, but Brad needed no name. The man was Musaka Mubende, Uganda's exiled Foreign Affairs

21

Minister. A sudden feeling that he was peeling away layers of time gripped him. Anticipation? Excitement? He was breathless.

A friend out of the past!

Brad's attention shifted from the floor to the video screen on his desk console; he zoomed in for a closer shot of Mubende. The Ugandan stood regally at the lectern, black tiger eyes flashing at the chamber's occupants. There—in the eyes—Brad saw it! *Fear!* Pure unadulterated fear from the most fearless man he'd ever met! Something was wrong. *Drastically* wrong.

He jerked his head from the screen, his eyes searching the cavernous room. Then he spotted them. Ugandan Secret Police. French SCEDE agents. Heavily armed Pentagon security guards and a few FBI men. His attention returned to the screen:

". . . There can be no doubt that a unique force does exist creating international turmoil through the proliferation of manufactured lies. Pure fabrication designed to pit countries against each other for profit. Now, more than ever in the life of man, a demonstrable need for unity and understanding is vital to existence. I put it to you, honored committee members, that in the not-too-distant past my own nation was targeted by these *invisible* men who wear many disguises. I attest to their visibility. Today, before I finish, I shall name these terrorists who sit in gold towers orchestrating the destruction of the world . . ."

Waves of hushed exclamations rocked the chamber. Astonishment immobilized their features. They tensed. Brad, startled into sobriety, leaned forward, cleared the screen, retuned his earphones for clearer reception. Instinct made him reactivate the video recorder, voice and ocular tapes. He zoomed in and focused on Mubende's dark eyes and felt a rush of adrenalin. He shoved his thoughts back a few years. The former World War II desert commando, Musaka Mubende, had risen from killer to top dog in Ugandan foreign affairs and deserved accolades for contributing to world peace. But today, something was drastically wrong! Unnatural paranoia emanated from him. Brad's attention riveted on the black man.

Was this to be the unusual day his senses had signaled on awakening that morning? He listened with every nerve in his body.

22

"They are an impenetrable force, secretly funding terrorists. They eagerly contributed to the destablization of my nation and all nations who jeopardize their clandestine efforts to maintain superiority. They are a force of such magnitude their powers extend to the creation and orchestration of every hostile act in the Middle East and Africa. They are a cohesive, *invisible* force—and, I dare say, protected in ways that defy the imagination. . . ."

Brad's brain worked triple time. Something struggled to emerge from his subconscious. Words triggered sights, sounds, images. Attuned to Mubende's voice, he raised the volume, zoomed in and out for a full face shot, focusing tight on burning anthracite eyes.

Less credible witnesses had hinted at these same *invisible* forces, but had failed to provoke the interest and curiosity engendered by this Ugandan statesman. Here, in the flesh, this giant had the courage to state positively what had heretofore been labeled hearsay.

Listening attentively, riddled with galloping uncertainty, Brad sensed a precarious geometry between what was said and what remained unspoken. Then, suddenly flashes of a vast array of images sprang from locked drawers in his subsconscious. A faint design strained to emerge from data accumulated and swimming every which way in his head. The nucleus of thought thrust itself upon him. Indefinable at first, like the hazy outline of a human embryo x-rayed five weeks after conception, one of low definition, yet pulsating with life it began to mature, triggered by key words: *Impenetrable . . . Invisible forces . . . Mysterious . . . Unlimited funds . . . Blind fronts . . . Corporate veils . . . . Protected in ways to defy the imagination!*

Fine lines of truth, woven into a bold design, began to emerge— wispy, a bit fragmented, yet, slowly solidifying into indisputable information; facts tying into Brad's forty-year career of warfare, espionage, intelligence-gathering and counterinsurgency activities.

Jesus Christ! From the beginning—before World War I! Before World War II burst upon the lives of man . . . before the United States had a nuclear monopoly in 1947! Was it really possible this power force had taken a stranglehold upon the world so long ago?

The split-second journey into his past cost Lincoln a fierce price—*a moment in the present!* He heard the commotion, thought his earphones had malfunctioned, until he saw it happen on the video screen. Musaka Mubende was suddenly propelled backward, lifted into the air by a swift impact, a bullet to his heart! Clutching at the dark crimson pool of blood over his breast, he was struck again between the eyes, and fell from the camera frame.

"Oh, my God!" Brad hissed, whipping off his headphones. Below him, on the floor, pandemonium exploded. Ugandan secret police rushed forward to the minister's side. Pentagon security guards, guns drawn, ran toward the lectern, forming a cordon around the dying Mubende. Committee members sat frozen in their seats, shocked at the appalling spectacle.

Brad's instinct for survival raced into high gear. He pushed the speed rewind buttons on all the videotapes, removed them from the console, and shoved them into his briefcase. Under cover of mass confusion and a rising hysteria as the committee chairman rapped for order, he swiftly departed the upper chambers before the exit doors could switch over to emergency control and lock him inside. Bolting through the door, briefcase in hand, he slowed his pace to a moderate, long-strided lope to the elevators. He pushed the down button and waited.

C'mon elevator, get cracking before the fucking alarms trip!

He studied the floor indicators—three on the up-flight, one on the down. Ah, at last! The door slid open, admitting him to a deserted car, and closed just as security guards stepped out of the other elevators.

Now to get your tail out of the Pentagon—pronto!

The elevator descended to garage level. Brad, calculating time and distance, began a mental countdown. Two minutes remained to depart the garage in his car before alarms sealed off all exits. Would he make it? How to secrete the briefcase and precious tapes, if he didn't?

He did, with four seconds to spare. He floored the accelerator, plunged the Datsun 310 through the last gate, made a sharp right on Washington just as the Pentagon's Mobile Security units rushed the forward gate.

He was sweating. In icy, near-zero-degree temperatures he was *sweating!* Brad eased along the road, turned right onto Arlington Ridge Road, headed due north before he noticed the darkening sky. Another record snowstorm in the offing? At midday it seemed dusk.

The next half hour was spent negotiating precarious, slippery roads in blizzard-like snow. Front and rear windshield wipers wouldn't work fast enough. On his left, Arlington Cemetery, hidden under thick swirling snowdrifts, appeared more desolate than usual. He turned on the car radio to monitor police and security calls.

PANIC AT THE PENTAGON! What else? Scramblers prevented laymen from learning what had happened to Mubende. Brad snapped off the radio, cursing the roads and lack of snow crews. Damn their priorities! The back roads were always last. He took a sharp right, crossed Key Bridge into Georgetown and negotiated his way through the bottlenecked traffic to his home.

What he needed right now was a good lay. The best he could find. Good thinking, Brad, ol' boy. In the clinches you always come out fighting. Who the hell was irrelevant. How soon can you get her is better.

Brad set a match to the kindling under the hickory logs on the hearth in his den. He poured himself a double Haig & Haig and spent the next few hours replaying the video cassette of Musaka Mubende's final death chant until he knew the speech by rote.

He recorded Mubende's speech on a separate tape console. Finished, Brad lifted out the slim cassette and snapped it into an electronic computer. In moments the electronic apparatus produced a complete readout of the text. Brad tore the data from the machine, stacked the sheets together and read the text again.

Now what, Major? How will you get proper evaluations on the voice and ocular prints without bringing NSA and Pentagon bloodhounds to the scent?

Brad gathered tapes and speech, placed them in a floor safe in a closet off the den, and engaged alarms hooked into the master bedroom and den. He had created several problems for himself and he had to sort out viable explanations.

Contacts would be made, questions asked. He would have to be ready for them. *Why, when,* and *how* had he left X-212, code name for Committee Chambers, without logging out of Central Control? The usual procedures, altered by Mubende's death would prompt an in-depth search through master computers for all the data processed through the desk consoles of each commit-

25

tee member. If Lincoln's were the only tapes missing . . . ? He'd cross that bridge soon enough.

He poured another drink, settled in a leather recliner near the fire, staring hypnotically at the mass of colored fire blazing brightly, experiencing the ebullience of a man at the edge of discovery. Bits and pieces of Uri Gregorevich's speech and of Musaka Mubende's last words filtered through his consciousness. He had made frightening decisions. Pray God he'd made correct assessments. In his business, he couldn't afford errors in judgment.

Bad, ol' boy, you've come a long way from your beginnings.

The eighth son of an impoverished immigrant Jew, he'd rejected his origins in the tenements of New York. He had run away from home at age nine, denying his heritage, turning his back on the imposed dogmas of orthodox religion. The abrasive city streets in the early thirties had shaped him as he scrounged about in back alleys, stealing, living by his wits for mere survival. Then realization nudged at him, convincing him that a streetwise savvy would fail to produce for him what he wanted from life. Hard-bitten criminals, underworld figures created in the depression's wake, had been his heroes until the awakening. A resolve to break from this mold forced him to struggle for a coveted high school diploma.

Sheer guts, determination, and a loathing for poverty blinded him to the ugliness of city life. He worked odd jobs, running numbers for a small-time hood, delivering bootlegged whiskey, and later as he developed into brawn and muscle, bounced deadbeats from whorehouses before age sixteen. He earned tuition to Maryland University, forgot Yosel Burnbaum's existence, and legally changed his name to Bradford Lincoln. It was a terrible time to be either Jew, Italian or even Irish, and he made the break, once and for all.

Benito Mussolini and Adolf Hitler, two power impresarios, were orchestrating political extravanganzas in Europe, forcing stunned observers to fox-trot to their tempo. War was imminent. Brad joined the Army.

His demonstrated penchant for ciphers, codes, cryptology, got Brad transferred to the OSS and soon it was off to Bletchley Park in England for orientation in the absorbing world of conspiracy, espionage, sabotage among the geniuses and brilliant warring men. His spirits soared. The experience of his early life had taught him to employ inborn craftiness, duplicity and silence. In this infinitely beguiling world, men's brains were reshaped into near-computer efficiency. His progress, lauded by exceptional men, fed his ego, inspired him to tackle anything. His daily fix of patriotism, Americanism, and dedication ultimately journeyed him through World War II, the Cold War, and the Korean and Vietnam conflicts.

His duties, now a function of the CIA, had propelled him through the fanatical fifties of McCarthyism, the scandalizing sixties of assassination and sexual and social revolts, horrendous drug trafficking, the spurious seventies of political upheavals, cover-ups, and world unrest.

Now, in the eighties, why this unexpected prick of conscience jolting him out of lethargy?

Mushroom clouds over Hiroshima and Nagasaki in August 1945 had spawned the germ of fear. Like the rest of the world, the cataclysm had anesthesized him, and regardless of the power placed in his hands, he moved trance-like through the next three decades into the eighties, blindly speedballing toward nuclear devastation without really daring to look at its lethal potential until . . .

The Pentagon Hearings.

Six months of fomenting discontent brought reevaluation because of this day's events. His entire career, the futility of it all, if in the long run it meant the annihilation of mankind, shook him to the core. If Brad's life had had a singular purpose, it was not to participate in the destruction. He was unafraid of death, unafraid of failure. He'd seen enough of life to be a deeply rooted cynic. Still he believed there was hope for mankind.

He had to believe this.

Outside a scrim of ebony pulled across the heavens had left a mottled darkness obliterating stars, moon, and planets. Subdued by his thoughts, Brad rose from his chair, turned on the patio lights. Snow had piled in high drifts, mantling a six-foot fence. He snapped off the light, pulled the drapes shut, checked the alarm systems and moved into the kitchen to fix a snack and brew a fresh pot of coffee.

Back in the den he munched on the sandwich, forcing himself to think slowly. He had work to do, ends to patch together if he hoped to complete the intricate mosaic forming in his mind. He

27

probed the congested battleground of his memory, dug back in time to World War II—four decades ago!

Four decades! He sorted, sifted recollections, isolating them, stringing together a chronology of facts, flimsy at best, but forming a working skeleton that he hoped would trigger events buried in his subsconscious. He lay back, eyes trailing about the room.

It was a reflection of his life: a room of leathers, heavy woods, bricked walls, plants, floor-to-ceiling bookcases and a highly sophisticated communications console. Books, war mementos, citations, ribbons, mounted shrapnel removed from his leg in a war injury, numerous artifacts, priceless art objects given him by grateful foreign chiefs of state, each tagged in bronze and dated, all a part of his life.

Faces from the past blipped across his mind, flowing like an army, until out of the milieu . . . one face . . . dominated all. One face!

A Corsicañ! A very special Corsican!

Brad breathed deeply. *Now think! Dammit! His name! What's his name? You know it. C'mon, Brad. The Corsican is integral to what's happening throughout the world!*

He knew it. Sensed it by the rushing of his adrenalin when he flashed on the man's image.

Compulsion drove Brad. He leaped from the chair, crossed the room, searched feverishly through desk drawers. He scanned the photographs on the shelves, peered at memorabilia. Nothing.

He quickly darted out the room, up the stairs, pausing briefly to shrug into a white cable-knit sweater as he scaled the next flight of stairs to an unfurnished catch-all room containing several foot lockers and crated material collected over the years. A half hour later the place was a shambles.

It's here, someplace! C'mon, find it! You've gotta solve the goddamned puzzle! He tossed more boxes about, tore into others.

Voilà! He found it at the bottom of a foot locker.

Old, frayed, yellowed with age, the scrapbook had been diligently assembled while recuperating from a war wound in West Berlin in 1946. Six years of his life compressed into a four-inch-thick book. Letters, photos, a curious collection of strange bedfellows who shared death, turmoil, fear, the DTs and a living hell!

He flipped through a few pages, stopped abruptly, suddenly

loathe to go back, terribly afraid that what he discovered would drastically change his life.

Downstairs in the den he poured Amaretto into hot eggnog, sat before the fire, and held the unopened scrapbook in his lap, thoughts spiraling in his mind.

Why, ironically, at the apex of his disgust and decision not to spend another day in committee hearings had a Russian's speech and the death of Musaka Mubende jolted him, erupting a floodtide of Brad's past life? He gazed across the room at the glass-enclosed cubicle containing two stunning bronze heads, circa seventeenth century Court of Benin, Bini Tribe, Nigeria, gifted to him by the late Musaka Mubende. Ousted in a bloody *coup* led by Major Idi Amin in 1971, the Ugandan diplomat had been placed in Brad's protection, flown covertly to exile in England. Three months later the art treasures arrived with Mubende's gratitude. Now his old friend was dead!

The ignominious deed peeled back layers of Brad's discontent.

Suddenly he remembered Musaka Mubende, a former SAS Commando in the North African campaign, had fought under the Corsican's command! Mubende had later elevated himself to political heights, not in Nigeria, but in his adopted nation—Uganda.

There's a tie-in, dummy! Find it!

Ready now, Brad opened the scrapbook, studied each photo—a hundred, two hundred, who counted?—paying meticulous attention to detail, faces, settings, backgrounds, dates, each stirring countless memories lazily awakening in his brain. Photos taken in Corsica, in Bastia, Ajaccio, Porto, a few in Marseilles along the waterfront, several at the Eiffel Tower in Paris with the French Underground forces. Victorious grins lighting up haggard, worn, frail faces. Rare photos taken in North Africa of those incomparable dogs of war—the SAS Commandos.

The Mozarabe! Of course! Now think, Brad, think! The Commander of the Mozarabe was . . .

His concentration was serrated by the telephone activating a recorder on his desk. He paused to listen to the call he had expected all evening.

". . . Major Lincoln . . . Brett Harris here. The time: 1900 . . . Date: one, zero, January . . . Code Purple Alert. Verify ASAP."

Brad checked the time, 1900 on the button. Brett Harris was Chief of Security at the Department of Defense—sobriquet: The Pentagon. At issue: Code Purple Alert. Essentially the message implied Brad had twelve hours to report in before the goon squads broke down his doors. The protection of committee members in times of crisis was paramount. *Well, Brett Harris, old buddy, you can fuckin' well wait. I've more important things to do.*

For an hour, Brad drank more Amaretto eggnog and black coffee; he turned on the television, watching news crews and cameramen with reporters hovering like vultures before the Pentagon, trying to pry information from departing VIPs concerning Mubende's death.

The "official" statement was a heart attack, but Brad knew that the cover story left too much open to speculation. Leave a minuscule crack open and the newshounds would find a thousand ways to pry open a can of worms. Bios on Mubende were flashing on the screen. A retrospective of his life, career. He knew it was a sham. It was all manufactured material! Ah, well . . .

Two hours later, a gusting wind wailed through the house, creating eerie sounds. Brad was no closer to identifying the Corsican than he was hours ago. The answer tottered stubbornly at the edge of his memory, refusing to unveil itself. In a spurt of anger, he removed three photos from the scrapbook, circled the heads of three men. The first was, then, Brigadier General Charles de Gaulle; the second, Lieutenant James Greer, Brad's *aide de camp*, actually his partner and sidekick in the OSS; the third, the nameless Corsican, a strapping man, handsome as a cinema star, dressed in the uniform of a British major, but his training, loyalty and life had belonged implicitly to Free France. He propped the photos up against a brass lamp and stared intently at them for long minutes.

Dammit! Nothing uprooted the key which would reveal the Corsican's name! Was it a psychological block?

At nine o'clock Brad called the Pentagon Security Chief.

"What's up, Harris?" he rasped, feigning a throat ailment.

"We are in crisis here. Weren't you briefed by Security Inter-op? Sector X-212 is under security wraps. Assassination . . . Mubende. Uh, Major, you logged in at 0900, but failed to log out."

"Sorry . . . I'm running a 102 temperature," he muttered hoarsely. "I left, failing to signal the Chair. Break in protocol, unintentional." He coughed, dissembled adroitly.

Brad got unconvincing sentiment and subtle innuendo from Harris. "Keep yourself available for interrogation concerning the coincidence of your departure to Mubende's death."

And fuck you too, buddy!

Three days later his discoveries, their scope and magnitude, staggered Brad Lincoln. He realized that *verboten* Pentagon corridors, containing *HIGHLY CLASSIFIED*, extremely sensitive data, must be trespassed if he were to find the substantiating evidence he desperately needed. But confidential sources within both State and Defense Departments must be penetrated at all costs.

Lessons from the past shrieked at him: *Protect your flanks*.

The questions bottomed out to: Whom do I trust? The answers: No one! This mission demanded the utmost secrecy and discretion. It must not fail, he repeated over and again.

It was four A.M. when he made his decision. Brad hadn't slept in three days and when sleep fell upon him it was hard, exhaustive, lasting only a few hours. It was enough.

He awakened bright-eyed the morning of the fifth day. He spent the entire day prowling trails through bureaucratic jungles between the CIA, NSA, and Pentagon strongholds in a desperate attempt to locate imperative files—files buried three decades ago by prudent, crafty, foresighted men.

Now, here he was, after five full days of intensified probing, at a dead end! Stopped before he had begun. Predatory, driven by fierce determination when sense dictated otherwise, he stood at a precarious impasse. The choice was his. He knew the price of mistakes at this level of secrecy—his own extermination.

Oh, Christ! His clandestine past dared him—his secure present deterred him. It was push—pull. Damned if you do—damned if you don't!

The cause of his frustrations . . . ?

He had located the desperately needed files, buried deep within the labyrinthian caverns of the Pentagon catacombs, buried in GAMMA 10.

GAMMA 10! No one penetrated GAMMA 10 and lived to talk about it!

Standing in a corridor at the Pentagon, Brad burst out laughing. He reached into his pocket for his cigarettes. How in damnation would he pole-vault this obstacle? Did he dare thwart Pentagon

31

rules? Lay his life on the line? He *knew* the answers, and he hesitated with good reason. The highest level of politics was involved. The risks, compounded by sophisticated electronic spying systems escalated to high-priced hit contracts put out on *any* man who dared buck the system.

A month ago Brad Lincoln would not have considered placing his life on the line after so long a fulfilling career. In the past five days something had changed. Discovery had infected him with madness. He must be mad to plot the penetration of GAMMA 10!

GAMMA 10, for Christsakes, was impenetrable!

Only the Director of Counter-Intelligence had access to this *verboten* crypt. And only the signature of the President could by-pass the DCI's. Without that signature Brad couldn't dent the electronic nightmare protecting GAMMA 10. Worse, unless he provided concrete facts to substantiate what might be labeled lunatic allegations, he stood no chance of ever convincing the President to sign the high-risk orders. He returned to his town house, deflated but unvanquished.

Brad stood at the window watching turtling crews blow mounds of snow into huge banks on both sides of the streets, obstructing private driveways. He stretched, tried to relax the building tension by limbering his muscles. He spent interminable time absently watching the snow crews at work, pondering his next move. He knew what had to be done, but he hesitated.

His gut instinct told him she'd cooperate. Trusting it implicitly, he was willing to pick up the phone this minute to complete the task, but conscience debated his *right* to involve her in the damnable sticky business. He tried to put himself in her place, think as she might, but how do you ever figure a woman?

He was exhausted from thinking about it.

He loathed dragging her into a foray of political barracudas on the basis of expedience. God! Brad had to reach this woman. His head throbbing incessantly, he padded back to the den, picked up the phone and was forced to wheel and deal to obtain her unlisted number.

He stared hesitantly at the numbers he had scrawled on a note pad. *No more stalling, old chap! Get cracking!* Setting scrambler devices into place, he made the call—protocol be damned—and held his breath. He would meet with her anyplace, wherever she wanted, it didn't matter, but they must meet. She had to be convinced of the dire necessity of complying with his extraordinary request, of the utmost discretion and silence required on the matter.

Two days after Brad Lincoln's call, she stood at the top steps of the Lincoln Memorial under darkening skies as snow flurries thickened the air.

Valentina Miles Varga Lansing, wife of Senator Hartford B. Lansing, was stunning. Jade green eyes, hair of burnished fire, unmistakable aristocratic bearing, framed by an expensive, superb designer wardrobe, the millionairess peered about the densely falling snow, searching for him. Her tall, slender body was clad impeccably in tailored avocado suede pants, boots to match, turtleneck angora sweater under a pullover matching suede jerkin, casually roped at the waist with a solid gold chain belt, blended perfectly under a full-length wild lynx greatcoat turned up at the collar.

He knew her at once, despite the passing years. It was there, all of it, better than when he last saw her—*how* many years ago? It was the authoritative way she stood, the subtle manner of elegance and class. He drew closer. Her hands were thrust into coat pockets, hugging the sumptuous fur to her body to ward off the chilling winds. Vagrant wisps of incredibly flaming hair were visible under the Cossack-style lynx hat.

For an instant as he approached she lifted her dark glasses, studied him scrupulously, the slightest glimmer of recognition in her viridian eyes as she placed him in her past.

Was she displaying the cultured immutable veneer women of her class employed among subordinates—or did she actually remember him?

"Major Lincoln . . . your description was perfect. I'd know you anyplace." She held her hand out to him.

"And I, you. Thank you for coming. You are more stunning than memory served me." They sauntered casually along the inner colonnade of the semi-deserted Memorial, past thirty-six Doric columns in the scant gathering of die-hard tourists determined, storm or no storm, to visit the Great Emancipator's shrine.

Valentina listened for a quarter hour without interruption, the imposing stone figure of Abraham Lincoln towering over them in the warmer center chamber. Undeniably jolted by Brad's urgency, his request triggered alarm and a hesitance to involve herself. She questioned him incisively. "Your reasons for not following protocol implies grave clandestine risks. Dangerous business, is it?"

"More than I dare hint. I debated at length before seeking this encounter. Your right to privacy weighed heavily on my mind. If word leaks of my intentions, all conduits to the man I mentioned earlier would atrophy. If nothing materializes and my efforts prove useless, no one need know of this encounter, that you interceded on my behalf."

Pensive, Valentina took the next steps in silence. When at last she spoke, her voice was firm.

"Major, you are or were an Intelligence officer. I assume your theories are substantiated by facts. I will act as liaison for you. Actually, I believe what you've hinted at. My beliefs are also based on facts. And Major, I am frightened at the implications."

Then Brad made a gross error. In a three-month journey, speeding over half the world, locked in combat with death, he would come to regret that he had lacked foresight to probe Valentina's enigmatic words. Elated by her acquiescence, the depth of her discerning statements went unmeasured.

"Will there be global war, Major?"

"A professional asking a professional? I know I can speak truthfully without alarming you. If it is not avoided, no one will remain to voice regrets or do fancy Monday morning quarterbacking."

Valentina sighed, a curious contemplative look creeping into her eyes. "I've never deluded myself—it is true that governments are crippled by insidious forces. The incredible, almost fictional events of the past two years merely underscore what you've told me. Recent attacks on various government officials— whom certain special-interest groups want out of office by election year—prove that treachery is cancerous. Attacks on the administration are frightening. Recent high-level resignations . . . proofs of enormous payments made them . . . ." She broke off in mid-sentence, guardedly. "I'll see your needs are met," she said, terminating their talk. "If your facts prove out, I might further enlighten you." A cold, knowing nod, as she pursed her lips gave him further insight to her character. "You'll hear from me within twenty-four."

He watched her turn her back to the gusting winds tunneling at her until she disappeared into the lacy filigree of falling snow. Brad eyed the inscription above Lincoln's statue. He read: *"In this temple, as in the hearts of the people, for whom he saved the Union, the memory of Abraham Lincoln is enshrined forever."*

And so was the lingering fragrance of Valentina Lansing's perfume, Brad thought. Two things struck Brad as he stood there; one, he hadn't dared ask her to identify the Corsican, she might have bolted. Two, as instant realization of doom shot through him, it dawned on him he'd just given Valentina Lansing enough ammunition to destroy him.

Brad battled demons all night. The next morning, when a courier arrived delivering a handwritten invitation, he put the demons to rest. He was ecstatic. It was more than he expected. His presence was requested on January 20, at the Virginia residence of Senator and Mrs. Hartford B. Lansing. Guests of honor: John Macgregor, the President, and the First Lady.

The affair was black tie, the parking catered, the setting and surroundings opulence personified. Security was meticulous, crash-proof. Brad was picked up at his home, transported by chauffeured Mercedes limousine to the Lansing residence, chilled Lafite-Rothschild champagne at his fingertips, and delivered to the red-carpeted entrance of the magnificent estate. Addressed by name, security guards examined his invitation under ultraviolet hand-held flashlight and graciously welcomed him. He was announced by walkie-talkie to the next attendant.

Moving foward, his expert eyes picked out the Secret Service watching him. Behind him, approaching limousines with glaring headlights reflected snowy banks. Music piped outside through speakers filled the night air while eagle-eyed guards clustered like parasites on a host.

A sign of the times, Brad thought, moving to the front door. Affluent Americans now had to beware of social violence directed against them.

Inside, wealth like nothing he'd seen assaulted his senses. Laughter, soft music, Paris perfumes, drenched the air. A butler took his overcoat, another welcomed him to the Lansing home, served him iced champagne in a fluted glass.

Brad nodded, glass in hand, calmly as if this were a daily

occurrence, and moved through plant-filled atriums to the salons designated on his left. He sauntered slowly amid a profusion of exotic bromilliads and dazzling moss-covered hanging baskets containing jewel-colored flora indigenous to Argentina. The hacienda, its authentic Argentinean furbishings, its architectural perfection, caught his fancy more than did the scintillating dinner guests decked out in glittering Galanos, Halstons, other designer originals adorned by Van Cleef and Arpel jewels, Chopard dancing-diamond watches and exquisite diamond solitaires. All exuded personalized aromas of Hermès, Chanel, Patou and a potpourri of countless others.

By the very nature of his profession Brad was not a joiner. He did not seek recognition, nor wish to be spotlighted. He skirted the edge of the gathering, heading for a collection of art objects displayed in lighted glass cases that structured a see-through wall between two cavernous rooms. The cases containing priceless Boehme porcelain pieces, rare Gunther Grangets, prismatic sculptures in Steuben glass by Peter Aldrige, fascinated him. Waiters wheeling gold and crystal carts moved among the guests like silent sentinels, programmed to please. Somewhere in a hidden alcove the orchestra struck up a continental air with Latin music.

Brad stared at everyone and everything with meticulous preoccupation. An irrepressible laugh escaped him. He shook his head at the absurdity of believing—however long ago it was—that he ever stood a chance with Valentina. This—her magnificent world, an inbred culture and breeding flowing from her—was but one of many impediments obstructing him from a relationship with her. From the moment she left him at Lincoln Memorial, disturbing memories had assaulted him. Viewing her now, in this setting against this lush backdrop, brought the fanciful dream in his mind to a skidding halt.

It was better this way he reminded himself. The serious business at hand precluded emotional junkets into the past.

From across the crowded room he caught Valentina's glance. His requested anonymity prevailed. She nodded, but made no attempt to introduce him to the galaxy of star-studded guests. Standing next to her was Senator Lansing, a tall, attractive man of Brad's age with a crop of distinguished gray hair, a toothy grin and an all-American, boy-next-door wholesomeness still charming the voters. Next to them, President John Macgregor and the First Lady engaged in social palaver with jet-set social-ites and several film personalities.

"Hello . . ." A sultry voice jarred him from thought. "If I've ever seen a more lost, forlorn, disenchanted look on a man, I can't recall. I'm Valerie Lansing, the irrepressible daughter of Hartford and Valentina." The beautiful young woman hooked her arm into his elbow and walked alongside him. "You must have a name."

"Do my eyes play tricks on me?" Startled by the introduction, Brad glanced across the room. "You are the image of your mother! It's incredible," he muttered, astonished.

"I always have the same effect on people. The age difference is barely detectable, no?"

"I am stunned, absolutely stunned. If I didn't know better, I'd swear I was seeing Valentina forty years ago."

"You knew Mother, then?" Her eyes lit up. "Truly? In the war? Oh, dear, we must talk. We must. There's so much I don't know. So much I want to know." She dismayed, "Darn! Here comes the man of the hour. The Russian, Gregorevich or something. I must play hostess to him. But please call my office. We must meet. I want to know all about"—she cupped her hand over her lips—"him . . . know who I mean?"

Brad didn't, but he was thoroughly beguiled by Valerie. She was whisked away toward the Russian—lucky stiff—but not before she glanced back at him, adding, "Sorry we're not at the same table. You seem the only interesting guest present."

"More so than Frank Sinatra or Cary Grant?" he grinned back, charmed.

She gave him a look of long suffering. "I'll see you after dinner."

He nodded, smiled and followed the other guests.

Dinner arrangements, six to each of several round tables, filled two sizable salons. Magnificent Royal Doulton China, Waterford crystal and Argentine gold service against an impos-ing well-coordinated decor in three shades of red, from pale cyclamen pink to crimson in the muted lighting, created a grand and intimate setting. The cuisine was Argentine, the wines in gold servers bore the label Vasquez-Varga vineyards, Buenos Aires.

Brad's name card placed him between two slightly inebriated Washington socialites. His seat provided him an overall view of the guests. He gazed about casually while feigning polite attention to the chattering women. The women on his left rhapsodized over the President's miraculous recovery following a recent assassination attempt. The woman on his right shrugged.

"You know how he stays looking so young—monkey glands, my dear."

"I heard it was GH-3 from Romania. I *know* for a fact."

"Is that why *they* sneak off to Baden-Baden?" They, meaning film stars, prominent people in the publicity spotlight.

From the next table Valerie Lansing flashed Brad a smile. The woman next to him caught it.

"Valerie Lansing, the brilliant Georgetown lawyer, owns the world. Not only is she the image of her mother, she heads her own law firm, a sky's-the-limit practice, if you know what I mean. Cases referred to her begin at the five figure level. Some people have all the luck."

Brad listened, but his eyes were on the captivating Valerie Lansing. Then, for an instant, he did a double take. The men seated at either side of her were *Company men!* Why should that astonish him? Before he dissected his uneasy feelings, dinner ended. Coffee and brandy was served in the next salon.

Valentina artfully disengaged herself from a circle of admirers. Sheer artistry, Brad thought, observing a performance of cultured grace and panache stemming from years of aristocratic breeding. For an instant the image of her in battle fatigues, as she dug her own slit trench in the Libyan desert alongside all the brave Free French soldiers at the Gazala Line, struck him. How she had existed on less than adequate rations in oven-intensity temperatures boggled his mind. He studied the stark contrast.

In her shell-pink Galanos chiffon, the only adornment a twenty-carat pear-shaped fiery diamond suspended from a platinum chain at her neck, she skillfully whisked Brad away from the party.

"Come see my collection of Spanish Masters," she said aloud, leading him through another plant-filled solarium, past a circular staircase toward a corridor leading to the east wing. Two Secret Service men in black tie lingering nearby nodded to them in passing.

Valentina moved languidly, gesturing as if she described a manificent sunset, but her voice urged caution.

"Don't keep him too long. I can manage fifteen, twenty

minutes without arousing the curiosity of the Secret Service. I arranged dinner for them in one of the salons." She smiled at her own cleverness. "How this takes me back to the ETO, Major."

Brad smiled. At the appointed place along the corridor she disengaged her arm from his, and calling to someone descending the staircase, left him to fend for himself.

He moved swiftly, opened the door, entered the dimly lighted room, closing it behind him.

"Lock it," came the firm command.

Brad complied. He turned to the man standing in partial shadow before the fireplace, staring at the portrait of Valentina Lansing. Brad coughed slightly. "Uh, Mr. President—"

"Yes, yes, come in, Major." John Macgregor turned to him, his hand extended in a warm handshake. "Good to see you again, Brad. It's been too long, old friend. Come, sit by the fire and get to the point. Why the hush-hush encounter? Why not the Oval Office? Is the matter *that* sensitive?" Undisguised annoyance crept into the President's blue eyes.

He sat down in a leather chair opposite the President. Carefully he began speaking the words he had rehearsed earlier.

"Documentation of a meeting between us would pose dangerous threats to both of us, sir. I'll need your ear for some twenty minutes. I'll tell you what I have so far."

The President listened in rapt absorption. Twenty-four minutes later he said, "You intelligence men work in strange ways, Brad." He marveled at and disputed Brad's tactics in one breath. "But why keep the White House at bay?"

"Leaks during the earlier stages of this operation could bring death to my contacts. I *know* you, Mr. President. I *trust* you. But the White House employs countless people." He cited names, dates, case histories, wiretapping, to prove his point.

"You speak of two crucial sources. One man, an enigma, by your own words—what guarantee have you of his willingness to cooperate, say if your theory proves true."

"He must—if I can identify him—or without him we go no further. You see, it's not just a theory. I've plenty of facts."

"I gather you need something urgent from me?"

"Uh, yes, sir. Clearance to *GAMMA 10.*" The explosion came on cue.

"Negative, Brad. *Negative!*" Macgregor shook his head

39

furiously. "I need no more enemies. One nearly got to me in my first year in office."

"Sir, before you became President, long before—I'm talking World War II days—the OSS and British MI collected thousands of files, *secret* files on matters that can prove embarrassing to many nations. I must have access to those files. I desperately need to contact *one* man, a friend, our *own* man, sir, *allegedly* buried in *deep cover*. I need to know *why* he was buried and *what* circumstances drove him to that fate. Moreover, *why* in Company files he is listed as deceased when in fact he is alive as you and me. This man can direct me to the Corsican."

"You realize what you ask of me?"

"Yes, sir. We could both end up at Arlington."

The President blinked hard. He exhaled a long, low whistle. "You *know* what to go for? I mean, there's a helluva lot of plowing to do before you strike gold. There might be a leak before you exit the file room." He shook his head dubiously. "I don't know about all this . . ."

Sensing uncertainty, Brad pressed on. "The agent I spoke of was a friend. The Company's *official* paper on him stinks to hell and back. The plus factor? I know *GAMMA 10* inter-op procedure by rote. I can handle myself. I promise."

"You don't buy the defection?" The President probed. "Brad, he disappeared, as I recall, in a twinkling, with all the earmarks of a pre-planned op."

"No, sir, I don't buy the defection. You don't share life-or-death situations with a man for twenty years without knowing something about him, his personality, his weaknesses, his strengths."

"Hell, Brad," the President chuckled. "I've lived with my wife longer. She's still a stranger to me."

"Not in life-or-death situations—"

"The hell you say! You've never been married. On a serious note, you are convinced the needed information is in *GAMMA 10*? No shredding of evidence took place to deny his existence, leaving him to sink or swim?"

Brad felt increasingly uneasy. He glanced about the room surreptitiously, his concern conveyed to the President.

"It's clean, Brad. The Senator is scrupulously meticulous in this aspect. No bugs. That *is* your concern?"

"Not exactly—uh, sir—I mentioned no names. Were you

briefed on the alleged defection? It isn't something any Chief Executive would know."

The President nodded.

"A fair question. No, I was not briefed. But, I do know the party to whom you refer. I have your complete dossier. In it is contained your personal and professional history. When I first stumbled on the name, I had every reason to be concerned in lieu of a recent assassination attempt on my life. Your next question is why did I find it necessary to study *your* dossier? Specifically, six months ago I altered your position from the NSA to a clandestine post of special advisor to the President."

"I beg your pardon—" Brad tensed. "I don't understand." But he did. The sudden *executive order* to attend Pentagon hearings!

"Six men—you, and five others—each unaware of his actual contributions to the Presidency for the past six months—were placed in strategic areas of government, to report without prejudice what is actually taking place. Information generally unavailable to the President, yet vital to his existence was funneled to me without the usual scrutiny of others who might have personal reasons to change the facts."

Brad's confusion was obvious as he listened intently.

"I've depended on your eyes and ears, your objective thinking, to funnel the facts to me via an undetectable pipeline."

"Forgive me, sir. I am not obtuse, but I don't understand."

"You're not supposed to, yet."

"I've made no reports to you—"

"You have, without knowing it."

His confusion total, he waited numbly for an explanation.

"Your eyes and ears interceded. Everything that piqued your attention at the committee hearings came directly to me through the electronic devices rigged in your console. Special apparatus, sensors, built into your desk console at X-212 provided me with duplicates of all your notations, all video cassettes, voice and ocular tapes. Every witness whose testimony provoked your interest, you underlined and I got the dupes."

"Why the secrecy?"

"To protect you as well as the President. Your earlier statement is one I appreciate. *The White House employs many people.* The question plaguing all Presidents has always been: *Whom can I trust?* Must I diagram for you the schemes of pressure groups leaning on previous briefing officers to present information supporting their own ideas?''

"No, sir," Brad acknowledged, then he decided to press his point home. "You are aware that Minister Mubende was killed before he could identify those special-interest power brokers?''

"You refer to Mubende's unscheduled apperance on the agenda?'' The President gestured his frustration. "Ah, yes. Unfortunately, news of his presence at the hearings failed to reach me in time to take measures to avert his tragic death. A foolish move on Mubende's part for not exercising proper protocol.''

"Perhaps with good reason, sir. I mean for *not* employing usual protocol. Before communiques reach the Oval Office, they pass several levels of influence—no?''

"Ah ha!'' Macgregor stared into the fire. "You mean there might have been a fatality *before* he arrived in D.C.? That might have been less complicated all around. *Damned!* Why did he have to be killed here? Why a Ugandan? It makes a stinking mess for us in the media.''

"Sir—about *GAMMA 10*—''

"That again, eh?''

"I see no other options open.''

"If you fail—my signature got you inside *GAMMA 10*!''

"They'll never know *why*.''

"Hah!''

"Mr. President, you *know* what I'm after. A basis does exist for the smoke signals sent up by various foreign embassies. I need time to prove or disprove them. After studying those *GAMMA 10* files, I'll know if I'm on the right track. If I am correct, I estimate a saving of six months. Precious time is evaporating.''

"You *really* believe that, Brad?''

"If I didn't, the personal risks I inflicted on a very special lady, by implication—''

"I understand.'' Macgregor raised a silencing hand. "The circumstances warranted drastic means.'' The President considered quietly, then spoke. "What in hell are you priming me for?''

"I don't know. God, I don't know. That's what makes it frustrating. We've gotta take chances, see where they lead.''

"Hopefully not to a Musaka Mubende exit. I don't want your death on my conscience.''

"That, sir, is an area of agreement I respect. But I am afraid if action isn't taken, global genocide will lay heavily on someone's conscience."

"You actually believe the organization Mubende alluded to exists?" the President asked somberly.

"Don't you, sir?"

The President sighed. "You know how highly I regard you, Brad. By the very nature of your involvement these past six months, I've learned more than I have in two years. What I'm saying is, you've always been a drum beater for justice. Fair, impartial. I needed that impartiality to steady the boat and keep it afloat in recent months."

"Do you have my complete dossier, Mr. President?"

The President, unaccustomed to being interrupted, nodded.

"My *military* dossier and Intelligence history?" The Chief nodded again. "From my early OSS days? . . . Good. Brief yourself on *OPERATION WHITE CORAL*. Circa: November, 1942."

"*White Coral?*" Macgregor searched his memory.

"I doubt you'd know it off the top of your head. Your war arena was the South Pacific. This was ETO. *WHITE CORAL*, code name for the Corsican Liberation prior to V-E Day—"

"What will I find in those files, Brad?"

"If I knew, I'd spell it out, sir. The man I'm seeking was integral in those operations *and* the North African Campaign."

"He was involved in *that* operation?"

"We all were. The Allies, I mean. Out of that era sprang a remarkable young man, an unsung hero. Rommel's books, his diaries give an accounting of him. Rommel refers to all his battles, but he praises the tactics employed by a young innovative man and his extraordinary associates, named them his most viable enemies."

"You've gone far afield, Brad. Back up. I'm not the military man of Ike's genre."

"Think a moment, sir. The thorn in Rommel's side?"

"Besides Hitler's failure to provide the needed supplies?"

"The most spectacular phenomenon of the North African campaign," Brad held firmly to the tack.

"Here sits the American President playing guessing games with a die-hard soldier *sans passemeterie*. What would the *Washington Post* make of this? Far more expeditious if you told me straight out. Wait a minute . . . I've got it. SAS crack

Commando units. Courageous, lionhearted daredevils spawned by the British Eighth Army—"

"*Bull's eye!* Humans turned into vicious killer dogs of war. Men who murdered, slaughtered the enemy daily in ways that paled Berber atrocities. Death squads, trained in secret camps in Britain, skilled in sabotage, intelligence gathering, plastic explosives, massacre and anything ordered by the top brass. Not all were British. A potpourri of all nations acclimated to desert conditions from the Foreign Legion were integrated into Free French and British 8th Armies. The SAS Commandos created such a groundswell that several world tyrants and power brokers recognized their potentials, their efficient, mechanized ability to obliterate—in essence to topple—governments."

"Major!" The President frowned, grew guarded, his voice dropping to a whisper. "Why are you telling me this?"

"The Commandos, those death squads, were led by an exceptional young man—"

"Not now! Don't utter another word. Understand?" He cautioned.

Brad understood perfectly. The matter was off the *official* record.

Then the lock sprung open. "You'll receive what you requested on Monday. By God, if you get my ass in a sling, I'll deny knowing you!" He grinned. "Uh—those liquor-filled Dutch chocolates you sent during my convalescence were spirited away by the Secret Service. I was damned lucky to lay my hands on one or two. How the hell did you get the contraband into the States?"

"If I answer, I'd implicate the President in a felony. Is this a request for another sampling?"

"If I confirmed your query, the President would be implicated in conspiracy. You decide."

"Glad you enjoyed them. I prayed for your recovery."

"So did I. I'm in hock to St. Patrick for the miracles performed on me. Some target practice, eh?"

"You will be careful, Mr. President. Look to your flanks at all times." Then Brad changed tack. "Did your experts analyze the Mubende ocular and voice tapes?"

The President nodded, his full attention focused on Brad's words. "What alerted you? Why did you record Mubende?"

"Facts. For the first time in chambers facts were stated

44

unequivocably—not rumors or ambiguities, but facts. I had to test his veracity.''

"You did. He wasn't lying. For the record, neither was the Russian, Greogrevich.''

"I agree. He took chances with that prepared text.''

"But he exercised proper protocol—he came loaded with personal protection.''

Quickly then, Brad wrapped up the briefing, while Macgregor scribbled on a white card. ''Rid yourselves of the tapes. Send them to this name and address. It's a blind, or as you chaps call it, a cover drop. You understand, Major, there can be no memorandum of what was discussed between us. If for any reason you stumble into trouble, the usual denials will be disseminated to the press.''

"You've described a dying man, Mr. President. Thank God I'm a former swimming champion.''

"Oh, for Christsakes, be careful!''

31 JANUARY 1983

Brad wheeled a rented VW van through the Pentagon garage, parked in the visitors' area, taking precautions to avoid committee hearing members. He approached Sector Five which was guarded by iron gates and two-fisted guards postured like a SWAT team.

The Sector, *GAMMA 10*, was soundproof. Two silent, stony-faced armed guards sat at desks banked against walls at either side of a portcullis, serving dual purposes as obstructors and electronic detectors. Brad stopped on command, submitted falsified, foolproof cover credentials to one of the stone statues. In lieu of a guard's accompaniment inside the file room, Brad subjected himself to an intense strip-and-search. Convinced he carried no concealed weapons or devices to photograph or destroy file contents, the portcullis was raised at the touch of a button, admitting him to an inner corridor, and descending with a loud clatter, locked shut behind him.

GAMMA 10! A death trap! An electric mausoleum spelling death to the unsophisticated, uninitiated trespasser! It was enough to send the blood pressure soaring.

Brad marshaled every ounce of clever expertise to outsmart the enemy. The *enemy*? Electronics! High-powered, dual-controlled camera-scanning apparatus working in tandem. There was ultra-sensitive equipment with zoom-in capabilities, and lenses capable of magnifying with clear definition any of the files he desperately needed to review. Beating the camera lenses at their game didn't fall into the category of child's play. High-speed electronic shutters could catch a *fucking* flea fornicating in flight! But this wasn't the only problem. The lethal aspect to be outfoxed— sensors! Clever, electronically controlled sensors recorded, upon entry into *GAMMA 10*, the subject's heartbeats, establishing a norm for his blood pressure rate. It was essential to maintain the same frequency, *doing* nothing, *thinking* nothing to interrupt the apparatus' established rhythm. Any deviation triggered a secondary apparatus with spying capabilities.

Cameras would swing about, fix tightly on the subject, setting off alarms in a nearby control booth. If that knowledge wasn't enough to jog the blood pressure, colored lights, synchronized with muted beeps, automatically set off panic buttons. Security guards, dispatched instantly to trouble spots, guns at ready, were primed to shoot first, *never* ask questions, later.

Forced to devise advance strategy to outfox the electronics, Brad came prepared. What he contemplated was tricky—deadly if he didn't pull it off. The trick was to stay cool, detached as hell, and bore the goddamned cameras into maintaining the established stats programmed on contact. Primed for every second spent inside this mausoleum, he wore tinted prescription lenses to throw off eye-print devices.

His plan was neat, simple and straightforward; he had seconds to engineer his strategy as thick leaded doors swung open admitting him.

Christ! Inside Gamma 10! It was awesome!

Aided and abetted by tranquilizers, Brad moved languidly along rows of file cabinets, ignoring the cameras as if they didn't exist. Peripherally he observed them taking their damnable statistics.

He inserted a plastic card into two slots. File drawers popped open at either side of him. Casually he set about his search, pulling out decoy files along with the actual files he needed.

He glanced at his watch. Twelve-ten. Good! Lunchtime was always the best time for clandestine shenanigans because guards were less inclined to sharper scrutiny when hunger pangs churned stomachs.

Gripping the files in one hand, Brad felt spying eyes zoom in, scanning the decoy files. Freezing all emotional responses, he stacked them together, highly visible decoys on top, and toted them to the desk at room center. He removed his jacket, stretched, yawned, feigning a leisurely stance before he sat down. His attitude was that of a bored bookkeeper. He picked up the first decoy, studied it intently. Cameras front and back began doing their work.

Brad controlled his breathing, a technique studied to perfection in Hatha Yoga. He probed the decoys, whistled airily, and marked time. At twelve-thirty he discerned audible reduction in camera activity. Following a perceptive silence, the scanners fell to a normal drone.

Very good! He opened the sought-after files stacked between the decoys, began to examine volatile information, unprepared for what greeted him.

In the next two hours, lessons of a forty-year career were tested. Words leapt off the pages, startling him. He was shocked by the infinitely lethal knowledge. Forced to employ extraordinary will power, he maintained composure while drowning in a staggering preponderance of complex material. Innocent men had been murdered, their deaths disguised as natural or accidental. *Concentrate . . . Memorize . . . Stay cool!*

The task of absorbing the deadly information infected him, giving birth to questions he should have asked himself in the past and had not. Had he devoted a lifetime of sham to his nation? Had he hypnotized himself into believing the American way was the *only* way? The *right* way? *You're no fucking cherry, Brad, you're the joke of the century!*

The *fucking* joke of the century!

Routed from a somnambulistic sleep, propelled by wild confusion, Brad fumed inward, damned and cursed the system, the men responsible for the file's contents. He found them out for what they were and felt sicker because he'd been part of them—an automaton programmed to move at the push of a button.

Don't play the god Momus, Brad, not now! This isn't the time to blow away your mental straightjacket!

He was finished. Three hours later he replaced the files, locked the drawers, rang for a release guard.

Outside—away from *GAMMA 10*—he did mental cartwheels

of joy. He had done it! He had outwitted the omnipotent electronic pharaohs of *GAMMA 10!*

Major Brad Lincoln drove home in the rental VW, taking a circuitous route to avoid possible tails. He took himself sternly in hand, forced himself to make no moral judgments, not until he had all the facts. Resentment and disaffection for the system served no immediate purpose and could prove lethal. He didn't believe his own hype, but the words had to sustain him.

Don't author your own paranoia, Brad!

The next logical step for him was to take a leave of absence from committee hearings, patch together some strategy and move the hell out of D.C. to his goal. By the time logic dovetailed into clear-cut answers he was aboard a 747 soaring over half the world.

Chapter Two

LONDON, PARIS, LUCERNE, SWITZERLAND

THE INSANITY BEGAN WITH TOUCHDOWN AT HEATHROW Airport in London. Brad enacted a ridiculous itinerary—the wanderings of a madman! After wading through customs at Heathrow, he turned around, boarded a plane to Orly in Paris. Deplaning at Orly, negotiating through customs, he picked up a ticket awaiting him and soared back over the Channel, returning to Heathrow.

Anyone observing the schizophrenic antics would declare him certifiable. Assuring himself it was too soon for a tail, he cast about wary eyes for that unmistakable face behind a newspaper or a dark look among the air terminal crowds and aboard planes that just didn't belong. He saw nothing intimidating.

The aerodynamic gymnastics continued to Rome, Madrid, West Berlin, until Brad was certain his role as a gawking tourist had attracted no one. Finally he booked passage on Air France to Zurich. From Kloten Airport he took the local to Lucerne.

A VILLAGE NEAR LUCERNE

Jim Greer, hulking, six-foot former CIA specialist, displayed increased agitation as he paced the wooden floor of his rustic chalet. The recluse, dressed in heavy mountain clothing exuded a sullen menace. Built like a Rams' linebacker, the added weight of a beer-belly paunch and unkempt shoulder-length brown hair streaked wildly with silver and a thick beard covering most of his face added to his threatening appearance.

He paused to stoke the fire, and dusting off his hands, watched it until the logs ignited. He glanced at the young woman seated on a nearby sofa working macrame and scowled fiercely.

A short-wave transmitter had relayed disturbing information earlier, from a friend in Allweg, a hamlet some six miles along a treacherous path of narrow, hairpin turns down the mountain. *"Eine Amerikaner* asking directions to *Herr* Zeigfried Manhauser's chalet just left the *konditorei,"* the friend had told him. The description given Greer could have meant anyone. He was taking no chances.

He gazed outside at the darkening sky, over a frozen landscape.

"A storm front is moving in," he said to the young *fräulein.*

"You have an hour. In this weather he's lucky to do five miles an hour." Berna sipped hot grog and glanced tacitly at the arsenal on one wall and at others strewn about the sitting room. At her side was a Belgian .9mm Browning. Greer wore a holstered Czech M52. Dragunov sniper rifles with telescopic sights, UZ58s, M-16s and other high-powered shotguns rested in niches on the wall. "You know who is coming?"

Greer shook his head. He turned to the slim, tall woman dressed in fitted jeans, knee-high fur-lined boots, and a turtleneck sweater. A perpetual insolence and mistrust darted from dark, penetrating eyes. Flaxen curly hair, pulled off her face, fell into a thick side braid over one shoulder.

"You shouldn't be here."

"Then I shall leave."

"No! I want you here."

"No. Yes! Stay! Go! Which shall it be?" She shook her head, repudiating his behavior. "Why do you disturb yourself? You have the advantage, *ja*? Guns . . . dogs. If he proves an enemy, do as you have in the past." She raised one hand, pointed her upraised thumb and forefinger at him. "Pow," she said softly.

"Thirty-eight notches in the stock of the Dragunov are enough. I don't ache for the thirty-ninth. I'm weary. Can you understand?"

Her brows lifted imperceptibly and fell softly in place; she stored sights, sounds, Greers's reaction under pressure in a nodule of her brain. She shrugged and deftly continued to braid and knot jute, twisting brightly colored wool skeins into unusual designs.

Greer, on edge, paced the floor, mulling over the disturbing news he'd received earlier and hadn't confided to Berna. A trusted conduit in a nearby village conveyed the approach of an American. Another leaked the news that a former World War II confidante was asking discreet questions concerning Greer. It had to be Brad Lincoln. Whatever complications brewed stateside, the inquiries only meant one thing to Greer. And he panicked!

"Twenty fucking years and not a word!" he blurted, burning a hole in the carpet with a neglected cigarette. He stomped it out, releasing some of the pent-up frustrations. "Now he has the gall to ask about me? Something is wrong. I don't like it."

"You told me you didn't know who—" Berna said quietly.

"I know," Greer snapped. "I know what I said. But I've been adding a few things up in my mind and I've got a sneaking hunch it's my old partner. It's gotta be! Someone knows he's the only man I'd trust. Now, after all the others, they picked him to do the job."

"You mean—uh—what's-his-name? You told me about him."

"Brad Lincoln. *Major* Brad Lincoln," he said snidely, pouring a tumbler of brandy, guzzling it all in a fell swoop.

"After twenty years? He should come now? It makes no sense."

"You don't know them. They'll strike when they are least expected."

"Tell me about him." She packed a bong with hashish, lighted it, and taking a hit, handed it to Greer. He helped himself, and began to speak.

"What can I say? We met at Maryland University, joined the Army, transferred to the OSS in the Guerilla and Resistance Branch, patterned after British Special Operations Executive. World War II battlegrounds initiated us in the blackest side of existence. Later, in the early 50's, we worshipped at the temple of the CIA. The mark of Dante's Inferno was etched on our minds indelibly."

"You were paramilitary. An SOD, *ja*?"

"On the button," Greer said, the drug relaxing him. "Special Operations Division—the animals of the Agency. We employed gangster tactics, dealt in force, violence and terrorism. When the SOD waged war, only the rules of war would apply. For me it meant *kill* or be *killed*. Failure to do our jobs meant death to me and my men." He took another hit from the bong. "Lincoln's classification was different from mine."

"He was non-paramilitary, *ja*? You told me his affiliation with the Agency was that of a covert operator who worked with unbloodied hands, whose crimes were categorized as conspiracy, bribery, corruption, *nein*?"

"Right again, *fräulein*. You remember," Greer said with a trace of sarcasm, "Brad was a fast-talking con-man who dealt in the creative plotting, orchestration and successful conclusions of clandestine political campaigns *without* resorting to violence. If he failed, he'd merely be expelled from the nation in which he operated."

"You have the distinct advantage over him, *nein*? So why do you worry if he comes here?"

"Don't kid yourself," he said harshly, "we're both experts in survival."

Berna switched over to French. "*Oui, je comprend*. But this man Lincoln remains inactive—at some desk job—*oui*?"

"Where did you hear that?"

"Where else?"

"Corsica?"

"*Oui*. I have studied both your dossiers at length."

"*Puorquoi*?" Greer stared hard at her, ticking his beard.

"Part of my training. Why else? Nothing is discounted."

Unsettled, Greer moved to the window, watching the huskies frolic in the snow. He rechecked the M52 for the fourth time, did likewise with the Dragunov. "If it's him—and we can't be certain—but if it *is* him, what does the son of a bitch want?"

Berna shook her head in mild amusement. "Poof! Men are all alike. Would it not suit you to wait and see? You are prepared for all eventualities. Why do you fret? *Je ne comprend pas*."

"That's right! You don't. How could you? You don't live here alone, isolated from civilization, practicing deception day after day, year after year, dreading that one moment when saying the wrong thing will draw attention. Anyone I meet could be a potential weapon aiming for my death. You come and go at your discretion. At least you can drop your guard periodically."

"Speak to Moufflon. He would help you."

"No. I pose liabilities to everyone with whom I come in contact. My crime is not a forgivable crime!"

"Honesty, dedication of purpose, loyalty to your nation is considered a crime in America?. . . *Mon Dieu!* I wish never to live there."

Greer smiled wanly. He turned from the treacherous snowy scene beyond the property lines, from the distant icicle peaks across the valley, then jerked his head around obliquely, listening.

Berna listened, her attention rapt. Her eyes followed Greer, watching him. "The dogs," she said quietly. "Someone approaches."

Outside, the Siberian Huskies, secured on thick link chains between two enormous pine trees, barked menacingly. Baring vicious fanged teeth, they growled deep-throated sounds. They strained at the chains, suddenly wild at the new scents. Greer peered intently through the steaming window.

A Land Rover approached. The barking, snarls and hissings became louder; the yellow-fanged canines could be depended on to intimidate the driver. He watched the driver cautiously open the door.

"Gutsy bastard! He's out of the car!" Greer snarled, rifle in hand. Most trespassers wouldn't chance encounter with the black-and-white killer dogs. "I can't make him out. Too much snow!" He cursed with renewed ferocity. Berna joined him at the window.

"He's carrying something."

"Son of a bitch! What the fuck can he want? I don't like it!"

Greer opened the door a crack, thrust the barrel of the rifle through it. His voice, loud, hostile, cried out in a crude German, "STOP! Don't take another step! Identify yourself!"

"Ich bin einer Americaner, Herr Manhauser . . . Brad Lincoln here." He was wary, economical with words, should the man behind the door prove not to be Greer.

The rifle barrel lingered a fraction, inched back a hair, Greer opened the door, wider, tossing Berna an 'I told you so' look.

Framed in the open doorway, rifle in one hand, the M52 in the other, his pose was ferocious.

"Is it you, ol' buddy? It's Brad. Can we *parle* a while?"

"Stop! I'm warning you! Move an inch and you're dead!"

The voice was cold, the expression deadly. "What's in the box?"

Brad glanced at the box—pastries purchased at the *konditorei* in Allweg. "Jesus! Just pastries. I remembered your sweet tooth—that's all!"

"Drop it! On the ground . . . that's it. Back up. Are you armed? Don't bother to lie. I'll know soon enough."

Brad complied instantly, nodding or shaking his head in answer. He observed Greer blow a silent, high-pitched whistle inaudible to human ears as he lumbered off the snowy deck, and descended the few steps to ground level. He ordered Brad up against the deck rail, spread-eagled. He did a quick touch and feel as an enormous German shepherd with long pointed ears came loping toward them.

"Fritz!" Greer commanded. "The box!"

The sable-colored sleuth, trained to detect weapons and ammunition, approached cautiously, prowling, sniffing, glancing tentatively at Brad. He grasped the string through his teeth, toted it to his master's feet, dropped it gently. He stared at his master waiting, panting, saliva dripping.

Observing the ritual, Brad's thoughts shaped around the sight. *What the hell had Greer endured since he left the States?*

Relaxing his disapproval, he understood Greer's caution and on his signal entered the chalet, momentarily startled by the presence of the girl. Greer stomped his feet outside on the deck and entered behind him.

"Berna," Greer spoke in German. "Not to worry. He is a friend, I think. *Ich erlaube mir, Major Brad Lincoln.* Put the gun away."

"*Einer Amerikaner?*" the word *Amerikaner*, dipped in vitreol, irked Brad, as did her disdaining manner.

He nodded. "*Fräulein, ich freue mich, Sie kennenzulernen.*"

Her dark incrutable eyes penetrated his as she strode past him in panther-like strides. She hoisted a rifle expertly into its niche in a wall case and set about making a pot of coffee at the far end of the sitting room, in the kitchenette.

Now that he was facing the man he had come so far to see, Brad stood for a moment, considering his next move. "We must talk, Jim," He glanced at Berna. "Alone."

"Talk. She doesn't understand English. Oh, a cuss word or

two, nothing else. She's fluent in French, German, Italian, Spanish and would you believe—Japanese? But no English.''

Struck at once by the combination of languages, Brad didn't believe she had learned no English. He kept silent; he would wait.

Over hot coffee and strudel, warmed by the fire on the hearth, he was unable to ignore the girl's penetrating eyes. The face could be handsome, but it remained hard, closed, the eyes shadowed with hostility. Brad took these moments to acquaint himself with the Bavarian-like rustic interior. Too Spartan for his own taste, it helped him understand Greer's position.

Finally, when neither Greer nor the girl were inclined to communicate, Brad floundered. ''Aren't you curious to know why I'm here?''

''Knowing you, you'll tell me when you're ready.''

''That's all? Not 'What the hell are you doing here after all these years?' ''

''That, too. I've learned patience. You're looking good.''

''I don't know how, after all I've been through—''

''Go ahead, cry on my shoulder—'' Greer's voice dripped contempt.

''All right,'' Brad snapped, seized the opening and began to dig for the information he sought. ''In your own words, tell me what happened in 1963?''

''Why? What's it to you? You still on the spook squad?'' Greer snarled.

''No. The NSA. Presently—'' he glanced at Berna—''liaison for the Chief Executive.''

Greer's smoky eyes sparked alive. He poured coffee, munched strudel, brushing the crumbs from his beard.

''Liaison for what?''

''Before I tell you, I've got to hear your version of that day in November.''

''What do you know?''

''GAMMA 10 files allude to your complicity in the Dallas tragedy—''

''*GAMMA 10?* You penetrated GAMMA 10?'' Greer instinctively felt the holstered M52. ''You *saw* the files?'' His voice turned deadly. ''Only the DCI sanctions GAMMA 10 penetration! You still work for them!''

''No! I told you no! How do I get through to you?''

"You won't. You're still a spook!"

"Negative. Listen—only one signature transcends the Director's. The President's."

"So tell me another fairy tale," he sneered.

"You're acting irrational. I'm telling the truth. All right, let me tell you what I learned and why my curiosity was aroused. The files indicate you either conspired in the main body of the Dallas plot or reported to someone high on the totem of command. By so doing you inadvertently placed associates and the Company itself in dire jeopardy. Included in the whereases, therefores, heretofores, and usual planted mumbo jumbo they alluded to defection. *Defection!* That tuned me out. I refused to believe you had sold out to any group hostile to America's interests. The way I summed it up was—that day spelled death for the President by assassins' bullets, and for you, Jim, extinction. I believed the first half of that scenario but not the second."

"Why rehash it? In twenty years reruns grow stale. I was a fool. Yet, if I had it to do again . . . ."

"I must hear the truth from you," Brad urged. "I can't negotiate if you aren't clean. If you're dirty or have gone double— nothing's possible. We'd be knocked out of the ball game before we got to bat."

"What in hell are you *talking* about?"

"I'm trying to tell you—"

Greer jumped to his feet, his temper exploding. "In twenty years I heard nothing from you! Now you trek halfway around the globe to determine *if* I'm a loyal American?" He was outraged, the tension caused by the unexpected meeting snapping his control.

Berna resumed her macrame, busy fingers tying, knotting swiftly. At her side, the Belgian Browning.

Brad lifted his hands, conciliatory.

"I'm trying to tell you—a remote chance exists to reinstate you—if you can be instrumental in a highly covert operation."

"*Bullshit!*"

"The Oval Office packs enough weight—"

"*Goddamit,* Brad, I'm no cherry!" Greer pivoted on one foot, stared at Brad, his face cool, curiously expressionless. What he saw in Brad's eyes caused his mind to spin out in the fast lanes of thought. "How? What can the Oval Office do when others with more clout failed? For Christsakes, be realistic! The man was a recent victim of an assassination attempt!''

"By a psycho-kid." Brad sipped coffee, playing down the incident.

Greer's contemptuous laughter bounced off the walls. "Believe that and you're a fool! Oh, shit! this is crazy! Why do I listen? You *fuckin'* Americans! *Fuckin'* naive—the lot of you! Let me tell you, ol' buddy, the last President I believed in was picked off like a *fuckin'* tin can off a *fuckin'* fence. And the *fuckin'* ostrich-Americans won't admit what happened! Don't care what happened! Else they'd have fired the fuckin' Warren Commission off their fat asses, and booted them outa their *fuckin'* fat-paying jobs! You want truth? I'll give you truth! *Your* man, like *my* man, can't do shit!''

"If I believed that, I wouldn't be here, risk my life or yours to talk with you. The only word I could get from anyone in the Company was you were *buried* in *deep cover*."

"And you believed it? After twenty years?"

"You would have, if you'd been in my shoes. You didn't turn sour until *after* November 23, 1963!''

The words hit home. Berna lit the bong and handed it to Greer. He took a hit, passed it to Brad who refused. "Look, I came to learn from you what happened. How you got to Switzerland? Who protected you? If I don't know the answers, we can't deal. The talk ends here."

Cagily, Greer asked, "How come you don't believe GAMMA 10?''

"I told you. Too much oversell. They painted you all black with no shadings. They bagged you for security leaks to the Kremlin. KGB ties. It was too pat for me to swallow. I sniffed the stinking fraud instantly. According to the reports, you were separated from the Agency, October '63—''

Greer's eyes widened in astonishment.

"—yet I found records of scheduled assignments someone failed to shred, up to and including November, through to December 1963. Someone before midnight on November 22, 1963 sent smoke signals out of Langley, coded printouts screamed: S.O.S.—James Greer . . . S.O.S! *SHOOT ON SIGHT!* Explain, please."

Greer studied his former partner, then spoke quietly.

"Simply . . . I made a dangerous enemy of the DCI. No small

fry for Jim Greer, he hadda bag the biggest game.'' Greer went to the cooler, brought out cans of beer, and slipping into a pair of calf-lined fur boots, tossed logs onto the fire.

"It was November 22, 1963 . . . Six P.M. . . . New Orleans . . . The Opium Den . . . A joint frequented by dissidents, dope dealers, foreign agents—the worms of the earth.''

Brad knew the place. Society's misfits congregated there and hatched harebrained schemes to bring world attention to them.

". . . It began there. That night the joint was packed. The back bar television was turned into the President's Dallas trip. Christ! What press coverage! His charisma lured people to him like pussy to hot cock. A ball-bustin' shit-faced slob I worked with in Korea put the arm on me, lured me into having a drink with him. Horned Toad Harry—Caligula''—Greer paused, but Brad spoke quickly; he didn't want Greer to stop remembering.

"I know that name. You refused to work with him following 'Nam.''

"That's the one! . . . Why did I listen to that cocksucker? . . . Insanity locked me into his frequency for forty minutes. When I left the Opium Den I possessed a terrifying secret. *Shit!* Like a *goddamn* jerk, Brad, I hadda drop a dime on him. When the music played—Jesus! *What* it played!'' His voice fell an octave. He stared into the fire. Brad waited for the words to continue.

"He was flying a death squad into Dallas the next day to waste the President! *My* President! President of *my* country! Ain't that a kick in the ass? My nation, *goddammit!* A nation I had sworn to serve and had in four *fuckin'* wars! They were gonna kill *my* President!'' In his raging renunciation he spun around, eyes fiery, skin reddened from the intense heat of the flames on the hearth.

He exasperated. "*Fuckin'* asshole! I should have forgotten it and split. For two weeks—*two whole weeks*—that S.O.B. was in Dallas laying ground work, planning alternative action in case the Secret Service made last-minute revisions in the travel itinerary. He got the itinerary straight from the Secret Service! Christ, Brad, if you'd heard that *muthuhfucker* shoot off his mouth in *Company* jargon, placing me in equal jeopardy . . . ! That S.O.B. *knew* what he was doing! I still see that cocksucker laughing at me in my nightmares! Sure—I was a *schmuck*. A real *schmuckaroo*. That prick unveiled the device. Fourth-level plotting—look alikes. Garrison in New Orleans had it right on the button. He cracked the assassination plot at the *operational* level. Seventeen—maybe more eyewitnesses—mysteriously dead, and the fuckin' Warren Commission perjures itself! Did Americans speak out against these men, supported by their own tax dollars! No. There was no outcry from the private sector! A few brave warriors attempted, but got shot down. Listen, you give the *fuckin'* apathetic citizenry jobs, welfare states, a preprogrammed television set that fucks their heads and you anesthetize them into zombies. Let a voice tell them to go buy Lichtenstein beer long enough—even if it's rotgut—and they'll march to the markets, scream and yell until they get the damn stuff. Even if they die!''

Greer stopped. He waved his arms in a disorganized gesture, implying the futility of digging up the past.

''Then you know the truth of that day?''

''The *truth*?'' Greer spit out the words. ''Is anyone really interested? The truth was a squad of programmed paramilitary spooks, free-lance mercenaries following assassination blueprints, were flown into the field of action, wasted the target and split. Concealed guns strategically positioned at intervals along the parade route as back-ups provided insurance if any of the five missed. That zaps the *lone-gun* theory! The Zapruder film told the story. The Commission wasn't interested. They *knew* the fuckin' truth! The President had no chance—none at all—of surviving. Like I said, following the kill, the assassins split . . . they were flown out of the country before the shit hit the fan. You know the rest.''

Brad's suspicions were confirmed, but he had to know more. It was imperative to his own mission that he track Greer's role to the end. ''No, I don't. You didn't tell me what happened when you left the Opium Den.'' he prodded.

''Oh, that . . . well, I got the hell outa New Orleans in a car rental, crossed the Pontchartrain Causeway over the lake, eased into Mandeville mulling over Caligula's venom. Christ! My mind became a *fuckin'* battleground. I reasoned, fighting enemies was one thing, but destroying *my* nation from within? Uh-uh! Call it a prick of conscience. But what decency remained in me after the crap I had pulled overseas in the services of *my* country, surfaced. Suddenly as privy to the Dallas conspiracy as that *iceman*—I couldn't handle it. My guts split wide open. I swung off the highway to a public phone and began a series of calls that sealed my fate forever.''

Suddenly uneasy, Brad looked at Berna, wondering about her identity, her relationship with Greer. The introduction had been minimal—he hadn't even been given her last name. Could she understand Greer's words, his indictment of his past? Her concentration seemed locked on the macrame. He sipped a beer thoughtfully, eyes fixed on the towering, lumbering man pacing the room.

"I called the White House. My call was transferred to the Justice Department, patched into wherever it was the Attorney General chose to be at that precise time. I was cautious, using only those numbers needed to pierce the top-priority communications channel. I should have fuckin' used Caligula's code, dammit! Time didn't permit me to think of using a cover and I couldn't risk having my call rejected. But I violated one essential lesson of survival: I placed the information before my own life. The fuckin' White House and the Justice Department was bugged! A computer at Langley picked up numbers, wholesaled my conversation with the A.G. to the top honcho—the DCI! Before the conversation ended—*before I finished*—my words were on the DCI's computer. My name and ID numbers popped up on computer readouts with the order to *TERMINATE!* S.O.S. *Shoot on Sight!*"

Brad's eyes trailed to the woman. Chills danced along his spine. She understood every word! He *knew* it! He didn't like this. Berna's expression, no longer remote, her eyes no longer hostile, he saw the workings behind them; wheels turning adroitly, assembling what she'd heard with precision filing. He frowned. *Why had Greer lied?*

Greer whirled around to him, eyes blazing. "I fuckin' *know* the assassins, the *power* behind them! All of those involved!" Greer raised a clenched fist and shoved it through the wooden wall, shattering his hand, splitting the skin, drawing blood. He cursed aloud, held his wrist tightly with his free hand until the initial pain abated.

Berna moved in like a sleek cat, examined his hand, cursed in French at his foolishness, then disappeared outside and returned with a bowl of snow. She forced him to immerse the injured hand.

"So the *Company* buried you?" Brad asked, wanting to end this.

Greer shook his head, his lips, pulled tightly over his teeth in

59

an unbearable grimace. "No. The A.G. He sent a helicopter for me, picked me up at the phone booth, just as a Company chopper arrived to gun me down. Ten hours *before* the Dallas tragedy I boarded a private jet out of Dulles, was given a new cover, ample funds in a Zurich bank, and burial in Lucerne canton. Yes, the A.G. provided for me, until they got him, too!

"Now, Brad, *ol' buddy*," he said with exhausted tolerance, appending *ol' buddy* to his sentences in a sardonic, patronizing tone, and despite the glowering glances from Brad, persisted in his taunt. He just didn't give a shit anymore. "Now, *ol' buddy*, convince me that *your* man, this American President, has the clout to hold *them* off! Presidents, *ol' buddy*, are not invincible! They don't stand a chance in hell to ward off this power cartel of former SOE experts!" Greer lifted his hand from the ice bowl, examined the injuries. He snapped his wrist once or twice, blew on it and immersed it again.

Brad controlled his reaction to Greer's startling information. *Power cartel! SOE experts! Christ!* This was it—the ramifications . . .

Greer relit the bong and took a hit.

"To wrap it up, I was here when the A.G. was wasted. The names, faces, locations changed, but the tactics were the same. Prime a loony, promise him immortality, ply him with enough goof balls to make him dependent on you, and he'll do the mule work. The rest is easy. You set him up like a sitting duck—a dead duck. And the dead tell no tales . . ." He sipped his coffee. "Remember all the times we faced death, Brad?" He inhaled on the bong. "In the war? The bottom line is: when death hovers over you, you hang on to any shred of life like a goddam fish out of water."

"You've been done a great injustice, Jim. None of this was alluded to in your file."

Greer's laughter was ascerbic. "The Company tagged me a fuckin' snitch! Try and live with that for a while on alien terrain! You get a rotten habit of looking over your shoulder every *fuckin'* minute of every *fuckin'* day." Jim picked up the rifle at his feet and flung it, stock first, to Brad. "G'wan, count 'em. Thirty-eight notches. Thirty-eight assassins that the Company sent to waste me. You sure you weren't tailed?"

Brad examined the notches in silence. He placed the weapon on the floor, barrel pointed away from him. "I'm sure," he said quietly.

"How did you find me?" Greer demanded.

"A computer. I ran a bio on you, then I cheated. I ran a facsimile of your m.o. in the OSS and early CIA days, cross-checked it against British M-I computers and—" he paused. "Something interesting happened. I was not prepared for what popped up on the screen."

Greer's lips exploded smoke, from inhaling hash from the bong. He stiffened perceptibly, glanced at Berna, his eyes smoldering.

"Don't work yourself into a stew, Jim. I destroyed the readout, deprogrammed the input, then checked with INTERPOL. It was done without trace, the source, covert."

Greer's face was ashen as he locked eyes with Berna, Berna pulled the magnum closer to her while he leveled cold eyes on Brad. "You—did—this—and—have—the—gall—to—tell—me—that—you—didn't—jeopardize—my—cover?" The words came out slow and deadly. He stared thunderstruck at his uninvited guest, his face contorting. "The input on the computers will alert someone that I am alive, for *Christsakes!*" He tossed the M52 on the sofa next to Brad.

"Go ahead, pull the trigger. I'm a dead man, now."

"How? Tell me how," Brad despaired.

"INTERPOL by mutual arrangement with British M-I transmits all inquiries on well-known agents, past, present, etc., dead or alive. London scans these microscopically. One slip—one query—provides them with plenty. *Goddammit!* You know the procedure!"

Greer threw the bowl of melting snow across the room, ignoring his hand. "Why, of all people, the British? Christ, Brad! London is their HDQS!"

"Who? Whose HDQS?"

Greer glared at him suffused with rage. Bloodshot eyes darted from Brad to Berna, to the fire, and back again. He trembled with the pent-up fury of twenty years of paranoia.

"I didn't use your name. I coded the words: *Corsican Jade.*

"You *what*?" Greer was speechless. "*Fuckin' goddamn*! You don't know what you've done!" He turned to Berna with a look of incredulity, slapping his hand against his thigh.

"For *Christsakes*, Jim, sit down. Let's talk this out."

"No! Goddamit! You had no right!"

"Don't treat me like an idiot, Jim. Each tactic was elaborately studied, meticulously prepared. *Corsican Jade* was a name you and I coined back in 1943—"

"—along with a half dozen others, still alive! The *wrong* people! I could kill you!"

"Would you sit down and hear me out? *Corsican Jade*, fed into computers, produced answers I desperately needed, I requested immediate clarification, and re-programmed my question, admitting I had erred by placing the wrong word into the query. I substituted the word *Jade* for the word *Coral* and with it an apology for the incorrect query."

"You asshole! British M-I are not *that* naive!"

"They bought it. The reply was instantaneous."

"And—"

"They replied, *Corsican Coral* is a cover name for a punk rock group traveling through Europe with a base in Zurich. Actually, they are skilled terrorists inciting the usual criminal activities attributed to the Red Brigades, Bader-Meinhoff, the P.L.O. and Carlos. I evidently touched raw nerves. British M-I contacted me asking for all data input on *Corsican Coral*." Brad mused over this, unaware of the changes occurring in his host.

Greer, fired with suspicious wrath zeroed in on Brad, the M52 reholstered but accessible.

Berna brought in a tray of freshly brewed coffee, poured for them and retired to her craft in silence.

"Will you ever learn Europe is *not* America?" Greer began. "The continent is a power-hungry snake pit. Power, *inestimable* power, high finance, Machiavellian politics and personal ambition cohesively holds Europe together. Here, assassination handles the dissident. Anyone voicing his thoughts against the power structure ends up a statistic. Here, a man gets an itch, he doesn't bother scratching it—he pushes a button eliminating it forever."

"That's precisely why I'm here, to identify the button-pushers who move Bader-Meinhoff, the Red Brigades, the Mossad—I need information to crack these *invisible* pharaohs of power."

"*That's* your objective?" Greer's bearded jaw fell slack. "You're crazy! You don't stand a chance in hell!"

"I must find a systematic way to attack these international moguls, and crack the entire apparatus, from the top to the lowest man! Or else there'll be nothing left of the world."

"*You're out to save the world*?" Greer's scathing voice roared with laughter. "You're fuckin' out to save the world . . ."

"Someone with itchy fingers is prepared to detonate nuclear warheads—"

"You? I've never known you to be altruistic." Greer rocked with mirth.

"I don't know what I am or have been. I, like you, followed orders in the service of my country. Suddenly I am strangled by all that's happened—no one has learned from the past! Power-crazed psychotics juggle the gold standard, control diamond markets, threaten OPEC nations. Global annihilation is in a countdown to zero."

"My, my. Brad Lincoln, a born-again human being? Tsk, tsk. What brought this on?"

"Cut the bull. I'm serious." He quickly explained the issues at stake, what he had gleaned in Pentagon hearings.

"Yeah, yeah, I heard about Mubende. Tough. He was an okay guy."

"Jim . . . We—uh—both knew a Corsican from *OPERATION WHITE CORAL* . . ."

Staring in the flames as he spoke, he missed the blanching of Greer's features, the alert, exchanged looks between him and the girl Berna. Brad continued. "He stood out like a beacon. Remember the *Mozarabe*? The Commando unit we linked up with in Corsica at the finish of Bir Hakeim in the North African Campaign? Don't you remember?" He fished out the three photos he'd carted over the North Pole and turned, hand out-stretched with them. He tapped the image of the Corsican. "Here—he's the one. I've gotta know *who* he is, *what* he is. Where he went *after* the war. And *where* I can reach him. I need straight answers, Jim. You're the one with a photographic memory, buddy."

Greer held up a set of car keys, jingled them in the air, signaling Berna. "Take a ride," he said bruskly. "We have a guest for dinner. We need supplies." He pressed a wad of Swiss francs into her hands. Brad watched Berna shrug into a fur-lined parka, pull a thick woolen cap over her head, turn on the short-wave radio to hear a weather report, slip a beeper into her pocket and move past them out the door without a second glance.

Greer waited until sounds of the four-wheel drive starting up reached them. "Brad," he began, photo in hand, "is—uh—he the reason behind this visit?"

"In a nutshell."

Greer nodded, mulling over the answer. He crossed the room, squinted through the front window, catching sight of the rear brake lights on the Benz disappearing down the mountain. "You sure you weren't tailed?"

Brad described the insanity of his travel itinerary to minimize dangers to himself and Greer. He wasn't sure Greer heard him or gave a damn. He watched him trudge over the plank flooring, pick up his shotgun, snap the breech, recheck his load, then do the same to the M52. "C'mon, let's go for a walk. Some son of a bitch on the next mountain a hundred miles away, working parabolics with a hand-held gizmo, can record our conversation. Can you handle a trek in the snow?"

"That's a mean storm brewing out there." Brad hesitated, skeptical of both the reason given and the chill factor. He realized then that he had no choice if he was going to learn what he'd come after. He shrugged. "It's your turf. If you say we walk—we walk."

Disquieted, nothing suited Brad. Not Berna, not Greer, certainly he was in no mood for a jaunt in sub-zero temperatures. He complied, slipped on a thick sweater and earmuffs provided by his host and his sheepskin-lined jacket.

Greer slung the Dragunov sniper rifle over his shoulder, shoved a flare gun and a beeper into his pocket. The beeper, a life-saving device employed in dangerous avalanches or precarious life-or-death situations, signaled ski patrols by giving exact location readings.

Outside he slid halters on the Huskies, each containing additional beeper devices, trackable by the same systems. "Twenty years living like an animal—man learns to adapt," Greer explained.

They hiked uphill in silence for twenty minutes, coming to rest at the precipitous ledge of an icy ridge. Behind them, half-screened by a ghostly latticework of snow-laden pines and oak trees, lay Lake Lucerne, like a bowl of blue cobalt framed by snowy drifts. High tors met like frigid spires against the overcast sky, imperious but lifeless in the dim light of day.

The short hairs on Brad's neck stood on end. He sniffed immediate dangers, his instinct for survival acute. He used the moment to vindicate himself when vindication was not sought.

"Cooperate, Jim, and I'll do my damndest to return you

stateside.'' His words, born out of fear, sounded manipulative, but he didn't give a damn—he didn't have any options from this height.

"Return to the States?'' Greer snorted. ''I'd be dead in a fortnight. I know too much.''

"An executive order would end the nightmares, reinstate you.''

Nodding, Greer blurted, ''I'd give an arm and leg to return, ol' buddy. Living like this fries a man's brains.''

Brad pressed his advantage. ''I need information about the Corsican damn quick or no man will live long enough to enjoy life as we've known it.''

"Life as we know it sucks. It's crap! *Fuckin'-A* hard to live. Especially in this frozen Disneyland. Berna doesn't live here—she comes once a month. Whacking my prick doesn't get it for me, buddy. When my dogs start looking good to me, I'll blow my brains.''

"Lousy as it's been, we're facing extinction. You want to gamble life away because it stinks at times?''

Something was happening to Brad. His testicles felt like frozen snowballs; his breathing grew labored. The stress from the climb, the thinning air, and the freezing temperature increased his urgency. ''Shake your brains, Jim. Fill in the missing links. I'm on a fucking timetable. The world loops the loop toward doomsday while you and I play *king of the mountain*!''

"Why is it always Armageddon with you spooks?'' His loyalties subverted since the Dallas tragedy, he faced his former partner tentatively, his manner ominous. He dabbed at the icicles forming on his mangy beard, and grabbed Brad's arm firmly. ''You're on the level? You really think . . .? Look, I won't promise bargains. Brad . . .? What's wrong? Christ! . . . You're turning blue!'' He whipped out a pocket flask, forced brandy down Brad's throat. ''You stupid son of a bitch! What are you trying to prove?'' Lincoln gulped greedily, his teeth chattering against the flask.

"You should have told me! Frostbite can be deadly! G'wan! Drink it down—all of it! Can you work up a jogging pace? . . . Sure?''

Brad nodded. He could not talk. His lips were blue, frozen to immobility.

An hour later, plied with hot buttered rum, he felt better, his numb feet thawed by a bucket of snow, to which water had been

65

added slowly until he tolerated heat. Brad sat before the fire listening as Berna rattled pots and pans in the kitchen, the aroma of cooking stimulating his appetite.

Greer, settled nearby, holding the bong. "Listen, ol' buddy, you ask for too much."

"Why is one man's identity *too* much? You forget, I know the Corsican."

Greer shot him a sharp, scowling look.

"For some damnable reason I am blocking him out."

"It's not a question of *one man's* identity. What you ask can trigger a volatile situation. It means exposing a *friend*."

"Earlier I showed you his photo. You turned green. Then we go for a trek in subzero weather and honest to God, I thought I was finished. That you deliberately—"

"—would waste you? I could have, you know."

"*Why*? For Christsakes, how would my death serve you?"

Greer was boldly audacious. "By bringing me a step closer to my goal."

"Goddamit, Jim! Level with me." He placed a hand on Greer's arm, forcing him to look into his eyes. "I admit my tactics were desperate, taking the risk of exposing your cover exceeded good sense. But I had no alternatives. Cooling my heels in committee meetings all this time—"

Greer raised a hand. "Don't say another word. You've given me an out. You showed me a photo. For reasons I fail to comprehend, you don't remember the Corsican. So, I'll point you in the right direction. But before I do, get this. You're on your own. You *haven't* seen me, got it? For all you know, *after* my disappearance twenty years ago, I could be dead. Make no connection to Dallas! If the name Jim Greer pops up in conversation, mourn me, for Christsakes, you hear. *Mourn* me!"

Agitated, he tossed logs on the fire, stoked it briskly until they flamed. Then he paced the floor, tugging nervously at his beard, running his hands over his face, smoothing his hair back in nervous, erratic gestures. He turned on the radio. Wagnerian tumult shook the rafters. Moving back toward Brad, he relit the bong, and inhaled deeply.

"Listen, I'll tell it to you once. In Paris you'll talk with Pierre Marnay. Remember him? Corsica . . . Marseilles . . . Paris . . . Play it cool. Do not, I repeat, do *not* tip your hand—tell him as little as possible. That son of a French whore owes us due bills from forty years ago. Make him cough up. But watch yourself, Brad. Watch yourself every step of the way. You'll be walking tightropes. Marnay's a wheel in the Surete, the SDECE.''

"Marnay? In the Surete? That feisty little waterfront rat? S-h-i-t! I figured he'd be head of some crime syndicate by now—or dead. *And* he's legitimate?'' Brad shook his head in disbelief. As he wrapped his feet in a hot towel, Greer hesitated, his glittering eyes probed for the reaction to his next statement.

"Actually, Marnay is Commissioner of the *Police Judiciare*.''

Throughout a Spartan supper Berna's eyes deliberately fixed on Brad's. He averted his gaze, unwilling to accept the message. After she cleared the dishes, she retired to the loft without a word. Brad watched her climbing the steps, every movement sheer animal magnetism screaming for seduction. Any other time . . .

Greer was talking, his voice laced with ominous circumspection and an undercurrent of prudence brought curious lights to his eyes. "Whatever you do—don't drop your guard.'' He saw Brad shiver. "What's wrong?''

"It's freezing here. How do you stand it?''

"It's a helluva lot colder where you're going.''

Brad sent him a questioning look.

"Since you played *king of the hill*, a new breed of player has entered the arena. You're batting in the major leagues—the biggest—nothing you've encountered before.''

"You think I'm a rookie, is that it?'' He was getting frustrated, everything about this encounter seemed pointless. It seemed to be all razzle-dazzle and nothing concrete. He pressed for more facts. "What are you trying to say, Jim?''

"You'll look like an amateur among heavyweights unless your story is pat and highly professional. Can the stuff about saving mankind.''

"It's true.''

"And out of place among man-eating barracuda. They'll squash you like a bug before you raise an antenna—understand?''

"They? Who are *they*? Look, I loathe speculation. Tell me.''

"Let them do the talking. They won't sit still while a stranger prowls around. They reserve big game for themselves.''

"Goddammit! You aren't listening. Who the hell are you talking about? *Who* won't?''

Greer waffled outright. "For fifteen fuckin' years I tried. I fucking near got killed. Because of you and old memories I couldn't get an inside track to the Corsican!"

"You *what*? . . . Fifteen years? Because of me? . . ." Brad did a fast reshuffling of years, raced back in time forty years. "Ah, I see. *Corsican Jade*, eh?"

Greer pivoted on one foot, eyes flaring wildly, his face flushed crimson. "Shut up!" he hissed. "Shut up, goddammit!" His eyes darted to the loft. He paced again furiously. "If I had any sense . . . Got any idea how much I'd net before you made contact with *Moufflon?*"

There! Finally unveiled—the name Brad hadn't mentioned! It was a code name—but it was a start.

Greer, realizing his slip, erupted like Vesuvius. He stumbled to the kitchen in a rage, rattled about creating a ruckus. Loud banging sounds, the opening and shutting of drawers, pots and pans tossed in loud clangor. He returned in moments carrying bowls of dog food, furrows deeply creased across his brow. Storming past Brad, he went outside, slamming the door behind him. Brad heard him calling the dogs. For an instant Greer ran naked, he had revealed what he dared not and the pain was acute.

Brad understood the other's chagrin, but his own exhaustion and frustration taking its toll, he hunched over, head in his hands, trying desperately to overcome the numbing effects of frostbite. What a devilish development.

An overwhelming scent of cologne hung heavy in the air. Brad, catching a waft of it, jerked his head up. He gave a start. Nude, Berna stood midway on the stairs, eyes smoldering. She crooked a finger at him, pantomiming suggestively, tossing damp mischievous kisses into the air at him.

Oh, Christ! She was gorgeous! Exactly what he needed. What he didn't need was a bullet to his head.

"Sorry, *fräulein*, nòt this time." Brad shook his head.

"*Nein?*" She cooed with unabashed temerity, sliding her hands over her firm breasts, downward, stopping at the furry patch of Venus. "*Ich bin fertig.*"

"*Es tut mir sehr leid,*" he apologized, one eye out the window.

Thudding sounds of Greer's feet stomping snow from his boots sent Berna sprinting to the loft. Jim entered, his fury unabated, knowing nothing of the miniscene enacted moments ago.

"Don't say a word! Not one word," he commanded acerbicly, thrusting his anger about him like daggers. "Why the fuck do I bother?" he blustered rhetorically, letting the German shepherd inside the house. The animal sniffed around, gazed at Brad, then curled up on the warm hearth.

Brad had to try to break through. "Because you care. Tell me who *they* are? This mysterious *they* who's got you riding strange horses in this three-ring circus?"

"If I have to explain, you fuckin' don't know nothing!"

"Did I come making like Solomon?"

"You're no goddamn temple virgin! You know as I know the roots begin with the old OSS gang and British SOE! Look, I've been outa it too long. My value is *nada*."

"Not to me." Greer unwittingly added another dimension to Brad's mission. "What's the tie-in to Zurich?"

"If I knew all the mechanics I wouldn't be alive. Zurich controls them all, they move to his drumbeats. It's that simple and so fuckin' complex you can't get near 'em to smell 'em. Prepare for the worst." Greer tested. "You gotta give to receive, buddy. . . ."

"Give what? Trade you for information? Dammit, Jim! If I were here to ice you, my style isn't walking in the front door! I refuse to feed your paranoia. I'm getting bored. With or without you, I've got plenty to do!"

"It could happen. I'm not indispensable. How sure are you you weren't set up to make tracks to me?"

"Because, *goddammit*, I *initiated* the project! It's my baby. Conceived and birthed in this brain." He tapped his head impatiently. "Only one man knows what I'm into and he knows virtually nothing. Without him—for the last time—*GAMMA 10* was impenetrable to me."

Brad stared at his host despairingly. It was clear that his defense hadn't penetrated Greer's paranoiac mind. He fumed.

"All right . . . All right. Have it *your* way. I *don't* understand, couldn't possibly understand the hell you've been through. Is that what you want to hear? You enjoy playing martyr? Where does that take us? Will it end here—a shoot-out at Alpine Village? I want to help you—"

"I don't need your help! Do your goddamned snooping and stay the fuckin' hell away from me! You're bad news!"

Brad's inner tension coiled, tightly. Nothing was going as

planned. Greer, too far gone, was locked in another world. Drugs? Who the hell knew? Greer had changed. He didn't know him.

He had the name he'd come for. Sometime in the middle of the night he would leave.

Sometime in the middle of the night, Brad awakened shivering. The fire was reduced to a few scattered dying embers. Rising from the sofa, he added logs, while from the loft came unmistakable sounds of libidinal joy. *Swell.*

Brad frowned thoughtfully as he warmed himself by the fire's glow. The throes of uninhibited sex jolted him. Not for obvious reasons, lack of participation, but due to the distortions running amuck in his mind. Greer and Berna. Berna and Greer. They just didn't jibe. Berna, a strange creature of perplexing personality, appeared awkward, ill at ease when they conversed. She acted like an ingénue, an amateur actress on stage for the first time, trying to convey mature emotions she had yet to understand.

The patter they had engaged in was cryptic, conspiratorial, deliberately spoken in several tongues, jumping from one to the next, disinclined to include Brad in their *damnable* secrets. He understood less of their esoteric pastiche. This disturbed him; her presence disturbed him; that Greer permitted Berna's presence when they discussed clandestine matters disturbed him greater. And *more* disturbing was Greer's inane remark. *Berna doesn't understand a word of English!* A vicious hawk feigning to be a cooing dove? Uh, uh. Berna's presence didn't compute.

Brad glanced at the luminous watch dial. One A.M. Too soon to take off. He would wait until an hour before daybreak. He crossed to the gunrack, selected a loaded pistol, checked the chambers, and kept it at his side on the sofa. He set his watch alarm to 4:30 A.M., pulled the comforter around him, and lay back, staring into the fires. He had a few hours to figure new strategy.

Greer was right. Desk duties had relaxed him. He had to prepare to outsmart, outguess and outdistance these men of the *new* breed to whom Greer had alluded.

Relax a moment and you're dead, baby.

He awakened, a sense of suffocation upon him. He blinked hard at the shadowy form over him. Reacting from instinct, he almost tumbled the girl from his lap. Berna, naked under the

70

comforter, sat on his erection, giggling softly, murmuring suggestively, the connotations unmistakable.

She wriggled sensuously, her warm throbbing body igniting his. Her low, throaty sexual ovations, subdued, but stimulating, her control was maddening. Brad panicked. His eyes darted to the loft.

"*Nein, nein, fräulein*," he muttered, trying to push her away.

"*Ja, ja*," she insisted, pantomiming sleep. "*Mein herr, er schlafen*." She moved slightly, affixing her hot wet mouth to his penis—he was too far gone. It was over in moments.

Control be damned! She had sucked him off, now stared at him triumphantly, mocking him with impertinence. "*Habem sei Amerikanische zigaretten, Leibling?*"

Catching his breath, he handed her an open pack. "*Nun weggehen abreisen*—go away, now. *Gute nacht, fräulein!*"

He thrust her gently but firmly from his spent loins. In the warm fireglow her allure was unquestionable. Unbraided, her hair fell in a mass of long, spiraling curls. Her eyes, darker, fascinated him. What a remarkable transition. He languidly caught a glimpse of what appeared to be a ribbonlike burn on her breast, close to the areola.

Rising, he pulled her to her feet, slapped her buttocks and sent her scurrying, amid protests, to the loft. She turned back, made an obscene gesture, and disappeared. *Christ!* All he needed was a jealous lover to waste him. Brad cleaned himself, began to dress, and reaching for his briefcase, took a notepad and scribbled a note, asking Greer to reconsider. He's call him in two weeks.

God, let the Rover's engine kick over!

He traveled to Zurich aboard the local, caught an Air France flight to Paris, and sipping a double Scotch on the rocks, brooded over the numerous changes in Greer. He believed Greer's story and had observed that the agonies of a thousand nightmares assimilated in a long perilous career had turned him moody, unpredictable as a savage constantly at war with inner demons. Ostracized by the Intelligence community, he was scared, his ego flayed.

Brad paid the stewardess for his drink, noticing a slip of paper tucked into the paper money. The note was written in European caligraphy. He read: *Imperative you contact Wolfgang Katz. Use conduits ORACLE CYCLOPS through known safe houses.*

Oracle Cyclops! . . . Oracle Cyclops! . . . Brad rolled the words over in his mind. World War II . . . Wolfgang Katz, West Berlin! Oracle Cyclops was a code name for a former Nazi officer, wrongfully charged of war crimes at Nuremberg forty years ago! *Forty years ago!*

What the devil? Berna! That perplexing, disquieting girl! It was her doing? *Why?* He unbuckled his seat belt, walked to the head, burned the note, flushing the ashes down the latrine, the words imprinted in his brain. Returning to his seat, he tucked the name Wolfgang Katz away in his head. First things first.

He spent the remaining flight time concentrating on Pierre Marnay. He thought of those cloak-and-dagger days in World War II, when Lincoln, Greer and Marnay were thick as bedbugs. They had shared Remy-Martin, women and song in a bloody living hell. Brad had never forgotten that day—never would.

December, 1943. A year before Seventh Army invasion flotillas and de Lattre's French Army B converged on their rendezvous off the French Riviera to begin the liberation of France.

Corsica, liberated by the combined Allied assistance of America's OSS, British SOE, the Resistance forces and those spectacular *Mozarabe* commandos, had driven the Axis soldiers back and in hot pursuit had landed along the Riviera, taking refuge in a few of the concrete pillboxes at the outskirts of Marseilles, prepared to infiltrate and move in on the German Wehrmacht Army.

For three days and nights Marseilles fell under a state of brutal siege. The battle raged between three indomitable forces, the Germans, Resistance and Allied forces, and the most devastating of all, nature. Thunder, lightning, and erupting black clouds made it hell for all. Bursting bombs, crumbling buildings, the Luftwaffe overhead strafing, dumping missiles, exploded streets into giant potholes, destroyed bridges, waterfront piers.

It was madness! Chaotic insanity. No one knew friend from foe!

On this day the Wehrmacht Army was out for vengeance. Their target: waterfront whores, brothels, bordellos. Their spy network had confirmed that the whorehouses were nests for daily espionage plottings and sabotage levied against the unwanted German invaders.

For six months these enemies had played cat and mouse

games. Today would mark a savage coup between enemies. Once frequent visitors to the illicit houses, it was learned their soldiers had been deliberately infected with venereal diseases and plied with drugs. German hatred for the whores escalated with violence on this day.

Meanwhile the people panicked. The air, rife with fear, bulletfire, and booming 88 guns, created pandemonium and the people fled. Small cars, stuck in the mud, were abandoned by their owners. Horns tooted frenetically, people yelled, scattering in all directions, seeking shelter from a lethal downpour of shells and bullets. Bodies struck lay bleeding, incapacitated, screaming, pleading for help.

Into this melee came the Advance OSS and British SOE, Resistance and Mozarabe commandos.

Captain Brad Lincoln took a squadron of his men along the narrow back alleys of Marseilles. The platoons had split up and made their way stealthily under full rain gear to their destination. Exhausted, debilitated, sleepless for four nights, Brad nursed a bullet wound where a sniper had winged him earlier. The weary squadron trudged on, knee deep in the mud.

At three P.M. it seemed midnight. The Luftwaffe had stopped divebombing hours ago. Then up ahead they saw the rendezvous point. Brad checked his communique in the pouring rain. The intersection of a crossroads to Martigues at the edge of Marseilles. Good. The building had undergone total renovation from unrelenting bombardment. Very little remained, a few walls, a partial roof . . .

It appeared abandoned. Earlier, decoy squads of commandos had lured the enemy in directions away from this area, diverting them with short bursts of gunfire. Finished, they were expected to circle back to meet with Resistance leaders, flown out of Paris that day.

Brad and his group of Resistance fighters hovered behind the broken walls of a nearby building, waiting, watching. He dispersed his men to the building rear while he crept forward, gaining access through an embattled door hanging ajar on broken hinges. Pain-ridden, wary-eyed, barely moving, encumbered by the rain gear and heavy artillery, he crept inside along musty, stench-filled corridors. Rats scurried across the floor, over his boots.

He eased on, hugging a broken wall, exposing torn plaster and

73

bare lath. He crouched low, shivered in the cold damp silence. A covey of predatory rats hovered over a dead man's remains. Brad turned from the detestable sight; he dared not send the rats scurrying for fear of exposing the presence of himself and the others. He stopped abruptly.

At the end of the corridor, a shaft of dim light pierced an open door obliquely, casting a fine ray on the rotted flooring.

Creeping cautiously forward, service pistol in hand, Brad reached the open door, his body flat against the wall. He leaped soundlessly to the opposite side of the door and tried to peer through the crack. In a sudden burst he kicked in the door, fell to a low crouch, gun at the ready to peel off a fusillade of bullets.

Desperately he took in the scene, focusing at dead center on the bed. Brad blinked. It took moments to discern the action.

A woman known as Chou-Chou in the Resistance sprang from the bed. Her face in the dim shadows, bloodless, without expression, distorted the usual picture of her he held in mind. She was pink-cheeked, robust, a buxom woman, seraphic-faced, available for pleasure to any man in the Resistance. You couldn't imagine Chou-Chou being angry with anyone.

WRONG! *She was the deadliest woman he'd ever encountered*.

The memory of his own sexual tryst with the woman flooded his mind, delaying proper action. She stood motionless before him, panting heavily, staring through cold, hard, calculating eyes, anticipating his action. Then he saw it!

An expertly wielded blood-stained steel blade glittered in the dim candleglow. Peripherally he caught sight of Pierre Marnay on the bed, bleeding profusely, half his nose gone. Within the same periphery Brad had failed to perceive the clear message in her eyes. Chou-Chou about to perform a lobotomy on Marnay, came at Brad, plunged her knife straight forward, a formidable thrust to parry. *Oh, Christ! He was a goner!*

Not quite. Simultaneous to Chou-Chou's insane but skillful thrust, a brute, whirlwind force coming from behind Brad shoved him to one side, the knife in Chou-Chou's hand sliced through Brad's rain gear, missing his heart, stabbing his right upper shoulder, saving him from death. The impact, however slight, staggered Brad. He sank to his knees, the gun spilling from his hand to the clapboard floor.

His rescuer leaped over Brad, felling Chou-Chou with a swift judo chop to the jugular, a stunning, controlled blow just short of

74

its usual lethal effectiveness. Later exposed as a Nazi collaborator, she would be turned over to the Resistance for interrogation and the usual for spies—extermination.

But Brad had lost consciousness. He came to moments later. The tall Corsican commander of the *Mozarabe* hovered over him, pulling the blade from his shoulder. He applied sulfa to the bullet wound as well and bound the injuries with strips of a soiled bedsheet. The scene was watched by the gutsy, courageous men and women of the French Underground.

A truck transported Brad to a secret, underground, makeshift hospital. His benefactor, the Corsican, he had later learned, carried Marnay on his back, sloshed three miles in knee-deep mud to a safe house under the live fire of German artillery. Enroute the Corsican had tarried long enough to singlehandedly wipe out four machine gun nests with grenades.

To convince Marnay they both owed their lives to the remarkable Corsican was like trying to convince a frog he didn't have a watertight asshole. Through an inexplicable association of ideas and memories, Marnay had credited Brad Lincoln with his miraculous escape from death. Marnay's reasoning contained a mystifying, albeit proud, appeal to Brad. Marnay steadfastly maintained it was the crucial moment of Brad's intervention—not the Corsican's courageous deed—that had prevented Chou-Chou from carving his carcass to the bone.

Argue with such emotional logic? Never. Not now, in any event, since he might manipulate this undeserved due bill to his advantage. Why wouldn't Marnay cooperate?

He wasn't grasping at brass rings from an imaginary carousel, was he?

The Air France 707 circled Charles de Gaulle Airport, waiting for word to land. Brad gazed out the window at the dismal rain blanketing Paris. Why had he recalled Chou-Chou and a thousand other incidental names and blocked the Corsican's from mind? His maddening subconscious refused to relinquish the name. Why hadn't he asked Valentina?

There were other inconsistencies. Jim Greer. Reference made to *Corsican Jade* had turned him green, among other things. Why? He mused over the trigger words.

CORSICAN JADE . . . Just before V-E Day all Europe scrambled for survival. The war had left immense devastation, frightening hunger. Black marketeering had reached pandemic proportions. Participation by enterprising top military brass had scandalized political higher-ups; yet, nevertheless, many ended up *beaucoup* rich with Swiss bank accounts. If published, the names would blow the lid off foreign relations.

CORSICAN JADE, code name for a few dozen French, British and American soldiers who had pulled off the coup of all coups. Numerous unscrupulous, predatory scavengers had brazenly burglarized, looted, and confiscated enormous caches of wealth from the people under siege, while before the Germans had sniffed out the stockpiled riches and hidden the loot for themselves. How convenient for the first; blame it on the Germans and *after* the war become instant overnight millionaires—yes? *No! Corsican Jade* got wind of the deeds, maneuvered themselves into positions of trust in the underground network and in well-organized commando fashion stole back the gold, silver, diamonds and precious art works. Most of them emerged from the ashes of war as powerful titans, respected business entrepreneurs, oil and shipping magnates, industrialists, financiers to whom the world paid homage. Egg-sucking ferrets! All!

Jim Greer's involvement with *Corsican Jade* lasted a year. The OSS HDQS at Clayallee 10 had received censored reports of *JADE's* activities. Brad refused to accept censored reports from British MI, demanding a clarification on *JADE* activities directly from Paris, London and Rome. He vividly recalled the communique:

Corsican Jade, a figment of deluded minds, does not exist. Repeat: IT DOES NOT EXIST!

Allied officials had closed the books on it; then the cover-up began.

Forty years later, through computer technology and a talent for cryptology, the entire scam finally would be spelled out for Brad.

Chapter Three

". . . There is a power, superior to all others, which
has arms and eyes everywhere and which today governs
Europe. It will govern the world one day . . .
                                    Monsignor de Savine, 1801

THE BISTRO, BOHEMIAN IN DECOR, muted in lighting,
nestled off Rue St. Germain behind a shabby, downright dirty
facade—merely a facet of French *snobisme* to keep out tourist
rabble. Sold out nightly, the management demanded advance
bookings for its gourmet clientele. For Marie Pierre Marnay, head
of the elite, *Brigade Criminelle of the Police Judiciare*, division
of the French Surete, a ten-minute notice sufficed.

The *Commissaire's* private table, at the center of a dimly lit
alcove, was slightly, but inconspicuously, isolated from the other
tables. A "reserved" sign, always propped up in a brass holder
next to the bowl of fresh flowers, kept trespassers away.

It was a very *special* table, indeed. Concealed in a niche
underneath was a heft snub-nosed .357 Magnum loaded with
semi-jacketed hollow-point bullets. A device knee-activated tape
recorders and silent alarms summoned outside help in moments,
if needed. Should the unexpected occur? *Voilà!* Instant eternity
to the offender.

The bistro was Marnay's office away from the office. Here he
entertained elite criminals, sophisticated snitches—even friends.

Brad entered the crowded, intimate room. Greeted by an efficacious headwaiter steeped in grand hauteur, he was led directly to
the alcove where the *Commissaire* sat in partial shadow. Brad,
totally unprepared for the changes in his friend, called out an
attenuated "*Frenchee?*"

"*Yankee?*" The slim fanatic whose singular desire forty years
ago was to annihilate every German soldier violating France had
acquired a modicum of unexpected finesse and polish. A shiny
pink bald pate had replaced his former shock of black, unruly

77

hair. Thick, white brows, coiled upward, matched a fastidiously waxed handlebar mustache. Save for a slight, barely visible paunch under a primly buttoned vest, all else was muscled steel. A Borgia mentality worked constantly behind lazy eyes.

Following vigorous backslapping and a French embrace, the two old friends stared at each other, bridging the four-decade hiatus. Marnay summoned the sommelier, demonstrated his lavish knowledge of wines. Finishing with courtly aplomb, Marnay turned in profile, touched his nose. "You like it, old friend? Better than the old one, no?"

"You never told me, did Chou-Chou cut it or bite it off?"

"Ah, you remember? I give the devil her due. She bit it off!" He followed with an animated dissertation of the damage done his old proboscis, the need for the implanted prosthesis. He laughed heartily. "Without it—no nose for Marnay. Imagine a sleuth sans a nose? *Sacre Bleu!*"

"You resemble a conservative but affluent banker, Pierre."

"And you? What changes do I detect, eh? Merely a touch of gray at the temples, nothing else. You are the same? Horny as always?" The laughter, raucous, a throwback to his former crudity.

They engaged in small talk over dinner of *Langouste froid, Jambon de parme* with melon, and spiced lemon slices topped off by *Camembert, Pont-Leveque* and *Boursin* cheeses, but only after continued consultation with the sommelier for the right wines.

"The correct wine is essential with each course or one is considered reprehensibly gauche," Marnay explained patiently.

Watchful, Brad noted the acquired affectations, recalling the Occupation when Resistance fighters had converted themselves into lethal war machines. Marnay had killed as many as thirty men without demonstrating a prick of conscience in each undercover operation. The runt of the litter among his Resistance brothers, Marnay possessed the honed perceptions of a skilled thief, the furtive eyes of a lean desert jackal, and the killer instinct of a jungle lion. The man had acquired polish, a genteel social manner and a soft-spoken voice. The eyes, no longer furtive, were masked, unreadable and as carefully veiled as his former colorful speech, affectations, and humor.

Brad, over demitasse and dessert, reeled out the bait slowly. Marnay's knee, under the table, activated the recorder. Disturbed by Brad's presence in Paris, the Frenchman masked his concern behind prim congeniality. The expertise Brad Lincoln wielded in casually searching the room—indiscernible to all but his trained eye—aroused the Frenchman's sleuthing instincts.

And that frenetic call from Switzerland! What infernal devilry consumed the American?

"Patience is a lost art to Americans in this supersonic age. In a mad world racing toward oblivion it is an invaluable tool. Employ it, *mon ami*, if only to maintain a modicum of equilibrium and keep Marnay's blood pressure down, eh?" He puffed on a Cuban cigar.

"I am here to ask questions only you can answer. I'll be brief and to the point. Tell me all you know of a man called Moufflon."

Smoke exploded Marnay's astonished lips. He coughed, reached for a wine goblet, agitated the smoke-filled air about him, his darting eyes probing the immediate area for possible eavesdroppers. He grimaced, gestured a silent apology, and moved his knee under the table to disengage the recorder. Fate worked against Marnay. His move fell short of its target and the device continued to record their words.

In the dimly lighted cellar of a building close to the bistro, massive electronic apparatus, including highly sophisticated parabolics and communication systems, walled the room.

Two rugged men sat at consoles listening through earphones. One of the men touched his companion's arm, indicating the input frequency. The second man switched frequencies to the other's, listened intently. Eyes flashed, sparking with excitement. Instantly alert, both men activated myriad dials. The second man employed a series of dials on the short-wave set and spoke in German into a microphone. "Triple-zero-110 . . . Prepare to receive transmission. Tripel-zero-110 . . . Are you reading me? . . . prepare to receive transmission. We are patching into your frequency in direct relay. A twenty-second delay . . . Confirm by coded signal . . . Over and out!"

Marnay's coughing spasm ended. At once aloof and edgy, his facade of *bonhomie* evaporated. He sipped his wine economically, dissembling to camouflage a newborn fear. "Moufflon? You said Moufflon? Ah, the Corsican goat, no?"

79

"You disappoint me, old friend. So frivolous a remark following blatant evasion? How unlike you!"

They parried back and forth, the American, insistent, determined in his perusal of truth. The Frenchman, vague, noncommittal and nervous. Careful to give him no real bones to chew on, Brad continued to bait him.

"The name *Moufflon* creeps into important matters of state— sensitive matters, too often to be deemed coincidence. Will you help me, Pierre? For old time's sake? But no games. Let me tell you what I have."

"You give Marnay no choice? He *must* listen to your laments? You are too serious, too dedicated. In the past it was always thus. You need a friend on whose back to cry, eh?" His English was accented.

"Shoulder, Pierre. Not *back*."

"*Oui*, shoulder, back, what does it matter? *Bon. Allez-y.*"

"*Moufflon*, Marnay, Moufflon, *s'il vous plaît?*"

Marnay raised a restraining hand, his voice dropped in volume to an annoyed hush. "*Parlez plus circumspection, si'l vous plaît.* For your health and mine, do not refer to that name. Restrain yourself, Yankee, *comprenez-vous?*"

A waiter served the *plateau*, a succulent assortment of cheeses. Brad put off his chagrin. Subdued elation coursed through him.

Voilà! One point scored for the American. Marnay *did not* deny Moufflon's existence. His minute victory dissolved under Marnay's affected officious posture.

"Why do you persist in creating dangers for us both?"

"Special covert assignment," he whispered conspiratorially. "Executive orders—from the top. Look, I've tried the usual diplomatic conduits. *Nothing!* INTERPOL's records allude to extraordinary feats perpetrated by an ambiguous underworld czar, code name: *Moufflon*. Yet, incredibly, nothing tangible showed up on computers."

"From Pierre Marnay you request a bag of tricks he does not possess." He made irresistible Chevalier-like gestures, gurgled low in his throat. "Listen, *bon ami*, forget that name eh?" He waved his hand in a flourish. "It would be much better all around."

"From one cop to another—I cannot."

Marnay melted a sugar cube in a demitasse spoon held over a

candle flame and poured the contents into his *café noir*. Pure terror flared in the Frenchman's eyes, mistrust, defense barriers shot into place. Disappointed, Brad halfheartedly spooned the delicious chocolate mousse without savoring it.

"You will not be dissuaded, eh?" Marnay made a feeble gesture of impatience. "Your silence screams at me—what good is life lived in fear? *Ecoutez-moi*, thirty years ago a career of spectacular feats attributed to uh—our man—made of him a giant in the eyes of a man highly placed in my government. *Comprenez-vous*? Our friend *was* and *is* highly protected. The facts are unavailable to me. I searched but found no—how do you say, *fourberie bouche*? *Oui*, snitches. No one for no price was brave enough to snitch on *our* invisible friend. Marnay, the old Resistance fighter, desired to learn more. *Alors! Commissaire* Marnay trespassed. *Oui*! Given pause to reconsider his actions by his superiors, the question put succinctly to him was simply, 'Which do you prefer, Marnay? Life or forfeiture of that life in exchange for a cause whose only rewards are death? Ehhhhhh?' " The gurgle in his throat grew more pronounced. "I leave to you, *ami*, which choice Marnay made."

"You are not the same *le tigre* who fought valiantly at my side forty years ago." Brad could not disguise his disgust and disappointment.

"We are, none of us, the same. You do me a disservice."

"Forgive me. I counted on you."

"You think me an insufferable, ungrateful bastard, eh?" He sighed. "*Mon ami*, inequities exist in my country. *Ecouter*, in 1965 my sleuthing took me to the Presidential Palace. Doors were slammed in my face. Summoned to the offices of my superiors, all doubts dissolved. If *Commissaire* Marnay desired to maintain his status quo in the elite Surete, receive his pension and remain alive to enjoy the fruits of his labor, he must never bring focus upon this man again. *Never*! Given a choice, a bullet at my own hand or at the hands of another, I wisely wiped the image of the man from mind. Now, some twenty years later, you appear from a long-ago past and expect me to expose myself to the only option open to me?" He shook his bald pate vigorously, exasperated at the crestfallen expression on the American. "*Ecouter*, you think I wouldn't give a testicle to learn the mystique surrounding *our* friend?" His voice dropped to a whisper.

There—references made to our friend. Why?

"Protected by the President himself? Still highly connected *after* de Gaulle's death?" He gurgled low and shook his hand effectively. "Ah, *mon ami*, I would consider such a coup to be the capstone of my career—if I lived long enough to claim victory. If I *knew* the answers, what would I do with such information, eh? Write Pierre Marnay's memoirs? Before the ink dried on the contracts, Marnay would be a memory." He grimaced. "In the Resistance I worked for ideals, purpose, a way of life. In the Police *Judiciare* I work for prestige, money, respectability and other fringe benefits." He wagged a finger at Brad. "Major, I am neither a virtuous man nor the noble warrior existing in your memory." Brad's contemptuous glare provoked a deep regrettable sigh from him. "You are alike, you and Moufflon. Curiosity never idles your mind. When you learn what you are determined to learn—but *not* from Marnay—do not make judgments, oui? Evaluate the facts." He poured champagne with panache as if he weren't affected by the conversation.

"Now you pontificate comparisons!" Brad blurted angrily. "You just said you didn't know *Moufflon*!"

"*Mon Dieu! Monsieur la renard!* At once you become the fox who hears not a word I speak? Did I say I did not *know* him? I merely emphasized my preference to live!"

"Ohhh, I see. I get it. O.K., Marnay, how much?"

Marnay wiped his lips daintily on a serviette, trying to check his anger. "I repeat, you do me a great disservice—"

"Five—ten at the most? Think what you can do with ten million—"

"Ten *million?*"

Not ten million, you numbskull—ten thousand! Brad wanted to shout his error, but the sum created so many changes in Marnay that Brad went the distance with it, hoping the truth would out.

Marnay's ferret-eyes narrowed. "What conditions do you attach to such negotiations?"

"The truth and all information supplied to do a complete profile."

Marnay's deadly eyes stared into Brad's. His fingers drummed the table in steady staccato. "So, *Mister CIA agent*, tell me, who sent you, eh? A rank amateur would demonstrate more descretion. You think to bribe Marnay with so staggering a sum? Hah! What good is *fifty* million American to Marnay if death prevents him

82

from collecting? You *dare* bribe me with one franc, when you, too, know Moufflon personally? Eh? *Why*? To entrap me?"

Brad shrugged it off as an obvious blunder, a tactical error made to test the other's loyalty.

"*Ecoutez moi, Mr. Intelligence agent,*" the voice still dripped sarcasm. "Complications surround *our* friend. One man creates a design, another performs, but not according to original blueprints. Dangerous improvisations resemble the original. Examine it closely to detect the fraud, just as I detected the fraud."

"Marnay—what the fuck are you talking about?"

"Another thing, Mr. think-tank genius, you have destroyed all illusions for me. If you think *him* to be the head of global strife, you are wrong. You, above all, should understand *what* he did and *why*. The method is irrelevant. But know, the moment he chooses to expose *them*, the apparatus of destruction aimed at him will resound throughout the world." A diabolical sneer, masking secret triumph, twisted his features. "If you attempt to reveal him, or contact him, hidden forces will spring from unexpected places to obstruct you. Special power groups to whom international political upheaval is essential to their existence will squash you like a bug. *Comprenez-vous?*"

Brad, damned if he did, kept it to himself.

Marnay's unassuageable anger spurred him on. "You think *you*, one man, can stop them? Not an army of two thousand men of your caliber will impede their progress. Not you, not your government! Billions upon billions of dollars are involved. Sums beyond your comprehension! Total governments! Nations, the world's resources! And you, *Mr. CIA man*, think to stop them?"

"My CIA involvements were terminated long ago, Marnay," Brad said in a steely voice. "You misinterpreted the sum I offered. My intention was to offer ten thousand American—not million. I only want Moufflon's identity, documentation of it—"

"You lie! You lie! You know him more intimately than you know me! Your purpose here is to trick me, expose me to dangers. You have reached a dead end, *monsieur!*" He whipped out the .357 magnum from under the table, placed it calmly on the table. "Now, go before I conjure up reasons to detain you. French jails are notoriously unfriendly to Americans. Go! My debt to you is paid."

*　　*　　*

You know Moufflon more intimately than you know me!

Marnay's enigmatic words confused Brad. He skulked broodingly through the rain-drenched Montparnasse, splashing through rain puddles scattered about the uneven sidewalks. Angry, disappointed, experiencing betrayal by a man who owed him more than he got. He'd been rewarded with riddles, a crazy man's rhetoric and an ulcer attack at his own stupidity. He'd played the scenario like a bungling sideshow barker at a carnival.

Marnay *knew* Moufflon's identity! Jim Greer *knew* Moufflon's identity! Worse, Marnay had insisted that Brad Lincoln *knew* Moufflon!

S-h-i-t! Why then was his own thinking apparatus failing to provide the answer? He set about sorting bits and pieces of the growing enigma, feeling like a dunce in a corner under a cone-shaped hat.

He understood Marnay's loyalty to his superior officers, his retirement dream at some lazy sun-drenched villa along the Costa del Sol, sipping *pastis* and *Manzanilla* with a bevy of women to satisfy his sexual longings. But he failed to understand the obsessive fear oozing from Marnay. The man was terrified. This from a cold-blooded killer—an insanely courageous man who conspired coup after coup against the Gestapo, his life in peril with every conspired deed? And Marnay had turned down a ten million dollar offer!

Uh-uh! Brad didn't buy it. Something was out of synch.

If, as Marnay had insisted, Moufflon's identity was known to Brad, he understood why the man had hurled panicked accusations at him. But Brad did not *know* Moufflon, *dammit!* *Why* would he *know* the man? Marnay's words burned his brain.

You know him more intimately than you know me!

Why had Greer and Marnay both refused to enlighten him? Unable to get off home plate, he'd made no *hits*, no *runs*, but enough *tactical* errors to detonate nuclear warheads from the Kremlin!

Something lingered at the edge of his mind, nagging at him.

He glanced at the luminous watch dial. He'd been walking aimlessly in the deluge for an hour.

An instinctive feeling of surveillance triggered built-in alarms and he hesitated. Shaking water from the brim of his hat, he stepped inside a shabby tobacco kiosk, purchased a pack of Gauloises from a sleepy-eyed clerk, lighted one from the gas burner on the counter, taking a moment to scan the area casually as he stepped back into the night. Observing no overt threats, he moved cautiously, with the clear impression that somewhere—not far away, unseen, unknown forces worked against him. He knew it—felt them.

Resuming his walk, he stopped abruptly before a shop window dotted with rain drops, his cat eyes sweeping through the dismal curtains of night. Shimmering oblique shadows played like celluloid strips in the drizzled haze of streetlights—nothing else moved. Yet . . .

Someone was out there, stalking him in the night!

A cab turned the corner, racing toward him. He hailed it. Ten minutes later he alighted, paid the driver and entered the brightly lighted George Cinq Hotel. He needed a drink! Ten to mollify him for exercising gross errors of judgment with Marnay!

Dabbing at his wet face with a handkerchief, he removed hat and raincoat, shaking the wetness from them, and snaked his way through the congested lobby. Glancing up ahead, he saw it.

The Crazy Horse Saloon! His favorite of all Parisian strip joints. Inside, the crashing discordant sounds of punk rock bombarded his senses.

The smoke-filled room, overflowing with mechanical, expressionless dancers lost in the vapors of hash, pot, booze, cocaine, French perfumes and traces of amyl nitrite, long a cover for a variety of dealings in contraband that included the trafficking of liquor-filled chocolates.

He checked his hat and coat, negotiated the room meticulously as he made his way toward the bar. Tonight Brad needed a woman. The Crazy Horse was as good a place as any to wheel and deal for one. Animated faces on all sides of him, laughing, talking, flirting . . . Christ! It didn't stop.

It was like entering a new dimension, a time warp of the macabre. Punk rockers with hideous, bizarre Mohawk hairdos dyed electric colors and their body tattoos increased his revulsion. Punk rock had infected the world! Whatever happened to good old Glenn Miller, Harry James, Sinatra, and music to make love by? Where were the normal, sane, everyday kind of people?

Onstage, dancers gyrated, peeling off garments to a throbbing staccato of drums. Brad moved past them, in pressing urgency to get to the bar. He craned his neck, raised an arm, signaling the bartender and mouthed the words, ''Double Scotch on the rocks.''

He downed the first, ordered a second, feeling warmer inside. *Forget business tonight!* Find yourself a sexy broad and . . .

He gulped down the second drink, ordered a third, plagued by doubt.

Who cares if you want to save mankind from nuclear obliteration? Look around you, the truth is scrawled on all their faces. They don't care. They live to appease momentary cravings. Future? What future? Now is the moment of truth. NOW!

Brad turned out the disturbing thoughts, his eyes drawn to the undulating energy onstage, and swept back along the sultry-eyed prospects propped up on bar stools. No one, not the assortment of broads draped around the bar, nor the honey blonde stripper at stage center negotiating her G-string for rounds of applause, stoked his passion. Tired, jet-lagged, his temples throbbing incessantly, he needed to rest. Instead he reevaluated facts in his head, sorting fact from fiction, trying to get back on a proper tack.

He picked up the third drink, eyes peering into the hazy back-bar mirror, jarred for a moment. The hairs on his neck did instant aerobics. The *face!* He knew it! Black hair created distortions, the face, changed exotically by cosmetics, the gown, revealing—he *knew* her! He couldn't place her, but no mistaking it—he *knew* the girl. Standing next to her was a tall, slender blond man who wore his hair in the chic, continental-styled Valentino check-point sideburns. Brad's head jerked around, he craned his neck, searching the faces at the bar. They were gone—both of them!

An overwhelming urge to tie up loose ends dictated his quick departure. He tossed off the drink, paid the bartender, prepared to leave.

The brunette, the same face in the mirror, slithered toward him, doe-eyed, lustrous red glazed lips parted seductively, negotiating silently. Brad swallowed hard. *Christ!* What a sensuous body. Something about her . . . Life squiggled in his groin. Desire and need battled with the short hairs on his neck and lost out to survival. He couldn't leave the Crazy Horse fast enough.

Brushing past the disappointed hustler, he picked up his hat and coat, tipped the hat check girl and rushed into the crowded corridor, crashing into an Arab dressed in desert garb. Instantly four menacing goons sprang at him. He raised his arms innocently, backed off apologetically and darted toward the front entrance.

An after-image of the hooker blipped a message.

A red, squiggly mark on her left breast had imprinted! Like Berna's! The rest of her didn't compute—or did it? If the makeup were removed . . .?

The Scotch curdled his stomach. He needed fresh air. Moving out the lobby doors into the night, Brad inhaled deeply while a uniformed doorman blew his whistle to summon a cabbie.

"The Bristol!" he snapped, boarding the cab. His thoughts wrapped around one repetitive theme. *Get the hell back to D.C. You've got no back-up here!* To make his short ride to the Bristol worse than the rising nausea were Marnay's words echoing in his mind.

Hidden forces will spring from unexpected places to obstruct you . . . They'll squash you like a bug . . . a bug . . . a bug!

Warnings couched between enigmatic words. He, the expert in ciphers, had lost his touch. His conversation with Marnay, ricocheting through mental corridors, fragmented other thoughts, confusing him. He'd reached a dead end and there were no detours in sight. Without Marnay, he was finished—or was he? There was the note concerning Wolfgang Katz. How would Wolfgang Katz serve him in his quest to find Moufflon? How, in God's name?

Brad strode through the Bristol lobby and entered the lift feeling awful. Pain assaulted his stomach as his nausea increased. Mopping the sweat from his face, he stepped out at the sixth floor, quickened his pace along the deserted hall to his suite of rooms.

Something was drastically wrong!

The key in his hand shook and several attempts to insert it into the lock failed. Everything blurred. Reaching for his glasses, he shoved them into place. Nothing helped. Groping for the lock, like a blind man, he guided the key into place. *Voilà!* He shoved the door open, felt for the light switch. Then the door slammed behind him. Brad heard a muffled commotion, a dull thud before his cranium exploded. Assaulted by shards of electrifying lights, excruciating, piercing colors, his eyes felt spiked by glass splinters.

Brad lurched forward, blood streaming from between his lips. He fell, reeling, stumbling blindly into furniture. Shadows attacked him. He flailed his arms, trying desperately to fend off his attackers, but a sharp needle jab to his right arm finished it.

He spun out, dervishlike, into dislocated arcs before tunneling in a bottomless pit.

Christ! He felt as if he'd been pounded into the concrete so hard, he was walking around on his balls. Then only merciful darkness.

Consciousness came slowly. A mental fog, chemical stench gave rise to nausea. He cracked open an eye, then the other. He felt life tingle in his lower extremities, spreading upward to his torso, arms, neck, then an energetic burst to the brain. Chest pains spread so acutely, he barely dared to breathe. The base of his spine telegraphed searing flame, his nerves were on fire. He felt immobilized by what seemed a ten-ton pressure.

Vaguely, as if from infinity, came clock chimes. Nine . . . ten . . . eleven . . .

Eleven o'clock . . . unconscious for an hour? Did it matter? It mattered plenty! I can't just lie here! Force yourself, dammit! Move! Goddammit! MOVE! Slow, now, easy does it. Pull yourself up, that's it. Grab hold of something, crawl, scratch, pull, tug!

He lurched off-balance, clung to chairs, walls, anything to get to his briefcase. He needed pain pills, amphetamines, anything to counteract what he'd ingested earlier. Copious sweat, nature's way of fighting off toxins, should have forewarned him. *The drinks!*

Yes, that was it! Drugged! He shivered, then turned hot as images distorted. He couldn't see the briefcase. He groped, and reaching for the black case containing the pills, he stared. He could see better from memory. He closed his eyes and unzipped the case, imagined the contents and felt for the bottle closest to his right hand.

Changing his mind, he took the case with him to the bathroom, each step dragging painfully. He fumbled for the light switch. Forced to shut his burning eyes from the sudden glare, he winced painfully until he adjusted to the shock of brightness.

He doused his head under cold water, feeling a slow relief as the water cooled his agonized skull. Now—the Percodan. He popped two, cupping his hands under the flowing tap, and slurped up the water, swallowing the tablets.

Slowly he rose to an erect position, the shock from brain to his spine sheer agony. Brad inhaled tremorously, increasing gulps of air. He kept his eyes lidded as protection against the light.

He looked into the mirror and blinked hard, arrested by the ghastly sight reflected in the mirror.

Holy Jesus! No! . . . No, it can't be! He spun around, leaning heavily on the basin, unable to focus through his glazed and dilated eyes. Aghast at what he saw, what he thought he saw, and what his brain registered finally, he tried to scream. Animal screams, sheep panic, hoarse shrieks glued to his larynx refused to dislodge themselves. He fell against the wall, shaking his head at the grotesque sight, convinced he was losing his mind.

He wasn't. He needed reassurance of his sanity. It came, dull at first, then perception returned as distinctly as the ringing of a telephone. Sounds of drunken laughter, boisterous goings-on from the adjoining suite drove him to reality.

This was no nightmare! It was real!

A few feet from Brad, suspended by an underarm harness, hung the bloodied, bullet-ridden body of an old friend. A man he had earlier condemned for a lack of guts. The man who had rejected his fraudulent ten-million-dollar bribe! *Commissaire* Marie Pierre Marnay! His neck slit by a wire garotte! The rest of him a sieve of bloodied holes—graphic testament that Brad had trespassed *verboten* waters!

Brad vomitted his dinner. the Scotch, and whatever else had frozen inside him.

The sight of dead men had never fazed him; he'd seen plenty in his lifetime, killed his share on assignment in war and espionage. But the unexpected, unwarranted desecration revolted his senses. The drugs administered to him created mounting paranoia. His head felt as if it were about to burst.

Chimes . . . again. Fucking, goddamn chimes, not bells, but chimes.

Reluctantly tearing his eyes from Marnay's mutilated body, he staggered into the sitting room, the hammering in his head unendurable.

He distinctly heard telephone chimes. Real chimes. His eyes darted to the beige-colored instrument on the desk, loathe to pick it up. *Friend or foe?* Who knew he was here? *The men who killed Marnay, you jackass! Who else?*

He picked up the phone, listening, not daring to speak. Two sentences got through to him.

"Get the fuckin' hell outa there and back to me. You've been marked for a hit!"

A loud click . . . then silence . . . the voice—Jim Greer's.

Brad fell heavily into a chair, repeating the sentences over and over in his mind. *Get the fuckin' hell outa there and back to me. You've been marked for a hit!*

Why, in God's name? Why? *Marnay spelled it out for you, dummy! You didn't listen!*

He pulled himself to his feet, the Percodan dulling the ache substantially left him light-headed. He unscrewed the silver flask in the briefcase, gulped greedily at the Scotch. A lousy combination, but the pain lessened. From the same black kit in the bathroom he removed two black beauties from a vial—uppers. He popped them, the combination still lousy, but necessary. From a secret compartment built into the briefcase he removed a new passport and cover ID. He glanced at the photo taken a year ago. It would do. Attorney Benjamin Lord of Phoenix, Arizona, was ready for action.

The mental fog was lifting. Brad knew Marnay's body must not be found in a room occupied by an American, *any* American. He had no time to rot in a French jail until an Embassy aide was contacted to spring him. Marnay was right about French jails.

Fifteen minutes later, the deed was done. Marnay's mutilated body, in full rigor, strapped erect in the express elevator, soared down to the basement. The poor slob must have resisted like hell for his body to be in full rigor so soon.

Brad was out the Bristol door, bag and briefcase in hand, one foot inside a taxi when the sickening wail of sirens approached. The cab shot forward on his orders. "Orly! An extra thousand francs if I don't miss my plane!"

So! A set-up! So soon? Someone along the way already had the information. Who? Who in hell knew his mission. *Christ!* He hoped to God he hadn't blown Greer's cover! Someone was trying to prevent him from meeting Moufflon! Marnay's words echoed from death.

Special power groups to whom international upheaval essential to their existence will squash you like a bug!

Two men in Europe knew what he was after. Jim Greer and Marnay. Marnay was dead; the atrocity calculated to produce a maximum psychological effect on him had nearly succeeded.

Jim Greer had no cause to set him up—did he?

Once at Orly, Brad ran swiftly inside the terminal. Stewards were already closing hatch doors at the boarding platform as he ran, flashing his boarding pass. They waved him forward inside the 707. Brad found his seat and sat down breathlessly.

He shoved his briefcase under the seat, buckled himself securely and closed his eyes behind dark glasses, praying for relief. Percodan and amphetamines turned to adversaries inside him; one dulled his mind, relaxed his body, the other forced him to think, tense up, and keep alert.

Images of Marnay's mutilated body wouldn't dissolve. The nightmarish expression, grotesque, etched vividly in his mind, persisted. Brad's roiling thoughts mushroomed. It *had* happened! The *who did it* and *why*, not apparent, yet he had to find out his own culpability. Had someone overheard their conversation? Picked up bits and pieces of it out of context, shaped them into a conspiracy? And who the bloody blue blazes was the illusive Moufflon?

Obviously Moufflon was known to Greer. To Marnay. *And* himself. But when—how? Brad tapped his head. When else, *Dumkoff?* World War II! Well, that narrowed it down to a few hundred thousand. Vindictive, bitter, hypercritical, he glowered inwardly.

Someone had tried to kill him! Instead they got Marnay!

Think, Brad! Think hard! Moufflon apparently stood at center stage of this scenario. Why would he want Marnay dead? Marnay hadn't revealed incriminatory information against the man. Then, *why*?

Thus far Brad's journey seemed pointless, and getting more pointless by the moment. He knew less about Moufflon than before departing D.C.

Why the hell am I here? Why was he trying to solve a puzzle that spanned forty goddamned years? Why? he asked himself, as he leaned his head back, aching.

A welcome cool breeze, an overhead tunnel of fresh air from the air conditioner, cooled the toxic sweat pouring from him. He dabbed at his face with a handkerchief.

Wait a minute . . . Wait just a minute! Something rang loud and clear. Now he had two goals to pursue. First, to find Moufflon; second, to identify the invisible forces spoken of in Pentagon hearings and definitely alluded to by Marnay. Marnay's death—his own close call with instant eternity confirmed the ominous power cartel. *That's who was stalking him—Zurich!* Without consciously dwelling on the subject, bits and pieces started to fit together.

The scent of freshly brewed coffee and hot croissants stopped the thought process. He was smiled at, handed a tray by a chic, voluptuous, blue-eyed stewardess. He smiled, aware her probing eyes studied his facial bruises scrupulously. He bit into the crispy, luscious croissant and was instantly assaulted by pain spasms. His jaws felt broken. He sipped coffee gingerly, breaking off bits and pieces of the cheese croissant, letting them melt in his mouth.

He concentrated again on the pieces of information he had collected. Had the brunette and blond man at the Crazy Horse Saloon, with the bartender's complicity, drugged his drinks? If someone wanted him dead, why hadn't they finished him off at the Bristol? Inwardly Brad fumed; the pieces weren't fitting together.

Then he knew. The events hadn't been designed to make sense!

Chapter Four

". . . The authors of the French Revolution are not more French than German, Russian, English, Italian. They form a particular nation which took birth and has increased in the dark amidst all civilized nations with the object of subjecting them to its domination . . ."
. . . Chevalier de Malet, 1817

Jim Greer, at once precarious and indulgent, got to the point over hot coffee and brandy. In Brad's absence his recollection of the immediate post–World War II era had sharpened perceptively: A succession of incidents, the numerous assassination attempts on the life of General Charles de Gaulle, initiated a public expose of those brokers in power who financed the secret army organization (OAS) in the 1962 attempts on his life.

"The lid was blown on the top-ranking wheels who masterminded the clandestine operation. It didn't stop continued attempts on the General's life. Each time the SDECE fought back masterfully.''

"Jim, you're reciting history I already know."

"Yeah, yeah, I know. But I have to tell it my way. Let me go back to 14 June, 1940, when Hitler marched into Paris. Marshal Petain capitulated and France split in two. De Gaulle, then a Brigadier General, formed the Free French Army from the remnants of the 13th Demi-Brigade of the Foreign Legion. He set up the French National Committee headquartered in Algeria and allied himself with Great Britain, Russia and the United States. In May 1944 he moved the FNC headquarters to London. Later, after the liberation, in Paris . . .''

Brad sipped the hot brandy eggnog, listening patiently, staring at the play of bright sunbeams forming oblique striations through the windows.

"Are you following this?" Greer snapped at him before continuing. "De Gaulle was made provisional president. The FNC was recognized as a de facto government. Now, get this. Two months later, this hero, who actually saved France, resigned. *Resigned!* His proposal for increased presidential powers, rejected by the legislature and the people, didn't deter the old war-horse from organizing a new political movement in April 1947. It fell flat as the proverbial hotcake. So . . . in 1953 this *hero* sought retirement. *Retirement?* From a man who had fought to the end for France? Ignored by the people he had liberated from German vassalage? Does that make for sinister plottings, Major?''

"Christ, Jim, stop this past history pavane and get to the point! You sent me a hot message over the wire! I didn't bust my balls getting here for a lesson in history!'' Brad was exasperated.

Greer wagged him silent. He was on a roll, and refused to acknowledge the interruption. The story would be told as he saw fit. "Got it, so far? Retirement in 1953? . . . Good. Five years later, in 1958, France recalled de Gaulle to help resolve the threat of war over Algerian independence. He was empowered to act as premier, to rule by decree for six months. He was later elected president of the new Fifth Republic and took office in 1958. In 1960 France acquired the atom bomb, strengthened ties with Russia and Communist China. Got the picture? *With* Russia against his former allies?''

Greer snorted cocaine through a slender, minuscule gold tube, cleared his nose, letting the cold, icy rush shudder through to his brain. A Cheshire-cat grin spread over his face. "Then, *ol' buddy*, came the succession of assassination attempts—not one, two, three—but a rash of attempts against his life. De Gaulle fought back; he used the *legal* instrument of the SDECE *and* the muscle of a very loyal Frenchman—a Corsican!"

Brad sat forward, tense, his coffee mug arrested in midair, ears honed acutely.

"I *knew* that would grab you, *ol' buddy*. A Corsican *and* a cohesive squad of trained specialists. Men *needing* no training in martial arts, the expertise of weaponry, and use of small, up-to-the-minute handguns. Men needing *no* training in arson, sabotage, demolition, explosives . . . No training in radio communications, kidnapping, slayings and assassinations . . ."

"*The Mozarabe!*" Brad hissed, above a whisper.

"Bull's-eye!" Greer's voice dropped a few decibels. "O.K., buddy, now we swing back to 1944–1950, the birth of a code word: *CORSICAN JADE*. For undiminished loyalty to France in World War II the Mozarabe were given the entire Cote d'Azur to wheel and deal in contraband goods *without* interference from the SDECE. The Marseilles waterfront and Corsica was theirs."

"And when we left West Berlin, you joined Corsican Jade. There was a connection? Between Corsican Jade and the Mozarabe?"

"One and the same, for a time. The Mozarabe was too well known in certain circles; it became unfeasible for them to operate under that code name, so they changed to Corsican Jade. Remember, I joined them only for one year. It was enough. I returned stateside, swore loyalty to the Company and became an *animale*—remember? I should have remained with Jade."

Dammit! Brad knew it! If any man knew how to fit the pieces of a forty-year history into place, it was Greer! He knew it in D.C. He knew it now. Greer was an integral part of this mission!

Berna was gone, and no mention was made of her absence.

Greer, no longer displaying the earlier hostility communicated during Brad's first visit, was relaxed, as charming as a friendly lion. He left the room, returned from the kitchen with a tray of cold cuts, cheeses, dark German bread, mustard and relishes. He constructed enormous sandwiches, poured cold German beer. Between bites, Greer continued.

"I know what you're thinking about de Gaulle, but it must be aired. His hostility to the United States and Britain in exchange for an alliance with Russia and China marked the beginning of the end for him. Why? He *knew* too much. He named the conspirators of the Dallas tragedy; they were the same men whose attempts on his life had been foiled. He passed the information on to the White House and to British M-I, but those in charge were too chicken-shit to bring charges—including the Warren Commission. Yes, I'm saying the Oval Office was scared to admit the truth. *Why*? Because the assassins lay within U.S. Government investigatory agency infrastructures. They have clout! I'm talking *tough* clout! Clout wielded by a power cartel who had financed and backed the careers of most politicians in government! They'll destroy anyone—any government who attempts to spotlight their scum-sucking politics! Check the record. Musaka Mubende got it! Poor old Katz got it in 1952 when he refused to buckle under them!''

Brad flinched. *Katz again! Wolfgang Katz! A name from the past written on a scrap of paper and shoved into his wallet during his last trip here.*

"Katz is dead . . .? You mean *Wolfgang* Katz? From West Berlin?"

Greer paused briefly.

"Nah. I don't think he's dead. But nearly. Twenty years of torture—something like that. But, back to de Gaulle. In 1966, backed by the Soviets, he advocated French-Canadian autonomy. He recommended a return to the gold standard and a replacement of the U.S. dollar as the chief monetary exchange standard."

"Jim, where the hell is all this leading? I know all this—''

"You Company men dissected all these moves cleverly by the *controlled* papers issued on the actions. But you failed to examine meticulously the chronology of events as objectively as I did for twenty years. Listen and learn . . . In 1968 de Gaulle withdrew from NATO, removed French troops from Indo-China—Vietnam, if you will. And then the old soldier faced the darkest crisis since he returned to power. Rebellious student protests, striking workers, economic instability and virtual anarchy! His power diminished. He retired in 1969 and died a year later from unnatural causes."

"*Unnatural* causes? Not a heart attack?"

"S-h-i-t! You don't get it—do you?" He slapped his thighs

95

loudly. "Damn! You don't follow me—the pattern? Jesus, did your brains *atrophy* in those Committee Meetings? Think, Brad—think! What would have been the consequences if de Gaulle *had* persuaded the Common Market to replace the U.S. dollar? World capitalism would have been shattered. The dope for dollar and diamond dealers would have gone belly up. Uh-uh, ol' buddy, they couldn't chance letting de Gaulle have his way."

He guzzled the remaining beer, opened a fresh can, and sat back, one leg over the arm of the chair. "Social unrest can prove fatal to industrial capitalists, Brad, but to international speculating capitalists, the same socio-politico-economic disasters provide opportunities for profit. Manipulators of money, if informed in advance, can profit from anything, *especially* if they happen to choreograph the global calamities."

Brad stared hard at Greer, thoughts stampeding across his brain like a herd of rhinos in heat. Greer observed him, anticipating, waiting for the lightning bolt of enlightenment to burst on his old friend. He repeated himself.

"Rebellious students, economic stability, virtual anarchy—all orchestrated. A recital of the SOD catechism? The Company's m.o.? *My* m.o.? Face it, it's a fucking conspiracy, Brad. All of it. All of it is manufactured. We stirred up the rabble-rousers, fired their radical, fanatical minds. The President is a figurehead, a *fucking* pawn in an international chess game controlled by the manipulators of money and power. The people of the world are innocent spectators who suffer by the chess moves, die in bomb blasts or heavy artillery fire in a war that fills the coffers of the rich! The President's got no more power than a bullet shot from a gun beyond its shooting range. He barely makes a dent in things—certainly his word is not lethal. But let him buck those power machines and he's stripped to the bone. Trouble with you, Brad, you always believed in sugarplum fairies."

"Cut the bullshit! You could have told me this before I went to Paris. You aren't concerned at Marnay's death?"

"Marnay is a dead issue. Drop it."

Brad refused. He pressed. "Marnay died because of me. Someone tried to inculpate me. They transported his mutilated body to my suite at the Bristol. I interrupted them and for my reward was shot with drugs—"

"And someone found you in time to inject the antidote to the poison!" Greer retorted hotly.

Brad was shaken. "Poison? . . . Poison! . . . How do you know this?"

"If you let me finish my spiel, you'll find out. Cool off. You've had a rotten go at it. You look awful!"

"I feel worse. About Marnay—did you discuss my meet with him to anyone? Berna, perhaps, whom you insisted didn't understand a word of English?"

"Will you forget Marnay until I finish?" Greer glowered.

"I want straight answers, Jim. Marnay was killed for nothing. Okay—tell me, who marked me for a hit? How you knew enough to warn me. Those were your words—not mine . . . *You* said I was a hot target! *Why?* To prevent my meeting Moufflon?" On his feet, Brad paced, flushed with frustration. It was the wrong tack to take, he knew it, but impatience wore him down. "Okay—okay, Moufflon's protected at the top. Protected from *what?* . . . Jim, shall I tell you why I am here? The sole purpose was to arrange a meeting between Moufflon and the Oval Office!"

"You're crazy! Have you gone mad?"

"I believe that Moufflon holds the key to the Middle East turmoil. America wants to avert nuclear war. It's that fuckin' simple! Does it warrant Marnay's death? The attempt on my life?"

"Yes, to those who'll profit by preventing such a meeting."

Brad, suffused with rage, stopped his pacing. He stared at Greer. Marnay's words broke through and suddenly made some sense. *Special interest groups to whom political upheaval is essential to their existence will squash you like a bug.*

His eyes were icy pinnacles. "Tell me how *you* knew I was marked for a kill! *Who* tailed me? How did you lean *where* I was, *when*, and with *whom?* Your call to me at the Bristol was *timed* perfection. I came here risking my life—for what? A recitation on de Gaulle? I need this garbage like—"

"Goddamit, you'll never learn! The one thing you lack is patience. All right, we'll play it your way."

Greer lifted his heavy frame from the chair and pressed a button engaging a tape recorder. The room filled with Marnay's and Lincoln's conversation at the bistro. Brad's reaction: a mixture of amazement, vapidity, speculation, then a slow anger.

Finished, Greer turned off the recorder. "Where are the photos you showed me last time?"

Brad fished through his pockets, produced all three. Greer

shuffled through them. "Here," he tapped one photo, indicating a scrubby-faced, gaunt kid, dressed shabbily in rags. Two enormous dark eyes stared out from him. "This is *Killer* Claude Montreaux of the Resistance, the owner of the bistro. Remember Paris? Marseilles? Corsica? A Resistance fighter trained by the *Mozarabe*?"

Brad stared at the photo, reaching into the past, vaguely recalling the lad. He nodded. Greer filled in the gaps:

"After Marseilles our detail moved northward to prepare for the Paris liberation. *Killer* Claude, a kid at the time, was eager to reunite with his family before the final coup and slipped away from our encampment, unprepared for what greeted him. His family, press-ganged by Germans into forced labor, were somewhere in Germany. Worse, far more devastating to Claude, was the shock of discovering that his three sisters had willingly sexually embraced Nazi officers. This knowledge unleashed a violent savagery in the boy's soul. Sickened and enraged at the sight, in the next hour all skills taught him by the Corsican commandos were tested. What followed was the howling, bloody, god-awful rampage—the slaughter of each officer and the vengeful butchering of his collaborative sisters. The final count when he emerged from the insanity of murder—five high-ranking Wehrmacht officers and two S.S. *Oberleutnants*, and three sisters. Ten in all! He buried the bodies in an underground wine cellar adjoining the ancient houses. In the process he stumbled upon a hidden cache of valuable art treasures appropriated and hidden by some crafty, farsighted men, not Germans, whose intent it was to return after the war and reap a profitable harvest. Unsophisticated, unaware of their real worth, he buried them in the same old wine cellar, barricading the entrance with old crates and wine kegs. He returned to the Resistance encampment without uttering a single word of his butchery.

After the war, Claude received commendations for bravery. From Marnay came the shattering news: his sisters, an integral part of the Resistance Underground, were missing. He told Claude of their invaluable contribution in obtaining vital information from the Nazis, information they in turn transmitted via sequestered mobile radios to British MI across the channel in London. Claude fell apart. He disappeared for a few years, retired to a military hospital to recuperate from frightening nightmares and mental aberrations. He confessed in confidence to Marnay what he had done that night. Following his full recuperation, Claude returned to the family house to find the art treasures gone. The skeletal remains of his victims lay strewn about, but not the treasures.

I am not certain what took place, but he confided in Moufflon. Soon after he appeared with enough bread to open a posh bistro on the Left Bank. A close association was formed with Marnay, a man he loathed for not telling him of his sister's brave contribution to the war effort. What followed was, Claude prospered, but Marnay, locked into his position as *Commissaire* of the Police Judiciare, was unable to elevate himself above that level of influence."

"I remember," Brad said solemnly when Greer finished. "*Killer* Claude was *CORSICAN JADE* with you and Marnay. Is that the picture? Why tell me all this? It merely confuses the issues."

"Killer Claude Montreaux is Moufflon's man in Paris. He saw you with Marnay, and called me directly, transmitting your conversation."

"Why, in God's name?"

"Marnay, inclined to play both sides against the middle, was baiting you. He stole the art treasures and dealt directly with the power cartel who accused the Nazis of stealing them. He had stolen from thieves thinking he had proper collateral; instead, he got the short end of the stick. He was cheated in the final count. How? I don't know. But he suffered politically."

Brad, about to dispute, stopped abruptly, the short hairs on his neck doing knee bends. Twenty years had passed. Did he really know Greer? Twenty years since he'd seen Marnay didn't qualify him as a friend. He recalled his initial shock at learning Marnay's position in the Surete. "What you're saying is Claude killed Marnay in a vendetta?"

"Brad! I don't give a shit *who* killed the bastard! He held the Commissaire's job as a payoff for his silence. Kept under scrutiny where others could watch him, he could be of service. Long ago Claude explained the rigged recording apparatus under Marnay's table at the bistro. While you and the Commissaire conversed, other ears listened and easily transmitted your conversation as simply as Claude's men patched into my frequency for relay."

Brad's face drained of color.

"*My cover's been blown!*"

"In spades."

"And *yours?* . . ."

"My name wasn't mentioned on the tapes."

"Marnay told me nothing to warrant his death—"

"Goddammit it! Marnay again! Marnay is *not* my problem! Why do you insist I deal with his death? Listen, there isn't much time."

Greer began to speak without letup. Brad listened in a contained silence. Two hours later the insoluble became soluble. Killer Claude had saved Brad's life. But there was more. Those men in white in the ambulance, pulling up to the Bristol as Brad hastily departed, were assassins after him.

"Who are they? Who's after me?"

"Can't say. The word's out. When I learn—"

"—who, it might be too late."

Greer raised the volume on the radio. He peered intently through the windows where the Huskies romped playfully in the snow. He tossed Brad a gun. "Check it out," he said gruffly, doing likewise to the M52. "Even a smart monkey can be felled from the trees," he said quietly.

Brad snapped the breech of the gun back into place.

"The fuckin' walls have ears . . . windows have eyes. Only the dead have no tongues."

"A lesson in Confucius say—"

"*Goddammit!* Shut up! Just shut up! Live in the wilderness long enough and nature teaches you plenty. One thing is to know when to keep silent."

Then Brad knew why.

He heard a beeping sound, faint at first, gradually growing more acute. His eyes darted to a panel of flickering lights on a bookshelf to the left of the fireplace. Greer shouldered the wall case, swinging it about to reveal a high-powered communications system powered by a concealed generator located on the property.

Astonished, Brad observed Greer in action, flipping switches, turning dials, inserting minute earphones and microphone disks into place, reading digital impressions on the computer screen. Listening intently to the transmissions, Greer responded in a mixture of German, French and Italian with the aid of voice-altering devices. Finished, he turned off the electronic goddess, mixed two brandy eggnogs in thoughtful silence. Obvious to Brad as he accepted one of the drinks was the relief in Greer's expression. He sat down in a leather chair facing him, the German shepherd moving from the hearth to curl up at his master's feet. Greer stroked the dog's head and began to speak. He began revealing the crucial information which had eluded Brad at the outset—the Corsican's name and true identity.

"The Corsican is Moufflon!"

Dammit! The revelation stupefied him. Brad was furious with himself for avoiding the real reason he had blocked the Corsican's name from his mind. He had been acting like a rank amateur! He had begun this assignment as a routine task. Now he was sickened at the complexities posed at every sinister twist and turn.

Fool! What madness had he embarked upon? He, a professional in his field, had failed to recognize the absurdities of his own strategy. To approach President Macgregor with Moufflon's true identity was tantamount to being declared mad. He'd be tossed out on his ass. The intricate mosaic that formed the Corsican's life was recognizable even in 1942 at the outset of their acquaintance. Had Brad made the connection between the Corsican and Moufflon, he would not be in Europe today! He would not have dared!

But he was here to gather pertinent data! If what Greer had just revealed was true, it meant Brad had to dig deeper, accumulate more valuable information.

An indefinable pattern buried deep in his mind was slowly coming into focus; it signaled dangerous grounds to be explored. He better understood Greer's paranoia, the circuitous route he had employed to spotlight the numerous obstacles Brad must be prepared to overcome. It became imperative for Brad to compile a documentation of facts, records—everything he needed to prove his allegations of the international conspiracy to President Macgregor.

Christ! He'd need a year to penetrate security vaults for the required data. Brad masked his unease with false bravado. "Whatever the outcome, Jim, something positive will come from your valuable cooperation."

"At least two stars on *your* shoulders."

Brad ignored the sarcasm. "You insist Marnay told me plenty. I assure you he gave me nothing."

"He told you plenty. You didn't pick up on it because you lacked the key: Moufflon's identity. Piece it together now. Come on! Marnay turned down ten million to identify one man? Hah! His refusal should have aroused your suspicions."

"Sure—if I knew what was in Marnay's mind. After all, I did *know* the Corsican!"

"Just bear in mind, Brad, you don't know everything! If you did, you wouldn't be alive. Knowing you, you'll piece it together before you touch down in D.C."

"*If* I get back . . ."

Greer's attention darted sharply to him. "Now who's paranoid?" He moved to the desk at the far end of the room, retrieved a fistful of glossy 8 X 10 photos from the drawer, thrust them at Brad, disgust on his face. "You thought I intended to toss you over an icy pinnacle . . . Well, old friend, I am not your enemy. Study these; memorize the faces and m.o.'s. All are known assassins—full descriptions and bios, including aliases, are on the reverse side. Look for them everywhere. Attempts will be made to terminate you every step of the way to your objective."

"Swell," Brad muttered, shuffling through the photos. He picked out three. "These have already tried. Do I waste them or lead them a merry chase?"

Greer glanced at the first photo, that of the tall, blond male, dark eyes, Valentino haircut. "Where?"

"The Crazy Horse at the George Cinq. He was with this melon-breasted brunette," he said, holding up another picture.

"They aren't into fun and games, ol' buddy. They play for keeps." He glanced at the third. "What about him?"

Brad nodded knowingly. "Charles de Gaulle Airport and later at the Bristol."

"He's the *Needle*. Tops in his field, he's a master at disguise. Don't make light of him. His expertise—toxicology."

"Poisons."

"*Exotic* poisons. Undetectable. Some without antidotes. His forte—deaths attributable to natural causes, cardiac arrests, etc. The other man is *Llamas*, a real bloody doozy. Assassins, hot for the price on you. It's their job to make certain you learn nothing. Them's orders from the top. They don't play games."

"*They*? Who—*they*?"

"The same *they* we spoke of earlier. *They* hide behind a hundred corporate veils in Europe, Canada, South America, Africa, the Middle and Far East and America. Tentacles of power? Canada, Liberia, Israel, Italy, Germany, Switzerland and the good ol' U.S.A."

"Everywhere—is that it?"

"Keep in mind what happened to de Gaulle when he tried to bring down the solid-gold walls of capitalism. These diamond-studded ivory-tower moguls, deep into drug bonanzas, will use all their resources to protect themselves."

"Has anyone explained the expediency of the neutron bomb to them? Those diamond-studded ivory towers aren't eternal. Oh, and another thing, Jim, the girl—" Brad pulled the photo, placed it on top of the pile. "Is she a *Corsican Jade* throwback?"

"No. *CORSICAN JADE* disappeared under the umbrella of *Partition Five*, the official tag given them by the SDECE. Before de Gaulle's death they became *Moufflon*, untouchable by law. The girl is *Corsican Coral*, a splinter group no longer connected to *Partition Five* or *Moufflon*. They are all programmed to kill the minute a dime is dropped on them."

"Berna, too?"

Greer flushed. "You want it straight?" He indicated to an obvious scar on the girl's breast. "The mark of *Corsican Coral*."

So, Brad asked the obvious. Was Berna Corsican Coral? Greer grew evasive at his questions, suggesting the girls were experts at makeup and wigs. Was Greer *Corsican Coral*? No, he had tried to hook up with them, couldn't qualify because of the *jacket* the CIA had dumped on him. They gave him a job now and again to pay the rent. That wrapped it.

"Now that you've snitched, are you caught in a web? What you've told me confirms a long haul of intelligence-gathering. How can I be sure, when I leave, you won't put that communications depot to work and put out an S.O.S. on me."

Brad leveled his gaze on the man seated facing him. "You can't be sure. For once in your life—no, it's the second time that I know of—you're out of the driver's seat. You can't stand not being in control. It makes you jittery and suspicious, right? You'll have to trust me. Like I must trust you."

The implied rancor harked back to *OPERATION WHITE CORAL*, Corsica, 1943. Brad had refused to relinquish full

103

command of the Allied effort on the island to the Corsican, now identified as Moufflon. Brad Lincoln's insistence on maintaining the American super-macho image had interfered in the special operations. Several deaths had resulted. The Corsican, containing his rage, had nearly stripped Brad of co-command. Later, well within his rights to do so, the Corsican officer leveled no charges against then Captain Brad Lincoln. In Marseilles, he had saved Brad's life.

Jealousy! . . . That was the reason his subconscious mind had refused to give him the Corsican's identity! Ah, frailty, thy name is woman. Valentina Varga—was woman. Brad's unrequited love had given all her love to the Corsican. Did she know he was the infamous Moufflon?

"We are—none of us—endowed with perfection," Brad said, struggling to keep his voice even. He was determined to pull every scrap of information before he moved on. But he was startled at Greer's next words.

"Your presence here is known to Moufflon. Your moves, reported to him, are analyzed, implying what you are after. He asks that I convey his inability to initiate an encounter with you for reasons even I dare not speculate." Greer turned up the volume on the radio. "You should know, for whatever it's worth, that the KGB are tracking you."

"*The KGB? Me? What the hell for?*"

"Beats the hell outta me, Huckleberry Finn."

"Nothing fits."

"Has it ever?"

"About *Corsican Coral*—?" Brad needed clarification concerning its connection to Moufflon.

"I thought I made it clear. No connection—none at all. *Corsican Coral*, like the Brigades, Bader-Meinoff, hire out as a whole or in part. They are bought and paid for, promised immortality."

"By whom?"

"The same power cartel responsible for shooting de Gaulle off his political perch. They are twelve in number: an outer circle of three protects the one madman in charge, a psychologically perverse fiend whose tentacles periodically send shock waves of fear to those he controls."

Brad's confidence wavered. "Can you identify them—any of them?"

Greer studied his guest before he spoke. "If I could, I wouldn't be alive."

The talk continued throughout the night. Early the next morning, prior to Brad's departure, Jim Greer dropped another bomb.

"How tight is the Oval Office with his new Secretary of State?"

"Harding?" Brad scowled. "Why?"

"Word is he's getting too much clout. He's been bad-mouthing your guy in the wrong circles. Building up kingdoms of gold for the next world."

"I don't follow. I need more."

"The money is being laid on him, backing him for the presidency next term. The kinda dough I'm talking, buddy, fucking blows my mind . . ."

Brad couldn't wait to leave. If what Greer had told him was true, then there wasn't much time before the whole thing could blow. . . .

Brad boarded the express to Zurich, enroute to West Berlin. There was a man there from World War II, a man he must see. Something Greer said, or failed to explain, sounded tocsins in his brain.

Wolfgang Katz knew something, something Brad desperately needed.

But before Wolfgang Katz, there was a woman he would see. If memory served him well, she was exactly what he needed. He had lived with her . . . Oh, Christ . . . he made a quick mental calculation. In 1946 she was ten years older than Brad. That would make her . . .?

No rutting around this woman's legs, Brad. He contented himself with memories of their boudoir gymnastics. Christ, she had been something in those days. There was a madness in her loins, a need to break through the horror of life during wartime. But now . . .?

Brad perished the thought.

Chapter Five

". . . It was neither parliaments, nor populations, nor the course of nature, not the course of events that overthrew the throne of Louis Phillipe . . . the throne was surprised by Secret Societies ever prepared to ravage Europe. Acting in unison with a great popular movement, they will destroy society as they did at the end of the last century . . ."

. . . Disraeli, 1825

WEST BERLIN
February 10, 1983

The enormous aircraft circled Templehof waiting to land in dense air traffic. The awesome aerial view of the Berlin Wall sprang up at the passengers, appalling them. One hundred miles of concrete manned by *Grenztruppen*, border guards stationed at firing-range intervals. Vehicle traps, beds of upturned spikes, barbed-wire fencing, floodlights, trip alarms and a dozen electronic spying devices designed to prevent people, living on one side of the wall, from learning how the other side lives.

Incredible? Crazy, perhaps? No—it was real and the passengers were chilled at the sight of what had numbed both East and West at the birth of the wall in 1960.

Forced to remain in his seat, Brad raged silently at the time lost pursuing vague offshoots from the central issue of his plans. This spiraling-off into complicated subplots merely disguised the main body of the plot.

Basic academics, dormant for years, sprang to life, guiding him.

Reverse positions with the enemy. Think as they think. Act as they would in given circumstances. Protect yourself against the unexpected, Brad.

How? He didn't know the enemy! The murder attempt on his life, and Marnay's death had not been made clear by Greer. Damn!

In Zurich, before Brad flew on to West Berlin, he had sent a ciphered message to a World War II conduit. The reply, received in cipher, when decoded, was terse, shaved to the bone:

Katz notified of your arrival. The meeting—locked into place. Study enclosed codes. One deviation and all is kaput.

Brad's mind worked fastidiously during the air time to West Berlin. He considered the man, Wolfgang Katz, formerly *Untersturmführer* of the *WAFFEN, S.S.,* a division of the *Schutzstaffel S.S.,* World War II Nazi elite guards acquitted of alleged war crimes in 1946, and protected by the Allied Control Council Law Number 10. Following the Nuremberg trials, Katz had worked with Lincoln and Greer. The German's cooperation in the reconstruction of Himmler's personal files resurrected from the ashes of the burning Reichstag had earned America's respect and appreciation. In 1950 Brad had separated from OSS Headquarters in West Berlin, returned to the states certain that Katz, under the terms of his acquittal from war crimes, had received proper protection and housing in a covert location of his choice.

Something had gone wrong! Drastically wrong!

The sketchy briefing was reminiscent of a Hitchcock whodunit. Abducted by the Soviets in 1953, held incommunicado in East Berlin for twenty years, he was sold to the Americans, delivered, and disappeared. *Literally* disappeared. Six months after leaving the East Berlin office of the KGB, the Soviets, as baffled as the Americans, were doubly baffled when Katz reappeared, a shadow of his former self, begging asylum.

Back to the Soviets, whom Katz loathed for killing his relatives during one of the warring coups? From whom he had attempted to flee in the past?

Uh-uh! Brad didn't buy it. He, the only man in whom Katz would confide, arrived in West Berlin to learn what had happened and how Katz tied into Moufflon.

The 707 finally swooped in for a perfect landing. An unmarked sedan sped along a VIP runway toward the giant aircraft. Brad deplaned, boarded the auto, sequestered behind smoke-gray windows. The driver sped out of Templehof's slushy snow-patched road, headed due west toward the Schöneberg district in the American sector. Brad swiftly changed into the clothing provided by the cadre of silent well-paid helpers who asked no questions.

Brad put on the heavy winter clothing provided him, thick woolen shirt, knitted sweater, a sheepskin-lined jacket and cap. He loaded the Czech M 52 pistol with Czech ammo, stored the cartridge box in his jacket pocket and meticulously examined the high-muzzle-velocity pistol. Good . . . all in working order. He shoved the weapon into his waistband under the sweater, then making certain no labels were in the boots, slipped into them. He also made certain nothing on his person identified him as an American. He was going in sterile.

He was exhausted. He'd had no sleep, and he needed it badly. He knew better than to attempt the mission while his embattled mind resisted caution, but his timetable permitted no rest.

"Do you have the instructions memorized?" the driver asked in German, turning off the main highway onto a narrow lane winding through a thickly forested stretch of snow-ladened farmland for approximately a half mile. "Up ahead a quarter of a mile," he cautioned, his eyes scanning the area.

The remains of his personal clothing stuffed into a backpack, along with a loaded minicamera, Brad left the sedan, slithered into the pack, slammed the rear door and watched the car and driver speed out of sight.

Shuddering in the icy wind, Brad tugged up the furry collar, and turned down the fur flaps of the cap, glancing at his watch, a cheap chronometer purchased at a shop in West Berlin. He set chartreuse-lensed snow goggles into place, and turning in the opposite direction, trudged along the narrow path along the Havel River edging Grunewald Forest heading for a point where the border runs midstream.

The icy pond glistened in the shaft of sunlight. He felt the hairs in his nose freeze. He trudged on. It was nearly eleven and he felt stirrings of alarm: had he taken the wrong turn? Then he saw him.

There . . . up ahead, under overcast skies, out of the sun. Brad watched a white-haired, bent-over old man, holding a fishing pole in an isolated spot of the winding riverbed bordered by a profusion of birch trees. Periodically he fly-cast a line into the swollen river rapids beyond the frozen edge. He was wiry,

108

emaciated and dwarfed by heavy winter clothing, certainly not fisherman's gear. Alert blue eyes lifted, fixed on Brad as he drew nearer. Brad saw the tinge of excitement, a glimmer of hope, then the expression was quickly concealed under lidded eyes. Brad spoke out in his most respectable German.

"*Guten morgen, mein Herr*. Do the fish bite well here?"

"*Nein, nein, mein Herr*. Not as they did once in 1946."

They faced each other, eyes searching eyes, testy, uncertain. Brad averted his glance, stared at the frothy white-capped river rapids. "You catch fish from both the east and west, eh, *mein Herr?*"

"You ask a complicated question."

"Simpler, then, can you differentiate between them?"

"From the east they swim downstream, spouting political rhetoric."

The carefully orchestrated pavane was about to end. "I take it you catch no Enceladus, here?"

"A moon of Saturn? Hardly."

They stared long and hard, the changes of four decades incredibly acute in Katz. The German, four years Brad's junior, looked eighty. Brad spoke tentatively. "Wolfgang—"

"*Ja, ja!* It's me, Katz. *Willkomen, mein Freund*, Lincoln." Tears steamed his glasses, and the two men embraced. "*Haben sie Amerikanische Zigaretten?*" Katz dropped the fishing pole, removed his glasses, waved them about to clear the steam and dabbed at his eyes.

Brad extricated the carton from his knapsack, handed it to his old friend, adding, "They cause cancer—don't you know?"

"*Das Karzinom?* . . . To me, what threat is cancer, eh? *Veilen dank*." Katz stared at the carton as if the contents were as precious as life.

Brad retrieved the pole, dissembled it, placed it neatly into its plastic case, and pulling the creel strap over one shoulder fell into step alongside Katz, shocked into cold sobriety.

Katz, utterly deformed, stooped, bore no resemblance to the young militarily braced German officer he recollected. The changes, acute, terribly graphic, he studied the man with oblique scrutiny to ascertain his authenticity.

"Come, my house is not far," Katz said warmly, communicating excruciating pain with each plodding step. Katz spoke randomly, his furtive eyes ringed with black shadows like a raccoon, darted about the area searching for an ambush among niches in denuded birch trees. Brad discerned the frequent pauses Katz took to catch his breath as camouflage to disguise his interest in the two hulking brutes following them at a respectable distance. American soldiers in plain clothing, M-16 rifles slung over their shoulders walked in bursts of action, their gait controlled by spirited Dobermans held back on choke chains.

The modest farmhouse was clapboard and stone. It was isolated from neighboring farms by a high concrete wall, manned by a few armed guards. The interior, warmed by a roaring fire on the hearth and simple, comfortable furnishings. A tray of hot coffee and *schnapps* lay on the table between two high-backed winged chairs. A robust, ruddy-cheeked woman in her thirties, in apron with her shirt sleeves rolled up, approached.

"*Mein* daughter, Marta. Marta, meet *mein gut Freund, Herr* Benjamin Lord, *Ja*."

She curtsied, helped Katz shed his overcoat, scarf, fur cap and galoshes, doing what seemed a mental inventory of the articles. She avoided Brad's eyes, took his jacket and cap, hanging them on wall pegs behind the front door in the small entry. Brad observed her critically. Something about her . . .

He felt a pang of uneasiness. She reminded him of Chou-Chou, the Resistance fighter who had reshaped Marnay's nose. Was he overworking his imagination? What possible threat could Katz' daughter pose to him? He stood before the fire rubbing his hands briskly. Katz poured coffee and held out the *schnapps*.

"You must come in summer, for the regatta on beautiful Havel River," he said, spinning off into pleasantries.

"You forget I spent five summers here?" Brad couldn't take his eyes off the narrow-faced, thin-bodied man, seemingly shorter than he remembered. Once a stickler for formality of speech, manner and dress, Wolfgang Katz no longer stood erect; now, he was a shrunken reflection of his former self.

Brunch of delicious shirred eggs, tasty German sausage, fresh bread and coffee invigorated Katz. Spyer, he actually glowed with provincial cordiality, the forty-year interim stripped from memory.

"When you were here the ACC applied their nonfraternization policy, denazification and demilitarization. That policy kept West Berlin weak and politically innocuous, *ja*? It took time, but now

110

West Berlin emerges strong as a bull, despite the four-color bridles integrated into one harness." He referred to the four zones of occupation.

Brad lighted a brier pipe, drawing on it, observing the white walled room, multicolored hooked rug, Spartan furniture, relics of the past—neat, orderly, everything in place. Leaning toward him, he spoke softly. "Katz, we must speak in private."

Katz understood. "Come, we go." He rose from the table, made short brushing strokes with his hand, motioning Brad toward a blank wall. He removed a brick from under the mantel, turned a switch, replaced the brick. A wall panel left of the fireplace opened, revealing another room. Katz stepped inside and flipped on a light switch, washing the room in bright candescence. Another switch engaged an overhead air circulator.

Brad entered and turned claustrophobic. The room was soundproof, insulated, windowless. A sophisticated communication terminal occupied a portion of a large desk. Overhead two closed-circuit video monitors focused on entrance and exit points of the farmhouse exterior. Brad scanned the room with critical assessing eyes. Glass-enclosed shelves on one wall contained World War II memorabilia. A second work area contained electronic typewriters and a word processor. In a corner was a raised hearth fireplace framed by pastel tiles. Two recliners and a table, functionally grouped before the fireplace. The table held a brass hurricane lamp, humidor, pipe rack, pencils and lined foolscap tablets. Katz, perfectly at home in his safe, cozy nest, gestured to the fireplace. "Matches . . . in the iron pot. Fire the kindling, *bitte*."

Brad removed a long match from the brass pot, fired it, held it to the kindling, jerking his hand back at the sudden burst of flames. Behind him, the sound of the wall panel sliding shut brought up Brad's head, a frown creasing his brow. "What happens, Katz, if the locks freeze—you know—*kaput*?"

"Marta pulls the main switch in the kitchen. We go to manual—"

"Why bother at all? You could lock up from inside."

"—and I release the mechanism from this room." Katz sobered.

"If something happens to you? Heart failure? A stroke?"

"*Ach, du lieber!* A remote switch at U.S. Intelligence Headquarters is engaged at the first sign of alert."

"You are, then, at the mercy of another when you are in this room?"

Katz, a formerly meticulous, well-organized man, studied Brad intently. Duty, responsibility, a total trust in authority had prevailed in his lifetime. He assumed it was the same with others. He still wore his stringed yellowish-white hair in military cut, dressed in prewar vintage country-squire attire, as if forty years hadn't elapsed. But those in-between years *had* happened and had taught him survival. Anticipating Brad's next question, he muttered quietly.

"*Mein* daughter, Marta, and her husband, Fritz, were cleared four years ago when I first found her."

"They have access to this room?"

"*Ja, ja.* But they do not come unless I summon them."

"In your absence, Katz . . .?"

"I carry a master key. Without it, electronics are *kaput*."

"Where do you sleep?"

"*Where do I sleep?* . . . But, of course, in the bed—in my bedroom. Where else—" Katz stopped, the picture forming in his mind. "But this is *verrict*—crazy! Nothing is touched. I would know."

"Master keys can be duplicated." Brad's caution created an ominous pause, the tension filling the room, electric.

"You allow speculation where none is permitted. Now old fears spring to mind." Katz stared unseeing into the fire.

"Don't ever drop your guard! It's a fuckin' mausoleum in here. No windows! One entrance and a peeping Tom!"

"Vas is das peeping Tom, *bitte*?" Katz spoke in his best English.

"A camera. Focused on us at this moment," Brad replied, his back to the mounted apparatus he'd spied above the fireplace.

"Part of a complicated alarm. Look here, this panel of buttons on the arm of my chair. If emergency arises, I depress it—so. Direct connection to Intelligence computers signals alert. You shouldn't worry, *mein Freund*." He depressed one button. A click brought Brad's attention to the wall cabinet behind him. "See? A regular arsenal for Katz. Handguns, high-velocity rifles, ammunition, even grenades."

Before asking the obvious *why* it was necessary to be this heavily protected, Brad was forced to point out the pitfalls.

"A *regular arsenal*, eh? Forgive me, old friend, but if some-

112

one deactivates the communication terminal . . . .? Cuts telephone wire . . .? What then?''

''Then Katz is *kaput*. The code directive: destroy all files, including *mein* manuscript.''

''*Manuscript?* . . .'' Brad got the answer to his unspoken question. He moved toward the gun cabinet. He'd realized that Katz was safe—as safe as possible—until *after* the manuscript was complete. He swung open the door, removed an M-16 rifle from its niche, examined the gun sight, reversed the weapon and peered through the barrel. He removed the ammo-clip, scowling darkly. *Empty!* He reached for a full clip, examined it, and snapped it into place, his temper flaring.

''Christ, Katz. Keep the goddamned guns loaded! How far along are you in the manuscript?'' He replaced the M-16 and picked up another, moving, talking, always with his back to the camera.

''Approximately halfway.''

''Is it outlined? *Keep your back to the camera, Katz!*''

''Only here.'' He tapped his head.

''Good. Do you dictate into a recorder? Type your own pages?''

''*Mein* daughter, Marta, types each day.'' He pointed to a shredder. ''The fate of my worksheets.''

''You *will* be permitted to complete the manuscript?''

''Upon that assumption, *mein Freund*, I am counting and pace *mein* work accordingly.''

Brad shoved a full ammo-clip into a Belgian-made 9mm Browning. He tossed it to his host. ''Keep it loaded at your side at all times.''

Katz understood. ''You have imported a paranoia I haven't experienced in many years.''

''In confining quarters claustrophobia produces in me profound paranoia, Katz. Especially when I do not command the situation.''

''You prefer we should go walking?''

''No. It is not my intention to aggravate your condition. With your permission, a few minor adjustments will do fine.'' Brad's gut instinct, dormant for years behind a safe desk job, kicked up a storm of protest in his belly. The old grooves that once communicated danger had grown rusty. The recent lubricant of thought and involvement had begun to remedy the defect. He felt for his gun, laughing at the absurdity of the gesture. Locked inside a mausoleum, what good was a gun except to shoot himself? He stepped on a chair, covered the camera lens with a doily. A quick assessment of the camera's peripheral capabilities included little beyond its focal point—the two chairs and table.

Brad turned the recliners around, backs to the camera. "My assumption is, they monitor what transpires between you and your guests. Do you control the audio? Turn it off."

"The apparatus is only video—not audio. I insisted on privacy for me *und mein* guests. The equipment is housed in the building adjacent to the house and is monitored by security guards. If trespassers dare enter, the camera immediately transmits the intrusion. Why go to such *behelligen*—so much trouble?"

"Let me stress a caveat—ever hear of lip readers?"

The German's jaw fell slack. "*Ich verstehe. Ach du lieber Gott!* Such fears you revive."

Brad explained it was not his intention to frighten him. He removed the doily from the camera lens and, setting his dark-lensed glasses into place, explained recent technologies, voice and ocular graphs and the hand-held mini-scrambler he had removed from his pocket. "You see this small case? It makes miracles. It scrambles any device attempting to tape our conversation. In a short while you shall see how much privacy you've been afforded. *Die Magie* works fast."

Before he finished the sentence, a red button on the arm panel flashed. It was U.S. Intelligence. Was everything all right? Stupefied, Katz assured them it was. Despite his protests, he was firmly instructed to call each hour on the hour until they determined the trouble preventing camera transmittal. His face ashen, hand trembling, he hung up the phone, furtive eyes on the device in Brad's hand.

"By the time they get a fix on the trouble, hopefully our conversation will have ended."

"What marvels we shall see in the future."

"*If* there is a future. The big money lays odds against it," Brad said bluntly. "That's why, old friend, I have come to you. I need answers. Shall we begin with *why* the Soviets abducted you, sold you back to the Americans twenty years later and *why* you chose to flee from them and backtrack into the arms of the Soviets?"

"It is safe to speak now?" Katz asked, visibly shaken. He opened cabinet doors under the table, removed a brandy bottle,

114

and two glasses. He poured economically in precise, equal amounts and handed Brad one.

Brad nodded his thanks, and prodded. "Now, tell me what happened in 1953 after I departed."

Katz began slowly. "The threats existed before 1946. For a time you were the sentinel of my life. Your departure prompted the dangers."

"Threats by whom?"

"You fail to recall my dossier?" Katz sighed. "How is it possible to remember so much so many years later? Better you should ask, who *did not* threaten Katz? All sides, enemies I didn't realize existed, assailed me night and day. I remember it all."

"The Soviets abducted you, held you incommunicado twenty years . . ." Brad tried holding him to tack. "Why?"

Katz shrugged. " 'Katz,' they asked repeatedly, 'what did you barter for your acquittal from the Americans?' I suggested they study the statement of records on file with the Allies. 'The files are fraudulent,' they insisted. 'Lies—all lies.' It was true, but I demurred, refused to give them anything of substance. Day and night, night and day it was always the same. Questions . . . Questions . . . Questions! Finally I tired. I fed them misinformation. Ach! Found out, I was punished accordingly. Ten years of nightmares and then a *Freund* said to me, 'Katz, feign senility. Display signs of mental aberrations. Forget things.' I saw the merit in this, so I did as suggested and the next decade became easier for Katz. I became a forgotten man. They fed me, exercised me daily like a pet dachshund, but received no human contact save periodic interrogation when a new adjutant replaced the former and wondered why Katz was kept alive at such expense to the Soviets. I, too, wondered in time. One day . . . a miracle. The Soviets in East Berlin realized the enormous profits reaped by clandestine underground movements from dissidents who wished to defect. So, they decided to cut out the middleman, and offered political prisoners directly to West Berlin for incredible sums. In spring, 1973, a miracle bloomed for Katz. The adjutant came to me. 'Katz,' he said, 'we have sold you to the Americans. Why they bought you—God knows. To us you are a liability, so, go! You are free.' "

"Free? *Ach, du lieber*! How quickly I learned! *Freiheit ist nur in dem Reich der traume!* Freedom exists only in the world of dreams. The KGB and military soldiers escorted me to Checkpoint Charlie. Money exchanged hands. I boarded a U.S. Army staff car and was driven directly into a living hell of nightmares. I was housed somewhere in old Berlin between the American and British sectors, but *not by Americans!*"

"*Not* by Americans? Clarify, Katz."

Katz sighed, deeply, the task of remembering etching harsh lines across his face. He snuffed out a half-smoked cigarette, placed the butt into a pocket of his corduroy jacket. "You held my complete dossier. You knew my background, the basis of agreement for my acquittal. You knew certain factions wished me dead and still do, for the knowledge I possess."

"Refresh my memory, *bitte sehr*. The records are buried in OSS files ."

"*Mein gut Freund*, Lincoln, why do I get the feeling my records were not buried in OSS files, but in the British SOE." He leveled his eyes on Brad in a protracted silence.

Brad's mind spun out like whirlwind. On his feet he paced in small arcs, his back to the camera, always aware of the seeing eye.

Forty fucking years ago, Brad! You've gotta span forty fucking years.

Delving into old history, Brad was forced to retrench. He needed more background. "Begin at war's end, at the beginning of our relationship," Brad suggested. "I must refresh my memory."

"*Gut*. At the end of the war I was an elite *WAFFEN*, *S.S.* But in 1938 I was *Einsatzgruppe*, part of an operational task force ordered to maintain law and order. Our primary occupation: liquidation of partisans and dangerous Bolshevist elements, including Jewish radicals. We were subordinate to the *Wehrmacht*, but the *Reichssicherheitshauptampt* retained functional control over us. From the *Einsatzgruppe*, I transferred to and received further training in the *Totenkopfverbande*—The Death Head Units."

"You were paramilitary, concentration and death-camp guards."

"*Ja, ja*, you remember." Katz thought a moment, and then shook his head vigorously in contradiction. "*Nein, nein!* It is important to make the distinction. The youngest, most vigorous of us formed the battle unit, *Totenkopf Division*. From this involvement I was elevated in rank and transferred to the *WAFFEN S.S.* Section *Schutzstaffel* Guard Detachment assigned to protect

116

officers of the Nazi High Command." Katz levitated his hand, muttering woebegone sounds deep in his throat. "Errors were made, grave errors, unfortunate for many Germans. You see, *Freund* Major, Death Head units and concentration-camp guards wore the same uniform as we did, carried the same pay books, and became a gross insult to those of us uninvolved in camp terrors."

"Then the war crimes charged against you were fraudulent?"

"*Ja wohl.* Precisely. At Nuremberg, the *WAFFEN S.S.* was dishonored by our commanders. The mixup arose because the bulk of troops, fifteen hundred in number, provided for the annihilation of the Warsaw Ghetto were *Einsatzgruppen* and the same squads who completed the atrocities at the deathcamps in those last days before Germany fell. Later, at Nuremberg, when that distinction became vital to our survival, no Nazi officer stepped forward to lift the sentence from our heads, to clarify the differences in our sections. The tribunal addressed all *WAFFEN S.S.* collectively."

"You wore the same uniform," Brad interrupted, "carried the same pay books, and they lumped you into one whole. I remember."

"It was unjust, humiliating, a travesty. Worse for me than most. In 1941 I was transferred to a lofty position of critical authority on the staff of *Obergruppenführer*, Reinhard Heydrich, Hitler's most promising aspirant—the man to who he entrusted, *Endöslung*—"

"*Endöslung?*"

"The final solution to the Jewish problem."

"Yes, yes, I know." Brad cut him short, anxious to keep him on the proper siding without countless detours. "You said in 1973 your life became nightmares. Yet, you *willingly* returned to the Soviets *after* the KGB ordeal. Why? Weren't you afforded proper protection in the American sector?"

"*Nein*, it was not thus. At Checkpoint Charlie the exchange *was* made. The staff car proceeded toward the Schöneberg District. We were intercepted and chaos followed. Held up at gunpoint by masked men, I was shoved inside a V.W. van."

"By who? Who were *they*?"

He shrugged in bewilderment. "Commandos, guerillas? Who could be sure? For twenty years I was not a part of humanity. The world outside was new, frightening—" He stopped. "Oh, *mein Freund, mein* words are not the whimpering fantasies of the demented.''

Katz, on his feet, moved awkwardly to the *safe* zone, away from camera scrutiny, and slowly began to disrobe. He painstakingly unbuttoned his coat sweater, peeled off two additional thinly woven sweaters and a shirt before dropping his trousers.

Brad's befuddlement ceased the moment Katz dropped his longjohns to his knees. His mind tumbled back to initial visions of Germany in 1945. The OSS advance forces, first to liberate prisoners at Belsen near Celle, now in West Germany, had expressed total revulsion at the camp atrocities. The memories and images ceased, for here, in the flesh, was the emaciated, fragile body reduced to skin and bones, scarred grotesquely, branded in the groin area. Katz's limp penis, a mere stubble and sacky hairy scrotum hung at the center in a mass of angry keloid scarring. The scarring—the Star of David, the Jewish emblem!

Wolfgang stared mutely at the appalling deformity, still not used to its repulsive appearance. His eyes contained a tragic vision of what had happened to him.

"Who did this to you?" Brad repeated his earlier query. His indignation spurred movement, and what seemed to Katz as sordid behavior. Brad reached into his knapsack and with mini-camera in hand began to photograph.

"You think Katz to be a freak?" Dumbfounded, utterly alienated by the American's crudity and insensitivity, he blinked, bewildered by the constant click of electronic shutters.

"I need these as evidence." *Click . . . click . . . click . . .*

"Of what use are pictures? It happened long ago."

"Talk to me!" *Click . . . click . . . click . . .* "Tell me *who*! *Why* this happened! You were acquitted of the war crimes." *Click . . . click . . . click . . .*

Finished, Brad removed the minicartridge, placed the exposed film in the hollow heel of a boot. He reloaded his camera as the dazed, submissive man began dressing himself.

The German tugged at his clothing like a child memorizing which article of clothing came first. He mouthed the words, *who . . . why . . . how . . .*, searching his memory for the answers.

"They found me at Nuremberg in 1945 through Gerhardt, Nazi Chief of Intelligence on Hitler's staff. You remember Gerhardt?"

"Gerhardt? The Nazi who defected to British SOE?"

"*Ach*, you do remember. *Ja*, the traitor to Germany long before the Battle of the Bulge. The British SOE owned him. In the final days he supplied the *Führer* with false charts, maps, misinformation. Hitler labeled them false instantly but resistance from advisors in those tense days in January 1945 was vigorous. Hitler moved against his inclination. Three days later, Stalin's promised three million Red Troops moved against the German Army. And so began the beginning of the end for the Third Reich. But why do I tell you, Major? You know the mechanics of those days."

"*Who* found you at Nuremberg? Tell me, Katz." Now Brad observed the man closely, listening not only to the words, but to the intonation of each. He studied the eyes, movements of the head and hands, his total body language. He searched for the sign of a lie. One lie would be the opening, the one breach in a wall for a barrage of grenade-like questions.

"Men who pressured me, threatened me—short of death—into testifying falsely at the trials. For this false testimony, gravely compounding the wrongdoings, I was promised the moon."

"Be specific. Tell me exactly what they asked—their terms." The wretched man was so overwrought Brad proceeded gently.

"Such a long time ago . . . What did *they* promise? . . . Immunity, a new life, new home, new country for *mein Fräulein* and children. But I refused to perjure myself. Germany had lost the war. I refused to subvert justice or compound the wrongs already done. The threats accelerated. First, the death of *mein Fräulein*. Second, *mein* children." Katz's pained eyes grew distant. Pitiful sighs emanated from his throat, the moans of the infirm who suffer chronic pain and learn to adapt. "Only *mein* daughter Marta survived . . . Only *mein Tochter*." Katz stared off into space. "They hovered over me like carnivorous bats eyeing their prey. One man—the leader, a man with colorless eyes, I shall never forget. He had such eyes—I have never seen such eyes before. When I refused to break he came to me in that stinking cell at Nuremberg. Such authority he had, Major. Like Hitler, himself. *Gott in Himmel*! I was spellbound by him as any man can be in the presence of madness. I have not forgotten the words he spoke to me forty years ago. That day he faced me with absence of emotion and said clearly to me:

" '*In the unlikely, ill-advised event you elect to reject our recommendations, know now, how open you leave yourself to*

119

repercussions and dangers beyond our control. We are growing in strength, for we have been taught well by history. And when the time is right, we shall hound you, day and night, until you pray for death to deliver you from suffering.' "

"Yet, you managed to escape them—"

"—or else they permitted me to escape to see where I'd run—"

"—and you ran back to the Soviets! Ah, diversionary tactics."

Confusion set upon the deep mask of misery lining Katz' face. He shook his head. "*Nein, nein, nein!* Those words were spoken in 1945, *before* I sought protection by the Americans. *Before* the ACC officers brought me to you and Lieutenant Greer at OSS Headquarters for interrogation. I ran to you Americans for refuge." He shrugged into the last sweater, buttoned it lopsided.

"Wolfgang," Brad said patiently, "you jump from 1946 to 1973, creating confusion in the chronology. Were you or were you not coerced into false testimony at Nuremberg?"

Katz nodded and shook his head alternately.

"The man with colorless eyes threatened you in 1945 at Nuremberg? Is that it?"

"*Ja, jawohl!* And again in 1973 when I was abducted from the Americans. He did not remember that I refused to testify according to his instructions. But I remembered. I remembered everything."

"Katz, please listen. In 1946 Greer and I completed our deal with you. We worked together five years. I left for America. From 1953 to 1973 is when you were abducted by the Soviets, correct?"

Katz nodded. "So, those atrocities done you were done by the Soviets?"

"*Ja, ja!*" He brightened, then scowled. "*Nein, Nein!* Not by Soviets. You confuse me. Atrocities were done to me by my abductors after the exchange at Checkpoint Charlie. He was the same, I told you, older, dressed like a banker, but he was the same man. He knew everything in the most disturbing details. Such an important man, *ach!* The eyes—the eyes were the same, without color. Who could forget such eyes? But he did not remember Katz."

"*Who?*"

"The leader. The one in charge of terrorists."

"*Terrorists*? What terrorists?"

120

"They are called terrorists today. Then? Hoodlums. Hooligans! One, Mosha Bauer, was an international criminal, I was told."

"Six months later you escaped these—uh—hooligans and fled back into the arms of the Soviets? I find this incredible. *Why*?"

"The KGB nursed me to health. Then one day they said, 'Katz, pay close attention.' They showed me photographs. Hundreds of photographs of men and women."

"Did you recognize any?"

"*Nein.*"

"Did they believe you?"

"Truth is indefensible. The KGB are *sehr gut, begabt.*" He touched his forehead with a finger. "They showed photographs of innocent men. Men I could not identify unless I was telling lies. *Ja*? Then, Major, the photographs became different. Men placed high in government, here and abroad. They observed me very, very carefully, with falcon eyes. But I retreated into feigned senility, forcing them to abandon all questioning. Later, much later, I was transported to the Americans—directly to Clayallee 10, then here to *mein* farmhouse. My new hosts—the Americans—like the Soviets, interrogated me, showed me photographs. I did not identify anyone. 'Katz,' they told me, 'you are exhausted. Rest for now. In time, when memory returns, you will be given a typewriter to write your memoirs.' They called it therapy to stimulate the mind."

"What then, Katz? Were you able to keep up the feigned senility?"

"What then? Then came company. Such company. Germans, Americans and Jewish psychiatrists, psychologists. Yes, yes, they visited with me, studied my writings, prescribed my diet. They gave me vitamins to build up my strength. Also to stimulate my memory, *ja*?"

Brad experienced sinking sensations. The tactics used on him growing more obvious by the moment. "Do they regress you with drugs or hypnosis?"

Katz winked broadly. "They think they do."

"*They think they do*?" Brad sat perfectly still. "My God, Katz, how do you fool them—beat the drugs."

"Twenty years in Soviet prison taught Katz clever tricks. When such visitors come to see Katz, I take a supply of *special* vitamins given to me by former prisoners in KGB prison. It counteracts their drugs. I feed them enough information to keep

121

them happy. See, *mein Freund*," he indicated to the video screen. "Security guards. Killer dogs protect Katz. One day will come an error. They will learn Katz's tricks and I will be *kaput*. Until then, I live with *mein* Marta. They tell me *mein* Anna, all my children but Marta, are dead . . . An accident, they told me. How cleverly they disguise murder as accidents."

Brad listened, a thousand questions needing answers. He posed this carefully. "Who are *they*? The Americans offering you sanctuary or those enemies dating back to Nuremberg?"

Katz leaned in close, whispered confidentially. "Are they—any of them—different, *mein Freund*?"

Silence punctuated by the droning of the ceiling air circulator, the sudden intake of breath filled the room. Shaken at the implications, at the terror tactics used on Katz, a tactic so pervasive it enabled power to be marshalled without opposition, filled Brad with foreboding.

Katz had fooled the power machine—the authorities. For how long?

Brad stoked the fire, staring into the flames, listening as the German made his first call to U.S. Intelligence. When the call ended, he asked quietly, "I know what they wanted in 1945, but in 1973? Even now, ten years later? Why are you so precious to them?"

"*You don't know what makes me precious to them*?" Katz expressed disbelief. "But, I thought—that's why you came." He picked up the house phone, requested a tray of hot coffee and pastries. He hung up, his eyes lifted to Brad's, expecting an answer.

"Katz, tell me what *they* want. *Who* they are." He stopped at the curious expression on the German's face. He saw that he would have to speak quickly to recapture the old man's trust.

Brad spoke confidentially. "My mission here is dangerous. Am I secure with you? If my cover is blown, it can prove disastrous to you, me, the world." He pointed to the minicamera lying on the backpack on the floor, lied adroitly. "Inside, Katz, is a homing device to keep my people apprised of my whereabouts. Should you or anyone attempt to entrap me . . .? Shall I spell it out, Katz?" He held up the miniscrambler. "You saw the magic this made? If anyone poses a threat, your guards—your servants—anyone, you will become past history." The lies were necessary

122

to test Katz. The German by admission had demonstrated a frightening control and awareness of intelligence apparatus.

Brad's answer came in a near cardiac arrest. Katz lacked an actor's theatrical flair to dissemble.

"Y-you a-accuse K-Katz of lying? You? *Gott in Himmel!* Why do you think I sent for you? You needed facts. I promised to supply them!"

"*You sent for me?*" Brad's bewilderment was complete.

"*Jawohl.* Through old friends. You were in Europe looking for Katz, they told me. They said you needed facts concerning vital matters. I sent word to you through old OSS conduits."

Riddled with galloping uncertainty, Brad paced furiously. He was unnerved by the suspicion that this meeting had been maneuvered by hidden forces. A fiendishly clever device—suggestion. Jim Greer, or was it Berna, who had implanted the desire to contact Katz in a vulnerable moment. A frightening juggernaut wedged between them. "Katz, listen carefully. I sent ciphered messages through an old friend to locate you. Confirmation of this meeting between us arrived. I think we have been set-up, but one thing is clear; someone wanted us to meet. Who told you I was in Europe?"

"An old conduit from a safehouse in Munich. *Who*, I cannot be sure. The codes were dated but precise as they were in 1946. I requested you to contact me through proper channels. You followed the elaborate code words on contact."

"A trap! We've fallen prey to a trap!" Brad's voice, laced with dread, broke into a cracked whisper. "A friend was killed making contact with me, recently. It poses a frightening speculation as to why."

Katz paled excessively. "A cleverly planned meeting, *ja*? We were thrown together to set an apparatus in motion? For what purpose, *Freund* Major?"

"I wish to God I knew."

They fell into silence.

A buzzer, abrupt, harsh and unexpected, startled. Katz pressed a button on the console, releasing the wall panel. Marta rolled a teacart into the room laden with cold cuts, freshly baked brown bread, cheese, tea cakes and hot coffee. She fussed over her father, brought his slippers and a lap robe from a wall cabinet, removed a few medicine vials, placed them on a tray, as a reminder for him to take them.

123

Brad contemplated their plight, his mind struggling to make some sense of the baffling events. He picked up a gold ball paperweight, tossed it in the air, caught it, and studied it cursorily, waiting for Marta to leave. It was a bas relief of the globe, not as he knew it. Under the rounding contour of what normally was Africa he read the inscription: *MONDO XX*.

Neither he nor Katz noticed the wall panel behind them was left slightly ajar, obstructed from closing firmly by a thin cardboard wedge. Juggling the gold paperweight, Brad approached Katz. "I think I've figured it, Katz. Regardless of who sought out the other, our meeting was goosed by the tactical planning of KGB." With an air of discovery, he tossed the ball into the air, caught it snappily and placed it on the teacart. "The question is, *why*? Before we solve the riddle, shall we determine the dangers posed us?"

"KGB?" Katz's white shaggy brows wormed into a scowl.

"Yes, KGB. To save you, me, or both of us from something sinister. Shall I prepare a plate of food for you?" he asked solicitously.

Katz wagged a finger and helped himself. "KGB engineered this meeting? *Ich bin sehr gespannt weswegen.*"

"I, too, am curious."

They ate in silence, each prisoner to his own thoughts.

"You steadfastly refuse to name your oppressors—those who tortured you?" Brad asked quietly. "You *do* know them. You lied to the Soviets. The Americans, too. You refuse to name them to me—why?" He held up a restraining hand. "No rebuttal, yet. I'm sorting the pieces aloud. I understand your fear. Your body is a testament to their brutality. But there's more—I know it. You must tell me everything. *Everything!* You understand? Else I cannot help you. I am prepared to offer you sanctuary in America—"

"No! *Not* America!" Katz panicked. "I am safer here." His eyes flared wildly, his face paled.

Shocked at the violent outburst, Brad displayed his astonishment. "Jesus! What are you so afraid of?"

"I tried to tell you, but you wouldn't listen."

"All right, I'll listen. I won't interrupt." Brad's watch read one-fifteen. He poured coffee, settled back, forcing patience, determined to hear Katz out.

"So, how do I begin to explain without appearing to justify

124

the actions of one man and a nation, which was condemned by a world fed on propaganda? One man rose from obscurity, shook the world on its foundations and nearly succeeded in reshaping it. For a time he brought unity, a sense of nationalism to a nation not yet recuperated from the previous war. He brought hope to the German people, restored their fallen pride, removed disease and decadence prowling through German streets after the Great War.

"Ah, you view me with distaste. You think I am justifying his existence on earth? Better you should hate the anonymous gods of finance who hid behind Hitler's shadow, as they hide today in the shadow of newer puppets, world leaders who dance to their strings. *Invisible* circles of power pulled the strings that animated *Der Führer*."

Brad Lincoln tensed. The coffee he sipped exploded from his lips. He dabbed at the liquid spilling to his chin with a napkin. He leaned in closer to Katz, his attention rapt, his eyes piercing, trying to find a lie in him. There was none.

"Hitler was *not* placed into power by the Germans. He moved under orders from London and New York. But then, *mein Freund*, you know better than I, no?" But Katz did not wait for his words to be acknowledged. He pressed on. "God have mercy on all of us. The truth is, Major, a conspiracy existed outside of Germany to rid the world of Jews. The British wanted no more Jews in Palestine. Eratz-Israel wanted only the rich Jews. Warnings came early in the war by galloping Paul Reveres who clearly conveyed the message to all affluent Jews—and they fled before the treachery commenced.

Brad held up a restraining hand. Disturbed, anomalous feelings shook him. "Why dote on the dregs of the past? I know—I know I promised not to interupt. It's best we concentrate on the present. Today. Tomorrow—the immediate future. At hand, as close as your panel of buttons, waiting to be activated are instruments of destruction. The past is over, Katz."

"Precisely, Major. What hope can there be for the future if we don't live in the present? How can we hope for peace?"

"Katz, listen to me, the anonymous men you refuse to name are in control of a terrifying apparatus of power. A nod from them, a wave of the hand, and the entire world is kaput."

"*Ja wohl*! You know them! What need have you to hear it from Katz?"

"What the hell are you saying? If I knew—would I be here demanding answers from you? I need names. Names, places, deeds! What did your persecutors want from you?"

The shriveled, tormented man popped pain pills. He rose, sidled to the fireplace, warming his hands before the crackling fires. Each movement was a ballet of unbearable agony. Lines on his face deepened, he looked haggard, defenseless, utterly devastated. When he spoke his voice could barely be heard. "That I was born, lived during the most crucial, mystifying events of this century is not the life I dreamed as a child. Is it my guilt to have been born a German? Must my fellow Germans and I drip forever in unendurable guilt for the heinous deeds ordered by a cabal of madmen outside of Germany? Madmen manipulate the world now, as they did then and before my time, and will continue until nothing remains of humanity as we know it."

"Goddammit! Name them!"

"No!"

"*What*?"

"*I will-not-name-them*!" The words came slow, emphatic and rapier-sharp. "If our friendship means anything, do not order me to the gallows." Twisting knots of stark fear contorted his face. "Look at me! See the effects of their labors! I am left with one kidney, a fractured spleen, punctured lung—so much! So much more. The miracle, rather the curse, is—I am alive."

Brad poured more coffee, added *schnapps*. Quietly, patiently he confided, looking for a way to get past Katz's defenses. "The men you shield by your silence are more dangerous than any past difference between us—between nations. Because these men dare do the unthinkable, they will explode the world with a hydrogen bomb. We face total annihilation. Katz, I beg you, name these men. We must counteract their terror."

"*Nein!* . . . *Nein!* I refuse to discuss it."

"You *what*? Then why send for me?"

"I have suffered enough!" Katz wailed.

Brad, furious and losing patience, rolled out the ultimatum. "Don't shove me into a corner, Katz. I'll come out using all the ammunition I have. The *protection* for both you and your daughter can be terminated, Katz!"

A four-decade encapsulation of agony became visible on Katz's face, triggering a nervous affliction. His false teeth clacked hideously. He shook tremorously, his features reflecting the fear born of experienced terror. "Nein, y-you d-do n-not m-mean w-hat y-you say."

Brad pressed harshly. "*Wei sagt man auf Deutsche*? How do you say in German, this is a craps shoot to the end?"

Chapter Six

"*. . . How dare the smooth talker, the clever official blabbers, open their mouths and boast of progress? Here they hold jubilant Peace Conferences, talk against war. But these same righteous governments who are so noble, industriously active to establish eternal peace are preparing, by their own confession, the complete annihilation of six million Jews and there is nobody, except the doomed themselves, to raise his voice in protest, although this is a worse crime than any war.*
. . . Max Nordau, Zionist Congress, 1911.
The New Judiah, Official Organ of The
Zionist Organization of England.

"*Ich verstehe,*" Katz said, arrested by the grim look in Brad's eyes. He shoved his bifocals onto his sweaty forehead. He resembled a cornered rat, desperate eyes searching for escape. He gestured toward the radio, and Brad immediately raised the volume.

Katz's eyes dulled to a cobalt blue. He fixed on the video monitors peering intently at the thickening snow flurries falling from overcast skies.

Katz made his second token call to U.S. Intelligence offices, assuring them he was fine, then, collecting fragmented thoughts, spoke up.

"Think, *mein Freund*, do you not consider it peculiar that the Jews who fought valiantly in the Warsaw ghetto made no attempts to fight off their oppressors? Regimented, herded into cattle cars like sheep, they make no attempts—no efforts to escape? Hah! And why not?"

127

Brad blinked hard, his face screwed in puzzlement. "Yes, but—"

"Listen, *mein Freund*. In Warsaw they numbered thirty-three thousand Jews who stood off three hundred fifty thousand Wehrmacht troops! In the end not one Jew surrendered! *Not one*! Yet the Jews in Hungary, rounded up in cattle cars like animals, *did not* protest? Thousands of able-bodied Jews, young, strong as bulls—Jews, among the condemned, many from a village near the border, and freedom less than three miles away—*did not* offer resistance! No one tried to escape! So tell me, my CIA friend, why not? The records show only twenty Hungarian police officers and one Nazi S.S. officer stood guard over twenty thousand Jews, and I am supposed to believe, actually believe, not one attempted escape! Shall I enlighten you, Major? Shall I tell you why no escape was attempted? Because someone they trusted fed them lies! Paid collaborators betrayed them, led them to believe they had nothing to fear. 'We are sympathizers' they told the unsuspecting. 'Trust us. Do not try to escape or fight. We have everything under control. We shall lead you to Palestine if you behave.' You see, Major, in those days the Jews would *not* have believed such lies from a German."

Katz paused to take his medication, sipped water and continued. "Is it not ironic? The Nuremberg Laws failed to include the war crimes of collaborators? I find alarming those masterminding the dastardly crimes got away with impunity. The stench of cover-up assaults my senses.

Brad sank heavily into a chair, runaway throughts gripping him. He decided to hammer it home. "Your information, I take it is based on solid, supportable facts?"

"Oh, *mein herr* Major Lincoln. *Who would be interested in Wolfgang Katz if he knew nothing*?"

Katz's words galvanized his senses. Brad, angry at his own ineptness reviewed Katz's story. He spoke firmly, logically, yet a tinge of fanaticism colored his words. So many years in prison. . . ? In this moment Brad considered his heritage, yet he was unprepared to lay claim to it—not yet. "We've gone far afield from the essence of our purpose in meeting," Brad said firmly hoping to get back on tack.

"*Nein! Nein!* We have not strayed from our purpose. It is part of the same problem."

"What has this to do with your abduction, your torture, the confining years in KGB detention? The man with *colorless eyes*?"

As Katz spoke, Brad jogged his memory back to those chaotic post-war times. April 1945 had ended. The deaths of three world leaders commemorated that month. First FDR died, then Benito Mussolini, killed by savage partisans, and lastly, Adolf Hitler, by his own hand. Coincidence? Then, as now, no self-respecting intelligence agent believed in the coincidence of triple deaths. Three deaths in a row had hastened V-E day. The E.T.O. had to shut down to defuse an international scandal or suffer the consequences of letting truth undermine the entire war effort. Big money had ended the war to avert scandal. Black-market profiteering in anything from dead men to megabucks ran rampant. The coffers of Swiss banks offering anonymity with numbered accounts had grown fat. Early in 1946, Wolfgang Katz, fraught with fear, hounded by an expertly authored paranoia, had burst into the newly christened offices of the American OSS. He told his story to Brad Lincoln and Jim Greer, and struck up a bargain for his acquittal.

Brad stared into the snapping, crackling fires as fresh logs ignited and burst into flames. Suddenly lights exploded in his brain and everything fell together. *Wolfgang Katz had had something to sell! Volatile, vital records!*

The Soviets *knew*. Their power play lost out. The French *knew*. Mistakenly they had appropriated the wrong records! British SOE *knew*—and killed for them! Utimately the American OSS had wheeled and dealed persuasively, and dangling acquittal bait for the alleged war crimes had lucked out.

Wolfgang Katz had not revealed the records' whereabouts! He couldn't have! Only Brad Lincoln knew where they were! Presently as he scoured the *tabula rosa* of his mind he experienced a maddening rush of agitation. His eyes still staring into the burning flames, he asked in a tightly controlled voice, "Where are the records, now, Katz?"

"Where they've been since 1946. Only you can locate them."

W-h-o-m-p! . . . a sound . . . dull, thudding, diffused by other sounds, crackling fires, the overhead circulator, a grunt, the exhalation of breath. *W-H-O-M-P*! . . . the sound louder, dominant, punctuated by his own fear, brought his head around.

"Katz!" Too late he called to the German. Brad fell to a crouch, whipped out the M52 pistol. The panel door clicked shut. Covering the short distance to Katz's side, he lifted the slack head. The frontal portion of the cranium gave way, the face hung to one side, a mask of bloodied flesh, exposed tendons and cranial gray matter seeping from the shattered skull, splattering, gushing from the open cavity like spouting geysers. Shot with a high-caliber weapon muffled by a silencer from behind, while he, Brad Lincoln, bright intelligence agent that he was, had over-looked some insignificant detail. The result—Katz's untimely death!

Suddenly he was crying, tears spilling from his burning eyes. He felt the changes before the noxious stench permeated the room, assaulting his senses. *Christ! Poison gas!* Ripping off his scarf, he dipped it in the remaining dregs of the coffee pot. He balled it, wringing excess moisture, and swiftly wrapped it about his head, covering his nose and mouth. A pall of claustrophobic fear snaked through him. He reached for the phone, banged the receiver, cursing aloud. *Dead! The fucking lines are dead!* His brain wildly signaled: *Get outa this windowless mausoleum or you're a dead man!*

Brad's clenched fists came down hard on the panel buttons, frantically, in an attempt to open the door. He coughed. Sweat poured off him. Beginning tremors, symptomatic of gas inhalations, coursed through him. His eyes bulged hideously. Sinking to his knees on the floor, eyes rolling upward, he remembered—the *air circulator*! Katz had engaged it on entering this burial chamber. His eyes raced to the wall, to the set of switches. He marshalled his strength, crept to the wall, racked by coughing spasms. Struggling to his feet, he lurched into a wild, propelling thrust, catapulted to the switch, disengaging the current. He pounded the control panel maniacally, panicked. He pulled at the panel control and . . .

Miraculously, the wall panel slid open. Brad lunged through the opening, rolling onto the floor, yanking down the scarf, gulping at the air. His eyes fell on the door, the message rang loud and clear. *Seal off the panel! Katz is dead! Save yourself!*

The poison gas, invading his sympathetic nervous system, created myriad changes in him. He felt his muscles go slack, vessels constricted, blood pounding at his temples. His heart-beats accelerating wildly; he felt as if his lungs, his heart would burst. The tremors began. He shook slightly at first then, his teeth rattled, eyes burning from the poison vapors. Convulsions a hair away, he garnered the last vestiges of strength, lurched to the mantel, removed the brick, turned the key and fell away sackily to the floor watching the panel slide shut. He desperately inhaled the fresh air, his vision blurring radically.

The screeching sounds of a vehicle's brakes, skidding to a halt, muted by loud, erratic horn blasts, crashed through his head. Somewhere a door banged loudly, a car engine stalled, started up, and stalled again. Oblique thoughts collided on an inner speedway of his mind. Too many things were happening!

Disoriented, his senses reeling, Brad went to the window. *A U.S. Army jeep!* Smoking exhaust fumes thickly engulfed the jeep. An edgy driver, barely discernible, leaned heavily on the horn. Vague shadows ran toward the house, shouting unintelligible words. Intercranial pressure confused Brad's thinking and he followed the sounds of a hysterically banging door, through the kitchen to the rear of the house, barely able to see through the hazy curtain that fell over each eyeball.

A storm door, left open, shuddered, thrashing blindly in the wind. He reached to close it, invigorated by the cold windy blast. Outside, nearly fifty yards away, he saw two figures entering a motorized vehicle. Brad fired the M52 too late! The Czech gun demanded close-range firing to be effective. He saw dark clumps in the snow. Vaguely he made them out—dead guard dogs. Thoughts were clearing.

Fucking assassins had Katz's daughter! Katz was dead!

Brad's eyes burned like hell! *Christ, not my eyes! Don't let me go blind!*

He dashed through the house to the front door. How to deal with Army Intelligence? Why were they here? To check out the electronics disturbances? Sounds continued to collide in his head, his impaired vision abating. A few feet short of the entry Brad stopped abruptly. His name, shouted over the incessant ringing of a doorbell, the pounding of fist against the door froze him.

"Major Lincoln! . . . Major Lincoln! For Christsakes, open the door!"

Major Lincoln! . . . Not Benjamin Lord or even Wolfgang Katz, but Major Lincoln! . . .

Who had identified him? There was no time for questions! The loud yelling, fierce pounding on the door, shrieking commands from outside could not be ignored. The hornblasts—nervewracking.

"Major! It's fucking Mayday! Mayday! MAYDAY! We gotta get the hell outa here!"

Grabbing the sheepskin jacket from the wall peg, he leaped to one side of the door, M52 in hand, turned the deadbolt and flung it open, scaring the living *bejesus* out of one Sergeant Bill O'Cady. Shaken, the frantic sergeant repeated his warnings, adding, "Christ! Let's shake a leg. The place is gonna blow!"

Reacting, Brad loped out the door, sprinted across the snow, climbed into the jeep with O'Cady. The driver, a black officer, floored the accelerator, skidding the wheels, fishtailing the vehicle out of control, and spinning the wheel in the opposite direction managed to stabilize the jeep. He reached a distance of approximately a hundred yards from the house when the earth exploded under them.

A barrage of M26 grenades hurled at them by unseen hands formed craters at all sides, propelling the jeep into a levitated spinout, ejecting its passengers before exploding in midair. It splintered, falling to the ground in pieces; the driver and both passengers fell into snowbanks like limp, rag dolls.

Behind them, lightning bursts of flame, flashing ribbons of fire unfurling illuminated the area for miles. The burning farmhouse, surrounding buildings ignited until only charred black embers remained. From nearby farms a few people emerged, huddled together witnessing the spectacle, shocked, fearful, worried that war had commenced.

Awesome, deadly silence, punctuated by the destructive sounds of a consuming fire, was followed by the *bise*, an icy, freezing north wind tunneling through the farmland, dissipating grenade smoke and fire. Three bodies lay prone in snowdrifts arrested by paralysis of shock.

Brad Lincoln brought his hand to his nose. *Broken*! His nose bled profusely. It *was* broken! Worse, he couldn't see! He groped close by, scooped a handful of snow and brought it to his nose and over his eyes, cooling the heat of pain. He winced, groaned aloud. Pain spasms tore at his body. Desperately he pulled himself to a sitting position, and through the blur made out giant plumes of black smoke trailing the horizon. Reaching for his gun, he struggled to his feet, forcing himself up. He grew dizzy, reeling sensations gave rise to nausea. Each sound brought his head about, cocked, listening desperately to get his bearings.

Sergeant O'Cady, not far away, was bleeding, his left arm torn to shreds. Captain Cassius Clay Washington picked himself up, miraculously unscathed, and rushing toward O'Cady, led him through clouds of black smoke toward Lincoln. They stared

132

at the skeletal remains of the Katz farmhouse, stunned by the devastation.

"There ya be, Majuh . . ." The Captain rotated his shoulders like a fighter shaking out the kinks. "Shit, suh, if anything happens to ya—it's the brig fer us. What in cotton-pickin damnation happened inside? Where's Katz? The servants? Can ya fill us in?"

Brad could not. He would not. And he refused to sit around like a sitting duck waiting to be picked off. He tried to distinguish the soldier's features, but couldn't. Sergeant O'Cady moved agonized about the wreckage picking up bits and pieces with his one good arm. Wincing at the pain, he manipulated a few wires, powered a communication device with a car battery and sent an SOS to Headquarters. A grin at his proficiency brightened O'Cady's blood-splattered face. He found two M-16 rifles and tossed one to the black officer shouting, "Help's on the way. Keep your eyes peeled, Captain," before he keeled over the rifle in a dead faint.

"Look at it this way, Majuh," the Captain told Brad on the ambulance drive back to sick bay, observing a medic easing Brad's burning eyes with drops. "Yuh coulda got us all killed. A man yer age shouldn't be playing cloak-and-dagger games. That stuff went out with Mom's apple pie." He flashed Brad an outrageous, toothy grin, one more insulting than consolatory.

Brad felt like punching him out. The narcotic in his eyes reduced the scorching sensation, but he felt terrible—catastrophe and death pursued him.

The droning, sickening, wailing sound of sirens precluded rebuttal to the black man's insults. If he talked to anyone, it wouldn't be to a razzle-dazzle army captain who didn't wear G.I. boots.

The son of a bitch wore custom jobs! At least five C's!

Brooding, assembling facts, Brad couldn't cake-dance around the critical issue. How did Army Intelligence *know* he was with Katz? *Easy, now, don't disregard a thing, buddy.*

A half hour later Brad was being prepared for surgery. Shot with procaine and a half-dozen muscle relaxers and pain-killing narcotics through rapier-sharp needles capable of penetrating elephant hide he cursed through clenched teeth at the masked surgeon who prepared to reset his broken nose. "Freaking *fucking* sadist!"

"Flattery will get you anything," the surgeon muttered, a pronounced Nordic accent evident in his speech.

Chapter Seven

He sat in a tilt-back surgical chair staring penetratingly into the surgeon's eyes. His sight was clearing. Yet, something was wrong. The pain was severely acute, accompanied by exaggerated breathlessness, accelerated heartbeats, aggravated thought and dulling vision. The eyelids fell heavily, lifted, fell again. He fought the opiates, stared into the surgeon's unwavering, sardonic gaze.

There! In the eyes! Victory was spelled clearly behind those eyes!

Brad recoiled in terror. The surgeon lowered his mask, grinned, self-confidence oozing from him. Brad saw it as an after-image, but he saw it! A small angry scar on the wrist: *Corsican Coral!* An assassin!

He was caught! Done for! . . . Fight it! Don't let it happen!

He plunged deeper—deeper into sedated euphoria. He screamed internally, but made no sound. In a last-ditch effort he jackknifed his legs, shoved them into the surgeon's groin. The man grunted, expelling air, bent over painfully. Brad pulled up on his weightless hands, locked them together and brought them down hard on the killer's skull. Balling his fists, he struck blows to the jugular. Shock and pain scrawled on the assassin's face gave Brad the edge he desperately needed. Lurching free of the chair, he groped through tunneled blackness, a fish-eye hole of uncertainty in what became the doors leading out of the surgery theater, zooming in and out of distorted distance.

Fight, dammit! Run! Save yourself! Get out those doors!

Any moment the drugs would overcome him. He shouted, screamed in silence. *Help! Help me, someone!* His felt his guts bursting. No sound escaped his lips, but inside he vented his terror. He flailed weightless arms about, thrashing, twisting lunging into gurneys, O.R. carts overturned, crashing loudly as instruments went flying. He lurched dizzily toward a hole he seemed unable to find, clawed blindly, spun helplessly in what seemed an endless whirlpool.

Panic left him. Faces leered at him, crowding, suffocating him. He couldn't die now! Not while the world spun dizzily toward doomsday. He sucked in his breath and cried agonizingly loud, "M-a-a-a-a-y-y-y-y D-a-a-a-a-y-y-ye-eeeee!"

Shock, fear, the greedy jaws of death opened, fangs dripping venom grabbed hold in a mystifying, muddled blackness.

The hospital room was white and silent, except for the gum-chewing, snap-popping sounds coming from a flashy toothed mouth surrounded by black. The mouth hovered over him.

"I keep telling ya, yer too old for such goings on, Majuh."

Brad was too weak from his recent ordeal to think of a smart retort. He sipped his clear bouillon in silence, wondering how long that wasteland of blackness had engulfed him. The return of energy and clear thoughts signaled his need to escape this confinement. He had much to accomplish and time was running out.

"All I hope is I get no moah assignments like you, suh." The rasping voice grated on Brad's nerves. "But, thanks to you, Majuh, we caught ourselves a biggie . . . Whassa mattuh, Majuh? You still feelin' rotten? T'aint no wonduh. Fer openers yer stomach was pumped out. You been shot with all kinds o' goodies. Life-support systems till the crap worked itself outa yer system. Tell me, hows come ya rate a big fish like *Llamas* to terminate yuh? He's some big cat muthuh!" Captain Washington shoved a glossy 8 X 10 photo at him.

Brad stared at the image, no flicker of expression on his face. *Llamas, eh? One of the photos Greer had shown him. So soon?*

"Just lucky, I guess," he muttered. His jaws felt broken.

"Howd'ja spot him? Kee-rist! That *muthuhfuckuh* slipped past security into surgery faster than a hot dick into a cold cunt. And there's hell to pay! How did he tip his hand? I mean, Majuh, that were no game of *peas, porridge hot* you done on him."

Brad's gut instinct signaled danger, and he didn't go for the bait.

"Ah get it, ya don't wanna rap. Is that it, suh?"

"Can't rap. Don't know the game you talk."

The flashy tooth grin dissolved and with it the Southern drawl. "The game, sir, is murder. How do we protect you, Major Lincoln, if we don't know *what* and from *whom*? We can't combat specters." The accent was British—South African, the tone frigid and hostile.

Brad played up an exaggerated astonishment at the metamorphosis in the black man's unmasking. The other found no humor in Brad's antics.

"Play it your way, Major. Your presence in West Berlin has cost Headquarters plenty. First Katz goes up in smoke and with him years of valuable work. The unraveling of a conspiracy, inches from our grasp. Now, *Llamas*! Clear out of nowhere a fucking SOE-trained assassin comes at you with *Corsican Coral* behind him. What the bloody blazes are you after?"

Uneasy at the insistant questioning, Brad stalled, "Who's the C.O. here, Captain?"

"*You* don't know?"

Too fast! The man was skilled! his instincts warned.

"I put the question to you." Brad's hand fell casually over the intercom button at his side. He depressed it, out of the African's sight.

"Ah, I see. Charades, again. Is that it? General Markham."

The son of a bitch made a stupid blunder! Or—was it planned?

"No offense, Captain. I'll talk with him. Them's mah orders, ya see?" He mocked the African with an affected grin. At once the short hairs on his neck stretched. Then, just in time . . .

The orderly entered the room, encased in an aura of efficiency.

"Major Lincoln—what can I do for you?"

Brad howled! He screamed in agony, writhing and twisting on the bed, startling the approaching black man, forcing him to back off. His enraged eyes, burning black daggers.

"I feel sick! I'm dying," Brad wailed, faking paroxyms. The orderly flew past the African, pushing alert buttons, turning on overhead lights, washing the room in stark brightness, and sounding alarms.

The glowering black fury eased out the door, anger etched into his features. Brad clung to the panic-ridden orderly, hissing

136

orders. "Get General *Mark Samuels*, Chief of Army Intelligence, on the phone! *My* phone. Then summon the Chief of Army Personnel! Don't ask questions, damn you! Do as I tell you. Wait—where's my clothing?" His eyes darted to the closet door at the end of one wall.

Discombobulated, the orderly nodded, then the young man picked up the phone, barked orders with cool authority. "Don't ask questions!" he shrieked, aping Brad's stern manner. "Do as you're told! *Code Red Alert!*"

Brad eased off the bed, stunned by weakness. He clung to sterile walls, his shuffling steps slow. He opened the closet door and turned the heel of his boot—the film cartridge was intact. Good. He dressed himself slowly, forcing himself to think.

His purposely designed strategy to avoid U.S. Intelligence scrutiny had been subverted. Who had put the finger on him? How had they known to pick him up at Katz's farm?

"What's your name?" he barkd at the orderly.

"Luther, sir. Corporal Miles Luther."

"Well, Corporal, get the *fucking* Chief of Security here on the double and let's get this game on the road." He wobbled to the bathroom. Luther moved for the phone.

Brad stood before the bathroom mirror appalled at the sight. Battered, bruised, misshapen, discolored, he looked as if he'd been through a meat grinder. How much more could he take? He was in alien territory. Why the fuck hadn't he worked under the protective umbrella of the military? *Why?*

Brad, about to learn why instinct had led him along other paths, washed his face with cold water, dotting it dry with a towel.

The games are over, Brad. *They* want you dead!

Fucking invisibles again. Who the hell were *they?*

General Mark Samuels, a brass-buttoned, blood-and-guts cardboard cutout of the original George Patton, glowered at Brad across the priceless antique desk plundered from an old German castle. Deploying words like Panzer tanks, he steamrolled Brad up one side of the office, down the other, faulting him security leaks, aborted intelligence missions, Katz's death and the near-misses on his own life. Adding insult to injury, he acerbically persisted in the verbal whiplash.

"For your edification, Major, an American M26 grenade is a

green oval sphere of thin metal sheeting lined by prefragmented, spirally wound steel coil wrapped around 155 grams of TNT-based explosive mixture. Once the safety pin is pulled, *Major*, and the pressure of the palm on the springloaded side lever is released, a four- to five-second time interim passes before detonation. For a radius of approximately fifty feet a casualty zone arises. The idea, *Major*, is to get the hell away in the opposite direction! Not drive smack into the middle of it!''

"I suggest you tell that to your man. I wasn't driving," Brad retorted.

"Five times that amount of TNT plus plastic explosives were rigged in the Katz farmhouse and—" The General fumed. "You realize that your presence there makes you an accomplice in a murder conspiracy?"

"The only atrocity you've omitted in this indictment is the volcanic eruption of Pompeii, General." Brad's indignation lay a hair below the boiling point.

"You are not amusing, Major Lincoln. *Llamas* penetrated *my* Command Headquarters because of you. I intend to learn why if I have to bust every ass from buck private to brigadier general. You, I'll charge with aiding, abetting, conspiracy to murder, collusion—every *fucking* thing I can dream up to keep you in the slammer until you rot! *Do you read me, buster*?" The man was livid, his eyeballs popping in white rage. "You've been sent to sabotage me! That's it! Another black mark against my command is what they're after! Katz is dead, thanks to you fucking spooks!" Violence bubbled under the surface, ready to explode. "Now hear me, and hear me loud and clear. No fucking Company man infiltrates my domain, disrupts the work of a career and walks away without explanation. I'll bust you if it's the last thing I do, you bastard. I've got your dossier. I know all about you," he screeched in apoplectic fury. *"Do you read me*?" He glared at Brad.

"Uh—which of the five dossiers compiled on me do you have?"

"What five dossiers?" Brad's words sunk in. "Don't fuck with me, buzzard-bait." He hammered a balled fist on his desk. *"Goddamn* spooks!"

"I never fuck generals. Brass asses don't get it up for me." Brad's maddenly controlled voice ticked Samuels off even more. "Before you court cardiac arrest, General, suppose you look this over carefully." Brad had to call his bluff despite the delicate arabesques he skated over thin ice. President Macgregor's words plagued him.

If you get into trouble, the usual denials will be disseminated.

About to place his credentials before Samuels, he spotted his coded dossier on the desk. The upper right-hand corner was rubber stamped with security markings: a royal blue, red and white stripe under it. "Ah, the Cambridge file. I was never really one of them, General," he said in honeyed tones. Their eyes met like lethal opponents before the kill.

General Samuels' reptilian eyes darted to the dossier on the desk, failing in the last attempt to control his temper. "Fucking spooks! You are all alike! But not free of my jurisdiction—get that?"

Rankled, losing patience, Brad neatly passed across his security clearance, taking perverse pleasure in observing the scathing cobra eyes blink in astonishment. Stunned, his features jerked, his jaw muscles slackened. He lifted his eyes, manacled to Brad's. "Bloody hell! I can check this out!"

"Let me accommodate you. Save us both precious time. Overseas Operator X-1000. Triple A-clearance. Area code 202. The number is 456-7639. Extention Z-zebra." Brad flexed his fingers, invigorated by renewed strength coursing through him.

Pray God he doesn't call your bluff, sport.

He didn't. Samuels deflated.

Brad turned the screws slowly. How to repair the damage? "For *your* edification, my mission here is covert. You have neither jurisdiction, nor the right to interrogate or detain me in any device I set into motion. Do *you* read me, buster? Now stay the hell away from me. If I need military aides, I fucking well know *where* and how to get them. Your Command Headquarters is a joke! Scum bags like the bogus Cassius Clay Washington penetrated your security! And *Llamas*! Explain how he slipped past security into a goddamn U.S. surgical theater!" Furious with himself for losing control, he pressed on dangerously. "Fucking asshole! Arrogant tin soldiers like you think the world trembles under your feeble clout. You and men like you fucked up the world—" Brad stopped short. "Yeah, yeah, I contributed my fair share to the screwup, but you, you fucking faggot, and the rest of your closet queens haven't the faintest inkling of the damage you've done the world. Worse—you don't give a damn!"

139

Brad retrieved his gun and identity cards from the desk, flung his jacket over one shoulder, and stormed out the office. He'd just committed a grave error by falling into that shouting match and had made an enemy of Samuels. He had pulled the most stupid blunder of all times. He had implicated the Oval Office! *Damn! Damn! Damn!*

Numbed by Lincoln's revelations and heated departure, General Samuels sat quietly for several moments, loathing the complicated scenario facing him. The fine print in his command gave him authority to waste Lincoln. He had every intention of doing so until he caught sight of the Triple-A clearance. The classification spelled clearly a *hands-off* policy. All protection, *like-it-or-not*, must be afforded Lincoln. Failure to insure the unwritten codicil could mark his own extinction.

He unlocked a drawer in his desk, which was bolted to the floor, lifted out a private telephone, dialed a ten-digit number, waited, drumming nervous fingers on the desk. His eyes fell to the golden globe encased in glass, resting at the rear of the open drawer. Dammit! A few more weeks and they would have had it all! Wizard electronics piped transmissions directly from Katz's typewriter to the machines on the premises, duplicating everything Katz had written. All that remained was the coding of his project and identifying the location of those *special* records! To submit the records, finally, to the Zurich consortium meant enough money to live an Onassis-like life. And this prick, Lincoln . . . *Son of a bitch*! C'mon—what's holding up the parade? "Hello . . . Hello . . . We blew it! Katz is dead! The agents Marta and Fritz inflicted the *coup de grâce*. Everything, save what we have here on file, destroyed. I don't know what he imparted to the American—transmission was scrambled . . . I tell you everything's a shambles . . . destroyed by bombs. Nothing . . . I got nothing from him, save a warning against interference of any sort. The bastard's got Triple-A clearance. Direct from the Oval Office. He escaped the gassing, Llamas missed . . . The African missed . . . Now it's my turn. I'll rip his fucking ass apart. Any implication, suspicion of a conscious conspiracy to subvert a White House directive, would end it for me. Listen, I want all available dossiers on Lincoln—*all of them*! Mine is obviously manufactured. We can't afford delays! You've got the clout—use it! Dig up all you can. What? . . . The KGB?

British M-I? . . . DGI—What the hell do the Cubans want? What the bloody fuck do any of them want with Lincoln? . . . I don't get it. Bloody hell! Get me the dossiers!'' Samuels snapped. ''I'll burn the son of a bitch! What's that? Yeah, yeah, cheerio to you, old chap.''

The General slammed the phone, returned it to its niche in the drawer. A soft knock on the door brought a scowl to his craggy pockmarked face, and he pressed a button to release the door. He glanced up expectantly. ''What is it, Lieutenant?''

The uniformed man whipped his right hand out from behind him, a Belgian-made, .9mm Browning affixed with a silencer aimed at his quarry. He fired three times. The shock on Samuels' face total, his head snapped back, the impact of three bullets forced him against the chair, then the body heaved forward onto the desk. Blood spurted from three holes between lifeless, glassy eyes staring at the ceiling.

The assassin moved in swiftly, removed the keys from the General's hands, his eyes falling to the partially open drawer. He removed the golden globe. Hunkering down, he yanked at a tape recorder affixed beneath the desk, removed a cassette, slipped it into his jacket pocket. He pushed a button on a panel on the desk, and a section of the wall swung open, revealing a private file cabinet. The assassin opened the top drawer marked *HIGHLY CLASSIFIED*, removed three files. The first, marked *LLAMAS*; the second, *CASSIUS CLAY WASHINGTON*; the third, *CORSICAN CORAL*. He closed the file and wall panel, and picking up Brad Lincoln's dossier from the desk, began to leave. Turning, he saluted the dead man, kissed the tape with exquisite delight. When he glanced at his watch, a coral scar shone lividly at the edge of the watchband near the wrist bone.

Llamas, the bogus surgeon, who less than a week before had attempted to waste Brad Lincoln, smiled triumphantly as he exited the U.S. Army General's office, closing the door behind him with gloved hands.

He was drawing close to his quarry, moving in for the kill. The psychology of fear had entered in the mind of his target and would create havoc. From havoc, errors would result.

And then he'd reign triumphant.

BOOK II

Chapter Eight

"Once when all the deep, unexplored mysteries in my life surfaced to cause numerous conflicts, I was compelled to fragment my personal dreams, give birth to a cold, brutal force chained inside me, a strengthening, sustaining, energizing force like that of a fireballing sun sent spiralling into the heavens. It kept me poised, alert as a man obsessed with premonition . . ."

. . . Moufflon

THE WOLF SPIDER OF SICILY bore no resemblance to the *lycosa scutulata* that feeds on insects, spins webs and boasts four pair of legs. The Sicilian Wolf Spider was human with no legs—none at all and singularly adept at spinning intriguing webs in the upper echelons of world politics.

Dealt a blow early in life, the loss of both legs, compensation for the shock done him came from specialization in a profession where legs were not requisite. He retailed a desperately needed commodity to a select clientele, power brokers willing to pay a stiff fee for highly classified information. A built-in guarantee of anonymity was provided each subscriber. Inquiries were held sacrosanct as was the information disseminated from the sprawling mountaintop aerie in Monereale, a few kilometers from Palermo, once the playground of European princes.

The dossiers of seventy-five thousand European and Middle Eastern billionaires, international politicians, businessmen, military advisors, intelligence operators and labor leaders were meticulously programmed into highly sophisticated computers in Wolf Spider's mansion. Manning the sleek computers and communications terminals were ten highly skilled technicians who received trusted information transmitted by global couriers, checking both the source and authenticity. Upon Wolf Spider's approval, specially coded clients making bona fide inquiries got answers within an hour in any of the principal European and Middle

Eastern cities. Others got direct calls by phone or telex communications. The clientele list, kept under vigorous security wraps, insured critical protection to source and client.

In his field Wolf Spider had no competition. One such organization, broader in scope, larger in concept, but not as informative, did exist—INTERPOL.

Why compile in-depth dossiers on purportedly respectable men? Why engage in the clandestine dissemination of information, so volatile in content it provided instant ground for Wolf Spider's annihilation and could bring down governments in a tidal wave of disgrace and destruction? The answer—a one-word explanation—*vendetta*!

A sworn blood oath to avenge two deaths, his own and his fiance's.

His own death? . . . Oh, yes. For the day his legs were cut off he died—he was born again a year later as Wolf Spider. No tragedy suffered upon him by God could have fired the vengeance he felt from the manmade malediction. A northern politician had robbed him of his beloved, his manhood and legs. He would be avenged!

The story, obscured by fear, spoken of only in the dead of a moonless night by balladiers and storytellers accompanied by heart-rending, passion-evoking music, recanted a modern-day Romeo and Juliet love saga of Vittorio and Marianina. Plucked from the groom's arms on their nuptial eve, Marianina, a tear-streaked, hysterical bride, was spirited away in the dark of night to the abode of the lecherous libertine who had lusted for her for many months. Marianina had plunged a knife into her breast rather than submit to his debauchery. Vittorio, the hapless groom, was abducted, beaten and transported by sinister men armed with *lupara*, to the *Bosco Ficuzza*, shot in both legs and tossed into a deep ravine to die. But the ghost of Vittorio haunted the libertine's villa and rolling hills of Monreale.

Wasn't it curious that ten years to the date of the infamy the politician fell to disgrace, catastrophe and financial ruin plaguing the years between. Scandalous revelations of his subversive plottings against the existing government through highly questionable banking sources in Zurich leaked to the newspapers. Scandals exploded into headlines. Abducted, the politician was held for ransom. Later shot, bullets shattering both legs, he was tossed into the identical ravine Vittorio had fallen fate to, and he tasted the same fear forced upon his victim ten years before. The local *carabinieri* received a note accompanied by an explicitly drawn map leading them to the body. Red Brigades admitted responsibility for the act.

The truth, more savage and melodramatic than the story chanted by roaming minstrels, amounted to this:

Vittorio, near dead, his lower extremities paralyzed and bleeding, had survived in the ravine for four days and nights. His agonized howlings went unheard, buried in the crypt of the long, nightmarish nights. By day he was fever-ridden and too parched from thirst to speak above a whisper. Each dawn found him growing weaker from the loss of blood, lack of water and food. Fever mounting, the gun wounds turning gangrenous, a total suffocation gripped him. Fired by an insane passion for revenge, he reached deep into a reservoir of strength, and literally clawed his way up the steep sides to the edge of the ravine, his fingers bleeding to the knuckles, a step away from death.

Destiny smiled on Vittorio that day. Three gentlemen hunters at *caccia* were quail hunting in the woods. A Corsican, a Moor and the local Sicilian *mafioso*, Don Lupo Ferruggio, stumbled upon him and rushed him to the Palermo hospital. The Corsican marveled at the man's stamina, and listening to Vittorio's wild ravings and accusations, measured his demonstrated survival instinct and unique brand of courage. If for nothing else, the chap deserved to live! Prognosis by the examining doctors was grim, indeed. Gangrene had spread to his upper thighs, amputation below the buttocks was mandatory to save the handsome nineteen-year-old's life.

For Vittorio the bewildering succession of events created a sequence of alternating reactions. Beyond the initial shock, excruciating pain and psychological trauma of drastic surgery fired a hatred so intense, it became his reason for existence.

Vittorio's first glimpse of daylight *after* surgery included the profile of a stranger, a hulking bull moose of a man in his fifties. The dark-eyed Moor, Matteus Montenegro, sat erect as a statue in a hard-backed chair, working colored prayer beads through the fingers of his huge umber-skinned fists. Large anthracite eyes above a multicolored reddish beard laced with silver intrigued the patient. Vittorio later deduced the Moor's eyes, masked by calm, belied the chained inner ferocity of the man. An intense awareness characterized him—an inner discipline lacking in Sicilians save for that special breed—the *mafiosi*.

Power oozing from the Moor commanded Vittorio's respect and curiosity. The nature of his words, spoken economically and without pity, comforted and steadied Vittorio, inspiring him with hope.

Don Ferruggio added Sicilian shrewdness to his personal assessment of the lad's plight. "Vittorio," he told the recuperating lad, "Signore Moufflon believes you are *molto bravo*. I, out of mercy, you understand, would have left you to die—such was your infirmity. What the Corsican sees in you, I have not witnessed with my eyes. So, I put it to you emphatically—only through the Corsican and the Moor can you ever expect to exact retribution for the *infamita* done you."

For Vittorio no further persuasion was required. He began to listen, watch and believe that his only salvation and the preservation of his sanity lay in heeding the Moor's advice. Matteus patiently explained himself. A certain kind of power was available to Vittorio if he dared to reach out to the world of computer technology and supra-communications systems. Mastery of such knowledge could lift a man without legs from obscurity to a lofty plateau to become king of his domain. His imagination was sparked.

But how was this possible? Surely his benefactors realized that with or without legs, if he lived and word reached the *scifioso* who had assaulted him, he was a dead man. Without legs, where could he go, eh? His every waking moment was haunted by his physical limitations. Then powerful friends spoke words followed by actions which provided miracles: a newspaper obituary notice, a mock burial at a *camposant*, a headstone engraved with Vittorio's name provided sufficient proof of death.

Vittorio Buonafortuna was dead! Long live Wolf Spider!

Computer technology in Sicily was as remote as spaceships, Saturn rockets, countdown to blastoffs and the moon shuttle in the late 1960's; as remote then as Pac-Man and computer games of the eighties. Thus, Vittorio was convinced he was talking to a madman. But never mind, the impossible had already provided a splotch of credibility in his mind. He accepted the subsidy, and in the next few years completed a mail-order course in computer technology from Munich, Germany and Tokyo, Japan. Gradually the world of split atoms, transistors, and micro-chips exploded into comprehension and spun fanciful dreams in his head.

The rage, humiliation, pain and discomfort felt for the next ten years culminated in the destruction of his sworn enemy. Revenge was sweet, but nothing was sweeter than discovery of his own self-worth. That the villain responsible for Wolf Spider's infirmity would die was a foregone conclusion and when it happened he had felt elated. By the time he was ensconced in the magnificent hilltop villa owned by the dead politician, Wolf Spider had no time to belabor his infirmity. The sheer effervescence of his power status in the clandestine world of political maneuverings occupied his every waking moment. How he reveled in the new-found power!

Wolf Spider's loyalty to his clients was indisputable, his loyalty and obeisance to Moufflon, absolute. The Corsican, Moufflon, and his factotum, the Moor, had swiftly and miraculously set up the entire communications terminal the moment Wolf Spider signaled his readiness. Monthly the Moor traveled from Corsica to Sicily to pick the brains of his protege on matters held *sacrosanct* between them. Special telephones provided direct communication between Sicily and another mountaintop aerie in Corsica.

And so on this day, when the special phone rang on Wolf Spider's desk, he answered it, subordinating all else to attend to Moufflon's directives. Within the hour a message transmitted to Corsica read:

Subject in question in dire jeopardy. Wolfgang Katz— dead. Subject survived poison gas inhalations. Hospitalized, he survived murder attempt; M.O.: LLAMAS, *Corsican Coral*. Subject recovered, dismissed from Army Hospital. Subject met with General Mark Samuels, USAAI (Army Intelligence Chief). Subject departed. Samuels found dead. M.O.: LLAMAS, *Corsican Coral*. Three-line bullet emplacements on Samuels' forehead. Subject has disappeared. He shook surveillance. KGB makes inquiries. From another source: LLAMAS offers dossier and tapes of Samuels' phone conversations to highest bidder. Shall I pursue? Advise . . . Wolf Spider.

BLOOD MOUNTAIN, CORSICA
February 12, 1983

Moufflon, ruler of an empire as powerful as a nation, a man of mystery, did not exist in the eyes of the world. No reporters hounded him, chronicled his life to make of him an international figure of intrigue, romance and speculation. He was never photographed with a bevy of clinging publicity-crazed actresses or members of royalty. No books were written about him exploiting his highly exploitable life. That they didn't was a triumph for this most unusual human being. Moufflon was a private man, a *very* private man. His fame proliferated among those unique circles of men who controlled the strings of government throughout the world. In such circles his accomplishments were viewed with a prodigious respect, laced by deep-rooted fear and awe.

Moufflon had dozens of close, loyal friends, trusted friends who would die for him; he had no need to put them to the test. Once a man highly placed in the government of France had told him, "You possess power, genius, the needed requisites to be the greatest among world leaders, but you must content yourself to remain an unsung hero, for the talents you possess are such, that spotlighting them will inevitably destroy those closest to you, and yourself in the bargain." Such words were not what a man of his abilities wanted to hear, but his profound love and admiration for General Charles de Gaulle uttering the words gave him pause to reconsider.

His decision to follow the proffered wisdom was not regretted. And so Moufflon picked and chose men like Wolf Spider, men discarded by life and instilled them with hope, uncovered latent talents and trained them. They emerged highly respected men, important cogs in the Moufflon global network. Wolf Spider was merely one of thousands Moufflon had resurrected from the dung heap of society's misfits to occupy vital roles in an army of trained specialists.

Today, Moufflon studied Wolf Spider's communique thoughtfully. Moving out from behind an ebony carved desk, he slipped into a sable-lined windbreaker jacket over a white knit turtleneck sweater, opened a glass sliding door, walked onto the snow-laden terrace and lifted his tanned face to the warm sun. He moved to the lionshead balustrade overlooking Corsica.

He was a tall, slender man, but not thin; his was the muscular stature stemming from years of discipline, a man in control of both mind and body. Broad shoulders, a strong, taut torso provided ample hints of a body honed to perfection. His well-defined features contained no hint of arrogance or self-indulgence. Uncommonly handsome, his unwavering viridian eyes were those of a man who had seen everything in life. A few silver hairs threaded into brown at his temples and his Raphaelian features drew second and third glances wherever he went. An aura of mystery surrounded him; far more intriguing was the magnetism he exuded.

The message in his hand, agitated by sharp zephyring winds disturbed him. He reread it, then shoved it into his pocket.

So! Zurich was closing in on the American, Lincoln! Moufflon could not permit this.

Moufflon breathed deeply, enjoying the panorama. Perched on óne of Corsica's highest peaks, halfway between Mount Rotundo and Mount Cinto near the timeless village of Niolo in the interior, the villa itself seemed carved from the mountain and afforded a breathtaking 360° panoramic view of land, sky and water surrounding the entire island of Corsica.

This man without global peer moved forward, shifting his attention to the *moufflon* and young bucks grazing nearby on the food provided them. Removing a sweet morsel from a bucket, he leaned over the balustrade, cooing to them. The animals, normally wary of man, pranced forward, stiff-legged, without trepidation. He leaned over and stroked the sable-coated animal, admiring its spiraling golden horns. He spoke softly, in French, as if addressing a human.

He thought of the animal as an old friend. They were alike in many respects; both had been bred to wisdom, caution, and survival instincts. Hunted, the animal for its splendid horns and fine silky pelts, the man for the contents stored in his brain, neither trembled or stood in frear of his enemies.

Today Moufflon was at an impasse. Decisions had to be made, the annihilation of a man and his insidious organization faced him. He sighed. He knew Zurich would advance innumerable obstacles and an avalanche of propaganda. His ability to openly negotiate would be jeopardized. Nations would turn against him and create a white heat of hatred directed against him until he was ground into dust.''

151

Moufflon fed the Corsican king of beasts more food morsels, speaking aloud.

"The task is full of dangers. It is not impossible, understand, but complicated, exacting, and may well mark destruction for Moufflon. All we've worked for these decades . . ." He snapped his fingers. "Pouf! Up in smoke. *Une tableau desagreable, mais non*?"

"Are you asking my opinion or ventilating your thoughts?"

Moufflon spun around, delight passing over his face like a beam of sunlight. He stretched out his arm, drew her close to his side. She laid her head on his chest, sighing with pleasure as he kissed her forehead. She gazed briefly at the animals, then beyond at the dimly shadowed Italian coastline separated by a stunning sweep of an azure Mediterranean sea.

"If Monsieur Igor Sikorsky and his predecessors had refrained from besting nature, how would we gain access to this eagle's lair? Why did you build in so remote a mountaintop, *mon cher*? Without helicopters, how would you be accessible to any of us?"

Moufflon lifted her chin forcing her eyes to meet his. "I find it inconceivable that your grandfather, *le grand raconteur*, resisted spinning that tale. Once, long ago, the *moufflon* saved me from death. Over there, beyond the terrace near the frozen lake at the foot of the icy pinnacle . . . you see?" He indicated the silvery fluted area around a flat mirrored ground at the center of a lacy snow scene. She focused briefly on it, turned back to him, face uplifted, dark luminous eyes reflecting love. "Oh, *cher*, how I love thee . . . let me count the ways."

His smile burst into infectious laughter. "And I, too, love thee, little one, but cannot take time to count the ways, *n'est ce pas*? Come, we have work to do, *ma bonne chere*." He paused to observe three helicopters hovering overhead. "They are on time as usual. Your friend is in grave peril. Three attempts on his life . . .? I hope he endures the rigors of his profession."

"Another Jim Greer he is not. They are worlds apart."

"*Vive la difference*." He sighed deeply. "*Vous et moi tulipe noir, ma belle*. But, back to business. I read your report. Excellent. I remember him from the war. A most unpredictable man, the Major." Moufflon's eyes narrowed in thought. "The immense project to be embarked upon overflows with calculated risk. If it fails, we lose everything."

"Never! You are not programmed for failure. You, *cher*, possess that *je ne sais quoi*, that undefinable something that precludes failure." She flirted outrageously with him.

"Behave yourself, Bernadette, else I shall forget you are the daughter of my beloved sister, Sophia."

"Why do you persist in that delusion? The same blood never flowed in both your veins. You say it to fend me off, I *know*!"

Moufflon paused en route to the concrete and glass mansion, held her shoulders, forcing her eyes to his. "Raised as brother and sister, not knowing the truth until catastrophe struck both our lives, alters the facts. What one believes in heart and mind becomes that person's truth. You could have been my daughter—"

"No! Never! What utter absurdity! Destiny saved you for me!" His amused paternal glances fanned her anger. She scowled fiercely as a soft breeze ruffled her wheat-colored hair. "She died before telling me the truth. *You* know my father's identity— why don't you tell me?"

He touched her cheek gently, caressingly with the back of his fingers, a sadness underlying his words. "*Oui*. It was her dying wish that you must never know."

"But *why*?"

He pulled a few wispy tendrils off her face. "You are the image of Dariana, your grandmother. Sophia's dark, sultry beauty is absent in you," he said wistfully. "It is Dariana who lives in you. Ah, what provocative intensity, what a vibrancy for life she radiated. Her beauty and charm singled her out and made her a very special Corsican. . . ." Then the moment ended. "*Allez*, we have work to do. Let us map strategy to bring Major Lincoln closer to his goal, *n'est ce pas*?"

She nodded, her face shadowed by a tinge of guilt, yet relieved. So far he hadn't reprimanded her, but then he fixed sternly on her.

"What is this potential for self-destruction running wildly in you? Your penchant for older men? *Alors*, inevitably curses, like chickens, come home to roost. . . ."

"*Oui*! It is precisely that—a curse! My professor at the Sorbonne called it an *Electra* complex. Never knowing *my* father, I am searching the world to find him. Why don't you answer this eternal riddle? Perhaps I would interest myself in a younger man—one my own age.''

''Bernadette! I don't threaten easily,'' he teased, laughter creeping into his voice. ''Ah, *chere*, consider yourself fortunate. My love for you blinds me to your indiscretions.''

The moment was awkward, what must she do to make him look upon her as a woman? She had loved him all her life—would love him to her death, as had her mother, knowing it could never be reciprocal love. ''Oh—oh, you *Corsicans*!'' she blurted angrily, unable to describe the emotions surging through her. ''When will you step into the twentieth century?''

Moufflon laughed tenderly, eyes lifted to the Sikorsky choppers overhead, only one remained to land. ''Pray God the twentieth century exists when this business is finished,'' he said quietly. He opened the glass doors. ''*Après vous, ma belle*,'' he murmured, lost in thought. He himself moved toward the helipad to greet the arrivals.

When Berna stepped inside, her demeanor became professional, as she concentrated on Wolf Spider's communique. She moved gracefully over marble floors among the outer corridor skirting the manor proper, headed toward the massive communications room. The plain *fräulein* Brad Lincoln encountered in Switzerland had emerged from her cocoon into an exquisite, colorful butterfly—the metamorphosis, stunning. She had learned the art of accommodating her looks to match the setting or to fade entirely in it, if necessary. Today she wore a revealingly fitted pale beige jumpsuit and matching suede boots. Her hair hung in loose, wild curls coiffed in that dramatic fashion which added wild abandon to her innate sensuality. Makeup skillfully applied enhanced her fine bone structure and luminous eyes.

Berna entered the impressive communications terminal, Brad Lincoln's predicament absorbing her thoughts. The damn fool was in trouble, *serious* trouble.

The sky over Marseilles was blue, cloudless, clear as a sapphire gem. A Sikorsky helicopter lifted off a helipad on a private airstrip at the outskirts of the city. It soared over the bay dotted with rows of colorful fishing boats, tugs, cruisers and luxury

154

yachts. The pilot set his instruments and headed in a southeasterly direction.

Seated in the passenger section with his hosts, Prince Youseff Ben Kassir and Dr. Jean Louis Delon, Jim Greer was on his maiden visit to Moufflon's secret headquarters. When he had received the summons, Greer shaved off his beard, cut his hair to a respectable length, and now dressed in a conservative suit. Looking years younger, he could pass for any prosperous businessman; the ferocity displayed to Brad Lincoln absent. A haunted expression lingered in his eyes.

"James, for your protection a blindfold will be set into position before we approach the compound," the Prince said politely.

"I understand, Highness."

"The view is indescribably stunning," Youseff rambled. "Perhaps, Allah willing, you shall return under less taxing conditions."

Greer wasn't certain what Moufflon expected of him. Actually he didn't care. For him it was a long-awaited move back into the center of action, to be alive again, instead of half-dead in that frozen hinterland of a prison existence he'd suffered for two decades.

The Prince, tall, lean, with skin of golden umber, wore a short sculptured beard and mustache. Dressed in apparel of the finest London tailoring, handcrafted Moroccan leather boots, solid gold watch and ring in the shape of a lionshead, he opened a bottle of chilled white wine, removed three iced glasses from a bucket, proffered a plate of canapes to his guests, and pouring the pale amber liquid, handed each a glass. He raised his in midair, toasting. "To global peace." They clinked glasses, sipped quietly.

Jean Louis removed a black silk scarf from his briefcase. "It's time, James," he said apologetically.

"You'll get no argument from me," Greer pacified. "I understand the necessity of sequestering a stronghold," he said as the scarf was set into place. No longer a forgotten man, Greer felt important. If he played his cards right . . .

Each visit to Corsica provided continuous pleasure and bafflement to Youseff. He was never able to locate the mountain aerie until the chopper hovered over it. The architecture, blending intimately with nature, was impossible to detect; he tried a thousand times in the past. Perched on a flatbed of rock amid the upper reaches of an icy pinnacle rising 2,600 feet above sea level, the

155

estate spread across the breast of a mountain, fortresslike, resembling a fortification in outer space.

"See yonder, Jean Louis—the entire coastline of Italy. Look to the south—Sardinia. And farther in the hazy distance—North Africa, my home."

"And to the west, Highness," laughed Jean Louis Delon tolerantly, "Gibraltar rises from the sea like a giant monolith. *Oui. Oui.* With you it's the same. Each time we fly here nature enthralls you."

"It is the abode of a king." Youseff flashed agate eyes.

"Your palace is the slums?" Delon, a petite, wiry Frenchman exuded cold, regal austerity. The former physician had paid his dues. Behind docile eyes hovered stockpiled terror and chained violence long restrained, which could be activated in a moment. Delon and the Prince were charter members of Moufflon's Council.

"For you, James, to appease his highness, I shall describe the view. You recollect Corsica from *OPERATION WHITE CORAL*, so I need not rhapsodize on its intrinsic beauty, for truly, Corsica is the tropical India of Europe. Nature protects Moufflon's fortress well. Intrusions are not possible from the lower reaches. A treacherous path leads from one village, ending at 1,600 feet. Beyond this point a winding trail, sixteen inches, perhaps less at its widest, corkscrews up the mountain face. Two years in construction, materials were transported to the site by chopper. Once called Blood Mountain, this became Moufflon's seat of operations for sentimental, but shrewd reasons."

"Why do I get the feeling you are trying to tell me something other than the description of Moufflon's redoubt, Jean Louis?"

"Ah . . . you're good, Greer. Merely advising you in advance, the disadvantages in attempting to locate this site through hidden electronic devices."

"You took my wristwatch, compass, used metal detectors on me—what else do you require? Shall I unscrew my brain, and expose its contents for a search?" Greer laughed, but his companions did not.

"Perhaps I can explain further," the Prince said quietly. "Years ago, before his mountaintop retreat was conceived, superstitious villagers told a story of a young Corsican lad lost on Blood Mountain while hunting *moufflon*. Legend claimed that the lad had taken a bad spill in a series of minor avalanches and hung suspended from a frozen promontory for hours until a party of hunters found him. A harrowing time ensued. The boy, apparently infected by a bout of temporary madness, had turned on the hunters, shot and killed three men. The search party returned to the village, more dead than alive, to spin fanciful tales of a sworn blood oath of *vendetta* to be visited upon the lad by the surviving members of the dead mens family. From clan to clan, the frightening word spread—*vendetta*! Kill the boy! Rid Blood Mountain and Corsica of the entire family.

"That young lad, James, was Darius Bonifacio—the man we knew in World War II with a spectacular military career is now Moufflon, a legend in a land of legends. No longer do the clans swear vengeance against him, rather, he is their unspoken king. You do understand how vital he is to Corsica, France and to the world . . ."

As he finished his story, the Sikorsky swooped down in a perfect landing.

Greer's blindfold was removed in the enormous living room. The Prince and Delon excused themselves as an aide indicated the cheery fire and an extravagant buffet. "Please help yourself."

Greer nodded, intrigued, impressed with the permeating smack of tremendous wealth. He noticed several servants casually moving about, and immediately realized they were trained guards, security, skilled in martial arts. On their white ski suits, over their hearts, was embossed a golden goat horn, the mark of Moufflon.

Greer, sipping champagne, moved about the spacious room amid oversized furniture in Spanish leathers, fur skins, richly carved rosewoods and ebonies designed by master craftsmen. Windows fifteen feet high formed a 45° arc at the edge of the room. Beyond them to the east was the hazy outline of the Italian continent. He searched for landmarks, but he couldn't pinpoint the exact location of Moufflon's retreat. The compass watch he'd worn had been removed the moment he boarded the chopper in Marseilles; it would be returned on his arrival back at the mainland. They didn't miss a thing.

He moved about, thinking of Darius Bonifacio, a touch of envy eating at him. To have risen in the ranks from humble beginnings as a recruit in the Foreign Legion was in itself a *fait accompli*. Only St. Cyr graduates, no enlistee, had ever advanced from shabby greenhorn recruit to officer. But France's critical posture in the war forced numerous reassessments. Darius Bonifacio, the boy wonder, had penetrated the time-long snobbery by sheer genius. An imposing figure then, even before he'd entered his twenties, Darius had signaled that he was a man destined for greatness. Greer actually knew very little of the Corsican except for those years spent in combat.

Greer morosely sipped champagne, brooding inwardly. What might he have become if instead of venting his passion for Coney Island red hots and Mom's apple pie, he'd remained with *Corsican Jade*?

He raised his glass in mock salute and pivoted around the room, "*C'est' a vie!*" Draining the choice Perignon, he refilled his glass, ambled past the grand dining salon—it seated fifty, he counted the chairs—separated from the living room by enormously tall sculptured glass panels at either side of a two-step-up level.

The decor, soft, muted earth tones, graduated the color spectrum of raw siennas, russets, taupes to pale pearly beige. Then Greer's attention riveted to a startling, and priceless art collection. He paused before a bewildering profusion of sculptures, oil paintings and art objects depicting war and death.

Deja vu, Greer. You've been here before, lived through the horrors. Emotionally stirred, he moved from painting to painting, mesmerized by scenes and portraits, memories seizing him as if it were only yesterday.

Captured realistically on canvas were the Battles of the North African campaign, grim portraits of Italians, Germans, French, Americans and British soldiers, including those skilled sappers of the 4th Indian Division of the British Eighth Army, depicting the ultimate horrors of war. Battles of the Coral Sea, Midway, Clark Field, Manila, the capture of Bataan and Corregidor!

Startled into sobriety, Greer frowned at the macabre recollections. Haunting, frightening brutalities of war! The Abbey at Monte Cassino, steeped with dead corpses, skull and crossbones piled in tiers amid the ruins; wounded, bloodied, maimed haunting human eyes staring at death; the massacre at Malmédy; doomed soldiers; battlefield executions; Death Camp at Buchenwald, depicting the deaths of millions systematically starved, tortured, murdered! What grim, bitter, but better reminder to any visitor to this incredible redoubt than to strive for peace?

Greer was stunned, his guts ripped apart by what he saw. Locked drawers in his mind sprang open, unleashing torrents of memories buried decades ago by the systematic mind-reprogramming ordered by the CIA. Greer, a cold, dangerous man, totally unpredictable, a man whose strange code of principles had labeled everyone else his enemy, momentarily shuddered with chills of revulsions. Then he forced the images to dissolve, reburied his feelings in the anger and bitterness amassed for two lonely decades. He was a professional—he knew it was a sure sign of death for a man on the run to indulge in the emotional past. He had never dreamed himself to be what he had become. This time around, with any luck, the fucking results would be different. He intended to seize for himself what Darius Bonifacio had achieved.

"*Bon jour, mon ami.*"

Greer spun around and stared. He recognized the voice but not the stunning woman standing before him. His eyes narrowed. "Berna . . .? I can't believe it. It's really you?"

"No—not Berna, her clone." she laughed huskily. "Should I express my surprise at the changes in you? *Mon Dieu*! Without your beard and long mane you no longer appear the ferocious snow leopard." Then she quickly masked further comment under a cloak of professionalism. "*Monsieur* Moufflon will be at least a half hour, James. Feel at home. Whatever you desire, please summon a servant."

Flabbergasted at the overt changes in her, he changed tack. "So, this is the world of Moufflon. I never imagined it—"

"—anything is an improvement over your self-imposed isolation."

"You are exceptional, Berna," he mused. "Somehow you fit into the picture, but not just as an ordinary courier, as I was led to believe." He gazed past her, his focus shifting beyond an inner courtyard to the glass-enclosed communications complex in the adjoining wing. Parabolics and satellite dishes were in clear view.

"I, too, take orders, like anyone," Berna purposely understated her position. Catching his line of view, she added, "I am one part in the giant network of the Moufflon apparatus. I merely do my work as best I can, as efficiently as I've been trained."

"I don't believe that for a minute. You are exceptional at what you do. As to your efficiency, I can attest to that," he said scorchingly. "You fooled me." His attention riveted to the technicians behind the glass wall.

"From one professional to another, the compliment is acknowledged. Let me, if I may, James, stress a point. Listen, and hear me well. Your presence here implies a certain loyalty. Make no mistake, once you've accepted a position of confidence and do anything to betray that confidence, you are a dead man." Her gentle, matter-of-fact tone triggered warnings.

Greer glanced sharply at her. "I fucking well know my options."

"Ah . . . It is *really* you, James. Your language as colorful as usual. And the word is option, not options. There is only one. Loyalty to Moufflon. You knew it before you arrived in Marseilles." Berna, suddenly uneasy, fixed piercingly on him. "It supercedes any previous commitments, *tu comprend pas?*"

Greer felt awkward, annoyed, betrayed, foolish. Here in Corsica under the aegis of Moufflon she had become a stranger—their previous relationship forgotten. He didn't like it, but realized he had no choice but to subordinate himself to her authority. "Suppose you brief me," he said coolly.

"Monsieur Moufflon reserves that privilege. It concerns your friend. He is in dire straits in West Berlin. Presently the Council sits in chambers determining the extent of dangers."

Greer acknowledged the words with a questioning expression, his interest in the communications terminal heightened. Noticing his eagerness, Berna smiled tightly. "All in due time, *liebling*. Control your curiosity. In your country there is a saying—it kills cats."

The air in the conference room was rife with tension. Twelve imposing men sat around an enormous thick-glass conference table, exchanging glances of annoyance. Beyond these men and seated along one wall sat three elder advisors—all bound together in fraternal fidelity. These men were members of Moufflon's Grand Council: discreet men of power and influence who kept low profiles, but occupied highly placed positions in the governments of their respective nations. All fought a common enemy, an enemy whose singular purpose sought to topple governments.

These experts, stunned by Moufflon's inflammatory words, demonstrated rare emotions. Skeptical of their leader's remarks, they demanded more information.

"*Mes ami*, permit me to clarify." Moufflon shifted position in his chair, his eyes fanning the table of ashen faces. "I speak from a position of caution and concern. A certain amount of risk-taking is mandatory at this juncture."

160

"You give us no choice?" Lucien Pascal, another Corsican demanded.

"None at all."

"You will need us," insisted the burly Irishman, Joseph "Dutch" O'Reilly. "You haven't explained why you underplay the significance of our roles and our past accomplishments. You no longer need us? Is that it?"

"I need you as never before," Moufflon admitted quietly, but firmly. "The matter is not open to debate. My decision stands. You will go about your business as usual. At the proper time, provided risks do not accelerate beyond reasonable safety zones, I will permit a referendum."

"Why this sudden wish to proceed alone, Darius?" Prince Ben Kassir pressed for answers. "Unity has bound us all these years. Now, you embark on this—on this insanity alone? It is crucial that you should explain."

"Very well," Darius raised his hand to silence the discontented rumbling about the table. "For better than three decades the Middle Eastern conspiracy escalates hostilities in that area. The question confronting us two decades ago was the extent of that conspiracy. We lacked answers then, but I assure you, *mes ami*, today, we have the answers. It stretches beyond credibility and *our* control."

The others sat forward in their chairs, eyes riveted on Darius.

"A brief recapitulation, *s'il vous plaît*. Twenty years ago, when you the council put before me the Zurich proposal, I declined. The offer for our *special services*, ten billion dollars— American—was persuasive. You recall I dealt harsh terms—"

"You hardlined every contractual clause," Jean Louis Delon acknowledged. "Your motive was to evoke our client's refusal."

"Precisely. I demanded direct contact with Zurich, and refused to work through any agents."

"But the matter failed to cancel itself," Lord Duncan Whitehall from London chewed his cigar to shreds. "It merely whetted Zurich's appetite."

"Exactly. A call came from Zurich. The conversation convinced me that the client was a madman. But the options Zurich offered produced interesting speculation. If we complied with Zurich, total control would rest in *our* hands. If we refused, the deal could be taken up by fanatics which would produce disastrous results. Zurich made it clear to me—with or without

161

Moufflon—he intended to achieve his goals in the Middle East. I never doubted him.''

Abu Bututu, a lean, tall, ebony-skinned Nigerian with black suns for eyes, held on Darius. "So for two decades Moufflon provided Zurich numerous victories in the Middle East—''

"—and failures when it became appropriate," added Pasquale Longinotti from Genoa, Italy, drumming his fingers impatiently.

Darius nodded grimly. "But recently Zurich refuses appeasement. He presses for the annihilation of his enemies. And so, a reassessment of strategies compels me to reexamine the imperatives and plan accordingly. We are presently at an impasse. Strategy implemented at this point excludes you for your protection. Should the plan fail, I go down alone. If I succeed, nuclear crisis will be averted and we will all emerge victorious.''

Longinotti protested in a harsh voice. "The exposure must not be carried by you alone, Darius. If fruits of this victory turn to ashes, as implied by your reluctance to implicate us, I, for one, am unwilling to let the risk be yours. *Ecco*, equally we shared the past—equally we share today and tomorrow. None of us would be here today if it were not for you, Darius.''

Darius raised a protesting hand, again silencing the dissenters. "Twenty years ago, the records show I was the one abstention. We debated, voted, debated, voted, until my abstention was nullified. But we agreed then, and the records show the final round in this conflict was to be mine to orchestrate as I chose. *D'accord*?''

The Council murmured disgruntled sounds.

"I paced the floor day and night before coming to this decision. I believe that the time for rhetoric is over." Darius poured *café noir,* paused dramatically, eyed his Council somberly. "Business of a personal nature unwittingly places me at the center of this power struggle. I cannot extricate myself. The objectivity of my former position enhanced my negotiating flexibilities. Now, my decisions, guided from a subjective position, influences me, forcing me to take up the gauntlet alone.''

His loyal advisors were not prepared for Moufflon's rejection and sudden alienation. Darius' reassuring calm failed to appease their confusion and they argued vociferously. Listening to the Council's objections, Darius thought back to their early beginnings in Sidi-bel Abbes, in North Africa. He smiled. They hadn't changed much, after all. Then silence ensued. The advisors looked to Youseff Ben-Kassir. Would he influence this craziness of Darius' thinking?

Puffing on a cigarette, continental-style, Youseff spoke in perfect French. "Darius, the world has no real knowledge that world-wide atrocities are originated and controlled by Zurich and Geneva. How will you, one man standing alone, bring this information to the world? How?"

Darius shrugged benignly. "Dialogue with Zurich is impossible. The man grows impatient, more irrational each day. We are not dealing with a normal man, Youseff. We all know he is a zealot dedicated to an insane cause. He does not create idols of stone in his image. He molds them, shapes them to his thought in diabolical ways. Facts about this fanatic have reached me. Something despicable takes place behind closed doors in Zurich, a satanic plan that demands immediate investigation. Trusted agents in his lair send reports of evil, *mes ami.*"

Eyes locked with other eyes, communicated thoughts and fears.

"To respond to your earlier query, Youseff, once Zurich is eliminated, the world will no longer be controlled by the Zurich apparatus, and I will be able to tell the truth."

"Insanity was not at issue two decades ago," Lord Whitehall said slowly, stroking his beard. "They are—all of them— madmen."

"The corridors of hell are not unchartered waters for us."

"True, Darius, but if you persist in perpetuating this personal vendetta—"

Darius interrupted skillfully, glossing over his displeasure. He had made no mention of a *personal vendetta*. "We are at a pivotal point in global security. *And Moufflon no longer controls the timetable of events in the Middle East!*"

The words, like soft-spoken velvet pierced like daggers. Council members' faces registered disbelief. The silence lasted five seconds. The lines were drawn clearly; they understood the ramifications of such a revelation.

"So, if to determine the outcome of the Middle East conspiracy, it were possible to meet Zeller himself on a battlefield, I would present myself in full battle regalia at once. Unfortunately, the entire earth is his battlefield. He and his kind are creators of a prodigious war machine that has poisoned mind and body;

163

professors of mass hypnosis and promoters of mass hysteria. This *invisible* cartel is the profiteer of international crimes which have established world dominion. And we have known it for decades, each integral part of the cog known to us. If we must strike—we know where to do the most damage." Darius sipped his coffee, his eyes trailing to the red flashing signal on the console before him.

Sheikh Ahkmud Zeki Zali, from one of the Arab Emirates, indicated his displeasure and concern. "Soon, Darius, I must take into my confidence members of the royal family to explain our role and objectives. We are not eager to fight the Israeli war machine after what happened in Lebanon in the summer of '82. But Zurich poses viable threats to all your blueprints for peace. How many *cease-fires* were violated? Six—seven? The Royal Family sees this as pure determination to exterminate the Arabs."

Serge Ivanovsky argued more adamantly. "We negotiated, convinced the P.L.O. to give up its revolutionary aims, dissolve terrorist activities. The rewards for their efforts? A veritable barrage of slander, manufactured misinformation hurled upon them."

Prince Ben-Kassir began, "And that indicates—"

"—how dangerous Zurich has become, Youseff," finished Darius. "His propaganda machine countermands our efforts. His zombies move to his command, strengthening his position."

"They are experts at creating illusions," offered Aba Bututu. "Outwardly his puppets cry for peace, yet they stealthily move in the night, conquering positions, but always when global attention is focused elsewhere. Yes, yes, I agree, the Moufflon apparatus no longer orchestrates the Middle East libretto." Bututu laid a wad of snuff in his cheek and chewed thoughtfully.

"It goes beyond that," the Sheikh insisted. "Zurich's tactic is to keep information from the public, especially *damaging* information. They censor anything that profiles them in a damaging way. We simply cannot compete with the support it receives from the United States without causing many deaths. Indeed, the hand of Zurich guides the—"

"Ahkmud, you are losing perspective, your objectivity. Hatred tinges your words. I have never known you to speak thusly."

"Is it because our intelligence forces reveal what you have failed to impart, Darius?" Sheikh Zeki Zali spoke warily.

Silence . . . ten seconds ticked by in electrified silence.

164

"Racounter, s'il vous plait."

"Should you defect, Zurich insures his own victory in ways that transcend propaganda machines and censorship."

Well done. The words designed to shock met their mark. Darius stared at Sheikh Zali, eyes narrowing to conceal his discomfort.

"Ahkmud, pray tell us this *insurance* you speak of."

Eyes orbited from Moufflon to the Arab chieftain. Clearly they had missed the statement couched in the sheikh's speech, but none mistook the coiling tension between the speakers. *Ahkmud* passed a sealed folder to the Prince, who in turn passed it to Darius.

"A complete report of my findings," he said, a flicker in his eye conveying no further discussion should ensue.

"Très bien. We dare not risk premature exposure to strengthen Zurich's position." He placed the folder before his console. "Now, then, a possible link paves roads for negotiations with the West. He must be protected at all costs. Recent attempts on his life by assassins, foiled, do not eliminate the dangers. Death stalks him. We must uncover the contractors—understand. The plan I spoke of earlier depends entirely upon the element of surprise."

"Darius, I insist we all go the distance with you to lessen the risk to you personally," insisted Youseff solemnly.

"I agree," said Lucien Pascal. "We—any of us—are expendable. Without you, Darius . . ." He shook his head.

The Moor signaled from one of the throne chairs. His companions, Chamois Barbone, head of the *UNIONE CORSE*, the Corsican Mafia, and Vivaldi Bonifacio, founder of the Moufflon organization, nodded. Darius acknowledged them. "If Zurich suspects our intervention, pushes and demands results as they did in Lebanon in 1982, then everything goes up in smoke. If attacked, Moufflon will survive, although it will mean high visibility and enormous vulnerability. Very well then, we will concede that Zurich controls the present. It is clear that attempts to bring peace to the Middle East are frustrated daily, but the final phase—the outcome of his plans—have held us captive for two decades. Well, no more. We shall resolve this infamy. I personally shall penetrate the area and learn for myself Zeller's goals in the Middle East."

Moufflon's console lit up again. He picked up the phone.

"*Oui*?" Darius swiveled his chair to face the enormous communications terminal in a room behind glass walls. Berna at the other end of the line read the message just received. "*Donnez-moi le communique, s'il vous plait.*" He replaced the phone, swung about and faced the Council.

"We are in crisis. A superpower summit meeting must take place to obstruct the madman of Zurich from reaching his goal."

The Council huddled while Berna entered quietly and placed the communique before Darius. It was from Wolf Spider. Darius read the decoded message:

Use extreme caution. One among your advisors has betrayed you. Information will follow.

Darius handed Berna the message without expression. She glanced casually in the direction of the throne chairs before exiting. Darius followed her line of vision imperceptibly.

Chamois Barbone fixed black piercing eyes—undulled by time or age—on Darius. Under that thick crop of snowy white hair burned the wits and animal intelligence of a stalking tiger. The chieftain of the formidable *UNIONE CORSE* observed in silence and listened to the exchanges with provincial cunning.

Vivaldi Fornari Bonifacio, the power source behind the Moufflon, the man who had raised Darius as his own flesh and blood, seemed lost in deep thought. Equally as mad as the man in Zurich, the aging, white-haired leonine figure, as powerful a potentate as any man in Europe, locked eyes with Darius. Demanding hazel-green eyes framed by thick white brows, fixed in silent scrutiny on the younger figurehead.

Darius focused on the man who had raised him, seemingly endowed with the capacity to read Vivaldi's soul. These two were bound together in a blood oath which had endured for decades, withstood the deaths of countless loved ones, created misery in the lives of innocent people. The oath was forged before Darius' birth, tying him to Vivaldi and Zeller in an unholy alliance of blood vengeance. Long before Darius Bonifacio discovered his true birthright, he had sworn a Corsican blood oath to destroy Amadeo Zeller, the madman of Zurich.

No one actually knew the story. Vivaldi Bonifacio had never told the tale, and the Moor, his lifelong factotum, would die before the truth spilled from his lips. But it was whispered that something diabolically frightening had taken possession of Vivaldi Bonifacio before he came to Corsica, that brewing inside him was a madness.

The truth was that Bonifacio was not Corsican at all. He was a Spanish noble, Francisco de la Varga, betrayed and left for dead in Spain, rescued by the Moor, Matteus. Together they had fled Spain to Corsica, adopted both the nation and the Genoan name of Bonifacio, and built a life on Blood Island, Corsica's ancient name. Here they marked time until they could bring to fruition the vendetta and sworn oath to destroy Amadeo Zeller—the man Vivaldi held responsible for reducing the de la Varga family of Seville and the affluent Valdez family of Buenos Aires to a graveyard of memories.

A flurry of excitement coursed through the octogenarian's body. Soon, now, thought Vivaldi, it would be ended. The painstakingly structured vengeance planned against Amadeo Zeller, having spanned five decades, would soon be consummated by his adopted son, Darius. The butcher in Zurich would finally pay for the massacre of his beloved fiance, Victoria Valdez! For the infamy done him! For the fraudulent appropriation of the de la Varga millions!

Exacerbating the ungodly story was the knowledge that the ill-gotten affluence had aided and abetted the felon, Zeller, in overthrowing the Spanish Government, paving the way for fascism and the Franco Government, and causing a proliferation of trade unions to demoralize Spain. Vivaldi was tired. Yes! Yes! He wanted it to end, to taste victory before he died.

The personal business Moufflon refrained from discussing with his Grand Council of advisors was precisely the blood oath of vendetta. *Vendetta!* Matteus, the Moor, recalling the Britisher's earlier remark, paled. Lord Duncan Whitehall had referred to a *personal vendetta!* How had he known? Captivated by these inner thoughts and more, the Moor hoped for Darius' sake the end was in sight. If for nothing else but peace and the unburdening of his own soul before embarking on his final journey into Allah's comforting arms. For only he and Vivaldi knew the truth.

From birth, Darius, adopted by a madman, was programmed to kill another madman in Zurich!

Moufflon's attention returned to the discussion at the round table. Listening to the open discussion, he clearly indicated there was a limit beyond which he could not be pushed.

"It is not our wish to disagree with your decision, Darius," said Jean Louis Delon. "But in this instance we agree unanimously you should remain anonymous until a meeting with the American President is secure."

Moufflon was touched. He knew what would follow. Prince Ben-Kassir did not disappoint him. "We will agree with your demands to speak before a world council, if your true identity is concealed until the eleventh hour. Your security must be guaranteed above all else. Will you concede to the wisdom and propriety of this move?"

Darius' silence provided them no penetration of his thoughts. The contents of Wolf Spider's message at so inopportune a time posed hellish complexities. *Treachery in his midst*? Disloyalty now—at so crucial a stage in their progress? Had Zurich bought a spoke in the Moufflon power-wheel apparatus? A sense of foreboding, masked carefully as he listened to his advisors sorting other business, turned his thoughts inward.

As they debated, at this very moment, thousands of tons of war materiel were being introduced to opposite sides in the Middle Eastern conflict, set to explode in mid-1984. The proliferation of nuclear arms, building to unlimited numbers in the itchy, trigger fingers of men programmed to deploy missiles at the first insult hurled over boundaries, was like sitting on a global timebomb.

And he must unite the world powers to defuse the timebomb. *Could he accomplish the impossible?*

Could he bring the walls down on Zurich without bringing the world crashing down on him?

He had much ground to cover before Brad Lincoln confirmed his suspicions with enough credible information to penetrate the barricade of the formidible political machine entrenched around John Macgregor.

Yes! President John Macgregor was the key! He would have to be convinced, and Brad Lincoln would bring the evidence to him.

Under the bulletproof vest President Macgregor wore in daily ritual there once beat a humanitarian heart. If it hadn't atrophied, Moufflon would provide Major Lincoln with tools to awaken it and restore its human heartbeats.

Turning in the swivel chair, facing the complex array of electronic computers in the high-tech communications systems terminal behind floor-to-ceiling glass walls, Darius marveled at their capabilities: electronics ahead of its time, bold in design, enthralling to witness at work. What outstanding capabilities! Approaching unidentified aircraft that activated radar and other signaling devices risked total obliteration if they delayed identification a fraction longer than the time permitted by international aviation laws. Computers with ECMs, jamming and anti-jamming devices, in the event of an aerial attack, could veer missiles off-course, forcing them to fall harmlessly into the sea.

That Moufflon operated under the aegis of the French Government was not a known fact, and if hinted at was immediately denied by the Republic. Vital to the Moufflon operation were the highly sensitive tracking systems permitting him access to Soviet and U.S. intelligence gathering. The eavesdropping capabilities of the orbiting spy-in-the-sky satellites launched by these nations, intercepted via complex tracking and transmitting systems, permitted Moufflon advance notice of *coups*, since each transmitted photos of the targeted areas in advance of planned military operations.

Darius shifted focus, his eyes rested on her. She was studying blueprints, exchanging dialogue with technicians. Berna was the best. The very best. The most trusted of his couriers, *and* to him the most precious. She was rapidly becoming indispensable. He studied her, while his advisors discussed his proposed strategy to bring Brad Lincoln closer to his goal, aided by *invisible* workers in the field. He had solved the larger part of his most pressing problem. Berna was his answer.

Now for the next step.

Darius politely excused himself from the Council chambers. He wanted to speak to Greer alone. Wolf Spider's communique bode an ill wind. Until the treachery was confirmed, exposing Jim Greer to any possible betrayal would be a grave error.

Once their business ended, he would send Greer back to the mainland covertly. He wanted neither Greer nor the Council to acknowledge one another—not yet.

Chapter Nine

MARSEILLES, FRANCE

THE NARROW WATERFRONT ALLEY WAS DESERTED. It was nearing midnight. A man, once known in certain select underworld circles as *Nightstalker*, stood languidly poised in a dimly lit doorway, his features indefinable in the shadows. Furtive, glazed eyes darted up and down the darkened street, searching. In the near distance the wharf sounds diminished in the late hours. Even the perennial stench of stale fish went unnoticed by the Nightstalker in these moments. His clothing was a mess: sloppy, filthy, spattered with ashes, cigarette burns, old food stains and vomit. His hands and legs trembled uncontrollably—not from the icy blasts of the cold, wet wind—from heroin addiction that immunized him to frigid temperatures. He shook compulsively, the desperate craving for heroin driving him, a criminal bent flaring in his eyes. Nightstalker searched for a victim, any victim to pounce upon and rob—kill if need be for the price of a fix.

Close by, piercing, critical, knowing eyes fixed on him, assessing his progressive debilitation, waiting . . . waiting. Holding Nightstalker in his sights, the Obstructor calculated how long it had been since the junkie had shot a load of heroin into his veins. The wretched man, in dire straits, his body and mind ravaged by dependency, dared death-defying means to satisfy his needs. A good sign, thought the Obstructor. Good, very good. In fact the Nightstalker, at the edge, was getting closer to the limit.

Plagued by a rising anxiety at the hopelessness of his situation, the heroin addict chewed on a sweet. Even better, thought the Obstructor: his mouth must be feeling dry, foul smelling, bitter; only sweets assuaged so awful an acrid taste. Judging from the skeletal look of the addict, good, nourishing foods hadn't touched

170

the man's stomach in weeks. The Obstructor would wait for just the right moment.

The Nightstalker, searching in vain for a victim, was unaware of the Obstructor's deviousness in diverting people from the area—cordoning off the alley—by posting sentinels at strategic areas. Pushers were paid to stay clear of this section of the waterfront. Soon, very soon, the addict would do anything to satisfy the craving: steal, cheat, even kill—anything but commit rape, for heroin robbed him of any sexual desires. The addict's only reasons for existence were the fixes and the stopping of the sheer agony of stomach cramps between fixes.

When shafts of light lanced through the dark purple recollections of Nightstalker's mind, spotlighting former days of glory, he'd remember those better days before heroin addiction had robbed him of everything, left him without honor or self-respect or enough ego to sustain himself. He was *merde*, the lowest of gutter rats forced to scrounge about in an addict's despicable existence.

At times he thought himself *cafard*. Look at him: Old friends had denied him, had put contracts out on him; and like any worm, he had buried himself deep into the rotting wooden hovels along the waterfront, hiding from them, from himself. It was true: Nightstalker knew enough to put dozens of men away. But he also knew that to survive he must not breathe a word or whisper a clue to anyone. Still, they sought him. So far he had eluded them all.

If only he wouldn't deteriorate so quickly. He could see it happening daily, moment by moment. He was on the brink of insanity. If he didn't score tonight? . . . Heroin coursing through his veins had transformed him into a pathological liar, and lying had become a facility he exercised admirably under certain conditions.

Nightstalker peered into the darkness. Where were the people who frequented this area tonight? To take his mind off the urgency of his mission, he thought of his fix, how after it he would dream of opium poppy farmers in the Gold Crescent of Pakistan and Afghanistan, and of the Lebanese, Syrian and Israeli middlemen making themselves stinking rich by dealing with their European and American counterparts—he having been the connecting link. Christ! What a brilliant catenation of buyers and sellers he had set up. Cops and customs officials looked the

171

other way while dope barons and respectable politicians plied their trade! They flourished in the markets he, Nightstalker, had set up. He had worked his balls off to organize, and ZAP! How fast he was eliminated the moment power brokers sniffed the billions to be made!

Nightstalker! Hah! The name once stirred prodigious fear in those with reason to fear him. Now he wasn't even a cunt-stalker. He was *nothing*! A *fucking* nothing who dared not even talk big. A deal set to net him five hundred million dollars had been in his fucking grasp. He came *that close*! Then he got it: his best friend double-crossed him, kept him high on heroin for three months, left him in some stinking mud cell near Beirut, hopelessly enmeshed in a more sinister living penance than from any death he'd dealt a man.

Why he hadn't been killed outright was a question that plagued him night and day until he couldn't think straight, and when he could, he stopped the self-persecution. For by then, it dawned on him that an error had occurred, a gross error in judgment—a miscalculation of his addiction. The overdose administered fell short of being lethal; and he went into hiding, for in his drug-saturated brain he realized he wouldn't live long enough to outsmart the man who'd cheated him from retiring on his dream isle to live out his life. If they *knew* he was alive, he was as good as dead: he knew too much.

Nightstalker's manliness and former fierce reputation was bound up in his greedy, drug-sucking, heroin-dependent arm. How many times had he contemplated cutting it off? He would have, too, until, somehow in his madness, he reasoned that he'd only shoot up the other, and if he cut that off, then he'd use first one foot, then the other. It was senseless to take out on the body what the mind controlled.

One day, asshole, one day you'll work up the courage and give yourself a hot shot, a mixture of rat poison and heroin! It's your only salvation, Nightstalker. Hah! Nightstalker! What a fucking farce!

Until then? . . .

Ah . . . footsteps! Shadows! He geared himself, counting the footsteps. Twenty feet away and coming closer was his victim. Gripped tightly in Nightstalker's hand was a blade. He prepared himself for the thrust. Sweat poured from him, his body shook, his eyes were distended, pupils dilated. He was in bad shape and growing worse. He was barely able to see. He strained, sniffed noticeably. Suddenly the victim stopped. Five feet away, he stopped! *Why, for God's sake*?

What the hell? Nightstalker saw him, saw the upthrust hand waving a plastic bag of white powder, disarming him. "Oh Jesus! God! Angel of Mercy!" He reached for the bag, clutching at it, clawing.

"Not yet, Nightstalker. First we *parler*."

"Are you some *cafard*? Why do you call me such a name? I do not know you. You are mistaken." At once galvanized by the stranger, Nightstalker blinked his bleary eyes. He eyed the dangling packet, searched the man's face in the slim shaft of light from an all-night café.

"And I am no angel of mercy. You want magic powder to make impossible dreams come true? First, Nightstalker, we talk."

"*S'il vous plait, Monsieur*. I beg you. I know no such man."

Before his agonized eyes the Obstructor tore open a packet, scattering the fine white powder into the air about them. Frantically the addict made fruitless efforts to grasp the bag and fell to the street, shrieking, eyes bugging as he licked the filthy gutter with his tongue to capture the ghostly remains of the heroin. "Bastard! Crazy, insane bastard!" he screeched in condemnation, in a falsetto voice.

His tormentor produced another packet and dangled it before him.

Nightstalker scrambled up on wobbly legs and reached for the heroin bag, his other hand tightening on his knife. The move was sudden, swift, but the Obstructor had anticipated the maneuver and in seconds he held the addict in a deathly grip, broke his hold on the knife. It fell crashing to the gutter several feet away.

"Now, we talk. And no bullshit. You'll get enough *horse* to keep you in clover for a year."

Nightstalker's bleary eyes tried hard to make out the other's features. "*Alors*, we know one another? From where? How do you know Nightstalker?"

"No, no, no, no! That's not the way it works. I ask the question, *comprennez-vous*? Perhaps you wish no golden dreams tonight?"

"*Monsieur, Monsieur! Quelque chose!* Anything," begged the half-crazed addict. "Ask me anything, but, first, I need a fix! For the love of God, *Monsieur*, whoever you are—a fix!"

Moments later they stood together inside a shabby hotel not far from where they met. The Obstructor, standing in partial shadow, observed in fascinated revulsion as the Nightstalker prepared his ritual of death. The heroin powder, placed in a spoon, was heated and diluted to a soluble. A rubber nipple attached to an eye dropper—to retard pressure so he wouldn't take the drug too fast—sucked up the solution. He made a tourniquet with a filthy scarf, popped a vein, and stuck himself with the needle, pumping delicately, a little at a time, teasing himself, moaning as he always did before the euphoric climax was upon him.

The Obstructor, an expert in these matters, waited for precisely the right moment. He leaned in, hissed the question.

"Where is Grünelda?"

Before the words impacted, sliced through the euphoric forgetfulness to a world of dreams and sand castles and bliss, the body stopped twitching and shaking, and paranoia dissolved. Panic registered briefly. But then fear, a world of terror, crashed inside the Nightstalker's skull, evincing an unmistakable frenzied expression. He glanced wild eyed at the stacks of white powder on the table, gulped at the excessive salivation in his throat.

"Answer my questions, goddamnit! How do I find Grünelda?"

The information dribbled from his lips. He used his expertise to lie. And each time he lied, the Obstructor slapped his face resoundingly, but in such a way that left no bruises. *It's all in the way you hold the hand. . . .* The death had to appear as an overdose—no foul play.

Then it was over. The Obstructor had gotten what he wanted. Nightstalker sat on the floor, unable to move, his back braced against the wall. He watched the other fill a syringe from a drug vial, jerked when the sharp needle pierced his debilitated hide. For an instant the hot rush, pitched at a fierce pace, jolted him, fairly levitating him off the floor. Then, aware it was over for him, he heaved a sigh and gasped. His eyes rolled drunkenly upward and froze into a glazed, sightless stare. Recognition had come too late!

"Rest, you fucking hophead junkie bastard!"

The Obstructor collected the heroin packets and left.

Nightstalker was dead. Next on the agenda—Grünelda.

WEST BERLIN
A WEEK LATER

Cafe Lili Marlene mirrored the ultra decadence of Berlin in the Twenties. The club, redesigned, nostalgically recreated the era and aura that made Berlin the naughtiest of European cities when adroit survivalists joined adventurous tourists and a coterie of Bohemian artists to convert the city into the hottest pleasure town this side of Paris, where perversion was the main bill of fare.

In those days of sexual depravity, the infamous Anita Berber stood at center stage enjoying adulation. Roaring through the fast lanes of Berlin's night life, she had danced nude on stage, indulged in cocaine and morphine, soared into lurid bisexual affairs, and consorted with thugs and pugs of criminal bent. Steeped in the putrifaction of venereal disease, she died at the age of twenty-nine.

In those Gay Twenties, powdered and rouged young men had sauntered along the *Kurfurstendamn* parading their wares to any who leaned toward the various jaded debaucheries. Worldly men of finance courted drunken sailors in the dimly lit bars. Transvestite balls provided expression for hundreds of men posturing as women and women posturing as men. Nudity flourished in clubs, on stage, on the screen, and at private parties where scantily clad waitresses in sheer panties were paid to be fondled by anyone offering the right price. Freaks skated about on the ice, completely nude save for earmuffs. Prostitutes paraded in the streets in boots, whips and garter belts. The era provided those with enough money to indulge every sexual fantasy known to man, and then some.

Until . . . Adolf Hitler vaulted to power, promoting puritanism and banning jazz as the devil's music. He jailed and shot homosexuals and herded prostitutes into officially sanctioned brothels.

Café Lili Marlene, born in the late fifties, flourished under the aegis of the West Berlin *kommandatura*. The birth of the Cold War inaugurated West Berlin's second industry—espionage. How it flowered amid tensions and international misunderstandings! Café Lili Marlene, the center for mysterious liaisons between unlikely people, promoted, as its main bill of fare, girls . . . Girls! . . . GIRLS! In the Sixties, the club became an equal

opportunity employer. The requests for boys . . . Boys! . . .
BOYS! escalated. Under the shrewd, clever management of Lili
Marlene herself, an equal number of young, ripe men sashayed
about. They were scantily dressed and bedecked with as much
glitter, makeup and perfume—and as beguiling—as any female
displayed. They offered equal, if not more, seductive lures.

Lili Marlene, born Grünelda, was eager to shed her sordid past
as a prostitute. She was a woman with an instinct for survival.
Wasting neither time nor money on a venture unless she could
turn a profit, and keenly aware of West Berlin's strategic location and its business potential, she developed a lucrative business.

Few knew of her sordid past as Grünelda. After the war she
had been involved in smuggling, jewel thefts, robbery and drug
trafficking, but she had finished with all that long ago. When
Lili Marlene was born, Grünelda and her shady wheelings and
dealings were buried, never to be resurrected. Plastic surgery,
followed by a new wardrobe, a different hair color and new
makeup—and *voilà!* She emerged as Lili Marlene, with sufficient funds to open Club Lili Marlene.

Upstairs in the renovated duke's palace that metamorphosed
into Club Lili Marlene, special rooms accommodated overnight
guests. International VIPs desiring anonymity got it at her club.
No one knew anyone's business unless Grünelda's past crept in,
forcing her to barter covert information for her own anonymity.
Early in life Grünelda had learned, nothing is for nothing.

Today the lesson was about to be driven home again.

Lili sat in her special alcove with her guest, a man who knew
her as Grünelda. In this alcove, she dominated the goings-on
inside her club, seated at a console which revealed the closed-
circuit video cameras as they monitored what was going on in
every room of the house. Here she kept a forcible hand on the
pulse of the operation. More striking than her nymph and nyphet
nymphos or their male counterparts, Lili, a dazzling barber pole
of glittering sequins, bugle beads and wigs, was a mountain of
contradictions. Face lifts belied her age. Her long, glossed fingernails served as a showcase for the numerous diamond rings worn
on each finger.

"I won't ask you how you found me—I already know," Lili
spoke quietly, without emotion, her eyes scanning the screens.
"What is it you want?"

"The tapes, Grünelda. Lord York's plans in the Middle East."

"Grünelda is dead. Stop using that name!" She flipped on a darkened screen on the console wall and angled in closer by remote control to a dimly lit room. Two men engaged in homosexual acts writhed and twisted passionately on the bed. She glanced at her watch, set the time for twelve minutes and darkened the screen.

Lili removed a string from around her neck, the key on it buried between her two enormous breasts. She unlocked a nearby door, revealing a large safe. Rolling the combination, she opened it and from a special drawer removed a video cassette. "When I received your call, I barely recalled you were part of Corsican Jade, *ja*? You made yourself very clear, old friend. What you ask of me is extremely dangerous business. Before you arrived, I managed to obtain a dossier on you, *ja*? Secreted in a very safe place is documented proof of your incupation in matters that will finish you in certain circles, should you dare betray me— understood? If you are thinking to do a Nightstalker on me, forget it. I am well protected, *verstehen*? I am finished with the past and intend to live out my remaining days without worrying if any of you are in pursuit. Now pay attention, I play it only once. Do anything that in any way arouses my suspicion and you are kaput. You see this counter? If I refrain from setting it every five minutes? . . ."

They spoke German. Her guest feigned innocence. "I don't understand your animosity."

"You . . . don't . . . understand," she dragged the words scathingly. "I am finished! *Fertig! Aufessen!* I want no part of your dirty business."

"You wish me to convey that message to Zurich?"

"Before Grünelda disappeared she told him she was through! Why do you think I went to all the trouble to change myself?"

"You were the best. Incomparable. Uh—Lili—you still are."

"Incomparable, hah! I no longer negotiate—"

"Except to the high bidder, eh, Lili? How do you manage to remain neutral in these precarious times?"

"By offering a dear commodity to the highest bidder. You aren't here to discuss my neutrality or Lord York's plans in the Middle East. What is it you want?"

"Not I, Lili. What Zurich wants." Her guest explained his mission. Lili listened. For an instant her dark eyes flashed behind the veil of remoteness, then fell to unreadable orbs again.

"No. I am not interested."

"So, I'll tell him you refused."

"No! He won't like it."

"Smart woman. You're absolutely right."

"Shut up! Let me think."

"Take your time. May I smoke?" He opened a pack of American cork-tipped cigarettes.

"If I agree—it's not a commitment, understand—but if I choose to involve myself, what's the tariff for me? Don't give me ballpark figures, I am not bargaining. Just the top."

"A few million, ten perhaps, plus a percentage."

"Why would I take risks? I have that and more, now."

"To live long enough to enjoy your affluence."

She cut him a sharp, glassy stare. "And your share?"

"The same. Why would it be different? We all risk the same."

"Your ass, you do! If something goes wrong, the pattern would be as usual. Lili goes down the tubes. I've worked hard for anonymity. I won't give up what I have. I can't." She glanced at the video monitors, snapped on an intercom. "Eddie, get that bitch Renois away from that john. He's *Polizei*!"

"But he's on *your* payroll, Lili," came the filtered voice. "Not any more he's not! Bloody hell, fire him!" She snapped off the sound, her eyes on the screen until she saw the man, Eddie, approach two men at the bar and break up the *tete-a-tete*.

Lili lit a hashish cigarette, ignoring her guest's proffered lighter. She inhaled deeply, expelled the smoke. "I enjoy being independent. I don't want to be owned any more," she insisted.

"Then pass this time. I didn't like ferreting you out. I respect your need for anonymity. But I work for the man. Face it, he is the tops."

She stared at him in disturbed silence. He was too willing to acquiesce. Lili worked the advantage every moment. She sat slightly apart from him, a bit to one side so as able to move swiftly in case of treachery. What was he really after? She didn't trust him, never did, never would.

"I'll think about it," she muttered, activating the video cassette. "You asked for the Lord York business—here it is."

The video screen lighted up. Two men sat opposite a table. Spread before them were a set of blueprints. The older man, tall, thin, white haired, set spectacles in place over his nose.

The other, medium build, dark skinned, dark eyes, pointed to the plans. Two men stood at either side of them.

"Look at these plans, Lord York. Examine them carefully, please. Make certain before you speak."

Lord York waved him off. "What is it you wish of me? You know I do not respond well under pressure and in the daytime." His eyes, glazed over from drug addiction, watered.

"I suggest you amend your usual routine and cooperate. The blueprints, Lord York. Is that your signature? Did you draw up these plans? Please answer if you care at all for the life of your daughter."

"Bring in more light. Let me see, here. What's that about my daughter? Alexandria? What of her? What is it you want? Can't you see I am in no condition to be answering questions?"

"Is that your signature?"

"Where is my daughter? What have you done with her?"

"She'll be dead if you don't cooperate."

"Yes, yes, see here—it's my signature. My Y is scribbled as usual. I demand to know what you've done with my daughter!"

"Sorry, Lord John. She's dead—"

"But you just said—"

"I know. I needed your authentication. Now I have it."

"Does London know about this? I demand to know."

"I cannot answer. I do not know."

"What good are the bloody blueprints, now? They should have been delivered—"

"To whom, Sir? To whom were they to be delivered?"

"I don't know."

"You are lying."

"Yes, I presume I am." Lord York replied at once, aloof. "There's bloody little you can do."

"You underestimate me, Lord York. I do not take kindly to liars."

"Nor do I. Alexandria is not dead! You can't feed me manure."

"Perhaps I do not make myself clear, Sir. My affiliations are with British MI–6. The blueprints are needed by the very men who killed your daughter. Our job is to duplicate these plans with certain changes."

"Changes, my arse! I shall accompany you back to London, and sit with British MI, myself."

"No, you shall not. All we need is authentication."

York pounded his bony fist on the table. "Authenticate! Authenticate, authenticate! By God, not only shall I authenticate, but I shall scream it to the Parliament, to Her Majesty's palace! These *are* my drawings. What I need know is where the bloody hell did you come by them? British MI! Hah! What a crockful!"

"Good. These are yours—the entire schematics, Sir?"

"The entire schematics, Sir?" York mocked the other's stilted Cambridge accent with the nagging voice of spoiled adolescent. "My dear Sir—"

"Falco, Sir. Falco will do."

"Ah. Clever. Falco, eh? Ferret would better describe you." York's bleary eyes narrowed, peering at his abductor. "You are Falasha," he spoke with a canny eye of discovery. "Yes, yes, you *are* Falasha. My, my, you *are* organizing. Since when does British MI embrace Falasha?"

"Make it easy on yourself, Lord York. The simple truth will do. To whom were these plans to be delivered?"

"You are Falasha . . ." York continued, blinking in recollection. "Your ancestry is Menelek, son of Solomon, King of Israel and Queen Sheba."

"You are a remarkable man, Lord York. You are as steeped in ancient biblical history as well as the high technology secrets of this age."

"My dear Falco, ferret, Falasha—whatever you are, whomever you are, I am many things to many people and perhaps fail to measure up to your ancient standards. When in saner moments I realize I may have sold out my nation to scumbags like you for the drugs supplied me, I succumb to an overpowering desire to vomit. Fortunately, the moments pass. In quieter moments I become total, absolute in my genius. My genius, as I see it, lies in the validation of these blueprints. I suppose I could deny it, but I don't. Yes, I designed the plan in the Middle East. If you possessed an iota of perception to which you and your kind lay claim, you'd know them to be originals. But I refuse to tell you where they go." York's eyes lifted, widened perceptively at the gun pointed at him. "Ah, a repeat performance of what you dished out to my dear Alexandria, I suppose? Here? Now? You wouldn't dare."

A muffled p-h-h-h-f-f-t! A gun, to which a silencer was affixed, fired one shot into York's shoulder. Lord York looked at his assassin. The bullet startled him, but it did not kill him.

180

"You are kind, a considerate Falasha. May you rot in hell. But not before you hear this: Without the key to the schematics, the blueprints are useless. The key is—" He tapped his forehead with a finger, grinned diabolically.

Three more bullet implacements fired in rapid succession made a line of three holes across his forehead. He fell over, splattering blood on the blueprints.

"Llamas!" muttered Lili's guest.

She snapped off the recorder, turned to him. "You picked up on the M.O. too, eh?" She searched his eyes closely for a hint.

"That puts another screw in the board," he muttered, wiping the beads of sweat forming on his forehead. "York died *without* revealing the destination of the blueprints?"

"You saw the action. You heard what I heard."

"Who were those men with York?"

"Friend, I don't ask questions, remember? That's why I've survived. Where do we go from here?" she asked cannily.

"Like I told you, he wants you there in the Persian Gulf. Perhaps in Sidon or Tyre? . . . In Lebanon."

"Not in the West Bank. Not Bashra or Qatar or near the conversion laboratories? Considerate of him," she spat scathingly.

"The choice is yours. I suggested Beirut, closer to civilization."

"Danke schön. How kind of you." The words were acerbic. "At the hub of activity, *ja*? Who will ask questions of another dead body, eh?"

"He suggests you spare no expense. He wants Lili Marlene outfitted with the latest in surveillance equipment."

"A surveillance whorehouse, *ja*? I herd the political whores into select pastures. You supply the junk, cocaine, hashish— tongue looseners. Then what? What's in it for Lili Marlene?"

"In addition to the millions? Your entire dossier, negatives, the whole kit-and-kaboodle of your past inculpation with Corsican Coral."

"In a horse's cock. What's the real mechanism?"

"He wants the princess as insurance. Then Moufflon."

Grünelda's checkered past, etched like acid on her features, turned her into a gargoyle of ferocious design. She wound her time clock, then stood up. "You have one minute to leave here. The girl means nothing to me, she is expendable. But I do not go near *Moufflon*. Got it? If you have anything to say before executioners chop you to bits and feed the pieces to the rats in Berlin sewers, you have—uh—thirty seconds left.''

"Fool! Turn off the fucking mechanism or your precious Club Lili Marlene will blow. If I am not out in ten minutes flat, *Fräulein,* it goes, you inside. Unless I leave in one piece with your assurance of cooperation—''

"You fucking turd! You are as degenerate as they are! How can I trust you if we are bound together in perversity?''

"Better perverse adversaries than deadly friends. One thing you are not, Grünelda—''

"Lili! Damn your hide, Lili!''

"—is besotted or without wits. Perverse at times, dogged in determination, but never did you subvert power. Commendable characteristics. He approves of you, else you wouldn't be involved.''

"That son of a bitch is still alive! Eighty fucking years and he won't give up the ghost. Goddamit, why doesn't he die?''

"Perhaps he's eternal—ever think of that!''

Silence . . . lung bursting silence in which she dare not breathe. She packed a cocaine pipe and lighted it, drawing on it deeply.

"Suddenly you are piano, Lili.''

"It's my age, you bastard. I'm growing older. Life, like wine, gets more precious with age. Now listen and listen good. I'll go along this last time. But in no way do I go near the Moufflon apparatus. The girl, the princess, is in Tripoli and poses no problem. But I won't touch Moufflon. That doesn't label me disloyal, just fucking smart. You tell him that—understand. I've lived a frightening life—afraid of day, afraid of night. Afraid of fear itself, but I survived. I survived and if I die I don't care. But *Moufflon* is *verboten.* Tell him. Tell him my exact words, if you dare. You hear?'' Lili, a fearless woman, experienced pangs of inner terror.

The Obstructor rose to his feet, fitting gloves over his fingers. "I shall convey the message as you recited it. You'll hear from me in twenty-four hours.''

"How, by diplomatic bag or electronic marvels? Oh—before you leave, shall I give you a taste of the bill of fare?'' Lili, growing bolder, turned from him, activated the video screen the moment the timer rang, and transferred the transmission to a larger screen.

The two homosexuals she had focused on earlier came into

focus were still engaged in salacious debaucheries. Their features grew more definitive.

"You know them?" Lili asked cagily.

The Obstructor gasped. He stared in stoney silence.

"You wonder at my trepidation, when *he* represents Zurich?"

The Obstructor did not reply. Mesmerized at the scene, he observed as lust-filled eyes met in an exchange of secret smiles: hands on each other's erections, probing, skilled hands on tender skin. The stars of the Sapphist scenario rolled, pitched, maneuvered each other into various positions with overt, libidinal audacity. The older man, quite distinguished even in his animal wantonness, was Anthony Harding, United States Secretary of State.

He turned the younger man over on his knees and, without breaking the flow of ecstasy, entered him rectally. The other shrieked, howled banshee-like, at the hard-raping thrust.

Lili's guest turned in revulsion. "I've seen enough."

"No! No, you haven't. Don't turn away now. It's time." She glanced at the timer set earlier. Less than a minute remained. You see? Here—now!" It was necessary that Lili teach her guest an object lesson.

The Obstructor's eyes trailed back to the screen. He saw Harding's upthrust hand holding a sharp blade come lunging down with ferocity. Time and again he slashed, cut, stabbed, the blood spurting up at him from the impaled body under him. For a second Lili's guest saw Harding's pupils dilate to glittering black orbs. His body jerked, he thrust himself in and out of the dead man's body; frenzied, soaked in blood and sweat, a shriek coming from deep inside him, he let out a demoniac howl as he ejaculated with sodomistic zeal.

The Obstructor whipped off his dark glasses, pushed the zoom-in button, and stared, fascinated by the satyr-like eyes. Lili watched him inscrutably. "What do you see, my friend? The eyes of Satan? Why do you pale? Is it because death accompanied the act of love? The victim, a willing pawn, served his purpose. Now, Harding can return to the mundane work of serving the world, sane for a time, to purportedly serve mankind. When the urge to annihilate comes again upon his cocaine-saturated brain, he will return and commit the act over and over, with impunity. Who concerns himself with the lubricity of such a man? An intellect like Anthony Harding mustn't be condemned if he chooses to take a few worthless lives to satisfy his demonic nature. Other murderers, if caught, are sent to prison and punished accordingly. Not Anthony Harding. His diplomatic immunity covers such atrocities. Besides, how many lives are lost on battlefields . . . in accidents?"

Lili's eyes were on the screen. Her guard was down. Her guest's hands were behind his back, pulling at a wire coil from a wrist band, grasping it firmly.

"I shall convey your message, Grünelda, and get back to you."

"Lili! Call me Lili. Do I call you Thunder? Or was it Lightning? Forget *Grünelda*! Before you talk with Zurich, would it not be wiser if you and I combined *our* efforts? Now you've seen the genre of men to whom he entrusts *our* lives, does it not give you food for thought?" While her eyes were still riveted to the screen, she wound the time clock.

"*Guten Tag,* Lili." The Obstructor moved behind her and in a quick move brought his hands holding the wire over her head and around her neck. He pulled, squeezed hard in a garotte, until she was dead.

Lili fell over her electronic console, her face a mottled purple.

The Obstructor peered at the video screen, noted the room number, and picked up a phone. He rang Harding. On the screen he saw Harding bolt up, glance at the phone, then pick it up.

"*Jawohl* . . . who is it?"

"Me. It is finished. I have the video cassette. The Princess is in Tripoli. . . ." Finished, he hung up. He noticed the VRC was working. Lili had recorded Anthony Harding in action. He stopped the machine, rewound the tape and slipped it into his pocket. Insurance! Great insurance!

Chapter Ten

"A madman is no less a musician than you or myself; only the instrument on which he plays is out of tune. The sane man to keep his sanity is forced at times to view things slightly off center. Who can perceive the torture of either soul?"

. . .Anonymous Writings

TWO DAYS AGO BRAD LINCOLN HAD LEFT U.S. Army Intelligence Headquarters at Clayallee 10 unaware of General Mark Samuels' murder, not knowing he was the primary suspect. Brooding internally, lost in thought, half-jogging, half-walking along the eastern edge of Grünewald, Berlin's Central Park, he glanced dismally at overcast skies, pelted by thickening snow flurries. He moved forward, alerted, always on guard for covert surveillance.

Traversing the length of Clayallee, he rounded the circle onto *Kurfurstendamm*, the business district, struck by the bizarre punkers in Mohawk cuts, rainbow-colored hair, wearing crazy space clothing. American G.I.'s wearing cowboy boots and ten-gallon hats; stunning Lolitas in revealing aluminum jumpsuits; Hare Krishna devotees cavorting about, their glazed eyes like those of heroin addicts. Bubblegum popping roller skaters, despite the inclement weather, wove in and out of snow-patched pedestrian lanes, scaring the hell out of an enraged citizenry. And those cyclists! Drivers shooting through traffic jams. It was the lunacy of a six-ring circus!

Brad sniffed the invigorating scents of freshly baked breads, German spiced foods, hot coffee. Famished, he realized he hadn't eaten since yesterday noon. He changed direction, headed a few blocks up the street to Schilling's *Konditorei*, number 234 *Kurfurstendamm*. He sidestepped his way around the nuclear arms protestors, his eyes everywhere.

How many times had he played this game? Stop. Peer nonchalantly in a shop window, eyes searching eyes, faces. Ears—all senses—working triple time. But there was nothing! Nothing tangible!

Brad sensed a glimmering retreat, blurred flashes of a face, a body—but nothing definitive. But everything he knew, experience told him:

Someone out there in chaotic West Berlin stalked him, marking time, waiting to kill him!

Strange how you learn to pick things out of a crowd. Years of training, learning to home in on countless incongruities the average person doesn't detect: the bulging outlines of a gun under a jacket; the wrong accessories worn with improper attire; an attitude seemingly alien to the subject; a look in the eye—the list was endless.

He loped through the crowds, his thinking fogged by the

residual effects of the drugs shot into him in the past week. His trained eye picked out a silver BMW from the sea of traffic flowing toward him. The car edged closer to the curb as if to discharge a passenger. The incongruity: one driver, no passenger. Brad moved toward it, cautiously drawn by it, his neck craning over the crowds to observe the scene.

The driver rolled down the window while Brad, tensed, hesitated, afflicted by mysterious awareness. Car horns tooted loudly, angry drivers cursed at the stalled traffic. Brad's gloved hand in his pocket tightened around the M52. The driver's hand thrust through the open window innocently handed him a slip of paper, and gunning the motor spurted out into traffic.

Brad lowered his head and tried to gaze into the face of the stranger, but it was too late. Alarms sounded split seconds too late. Two men, blurred figures in motion, came at him, impacting with sharp, swift blows crashing down on his skull. Excruciating agony radiated from the base of his skull, collapsing his chest, crumbling his spine, and extending pain to his feet. He shriveled up and felt himself lifted into the air, hurled through an inky blurred nightmare.

He awakened to sounds more excruciating than the injuries he'd suffered. Pulsating images surrounded by pulsating color played havoc with his eyes. Clangorous onslaughts shuddered through him, exploding his ears. Panicked, he covered them, anticipating the resounding crashes.

Christ! . . . Fucking bells! He was going mad! Mad!

Crashing vibrations deafened him. He forced himself to move. *Where in God's name was he?*

As he peered around the inky enclosure, he saw overhead a black mass swing toward him. He recoiled as it passed over him and swung to the opposite side. More explosions blasted his eardrums. He stared thunderstruck in the shadowy confinement, at the bellowing mouth of an enormous bell.

The Freiheitsglocke! The bell tower of the Freiheitsglocke!

It was Germany's equivalent of the American Liberty Bell! He was in the American sector—not far from where he had been struck.

Get the hell outa here! How? He felt like jelly. Could jelly crawl to the tower door, open it, pull itself up and press enough weight against it to release the doorjamb?

186

It did. He made it! The bells, again! He lurched through the opening savagely, holding the wall unsteadily, half-blind, half-dazed, groping in the semi-darkness, clutching at his ears.

He stood at room center in the tower's base. He remembered as he entered the area that seventeen million Americans had affixed signatures to a carved text stored behind locked glass doors. He recalled past history clearly, so why couldn't he patch together the events landing him in this belfry? He caught sight of his reflection in a glass panel. Christ! He looked awful. Worse than on his discharge from sick bay two days ago.

Two days ago! Memory returned in bits and pieces. Instinctively he felt for his gun. Good. Intact.

He exited the door, leaning on marble pillars, dabbing at the excessive sweat dripping from his face. Images came at him. The silver BMW. He held his temple, felt warm blood trickle from a wound into his fingers. He stared at it, unable to think. He reached for his handkerchief, noting as he did a slip of folded paper fluttering to the floor. He stared at the paper, considering, if he leaned over to retrieve it, could he stand erect again? It took moments to figure strategy for the task. The thought frightened him.

Diminished capacities—now?

Brad inched slowly lower, supported by the pillar, sliding his back down the smooth marble column. Hunkering on his heels he retrieved the envelope. It took enormous effort and time to get back to his feet again. Then, suddenly, action went into accelerated time. Before Brad unfolded the paper, he felt himself propelled out the door and into a taxi. A white-haired guard snapped orders to the driver. *"Schillings 234, bitte!"* To Brad he hissed, "At Schillings ask for Otto. He is safe, *verstehen? Das Kompliment der Zeigenbock. Gutan Tag, mein Herr."*

The driver took off in a tear. Brad glanced behind him, but the guard had already disappeared. *Das Kompliment der Zeigenbock!* Translated it meant: Compliments of the head goat! Goat! *Moufflon!*

Brad unfolded the note, his hands shaking. He decoded it:

General Mark Samuels assassinated 9:45 A.M. following your departure from his office. Cover your flanks. Do not communicate with *die Bienenkonigin.*

Bienenkonigin! Queen Bee! One of countless code names for Jim Greer! Greer again. *Do not communicate with the Queen Bee!*

Samuels was dead! The bastard's death complicated his work. Christ! He had been there at 9:40 A.M. A fucking five-minute differential made him a prime suspect in a homicide. *Think, Brad.* Whoever killed Samuels must have reserved a neat place for you alongside him. The thought sobered him.

He had not come this far to face defeat. He must penetrate Clayallee 10! He must or he'd never know the truth. Katz's words returned and fired him.

But how? God Almighty, how? How to regroup tactically without assassins pouring through West Berlin taking potshots at him.

By the time Brad arrived at *Schillings 234* he knew his next move.

He waited five minutes, then walked to the telephone and made his call.

The wailing sirens multiplied, coming closer. Outside Schillings four U.S. Army staff cars loaded with armed GIs came to a screeching halt. They poured from the cars and jeeps, guns at ready, like swarming SWAT teams prepared for a shootout with the nation's most wanted criminal. Brad stepped forward, hands upraised.

"I am Major Bradford Lincoln. I was with General Mark Samuels from eight hundred hours to approximately moments before his death. How may I be of help?"

Chapter Eleven

THE RAPE OF CONCATENATE-ALPHA on the night of February 28 exploded disbelief in the Intelligence communities of West Berlin sectors and became a subject of great concern at the Pentagon. The insolvable mystery gave rise to tightened security measures at Clayallee 10.

A computer raped by specters? By someone who didn't exist? Hardly. This statement, issued to Chiefs of Covert Operations, nevertheless instituted a severe tightening of security and the application of more ingenious measures to prevent penetration of its sacrosanct files.

But three days before, at noon on February 25, no one at Intelligence Headquarters entertained the vaguest hint of what was about to transpire at Clayallee's catacombs. Security was minimal.

Milford Race Meadows paid the taxi driver and stepped from the cab. Pausing briefly, he nonchalantly scanned the area, tugged up on the beaver fur collar of his coat, and reset the bowler on his white-haired head. The disguise was perfect; dark pancake makeup covered all bruises; false white brows affixed by spirit gum covered his own and flared over tinted bifocals. A thick brush mustache and stooped walk added ten years to Brad's age. He carried an expensive crocodile briefcase in one hand, walking stick in the other, reflecting the very height of fashion for a respected author. He looked up, impressed as he always was at the familiar sight.

Clayallee 10. A German baroque, graystone building, it had once housed the highest German Appellate Court, the *Kammer-dericht*. Following World War II it housed the Allied Control Council. Few knew the contents of this building, the nightmarish history of intrigue born within ACC and OSS walls from the moment the Allies marched into Berlin in 1945 to cut up the luscious pie that was Berlin.

Intelligence files on every Allied Military and Intelligence operation had been microfilmed to conserve space; many had been transferred to Pentagon crypts in D.C. Some were still contained in the subterranean vaults here at Clayallee 10. Countless secretly coded operational records of injustices done to a race of people the world seemed bent on destroying, Germany, the Germans themselves and a portion of their history were buried inside.

Meadows walked slowly through the glass doors. At precisely twelve noon, a time when security checks grew lax, he quietly presented his credentials to the first battery of guards. Approved, he was sent on to the second, where a cursory check admitted him to the third phase. Armed uniformed guards rechecked his papers and treating him with deference pointed him to the caged lift. The author entered and descended one floor below. He stepped out into the corridor, busy eyes noting the few changes.

Not nearly as intimidating as GAMMA 10!

Treated as a benign author, he was permitted to work at his own pace. He worked ambitiously, sorting through essential data

189

trying desperately to bridge the four-decade interim. The work was repetitious, time-consuming, and unproductive. Nothing earth-shattering emerged. Driven by Wolfgang Katz's provocative statements, his final words burned vividly in his memory, prompted him to work late into the night.

The records are where they've been for forty years! Only you can find them! Only you . . . only you . . . only you . . .

Brad worked steadily, realizing that *unknown* parties had kept him directed on course. But he berated himself; where was the key and how to get the unidentified force to reveal himself?

It was midnight. Brad sighed. He was hungry, fatigued and surprised he'd been permitted to work so late into the night without reprimand. He peered about the cavernous mausoleum, stacked high with metal cabinets, photocopying equipment, records filed ominously under thousands of codes to throw the uninitiated off track. Sheer lunacy had led him here. The idiotic involvement could absorb a year's time. So much ate away at Brad. He, the dim-witted American, had led the enemy to their target. Poor Katz hadn't endured agony and hell for forty years so an old, trusted friend could betray him. That was the rub! He'd drawn the bloodhounds again! Marnay, Katz, Samuels, not to mention his own brushes with death. Death stalked him everywhere! A goddamn cat possessed nine lives—how many did he have left? The unanswered question provoked cold sobriety, forced decisions. He was tired—dead tired.

Three days and nights spent in the protective confines of Army Intelligence Headquarters had provided him with time to think. He had walked away, imparting less than he received. The absence of the Cambridge dossier which he had last seen on Samuels' desk and General Samuels' dossier posed numerous questions—many unanswered. According to the dossiers of accredited assassins provided by Jim Greer, Samuels' death clearly pointed to the murderous hand of *Llamas*. Questions concerning Brad's presence at the Katz farmhouse at the time of the devastation were passed off as coincidence. He was visiting an old friend. A Nazi? they asked. Brad harked back to his OSS days in World War II when the Nazi Katz worked under the aegis of the ACC. They were working acquaintances—that's all.

Author Meadows bid the guards good night and left Clayallee 10, dejected at the slow progress. He hailed a cab and drove to the Berlin Hilton, to the room booked to Meadows.

He arrived at his suite at the Hilton, paced the floor furiously, his melancholy deepening. He had trusted no one in his life. No lovers, only whores had serviced him. Whores for a fee demanded no emotional involvements, pulled no strings to keep him in line. Always the loner, dedicated to country and career above all, he had not allowed family ties in the strong Jewish tradition to take hold of him. Now, in these moments, he felt more alone than at any time in his life. He moved to the table, poured a double Scotch from the pinch-bottle, downed it, poured another and walked to the window gazing out at the *Kurfurstendamm*, alive in bright neons. At the depth of his impression, he was struck with lightning-bolt hope. He remembered . . .

Concatenate-Alpha!

A change in strategy was mandatory. Adrenalin rushed his senses as his thoughts knifed forward. Of course, *Dumkoff*. It had been right under his very nose and he hadn't seen it. Dressed as Meadows, he left the Hilton, walked rapidly along the *Strasse* to a nearby liquor kiosk. He made several purchases, returned to the hotel, feeling ebullient. The strategy counted on several factors; precise timing was the most crucial element in the overall plan.

At precisely 9:00 P.M. on the evening of February 28, author Meadows entered Clayallee 10, passed through the usual security checks, descended to basement level, heading toward the two guards manning former OSS files. He nodded a greeting, was waved through the portcullis opening and scanner.

Then all hell broke loose! Alarms shrieked and flashing red lights lit up consoles like Christmas lights. Leaping to his feet, the first guard immobilized him with a drawn gun. Meadows feigned confusion, tapped his head in a gesture of forgetfulness. Pointedly ignoring the gun, he ambled back to the desk, apologized and opening his briefcase withdrew two bottles of Camus Cognac, presenting one to each guard.

"The cold weather in Berlin atrophies an old man's brains." he laughed. "This is my last night, so I bring you each a token of my appreciation. You've been helpful."

The freckled, bright-eyed guard named Wally searched the case, removed further offending items—three silver cups. He closed the case, flung it through the scanner. It cleared. He shook his head.

"Jee*sus*, Professor, you scared the shit outa me."

Holding the doctored cognac in one hand, Brad quickly tore off the gold foil, shoved a corkscrew into the cork, popped it open and cordially insisted they join him in a drink.

The guards exchanged dubious glances, peered about the corridors, stared thirstily at the liquor. "I dunno, sir," Wally said halfheartedly. "We aren't supposed to drink on duty." The guard named Monroe added, "We aren't supposed to take gifts. Oh, what the hell! If you don't tell, we ain't gonna broadcast it."

They clinked silver cups, failing to notice that their host's contained only a few drops. Brad poured generous refills, recorked the bottle muttering, "Back to the old grind for me. If people only knew how diligently authors researched their material . . ."

The guards polished off their second drink. Brad took their cups, wiped them clean and handed them to Monroe. "I'd better leave them with you. Can't risk a cardiac arrest from those damnable alarms."

Meadows entered the microfilm library, turned on the bright overhead lights, washing the sterile area in flickering neon. Shoving aside the mental cobwebs of the previous days' failures, he play-acted his way, searching microfilm spools, waiting for the drugged drinks to work on Wally and Monroe.

Beyond the guards at the far end of the corridor, another impediment; a maintenance man swept floors, rattled buckets, emptied debris into rollaway cannisters.

Turning on the viewer, Brad pressed a forward button, fanning through random material. He stopped abruptly as a title flashed on the mini-screen. *OPERATION SQUAWK.* How the devil had he missed this? He backed up the viewer and studied the screen, slowing down the rotation. He read:

INTRO TO OPERATION SQUAWK THROUGH OSS CHANNELS LIGHTNING AND THUNDERSTRUCK. DEFER TO NUREMBERG. REFERENCE FILES DECODED. IMPLEMENTED CAMOUFLAGE SECTIONED BY LIGHTNING AND THUNDERSTRUCK.

Brad smiled. Lightning and Thunderstruck were his and Jim Greer's code names, among others. Thumbing through the coded files, he fished out the designated microfilm spool, threaded it patiently. He pushed the operational button, spinning the reel.

Whoa . . . back up! There—right before his eyes. It happened

so quickly he was unprepared, and backed up the spool slowly
. . . slowly . . . Stop! He read:

OPERATION SQUAWK: See Nuremberg Trials.
NUREMBERG TRIALS 1945–1946

The trials came under the authority of two legal instruments.
THE LONDON AGREEMENT and ALLIED CONTROL
COUNCIL LAW NUMBER 10. THE LONDON AGREE-
MENT provided for the establishment of an International
Military Tribunal; one judge and one alternate judge from
each of the signatory nations, Great Britian, France, Russia
and America, would try war criminals. Under this legal instrument war crimes fell into three categories: planning, initiating,
the waging of aggressive war, violations of the law and
customs of war as embodied in the Hague Convention as
crimes against humanity. The most important of these trials
were held in Nuremberg, commencing in October, 1945.
Judgment was handed down on October 1, 1946.

In December, 1945, the second instrument was promulgated
by the ACC.

ALLIED CONTROL COUNCIL LAW NUMBER 10

This instrument provided for war crimes trials to be held in
each of the Occupied War Zones in West and East Berlin.
Under this law war crimes fell into six categories, including
acts performed by war criminals:

1. Doctors engaged in experimental medicine on war
   prisoners in Concentration-Labor Camps.

2. Judges who complicitly committed murder under the
   guise of judicial process.

3. Industrialists, businessmen or any Nazi who looted
   occupied nations.

4. Any person or persons involved in forced labor programs.

5. S.S. Officials, Prison Administrators, Concentration Camp Commanders who enforced racial laws and promoted genocide.

6. Any High-Ranking military or civil officials responsible for criminal acts of the Third Reich.

Brad mulled over these words carefully, recalling Katz's haunting words. *"The laws failed to include the war crimes of Jew collaborators."* Strange . . . Brad flipped the button and continued to read the screen printout:

Results of the twelve trials held under the authority of ACC LAW NUMBER 10 produced the following statistics:

INDICTED 185
   SENTENCED TO DEATH BY HANGING 30
   INDETERMINATE SENTENCES 120
   ACQUITTED 35

SEE: *OPERATION SQUAWK*—1956 to?

Summation: Operation Squawk dealt with a rash of protests from Special Interest groups dissatisfied with the categories of war-crimes covered in THE LONDON AGREEMENT and the results of the aforementioned trials under ACC–10. By mid-1956 each of the Allied Sectors of West and East Berlin were deluged by Jewish Agency, Ira Baumgartner, an active Zionist leader and his followers demanding a thorough examination of the atrocities done in Concentration Camps to the millions of prisoners. A court stenographer present in each sector documented the protests and allegations hurled against the Allied Military Government for their inhuman disregard for the lives of millions of Jews integrated in those camps amidst other prisoners. (SEE OSS FILES for complete stats on OPERATION SQUAWK)

OFFICIAL SUMMATION: 1945–1956

With more to do than concern themselves with a handful of defeated Nazis, the Allies in each Occupied Zone fell to the monumental task of pulling together a war-torn Germany. Disparities with the Soviets increased daily. A business-as-usual-procedure was adopted, a growing alienation by Jewish agencies over the disposition of war-criminals temporarily set aside caused discontent.

OPERATION: EYE SPY: 1946–1953

A forced alliance with ex-Nazis vital to Allied needs in alien Germany has encouraged a conciliatory atmosphere in each Allied sector. Imperative is cooperation from former high-ranking German officers able to assist in the reconstruction of crucial records. In addition to assistance in gathering special intelligence, a unique relationship has germinated between conquerors and vanquished. Existing dangers preclude caution.

SPECIAL SERVICES:

In exchange for *special services*, the 35 acquittals were given new identities, passports and funds to begin new lives in foreign nations of their choice. Those 120 given indeterminate sentences proved extremely important to the Allies, and in exchange for special services were summarily dispensed in like fashion. Secret documents revealed pacts made by Hitler and other nations became of special concern to each Military Command, and a growing need for highly sophisticated intelligence-gathering has commenced. The Allied Control Council, increasingly aware of its lack of sophistication in espionage and the dire necessity of same is accelerating its clandestine operations.

The race in each sector to seek out the most knowledgeable of war criminals commenced in OPERATION: EYE SPY. A judicious combination of policies designed to prevent discontent has endorsed a covert apparatus dividing war criminals equally.

NOTE: It is documented that the OSS failed to foresee the number of alleged war criminals requesting American jurisdiction. A rash of protest from each sector created pandemonium. Thus, an equal division of prisoners will be made—not adhered to in totum, but nonetheless the division is formal in substance.

Brad turned off the viewer light. He lighted a cigarette, drew on it thoughtfully. Through the smoky haze he saw the guards yawning. Good. Turning to the business at hand, he played with trigger words, notations, dates, hoping to spark his memory.

Forty years ago insanity prevailed following V-E Day. Global power plays had disrupted Allied efforts to reconstruct war-torn Germany. The four powered *Kommandatura* had staked their claims, driving the German nation into schizophrenic nightmares. Each sector had reflected the independent viewpoint of that nation empowered to administrate each bailiwick. Madness had ensued. Mounting tensions had fired Russia's temperamental blockade in 1948. The Cold War followed a valorous West Berlin airlift.

But, just before the Cold War took hold, protection in exchange for information became the order of the day. War games were played every minute of the day.

It wasn't until *after* Brad had left for the States that Jewish agency factions angrily protested the slap-on-the-wrist punishment given war criminals. They had stormed ACC Headquarters demanding a special brand of justice. Court judgments of guilty or not guilty did not appease them. "Those men whose names appear on our lists shall be singled out, hunted down, persecuted, brought to justice, if it takes forever!" became their battle cry. The OSS, British SOE, French SDECE, even the Soviet OKRANA, were inundated by crank calls, threatening mail, waves of violence and promises of retribution. They merely processed the complaints and filed them away, according to OPERATION SQUAWK.

Reviewing the information four decades *after* the fact clarified a few intriguing ploys of yesteryear. Given a fresh perspective, a chronology of events for the interim years, and Brad witnessed a cleverly executed pattern emerge, invisible in the postwar era, but one that explained the terrorism of the Irgun, Shin Beth, Haganah and what later evolved to the present day Mossad. The pattern pointed to the existence of a low-level conspiracy. The question was *why?*

A glance at the wall clock jolted Brad from his reverie. Time, his enemy, approached the witching hour. The guards were sound asleep, their heads lay slackly on their desks. *Perfect!*

Now, the trespass.

But something nagged at Brad, Katz's name echoed in repetitive refrain, trapped him into immobility.

GAMMA 10 popped into his mind. Why? Why *Gamma 10*? Something wasn't computing. Momentarily forcing the timetable from his mind, Brad scanned the massive accumulation of data in his briefcase, digging deeper into his skull, haunted by Katz's words.

Only you, Major, can find the records . . . only you!

Goddammit, Katz! How the hell do I find them after forty years?

He screamed his frustration internally. The moment eluded him. He almost had it—it tottered at the edge of his memory and it slipped past him, thumbing its nose at him.

Well, screw it!

Don't push, Brad. The slide rule, an instrument of fact, doesn't always solve the equation. Leave something to intuitive faculties!

And then, as elusive as oblique shadows of night creating vague shapes and forms, as miraculous as the unfolding petals of a rose, the answer bombarded Brad's thinking.

Katz! Goddammit, Katz! You son of a bitch! You should have reminded me! Katz was a cover name! No records existed in OSS files in that name!

Wolfgang Katz had not existed before 1946! An outpouring of information fired his impatience. The key had not been Wolfgang Katz at all. It was Wolfgang *Kaltenbrunner* who existed as a Nazi officer!

And so Brad paced the floor, the revelation mind-boggling. When he finished putting it together, the rape of *CONCATENATE-ALPHA* was inevitable. And so was a splitting migraine.

In 1946 Wolfgang Kaltenbrunner, WAFFEN S.S., had personally turned over to Captain Brad Lincoln volatile records, an accurate accounting of concentration and labor-camp inmates at Belsen, Dachau, Ravensbruck and Auschwitz in Poland: the *actual* body count, listed by name, number, age, gender and nationality and the final disposition of same. Brad, himself, had personally authored a top secret, highly sensitive scenario, deliberate in its attempts to conceal the whereabouts of this sought-after material until proper safeguards, like those employed at GAMMA 10, could be facilitated. Of intense volatility were names of Jewish collaborators, held sacrosanct by the Nazi High Command.

The file title . . . ?

ARBEIT MACHT FREI-10! Work makes man free! The very words engraved over the entrance to Auschwitz Concentration Camp! The number 10 referred to ACC Law 10, the legal instrument responsible for having saved thousands of wrongfully charged Germans from undeserved death.

He glanced at the sleeping guards and walked quietly along dimly lighted corridors toward a virgin area: *DIVISION FIVE.* He approached the first level of entry, a microfilm library similar to the OSS Room, containing extremely sensitive material, posing numerous security risks. What lay beyond these parameters was far more intimidating than GAMMA 10!

Two armed sentries in glassed-in booths guarded the entry. Their eyes widened perceptibly at the TAC ID pinned to Meadows' jacket.

Triple A Clearance! One of the men punched Brad's card into a compact desk computer. The mini-screen lighted up with coded digits. "Yes, sir!" he came to attention at the confirmation on the screen. "Prepare yourself for SOP (Standard Operating Procedure)" He inserted the card into an electronic detector. Instantly the iron gates opened, sounding like the mating shrieks of baboons reverberating off the walls of the tomblike catacombs.

Brad shoved a ten-spot through the bars. "If you'd be so kind, can you scrounge up a large pot of black coffee?"

"No need for that, sir. Uncle Sam picks up the tab. Why ya working so late?"

"On my line there's no early or late, just all the time."

"Gotcha. A bust in the balls, ain't it?" He snapped on an intercom and ordered coffee. "And make it fresh. We got a VIP down there, Charlie."

Brad frowned, irked at the attention. He moved through inner corridors to a glass-enclosed room, guilefully avoiding the closed-circuit cameras. He knew that if he moved a certain way, kept his head in profile he could avoid the lens. He inserted the plastic card in the proper slot. *Voilà!* The door swung open and admitted him to cardex files and a more impressive microfilm room.

198

Brad's trained eyes scanned the room. No surveillance equipment? Interesting. He moved to the files, injected his card and sprung open the correct file drawers.

He flipped through the K cards slowly: Kalt, Kaltenbrock . . . Kaltenbrude . . . Kaltenbrun . . . Kaltenbrunner! At least two dozen Kaltenbrunners . . . Ernst, Fritz, Heinrich, Tovar . . . ah—Wolfgang. He read:

Kaltenbrunner, Wolfgang, *Untersturmführer*, *Schutzstaffel*, *WAFFEN*, *S.S.* Elite guard detachment, attache to General Reinhard Heydrich, terminated May 29, 1942. Cross index, search K-646-S.

He nonchalantly yanked the card from its central pole alignment, shoved it into his pocket and moved casually to the file section indicated on the card. Once the cross-checking ended, he searched the S numbers and title: *ARBEIT MACHT FREI-10*. He engaged the search button, observed the whirling motion of a long, tubular disc as it zeroed in on the material. He jotted numbers on a pad, returned to the cardex file, dismayed at the size of the celluloid spool. The tedious process commenced; he loaded the spool into the viewer sprocket and began the search for one operation logged among thousands.

The payoff came twenty minutes later. So did the pot of coffee.

"Take what you want, sir, we'll drink the rest."

Brad accepted the tray, carried it to his work area and gulped a fast cup of steamy black liquid, poured a hasty second. Swiftly, unobtrusively, peering at the occupied guards, he poured a remaining vial of Flurasepam hydrochloride into the pot, the same drug used in the Camus cognac. He returned it to the guard. "Drink it while it's hot," he said in that quiet, cultivated Meadows voice. "Too much makes me nervous."

Brad moved deftly. He removed the film from the loader, marked the imperative area with colored clips, sliced out the portion needed, and splicing the free edges together with a splicer conveniently left on the work counter, he coiled the strip tightly, pressed a spring on his gold watchband, placed it inside the hollow and snapped it shut.

Next he photocopied dummy stats on a strategic World War II project entitled: OPERATION BARBAROSSA. Hitler's obsessive military strategy calling for the destruction of Russia.

Let the fucking bloodhounds figure this bit of business!

As he photocopied the decoy dupes, each were duplicated and collected by electronic apparatus, his ID number appearing on each printed copy for future reference. For this reason, he had pirated the crucial microfilm outright. Years could pass before the pilferage was discovered.

The guards were lighting up cigarettes. *Pour the fucking coffee. C'mon, I haven't got all night. That's it, drink it . . . drink it up.*

Ten minutes later they were in lullaby land.

With no fixed plan in mind, and at all times conscious of the time, Brad played the next phase by ear. He moved swiftly on the balls of his feet toward the dimly lit T-shaped room at the end of the corridor. The moment had become implicitly provocative.

Standing outside the glass-walled room, he stared at the imposing electronic computers, a high technology with incredible capabilities. The thought of penetrating the *verboten* area sent a rush of excitement through him. Simultaneously, fear of discovery dictated prudence.

Fear is not part of my mental landscape he muttered over and over again.

Still he hesitated. The shrine of complex technology spread over three cavernous rooms. *He was actually here!* There seemed to be a living intimacy between himself and this iron goddess. Only a man steeped in codes, ciphers and electronics would understand his virginal approach, like that of a bridegroom to his bride on a nuptial eve.

Concatenate-Alpha, referred to as the Cat in D.C. backrooms, was proficient at tapping into the secrets of foreign governments, code-breaking, and the dissemination of misinformation. Hell! It could make or break any Intelligence apparatus in existence. *Enough reverence, Brad,* he urged himself forward. *Now,* penetrate! He felt no reluctance, he simply had no desire to be caught in the rape.

It lay before him, unattended, its brain turned off by a switch. Brad inserted his card. The gates slid open, closed silently behind him. He moved forward cautiously, eyes everywhere, heading toward the main terminal. He studied the controls, scanned the switches and flipped one. A high-intensity beam washed the work area in brilliant light. He peered about, searching the control area and readout screens for alarms. He pulled a rollaway chair into position, placed his briefcase on the floor at his feet and stretching his fingers, rubbed them gingerly like a safecracker limbering up before a caper. He had to work swiftly before some buck private pushing for captain's bars stumbled on the trespass. He searched for the on-switch, shoved it slowly toward mid-capacity, listening to the terminals coming alive in the electronic brain. He punched in coded numbers on the keyboard, unprepared for the vocals. A synthesized Darth Vader voice reached out, shaking him to the core:

YOU ARE INCOMPLETE. LOG INTO MAIN TERMINAL FOR EXTRACTION OF CODED DATA. . .

A goddamned talking computer was all he needed!

The bewildering moment passed. Sweating bullets, he lowered the master decibel range. He brushed the drops from his brow, punched out the required code, adding: EXECUTE ALL VISUALS ON FILE.

YOU ARE OPERATING IN ERROR . . . CODE IN SUBJECT . . . REPEAT . . . CODE IN SUBJECT!

Dammit! He reduced the decibel range again, complied with the request, coded in his subject: MOUFFLON.

A flow of mechanized perfection followed. *Concatenate-Alpha* blipped a series of ID numbers, file codes, followed by a flurry of additional blips with which he was unfamiliar. Printed material skirted across the screen. The voice, adjusted to minimal velocity, unnerved him. If the computer voice was automatically logged in a main control booth, piped Sphinx-like through security channels or transmitted its oracular powers to unseen monitors, his goose was cooked.

Speculation ceased abruptly. His eyes on the screen readout widened perceptibly, his fears dissipating by the ebullience of discovery shooting through him like adrenalin.

Sweet, sweet Jesus! It was here—all of it! A bio on Moufflon! . . . C'mon, dear lady, put your bill of fare up on the menu for Brad to digest. Atta girl, make with the entre, dessert and coffee.

Like a child with a brand-new toy, he muttered over and again, *"I'll be damned! . . . I'll be double goddamned!"*

The rising excitement ceased. Something was wrong. *No information prior to 1950 on Moufflon?* That's crazy! Brad had met him in 1943 prior to *OPERATION WHITE CORAL*! Yet, the infallible *Cat* contained no information prior to 1950? If a man's past can be deleted thusly . . .?

That, Brad old boy, is power!

He recoded the subject and read it again, marveling at the scope and magnitude of the Moufflon network. Unable to define his reaction to the astounding information—it took several impatient blips from the Cat and an excoriating remark to jar him.

. . . IF YOU ARE A NEOPHYTE, GET TRAINED PERSONNEL TO ASSIST . . .

And I'd like to punch you in the nose!
On impulse, his hands flew over the keyboard. The request printed:

KALTENBRUNNER, WOLFGANG . . . WAFFEN S.S.
. . . EXTRACT ALL DATA ON RECORD . . .

And so began the complete bio on Wolfgang from birth through his formative days in Nazi Youth movements, including the military stint to war's end. The screen went blank, then printed:

. . . CROSS-CHECK AKTION 4 *f* 15. SEE REINHARD HEYDRICH. SEARCH AND LOCATE BRITISH M-1 FILE 999 000 989 010 . . .

Frowning, Brad keyed in: CLARIFY.
The computer repeated its previous instructions. Glancing at the wall clock, he synched it with his watch, set his alarm to ring in an hour. Firmly he keyed in the word:
AKTION *f* 4.
JACKPOT! He read it all, storing it in his memory.
AKTION f 4: Hitler's secret order in 1939 calling for the death of 150,000 German prisoners and mental cases labeled incurable. The importance of AKTION *f* 4 was not the case itself, but that it led to subsequent AKTIONS 13 15. Application of the tactics conceived in AKTION *f* 4 at labor and concentration camps housing confined socialists, Communist Jews and other anti-state elements, meant eradication. First, the sick and criminally insane; second, the anti-state elements; third, the Communist Jews. Specific orders signed by Hitler authorizing AKTION 13 *f* 14 had never been located, complicating the subject. In 1941, an alleged order from Hitler conveyed to General Reinhard Heydrich through Goering, commissioned Heydrich to solve the Jewish problem. The procedure: Emigrate, Evacuate and Confis-

cate properties. For some unknown reason, mystifying historians ever since, Heydrich, charged with the monumental problem of *endlösung*, had not proceeded with the order. Brad shook his head, glanced at the clock. He was working against time. There was so much—too much!

Now the data output confused him. Seemingly unrelated blueprints, codes, and ciphers dating back to primitive intelligence-gathering days clouded the issue. The screen flashed with data referring to Nuremberg, then made a quantum leap to 1953 and back again to ACC Law Number 10. Redundant, time-consuming perplexing information robbed him of precious time. Dammit! Less than twenty safe minutes remained. He needed time!

Green arrows flashed at screen left, then the miracle code appeared:

GPBM—LIDICE- ZERO—BRITISH M-1 TRIPLE TEN-ZERO.

What the devil! British M-I? Intercept and trespass in a fell swoop? Shit!

Brad knew the consequences, if alarms tripped, but he had no choice. He sucked in his breath, keyed in the code, unsure what he had until the readout commenced. Jumping from word to word, he absorbed the information, forcing the hysteria gripping his solar plexus to abate. Did he dare switch the transmit key to *printout*? He did not! He reread the screen's contents, committing each word, line, phrase to memory:

DATE: 29 May 1942
GOVERNOR PROTECTORATE OF BOHEMIA AND MORAVIA, GENERAL REINHARD HEYDRICH STRUCK DOWN BY BOMBS EXPLODING OPEN MERCEDES SUCCUMBED TO INJURIES. HE DIED TWO DAYS LATER. AIDE KALTENBRUNNER, WOLFGANG, WAFFEN S. S. SURVIVED. SPECIAL COMMENDATION FROM HITLER FOR RETRIEVING HEYDRICH'S PERSONAL ATTACHE CASE CONTAINING VALUABLE RECORDS EARNED KALTENBRUNNER PROMOTION AS KEEPER OF RECORDS UNDER HIMMLER COMMAND. VILLAGE OF LIDICE DYNAMITED IN RETALIATION FOR ATROCITY. MEN OF VILLAGE, SHOT. WOMEN SENT TO RAVENSBRUCK CONCENTRATION CAMP. CHILDREN, INTEGRATED INTO NAZI YOUTH GROUPS IN GNEISENAU, GERMANY. NOTE: DISTINCTION MUST

BE MADE. WOLFGANG KALTENBRUNNER UNRELATED TO GENERAL
ERNST KALTENBRUNNER WHO LATER REPLACED HEYDRICH. REPEAT:
NOTE DISTINCTION BETWEEN MEN.

That's it! He'd done it! Further proof of Wolfgang's veracity
was contained in the microfilm secreted in his watchband. The
screen went blank, then printed:

CODE RED ALERT . . . IDENTIFY . . . IDENTIFY!

Brad pressed the erase button, pulled the switch on *Concatenate-
Alpha*, listening as the formidable computer groaned to a protracted,
whining halt. He snapped off the overhead intensity light, picked
up his briefcase and paused for a backward glance.
If the boys in the backroom at Bletchley could see me now!
He swung out of DIVISION FIVE with his TAC clearance and
his silver cups.
It was time for Milford Race Meadows to disappear!

As he boarded the 707 to London, Brad felt a sense of
satisfaction. If the OSS had pulled the plug forty years ago on
Wolfgang Kaltenbrunner, he might be alive today. Those terrible
years of the sixties and nightmarish seventies and the inevitabili-
ties of the eighties might have been circumvented.

Chapter Twelve

WASHINGTON, D.C.

"YOU'RE BEYOND BELIEF!" BILL MILLER LEVELED A BARRAGE OF EXPLETIVES at the caller. "You asked your questions. Three times I replied in the negative and you keep insisting! My dear Charles, this conversation is getting us nowhere." He snapped the mute button on his cordless, and flipped another key. "Bobbie! Where the fuck is Kagen? Get Kagen here on the double!" He got back to the caller. "I categorically deny Oval Office involvement! No! I wouldn't think of taking the matter to the President! The idea is preposterous! Offhand I've never heard of Milford Race Meadows! The ID number belongs to a dead man . . . CIA clearance . . .? Well, Charles, that's not my avenue of expertise. Take it up with the spooks—with the DCI. Yes, goddammit, I am annoyed. You'd be annoyed, too. I have no knowledge of this—you insist I do, and that rankles me. Get it! I don't like to be rankled, buddy!"

Bill Miller slammed the phone, glanced up as Tom Kagen, a red-haired, freckle-faced liberal with an overactive sexual drive, rushed into the room, putting final touches to his attire. Deceptively stocky, the physique of the former Notre Dame linebacker was solid brawn. "Ya hadda interrupt? Ya couldn't have waited, Bill? The best goddamn piece of ass I've had in God knows how long . . ." began the aide, finally getting his clothes in order. He sat opposite the glowering chief presidential aide, caught the file tossed at him.

"Read this, Don Juan, and dig deep for some fucking answers or else our heads will roll." Bill Miller, a tall, angular, prudently conservative man in dress and manners was in his forties. A Harvard graduate with a Masters in Poly Sci from Cambridge University in England, a summa cum laude graduate stared at his partner with exaggerated patience, fairly fuming as Kagen scanned the report, cursorily at first. He poured a cup of black coffee, drained it, eyes still on the pages.

These two, as mismatched as the tortoise and hare, as unlikely a team in President Macgregor's political covey of confidants, were unbeatable. Bill Miller's impeccable logical approach to issues evaluated and analyzed a subject to death before rendering a decision. The Irisher Kagen, trained in law by the Jesuit Fathers at Notre Dame, possessed both a rapier-sharp intellect and an uncanny gut instinct for honing in on a matter after a quick run-through.

Miller waited for Kagen's reaction. Kagen took a Percodan, washed it down with coffee, to soothe the ghost of a football injury done to his back. Miller played back the morning's phone conversations. Once through, Kagen demanded, "Play it back."

"Why the hell for? I know it by rote! The phone hasn't stopped ringing since you left to bang Miss What-ever-her-name in Communications! Look at the facsimile reports! Telexes from Clayallee 10! The son of a bitch, Meadows, alias whoever the hell, forged TAC! Triple A-Clearance! And that puts us in the middle. Tom—are you involved in these charades?" he asked testily, hoping for negation.

"I should resent that, Bill. Coming from you, I'd feel slighted if you didn't include me in such a conspiracy," he added wryly. "I'd reciprocate, my good man."

"Swell. And don't my good man me."

"Track it down! How difficult can that be?" Tom shifted into higher gear. "Who in the Company, if the rape was U.S.-originated, has had love affairs with computers?"

"Good thinking, Casanova."

"Put a trace on all Company men. If we come up empty, put Intelligence men to work. Trace the m.o. of all KGB, British, French and Mossad agents."

"The trouble is motivation! The reason behind the rape of *Concatenate-Alpha*. For Christsakes! He probed *OPERATION BARBAROSSA!* Who the devil needs to unearth those skeletal bones? Everything this Meadows duplicated was subterfuge, designed to conceal his real motive. Dammit to hell! What was he after?"

Kagen, in the harness, with all thoughts of his *coitus interruptus* on the back burners, sifted through the reports, picking out highlights.

Bill Miller and Tom Kagen, top presidential aides, staunch party men of the new breed, steeped in computer techniques of politics, had been on Macgregor's Special Team of Advisors since his governorship days in Illinois. Both men knew all too well how popularity polls, and speeches made to the *right* people at the *right* time figured into decisions made in the Oval Office. The exceptions occurred when the President initiated measures he sincerely believed to be for the good of the nation—special-interest groups be damned! He usually got his way.

"I am boss," he stated firmly on such occasions. "I don't give a damn about popularity polls! Now let's roll up our sleeves, get down to work and see what the *presidency* is all about!"

The recent subtle changes in the President was not lost to either of his aides. He shot from the hip less often in heated cabinet meetings, hedged, grew testier, answered harsh press criticisms with barbed answers and deferred frequently to countless questions, declaring the matters too sensitive to discuss.

"Bill—did you read this report from West Berlin Intelligence following the death of General Mark Samuels?" Kagen tossed it to his partner. As Miller perused the report, Kagen tapped his head thoughtfully. "Lincoln . . . Lincoln," he mused. "Major Brad Lincoln! Wasn't he a former briefing officer? I thought he was with the NSA."

On impulse he picked up the phone. "Get me personnel, Jim." He waited. Miller was engrossed in the report. "Yeah, personnel. I need a file on Major Bradford Lincoln, yeah, B-r-a-d-f-o-r-d—you got the rest. On the double. Bring it to Bill Miller's office—the full computer readout!"

Two hours later the two aides stared at one another, long, hard, fitfully. They had patched together bits and pieces, deplored what it signaled.

"I fucking thought we knew the President," Miller said, deflating.

"Don't jump to conclusions," Kagen remonstrated. "Despite our untenable position, we must permit him an opportunity to explain. If the chief chose to keep covert a matter capable of blowing foreign policy sky-high—he had sufficient reason."

"Well, dammit, I'm pissed. To be eliminated from covert foreign involvement signifies lack of trust. I want answers, Tom. *Why, when, how* and *who* coerced the Chief to depart from the usual protocol on matters concerning COP (Clandestine Operational Procedure)."

"It's stupid and damned counterproductive to engage in hypothesis. There's only one way to clear the air. What's the Presidential agenda?"

Miller grimaced. "Jammed tight. Only open time is Saturday. Know what that means? My wife, yours and the First Lady will send up smoke signals. War clouds, buddy."

"What's your thinking, Bill? Any idea what the Chief will do if the facts prove false?"

"Resurrect the guillotine. Heads will roll. Never thought much of that device. Did you know bodies don't actually die instantly— bodies have often sprung to their feet and moved around—"

"Bill!" Kagen grimaced. "Spare me the gory details."

Saturday morning, following the wake of domestic discord, Miller and Kagen ambled through deserted White House corridors toward the Oval Office. Both men had spent too much time reviewing covert dispatches and the remarkable personnel files of Major Brad Lincoln.

"For Christsakes, what a dossier! A Company man, CIA, and NSA! The possibility of Oval Office involvement is no longer remote!" Miller exasperated at one point along the way. Both had expressed exaggerated shock and disbelief. Their thoughts communicated to the President two days ago had led to this Saturday meeting.

Both brilliant organizational men, they possessed unique talents in administrative skills. Their stature and solidarity with the President, their ability to influence his priorities had earned them unique respect and extreme deference from all White House staffers, and special interest groups.

Today both Kagen and Miller felt abandoned, deserted, betrayed.

President Macgregor acknowledged his aides, waved them forward, and ending his phone call, shuffled, stacked bulletins and memos neatly to one side for later perusal. He plopped a gold globe paperweight on them. "Well, Tom—Bill," he said brightly. "What's this all about?"

The President listened to Miller's prepared litany for an hour. Macgregor, a superb actor demonstrating controlled charm, the animated verve of a courageous man play-acting his way through office. Under handsome comely charm was solid steel, the personality of a man who knew what he wanted and how to get it. In the clinches, no one ever soft-soaped him and got away with it.

Now the President stared into space, forming pictures that Miller painted. He expressed a mixture of amusement, delight, disbelief and incredible respect at the involvements. Realizing his men needed answers, he shoved his glasses onto his forehead. "What exactly do you want to know?"

"Well, sir, for openers, is it true?"

"How the hell would I know that, Bill?"

"I mean did you order the clandestine operation?"

"No."

"Do you know *anything* about Lincoln's charade in West Berlin?" Kagen asked, lighting his Meerschaum. "Do you mind if I smoke, sir?"

"Yes to the first question. No to the second."

Miller frowned petulantly while Kagen puffed on the ostentatious pipe.

"Suppose I tell you how it began?" The President leaned back in his swivel chair, sipped a glass of diet cola. "Brad and I go back a long way, to World War II, when politics was hardly a glimmer in my eyes. From active duty he gravitated to the role of briefing officer in two administrations. He's a thoroughly professional military intelligence officer who earned promotions in confidential roles in high-level intelligence. I found him knowledgeable, properly circumspect, and loyal. Loyalty to me is a precious commodity the world lacks in great abundance.

"Shortly after taking my oath of office, these damnable Pentagon hearings began. I remembered Brad, located him with the (National Security Agency), the most secretive, high-technology snooping agency in government.

"His position, essentially a desk job, placed him on investigatory and advisory boards, moving in and out of power circles, hobnobbing in confidence and trust among giant decision and policy makers. I found him to be strong in crisis, decisive in judgment, skillful in bureaucratic infighting, indefatigable in his labors. So, I requested his transfer to Pentagon committee hearings. What sold me on him was his lack of addiction to *flash-intelligence*. He deals only in cold, hard facts. His reports are accurate, informative, and without bias. He is not, never has been, a man easily used by higher-ups in the intelligence community."

The President sipped his cola. "I detect doubt and disconcertment in you, Bill."

"Doubt, perhaps, Mr. President. We can't afford to be victimized by *official lies* foisted on us without basis in fact. Company men are ingenuous in the manufacture of *cover* stories."

"A point well taken. Let me explain. Major Lincoln approached me on a matter he considered *earth-shattering*. I know . . . I know . . ." He shook his head, raised a protesting hand. "We in the Oval Office aren't prone to melodrama. Neither is the Major. I listened, considered carefully the implications and complications, should his evaluations prove incorrect. Years ago, he was instrumental in establishing an international network of American agents, counterinsurgents and special operatives concealed in various military compounds throughout Europe, the Middle and Far East. He knew *where* to go, *whom* to contact and *how* to expedite matters. He searched for facts—not rumors—at great personal risks. His request for a totally covert operation centered primarily on his desire to protect sources of information. A slip of the tongue, a hint of his purpose would have meant disaster."

"From the looks of things, sir, disaster dogged him at every turn. My God, Mr. President!" Miller spoke rapidly, barely pausing at the end of a sentence, as if he were pursued by devils who gave him ten seconds to narrate an hour-long story.

"Concatenate-Alpha?" The President leaned forward, amused. "He did that? Lincoln broke the code and *raped* the computer?" He laughed in delighted amusement. "You've got his dossier. He worked with the backroom boys at Bletchley, breaking the Nazi code, ULTRA. If he could do that—. Well, he's a master at codes and ciphers."

"Well," Kagen added quietly, "his dossier indicates he's the best man for the job." He watched the President pick up the golden globe paperweight, toss it from one hand to the other, and stroking it with his thumb, finger-polished the inscription *MONDO XX*. He tossed it into the air, caught it quickly and placed it back on the stack of papers.

"In any event, you'll hear Lincoln's report in a week or so. He's due back shortly."

"Any objections if I initiate tracers on Lincoln's route? Covertly, of course." Miller removed his glasses, fixed solidly on startled presidential eyes.

Tom Kagen masked his disquiet at Miller's impudent remark. He fell into his usual posture of listening.

"I suppose you have basis for such a request, Bill?" the President asked candidly.

"None, Mr. President, save my penchant for neat and orderly planning. Whenever it's threatened, I grow skittish. Better to lock the barn doors before—"

"Tom?" Macgregor glanced at Kagen.

"No objections, sir, provided Major Lincoln and his sources are protected. Additional covert efforts could alert the *wrong* people for the *wrong* reasons."

"I agree. Bill, what protection do we offer the sources?"

"None, offhand. Not until inquiries are made."

"*Negative!* My answer is—I repeat, *negative!*" Noting the flicker of displeasure in Miller's eyes, he added, "I'll go this far. We wait for the Major's report. Evaluation will follow."

"You're the boss." Miller shrugged, his expression deadpan.

"Bill, I refuse to make the grave errors made by my predecessors. Absolute control in covert operations *must* rest at the top. Let me be clear on this issue. Only the President approves, disapproves or cancels any and all covert operations as *he* sees fit. Clandestine operations in my administration will not be permitted to grow out of control as they did two decades ago."

"Three murders, several attempts on Lincoln's life, tampering with government property—*Concatenate-Alpha*—and you say you won't permit clandestine operations to get out of control?"

"What's the point in overdramatizing, Bill?" The President's repudiating voice turned frigid. "We wait on Lincoln's report. If he pulls it off, America becomes more credible to our Allies in future confrontations."

"I suggest, Mr. President," Miller spoke up, his voice harsh, "you wear your bulletproof vest more often. You do realize who Lincoln's *aide de camp* was in the ETO?

"Mr. President, twenty years ago John Kennedy rode grandly into office with remarkable naivete. Abruptly awakened to stark realities, the hazards of secret operations, he discovered dangers, knew what went wrong, but suddenly found himself captive to counterinsurgency—"

"—he *learned* never to trust the experts again," the President retorted slowly, evenly, speaking each word with unmistakable emphasis.

"Mr. President, Major Lincoln's ties are with men implicated in the Dallas tragedy. It's in his dossier. Both men were trained in *OPERATION WHITE CORAL* in the ETO. Lincoln has used them all, codes, contacts, safe houses, cells all taught in the *CORAL* operation." Bill Miller observed the changes in the Presidential expression.

And John Macgregor recalled Brad's emphasis on *OPERATION WHITE CORAL*.

If anything happens to me, study the Coral operation. We were all connected. The man . . . unsung hero . . . death squads . . . SAS Commandos!

"Suppose we study *OWC*? You infer I'm a possible sitting duck? Yes? Bill . . .? Tom . . .?"

"There's a hitch, sir," Miller said tightly. "The files are in GAMMA 10."

"For Christsakes! You want me placed in competition for assassin's bullets?"

"It won't do," Kagen broke in. "By penetrating GAMMA 10 ourselves, we'd only bring additional attention to Lincoln. I suggest we wait for his report before doing anything."

"And I further suggest we send a back-up team to insure his safe return to D.C." Miller urged, scanning the reports.

"You're that concerned over his safety? I warned him he'd get no validation from the White House."

"Read the reports, Mr. President. The man's in serious trouble. I suggest we help him out."

"By all means, if you can trace him. But I urge you to use discretion." Macgregor scanned the U.S. Intelligence reports from Clayallee 10. "You think Lincoln was responsible?"

Bill gave the Chief a brief rundown of Lincoln's activities. "Nothing positive—only circumstantial. He was present at the death of a former Nazi officer suspected by our men as being a double agent for the KGB. What do you think?"

"What do I think? It's a waste of time to speculate."

"Who or what is Lincoln after? To strip valuable data from the *Cat*?"

"Well, we really don't know that, do we?" the President hedged.

"Trusted sources reveal he attempts to rendezvous with a powerful European figurehead, a legend, so to speak, with enormous wide-reaching powers. Any thoughts along these lines, sir?" Miller asked.

"Not the vaguest." Macgregor lied adroitly with a bland innocence that did not pass unnoticed. "Whoever you entrust to track Lincoln must be without blemish—totally trustworthy—"

"That narrows it to zero." Kagen stated with brutal candor.

"Errors this late in the game plan might prove disastrous," Macgregor said, bypassing the remark.

"Have you a suggestion, sir?"

"Hell, no, Bill! You're the experts at charades. Let me tell you— you'd better cover your asses. If Company boys sniff us out, or the NSA, leaks to the press will barbecue our butts. For God's sake use every precaution to protect *our* man. Risk of exposure is lethal."

Miller and Kagen left the Oval Office depressed, knowing less and feeling worse for their efforts. They padded through the halls in the West Wing, past deserted press rooms, out through the First Lady's Garden, to their cars in a morose, studied silence. Not a word was exchanged until they boarded their cars.

"We'll think on this, Bill. No talks, yet. O.K.?"

Miller nodded, climbed into his silver Mercedes sedan, drove off White House grounds, nodding to the posted sentries, and wheeled onto Pennsylvania Avenue lost in thought. Uri Mikhail Gregorevich was due in from Moscow. Dare he make contact before his arrival?

Chapter Thirteen

CAIRO, EGYPT
March 15, 1983

TANKS, MARCHING FEET, SURFACE-TO-AIR MISSILES, paraded in the streets.

Cairo was a flea market of ancient gods, a conquered people, a bargain basement on two floors, earth and heaven, and a mass of filthy beggars. Nonetheless, a show of military strength dominated. The stench of war drifted over the Red Sea from Lebanon and Israel, ballooning tensions already tightly coiled inside Egyptian Arabs. Inscrutably silent as the Great Sphinx at Gizeh, Egyptian leaders believed what they had tried to dismiss from mind in recent months. Israel had gone mad! Quietly, unobtrusively, they prepared for the final assault when Israel renounced the Camp David Accords, scuttling the Middle East peace process.

Brad had arrived in Cairo three days ago following several depressing, unfruitful visits to London, Paris and Rome, where he had gone to search for the evidence he wanted to bring back to his president.

Today, he hailed a cab en route to the Cairo Hilton on Tahrir Square, to keep his appointment with an old friend. As the cab merged with traffic in the hot city, he reflected.

In London, British MI were reserved, cool, demanding, highly suspicious and downright hostile. Kept on a taut leash by this unexpected treatment, he sensed a growing discontent by top-level executives within the Embassy toward American foreign policy. Their unwillingness to cooperate had terminated his business abruptly. Former contacts with British SOE, either unavailable or dead, their dossiers, clearly stamped; *WHEREABOUTS UNKNOWN,* signaled dangers.

In Paris he was read the riot act. "Power cartels have brought humanity to a plateau where insanity is a greater problem than world hunger," the Minister of the Interior told Brad. "Human beings don't want to be leaders, only followers. Find them a nut to tell them *what* to do, *when* and *how,* and everything is lovely."

Brad had found the French less hospitable than the frosty British, yet eager to add their disgust with American foreign policy. The Minister had raged, "We've lost respect for the United States for the weak, milksop manner in which they cavorted in the Middle East peace process. Those butchers will not be punished for the massacre," he had railed. "They want control of the Golden Crescent!"

The Golden Crescent! Another fucking impediment.

Two days spent in Rome, equally as disastrous, where high-level diplomats, former W.W. II friends, aired their discontent over U.S foreign policy. However much he tried, he couldn't get them off the subject. Their silence beyond certain parameters

214

spurred Brad to fly to Cairo to arrange a meeting between himself and General Abu-Qir, Chief of Army Intelligence for the Arab Republic. Both had fought alongside the other in the North African campaign.

The cab driver pulled up before the opulent Cairo Hilton. Brad paid the driver, entered the hotel, heading for the El Nile Rotisserie—the main dining room.

Brad entered, greeted by a familiar voice. "Ah . . . Mustafa! What a pleasure to see you again." He embraced the tall, umber-skinned Egyptian fraternally.

"Likewise, my good friend. Too many waters have passed under the bridge of our friendship. Come, let us drink a toast to friendship and thank Allah for bringing us together."

The reunion got off to a pleasant start, but floundered before lunch was served.

The dining room was crowded, smoke-filled, overflowing with jet-set entrepreneurs, wheeler-dealers, sharpshooters of all creeds and colors playing for high stakes. Brad found the atmosphere confusing; the vibrations were so mixed, he was on edge, discomforted.

The General leaned in close, his black piercing eyes holding Brad's. "Take a good look, old chap. You may recognize a few faces. Most are protected by the financial umbrella of international titans intent on carving up the spoils of the Golden Crescent. The hunt in the Middle East is no longer for oil—but for the immensely profitable opium poppy."

Again Brad heard the words: *The Golden Crescent*, and was perplexed. It seemed the drug network was much more firmly entrenched than he had imagined. But he brushed aside his disquiet and went after the primary purpose of this meeting.

"Actually, General, my concern is the nuclear threat." Brad launched into a sell initiative, desperately using feelers to get Abu-Qir's reaction to the threat.

"I share the overt concern over our vulnerability here in the Middle East, however I doubt nuclear war is a viable threat."

"Really? Interesting." Brad was surprised. "Europe feels like they're sitting on a time bomb and you, in the thick of things, seem unconcerned."

"I say, old chap, you fail to understand me. We are quite concerned. My dear Major, you so understand that the underlying wealth has shifted from rich oil fields to the precious opium

215

poppy. The Golden Crescent is highly coveted and they mean to control it, reap the enormous wealth. Dope is sold for dollars and diamonds which in turn are used to buy weapons arsenals. It's the three-D syndrome, a highly infectious malaise of greed that eats at the heart of that Middle East nation. Weapons are power—and power is their god.'' He sipped his Scotch and water calmly.

''In the thickening vapors of hash and cocaine the dope dealers and arms peddlers are not easily distinguishable,'' Brad said quietly. ''But getting back to the main thrust of my visit, Mustafa—''

Mustafa Abu-Qir, seldom one to mince words, despite his British-trained detachment, made apparent his vitriol. His words held Brad in shocked silence.

''Not only does Egypt consider their acts barbarous but a direct insult to American diplomacy and American generosity. We, you and I, do not invent policy. But if you carry anything back to your chief, advise him of the clandestine acts conducted here and abroad by the Mossad who no longer conceal their actions to gain control of the entire Middle East. U.S. support makes them brazen.''

Brad's stomach engaged in a series of sinking sensations. The Egyptian's words doomed all hope as he leaned over his salad, gesturing with a finger under Brad's nose.

''With America's help Israel's goal to dominate can become reality, old chap. But take this back to your President, also. With that reality shall come devastation! The Arab world will not permit it. If, to prevent such a happening, we must unite with Eastern nations, for *baraka* we shall do as Allah decrees. You see, Major, old friend, what must be done has already been written. We Arabs, too, await the final countdown.''

''Therefore, your prognosis is—'' It was an inane interjection, but Brad was scrambling to make sense of what he was hearing.

''*Inch'Allah*! We shall meet in eternity if so lofty a place continues to exist after thermonuclear warheads are set off.''

''You're insane if you believe this, Abu-Qir. Out and out *cafard!* But not as mad as I for listening to your dismal forecast.''

''It is expected. One does not oppose destiny. What will be will be. You are American, I, an Arab. It is impossible to understand the ways of each people.''

''*We could try!*''

''We did. We made every effort, time and again. But we will

not stand aside and let Israel with U.S. aid wipe out our very existence."

"I deny such intentions are promoted by my government!"

"Deny what you will. Others dictate American policy. America lacks effectiveness in exercising constraints over an Israel searching for power. And because it does, the world believes it sanctions their aggression."

"It isn't true!"

"You adopted Israel, support her with billions of taxpayer's dollars. You identify with Israel. I point to the United Nations fiasco in 1982. So? How then is it possible to maintain objectivity with Arab states?"

Brad deflated.

"Don't despair, old chap. We here in Egypt live with the daily threat of war hovering over and around us. You Americans, untouched by war since the mid-1800's, are not as conditioned."

"I had hoped to bring far more encouraging information back to my President—"

"Musaka Mubende was killed for trying to tell your government—" he broke off in mid-sentence. He dropped his voice an octave. "Mubende tried thirty times to rendezvous with your President, your Secretary of State—"

It was the way he said *President*, the same scathing unspoken indictment as when he said Secretary of State, that alerted Brad. Unmistakable revulsion colored his tone, as if he were speaking of some diabolic obscenity.

"—he bloody well had to pierce the Pentagon hearings. Unfortunately, by then, someone heard of his mission and assassinated him. My recommendation to you is leave Cairo, return to Washington and be bloody careful with the information you have already digested."

Brad's lips parted in astonishment.

"Your scent is properly coordinated, Major. Our old friend is no doubt the key to this nuclear prognosis. Just be bloody careful."

Our old friend? Brad tensed, his eyes darted about the area, on the alert, at once uncomfortable.

"Relax, old chap. At least two dozen *Mokkadem* are guarding us. Four are assigned to your case, to watch over you until you depart our land. Yes, yes, *our* old friend. Captain—what was his name?"

"I haven't the vaguest idea of whom you speak."

"Good, for a moment I thought you'd deny it and you did. For the record, I pray Allah will assist you in your plight, Major."

"For the record, if I had the vaguest notion of what it is you are prattling about, *old chap*, I'd pray to your Allah or whoever it is out there to solve this fucking manmade dilemma."

They shook hands in parting. Brad left the pub, walked the busy Hilton corridors out the foyer into the hot, dry desert air. Abu-Qir had deleted portions of a painful scenario, thought Brad. Either he was professionally unable to reveal what Brad had learned in Sicily or he wished to spare his friend profound embarrassment.

Brad hailed a cab to the flat of an old friend, where he'd stayed for the past days, avoiding the mainstream, close to the old Shepherd Hotel, a favorite water hole of World War II fame where cloak-and-dagger games were conducted by global espionage agents.

Brad's report to the President bulged with frightening facts. He reflected on all this as the cab drove through narrow back alleys to the flat, aware that four *Mokkadem* agents tailed him.

He was finished, his flight scheduled to depart Cairo International Airport to London in less than an hour. Dressed in beige desert khaki shorts, short-sleeved safari jacket, knee socks and desert boots, Brad packed his briefcase, tucked his automatic into his waistband. He hoped the flight time from London to D.C. would be sufficient to sort the massive disconnected data he had amassed.

The phone rang brashly. Startled from his thoughts, he let it ring three times, hesitant to answer. Who the hell . . . ? No one knew his whereabouts. *Answer the goddamned phone, dummy!*

He picked up the receiver. *Jim Greer!* History repeating itself?

"Get the fuck outa there! You've been marked for a hit! Right now! Move! Call me from a safehouse! Got it? Now *move*, you son of a bitch, *MOVE!*"

Brad, briefcase in hand, got as far as the door when loud, crashing explosions collapsed the walls. He flung himself to the floor, covered his head protectively from the glass shards, plaster chunks and shrapnel raining down on him. Two warheads spun like pinwheels on the floor, burning a trail on the carpeting, but

218

failed to explode. Brad didn't wait for the phenomenon or further assault.

Christ! It was insanity again! Brad leaped to his feet, bolted over the stairwell, clutching the briefcase.

Three shattering explosions crumbled the walls, thickened the air with dust and debris. Caught on the landing between the second and first floors, Brad choked on the smoke blackening the hallway. Greedy flames and blistering hot smoke obstructed his exit. Steeling himself, he lurched through the flames, singeing the hair on his arms and legs, and scaling the steps three at a time crossed the foyer, out the door.

Outside at last, in a hot, dusty courtyard, he beat at his body, suffocating the flames. Coughing, squinting up at the swirling tunnels of black smoke escaping the terrace windows of the gutted apartment, his eyes burned, smarting painfully in the smoldering haze. Brad peered about, measuring angles and distance, trying to get a bead on the direct line of assault. He trailed the line across the street to a second floor window.

Suddenly from nowhere a figure raced toward him, yanked his burned arm savagely, shoved him forward into the blackened air. Brad tensed, but arms held high came crashing down on him. Shock exploded his cranium. Pains, spiraling down his spine, turned his legs to water.

Jesus! Sweet Jesus! Not again! He fell to oblivion.

The pain, excruciating, his eyes burning like liquid fire, he peered through narrow slitted eyelids, trying like hell, but unable to lift his head, the assaulting pain staggering him. *Lay back, take it a step at a time, Brad. Easy, now. that's it.*

Spills of light from perforated brass wall lamps, playing weird shadows on the walls, disoriented him. He blinked, and his vision cleared. Where the bloody blazes was he? Had he been here long? A day—two—three? Unanswered questioned unnerved him and as memory slowly returned, with it—panic! His watch dial read: eleven hundred hours. The crystal was cracked; it had stopped running.

Christ! His flight! He'd missed his flight! Brad jerked his body upright too soon. The aftershock jarred him, pain tortured his head, neck and spine. Forced to drop his head into his hands for support until the painful spasms abated, he picked out patterns of flamingos on the carpeting. Low oriental tables, sofas, empty coffee cups strewn about, he gazed at the thick patterns of colored, melted wax dripped from old wine bottles used as candle holders. Mounds of hash and Turkish cigarette butts in countless ashtrays dotted the room.

Where the fuck was he? His tattered briefcase lay at his feet, unopened, his gun nearby. A cell? A *safehouse*? It had to be. He remembered the watchband clasp containing the microfilm, hollow heels containing the film on Wolfgang! Did he dare check them out? Instantly paranoid, he resisted the desire to check their safety. Eyes peered out at him, he felt them!

Brad reached slowly for the M52. The chambers were empty. What else? He moved to the briefcase, snapped open the clasps, searching for the box of Czech shells. Gone! Dammit! They'd been lifted! He flung the useless weapon on the table, watched it spin in a circle to a halt. And then he heard voices! Muted sounds . . . an argument from somewhere in the building . . . the slamming of doors. Brad sprang to his feet and immediately collapsed in agony on the sofa, the weight of his head intolerable. God, what *fucking* pain! He had to move—he had to!

Slowly, he turtled toward the door, drawn by the voices. *No more carelessness, Brad,* he warned himself. He knew he'd be a goner if assaulted one more time.

Then he saw the languidly posed shadow in the doorway. Instinctively he tensed, then he realized he *knew* that voice.

"Six Soviet-made Katyuska anti-tank rockets fired automatically by an electronic timing device set into place hours before your arrival left few traces, Major. You were lucky."

Specters! Goddamned specters! If he didn't know better . . .

Jesus! She spoke English better than he. His strength dissipated and through lidded eyes he watched helplessly as she opened a small black case, removed a hypodermic syringe, filled it with the contents of a glass vial.

"It's morphine—to kill the pain. You must be ready to travel in less than a quarter hour." Berna cautioned him quietly.

"T-travel?" He backed away. *Berna!* Greer had called to get him out of the exploding house and then Berna showed up! How could they know what was happening in Cairo?

"Trust me. Don't ask questions. You'll get answers in due time." She plunged the needle into his arm, emptied it and withdrew it. "You *must* walk out of here with me, understand?"

"Have I a choice?"

"No." She glanced at her watch nervously, tossed the empty syringe into a waste receptacle. She tossed him a pair of dark glasses and a *jellaba*. "Put these on. We've no time to waste." She loaded the M52, shoved it into the upper part of her khaki-colored flight fatigues. "Do anything foolish to bring attention to us and I'll kill you, Major. I promise," she said harshly.

He didn't doubt her for a moment. His strength sapped, he succumbed to the morphine. "Are you expecting trouble?"

"You ask that *after* the insanity dealt you these past weeks?" Her voice was deadly. "How many lives are left to give your country?" Berna stood at the window peering down into a glaring, sun-bleached white courtyard. Her skin was darker, tanner than he remembered, her dark eyes flecked with golden amber glints. Seduction poured from her effortlessly. The flight fatigues, boots—what an appealing sight—hinted at every curve of her body. Vivid images rushed at him, mingled with the lulling effects of the morphine, desire, stirring a mixing bowl of semen inside him.

"Now,!" she hissed. "Down the stairs, into the waiting sedan! Move, dammit!" she snapped.

Berna steadied him out the door into the waiting dusty sedan. The auto bolted forward like a torpedo. The vintage Daimler, a World War II relic, a mass of nuts and bolts held together by wires and pure faith, swerved sharply, careened around corners, headed out of the city. Frenetic navigation by a wild driver was sheer torture. Seated alongside him, his leathery skinned, swarthy companion with black reptilian eyes orbiting in all directions at once seemed unconcerned at the hair-raising driving gymnastics. The security of a Kalishnikov assault rifle accross his lap, its curved magazine load intact, was a courage-booster in any language.

They chattered like mad hens in an incoherent Arabic dialect. They shrugged, grunted, gestured animatedly, using no names, snorting cocaine intermittently. They were good. Insane, but good technicians.

Lulled by the morphine, Brad dozed off and immediately was trapped in so savage and crushing a dream that he experienced paralytic fear. He saw the wrathful face of God conceived and born in the vast space of desert, casting an immense shadow upon the face of the globe.

Gripped by sensations of terror and breathless fascination, he tried to peer beyond the blinding penumbra. And then he saw displeasure on the face of the wrathful Deity. With a giant fist He scooped up a handful of sand, blew on it, converting it to a *ghilbi* and flung it upon the world; with his other fist he scooped up a fist of mankind, crushing them in his fury.

Caught in an omnipotent force he seemed unable to circumvent, Brad screamed, shouted, begged to be heard. "I'm trying to save them, but they won't listen!" The words echoed emptily, swallowed up in the howling of mighty winds. Temperatures zoomed to a fiery-coal intensity, dropping suddenly to frostbiting ice. Huddling among the fleeing, screaming, wretched people, he covered his head, staving off the sounds. He lurched, fell, burrowing himself into the ground as deafening sounds of explosive jet streams springing from the very feet of God shot over the poles. Then brilliant, blinding violent reds, blood crimsons, flamed around him. The earth roared, trembled thunderously. Black puffs of smoke erupted. Small bursts growing larger until the mushroom shape took form and swelled upward, leaving the shallow earth's bowl, empty, barren of humans.

Brad awakened, a loud yell escaping his lips. His body jerked forward, restrained by a seatbelt. His ears popped.

Airborne! For Christsakes, he was airborne. To where? His eyes assessed everything. He was in a Sikorsky Jet, plush, customized, a luxury only royalty afforded. Over the bulkhead was an unmistakable emblem, one he hadn't seen in nearly forty years since the days in North Africa. *The Black Lion of the Desert!* This was the private property of Prince Youseff Ben-Kassir of Algeria!

"Bad dream?" Berna asked laughing, startling him. So, his guard—guardian?—was still with him. "Morphine and *gat* do take control and force you to travel in many directions," she said. "I trust the *houris* pleased you? The dreams usually produce the rarest demi-mondes."

"If I described what I saw, you wouldn't believe me," he hedged, struggling to get his bearings.

She tossed the M52 at him. "It's yours. Use it if you must when we land."

"May I remove the *jellaba*?" Berna nodded. "I suppose somewhere in this floating sky hotel there's a restroom?"

She pointed him in the right direction.

Moments later Brad critically examined his reflection in the mirror. He checked the gun and satisfied, he shoved it into his

222

waistband. He dashed cold water on his face. Was this a two-way mirror? He couldn't tell. He wiped his face and hands, and faking a dizzy spell turned his back to the mirror. He hunched over, sprang the watch clasp and breathed easier. The microfilm was intact. He bent over, feigning cramps. Another quick movement, checking the heel of his boot, assured him the Katz film was equally safe.

Guarded, always guarded, Brad laughed at the absurdity of his caution. Christ! Berna had saved his life! Greer's hairy warning demanded scrutiny, still it was Berna who yanked him out of that death trap! What role did she play in this impossible scenario? And now—out of a four-decade past—Prince Ben-Kassir!

He studied his reflection, the changes in his appearance. He was gaunt, tired, overstressed, fatigued. Pyramiding complications, totally incongruous characters playing out a stark drama, with him the target at center stage multiplied the dangers with frightening consistency. Fleeing a highly invisible enemy was worse than facing a visible battalion of well-armed soldiers on a battlefield! All this because he wanted to find the means to end global inhumanity.

Brad reset his aviator's glasses into place, and returned to his seat next to Berna. "I owe you my life," he began. "How do I repay you?"

"All in a day's work," she flipped, lighting a cigarette.

"You work for Greer? Is that it? Perhaps I should have enlisted him to run interference for me."

"You take all this calmly enough."

"*Calmly?* Inside my guts are twisting, ulcers screeching. Let's see, how many attempts does that make on my life? Three? Four?" He gazed below at the scorched, endless stretch of Libyan desert.

"You create death traps. The staggering price on your head entices sewer rats out of hiding."

"Does the staggering sum entice you, Berna? Or the others in *Corsican Coral*?"

"*Corsican Coral?*" She laughed, her brows arching in mocking scorn. "I trained with them, but the ties were severed, Major. *Corsican Coral* are freelancers. My oath is to one man. A man who raised me, educated in egalitarianism, epistemology, theology, morals, ethics, and oh, yes, the subtle, triple-edged sword of international politics."

223

"Sure. Fine. That's dandy. He turned you into an assassin and you worship the ground he walks on."

Berna stared at him momentarily speechless. "You dare make so unfair an assessment when you lack facts? Opinion and speculation do not ensure the truth. Complications fall at all sides of him. One creates a design, another performs—"

A light flashed in Brad's mind. He'd heard those words before! From Marnay, that night at the bistro. Brad interjected, *"But not according to the blueprints, rather a dangerous improvization resembling the original. Look close, you'll detect the forgery."*

She stared at him in silence.

"Someone quite dead spoke those words to me before his demise. I didn't understand then—I still don't."

"Marnay added a caveat, did he not? 'Beware the fanatical forces determined to keep you from Moufflon.' "

"Your life is in equal jeopardy if you know what I know."

"Danger and I are compatible." Berna stretched her long legs, kicked off her boots, wriggled her toes contentedly. "You amaze me. Greer insisted that by now, you'd know all the answers. You *don't*, do you? No . . . you don't. How you dallied in detours! In the pouring rain of Paris, up side streets, down darkened alleys, in and out of airports, hopping from one nation to the next, curiosity luring you closer to death. What drives you—a fixation with death?"

"No one *wants* to die."

"But you approach death as an enemy. It stalks you at every turn. Take time to let her join forces with you."

"Where are you taking me? What's our destination?" he snapped irked by her all-knowing attitude.

"You don't know the answer?"

"Black lions of the desert are a rarity. I've known only one. Is there a connection?"

"I see, answer a question by asking one. A boring tactic. Greer described your memory as photographic, infallible. He erred. If you had honed it, half the world would not be in pursuit."

"Forty years is half a lifetime," he muttered sotto voce. "How did you get caught up in this?"

"I owe it all to him. He took me under his wing, taught me everything." She gazed out the starboard window pensively.

224

"Including giving head? Then you are Greer's property?"

He accepted her disapproving look, but not her outburst of merriment. "Greer? I was not speaking of Greer!" She laughed. "You Americans! What a simple lot you are. You know nothing of life." She poured champagne for them. "What idiotic ideology you espouse! What a man does or does not do in his bedroom is not what makes that person a fine human being or a lout. No wonder your nation can be had. You do not know how to make the division between a man's politics and his sexual life." She shook her head in exaggerated disbelief.

"Tell me about the Marquis de Sade, *chere*!" he said pointedly.

"*Le Marquis de Sade*? You are the last person to preach morality! *Mon Dieu!* You have seen all sides to the coins of life!"

Brad bit back the desire to impart a few object lessons. "Berna, *chere*, that night in Lucerne, you determined to seduce me. You calculatingly accomplished your desires very efficiently."

"That night I did not seduce you. I merely relieved you of your tensions. Seduction, *mon cher*, is a two-way street; a symphony that unites two souls for a moment suspended in time. You attach too much importance to the act."

Brad turned from her, sipped the Perignon, his attention suddenly focused inward, rifling through the baffling information he had unearthed.

How had Wolfgang Katz's dossiers fallen under British MI jurisdiction? Why were the Soviets, French and British interested in records forty years old? Why later did U.S. Intelligence snoop around? When had Katz become a cause célèbre between the four-power Kommandatura reigning over Berlin? Why? . . . Why? . . .

Concatenate-Alpha had told him part of the story. The leaks to the Soviets came from the British. Why? Twenty fucking years of torture by the Reds—for what? His acquittal in 1946 from war crimes had ensured the rerouting of his files, those highly sensitive OSS files, to D.C. with subsequent burial in GAMMA 10.

But, someone had changed all that. Who had leaked information of Katz's sale back to the Americans in 1973? Who had intercepted the staff car? Who had access to the files? Who was powerful enough to push, pull, manipulate and control the strings? Wolfgang had told him—and he had not listened.

His only lead—*a man with colorless eyes!*

Brad considered. U.S. Army Intelligence had cleared Marta

and her husband Fritz. But the Cat's files on Wolfgang clearly stated he had three sons—no daughters! Why had Wolfgang lied to him? Or, after so many years, did Katz actually believe or want to believe he had a daughter? Brad knew that psychiatrists shooting Katz with a dozen or more mind-expanding drugs were able to induce psychosis or any state of dependency to achieve a desired result. The brain, its endless bag of tricks, could be forced to make adjustments and readjustments, depending upon stimuli. In Wolfgang's case the perfect tool had infiltrated his subconscious to create the belief in the existence of a daughter to compensate for the loss of a wife.

Mind-altered states, an often employed Company tool, were beyond Brad's ken, beyond his desire to participate, but not beyond his ability to recognize the apparatus in use. Foreign Intelligence agencies, experiencing growing pains of power in the expanding spheres of world influence, had forced the birth of highly sophisticated technologies to seduce the human brain. The methodologies were appalling.

One thing was clear, Brad thought. The same bloodied hands responsible for initiating the First World War had activated conspiracies to implement World War II, and at war's end had prepared for the final holocaust of the eighties. Those same hands had sealed Wolfgang's fate. The pity of it was those vicious men went unnamed—unidentified. Brad's only lead was a man with *colorless* eyes!

How extraordinary! *Colorless eyes!* The notion made him uneasy. He muttered above a whisper, yet loud enough for Berna's ears. "British based collaborators killing their own people? My people? Innocent people led to their death?"

"Collaborators killing their own people is nothing new. But Major Lincoln, you are squeezing the blood supply from my hand."

Startled, Brad glanced at her, released her hand abruptly, apology on his lips never uttered, for he was struck by another outpouring of thoughts. He locked himself in again, shutting her out.

Wolfgang had spoken one name . . . Mosha Bauer. It was the name of one of the terrorists who held him captive in 1973. The *Cat* had cited names, incidents and a rash of activities which burned vividly in Brad's mind. Still, this one man, this one name—Mosha Bauer, presented a disturbing point. What made

226

Mosha Bauer *special* to Brad was not the dossier on him, but its disappearance. According to the *Cat*, all records of his entire criminal career had been deleted from every law enforcement agency in Europe. Not INTERPOL, not BRITISH MI, not the French SDECE, nor the Italian Intelligence files contained a shred of evidence of the bloody assassin's rash of crimes. Interesting? Mosha Bauer's existence had been wiped off the face of the earth as if he had never existed.

That, Brad is real clout!

His head ached as the morphine wore off. He knew he was pushing too hard, that the data crammed into his head needed settling. Priorities existed: his life, above all. He came out of the tunneled thoughts and glanced below at the passing terrain. "Look! The Kasserine Pass!"

"Yes," Berna replied. "See there—beyond the mountains? We will be over Algeria in a few moments."

Brad turned to her, sobering. "You know a helluva lot. God, if only you knew a man with *colorless* eyes!" he muttered dispassionately, his voice trailing off. He admonished himself for speaking aloud.

"I do."

"*What?*

"Know a man with colorless eyes." She glanced at the flashing lights on the bulkhead, snapped her seatbelt on. "We are almost there, *mon ami*. Buckle up."

Chapter Fourteen

**ALGERIA
THE NEXT DAY**

HOUAHOURI BOUMEDIENNE AIRPORT CONTROLLERS cleared the Sikorsky jet to land. Taxiing to a private airstrip, the passengers deplaned and boarded a waiting Sikorsky helicopter.

Airborne in moments, the chopper followed the Mediterranean

coast to a private estate partially hidden by enormous date palms in a secluded cove of an isolated stretch of shoreline.

Bearded, armed sentries wearing cuffiahs manned enormous palace walls, watching the chopper land on the helipad adjacent to the villa, communicating with the pilot through hand-held receiver-transmitters.

"Come, follow me." Berna ordered. They headed through to a courtyard overwhelmed with lush foliage, colorful blooms, squawking macaws and parrots, chittering monkeys, all screeching in wild cacophony.

Berna led him through tiled, gilded porticos to the main villa. Beyond them, past a white sweep of sand, the azure sea was dotted with boats. A brown-skinned servant with enormous anthracite eyes appeared, bowed to Berna with extreme deference. Handed an envelope on a silver tray on entering the foyer, Berna broke the seal, eyes skirting the contents. *"Merde,"* she cursed softly. "Our host is away . . . pressing business. He'll return in three days."

"Why did you bring me here?"

"You need a rest. In addition, your objective, the reason for this insanity, is to meet with Moufflon. Youseff will arrange it."

"Ah! Then he is not a phantom . . . Good. But how—"

"Greer made the contact. We jockeyed pawns about to clear the way after the third attempt on your life."

Brad sizzled. *"He* had the clout to arrange this meeting at the outset? *Damn* him! *Damn* him to hell! Three needless deaths! Marnay!" he sputtered following Berna through the floral courtyard to the main villa. "Wolfgang! Samuels! My death runs!"

The setting was something right out of the fabled Arabian Nights: relics and artifacts of Phoenician, Carthaginian, Roman origins of Arab conquests and French Colonialism graced the high marbled walls; golden archways; open grillwork balconies; sparkling mosaic inlaid floors; low sofas and ebony tables; spacious water pools filled with turquoise waters and floating flowers; lush atriums overflowing with jewel-hued blooms; scented incense. It was intoxicating, opulence personified, but it failed to assuage Brad's fomenting displeasure. He could wring Greer's neck.

Berna paused before an open door, swung it wider. "A guest room. "You'll find shorts—trunks, whatever you need. Shaving supplies are in the adjoining bath. You burst with curiosity, *oui*?

228

Très bien. Meet me on the terrace in ten minutes we'll go for a swim. You are safe here. Take time to rest. You need it."

"How long must I remain?" His impatience, tinged by irritation was clear.

"Until Youseff—His Highness returns."

"Berna, I'm pressed for time. I'm overdue in Washington . . ." He stopped, hesitant. It still wasn't established whether Berna was *friend* or *foe*. "Why the disguise when we met?" he demanded.

"*Mon Dieu!* More questions? *Allez.* Can they not wait until we *both* relax?" She closed the door behind her, opened it again. "You are under Youseff's protection, Major. You will not be harmed else those responsible would not live to boast of their deed."

"Swell. That's great comfort," he said dryly. "It is a splendid retreat—"

"—for us, *cher.* Not to unwelcome intruders. Remember that."

Brad had seen Berna nude before; details of her near perfect body were imprinted in his memory. Clothing was mere adornment, at war with her sensuality. Naked, she possessed animal magnetism and a certain *joie de vivre.* It was the attitude, the way she held herself, her voice, and the way she moved her smoldering eyes to reflect every sensation she wanted to impart. She stood before a portable bar, wearing a hand-crocheted cyclamen pink string bikini bottom, so abbreviated it was barely noticed. Thick, lustrous, flaxen hair hung in spiraling coils below her shoulders; dark walnut eyes glistened with golden flecks in the sun; the legs, long, shapely. Her body was sun-kissed, tanned to a tawny bronze that was so appealing Brad felt a profound awakening, a moving seduction stirring his loins. His reaction was electric.

She beckoned him to the bar, a gold and crystal serving cart laden with wines, whiskeys, Scotch, cognac and brandy. Her slender fingers played over the assortment, her eyes questioned silently.

"Scotch on the rocks."

"*Voilà.*" She handed the drink to him and poured Lafite Rothschild for herself. "Your disturbance is obvious, your anxiety, infectious. We shall be here three, four days at best. If my presence disturbs you, I can lose myself in the palace."

"Fat chance," he chided, clinking glasses.

"Take your time. When you are ready to talk, I am but a moment away," she said, an ineffable smile playing at her lips. She kicked off her sandals, descended sand-swept stairs onto the beach to the sea.

Beyond her the famed Turquoise Coast under a dazzling crystalline sun reflected diamond facets on the whitecapped water crashing to shore. Gray and fawn-colored rocks plunged straight to the sea on both sides of them. Behind the palace, like a circle of protection, the *Corniche des Dahra* wound between high cliff, sea and forest. The setting was idyllic, marred only by constant reminders of danger—the armed sentinels posted about the private estate.

Brad watched her enter the water like a sea nymph. She was sensational, just perfect for him, now, when he needed her desperately.

They began quietly, strolling the hot sands, toasting their bodies to a deep honeyed amber. Brad hadn't realized the extent of his exhaustion. By the second day nature began to heal him, restoring the imperative *third-eye capabilities* so vital to men in his profession. He detached himself. There was no shop talk, no questions, no answer sessions. He wasn't ready, yet. Berna, understanding his need for solitude, didn't worry when he escaped into deep pockets of silence. She busied herself planning meals, moving about unobtrusively.

But not for a second did she escape his oblique scrutiny. Exciting facets abounded in her. He found her amusing, intelligent, logical, discreet. Baffled by her, awed in a sense, he wondered at the ease he felt with her here when he had mistrusted her at the outset, considered her dangerous. She was growing on him; with little effort he could ease her into his life.

He sat on the chaise on the hot sunny terrace contemplating the two personalities; one the formidible iceberg he met in Lucerne, sullen, unyielding, suspicious, retiring, coquettish, a downright Sheba of seduction; two, the warm, compassionate, attentive companion who innately sensed his needs before he did. Both, totally woman, fearless, tough, remarkably disciplined, who under live bullet-fire had demonstrated unique skill and exceptional courage. She'd saved his life.

What a woman! Enough to make Byron and Napoleon roll over in their graves, green with envy. She remained an enigma to Brad. Her effect on him was liquid fire coursing through his blood. He made no move toward her until the afternoon of the second day.

They strolled the isolated beach to the high walls and buoys marking the Prince's property at water's edge. An enormous tangerine sun reflected flaming waters, giving a glow to the earth and sky. Brad scooped up a handful of flat, smooth pebbles, flung them one at a time over the water, watching them skip over the jeweled surface before sinking from sight. He smiled, peering about, searching, listening. Finally he broke the silence. "How all this makes World War II seem so remote." He gestured widely with his hands. "Before the United States officially entered the war Greer and I came here gathering intelligence. I was stationed in London. In my off-time at Bletchley we wandered about North Africa. We knew a war would be fought in the area. See, there—beyond the yacht?" He pointed past the sleek luxury ship, the *Zhahara*, at anchor in the bay. "French and British man-of-wars dotted those waters like mosquitoes. Under their bellies, German U-boats maneuvered the waters like man-eating sharks, escaping depth charges hurled at them. God! What audacity! For a time they were incomparable, Berna. They led the Allies a merry chase. Thundering anti-aircraft guns, superior to any the world had seen—and *blitzkrieg!* What terror for those who experienced and lived through *blitzkrieg.*"

Brad sighed heavily. "It's all gone now, locked up in some strange time warp. The Germans are a forgotten people! Pity they were geniuses. Did you know Hitler had jet planes at the beginning and failed to develop them? He did. The real pity is if we human beings put our heads together there's no telling what miracles mankind might have uncovered. Why must it always be war?"

"The place reeks memories. Are they all bad for you?"

Brad shook his head, tossed the remaining pebbles into the sea, dusted off his hands. "Memories . . . images . . . sounds . . . utterly ridiculous nostalgia. You think me a fool?"

Berna lifted those smoldering eyes, her gaze unwavering. He reached out, drew her close into his arms, holding her, smelling and nuzzling her, the tingle of life stirring. "I've never forgotten you—that night at Greer's place, creeping down the stairs—awaking to find your head buried in me."

Berna, suddenly coy, flushed, her expression innocent, eyes

widening, roaming over his face like a gentle caress. Her head tilted back, away from him. She studied his expression. ''What a strange man you are—full of contradictions.''

''And you act like a virgin.'' He laughed, amused with her.

''Once lost, innocence cannot be found. If I act virginal, it is not in the way you mean.''

''Be what you are. Admit you've given me a few bad moments. It was *you* I saw at the Crazy Horse in Paris the night Marnay died?''

''No! You are in error.'' She turned abruptly, slid from his arms and ran toward the terrace, scuffing up flurries of sand with her bare feet. He ran after her, catching her, pulling her toward him and kissed her longingly, achingly, in breathless silence.

The backdrop was storybook magic, the only sounds, waves crashing on the shore, punctuated by rapid heartbeats, short gasps between protracted mouth-swallowing kisses.

Moments later, they tumbled together on an oversized bed, making love, releasing pent-up emotions. Brad ravaged her, unable to stop himself. New, uncharacteristic experiences coursing through him came at the *right* time, erupted and he was unlike he'd ever been before, moving over her skillfully, unaware of the venting of his deeply rooted needs, aware only that he wanted her totally as he'd never craved a woman in his life. For Berna the release was curiously incomparable, firing her senses. To be desired subliminally and be taken up wholly by a man overwhelmed her. Together they moved in infinite pleasure, locked in the sensation of the moment.

''It was paradise,'' he muttered huskily, holding her close.

''*Mon Dieu, cher!* Paradise is a place with many exits but no entrances.''

Jarred back to reality, he insisted they go for a swim.

Later, over champagne and Beluga caviar, Brad stroked her face gently, resurrecting a time-worn cliche. ''How did a nice girl like you fall prey to evil, sinister men?''

''Don't call me a *nice* girl. I find my companions neither evil or sinister!'' she snapped defensively, moving away. She stormed through the palace, past aviaries filled with cooing white doves and exotic lovebirds.

Brad couldn't be angry. He didn't know her well enough to take umbrage at her histrionics. ''You're a miracle worker—a regular Florence Nightingale,'' he cooed after her, maneuvering the mood to a lighter vein. He caught up with her along the corridor leading to the library. "For a man whose atrophied brain and body bounced back to life at your touch, I am humbly grateful." She glared at him. He fell into step alongside her, past fountains splashing perfumed waters into lower turquoise pools floating water lilies.

"How much of my business do you know?" he asked quietly.

"Enough to label you insane or suicidal for working alone."

They were in the library now, a massive man's room, adorned with animal heads, furry skins, soft, comfortable luxuriously crafted sofas and ebony tables. Tall, high-ceiling walls were filled with portraits of Prince Ben-Kassir's ancestors, kings, emperors, American Presidents, Allied Generals Patton, Montgomery, Eisenhower and de Gaulle. Brad stopped abruptly, his focus intent on the portrait of a woman with hair the color of a fiery sunset, eyes of crushed viridian jewels. It was Valentina Varga Lansing! Berna, cautious, brows arched questioningly, spoke up. "You *know* her." Not a question, a statement.

"I'm not certain," he lied. "Who is she?"

"A woman of mystery. No one will identify her. But I know," she muttered with a whisper of petulant indignation. "Lovers. They were lovers once." She pointed to a tall, handsome man in the uniform of a British major. The visor of his cap fell in a shadow over his lean good looks. "Countless others adorn his study in Corsica, *and* in Paris! I'd give anything if he looked at me with the same eyes he has for her."

Brad, surprised at her candor, blurted, "You love him!"

"All my life. As a baby he bounced me on his knee. As a child I grew up adoring him. As an adult, he patronizes me, treats me as a child. My love progresses nowhere."

"You love a man who exposes you to incredible dangers? Places you in jeopardy each moment you live?" He bridled angrily, aware he repeated himself, and that incurred more wrath.

She countered savagely. "I warned you not to judge matters about which you are ignorant. You think you are any different?" Her wrath steamrolled him. "The only difference is in the color of the flag we salute. Man is a pathetic, gullible creature, too lazy to learn for himself what being human means; he lets others wind up his brain—think for him. The tragedy of our world, *mon cher*, is man's apathy. It is the reason—what is the word? your American word that describes so much? Ah, *fucked-up*. The

233

world is fucked-up, *oui?* One *real* man stands out among all others and he is attacked.''

Brad sidestepped her verbal line of fire, struggling to conceal his amusement. ''I know *why* the world is fucked up. Do you? Terrorism merely compounds the sickness.''

''*Mon Dieu!*'' she exasperated. ''You cannot be so stupid! You? Counterinsurgency! Covert operations is your life! OSS! CIA! NSA! You are not to be believed. Such words from a *specialist?*''

''You've done your homework well. Did Greer unveil my entire life?''

''Terrorism!'' She mocked derisively, engaged in audacious tirade. ''Terrorism is a desperate need by desperate people, as old as civilization itself. If there were no wicked, evil men, there would be no terrorists. It is a tool of the people to fight tyranny! Despotic governments do exist in this progressive twentieth century and deserve to be toppled. Without the will and support of the people, terrorism could not exist. Oh, *merde!* This is ridiculous!'' She scurried about the room picking up objects, replacing them to appease her frustration. She spun around, livid. ''We are both sophisticated enough to know the world is in chaos. The plaguing question is: how to remedy the situation. To that I shall address myself later. *Allors, s'il vous plait,* I shall see to dinner.'' She stormed from the room muttering a string of French curses, leaving in their wake a smiling man.

Brad poured himself a double Scotch and sank heavily into a deeply cushioned chair. Some trigger-word had set her off. Brad smiled, suddenly tired. He relaxed as mass emotions fell upon him. He had exceeded himself in the bedroom earlier—but what a way to go.

He laid his head back, closed his eyes listening to sounds; cooing birds, zephyring sea breezes, breakers on shore, a distant horn from a passing fishing vessel and voices . . . soft, whispering voices lulled him.

So much had happened. Plucked from near fatality in Cairo, he'd had neither the time nor strength to guess at the identity of his would-be assassins. Berna promised answers to some of his mystifying questions. But thus far he'd succeeded only in firing her indignation, incurring her rancor and a verbal whiplash of condemnation. What a strange bird—Berna. She disturbed him.

234

What he didn't understand eventually disturbed him and he pondered. Who was she, really?

Her relationship with Prince Ben-Kassir was curious. Permitted free run of his palace, servants, air power and men? Such liberties seldom sprang from casual acquaintanceships. Rankled, jealousy sprang from dark corners of his mind, increasing his displeasure.

Jealousy . . . His eyes snapped open, he turned slightly, gazing across the room to Valentina Lansing's portrait. Something was shaping in his mind, disquieting him. Holes existed in his memory where none should exist. He sipped the Scotch, quietly assembling his thoughts. Questions formed, faded swiftly. Gaps of information eluded him.

Brad realized that the possibility of accomplishing the impossible before he returned to D.C. lay in scrupulously examining every piece of the giant puzzle. Could he wrangle newborn strategy to tie the ends together before he met with the President? *Dammit!* Where the bloody hell was Youseff Ben-Kassir? His Royal Highness? He was getting better, his thinking cleared. Yet, he was so tired . . .

Brad awakened two hours later, lured by aromatic scents of succulent food. He showered, shaved, slipped into fresh shorts and sandals, made his way to the terrace where Berna and dinner awaited. He ate ravenously.

Berna drifted into congenial patter. Brad attempted to isolate the feelings he felt for her, tried desperately to define them, but they eluded him or else they were indefinable emotions.

Over Remy-Martin and coffee he treaded lightly, taking the first concrete step after the earlier rift. She interrupted him from time to time, asking questions he should have asked himself. But as he listened, he witnessed the unfolding of a remarkable woman, a multifaceted woman of unique abilities.

"Youseff will not be coming. He is detained by previous commitments, and empowers me to brief you on recent events and speak on his behalf." Berna sipped her demitasse. "Your presence in Europe creates numerous complications. Moufflon is inaccessible to you through usual channels." Brad blinked hard. "Your government must initiate the move. . . . You don't understand," she added, catching his disappointment. "Permit me to explain. Too many factions, observing any meetings between you and Moufflon, might jump the gun, upset the timetable.''

"*Timetable!* . . . A timetable does exist?'' He knew it! His assessment was proving correct!

"I promise, Major—''

"Brad.''

"—to clear all doubts before you depart.'' She commenced. "You extracted sensitive data from *Concatenate—Alpha.*''

"You continue to astound me.'' He was unable to mask astonishment.

"Presently, Clayallee 10 authority and other potentially dangerous sources are combing the continent for the spectral Milford Race Meadows who tapped the *Cat*'s brain, using what has been confirmed in Washington as forged TAC. Nice job of sabotage. You are a real professional,'' she applauded him. Brad seized the opening.

"Berna, tell me what you know. It would simplify matters. We are on the same side, are we not?''

She gave him a look that could mean anything. "Patience. You will find *Colorless Eyes* soon enough. First, Youseff suggests you return to your President, submit only that which *must* be submitted, and be circumspect at every step. *Comprenez-vous?*''

"You imply dangers exist in the Oval Office?''

"Eyes and ears of subversives have infiltrated the White House. Some are among the President's most trusted advisors.''

Brad's brows arched cynically and dropped. "Swell.''

"Take caution. They maintain low profiles, and influence the puppets placed high in government. They are not the quote, unquote, 'terrorists' who risk life, limb and property,'' she said with a smack of sarcasm. "They are powerful financiers, hiding under protective umbrellas of respectability. Major—uh, Brad— their power is they *hold* paper. *Comprenez-vous*? Mortgages, loans, and so forth. In their minds are birthed the bloody coups orchestrated directly from Zurich, Basel and Geneva. The actual bloodletting is left for the *animales,* and *mechanics,* the robot psychotics who perform like windup toys.''

"Marnay—''

"—Marnay? *Mon Dieu!* Greer is correct. It is some fixation you have for him! The man was weak, totally unsuitable—''

"So he was wasted?''

Berna paused patiently. "No one connected to Moufflon killed

236

Marnay. The invisible power hierarchy from Zurich contracted his death. Greer set you straight. Marney was innocuous. On the other hand, Wolfgang Kaltenbrunner—''

Brad's attention riveted on her, critically.

''—is another story.'' She puffed on a Turkish cigarette.

Brad, unnerved at her disclosure, poured champagne. *She called Katz by his right name—Kaltenbrunner!*

''Do you know why Marnay was wasted by the *invisibles?* They wanted what Russia, France, Britain and the United States failed for four decades to obtain. What you finally obtained—the damaging records from Kaltenbrunner! Marnay was their link to Katz. As a member of the French Resistance, he knew intimately what followed after the war ended; his access to records within the SDECE was invaluable . . .''

Brad's features were unreadable, solidified in thought. *So they thought—whoever they were—he had obtained Wolfgang's precious records? He had not! He had succeeded in locating them— presently buried in GAMMA 10 at the Pentagon. Brad still didn't know whether or not he needed the actual records, yet. He had accumulated enough to make his point in the Oval Office—hadn't he?*

Berna was still speaking. Brad listened intently. ''With your permission may I recapitulate Wolfgang's plight? In 1973, after twenty years Wolfgang had outridden the storm. The Soviets, bored with him, sold him to the United States in West Berlin. Wolfgang had triumphed. He had kept his bargain with America, with you, the OSS. His reward—freedom, at long last. But the odyssey of Wolfgang Kaltenbrunner began long before 1973. Much died with him, a great deal was conveyed to you. But in 1973, no longer a forgotten man, he was groomed, transported to Checkpoint Charlie under heavy KGB escort. The exchange was made. One hundred thousand dollars—American—for the former Nazi officer. *Voilà!* He boarded the Army staff car. Across the street two KGB agents disguised as West Berliners sat in a parked V.W. bus observing the transaction.''

''Wolfgang never mentioned this.''

''How could he? He knew nothing of the KGB's curiosity. Think! What crossed their clever Soviet minds? *A hundred thousand dollars American for a senile old man?* Without the usual negotiations for a lesser amount? Bargaining always accompa-

237

nied such deals—but not in this case. *Why?* How curiously whetted were those Russian mentalities, eh?"

Brad and Berna strolled along the beach, a midnight-blue sky overhead, studded with brilliant starpoints, a lemon-sherbet moon for light. She continued, editing as she spoke:

Wolfgang's destination became infinitely vital to the Soviets. Their original assessment of Katz's value, now, two decades later, could not be ignored. But no one, not the Americans nor the KGB, could speculate on the fate awaiting the German. Something went wrong. Wolfgang recalled driving along the Kurfurstendamm, electrified at the changes of twenty years, bewildered by the unfamiliar. Then a feeling of terror permeated his senses. Living through two decades of torture by his wits had signaled dangers. Suddenly the staff car lurched, swerved off to the right of the *Strasse*. Another U.S. staff car pulled across its bow, obstructing it. In whirlwind action, Katz, forced out of the car, was shoved into the second. It took off like a rocket. Katz was blindfolded. "For security measures," he was told by these men.

Security for what? Who knows Katz after twenty years? He got no answers. He was taken to an apartment in the older section of West Berlin in the British sector. The blindfold was removed. Katz stared at the soldiers. The Americans had paid for him—but these were *not* Americans! He saw hatred and arrogance in their eyes and knew them at once. They were his enemies.

His enemies had lain in wait for twenty years, now they would eat him alive! They began politely asking discreet questions, progressing impatiently to mental and physical abuse. He refused foods, certain they contained drugs, perhaps poison. He fell back into the same posture he assumed with the Soviets, using the same tool—senility.

There were six captors, five were subordinates, and one was an egomaniacal man with animal instincts and superior brain—who possessed nearly *colorless eyes*. Yes, Major, he is the real power behind all this world unrest. A crafty, egocentric who came and left the apartment often, and for a time disguised his loathing of Katz.

Somehow an error was made. For some unfathomable reason they mistook Katz for a Jew! Katz failed to clear this confusion for fear his real identity would move his abductors to more horrible atrocities than what was ultimately done to him. Attempts to break Katz failed, all seductions were foiled by Katz's well-practiced bewilderment.

Colorless Eyes took pains to paint pictures of a heavenly valley, riches at the end of a rainbow, a new life free from care and worry. He soothed Katz, smiled on him as a fellow Jew who knew well the feeling of being compromised. Since Katz had failed to disclose his secrets to the Soviets, it stood to reason he had endured torture to preserve and turn over the precious documents to his fellow Jews. "The mark of a true Jew! A true Zionist!" *Colorless Eyes* boasted of Israel's accomplishments since Statehood had flowered. He impressed upon Katz the value of such documents to be used as a bludgeoning instrument against an anti-Semitic world where the Jews had been persecuted for centuries. *"Soon, the world will pay for the deaths done to millions of Jews!"* Not only those killed in World War II but for all time. Now, Katz need only reveal the location of the records—he need not be involved in the theft.

Katz wanted to shout, "Lies! . . . Lies! . . . Lies!" But he couldn't jeopardize his position by feigning anything but total senility. He wondered, where were the Americans who had paid his ransom? Would they search for him? Or had the purchase for him been negotiated by *these* men? Had they fooled the KGB? Lured them by willingly paying so dear a price for him? Katz's fears multiplied.

Under the mask of incoherency, Katz memorized their faces, each were traced indelibly upon his mind. Intrigued by, and as fearful as he became, of the colorless-eyed titan, he noted the homage and extreme deference paid him by one man in particular whom he identified later to our contacts as Mosha Bauer. But before he had managed to escape he was hideously tortured. Invectives were hurled at him; he was labeled a collaborator who had sacrificed his fellow Jews for records he refused to surrender. His pretense—passing for a German among Germans at a time it had been unpopular to be a Jew—hadn't fooled them. When they finished with him, they admonished, he would never forget he was a Jew!

They were on the terrace again. Brad opened a fresh bottle of Lafite. "And so they branded him," he said flatly, flashing on the ugly mass of keloiding he'd seen and filmed. He poured the frothy amber liquid into iced glasses. "These same men, *Colorless Eyes*, were among the same men who pressured him at Nuremburg, coercing him to falsely testify. But you say that *Colorless Eyes* failed to recall Wolfgang's true identity? A man of *his* calibre guilty of memory failure? Uh-uh! I don't buy it."

"Such curiosities occur periodically, proving that man is not infallible. Only in fiction do the facts tie up neatly. In life?" she shrugged, then continued. "Recall the *Cat's* readout. S.S. General Ernst Kaltenbrunner succeeded Reinhard Heydrich. A caveat appeared not to mistake Ernst for Wolfgang, *oui?* General Kaltenbrunner, an avowed Jew-hater, turned his back on the Buchenwald corruption, thereby incurring the wrath of the Jews. Moufflon believes the confusion over the names occurred."

"And Wolfgang, assuming I knew his real identity, failed to enlighten me in that aspect." Brad reflected, jumping ahead. "Why, tell me, why does Wolfgang become pivotal to my purpose here? It still isn't clear to me."

Berna sipped the remains of champagne, excused herself, returned moments later carrying a leather briefcase. She dialed several numbers on the combination lock and it sprang open. She dug out a manila file, placed it on the case on the low table before her.

Brad watched her, flashing on the name Mosha Bauer again, the assassin whose files were deleted from INTERPOL. He'd been one of Wolfgang's persecutors. Interesting.

"The woman, Marta, was not Katz's daughter. Both she and Fritz cleared security on General Samuels' signature."

"Patient assassins."

"You know?"

"I believe Katz was made to believe the existence of a daughter through drug induction—he needed to believe in something."

Berna seemed impressed, then went on. "In time, Marta might have succeeded. But your presence panicked them, and by foiling their monitoring devices, they assumed the worst—that Katz had confided in you. Buttons were pushed. Calls via clandestine channels exposed your assignment as covert. D.C. denied involvement. The denial itself proved you guilty—that you were with Katz to uncover his secret. I know . . . I know . . . your next question is, how do I know all this?

"Someone else had tapped into Marnay's recording device at the bistro. Your identity was known at once, your cover blown even as you paraded through the Paris rain. The identity was forwarded to Marta and Fritz. They learned about you through Katz in measured sums, but enough to check your dossier with General Samuels. And so, *mon ami*, measures were drafted to terminate you, after pirating the information Katz gave you."

Berna poured more champagne while Brad leaned forward, staggered by the explanation. "So, we come to General Mark Samuels. The General dispatched the African to dismantle the jamming devices at the Katz farmhouse, unaware of Marta's efforts to retract from you what Katz gave you—"

"If he gave me anything, it was destroyed in the bombing."

"Perhaps she saw the KGB and fled. We are uncertain in this. In any event, you were saved by the very assassin hired to waste you. The African. Then, again, the unpredictable. Explosions, injuries to you. Rushed to sick bay, to face near annihilation by *Llamas*. How incredibly you managed to foil *Llamas* you must tell me, later. You escaped his clutches, and were rescued by the African, whose job it became to extract Katz's secret from you. Whatever you had working for you, Yankee, saved you, miraculously. Then, once again, you navigated into perilous waters—General Samuels' domain. A piranha, that one," she shuddered, for the first time reacting to the events.

"Who killed Samuels?"

"You won't believe it. Even I needed substantiating evidence before the pieces fell together. The KGB."

"*What!*"

Berna shrugged. "I told you you wouldn't believe it."

"How the bloody devil. . . ? What stakes do the KGB have in Katz?" He asked the question, needing facts to back his own theory.

"Why would any nation's intelligence community seek the truth?"

"ALL RIGHT! The question was naive! The KGB ordered Samuels' death. Who pulled the trigger?"

"For the record?"

"Yes, dammit, for the record and any own edification!"

"Aren't you going to ask why they ordered Samuels killed?"

241

Brad felt the question even as she asked. He nodded in pantomime.

"To keep you from being killed."

"Me? . . . ME? . . . Why should the KGB care if I survive or die?"

"You are important. A vital part of an interesting mosaic. Moufflon assessed your intrinsic worth at once. Accordingly, he has made your path less turbulent than it might have been without him."

Brad grimaced balefully. "Very well, we have a new mystery. Now, who wasted Samuels?"

Berna smiled wanly. "You will never pass an adjutant outside a general's office again without exercising more caution than you did that morning. Perhaps it was the early hour. You don't remember? Dear Major Lincoln, the adjutant was *Llamas*, the assassin you foiled in surgery!"

Amused by his obvious disconcertment, Berna lighted a cigarette, sipped her champagne, taking a momentary breather.

"Two separate contracts on me? And he made no move to nail me in Samuels' office?" He tilted his head, his skepticism clear.

She held up three fingers. "Three contracts. Following his aborted attempt, he was paid exorbitantly *not* to exercise the first contract."

"Who negotiated the first?"

"General Samuels. You threatened their project with Katz," she said calmly.

"The United States? *My* government?" Expressions of belief stabbed at him.

"Negative, Brad. The United States isn't involved in Samuels' dirty business. He's a pawn of Geneva and Zurich, long a suspect in the business of laundering dirty funds for the illegal purchase of arms and ammunitions and nuclear arsenals for certain nations in the Middle East." She held up a restraining hand. "Don't ask me to brief you. It's not my bailiwick of expertise. Moufflon can and will do so at the proper time. I am responsible only for imparting certain data to you. *Llamas* infiltrated Samuels' command post under KGB directives three months ago to get close to him. He became the General's factotum, confidant and aide. They—uh—shared—"

"Homosexual perversions and proclivities," Brad interjected. "I didn't think you Europeans blushed over sexual matters."

242

She clucked her tongue and moved to a fast forward. "Samuels belongs to Zurich. Your disappearance following submission to Intelligence interrogation caused flurries of worry in all Berlin sectors. In East Berlin the KGB and Soviet hierarchy went crazy. They pulled strings to locate you. When hotel registers indicated no trace of a Major Lincoln or Benjamin Lord, the professionals surmised you'd adopted a new cover. An associate of Moufflon sent out feelers, transmitted his findings, and the network went into operation. They found you. Transmitted news of Samuels' death and you handled it well.

"And then one night, in the wee hours of the morning, a sophisticated computer on top of a Corsican mountain intercepted your trespass of *Concatenate-Alpha*. The *Cat*, Major, is a microbe compared to the colossus in Corsica."

Brad paced the terrace, allowing the sea breezes to cool his indignation. He was speechless. Big Brother was upon us in spades!

"The moment you requested data, Moufflon's technicians activated powerful neutralizing electromagnetic fields, jamming the signals preventing anyone else from stumbling onto the trespass digitals. Simultaneous to your receipt of all extracted data from the Cat, a readout of the same data appeared on the Corsican computers. Moufflon was alerted at once, and aware of your formidible m.o. in coding ciphers and Ultra at Bletchley Park, ferreted the rest. He ordered the Code Red Alert to flash across the Cat's screen. He could only jam for so long. Wisely you terminated, passed through security with the decoy dupes— *OPERATION BARBAROSSA*—intact. Ten minutes longer. . . ? A computer high atop a Zurich mountain would have picked up the jamming alert. Your exit would have been obstructed."

Berna paused a moment. "I have learned a great deal from studying your m.o. One—this is certain—you have none. You are inconsistent."

"Consistency in my profession terminates careers. The rule is: *do* the unexpected. Never be where you *are* expected."

"I gathered as much. Paris. London. Rome. Why Cairo?" she probed.

"Why not? One place is as good as another."

"You don't trust me. Still? Never mind. I'll tell you. Doors slammed in your face where you least expected them, you arrived in Cairo to confer with Major General Mustafa Abu-Qir.

243

When I lost you at the Cairo Airport, I called Greer. He figured it on the button: that you'd stay at Abdul Gamal Bassam's flat, a conduit from World War II days. What you learned may or may not be as important as your purpose in Youseff's villa now. It is for you to decide." She handed him the file. "For you, from a friend. Moufflon. These are Wolfgang's records—now you'll know why Katz was pivotal to your global meanderings. There was more, the real reason for the terror permeating his reasoning. Katz had records of a massive cover-up; records of atrocities by *collaborators* who permitted the unsuspecting Jews to be sacrificed in the camps without lifting a helping hand."

Brad spun around. He stared at Berna as he had stared at Katz when he first heard the story. Curious sensations rushed his senses. Berna's voice cut into these feelings.

"Katz worked with Moufflon. Unable to locate the records you cryptically filed, cross-filed and buried in some catacomb, he began to reconstruct from memory what he chronicled four decades ago."

"The records, if published—"

"—might not do the damage done by those who covet the information, to distort the truth and so augment a frightening apparatus of power. Now do you understand why you are targeted for death? With such records he can rewrite history, control all global machinations."

"Who?"

"Colorless Eyes!"

It sank in, and turned his stomach queasy. But something was happening to Brad Lincoln, who once, long ago, was Yosel Burnbaum. For the first time in years he thought of his mother, father, brothers with whom he'd made no contact—none at all.

"You traveled the length and breadth of Europe to test the reality of nuclear war, unaware how close you are to the answers you seek. You've stumbled upon the perpetrators and are unable to identify them. You will never be able to identify them, Major. Only one man makes miracles—one man alone—Moufflon."

"You ask me to trust a man who has no past before 1950?"

"How do I respond? It was before my time."

Brad winced. "How young you really are."

She didn't want to hear how young she was. She had a role to play. "Pity, Greer isn't here to run interference for you. You need an SOD specialist to keep the other *animales* away."

"Greer is in no position to expose himself." Brad felt relaxed as he poured two glasses of champagne.

"I know, Greer's presence is simply a hedge against possible assassination—to provide you with needed support."

"I repeat, he is in no position to expose himself."

"And I agree. How about me?"

"How about you—what?"

"Let me be the hedge against any ambitious assassin."

He stared at her. His expression wrathful.

"*Très bien! Ca va bien!* Forget it! The offer was made, your scowling looks declined. It shall be reported so. You are free to leave whenever you desire. Shall we spend this last night as friends?"

"Just like that. I am free to leave. No more briefings?"

"*Oui.* One more. It will wait until your departure. Whatever else you hear, believe, Brad, Moufflon does not see the final battle of mankind between democratic good and communist evil. Liberation from myths, stereotype and fanaticism is man's only salvation. Man must be free of tyrants, despots who impose their will in low-level conspiracies."

"I accused you of dealing in low-level conspiracies," he snapped.

"I refuted you," she countered. "At the right time you will be presented with the logistics of the conspiracy—and you will be staggered." Berna unhooked her halter, stepped out of her shorts and stood before him, naked. "Join me if you wish."

Join me if you wish! Hadn't he made himself clear yesterday, the day before, even today? She hadn't ignored his hunger earlier that day.

In the moonlight she ran to the sea. Brad turned on the stereo equipment just inside the terrace door and music filled the night air. He stepped out of his shorts, and toting blanket, Lafite-Rothschild and two fluted glasses, followed her. A short distance from shore he dropped the blanket, propped the bottle and glasses into the sand and ran to the sea, swimming toward the moonlit body bobbing up and down on the waves.

He sliced expertly through calm, silvery waters, catching up to her. Her attempts to elude him failed. Succumbing at last to his strength, she cupped his wet, cool face, kissed him, her trembling body firing his. He locked her arms around his neck and swam her piggyback to shore. They frolicked in the shallows for a time, then, Brad picked her up, carried her to the blanket, laying her on it tenderly. She looked up at him.

"Shall we fuck again? As we did earlier?"

For answer, Brad covered her mouth with his. Her breasts swelled, heaved, trembled acutely as she came to full passion.

In the moonlight he saw it—the scar—Corsican Coral. It no longer disturbed him. He touched it, lightly, caressed it with his hot tongue. Instantly Berna's hand guided his tongue elsewhere, his hand to a hot, pulsing cunt caressing the tight curls and velvety lips. She felt cool to the touch, while inside her burned a brightly stoked fire.

"Twice in one day? Why wouldn't you let me love you the first day?" he drew her closer to him.

"You didn't need me as you did today and now."

"Are you always so accommodating? Do you know all the answers?"

"Yes." She apologized softly, electrifying him with sultry eyes; he melted inside. "At times I wish—" Her words were silenced, covered by eager lips over her.

Brad held her tighter, closer, skillful hands exploring, stimulating, kneading her throbbing breasts gently. He felt the subtle restraint once again, her hand over his, reguiding his hands or lips elsewhere when he made contact with her left breast. Later, much later, he would be forced to recollect this oddity and when he did it would be too late.

Now, body trembled ecstatically against body, both inflamed with passion. She was shaking, quivering in climactic spasms. Brad's urgency was such he permitted her to engineer the scene against his macho inclinations. His tenderness was such, she gasped wantonly, his artistry, impeccable. Berna pulled herself atop his warm body, straddling him. Thoughts subordinate to feelings hung suspended, emotions rode herd in full acquiescence, both intoxicated by erotic sensuality. He gave her head to do what she desired; she was willful, demanding, insatiable.

Berna, a strong-willed, aggressive feline, controlled her sexual needs as she controlled her life. She performed magnificently, using slow, precise, studied, erotic movements, riding him as she might a champion stallion. She knew *what* to do, *when*, *how* and sensed precisely the *right* moments to pull back to stimulate his desire.

Release came in torrents, and Berna's frenzy unleashed exquisite delight. She climbed to plateaus of multiple climaxes, shuddering from one to the next ecstatically. Brad's body arched in a final thrust, his eyes fired; he writhed, twisted, groaned deeply in his throat. Pretense and resolve shattered, a delicious euphoria embraced them. Berna shoved the damp, curly tendrils of hair from her flushed face and curled up guilelessly in his arms like a baby fox cub; a vixen.

"Sex reduces everything to the lowest common denominator," he whispered huskily, holding her tighter. "How easily everything falls into perspective . . . God! You are beautiful!"

She laid against his heart unable to still her own until earthly senses returned and with them awareness; sounds of breakers on shore, rustling palm trees, musical phrases of birds, lingering night fragrance of desert blooms. Suddenly chilled, she raised up on an elbow, poured champagne, sipped from her glass. "In the desert you become mindless, affected by eternity," she whispered softly, absorbing the curious luminosity of the moon against the midnight sky.

Brad, fully awake, stared at vast formations and shadings of fiery lights around the moon, listening to revivals of old ghosts.

"You think we'll take refuge up there soon?" she asked.

Reality struck him full force, crash-landing him to earth. What was he thinking? Fully pleasured by this half-nymph, half-killer, he was patching together a future for them. A few more seconds and he might have wrangled her back to D.C. with him.

"You're too young for me," he said sternly in an extension of his thoughts. "Someone closer to your age would be more suitable."

"Suitable for what?" Perplexed, then understanding, a shadow of a smile flickered over her face. "To build a life? Make babies? Perpetuate this insanity? What will happen has already begun. How can two people attempt to build a life on the knowledge we both share? You Americans! You anticipate the future with dedicated ferocity and fail to enjoy each day. What life is so sparkling, what is so fragrant and intoxicating as life lived moment by moment?"

His earlier exhilaration deflated. Brad felt the fool who had roamed the earth and saw nothing. He watched her gulp champagne wantonly, tilt her head back, stretch her body to the moon. In a quick movement, Berna turned the champagne bottle on him, spilling the amber liquid over his body. Flinging the bottle from her, she pressed her face against his wetness. About to protest, Brad, thoroughly galvanized, shuddered pleasurably.

She had surpassed herself and now created new designs in his memory to be relived at a later date.

A mad rush of images and jealous daggers struck at his heart. *Who had enjoyed her before this? Stop the crazy thinking! The excitement you feel is due to the perfection of her skills. Enjoy her! Enjoy every precious moment. God only knows if there'll be more.*

Before emotion annihilated thought, he raised himself on one elbow, watching her bring him to full power. The vixen! She delighted in it, derived pleasure and power from control! Why resist?

"Let me give you equal pleasure, *man petite*." Attempts to shift positions, take control, increased her frenzy. "Oh, Christ! Christ! . . . You are something . . ." Her lips, tongue, expert fingers sent him into orbit. He ejaculated vigorously like a howling animal in heat. He felt as if his soul has left his body and from the lofty heights looked down on Berna and himself in a frenzy of tangled arms and legs, floating down to earth, spiraling, sinking into the sands.

He was silent until his heartbeats subsided. Then thoughts pierced the euphoria. "Berna, what does *MONDO XX* mean?"

She stiffened, tensed, lifted herself off his body, her hands pressed against her face, brushing back the coiled wisps of hair.

"Qu'est-ce que c'est que?"

He repeated, *"MONDO XX*. Engraved on a gold paperweight in Katz's study."

"Kaltenbrunner had the globe? He showed it to you? It was his? *Oui*? Where did it come from?"

"Yes . . . No . . . We had no time to discuss it."

"You have seen such a globe before?" She fished about for a hashish cigarette. Brad shook his head. He lighted the smoke for her. "Did you look carefully at it?" She puffed nervously, inhaling deeply.

"Yes. Half of Africa was missing. Portions of North America, too."

At once aloof, she spoke economically, her eyes darting about the darkness like an skittish animal. "Translated, the words read: GLOBAL 2000. It is a plan conspired by the power cartel to rid the earth of two hundred million inhabitants. Simply, genocide."

"Decent of them to permit us to live to the year 2000."

"You think it to be humorous? It is not."

"Yet you offered to swim along with me in perilous waters."

"I could help."

"Negative . . . Not because you wouldn't be appreciated. Christ, you've tied a mass of loose ends together into a neat package. You've saved my life and precious time."

"Why not, then? You make no sense."

"You won't laugh? I think I love you. It's never happened like this before. I feel like a child—"

Berna's mood altered noticeably. She stopped, placed a finger to his lips, cocked her head, listening acutely. Brad stopped, caught the expression on her face, and caught up in her mood, he rose to his feet, pulled her up. "Come. Let's go inside."

Leaving everything on the beach, they moved wordlessly toward the terrace, scaling the steps. Brad hesitated, he reached for the terry robe on the terrace chair to wrap around her.

It was the *wrong* move at the *wrong* time.

Berna saw the spurts of blood erupt like craters on Brad's chest and shoulders long before she heard the shots. Two split the night air, muffled by the darkness. Two more shots, then silence as she pulled Brad to the terrace floor and fell spread-eagled over him protectively. She did not move. Her trained ears identified at once. *Merde! A Dragunov sniper's rifle!* With telescopic sights able to pick a man off at 900 meters!

Très bien, Bernadette. What use is this vast knowledge of international weaponry to you, now?

She leaped off Brad's body, snaked swiftly, cautiously across the terrace, entered the main salon, flipped off the light switches, thrusting the room in darkness. She tripped a series of alarms, and crouching low crept back to Brad's body in the darkness. She tugged at the terry robe, mentally counting down, three . . . two . . . one . . . She tugged the sash into a knot. NOW!

Blinding floodlights shot up into the dark sky. Droning alarms shrieked piercingly, alerting the palace staff. A chopper's rotors overhead caught Berna's attention. She retreated into the shadows, dragged Brad's body inside, locking the terrace doors behind her.

She fell to her knees over Brad, listened for heartbeats, felt his pulse, and biting deeply into her lower lip, turned him over gently on his back. He was unconscious, but alive!

Servants scurried to her side. Taking full charge, Berna snapped orders in Farsi. Behind them, nervous security guards rushed in, confused by the unexpected catastrophe, muttering landslide excuses. "We saw them! Yes, we did. Did you identify the chopper? Not even with telescopic sights in floodlighted night, nor by radar," they admitted shamefacedly. "Two assailants, madame, suspended from ladders on the helicopter. May Allah have mercy upon our foolishness."

Berna shooed them from her sight unleashing curses, admonishing them. "You had best prepare proper alibis for His Highness or else!" She drew an imaginary line across her neck, slamming the door after them.

She finished an hour later, sweating profusely, fully exhausted. Wrapping the last of the bandages, she dictated into a tape recorder:

Both bullets penetrated flesh, missing clavicle by hairs. Two perforations inflicted so precisely indicate expertise in weaponry. Distance of miss—approximately twelve inches off two conceivable bull's eyes, the heart or head at dead center implies either deficiency in telescopic sights, barrel warp, improper balance while firing or intentional misses. I discount the last probability. *Note:* No rotors heard at moment of impact or slightly before. *Added note:* Subject evidences several previously inflicted bullet wounds by low-calibre weapons. Wound expertly treated and healing well advanced. Chart to accompany report, indicating precise point of penetrations.

Berna yanked off surgical gloves, snapped off the recorder. The night of seduction had ghoulishly metamorphosed into a life-or-death operating theater of the macabre.

Brad vaguely recollected what happened. But the smell of blood was in his nose and throat, it choked him, nauseated him, it swirled to his head, made his eyes swim, his ears ring and inside he felt he was dying, slowly but surely dying.

A three-day convalescence was spent reading the Moufflon brief. Sobered by its contents, Brad considered his prospects of returning to D.C. He barely noticed his infirmity was healing, that he was ready for travel.

They breakfasted on the terrace, shortly after dawn, sipping steaming pots of *atai benaana* and tasty *pastilla*, a stuffed pancake with *Mille feuille*, a bit rich for his taste, but excellent. Berna poured the mint tea, expounding on the two empty bullet casings on the table before him.

"Where did you learn international weaponry identification?"

"At age ten I identified aircraft by the blips on radar screens. Each are uniquely distinct in frequency penetration of the atmosphere. Be grateful our assailants didn't hurl Dutch v 40 fragmentation grenades or use Kalishnikovs as they did at Katz's farm, or we wouldn't be here discussing a future. When do you leave?"

"Three this afternoon." He joined her at the balustrade.

"You are to use Prince Ben Kassir as your diplomatic liaison if you encounter snags in convincing your President. On the table is a box. A token of our friendship." Brad, awkward, about to decline, was cut off. "It is not what you think. Thank me only if you find it effective." She watched him open the box and examine the slim, solid gold pocket pen. "Study it carefully as you handle it. It dispenses a mini .22 calibre bullet. Should the firing mechanism fail, pressure applied to the clip releases sufficient poison to finish the job. Handle it with caution. Compliments of Moufflon."

"Shades of James Bond."

"But, of course," she said impishly. "All innovations come from the screenwriters. Seriously, be circumspect. You face many dangers. Your enemies know we've liaisoned."

Brad fingered the shell casings. "Soviet? I thought they wanted me alive." He smiled at the innocuous statement. She tossed him a look of long suffering. "I've dispatched the m.o. to Corsica and Sicily. I'll forward the report to you in D.C."

"You're talking, but I don't hear a thing. I'm sitting here watching the wind and sea in your hair."

"Be serious, there's little time. You do believe Moufflon's

influence can halt the proliferation of nuclear madness in the Middle East, restore peace and stability?''

''The *Cat* and you have made a believer of me.''

''Cling to that belief! God knows propagandists will move the firmament to dissuade you *or* waste you.'' She sipped her tea. *''Allors,* Moufflon is your only hope.''

''You are sold on that premise. Yet I detect a modicum of doubt. What is it you are not telling me?''

Berna picked up the teapot. ''Come, it's time for the moment of truth. The library, please.''

In the library Brad's attention trailed to Valentina Lansing's portrait. Berna, aware of his shift of attention, flushed back her displeasure. She opened a bottle of Dom Perignon, poured two glasses and walked toward him.

''Isn't it early for celebration?''

''Our farewell drink.'' They clinked glasses. ''Before we continue, tell me how you really feel in hearing contradictions about your own people?''

''Americans are a sturdy stock. We're used to being assailed. *'Yankee Go Home!' 'Ugly Americans!'* Yet they beg for our food, money, and assistance.''

''No, no, no, no, no! I am speaking of *your* people. The Jews.''

Brad spun around, blanching. About to deny what sounded to him like an accusation, he faltered and spoke out honestly. ''For no special reasons I can articulate, I've never practiced the religion.''

''No, Major, not the religion. The political Jewry—Zionists.''

''Sorry, I am interested in neither. Next question, please.''

Smoldering eyes dug deep into Brad's soul for ten seconds. He felt stripped, laid bare for dissection.

''Berna, religion is a bore. I talk politics only because it is my livelihood but it doesn't border speculation. I deal only in facts and I have my share of those. Now, tell me, what has being Jewish or not being Jewish have anything to do with Moufflon, my mission here?''

''Did Wolfgang know you are Jewish?''

''No, *goddammit!* And I am not Jewish. I don't know the first thing about being Jewish!'' He was angry, short of temper. Worse, he didn't know why. ''You can be very aggravating at times.''

Berna moved to the sofa, still in her sheer silk dressing gown, her body outlines unbearably disturbing. She lighted a hash cigarette, inhaled deeply, holding it inside her.

"Suppose I continue. You've heard the overture, now for the melody. Over the past two decades you've witnessed a slick orchestration of hostilities in the Middle East escalate to what is now pandemic in proportion . . ." She continued to articulate, unravel the complexities.

Briefly Brad's gaze shifted again to Valentina's portrait, nagged by the implication of its presence on these royal walls. An abrupt silence startled him, brought him out of reverie. He flushed, his attention shifting back to a stern-faced Berna. He made a disorganized gesture. "She reminds me of someone I knew long ago. You were saying. . . ? Christ! Am I going bonkers? I thought . . . What I thought you said a moment ago was . . ." Her somber-faced silence screamed at him. Brad blinked hard, placed his glass on the table.

"I repeat, Moufflon has orchestrated all military altercations in the Middle East between Jews and Arabs for two decades, under the strict orders of Zurich."

Brad sank heavily into a nearby chair, the pins knocked out from under him. His free hand rubbed his left arm secured by a sling. He let it all sink in. Finally he spoke, "Clearly I misunderstood you—something I missed—"

"—when you were daydreaming of a redhaired woman?"

"*Berna!* I misunderstood, didn't I?"

But Brad had not misunderstood. In a sudden rage he flung the glass across the room at the fireplace, shattering it to pieces.

The phone rang. Berna quietly sauntered to the desk, picked it up, and speaking in French, spoke in low whispers. She hung up and moving toward a door, opened it, revealing a walk-in safe. She dialed the combination, swung open the door and turned on a light. Inside were files. She went to one, opened it, sorted, and pulled out a folder. She returned and stared at Brad's ashen face almost apologetically. She demonstrated a softer cordiality.

"It was Youseff. He insists you must be aware of this before you return to America." She laid before him an assortment of photographs, statements, confessions that proved the inculpation of a high-ranking U.S. statesman in the assassination of two European figureheads.

Brad stood mute, stunned by what he saw, read and heard.

Photos of Anthony Harding, Secretary of State, in secret liaisons with men of questionable character, were studied with intense scrutiny. The information overwhelmed him. In his profession he had seen everything—he thought.

"Photos can be doctored," he said unconvincingly.

"Why is it so difficult to believe your Secretary of State has committed such outrageous deeds?"

"Perhaps for the same reason I find it difficult to believe your earlier statement concerning Moufflon. Oh, Christ! This is too fucking incredible! What would motivate Harding to involve himself in this?"

"Well, you've got me. I can't tell you because I don't know. I only know your Anthony Harding is up to no good in the Middle East. And it isn't an overnight plan," Berna continued, her eyes never leaving his face. "You are shaken by the revelation. You don't know where to turn, perhaps? How to convert the information to your advantage—"

"Don't tell me what I think or feel!"

"Your heart is not encased in rhinoceros hide, *cher*. When all this settles you'll know what must be done. I shall offer you a brief summary. What I said earlier was true, concerning the Moufflon apparatus. But suddenly, since the Lebanon War, Moufflon feels another force at work, as if Zurich *knew* in advance what Moufflon's motivation was and in some way uses Anthony Harding as a hedge against Moufflon. Moufflon will be in the Middle East soon to see for himself what is happening. The rest is for you to assemble and make fit as you see. Now, for the ironic finale. The man you seek in Zurich is *Colorless Eyes*. He is the Zurich titular head of the *invisible* cartel. This man is so important, he does not exist. He controls the entire world, but he does not exist. Imagine. *He does not exist*—yet the whole world fears him. This man with *colorless eyes* who does not exist is both Moufflon's employer and his mortal enemy!"

"*HE WHAT?*"

The image was vivid.

The rug suddenly yanked from under him, Brad saw the guillotine blades descend; his head lopped off, rolled out before him on the carpet, staring sightless up at him. He sank deeper into hopeless quagmire.

*   *   *

In London, a reshuffling of flight plans due to cancellation of a scheduled Concorde flight forced Brad to connect with an Army transport and fly directly to Dulles Air Force Base. He used flight time to mentally replay the stupefying narration Berna had recanted.

Battling the thunderstorms of his mind, Brad removed each emotional spike until his thoughts stopped cartwheeling. Logic returned and with it pyramiding doubt.

How would he sell the package to the Oval Office?

He realized that further excursions into Moufflon's domain would be impossible. It was clear that the next step in this masked power play would be direct contact between Moufflon and the highest echelons of U.S. Government. Major Brad Lincoln was to be the conduit.

BUT HOW? Sweet, holy Jesus! HOW?

He arrived in Georgetown fatigued, jet-lagged, and barricaded himself behind locked doors. He fell asleep battling demons and gargoyles in recurring nightmares, unaware of the drama taking place across town.

Brad had missed the Concorde flight, but the *Needle* had not. Bristling impatiently aboard the giant bird without a target, the assassin left the plane at Washington National, trekked through customs and moved swiftly to the phones in the terminal. He placed an overseas call to Paris. Speaking a German-accented French, he vented his spleen. The voice at the other end was caustic, emphatic and deadly.

"The American must not rendezvous with the President. If, through inexcusable slip-ups the connection is made, render all plans obsolete. New strategy will be implemented. Use all available conduits to delay him, or waste him."

The *Needle* hung up, his mission spelled out in no uncertain terms. Heading out the terminal exit, the well-dressed blond assassin was arrested by the message playing over the airport intercom.

Inside a soundproof room adjacent to the VIP lounge a Concorde stewardess stood with two State Department officials from the Office of Security peering intently at overhead video consoles. They listened to the intercom: *"Mr. Zephyr, please report to Concorde Customer Accommodation desk . . . Mr. Zephyr . . ."*

Downstairs the Needle spotted terminal in-phones a few feet

from the Concorde desk. He scanned closed-circuit video cameras sweeping incoming and outgoing passengers. Avoiding camera range, he ducked behind passengers and entered a deserted men's room, moving toward a closed stall designated for the handicapped. It was larger than most stalls—perfect for him.

Less than six minutes later a different man emerged. Wearing black pancake makeup, an Afro wig, tweed suit turned inside out to a solid color, a compact slicker over the suit, black contact lenses over blue eyes—all traces of the Needle had vanished.

Before the mirror he tugged up on a turtleneck sweater, covering the makeup line, slipped into a pair of gloves, and engaging in a series of bodily contortions, at once appeared inches shorter and added thirty years to his appearance. Satisfied, he exited, lumbered slowly to the accommodations desk, and in a cleverly disguised voice announced, "I am Zephyr." The attendant directed him to the house phones while unobtrusively engaging a lever under the desk.

Upstairs the Concorde stewardess studied the bent-over old black man. She shook her head vigorously, denying him as her passenger.

"Mr. Zephyr was tall, slim, a white man, Nordic in appearance. At least six inches taller. His fingers were slender, aristocratic. Oh, yes, he had a red scar over his wrist bone. Obviously you have an imposter."

"Was *this* man on your flight? Perhaps you had two Zephyrs?"

"There were no blacks in my section at all," she insisted in her very British accent. "I say, something is bloody strange." She approached the screen, peering closely. "This man is wearing the identical shoes my passenger wore. Yes, yes, I'm certain."

As the frustrated State agents perceived the importance of the seven-minute delay before Zephyr answered the page, they bolted out the door, flew down the UP escalator, elbowed their way past irate passengers, unable to flash badges and dramatically cry out, "FBI!" Plowing forward, they lurched out the doors, dodging passengers, and stood like dummies on the sidewalk, searching every which way.

TOO LATE!

The Needle was lost to them. He had boarded a cab and now wheeled into streams of bumper-to-bumper traffic off the concourse onto the George Washington Parkway, the cab's license obscured by swiftly paced autos moving in behind.

"Son of a bitch!" Cursing overtly, the agents flagged their drivers with hand-held receiver transmitters. They communicated *failure to apprehend* in embarrassed silence.

Given four hours to make the arrest, they had lost their target, a prize catch, and what remained of their self-respect.

Worse—how would they report the fiasco to their chief?

Chapter Fifteen

JOLTED FROM A NIGHTMARE BY THE BRASH RINGING on his phone, Brad rubbed his eyes, groped for the receiver in the darkness. Before he could speak, the caller shouted, "Don't talk. Just listen!"

Brad obeyed implicitly, still drowsed with the intoxication of the whore curled fetally next to him. He fired a cigarette with his free hand and sat up swiftly, fully awakened by the caller's message. "Thanks, ol' buddy," he muttered. He swung his legs over the side of the bed, groaning at the same time. Six in the morning! *S-h-i-t!*

He glanced at the agency whore. Not bad. Not great, but not bad. She was no Berna, but if he'd been in the right frame of mind it could have been sensational. He poured hot coffee from the timed brewer, moved to the bathroom and turned on the shower. He switched on a sunlamp, sipped his coffee as he hot-lathered his four-day beard.

Goddamned Oval Office! Delays . . . delays . . . delays!

He frowned. The call disturbed him.

Still a goddamned target, was he? Stalked in Europe, it hadn't stopped, not even on home turf.

Men will stop at nothing to keep you from the Oval Office! Corsican-Coral! Zurich! Fanatics! Terrorists! Assassins!

Becoming some asshole's target, the bureaucratic delays preventing him from rendezvousing with the President blistered his anger. The goddamned scenario played like a threepenny opera! Hadn't everything so far played like a bloody melodrama?

Brad stepped into the steamy shower, lathered his body and

257

squeezed shampoo from a tube onto his head, soaping it vigorously. The tube slipped from his hand to the tiled floor, momentarily ignored. He luxuriated under five fine jet sprays, rinsing off the soap, letting the invigorating hot water, fine as needles, penetrate his aching body.

Washington! It was a maddening city! From the moment he'd touched home base, he'd shoved, pushed, pulled, damned near parted the Potomac to cut through governmental red tape. Getting past presidential aides to the Chief Executive had drained him. Relegated to standard protocol, his appointment with Macgregor was two weeks hence. *Two fucking weeks—hence!*

The goddamned world tottered on the brink of disaster and he—with the knowledge he carried—had to wait *two fucking weeks!* He'd risked his life, including those of countless others, and these jerks insisted on adhering to protocol. It made no sense—none at all.

What had cooled Macgregor's enthusiasm?

Questions plagued him. The caller's message churned his guts.

An assassin, identified as The Needle, just missed you, ol' buddy!

So? What else was new? He hadn't come this far to be picked off by some scumbag. *Dammit!* Nothing warranted his playing *sitting duck* for two weeks while a psycho-sickie, roaming D.C., took potshots at him. The caller had graphically described the faux pas at Washington National and how the assassin had escaped.

Forced to wait out protocol's timetable while fitting into an assassin's prearranged schedule boggled his mind. Voices from the grave worked him across the barriers of death: *Special interest groups to whom political upheaval is essential will prevent you from reporting to your President.*

In a sudden burst of frustration, Brad leaned down to pick up the shampoo tube.

A crashing explosion shattered his eardrums and the glass shower doors, sending him flat to the tiled floor. The whine of ricocheting bullets bouncing off the splintered tiles caused him to flinch and cower low. Exploding shards of dagger-sharp glass bit into his shoulders, lower back and butt, like porcupine quills. Pain and panic be damned! He couldn't just lie there!

Gathering his strength for one assault, he sprang from the

shower, bleeding copiously and flung himself against his assailant. He knocked the Browning 9mm from her hand. She parried blow for blow, kicking, chopping, kneeing his balls, using every dirty trick in the book. Brad at a slight disadvantage, his body slippery and wet, couldn't grasp her firmly. Finally he pulled back his arm, connected with a powerful uppercut to the jaw, knocking her flat on her ass. She sank to her knees, eyes rolling upward. Brad caught her as she collapsed and lowered her on the carpeted floor, his own blood dripping all over her.

Barbie! The hooker! The goddamned hooker who had pleasured him last night! Why hadn't she nabbed him in his sleep? Why now?

Sharp dagger pains assaulted him. Christ! This Double 0-7 horseshit had to end! He picked up up the Browning automatic—a heavy *muthuhfucker* for a broad to tote—and checked the clip. Three shots fired, ten remained. Why stop at three? She could have wasted him. He stared at her crumpled body, oblivious to his own injuries.

Hard to believe they had made love last night. No, Brad—not love, sex! Then, under the ultraviolet lighting, he saw it and froze. On the left breast—to the left of the areola—a scar. *Corsican Coral!*

Reaching down, wincing at the pain, he grasped her head off the floor, searched her features. Releasing her, he tied her hands behind her with the sash of his terry robe. He adjusted three-way mirrors to assess the damage done to his shoulders and back. Reaching into the medicine chest, he popped a Percodan and tried with clenched teeth to pick out the larger glass shards from his arms. Christ! What pain!

He dialed a number on the wall phone, an eye on the girl.

"Jubilee? Is my number lighting your board? . . . Good—tell me the number. Who was the broad you sent last night? I did call—nine or thereabouts. *You—sent—no—one?* . . . Are you certain?" His eyes darted to the girl, Barbie or whatever the hell she was called. "O.K., gotcha." He yanked the terry robe from his caddy and ran out of the room.

Twenty minutes later, he'd swept out all the rooms of the townhouse and found the bugs, wiretaps, the whole kit and kaboodle! One tap tied into the main utility and phone lines; it was ingenious—barely detectable. The next was found where he least expected it. On a top book shelf in the den, amid a dozen handbound leather editions of the classics. Inside the belly of *HAMLET*! The pages, scooped out, made room for a sensitive device able to pick up what the others might fail to do.

Well, well, well! How all occasions do inform against us!

The familiar quote from *Hamlet* suited the occasion but failed to appease his outrage. His neglect in failing to secure his house was inexcusable, and he spent the next half hour removing the fucking devices. The Percodan dulled the pain, made him groggy, but not groggy enough to ignore the nagging in his brain.

He picked up the phone, engaged scrambler devices, dialed the Agency. "Lolly—put Jubilee on again. I gotta talk with him."

"You ain't the only one. And please, no names, Mr. 711."

"Look, I just talked with him—"

"Uh-uh! No, you didn't. Not from here. Jubilee ain't shown up for work for two days."

"What are you talking about? He sent Barbie to me last night."

"Uh-uh! We got no one by *that* handle. Yes, suh, I'm looking at your number. 711, all right. We ain't heard from yuh in a long while. If you hear from Jubilee, tell him Madam's hotter'n a pistol!"

"Yeah, yeah, O.K." Brad hung up.

Goddamn! A fucking intercept on the line! You'd think he was a fucking cherry. He had ignored a basic rule. *Protect your domicile, bright boy!*

He bolted back up the stairs, at each move star points stabbing him. The whore on the floor hadn't budged. He reached for the wall phone, punched a programmed number, and waited. "Doc! Flip on your scrambler. This is MOCK ORANGE III. I need help!" He hung up, moved gingerly over the broken glass, to his bedroom.

Fifteen minutes later an intern from Johns Hopkins Hospital arrived. Tall, clean-cut, dark bright eyes and black hair, he shot Brad with Demerol. Inquisitive eyes darted about the blood-spattered room, at the girl lying prone on the floor. Playing at unruffled composure, he shrugged to conceal his amusement. "What the hell is this? New S & M games? Glass stilettos? What the fuck is next with you spooks?" He picked out the shards carefully.

"Very unfunny, Doc. Anyone ever tell you you're a ringer for Digger O'Dell?"

"Digger O'Dell? Never heard of him."

"Just finish the goddammned job!" Brad snapped without humor.

Finally regaining consciousness, the Barbie-doll struggled against her restraints, screaming loudly. Brad broke away from Lou Hadley, stuffed a washcloth in her mouth. "Can't have you waking the neighbors," he chastized.

Brad winced while Hadley finished sponging the bloodied pits with alcohol. The lean, hungry intern had financed his internship with extra money earned by doing odd jobs for Brad. An American Indian by birth, he became more white man than Indian through education and a half-breed mother who had married a Yankee. Luckily he had retained a valuable ancestral instinct—silence. He could be trusted.

"White Bear," Brad asked sotto voce. "What do you make of the scar on the girl's breast?" Using Lou Hadley's Indian name signified a certain intimacy. Glancing obliquely at the scar, Doc did a double take. He placed his instruments on the counter, focused the bright sunlamp over her, illuminating the breast. He examined the heaving breast with professional detachment, then frowning, cupped the globular breast in one hand, probed the scar with his right forefinger, feeling, rubbing, studying intently.

The wide-eyed girl squirmed, wriggled eel-like, backed away from him, muffled gurgles in her throat. Brad moved in, pinned her to the floor. She shook her head in muffled protest. Restrained by Brad's arms, she shook her head vigorously, thrashed her legs about, kicking viciously at him. Brad increased the pressure, pinning her knees and shoulders flat.

"If I remove the gag, will you identify yourself? Stop screaming? Who sent you? Are you Corsican Coral?" She shook, trembled under Hadley's probing, her pleading eyes begging him to stop.

Hadley rubbed the scarring, pressed hard, released the pressure, observing the elasticity of the tissue. "Hello . . . what have we here?" White Bear peeled back the scar tissue, studying it, puzzled. "Damned! It isn't scar tissue at all."

"What is it?"

"Damned if I know. It *resembles* tissue graft, *acts* like it, but it's not." On his feet, Hadley lumbered over to the bright daylight at the window. Brad moved in closer, both peered curiously at the coral-tinted tissue. So intense was their concentration they failed to note the changes occurring in the girl.

Panic-striken eyes popped from their sockets, fear grotesquely reflected on her face, the body stiffened, then fell limp, eyes staring out into space, sightless.

Brad turned casually. "Doc!" he shouted. "Doc! Look!"

He reached her first, turning ashen. "She's dead!"

Hadley, on his knees, checked her vital signs. "No pulse, dammit! Help me!" They laid the nude body flat, then Hadley thumped her chest. Mouth-to-mouth resuscitation followed. Hadley searched his bag.

"Goddammit! No adrenalin!" He was incensed. "Major! You've got a problem! What the fuck did you do to her?"

Brad ignored the emotional outburst; he contemplated the situation with maddening detachment. "Can you do an autopsy?" he said calmly.

"No! I'm through! . . . You ask too much! My career's at stake, Brad. For Christsakes, if I go down the tube, you won't be there to bail me out! It's like you *fucking* spooks don't exist. I've gotta look out for number one or its back to the reservation, a lonely white bear among redskins."

"You got it wrong, Lou. It's not what I did to her. She used me as a human dart board. She shot at me through the shower door. You're looking at a bona fide, international assassin."

Hadley's eyes widened in astonishment, darted to the girl as if she were some new, unidentified specimen under a microscope. Brad continued the hard sell. "I know what's at stake. Do this for me and I'll push for a Pentagon staff assignment the moment you complete your internship. You'll be guaranteed a three-day-a-week golfing career, or tennis if you prefer."

Hadley listened, the wheels of seduction churning.

"She was alive when you arrived, wasn't she? Now she's dead. I've a hunch her death is connected to that stuff—the tissue graft. Is that a reasonable assessment?"

Hadley pursed his lips contemplatively, eyes searching for the coral tissue. "Where is it? What did you do with it?"

They searched frantically, combed the shag carpeting. "There, right by your hand. Pick it up carefully."

Doc held the tissue under the lamp. "It resembles keloid scarring, it has the texture of a cockscomb. Actually, it looks like tissue from the labia—in the area of—"

"I *know* what labia means, Doc. Make your call. I need a lab analysis and get back to me fast. How soon can you push the autopsy?"

"Pathology is backed up to Christmas!" Hadley flared in annoyance.

Brad pulled out his money clip. He pressed two hundred dollar bills into Lou's hand. "Two more bills when you tell me the cause of death. Now, let's get her the hell out of here. Tag her Jane Doe until after the report. I'll notify homicide—no, Lou, not the local fuzz. Our *own* boys. This one needs top security clearance. She isn't the usual piece of ass."

"You mean—"

"You got it. Upper echelon stuff." Brad lied to abate the Doc's squeamishness. "Look, White Bear, we don't pick *anyone* for trustworthy missions. And, Lou, we take care of our own." Brad's manipulative voice dripped with sincerity. *The stupid son of a bitch believed him!*

How easy it was to orchestrate lies and deceptions under the guise of national security. Brad knew a medical record of a Jane Doe would be processed, cause of death—unknown. An autopsy ordered by a discerning intern would be filed, the records later lost in the milieu of hundreds of thousand files. In time it would appear that the girl had never existed.

But, *someone* did know. That *someone* still prowled the streets of D.C. waiting to kill Brad. The dead girl, one venomous fang on a powerful international trigger had been pulled. Her absence, beyond reasonable time allocated to the job, would communicate her fate. Renewed efforts to waste Brad would gather momentum.

Brad put his minicam to work photographing her from every conceivable angle. He took Polaroids of the scarring, close-ups of the area around the scarring. Hadley watched in fascinated awe, marveling at Brad's composure.

Moments later he backed his Datsun out of the garage, parked it on the street, drove Hadley's battered V.W. van inside, closed the doors. Together they transported the girl's body, wrapped in a tarp, into the van. Brad slammed the doors shut.

"O.K., White Bear, she's all yours. Nothing must lead back to me. Don't tell me how you book her, got it? You've handled enough stiffs to know the procedure. Remember, you aren't remotely connected to this—got it? Drop into the morgue casually. Make it look like routine curiosity—you know about the breast—"

"Don't dictate procedure, Major. I can handle it."

"Do it."

Her name was Cerulean. When Brad checked the glossy 8 X 10's Greer had provided he knew she was Corsican Coral. The next day he received the lab's conclusions on her clothing and personal effects. The clothing: strictly Sears. The perfume: Paris, two hundred bucks an ounce! Incongruities abounded. She was a real pro—carried no ID in her bag. A few cosmetics and a hairbrush.

Cerulean, eh? So what? She was dead. Did it matter who she was? Did it? *Only to someone else!* The enemy was closing in, for God's sake! Here on his own turf!

And the White House kept him waiting!

Were they trying to drive him mad? How much more punishment could he take? He raged as he studied his prepared brief to the President.

Two hours laters, he realized he had one option which would accelerate the scenario—an ace-in-the-hole option. Using it was anathema, but so was being targeted by killers! Compelled to replay the trump card to gain the essential advantage in this deadly game, he stalled until he could stall no longer.

He opened the safe, caught sight of the photos taken of Wolfgang Katz. Spurred by the sight of the atrocity done him, Brad took the offensive, telling himself he had no choice.

Death stalked him. Death stalked the globe—and he stalled?

He sat at his desk and made the call. The phone video screen lighted up. Her image smiled at him.

"What a pleasant surprise," she whispered huskily.

Chapter Sixteen

VALENTINA MILES VARGA LANSING STOOD at the beveled-glass picture window staring at the frothy rapids of the stream in the beginning throes of spring thaw. Robins chirped. A large, roaring fire on the hearth buffered the tinge of frost clinging to the air.

Valentina gazed about, making sure the last-minute preparations were in place. The studio, as she called this renovated two-century-old grist mill of stone and brick, was more than a retreat. Nestled in a remote corner of the five hundred Virgina acreage known as Camelback Ridge, perched on a picturesque knoll overlooking the babbling brook, she was safe from the restrictive, loathesome, confining social protocol demanded by Washington cliques and their tiresome game-playing. Here in her sanctum sanctorum, hidden from the main road by thickly clustered denuded birch in a woodsy area known as Fox Hollow, she could be herself, and relive fond memories of a most unusual past.

Twentieth-century intrusions: solar heating, eight bronze bubbled skylights spaced on a high pitched roof; an artfully concealed underground carport, vis-a-vis a wide visible sundeck, were occupational necessities to ensure visitors' privacy from prying telescopic lenses. Inquisitive reporters and their revealing cameras, eager to compute two plus two into four hundred secrets, were foiled. To outwit the D.C. paparazzi one had to camouflage what couldn't be camouflaged and do it with exquisite and unquestionable propriety. Valentina smiled enigmatically as she padded quietly inside the four thousand square feet of contemporary living that formed her private world. Here she engaged in sculpting, oil painting, the cultivation of exotic cacti, ferns, fronds, succulents, jeweled bromeliads, rare species of hothouse orchids.

A geometrically precise staircase of quebracho wood, imported from Argentina, rose from the center of the structure to an open three-sided loft overlooking a floor-to-ceiling stone fireplace. Valentina had analyzed and judged the reconstruction with the judicious discriminating taste of a connoisseur. Since Valentina had cultivated a unique taste and admiration for ethnic art, the studio served as a perfect background for a unique art collection. Silver, copper and bronze plaques, Colombian artifacts adorned the walls. Illuminated wall niches displayed Huaca Prieta carved gourds, Acon-painted jars, Cuspisnique incised bottles, Mazca, Recuay jars, Moche portrait pots and effigies, Chimu black-ware bottles with edified carvings, Chancay-Inca vessels, Inca Polychrome jars. Numerous high colored Indian tapestries and priceless fierce-eyed flaming masks of indescribable grotesqueness adorned other walls.

Valentina completed the last floral bouquet when a short buzzing sound called her attention to the closed-circuit video screen mounted in a wall case. She watched as Brad Lincoln drove through an electronically-controlled gate and approached the house a mile up the winding path to the underground carport. A half dozen armed guards with Doberman pinschers on choke chains at either side of the snow-dotted lane paused to observe the passing car with professional curiosity.

Valentina loathed the tight security forced on U.S. Senators and those holding key positions in government, but daily mail-bags swelled with hundreds of threats to them. She glanced at the unique grandfather clock, its visible, intricate wooden clock-work sprockets turning in fascinating motion. Eleven fifteen. He was early.

She moved past the warm fires on the hearth, dressed casually in designer jeans, white silk shirt and white angora cardigan over her shoulders, sipping the remains of Perrier water. Dramatic bronze lights from the skylights added luster to that whirlwind mass of curly hair. Chiseled, aristocratic features, the forehead high, the nose slender, well formed with a tilt at its end, and eyes of viridian jewels set off the full glossed lips above a defiant chin. A fresh, colleen beauty, complemented by the blood of an impassioned Argentine, produced startling contrasts, beguiling, tempestuous, yet, cool, remote and unyielding. Valentina Lansing was an enigma to Washington where enigmas inevitably were shot down and destroyed. Above all, she was a survivor.

Valerie swung open both carved wood doors just as Brad rang the door chimes.

"Major, how good of you to come," she said huskily in the same impossible-to-forget voice. She stood still for a minute, framed in the doorway, simply the most beautiful woman he'd ever seen.

The beauty of her face in no way diminished by the years; he found himself noticing her body as she led him through the unique residence. When last they saw one another she was wrapped in the demands of playing hostess to the glitterati, and he in establishing covert contact with the U.S. President. But now, she simply glided over the carpeting sensuously, a fluid motion of thighs, stomach and pelvis in total coordinated rhythm. Brad warmed his hands before the brisk fire, watching her pour two mugs of coffee with unmistakable finishing-school grace, observed as her jutting breasts under the silk blouse heaved with each breath, each movement.

"You're a black-coffee man, I know. Try it my way with ice cream and cinnamon. *Café angélique*." She mixed the ingredients at a serving cart, then sitting deeply in the mocha-brown suede sofa, patted the space alongside her. "I'm yours for as long as you need me."

Brad smiled obliquely at what could be misconstrued as seduction.

She returned his glance. "You're thinking, what an impossible ending to a love story equally enduring, as tender as Romeo and Juliet?" Before Brad agreed or refuted her, she rambled. "There can never be another like him. Ah, you like the *café angélique*? Good."

Brad studied her over the rim of his cup, oddly moved. "No matter what I think, you endured. No residual effects of those years remain. How do you do it?"

She laughed throatily, shrugged. "Each day you awaken, do what's expected, and fall asleep each night hoping you've done your best. You plod along, some days worse than others. Years roll by, you think you've got it knocked until some silly little thing, a sound, the braying of a camel on a television program, transports you back in time to a place you were once a part of and *voilà*! you relive the tragedies and good times. Or you go to a movie and see actors playing out the very experiences you've lived. A thousand memories prod you alive, haunting you. The trace of a familiar, fragrant scent, and suddenly it's Corsica. Corsica, where love flowered, bloomed and turned to nightmares." She sipped her café.

She turned to him, her eyes, trapping his. "The saddest thing, Major, is to discover it's all gone, save the memories. Tell me, how is it you content yourself with memories for a lifetime?"

"If I possessed the power to divine an answer, I'd help myself," Brad replied in a voice locked into her emotional frequency, for suddenly he, too, was transported back in time, recollecting far too much, spending more emotion than he could spare. "But, like you, I work, pace along with the mad, mad, mad world quickly running short of time. My commitment—my work—is therapy. Speaking of commitments," he interjected, breaking the spell, "to function I again am forced to ask you to intercede on my behalf." Brad explained his dilemma. He paced, moving to the large picture window overlooking the brook and fading winter scene. He detailed his recent European jaunt graphically, spelled it out clearly, withholding TTS (Top Secret Stuff).

Listening attentively to the unfolding of the volatile odyssey, she trembled at the mention of Moufflon, her expression varying; at times her eyes sparked with fire, then grew subdued, her face paling, then alternating hued with crimson.

Over luncheon, succulent chilled lobster and wine served at the picture window, forcing himself to avoid comparisons with Berna, Brad observed her inscrutably. Valentina had the look of vital worldliness, of one who has lived fully, laughed loudly, told off-color jokes, drawn to inside straights, danced all night, driven too fast, hammed it up on occasion until horrid reality intruded on her fantasies, forcing her to revert to fancy finishing-school artfulness. Overshadowing it all he detected a curious urgency in her, a profound, almost resolute determination to contribute to the intrigue.

Brad had to think. You don't ask a woman like Valentina Lansing a direct question—not if you want straight answers. Then Valentina shifted in her chair, pressed a lever on a console. Instantly the room filled with the velvety tones of Doris Day:

Kiss me once . . . Kiss me twice . . . Kiss me once again . . .

"Do you dance, Major?"

"Only the old-fashioned way," he answered, startled by her question.

"Is there any other way?" On her feet she beckoned with outstretched arms. He rose hesitantly, forcing the suddenly smoldering memories back. For too long Valentina, the unrequited love of his life, had haunted him. Now, for the first time he held her close, her perfume intoxicating him.

It's been a long, long, time . . . Never felt like this before—

They moved slowly, dreamily, dipping into the mood music. Valentina's mind backtracked to another time, another world, another man. She lay her head on Brad's shoulder, snuggling against him, dreaming of the only man in her life, the man called Moufflon.

"What are you doing to me?" His voice smacked of sentiment. "I don't listen to this music anymore. It stirs a beehive of memories." He trembled against her, desire mounting, hardening with uncontrollable passion.

Valentina backed away from him, eyes searching his, momen-

268

tarily startled. She slipped from his arms apologetically. "I didn't realize your memories, too, would be stirred."

She returned to the table, poured more wine. Brad followed her.

Any other time . . . Any other woman . . . He would not have let her go. Their eyes locked. Through magical metamorphosis she was again Mrs. *Senator* Lansing, an enchanting creature of rare beauty, unique sex appeal—*a woman of iron*.

"Some memories must be resurrected," he began firmly, as if no break in the conversation had occurred. "It is imperative I get through to the President, but I can't get through his damned aides! Worse, I'm not certain it isn't a deliberate ploy to keep us apart."

She flashed him a sharp reproving glance. Brad knew at once it would take enormous conviction, more than the truth to convince her.

"I was cautioned in advance, warned of forces determined to prevent me from a liaison with him." Briefly Brad stared at the amber liquid in the delicately hand-blown glass. When he looked up, Valentina no longer sat opposite him. She stood before the fireplace studying the oil portrait over the mantel.

"My grandmother, Major. Victoria Valdez de la Varga. Born in Buenos Aires, she marred a Spaniard in Seville, Spain—my father, a man I've never met or seen."

Brad approached her silently. "I was certain it was a portrait of you." He studied the likeness critically. "The resemblance is uncanny."

"You met my daughter Valerie. She is a replica of her grandmother. Uncanny, as if in reincarnation."

"More so than you?"

Valentina nodded. "Even in temperament. When did we— you and I—last see one another in Europe?" She turned from the portrait, her cool green eyes on him. "You are very handsome, you know."

"If I told you the exact date, it might reveal my feelings for you." He flushed.

She studied him somberly. "I didn't know. I'm sorry."

"How could you? You were in love. Blind to anyone else."

"I was in Paris before V-E Day, in Berlin in April, 1945. I returned in 1946. In 1958 I flew to Corsica. My daughter Valerie is twenty-five. I married Senator Lansing two months *after* I

269

returned.'' She fixed her eyes on Brad until the implication registered in his eyes. ''Woman like *my* mother and *my* daughter, a breed unto themselves, *always* get what they want. What determination!''

It was *crazy!* He wanted to tell her he'd love to listen to her story another time, another place, when timetables failed to exist, when fanatics stopped wanting to destroy the world. Something prevented him from speaking up. He frowned.

Mild alarm sprinted across her eyes. She returned to the table, poured espresso, ignoring the question. ''Despite the history between us, I deeply cherish my memories of him. I refused to compete with Destiny for him. It would have destroyed us both. I do regret ceding him without a fight, but I chose to leave Corsica. He is all right, isn't he? Tell me these unsettled feelings are purely imaginary.'' She poured brandy for them. ''Are you going to tell me his life is in danger?''

''It was always so. Danger is his life-style. Was, has been, always will be. Don't be alarmed. He's powerful, well organized.'' He knew she ached for information. He dribbled it a bit at a time.

''I failed to establish contact with him, there were too many obstacles. My duty as I saw it was to return here, report to the President.'' He paused, voice husky. ''Perhaps if you had married him—''

''—instead of jumping from frying pan into fire?'' Her laughter disarmed him. Confined to the hidden side of her life were secrets she confided to no one. ''It's too late for regret, Major. I shall do my best to expedite your appointment with the President.''

Brad sensed the urgency he'd detected earlier, a desire to confide, and almost saw the mental chains of will and determination preventing her from doing so. Her reputation, a *special* status earned in D.C., placed her above the crowd of spotlight-grabbing socialites. He'd never seen or heard of a chink in her armor.

Valentina moved without the arrogance afflicting most woman of lesser status, rendering her very *special*. Now, languidly moving about the room, thoughtfully rubbing her hands together as if she were kneading clay, she paused before the wall of Incan artifacts, her voice above a whisper.

''In all you've told me one essential name is flagrantly missing.''

Numb with shock, Brad stood perfectly still. *God! No more complications!*

Valentina spoke slowly. "No one, Brad, especially not the President must know, but if I don't confide in someone I'll go mad. If word leaks—if it gets to certain circles in Europe, Valerie's life will be greatly imperiled."

"Then *don't tell me*! Please! I cannot assume the responsibility." He felt awkward, overtly cautious. "Even the walls have ears," he hissed.

"And a woman with a three-inch tongue can slay a giant," she said, regaining composure. "In this instance I'd be delighted to slay the giant," she quickly reiterated. "It's not what you think." Pressing her slender jewelled hands together, tapping her lips contemplatively, she approached him, took her hand in his, led her to the sofa before the fire. "I have no right to implicate you in Valerie's business, but I must. In a way, you are both pursuing the same thing. But you, Brad, lack the essential ingredient to achieve your goal, so precious time will be wasted. One man is the missing link—Moufflon's enemy. I know that man, Brad. *Really* know him."

He was hooked. Eyes locked in tremorous silence. He held up a restraining hand. "How safe is it to talk?"

"Men with noisy boxes sweep it once a week."

"The D.C. syndrone," he muttered, aware suddenly that the lights had dimmed. Valentina, busy at work at the console at her side next to the sofa, made a screen appear from the floor. Another switch pulled the draperies, lighted the screen. She snapped a video cassette into place and flipped the play button.

"*What the hell?*" For a moment, Brad was stunned.

"Don't make it more difficult. It's not the usual porno flick. Please pay close attention. Tracking isn't as sharp as it should be. In moments you will recognize the stars . . ."

Brad squirmed, discomforted. He didn't like what he saw, and when he recognized the performers, disliked it more. The implications were too horrendous to contemplate. A man and woman on a bed in various stages of sexual play loomed larger than life. Valentina stopped the frames, zoomed in tighter. The stars, unmistakable, identified beyond shadow of a doubt, brought a fierce scowl to his face. The dialogue between the couple in the erotically staged scenario was unintelligible at points. Who said a *picture is worth a thousand words?* Between orgiastic sighs, sexual exhortations, between repasts of cunnilingus and anal debaucheries in which Geralee Macgregor protested, but willingly complied with Anthony Harding's bestial commands, enough was said and done to turn Brad's stomach.

He swilled down a large brandy. "Where did you get these? My God! You realize what you've got? The implication is grotesque, in lieu of recent Middle East developments! Jesus Christ!"

"Don't ask me to reveal the source. I will *not* tell you. But if you think these are dynamite . . ." She removed the cassette, inserted another in the VCR. "This was taken approximately two hours ago at the Watergate."

The film exploded on the screen. The interior, a luxurious suite. At center on a bed, two men engaged in salacious homosexual acts.

"A switch hitter! *A fucking switch hitter. Some Secretary of State! He fucks the First Lady, then more to his liking but against his religion, an Arab!"*

"It's not what they're doing. Listen . . . Listen. . . !"

"So, Anthony, the plan put to you by Zurich is to hasten a bona fide sale of the lands in question. You understand?" the Persian told the Jew. *He was not an Arab*, Brad realized at once. Grunting, groaning erotically at the masterful fellatio done his fat Jewish cock, Harding murmured in assent, the pleasure too enthralling to despoil it with business. He waited for release, glorious climax, punctuated by hoarse groans and animal vaults over the bed, over his lover, until he was spent.

They both lay back, the Secretary of State and his Persian factotum, presently leader of a puppet government in the Middle East. They sipped Dom Perignon easily, shoveled caviar hedonistically into their mouths.

"*Purchase the goddamned lands!* What a master stroke of genius! Now who can accuse the aggressors of militant warfare? They'll own the fucking lands outright! Christ! Zurich never fails us! If we own the West Bank outright—"

"But it is illegal for Jordanians to sell lands to the Jews!"

"My friend, why do you worry? We'll cross that bridge in time. Haven't our people always excelled in maneuvering the craftiest of men? You do want to be on the winning team, no?"

Harding pushed the other's mouth on his flaccid cock, laid back languidly.

Valentina snapped off the video cassette. She turned on the stereo and a songster cooed through the speaker system: *I can't begin to tell you how much you mean to me . . .*

Immediately Brad was on his feet, electronic counter in hand. "I'd feel better if I had a look around." Palming the device, he covered the entire lower floor, missed nothing. Valentina observed his professional scrutiny; he peered into areas she hadn't dreamed were vulnerable to bugging.

Brad walked the length of the brick walkway at the rear of the house past three studios. He paused before a locked door, turned the handle, glancing at his hostess questioningly. Valentina flushed.

"It's private—uh, quite private." Her eyes sparked defiantly.

"I gathered as much. May I look inside?"

"I'd rather you did not," she avoided his pressing glance.

"Then don't utter another word—understand?" The command was clear.

"It contains no parabolics—no electronic wonders—" she offered.

"I can't take the chance."

Valentina hesitated, a wisp of annoyance flickered in her eyes. She tugged reluctantly at her shirt, reached under it to a gold chain around her neck, pulled out a gold key. She inserted it into the deadbolt lock, opened the door, turned to him. "Promise you won't think me daft." She flipped on a light switch, flooding the room with brilliant illumination.

Brad made a playful gesture over his heart, entered and stopped abruptly, stunned. He panned the room inch by inch, from floor to ceiling, totally dumbstruck. Wall shelves filled with disquieting memorabilia, revealing photographs, chilling mementos of an era past, another lifetime ago. Disguising his true feelings behind masked complacency, he moved stoically about the room, pretending indifference to the contents.

A French Legionnaire uniform complete with backpack was draped on a store dummy, contained in a glass wall case. Nearby, another dummy's regalia was that of a British Major, vintage World War II. Speechless, chills slipping along his spine, Brad felt in the grip of inexplicable emotions. Muzzling the questions threatening release, he muttered a quiet thank you, turned, anxious to leave the disturbing room. Before exiting, his attention

273

focused on a photograph of the *Mozarabe*, circa 1943, in Corsica. His and Jim Greer's image grinned at him. In the center— Moufflon. For an instant he stood mesmerized. Then, suddenly afraid for Valentina Lansing, for possessing so incriminating a photograph—and *those* volatile videotapes, he exited. Valentina locked the door behind them securely.

Two hours later, Brad ready to depart, she added to her story.

She sat at her desk, scribbled a note on eggshell pink stationery. She folded it, handed it to him. "Safer all around."

Brad glanced briefly at the words, flushed, and stared stonily at her. He thrust it into his sweater pocket, his eyes demanding explanations, a sense of weariness and frustration enveloping him. It was too fucking complicated!

"Before World War I a conspiracy to alter the direction of European and Middle Eastern politics commenced with the systematic assassinations of international political figureheads. We didn't learn of the atrocities as swiftly as we do today. The name I wrote is the leader of sabre-fanged political tigers. Something strange and profound is taking place, something you and ten thousand like you cannot combat. But he can. The man you call Moufflon."

"Your words are echoes of other words," he said incisively, recalling Berna's godlike worship of the man. "My problem is gaining audience with the President. I must convince him."

"That's the simplest of tasks. I warn you, too, be wary of those around him. *Advisors* is what they are politely referred to. I personally call them *trigger-men!*"

"You are incredible. How is it you possess more insight than any of a dozen men with whom the President surrounds himself?"

"Haven't you guessed? I'm a sorceress—"

"—no doubt ever existed."

"—who at times out-sorceresses herself." She sipped her drink. Valentina spoke succinctly, zeroing in on salient points. She displayed a cool, brutal remoteness when dealing with facts. Her tone projected confidence, adding credibility to her story. She was eager to explain, tried not to mislead. She condensed her presentation, adhering to facts.

Three hours later, her eyes dimming from exhaustion, she walked Brad to the door. He didn't want to go but he forced himself. Reaching up, she placed her arms around his neck, laid

274

her head against his heart, then her lips parted and she lifted her face to his, accepting his kiss. Her fragrance stirred his sensuality; her nearness, the sudden vulnerability communicated to him, threatened to expose his own hunger for her. He had loved this woman the moment he set eyes on her in London, 1941, at one of those secret officers' camps where the British vigorously trained soldiers and *special* intelligence teams for the war against Hitler. All this lingered at the back of his mind as she trembled against him; her warm, sweet, coffee-cognac kisses mixed with his juices and brought instant reaction. She felt it, placed her hands on his trousers, groping for his penis, felt its urgency . . . hard, harder, even harder. She moaned, fell against him, pressing her flesh against his.

Alarms sounded in Brad. God Almighty! He wanted her! He'd have done anything not to be who he was at the moment. Her feverish kisses persisted, then, suddenly, feeling his resistance, she slid her lips off his as if an icy wind had chilled her responses. She pulled back abruptly, looking like a schoolgirl caught doing something naughty. Worse—like an unfaithful wife.

Dotting the sweat from her flushed face, she mumbled incoherent apologies. "There's been nothing between the Senator and me for years," she said quietly, reaching to help him with his jacket.

"It's not you. The nature of my work, the complexities . . . I dare not expose you to any danger, understand?"

Valentina was silent. She opened the door, then closed it swiftly, in afterthought.

"The man whose name I wrote down is *Zurich*, referred to by Anthony Harding and his paramour. Oh, yes, something else—he has an unusual characteristic, quite rare, according to my grandmother—near colorless eyes."

Valentina, wrapped in a quivering silence, watched Brad leave the carport. Had he suddenly paled at her last remark? Or was he regaining composure? What a foolish thing she did, losing control.

Then she returned to her sanctuary, the private salon of dreams and memories earlier introduced to Brad Lincoln.

Valentina hesitated before the door, a hint of defiance in her eyes. When she stepped inside, she secured the deadbolt and approached the large portrait on the wall between glass cases. Eyes misting with tears rested on the exceedingly handsome man wearing the full regalia of an officer in the French Foreign Legion seated on a camel. She reached up, touched the face caressingly, and inched along, glancing lovingly at every framed photograph of the two of them together; she in her uniform, he in his, their faces radiant, the aura of love oozing from them. Photos in Egypt, standing at Ghiza before the Sphinx; some taken in her jeep along the Gazala Line, from Tobruk to Benghazi, and Bir Hakeim; photos aboard Rommel's captured Panzer IV tanks in Tripoli; at the parade grounds at Sidi bel Abbes in Algeria, with General de Gaulle, General Koenig and countless British and Free French officers and soldiers.

The *Mozarabe*, incredibly brilliant SAS Commandos, smiled back at her from gold and silver frames. A glass-enclosed chest between two glass wall cases containing the uniformed store dummies displayed the honor medals Valentina had been awarded. The French *Croix de Guerre*, pinned on her personally by Charles de Gaulle, at the center of others received for bravery in the performance of duty in the line of fierce battle fire.

Valentina's past, so much she'd been unable to part with, lived in this room, came alive with memories to stimulate her. It was all there—the good and the grotesqueness of war.

Valentina flipped on the stereo. *Lili Marlene* echoed in the silence, sung by the incomparable Edith Piaf. How appropriate. She unlocked the glass case containing the French major's uniform, picked it up bodily and rolled it forward out of the case. Gently she placed her head against the mannequin's chest, closed her eyes, at once assailed by swarms of images.

Lieutenant Valentina Varga digging her own slit trench lay huddled inside it along with desperate men barely existing on iron rations, fighting off scorpions, Rommel's incessant barrage of gunfire and the worst enemy of all—the *khamsin*, what the British called hot raging winds blowing up to 90 MPH, and the *ghilbi*, named by Arabs and Germans; a wind capable of driving the soldiers mad and one which had oftentimes buried an entire company under sand.

Why had she subjected herself to so abrasive a life? The daughter of a multimillionaire? An American-born citizen, before American commitment to the war? It wasn't a subject Senator Lansing's wife discussed with anyone. Few in Washington knew of her World War II days. In this room, in her world, the one to which she belonged in heart, spirit, mind and body, she could relive those days. No one could take this from her.

Valentina's arms snaked lovingly around the mannequin's neck. She sighed, readjusting her position to a more comfortable one. When the moment passed she brushed aside her tears, and reset the mannequin in its niche. She locked the case, turned off the lights and left the room, seized suddenly by thought. She had work to do.

Locking up her treasures, Valentina returned to her desk, thumbed through her personal telephone book and using her automatic dialer, pressed the required number. She waited. "Hello," she chirped brightly. "Do I have you at a disadvantage, John?"

Brad Lincoln, about to become a basket case before he got back to Georgetown, had made love to Valentina—mentally, frantically, maniacally, a thousand times over. He fantasized fever-pitched sexual outpouring, shackled in mind all these years, never dreaming the moment would arrive when he, Mr. Strong-Macho, iron man, would bow gallantly and say, 'Nay, nay, fair princess, we are honor bound to higher causes.' *BULLSHIT!* He was furious with himself. Worse, he felt he had betrayed Berna, of all people!

Methinks, Brad, schlemiel, you should see a shrink!

He drove along the causeway mentally sifting, sorting extraneous matter from the essential facts, gluing together bits and pieces of the gems. It was impossible to blink away the contents of the volatile video cassettes, the implication of the participants as their roles fitted compactly into a grotesque global scenario.

Brad swerved unexpectedly and intuitively off the causeway ramp, searching for a service station. Behind dark glasses he peered for possible surveillance. Why had he pulled off the highway? In moments he'd be home.

He pulled into a gas station and ordered the attendant to fill his tank while he went to the men's room. Inside he locked the door, fished Valentina's note from his sweater pocket and read: *Valerie in Paris. In grave danger. Please, please help her.*

He scanned the names: *Amadeo Redak Zeller, Victor Zeller, Suisse Banque Nationale, Zurich.* The last name was: *Vivaldi Bonifacio, Ajaccio, Corsica.*

Brad committed the note's contents to memory. He snapped

on his lighter, flushed the burning contents down the toilet, watched the ashes swirl around the bowl before the gurgling waters swallowed them.

So! *Amadeo Redak Zeller was Colorless Eyes!* The name by reputation burned vividly in his mind, by implication and the manner in which Greer avoided the subject. Victor Zeller must be his son.

Brad buttoned his jacket, puzzled. He patted his chest at the unexpected bulk. *What the hell?* He fished through his inner pocket. The fucking video cassettes! Valentina had slipped them inside his jacket. Oh, Christ!

Anthony Harding, *Secretary of State,* and Geralee Macgregor, the *First Lady* in compromising situations! And Prince Mumuhud! What an unlikely *ménage à trois.* Brad paused for a moment to consider: was it just possible that Harding manipulated the clever, highly improper sale of the West Bank? What a goddamned unexpected coup for America's enemies!

About to leave, Brad took time to urinate.

The act saved his life!

An explosion blew up half the gas station and with it Brad's Datsun. He emerged from the falling debris, coughing, sputtering, shielding his eyes. There's wasn't enough left of his car for identification purposes. He ran down the street to a phone booth, placed a call for an ambulance and the police, then another for a taxi. He crossed the congested street, joined the stunned crowds who poured out of a coffee house in droves staring at the flaming spectacle. He made himself inconspicuous, eyes wildly searching for a face, an eager face in the crowd that might have tailed him.

A bomb! A fucking timed plastic explosive planted in his new car! If he'd stayed to romp in the hay with Valentina. . . ? Christ! another nightmare!

Brad saw an opening among the crowds as flashing sirens, fire engines, police black-and-whites, howling ambulances converged on the scene. He took the path between the café's side entrance to the next property. He could not involve himself. If the police got lucky and salvaged an ID—he could say the car was stolen. Up ahead he saw the cab. He knocked on the window. "Are you free?"

"How far ya going?" asked the driver, engrossed in the accident.

"Georgetown."

"Get in." The driver shoved down the flag, and took off easily, heading up the ramp to the causeway. "Can ya beat that? Ain't enough lunatics in the world, someone's gotta lay on a bomb on the poor guy. I wonder who it was? You see it?"

Brad turned in his seat, glanced back at the receding smoke plumes trailing across the sky. "What happened? I heard a noise . . . Too busy to ask . . ." He settled back, listening to a detailed—and embellished—play-by-play description.

"Must have been some union boss. Or a congressman. You know how many get knocked off and the public never hears the truth? Well, let me tell you . . ."

Brad paid off the driver at the University entrance, watched him drive off, then, turning in the opposite direction, jogged the back roads and alley behind his townhouse, the sights and sounds of late afternoon somehow calming him.

Before he unlocked the rear gate, the raucous, vicious snarling began. The Dobermans he'd recently purchased gnashed fanged teeth on cue, snapped and barked in rising crescendo. Brad cooed to them reassuringly. The security of knowing that intruders opted for a deadly fate, should they combat the killer dogs, sat easier on his guts.

Inside he secured the doors, considering how differently his European travels might have been had he lunched with Valentina Lansing beforehand. Christ! His head ached with so much crammed inside it. Zeller the octopod! Zeller the Zurich beast! Zeller with colorless eyes! How fucking far did his tentacles reach?

Brad placed the video cassettes next to his VCR. He lighted a fire, ambled to the front door, rechecked the locks and deadbolts. He glanced casually out the beveled glass-windowed door, beyond the wrought iron enclosure, up and down the street.

About to pad back into the den, he stopped. A *distortion!* He scurried to the living room, peered out from a narrow slit between the blinds. Son of a bitch! It was there, across the street. A blue Ford van in the same spot as before he'd left for Virginia. His eyes widened at the emergence of a periscopic roof antenna, swinging about, opening like a wire dish. His knees buckled slightly, brows frowning. They had beamed in on the activity inside his house!

Parabolics! Fucking parabolics!
Had they tracked him to Virginia? To the Lansing estate?

Asshole! He'd overlooked the most fundamental method in the book—homing devices! Sophisticated tracking equipment! *Sons of bitches!* Brad raged at his sudden feeling of impotence. Valentina Lansing's life was in danger! *Damned fool!* He cursed himself up one way and down the other, until he calmed down. Then he moved swiftly, sweeping the place free of electronic devices. Lately it was developing into a daily chore . . .

Was he protected from parabolics? Was he? He paced the floor angrily, occasionally striding to the front window to peer at the accursed electronic nightmare. *Christ! How dare they?* How fucking *dare* they? The answer rushed his senses.

He loped to the den, picked up the phone, punched away at digits on the automatic dialer and waited. *Go ahead, crank it up to eavesdrop on me, you bastards!* "Hello . . . Senator Bainsbridge here. Now listen, there's a blue Ford van parked on N Street in violation of all city codes. All day! Dammit! If you men in blue did your jobs once in a while . . ."

Brad slammed the phone and scurried back to the front window, a Cheshire-cat grin spreading on his lips.

DOWN PERISCOPE! HALLELUJAH!

The hostile van moved, but not before Brad caught sight of the plates. He returned to the den beaming satisfaction.

He dialed.

"You know me. I won't use names. Imperative you know my car was blown up. Academy awards material viewed is safe. Surveillance is heavy. Exercise caution. Admit no workmen to the studio or your home without the strictest security clearance. Be alerted to blue Ford van, Virginia license SOJ-153. Do you read me?"

"Message confirmed," Valentina said in a stalwart voice. "I read you perfectly."

Brad hung up. He rummaged through his file for the next number. Hooked into scrambler devices and voice-alerting mechanisms, he made his call on the video phone awaiting a familiar face to appear.

"Aaron, buddy. I need a favor. Run four names through the computer. Read me: the first is Z-zebra, E-elephant, L-lion, L-lion, E-eel, R-rhino. Yeah, that's it, Zeller. Do it twice. First to Amadeo Redak Zeller, then Victor Zeller. Oh, I dunno, begin with Zurich, then try Geneva, Rome, London, Paris, what the fuck—Tel Aviv." Brad clarified in the same manner the

280

name Vivaldi Fornari Bonifacio. He emphasized the importance of a covert approach. "That's right, buddy, highly classified, Executive level. Impossible to use the usual channels. Got it? O.K., listen closely for the *open sesame* numbers: 0044550-96-111-00053-AAA." Brad repeated the coded numbers, heard a loud gasp at the tag end of triple-A clearance. "Now, buddy, read it back to me. Listen, I can only tell you once. Bring no—repeat, no—focus to subject matter. No identifying requisitions, no duplicates, got it? . . . I'll tell you how . . . In your off-hours, just before you reload, let the perforations come at the end of a roll. A few torn pages are meaningless—accidents can happen . . ."

Brad held the phone at arm's length. The expected outrage came over the phone, followed by colorful expletives. "You won't be satisfied until my ass's in a sling. You're fucking crazy! They'll fry my balls, and you, you son of a bitch will be on hand when they're served at the banquet. No! No! They'll castrate me if I'm caught."

"Don't get caught."

"Easy how you spooks play with another guy's life."

"Would a pass for the World Series ease the pain?"

"Make it two. All expenses paid and you've got your patsy."

"You got it. Uh—one more thing."

"Shit! It's *never* a clean bill of goods."

"One more name." Brad sucked in his voice. He spelled it softly. "L-a-n-s-i-n-g, V-a-l-e-n-t-i-n-a," waiting for the fireworks.

"Negative! Negative! N-E-G-A-T-I-V-E! The Senator's got enough eyes and ears on the payroll to crucify me. Coming from a Jew-boy, that ain't funny. No! You heard me—no! Not in the middle of a fucking Senate investigation scam."

"Two passes, including air freight to California. Listen, it's not the *woman* I want—" he paused, hyping himself. *You've done it before, Brad! Do it again!* "The lady's life is in jeopardy. We gotta know all about her to track down possible suspects. Two attempts, Aaron, buddy. Can't chance the third, unprepared."

"Use your own goddamned resources." The voice was surly.

"Can't. It's a possible *inside* job. Do you read the implication?"

Brad sucked in another pigeon. *See how easy it is?* He stressed further caveats of secrecy and pressed down on the lever severing the connection. The relationship with Aaron and White Bear and a dozen other *silent* men could not be solidified beyond a business relationship. He could afford no allies, or friends. They worked in coded names, received monies depositied in safety deposit boxes in covert names. They kept their end of the bargain, he never failed to keep his. This way no one got burned.

Brad sat in the darkness, drinking Scotch, thinking of Valentina, how close he'd come that afternoon to taking her as a woman, as he'd dreamed of having her for so many years. *What a woman!* The millionaire, socialite wife of a headline-grabbing, misguided, egomaniacal Senator involved recently in numerous questionable causes, corporate blinds affording him anonymity in shady dealings, she had miraculously held herself aloof to scandal. Alleged charges of collusion, conspiracy and a dozen judicial infractions hurled at the Senator had proven ineffective, dismissed for lack of evidence.

When was it, Brad tried to pinpoint it—early in 1960. A love affair between the press and the Senator's wife had ruptured, following two assassination attempts on Hartford Lansing's life. His politics, as subdued as his personal life, his reelection against formidible opposition, hinted at the power of Valentina's wealth. Recently linked to several Middle Eastern potentates in connection with flagrant anti-trust violations and suspicious morals involvements, the plot against him smelled to high heaven of subversive shenanigans aimed at removing Senator Lansing from politics. He was referred to among Washingtonians not as the lame duck, but a *dead* duck!

Valentina's failure to mention the Senator's plight might have explained the separate quarters ten acres away from the hacienda, her isolation, and her remoteness to D.C. social life. And that secret room! Her preoccupation with the past was dangerous.

His thoughts of Valentina progressed to the video cassettes she'd given him. He turned on the VCR. How the devil had Valentina come by the tapes? The question plagued, irked and tugged at his curiosity. *Dummy!* All you had to do was put your lips together and ask.

The screen lighted up and he replayed the tapes.

Geralee Macgregor and Anthony Harding! Incredible.

And the Persian Prince. He was more Harding's style. Harding, a closet queen, was married to preserve his image and politics, but those in the cloistered and hallowed circles of D.C., who possessed the innermost problems of its gilded stars, *knew* the inside dope. Harding had kissed asses all the way to the top, and done a few extra calisthenics en route to get him to a position of strength.

But was it all in America's best interests, Brad pondered? He knew he'd get better odds by betting it was all for Harding's interests. Trouble was, why the fuck Macgregor permitted him to bask in the glory of the State Department!

And that revelation about buying the West Bank!

How possible was it?

Brad kicked himself for not majoring in economics and banking! That's where the money is, old boy! And no puns intended!

He jogged his memory. Harding was too *charming*, overly solicitous, in the way confidence men exude obsequious pandering when soliciting prospective suckers, the overt signs of a power-mad Nero. There was much more to Harding than this thumbnail sketch, and Brad was forced to dig deeper. He turned off the VCR.

The more Brad dwelled on the material imparted to him by Valentina Lansing and the involvements of her daughter, the more aware he grew of his untenable position. Marnay had spelled it out for him. *There are those who will stop you, prevent you from meeting with your President . . .*

He honed in on Zurich! Zeller! The man with the colorless eyes!

What devilry had Valerie Lansing skinny-dipped into to cause such consternation and fear in her mother?

He thought of Valentina again, and that monstrous studio.

Christ! The obsession he'd witnessed earlier that day created doubts in Brad's mind. However spellbinding, however unique she was among woman, he had to place things in proper perspective. But how?

Stop it, Brad! Stop it! What matters is that Valentina Lansing has the President's ear! And that, by God, means catching the brass ring on the merry-go-round. Nothing else matters! Not for the time being. The imperative is to get to the Oval Office.

But now he could no nothing but wait. He loathed interminable waiting.

That night, after a light snack, Brad's attention repeatedly returned to Valerie Lansing. Intrigued by her, he considered the mysterious involvement to which she dedicated herself. Why did he get the feeling she played a part in this Zeller business? That something evil and dangerous colored her European incursions.

Obviously, since she hadn't the sense to experience fright on her own, Valentina had manifested the required fear absent in her daughter's nature.

Brad poured more Scotch. He was celebrating. He knew the identity of *Colorless Eyes!* Now, he *knew* why Berna had kept the truth from him. His confusion might have blocked out essential data that must be understood every step of the way. Each segment fitted into place like an intricate mosaic, and demanded painstaking effort to fit into place. He was sweating it when the curtain lifted.

Dummy! You pure, unadultered dummy! he railed himself.

Brad moved to his desk console, staring at his own personal, complex computer. For Christsakes! He'd suffered enough headaches trying to piece the fucking unending pieces together! All the while *Apollo's* brain was ready, willing and able to accept the collected data, and render him the needed answers!

Brad got to work, forgetting time, the entire world as he imparted to the *Apollo* brain all that had had been stuffed into his for the past many weeks.

Friday at six P.M. the President's stern voice on the telephone broke through his concentration. "All right, Major, you got through to me. What's the big rush? I'm up to you-know-what in international furor, domestic political mayhem, resignations and God knows what else. It's a goddamned cancer!"

"When you read the reports, you'll consider it top priority, sir."

"Can't it wait until Monday—next week?"

"No, sir." Brad heard shuffling of paper, slamming of books, the echo of muffled curses.

"Tonight or tomorrow, Major? Tomorrow . . . lunch . . . informal . . We'll chat. Bill Miller and Tom Kagen will be here."

Valentina Lansing was not mentioned.

Chapter Seventeen

LUNCHEON IN THE WEST WING OF THE WHITE HOUSE was a total bust. A hot and heavy global anabasis viewed on six video monitors had racked up enough negatives for Brad's briefing to ensure failure. The urgency of his business took an immediate back seat to the explosive action on center stage. The added impediments of *flash-intelligence* memos delivered by communications aides prescribed doom. If he had any sense, he'd leave . . .

On the screens they watched the fiery glow of exploding shells, flaring rockets zephyring across ghostly cities. Artillery pounded away as Scorpion tanks armed with .8mm guns lumbered over the desert terrain, crushing everything in sight. The situation in Lebanon was intense. American involvement in confrontation with the Israelis pitched at a high peak. Infantry soldiers fired blistering surface-to-air missiles at invading aircraft. Electronically astute flying nightmares, F-15's F-16's in aerial combat with MIG-21s, MIG-23s, MIG-25s equipped with ECM, jamming and anti-jamming devices, soared and dove in graceful arcs before exploding in midair. Others escaped. Guerillas armed with Kalishnikov assault rifles, grenades, recoilless rifles and rocket launchers moved with uncanny precision to advance posts. The faces of the guerillas were different on three of the screens, for these transmissions emanated from separate warring arenas. Three from the Middle East, yet the staccato of rifle fire, aerial gymnastics, deafening burst of weaponry and sophisticated war materiel presented deplorable consistency in performance. The international guerillas curiously bore uncanny similarity in training precision.

Judging from President Macgregor's tight-lipped expression, he *knew* the scenario. He tossed the napkin down on his plate fiercely.

"Where is it written on tablets of gold that Americans must be guardians of the globe?" He rose to his feet. "I'm going for a swim to cool off. Join me, anyone?"

For nearly a half hour Brad sat at the edge of the enclosed pool observing the President and his aides swim the length and back of the Olympic-sized pool. Brad cooled his own anger and used the time to forcibly obliterate all images of Geralee Macgregor and Anthony Harding from mind. How could he face the President, prevent this shocking incident from creeping into briefings to the Chief? *Did he know? Could he possibly be ignorant of his wife's indiscretions?* The implications of their boudoir liaison was like uncovering a pit of anacondas at the edge of a precipice with nowhere to go but over a high cliff into oblivion.

A half hour later they returned to the Oval Office, refreshed, momentarily free of frustration, disenchantment with Middle East routings. Dressed casually, the President mentioned Camp David. He saw no reason why they couldn't adjourn to the retreat to take advantage of the beginning beauty of the early spring. Resigned, however, he tossed Brad's lengthy brief on his desk, sat down behind it, gesturing to the others to do likewise.

Without preamble he nodded to Brad. "Suppose we get this show on the road. I've briefed Tom and Bill on the nature of your mission."

"The Committee hearings transcripts?"

The President nodded impatiently.

"I'll begin with penetration of GAMMA 10."

"You penetrated GAMMA 10?" Miller's curious glance connoted a glimmer of respect.

"If you react to everything the Major imparts we'll be here all day," the President said, forcing a tolerant smile.

"Suppose we get all the shockers out of the way? *Concatenate-Alpha* was also my doing."

The triumvirate exchanged glances of respect, astonishment and trepidation.

Losing none of the magic in that moment, Brad launched headlong into the meat of his dissertation. "Mr. President, Bill . . . Tom . . . I am convinced nuclear destruction is imminent. Your administration is targeted for political disaster, annihilation, if you will, by *invisible* forces alluded to in Pentagon hearings, and described succinctly in my brief. A conspiracy is at work to discredit the United States."

Having stunned his captive audience to stark attention, he poured on the facts, beginning with Uri Mikhail Gregorevich's speech, so curiously slotted before Musaka Mubende's unscheduled speech, his findings at GAMMA 10, Greer's subsequent revelations. He imparted how Greer's story led him directly to *Commissaire* Marnay. He graphically described the Frenchman's fears, his fiendish death at the Bristol, the attempts on his own life. He journeyed the rapt trio back to Greer's chalet, on to West Berlin, and using cover names to identify his sources, described his encounter with Wolfgang Katz. A delineation of Katz's background and death ensued. He described his own near-fatality by poison gas, the rescue and near-lethal encounter with Llamas. General Mark Samuels' arrogant temerity, he suggested, best described his curt dismissal of the man's death. "A separate file exists on Samuels and his real involvements in West Berlin. I won't take precious time to peel back the dirty layers of his involvements—yet."

Brad supported his reasoning behind his incursion of Clayallee 10 and penetration of *Concatenate-Alpha*.

He prudently refrained from describing Moufflon's effectiveness in jamming the Cat's trespass signals, minimized Berna's life-saving tactics in Cairo and Algeria, referring solely to the incident and one of Moufflon's agents. He repeatedly underscored the efficacious, unseen, unknown silent forces providing him *protection* against the overtly threatening forces assailing him, in their effort to diminish his chances of success.

"Can you identify those forces?" Miller asked, puzzled.

"No. I established the existence of the *invisible* power cartel spoken of in Pentagon hearings. A highly evolved aureole of power exists. The massive organization is expert in the dissemination of manufactured propaganda. Their tentacles grip the globe."

"You *identified* them? Kagen subdued a glimmer of excitement.

"Don't I wish . . . The apparatus is concealed behind multinational corporations thickly veiled by holding companies reaching into every area of control. They possess more sides and clever combinations than are found in Rubik's cube. And why not? They've spent generations perfecting clandestine intrigue."

"All this? So many risks for nothing?" asked a crestfallen Chief of State.

"No—not exactly nothing. I learned the identity of one man who can expertly detail immediate and maximum dangers. He can fix the proximity of nuclear war. He can identify the author of the Middle-Eastern scenario for the past two decades." Brad was deliberately vague, underscoring Berna's parting warning. *Beware . . . beware . . . Beware of those close to the Oval Office.*

"One man?" Miller's contempt was visible. "One man can identify what our intelligence community and spying satellites are incapable of doing?"

"I didn't clank sabres with death to spout fairy tales in the Oval Office, Bill." Brad was firm, repudiative, equally as forceful.

"Mr. President, no one wants to believe America to be less powerful than any nation, yet, an undercurrent of belief abroad suggests the United States has fallen prey to a *control* apparatus that robs us of prestige and power among our Allies. Europeans highly placed in government express dismay. Why, they ask, aren't efforts taken to crush this dangerous force swarming everywhere in American politics?" Brad sipped his coffee, noting the prodigious interest in his words before segueing jarringly. "Mr. President you are known globally as an anti-communist President—"

"What has *that* got to do with—" Miller's words fell to silence by Brad's restraining hand.

"—our Allies contend you are so far to the right, the stabilization of our government is barely possible."

"The Soviets must get the message," said Kagen, relighting his pipe. "They cannot repeat—puff, puff—Afghanistan, Czechoslovakia, Poland—"

"And so begins the pavane?" Brad countered. Meanwhile, the Soviets say the United States must get the message; it cannot do as it did in Tibet, Cuba, Africa, Vietnam, South America, Iran. That puts us back to square one." Brad was exasperated. "For the world to survive, U.S.-U.S.S.R. hostilities must cease. Unity between the superpowers would destroy subversives, those evil-boding *voices* in our nation. Make no mistake, a *voice* has dictated the American way of life for too long. . . . A cleverly concealed *voice* of destruction shapes the mind of our youth through carefully *controlled* media. Skilled agitators, they are instigating lethal damage to the core of America."

Miller's protest froze on his lips. Kagen pondered his pipe. Macgregor glowered. Brad plunged in deeper.

"Historically, the bearer of bad tidings was beheaded, tossed to the lions. Recent attempts on my life clearly suggest the volatility of my mission. The nuclear icing on the unpalatable cake of impending nuclear war is melting.''

"Major, you're floundering," Miller snapped. "Get to the point."

Brad continued, as if he hadn't heard the protest. "Think. Two former Allies in World war II became adversaries at the end of the war. The contributory causes . . .?''

"Any of a long list of grievances," Miller insisted. "Berlin Blockade, Berlin Airlift, the U-2 spy mission, the Cuban missile crisis, Vietnam? Take your pick.''

"Or," said Kagen, "perhaps it dates back to Stalingrad? Refusal of the Allies to open a second front and take the bludgeoning burden of Hitler's troops off Russia! Who knows?''

Brad shook his head. "You think any of these contributed to the alienation? Perhaps. I put it to you, insidious propaganda turned these nations into bitter political adversaries. Brutal anti-Communist flag-waving underlined every aggressive act on foreign soil as Communist-inspired when Communism had no bearing whatsoever on the issues at stake. You might be justified in asking, did Russia spread the toxin? *No.* Did America? Not *exactly.* Then, who? In four decades anti-RED propaganda does not cease. Who will ferret out the root cause?''

Brad shuffled through some papers in his briefcase.

"What of your own inculpation, Major?" Miller asked guilefully. "In the CIA you waged clandestine counterinsurgency defining Soviet and World Communism as the enemy. How exactly do you define your participation today?''

"Without sounding treasonous?" Brad smiled. "Very carefully." The others found no humor in his remark. "Very well, viewed three decades later, reprehensible, Bill. A major contributor to present-day global crisis. You want me to cop out? Blame my government? Insist I only took orders—did what I was programmed and ordered to do on penalty of death? It won't wash." Brad shook his head, his eyes remote. "I sat in judgment of the losers of World War II. Those men labeled *war criminals* by a *controlled* media also took orders from their leaders. Hell, I'm not talking psychopaths who enjoyed the power and blood letting—I'm talking of those admirable German officers who followed their commander's orders and were summarily placed on trial and executed for obeying their superior officers.''

Miller resisted. "Nuremberg magistrates suggested the alleged *war criminals* could have refused to take orders—"

"Goddamnit! No soldier in any army in the line of duty disobeyed orders from the top! Not you, Mr. President, nor I refused the dictates of our superior officers in the war!"

Brad sipped ice water. Then with the panache of a trained prosecutor he picked up the action. "For centuries losers of wars, leaders of defeated states, faced no executioners. Not even Napoleon! Never—not the first or second time he lost a war! Exiled, yes. Executed—no! Yet in 1945 the Allied victors executed so-called *war criminals,* the political and military leaders of Germany, Italy and Japan."

Brad lighted a cigarette, puffed thoughtfully. "No matter how the Allies dressed the atrocity, it came down to the same thing— victors killing off the losers! Conscience promoted the implementation of Allied Control Council Law Number 10 and the world had found their patsies—their fall guys—the Germans. Blame everything on the dirty old Nazis! Kill off all dangerous enemies— anyone who knew the truth—and blame it on the Germans."

"Major, exactly where-the-hell is all this leading?" Kagen sulked.

"You'll see in a moment. Western leaders, prompted by the established propaganda machine, established a precedent, a *noble* precedent!

"The winner of any war, moral or immoral, could exercise the right to execute the losers—all of them, if it suited their fancy— merely by labeling them war criminals or terrorists!"

"Major! You realize the implications you pose?"

"I pose nothing. It's in the laws and by-laws of ACC Law 10 and of the General Assembly of the United Nations." Brad fished out the Katz photos, placed them before the President and his aides, and harked back to his thumbnail sketch of Wolfgang Katz. When he finished he waited for their reactions. Nothing.

"You don't find it bitterly ironic? Not even devious when the suspects, highly placed collaborators, became party to the mass genocide of prison camp internees and actually got away with it, shoving the burden on the Germans themselves, some of whom may have not been inculpated? What magnificent scape goats, eh?

"Major! I object to all this," Kagen declared bitterly. "The implications and complications of such a wild exaggeration are indescribable. You realize what you are saying?"

The President and Bill Miller stared aghast from one to the other, shocked at the mild-mannered Kagen's unusual emotional outburst. The President held up a referee's hand. "Arguing is counter productive. Let the Major complete the briefing, Tom." The patronizing tone rankled Brad, but he moved on.

"Very well, Tom, since Katz's information offends you, let's go on to the post-war era. America, forced to sharpen its wits, broadened its intelligence forces and traveled the precarious journey of counterinsurgency. What good was it? Today we face a colossal enemy—thermonuclear war! Measures must be taken to circumvent global catastrophe."

The President growled. "I advocate new policies, strive for clearer international understanding, but our allies fail to see the urgency."

"Mr. President, the dissemination of false propaganda to *out-psyche* a purported enemy must cease. We must rid ourselves of the ignorance and fear of Communism!"

Oppressive silence, steeped with mixed emotions, accelerated the vibrations in the Oval Office. Brad sipped water studying the triumvirate's smoldering glances under lidded eyes. Miller dove in tersely. "This man—the man you spoke of earlier—uh, *Moufflon?* Can he identify these—uh—I feel ridiculous referring to them—*invisible* power brokers? . . . You're sure?"

"I'm sure."

Again, interminable silence, was followed by the sounds of heavy breathing, punctuated by loud sucking sounds as Kagen relit his pipe. Brad stretched his shoulders, rotated his neck, to limber up.

"Mr. President, a goddamned timebomb ticks to a countdown in the Middle East—"

"—and that timebomb is?" John Macgregor leaned forward eagerly.

Brad cleared his hoarse throat. "The fuse to that timebomb," he began, slowing the tempo, "is one nation. Not the people—that point is emphatically made—but the existing government of *that* nation, whose helmsmen are controlled by the propaganda machine. They make unreasonable demands upon the United States, upon mankind, and force escalation of nuclear war.

"Our allies ask, 'Why does America permit them to proliferate such evil? How dare the United States dictate policy to other nations when they remain inefffective against so insidious a force? The United Nations are mere errand boys for a moneyed lobby.' Rumors abroad proliferate. They say the Zurich cartel contributed to your campaign, ensuring your enslavement to their dictates.''

Kagen on his feet, voiced his outrage. "You dare—you dare make that insinuation—?''

"Not my insinuation, Tom. And where better than in the Oval Office to let our President know what is echoed overseas in high places?''

"The Major is not out of order, Tom,'' the President intervened. "In dealing with allies and enemies alike it's vital to know what they think.''

Brad paced the floor, growing wearied. He gestured in wide arcs. "Back to the Middle East . . .'' How the devil could he look Macgregor in the eye, convey the ignominious plans of his Secretary of State?

"A careful analysis reveals that *certain power factions do not want Arabs and Jews to live together in peaceful coexistence!*''

"That statement is unintelligent!'' Miller snapped.

"Not when viewed this way. First, the monetary gains from enforcing a perpetual state of war. Second, obsessive *control*. Consider the billions upon billions of dollars spent on arsenals, bringing enormous profits to the arms sellers. Let's not ignore the means by which the majority of arms are purchased. Dope, sold for cash, diamonds, gold and oil, laundered through European and Middle Eastern banks, pay for contraband weaponry. Who suffers? American drug-addicted youth runs epidemic! Corrupt government officials, captive to dope dealers, fall prey to their slightest wishes.''

"This gets worse by the moment. What exactly are you driving at?'' the President muttered gloomily, glancing at the ormolu clock on his desk. "You're covering a helluva lot of territory in one briefing.''

"No President can right the wrongs of previous administrations overnight,'' Miller said consolingly.

"Where will it end? Who'll steer America back on course?''

Brad glanced from one to the other. The battle lines were drawn. He sensed it. Did he dare skate over thin ice?

He did. His focus on the President, his manner ominously oblique, he urged, "We must not, Mr. President, permit America to fall captive to any foreign government or power machines.''

292

"You dare dictate policy to the President?" Miller's rapier voice sliced frigidly through the tension, astonishing the Chief.

Brad wanted to shout, "He has a staff of *hardliners* to do it for him," but instead he checkreined his fury, forced an exaggerated smile of bland innocuousness. "What utter absurdity, Bill! My purpose here is to uncover the malignancy eating at the core of this administration. Can we afford to ignore our allies? Think carefully, Mr. President, before you send them into Soviet arms. They do, *after all,* share the same continent."

They share the same continent!

The facts, indisputable, it was this statement summing up an inner reality that struck home. The pause was ominous, the tension worsening. At this point Brad glanced at his watch, and began wrapping up the session. When he finished, Brad, unable to gauge friend from foe, studied the trio. Miller vacillated. Kagen's expression contained less contempt. The President rode the rail, middle-fencing it all the way. Brad detected in each a calculated scorn, disbelief, and glistening at the apex of their discontent, wounded egos.

For hours Brad had run in downhill patterns with head and body feints, cutbacks, hooks, crossovers. He was learning how, when it came time for the ball to be tossed to him, to get past these, the President's men. For surely then, he would become a lion in a den of Daniels to the NSC and Joint Chiefs of Staff.

Through the briefing the point was made often enough, "You'll be obliged to edit the briefing, Major, to one third it's size."

The President intervened. "Why is it necessary to deprive ourselves the beauty of Camp David? We can easily continue the briefing there. Agreed?"

Calls were made to their respective families and in a quarter hour the foursome and Presidential entourage of Secret Service men strolled the short distance from White House to the waiting helicopter.

Brad used flight time to reflect on the Presidential aids. *Friends* in the intelligence community had prepared for Brad a psychological analysis of the two aides who strongly influenced the Chief Executive. Brad's careful study of these men made him less vulnerable to their sting. *But something distorted the picture. What?* Brad got the distinct impression, however much they appeared otherwise, that they weren't solidly connected in thought. Miller hit the hardest, Kagen with vitreol. In the final wrap-up *who* would become his ally?

Below, in the early twilight, he saw the splendor of Camp David at the tall end of a winter thaw. The Catoctin Mountains, still dotted with snow patches, resembled a Currier and Ives painting.

The Secret Service men, in touch with ground forces, cleared the chopper for landing. They exited first, assigned the trio their quarters at Dogwood. Their overnight stay limited their distance from Aspen, the Presidential quarters.

The Maryland air was cool, nippy, clear and invigorating, the accommodations rustic, homespun and relaxing. Following a brisk walk, they dined at Aspen, rather than Laurel Lodge, and sipped coffee and cognac in the Presidential study.

Briefing continued as if there'd been no break in continuity. The atmosphere, more relaxed in the wood-panelled den, brought an aura of calm to the foursome. Major Lincoln's opening statement galvanized the room and its occupants.

"There is a timetable. A plan for the reorganization of the Middle East. A plan to undermine the sovereignty of all the states in that region, transforming them into lawless tribal fiefdoms of organized crime."

The astonished expressions, mouths agape, wide-eyed disbelief stretched into throat-clearing spasms, crossing and uncrossing of legs, thigh slapping, a series of exchanged nervous glances.

"The hell you say, Major." The President clutched his brief. "It's all in here? Detailed? Including the fine print?"

Brad nodded.

"I believe it's in order, then, for the brief to be duplicated? A copy for Bill and one for Tom. I suggest they read it fully—then we can discuss it intelligently."

"I have no quarrel with that, sir, on the condition that no extra dupes are made. It would prove disastrous if the file should fall into enemy hands."

"Here at the White House—Camp David?"

"Especially here." Brad's eyes conveyed his caution, his concern.

"Very well, I'll assign the Secret Service to the task." He handed Miller the file. "Do what has to be done, Bill."

Brad sat uncomfortably with this decision, but waited for Bill to return before he revealed the denouement. "What I am telling you is not detailed in my report. Consider it a verbal addendum." The President raised his eyebrows at what this statement inferred, but listened intently to Brad's words.

"What I am here to tell you is that the West Bank is being purchased and developed at an alarming rate of speed. When one owns land, annexation becomes unnecessary."

He felt the venom hanging cloyingly in the air. Six frigid eyes focused on Brad. Six sharp ears listened for him to make a serious blunder. Unspoken questions frozen on their lips should have warned him to stop, regroup and assess his position. Instead, he plunged deeper into uncharted waters.

The look of Miller moving in for the kill caused Brad a moment's uncertainty, left him open to errors of judgment when he should have exercised rapier discernment. Making no excuses, he lowered his chin, narrowed his eyes and peering out under a projecting brow ridge, rocked heel to toe, his hands stretching and balling fists behind his back.

"We, the United States, the American people, are at a point of impasse. We are victims of *cover-ups.* *Cover-ups* that make Watergate pale and fall by the wayside. Our allies regard the prospect of placing nuclear arsenals in the hands of fanatics with mounting fear, while never has America's image abroad fallen to such low depths." Brad snuffed out a cigarette butt, continued.

"Mr. President, you can't give birth to a dream while you languish in the midst of nightmares. Like a godawful, horrifying nightmare, the sinister power machine pervading every aspect of government affects us all, our way of life, the welfare of the entire world. What do we do? Roll over and play dead?"

A pervasive silence met Brad's volatile summary. Finally the President spoke.

"Well, it's easy to see that we, unfamiliar with the entire scenario, must retire to our quarters to review the brief."

"Agreed," said Miller, donning a mask of diplomacy.

Kagen nodded in assent. "You composed a complex scenerio, Major. I dare not challenge you until I study the facts in detail."

On that note, they adjourned for the day.

Sunday they returned to D.C. "How much longer before we wrap it up, Major?"

"Give me an hour tomorrow. By then, you'll have had ample time to study the brief, become better acquainted with its contents."

The President's growing concern over the information imparted exploded in irritation. "What has all *this* complex rhetoric to do with impending nuclear war and U.S. culpability? The deaths of Musaka Mubende, the attempts on your life—the deaths of others?"

Even the aides indicated their astonishment at so naive a question after even a brief perusal of Lincoln's brief.

Brad, more lenient in his attitude toward Macgregor, replied calmly, bluntly. "Everything, sir. Those men died because they *knew* the truth. My own death is scheduled because I am a threat to *their* plans. This encounter, my meeting with you, was delayed by silent, unseen hands at work. The dead were silenced by assassins hired by Zurich, the same power cartel that wantonly orchestrates a bizarre symphony of global strife. They plan the worst bloodletting in the history of mankind."

"Pray to God, Major, you have proof of the allegations made these past two days."

And Brad paraphrased the words of a dead man, Wolfgang Katz. *"Oh, Mr. President, why would anyone want me dead, if I didn't know the truth?"*

Each parted in morose silence, their faces drained of color.

The next day Brad received a call. A meeting was scheduled at 4:30 P.M. Juggling of the Presidential agenda had swept aside all insignificant duties of his office; the priority was Lincoln.

Brad paced the floor of the Oval Office. His eyes trailed behind the President, rested briefly on the flagstaff and the flag between the blue-tinted windows, traveling upward to the fierce-eyed, golden eagle perched atop the pole, its wings outspread. He stared interminably at the fierce eagle eyes. "Approaching the last leg of my journey I needed more than a professionally acceptable reason to relentless track and pursue a man whose life I found contradictory, controversial and anathema to most American mentalities. I am speaking of the man, Moufflon." He continued, speaking cautiously, finished his spiel amid mounting pressures, omitting only Moufflon's true identity, his Corsican based operations and the story Berna had revealed of his ties to Zurich.

Yielding to instinct, he sat down. He found himself appending *sir*, to his answers, in sardonic, patronizing tones, and despite

296

a glowering Presidential countenance persisted in the deliqnency. Brad glanced at the mini counter in his cupped left hand. The needle was going berserk.

Miller pressed. "You mentioned certain silent forces covertly assisting you as you trailed through Europe and North Africa. You insist you cannot identify them?"

Brad reluctantly slipped the detector into his jacket pocket.

"To do so would venture us into speculation," he said, deliberately vague.

"Obviously a crisis is impending. Hopefully, Moscow will listen. We must move for a summit meeting, for more reasons than nuclear arms reductions," Miller said emphatically.

The President's quizzical gaze emphasized his disquiet.

"Implicit in your briefing is an admanant recommendation, since we stand on the threshold of the twenty-first century, that we desist placing nuclear arsenals in the hands of people not yet attuned to the twentieth century?" Kagen spoke up.

"In a nutshell, Tom. No matter how we attempt deception, the sobriquet of the next century is thermonuclear war, my friends, unless the super powers take steps to circumvent such a catastrophe. Certainly the Third World nations won't agree to give up their playtoys."

"Christ," muttered Kagen. "They must all know the after-effects of nuclear warfare!"

"Do they think—any of them—do they believe they can destroy their neighbors without suffering domino effects of radiation, fallout, toxic fumes—"

"Mr. President," Brad continued, clearing his throat. "We— America must take a stand or we shall be at a dangerous impasse with the world. What America does in the coming days will determine mankind's preservation or its extinction."

"Brad," the President sounded fatigued, "The infectuous malaise eating at the heart of our nation is not autochtonous to my administration. I'd appreciate *your* acknowledgement that an imperfect nation existed long before I took office. I grow weary of the excoriation done me for the blunders of my predecessors.

"Mr. President, you forget I was briefing officer to several before you took office. I do understand the problems. To these proud, stubborn, competitive men, accustomed to dignity and public respect, admission of oversight or contradictory action would be at odds with the image each had of himself, the image of careful appraisal and flawless wisdom. The Middle East is tottering in the hands of a very dangerous clique. Men playing lethal games of international monopoly have inborn hatred for mankind and want to dominate by *controlling* the world. And once they succeed in their ends, they will control the world's oil supply and the worst danger of all, the Golden Crescent! and its addictive opium poppy. From which,'' Brad lowered his voice even further, ''stems more control than the desire for oil!''

''We must discourage precipitate action,'' the President said glumly.

Brad, afflicted with the need to wrap it up, closed his briefcase, glanced at his watch. ''I must urge you to contact Moufflon through proper channels. It is my belief the future of all mankind rests solely in his hands.''

The future hope of all mankind?'' Macgregor uttered a throaty exasperated sigh. Miller and Kagen, as inscrutable as the Sphinx, studied the President. ''I find that remark a bit much to swallow, wouldn't you say, Brad?''

Brad *wouldn't* say. He submitted the remainder of photographs, microfilm, pictures of the atrocities done to Wolfgang.

''Any idea who wants you dead, Major?'' Miller spoke with brutal candor, his head cocked speculatively to one side, forehead corrugated in query. ''We must assume the assassins— whoever they are—place esteem on your death. Now you've briefed the President and his aides, a shift in focus must include the President, Tom and I as targets. Surely Major, you have an inkling of their identities?''

All eyes were on Miller. Brad critically studied the lanky intellectual. Miller's command of foreign affairs—short of spectacular, including direct pipelines to foreign embassies and key emissaries—enhanced his value to the Oval Office. Brad understood, although he loathed his goading and oppressive attempts to protect the President. He also knew what Miller implied and rebutted abruptly.

''Not Moufflon's people. I'd stake my life on it. Meeting him on a one-to-one basis is viable through State channels. You see, we served together in the war as allies.''

''You *know* his identity?'' Miller thumbed through the brief.

Brad, nodding, addressed the President. ''Until your decision to confer with him is finalized through his advisors, I swore to make no identification, for obvious reasons.''

The aura in the Oval Office metamorphosed. They stared at Brad as if he were a traitor. Worse—he felt like one. He took a firm stand. He could not betray the confidence, more than just one man's life was at stake. Brad suggested they reread his report, study his recommendations to better understand the complexities.

"This suggests something ominous, Mr. President." Kagen's tone communicated urgency. "We must proceed with the assumption that his alleged assassins *know* of these briefings. The buck has just passed from him to the Oval Office."

Miller obliquely scrutinized Kagen. "Am I hearing an echo, Tom? Didn't I just imply the potential hazards?"

"Yes. I merely emphasize the menace. The Secret Service must be alerted—perhaps the FBI."

"No!" Macgregor was adamant. "My present concern is the level at which we become expendable. First, we analyze and evaluate the Major's brief. I insist the briefs be kept under tight security wraps. Agreed? The briefs do not leave the Oval Office—got it?"

A little late for that, Mr. President. God knows who has the dupes!

Brad listened as the Chief Executive outlined his plans.

"We four are responsible for numerous lives. If one word leaks, one of us will be faulted. And may God have mercy on his soul! Brad, did you obtain the Kaltenbrunner records in their entirety?"

Kaltenbrunner!

He stood for a moment considering the implication. Nowhere, not once in his rambling, nor in his brief, had the name *Kaltenbrunner* appeared! He felt sick to his stomach. Marshaling his wits, he was dealt another low blow. As the President referred to the thick brief before him, he shifted its position and Brad caught sight of a golden-globe paperweight; it was partially covered by the file.

Struck suddenly by massive incongruities in the behavior of these men, he had to flee. Uncertain how he had exited the Oval Office, he recalled making some lame excuse, an imperative to keep a nonexistent appointment.

The paranoia was not unjustified. In his rental car Brad left the Pennsylvania Avenue address, making his way homeward, past

Washington Circle to N Street, his eyes in every direction at once, yet seeing nothing.

Holy Christ! John Macgregor had pointedly asked for Kaltenbrunner's records in their entirety!

Inside the townhouse Brad fed the dogs, checked the alarms, swept the house for covert electronic devices, and sat down before the television set with a freshly uncorked pinchbottle. He began sipping, progressed to gulping it until he got stinking drunk.

Chapter Eighteen

FLASHING RED AND GREEN LIGHTS ON THE COMMUNICATIONS console in the den had gone berserk. The answer phone, glutted with messages ignored for days made swishing sounds; tapes spinning on spools flapped chaotically.

Brad awakened hung over. He mixed a fast Bromo, popped a few Tylenol capsules, fixed an icepack for his head and set a fresh pot of coffee brewing.

Padding into the den he slipped off the cacophony of lights, recorders, and switches, reversed the tapes and holding his aching head until the room's momentum abated, delicately depressed the play button on the message machine, wincing at the slightest squeak.

The first message: Mr. 711 . . . Jubilee is dead . . . Drug O.D. . . . Police are asking questions. I told 'em you spoke with him that morning. They says it's impossible 'cause Jubilee was dead twelve hours before. Sorry, I hadda give 'em your name. This is Lolly.

The second message: H'ya . . . White Bear here. You wanna know what happened to Jane Doe? Call me. You won't believe it . . .

The third message: Hey, buddy . . . Aaron, here. I got the data you ordered. S-H-I-T! What are ya on to? This is dynamite! . . . Be expecting a parcel from me via Speedee Delivery. Listen, why don't ya send me the tickets in advance? I don't believe you're still walking around snug as a bug . . .

300

F-u-n-n-e-e-e-e, Aaron. Brad pushed the lever again.

Sounds of the door chimes interrupted him. Brad squinted painfully above at the closed-circuit video screen mounted on the wall. *Speedee Delivery*—already? He padded to the front door, peered through the peephole, opened the door, signed for it and took the package inside, glancing at the secret coding Aaron used on the upper left-hand corner: Three circles within a triangle.

Coffee pot in one hand, parcel in the other, he returned to the den, placing the items on his desk. He pulled back the drapes, shoved open the sliding glass doors, muttered a greeting to the two Doberman guard dogs, hand-signaling them to silence.

Beyond the fence, spring was in blossom. The university grounds abounded in greenery. He inhaled deeply, wincing at the ache in his head, rubbed gritty eyes and yawned. He needed a hot shower, a shave, *and* coffee!

He returned to his desk, gulped down a full cup, tore open the package, tossing the wrappings into a trash container. He scanned a few pages. Good. Very good. He felt the inner coiling of tension of a man on the threshold of discovery. He sat down, continued to read. Better. Getting better all the time. He lost track of time.

Four disturbingly unique human beings—Amadeo Zeller, Victor Zeller, Valentina Varga Lansing, Vivaldi Bonifacio—and their innermost secrets leaped off the page at him. Four key people who figured prominently into the Moufflon scenario and the impending threat of nuclear war! *Oh, Christ! Jesus Christ!*

Brad Lincoln waffled outright. For days and nights he took uppers, comsumed gallons of black coffee, forgetting to bathe or shave. He barely ate.

The Amadeo Zeller file was the profile of a demon!

Ruthless, domineering, egomaniacal men had abounded in his lifetime, but as he read and tried to form an image of this man, he couldn't. He read and reread the dossiers wondering, had his imagination created a monster? The evil of the man became increasingly apparent. Sifting fact from fiction, he wondered how the hideousness connected the lives of Zeller, Bonifacio, Valentina Lansing and Victor Zeller. It was enough to send him into borderline shock.

Who'd believe him? The Oval Office, already viewing him through jaded eyes, would label him certifiable if he presented these files!

Driven inescapably by phantoms to cover his tracks, Brad photocopied the files, stowed the originals in a bank vault.

Christ!

Zeller had dismantled governments! Thrown nations into utter chaos! Created enfeebling wars that sapped the life's blood from countless nations! Tyrants raised up had been toppled and slain when their reason for existence no longer served his purpose! He had destroyed the validity of a nation's currency! And none of his ignominious deeds were traceable to Zeller—not legally or on paper! Brad needed no verification, he *knew* because it was his business to know.

Wolfgang had given him the key—a man with *colorless eyes!* Valentina had identified her grandmother's tormentor—*colorless eyes!* Berna had validated Zurich as the man with *colorless eyes!* How many men existed with such a trademark whose deeds and manipulations formed a perfect m.o.?

Brad envisioned the man's soul glowing, an internal core of fire primed to burst into conflagration! Amedeo Zeller—a beast!

He punished himself for not paying more attention to Major Victor Zeller's dossier in World War II in the *White Coral Operation.* No prognosticator could have guessed what had evolved since then.

Brad was exhausted, tired of flimsy glossed-over clichés and patriotic euphemisms, tired of probing, searching, knitting complicated mosaics into intelligible patterns for others to dismantle. He felt like burning the files, fleeing the country, dropping his identity to live out his remaining days on some Edenic paradise, an island in the sun, away from man and all his hideousness.

A week later Brad was summoned to the Oval Office. Subdued, showing signs of strain, yet, astute and far more trenchant than in the recent past, he met with the President in private, answered questions put to him as best he could, always crimcumspect.

Two weeks later Brad's world exploded.

Chapter Nineteen

IF THE OVAL OFFICE WAS THEATER, the President's Conference Room was Grand Opera, where the arias sung seldom subscribed to authored librettos. Improper emotions corrupted the control and elegance of the production, no matter how skilled were the divas and tenors.

Daylight was totally suppressed by draperies in the Colonial decor, the only whisper of the twentieth century was the air conditioning. Courtesy—*Thank you for Not Smoking*—cards lay in gold holders before each place setting. Compotes filled with candy-anything to alleviate nicotine withdrawals—graced the table.

Brad watched them file into the room. What's the emergency? they asked. Who the hell is Major Lincoln? Never heard of him! What are his credentials? Why hadn't the Chief briefed them in advance? I was parring the ninth hole when my aide reached me! *Dammit!* No smoking. Again? Don't tell me the fucking Middle East is exploding again! Damn!

Brad avoided their eyes, glanced about the room at the American flag behind the President's chair, at the golden fierce-eyed eagle perched atop the round globe, listening to their idle chatter.

These, the President's Special Secret Team of Advisors—members of the NSC, Secretary of State Anthony Harding, the Joint Chiefs of Staff and other advisors—took their places on signal from the President. Macgregor chaired the meeting, keeping it subdued. He introduced Brad, backgrounding his work and credentials.

The tense, hostile atmosphere grew stifling. Hard, appraising eyes glared scathingly at Brad, furious at the interruption of their pleasures. Under lidded eyes Brad studied Anthony Harding intently.

Once the diplomatic strokes were gotten out of the way, a beguiling *corrida* commenced. The scenario played with the cleverness of an impassioned bullfight.

At times, Brad, the matador, performed brilliant *veronicas* with Belmondo expertise; then his role changed and he demonstrated the mercurial skill of an enraged Miura bull charging against the *picador's* knife thrusts; then once again he became the matador, swallowed by the butchery of blood-thirsty spectators. When pushed to the moment of truth, none displayed courage enough to thrust him through with the *muleta*. Brad admirably resisted their attempt at his annihilation.

A barrage of insulting, insinuating questions was hurled at him rendering him dazed, perplexed, and anxious.

"I expected a battle," he said easily, "not a massacre." But, as they spoke and he listened, replying economically, seldom belaboring the points, reserving his answers to "yes" or "no" when possible, there began to form hidden messages he couldn't ignore.

Brad held the distinct advantage. He *knew* them. He *knew* the contents of Amedeo Zeller's dossier and it made these men more visible in his eyes. How cleverly they disguised ignominious deeds behind innocuous expressions! Behind veiled eyes and a surface politeness, how they scrutinized him!

Marvin Pressman, Secretary of Defense, a tall, blond man with graying hair and deceptively young features, was carefully barbered, casually but expensively dressed, and looked as if he'd mosied in off the ninth fairway. He put a question to Brad, bluntly, as if he expected contradiction. "I find it extraordinary that you should find things where our *own* men have failed."

"What the devil does *that* mean, Marvin? *Our own men?*" Macgregor intervened. "What the bloody blazes do you think the Major is—if not our *own* man?" The President's inclination to anger was unmistakable.

For a time the *advisors* scanned the briefs. Pressman dismissed the President's remark as rhetorical. They sipped their drinks, and Brad watched them wind up, prepared to fire stormy salvoes at him. He subjected himself to their probing barbs, parrying skillfully without letup.

One of the NSC advisors, a *summa cum laude* graduate who broadcasted the fact with every word, was a man of seventy who looked fifty. A few face lifts, eye tucks, collagen shots—what the hell, he even walked twenty years younger. Oliver Gillman picked up the tempo. pausing periodically to wipe his glasses as if he'd learned the technique to unnerve an opponent. After firing off a number of questions, he listened to Brad's reply.

Leaning in, catching Brad's eye, dramatically he patted, "I've never heard such rot since the Apollo theory was promoted at Delphi." This in answer to a question concerning Moufflon.

"I didn't realize you were *that* old, Gilly," the President said buoyantly in an attempt to lift the pall of gloom hovering over the conference room. The President's slickly quarterbacked plays moved the team strategically in an effort to zero in on the subject of *Moufflon*. His aides, like loyal linemen, attempted to protect his flanks, some ran interference, others evidenced frustration when he failed to heed them.

"Major Lincoln, a specialist devoted to the service of our nation, deserves to be heard without restraints. You've placed him on the defensive, deliberately obstructing his efforts. Recent assassination attempts created hell for him."

Brad tuned them out, his condescension obvious. Rapier questions, designed to pierce through Moufflon's identity, chipped away at him until the jacket of *traitor* hung oppressively over him. He flat-out refused to document Moufflon's identity until *after* a Presidential decision was reached.

Hell broke loose!

Storms of protest by men unaccustomed to outspoken subordinates stopped short of personal attacks and overt threats. Brad, visible now to all of them, had avoided visibility in his career. Now, he committed names and faces to memory, for as they spoke, Brad's resentment of them grew. He distrusted their opinions and ideas, for most were stereotypical of the political malaise eating at America in the fifties. They promoted outdated political rhetoric with no concept of what was happening in the world. How in God's name were these men placed into cushy jobs?

They vetoed initiating dialogue with *Moufflon*. Stunned, Brad asked if they offered any alternatives. Yes, they would sit it out, wait for something more threatening to occur before taking any action. They accepted the statements of American ambassadors presently wholesaling American proposals in the Middle East assuring America that no real or immediate dangers threatened!

No real and immediate dangers exist!

Brad exploded. "You are supposed to be reasonable men entrusted with the leadership of our nation! What you are—" At his vitriolic words every head jerked up, riveted on him. The President's eyes telegraphed warnings.

The moment was irresistible!

So Brad bit the dust. "Uh—what you are is—well, you *aren't* experts! . . . Uh . . . not trained intelligence men." Macgregor breathed easily at the manufactured balm. But too soon!

"Knowing what I *know*," Brad continued, "risking what I've risked in meeting with international ambassadors, I listen to you discharge awesome responsibilities with irresponsible lack of intergrity—and I want to retch! You *dare* sit here, in the shadow of government, negating in detail the existence of a global power apparatus aimed at mankind's annihilation? Christ! The least effective buck private knew this as fact forty years ago. You know intimately the ploys of this cancerous malaise undermining the heart of America! You blatantly deny its existence?" Brad stood up, kicked back his chair, a look of pained apology shot toward the President. He collected his briefcase, and, nodding to Kagen and Miller, braced and strode out of the room.

The *Company* had made him a cynic; his work a disbeliever of men, but the Zeller files had rocketed him to a plateau of violent hate for the breed of man for which Zeller stood. He now believed that the system to which he had devoted his life was foul and needed a thorough expurgation.

Something had to be done—soon!

How could he tell these men, any of them, what Abou-Qir spoke about, the Golden Crescent, and plans to redraw the Middle Eastern boundaries? Better keep it under wraps, Brad, old chap, until you know these men.

BOOK III

Chapter Twenty

BRAD LINCOLN HAD AN UNKNOWN ALLY IN D.C. Uri Mikhail Gregorevich, in contradiction to Soviet politics, firmly believed an expedient, vital in solving the Middle East crisis, was crucial. Seated in the plush offices of the Soviet Embassy at 1825 Phelps Place, Northwest, he flipped the replay button on the tape recorder concealed in the Grand Baroque desk, listening as the tape swished back to the "start" position. A thick, frayed manila file lay on the desk—a KGB report labeled: MOUFFLON.

Uri was tall, slim-hipped, instantly identifiable by his sultry dark eyes and handsome features, the military swagger, and Bond Street tailoring. His well-muscled athlete's body, gleaned from a lifetime of fencing, expert horsemanship, and soccer, barely concealed under the impeccable fit of his clothing, drew second glances from both sexes in the nation's capital. His education was formidable. He was admired in D.C. political circles for his demonstrated, keenly honed intellect, enhanced by a sharp, charming wit.

Uri Mikhail, no theoretician, despised abstractions. He believed they held no place in politics—perhaps in science and the management of human lives, but not in politics. Politics to the young Russian was a battleground of tactical planning, strategy, not conjecture or hypothesis. His political advocacy implied explicit knowledge of one's opponents, honest fact assessments, then forthright battle, but always, always an avoidance of military incursions. Unfortunately, Uri at thirty-nine, was unjustly victimized by his youth. The Junior Politburo's member's belief bore little weight and no similarity to those expressed by Senior Politburo members except in certain power circles.

Uri ran his slender fingers through his dark, closely cropped curly hair. He removed his gold-rimmed glasses worn more for effect than for functional purposes and sat back in the hobnailed, carmine saddle-leather chair. His eyes ran over the neat clutter of his desk, fell on the vodka-filled lead crystal decanter. He poured a tumbler full, reflecting momentarily. As innovator of daring, untried political vistas, he had transcended Soviet diplomatic decorum with audacious honesty seldom flaunted in political and diplomatic corridors. Political VIPs knew when you asked Uri Mikhail Gregorevich a question you got straight answers. Question the intrepid Russian concerning affairs of state, his stock answer—preceded by sardonic, exaggerated amusement—seldom varied. "To speak candidly of any woman, including Mother Russia, is the height of dastardliness."

No smug political rhetoric hung seven veils on every fact.

The tape recorder ground down to an abrupt halt. Uri pressed the play lever. Bill Miller's smooth voice intruded on the silence.

"Uri, the Moufflon apparatus is incredible. The question is: can he deliver? The unification of the superpowers in this joint venture will create hell in the lion's den. The fur will fly here and abroad. The iron barricade around the golden eagle must be penetrated. Rest assured your role in this mission will not be seen as subordinate to the United States. I will get back to you soon. . . ." The tape swished noisily and Uri turned off the switch.

Whistling low, he lighted an American filter-tip cigarette, smoked it Russian style, holding it between his thumb and forefinger. He sipped his vodka, glancing at the MOUFFLON file, marveling silently. *That Andreevich Malenekov!* Born with a bloodhound's nose and instinct, when was the KGB Chieftain ever wrong?

"The Americans are contemplating covert action with Moufflon!"

These words spoken six months ago by Malenekov were relegated to pages of history moments ago by Bill Miller's testimony. That Uri Mikhail would prove a valuable instrument of negotiations in the *Moufflon* initiative was unknown to the Americans or to Uri himself, but not to the crafty KGB Chief. Uri's burning desire to meet the enigmatic *Moufflon* heightened the intrigue. Wisely, Uri had kept this desire to himself. How incredible! Fate had mixed the proper ingredients in this bowl of intrigue and was about to deliver the finished product.

Uri, destined for spectacular achievement, was born February 8, 1945 to General Mikhail Gregorevich and his remarkable wife, Zahara, at the family's summer estate in Zhukova. As the son of a distinguished, staunch Party member, winner of Soviet medals of honor in World War II, he was schooled in the highest academic universities in Russia and did his stint in the military forces.

Before age five, Uri had memorized his primer and rode a horse as expertly as any cavalry officer. At age six, his clever agility and physical coordination drew raves from his fencing master. At age eight, he sailed a skiff along the Moscow River in regatta competition. At age ten, when stories of Stalin's repressive leadership piqued his curiosity, Uri asked hard, intelligent, deeply probing questions. Marxism and Lenin's Communism were not easy for Uri to comprehend; Stalin's death—a shocker. It was later, during the de-Stalinization of Russia, that Uri's political vistas broadened. During Khrushchev's reign, Uri, well-steeped in academia beyond his age, went abroad to study at Cambridge in England, later Harvard in the States. The political contrasts intrigued and puzzled him.

As a future contender for the highest office in Russia, Uri bridled at, yet purposely maintained a low profile among the hierarchy of the elite Soviet Politburo. Uri recognized the perils—to antagonize the ruling moth-eaten political tigers, ravaged by their own bitter jealousies of the younger fledglings—was to commit political suicide. To alter the thinking of this antediluvian body of men would take a major revolution of thought, one not on the current agenda.

This critical observer of Russian politics roamed freely through the Kremlin political arena, assessing both assets and pitfalls of the system, noting the sharp contrasts between East and West, and retaining the positive aspects of each, kept his silence.

In the later years of this decade, possibly in the 1990s—if the world still existed—middle-level Russian officials would be jockeying about for power in the inevitable transfer of authority to men of Uri's generation. Premier Vladenchenko's protégé must be prepared. If the Russian Premier's clout prevailed, Uri Mikhail would become Premier following his demise. But the Premier, as tough a man as he was sentimental, conveyed the message to his protégé with brutal candor. "If you, Uri Mikhail, were incapable of dignifying the helm of Soviet politics in these troubled times, I would defeat you, if forced to return from my grave to accomplish the feat."

Doubt the Russian Premier? Never!

Uri butted the filter-tip, poured more vodka, and sipping it walked to the window. Crowned spokes of illumination projected over the Capitol dome, lit up the night sky like a giant midway. Uri sighed, the slightest hint of wistful homesickness evident. *Concentrate, Uri. Concentrate.*

Bill Miller. Their paths had crossed often at diplomatic functions and a friendship had evolved. Both had freely engaged in personal, political and diplomatic rhetoric, finding each shared common grounds of thought. Uri weighed the importance of Miller's call. It had confirmed more than Moufflon's existence! It confirmed the Middle East menace: the proliferation of illicit narcotics saturated the Middle East, rendering income from the Golden Crescent more lucrative, more tempting than the billions in oil revenues. Every nation covertly scrambled for control, hiding their greed under various guises of humanitarian endeavors. Oh, how the greed dripped from their wet, venomous fangs! KGB Chief Malenekov believed in Moufflon.

"He is a sorely needed catalyst, Uri. He could expose the proliferating conspiracies which shroud nuclear perils, yes, yes, and which for Soviets present viable menace. Worse, Uri Mikhail, word reached First Chief Directorate of new redesignings of Middle East boundaries!" These words spoken by Andreevich Malenekov shocked Uri into realization of the severe gravity underoot.

A redesigning of Middle Eastern boundaries!

What an ambitious, but deadly goal! Did the perpetrators know the extent of their madness? Uri had spoken with Miller. They agreed that the next step depended upon the President's ability to assess the value of Soviet participation. The stumbling blocks: *Presidential Wooden Soldier advisors! Formidable puppets!*

Uri shuddered. To control the Golden Crescent and oil-rich Middle East, Zurich was prepared to risk nuclear war. *NUCLEAR WAR!*

They were mad! Uri paced the room. Thermonuclear war was not child's play! It was a global incinerator!

"Malicious propaganda paints Soviets as aggressors," Andreevich had told him. "Why, Uri, because when our borders are threatened we take immediate action? Yes, yes, it is a false profile given to us by deployers of vicious anti-Red rhetoric who spread it to the Western world. It is a plague to us, it strains

312

relations with the United States. But we shall not play so foolish games, yes?''

And Uri wondered why *America refused to expose such subversive manipulators.* He was confounded why, if Russia sneezed, American heartbeats stopped. If America hiccoughed, reverberations resounded throughout the Kremlin. Each nation was perfectly attuned to the other's bags of political shenanigans, knew intimately the other's intelligence-gathering apparatus and networks of information. CIA and KGB agents outdid the other to cover their footprints in global operations, and each knew in advance what the other intended. It was fiasco!

These two superpowers could not establish a foundation of friendship based on mutual respect and human needs instead of a schizophrenic need to out-psyche the other. Rather vicious propaganda manipulated by independent global titans aimed at breeching their relations struck at the very core of their nerve network, deteriorating possible accord between them.

The American President, thought Uri, a puppet, manipulated by these silent, *invisible* forces, was too deeply entrenched to exit gracefully. One of two options remained for him, assassination or impeachment on trumped-up charges. In an effort to obtain a more intimate profile of the man in the Oval Office, Uri had cajoled Bill Miller into giving him his personal impression of the President. Uri gained no insight from Miller regarding the man at the helm of the ship of state. On the subject of John Macgregor, Miller was mute.

Uri's respect for Miller grew over a shared concept: a dream of alliances, trust, and understanding between their nations. However improbable the dream, the concept was not abandoned. Both adamantly opposed those invisible forces prescribing global genocide. Why, for the love of God, did they persist in wholesaling nuclear destruction? Had they coveted plans of a secre escape hatch to the next dimension?

Telephone chimes shook Uri from his reverie. He returned to his desk, glanced at the flashing red light; his private line. Eagerly, a tinge of elation in his voice, he picked up the receiver.

"Valerie? . . . I see. . . . If you will—tell me where Miss Lansing can be reached. . . . I see. Thank you, you are most kind.'' Uri hung up the receiver, sat back, brooding at the inner design forming in his mind. Was it possible? Was Andreevich

Malenekov correct as usual? Deeply disturbed, he reflected on Valerie Lansing, on their first encounter.

It was January, shortly following his address to the Pentagon committee hearings. Uri Mikhail Gregorevich had become a *cause célèbre* in D.C. His speech had shocked the committee members. Leaks of his audacity and bravery spread. Suddenly, he was a sought-after commodity. Washington socialites and hostesses were determined to glitter their tables with this *in* luminary.

Uri considered declining the hand-delivered invitation to the gala in honor of President John Macgregor given at the Virginia home of Senator and Mrs. Lansing, but his curiosity over the President lured him like a shark by live bait.

Valerie Lansing swept him off his feet. Her beauty, striking resemblance to her mother, was astonishing; she exuded warmth and cordiality. She had done her homework, read a brief bio on their guests and, with amazing recall, engaged him in conversation about his favorite hobbies other than politics.

Valerie, a knockout, was everything Uri dreamed of in a woman. Enchanting, delightful, witty, gay, extremely intelligent and totally lacking in that empty-eyed, posed affectation plaguing the bird-brained chits flitting about D.C., available to anyone in the diplomatic service.

"I love parties, pretty women, vodka, caviar, champagne and gourmet foods. Does that make me enough of a capitalist to stir your interest?" he asked Valerie. "I wish to know you better."

Valerie laughed merrily. "Your life is regimented and centered around your diplomatic role. I would find that weary and increasingly boring."

"How well you know me," he chided gently, then on a more serious note, "I mean what I say. Will you have dinner with me tomorrow night?"

"No, thank you. No. I'd loathe the heartaches. Besides, I will not play second fiddle to any man's career."

"Your mother seems to have fared quite well adjusting to her husband's career."

Valerie flashed defiant azure eyes on him, caught herself, smiled and bypassed him momentarily in favor of another guest.

Valerie was smashing. She was perfect. Smitten with the ravishing, fiery-haired, blue-eyed Georgetown lawyer, he observed her at a distance. How she glowed in the circle of her parents' wealth and clout! Jarred by inconsistencies, he felt certain she, as a woman, was equally attracted to him as he was to her, but when he turned on the charm, she wasn't buying. He persisted throughout the evening, amid the gaiety and excitement of visiting film celebrities, to reach her, unable to penetrate that superficial hostess manner in which she conveniently cloaked herself when it suited her purpose.

She spoke guardedly, laughed as if in afterthought. She was remote—infinitely remote when she chose. "Let's dine together tomorrow," he insisted. No! "The next night? The night after? Lunch, even breakfast?" She declined.

"Perhaps on your next trip to Washington."

A refusal—but she hadn't slammed the door in his face. She had left it ajar.

Uri called her the next day, the day after, and the day after that. A secretary at the law firm vaguely insisted Miss Lansing was away on sabbatical. "Miss Lansing is *not* accepting clients presently." Uri insisted he wasn't a client, but a friend. "Then you should know where to reach her," came the sharp retort.

Uri continued to call her on each trip to D.C.—he even called her from Moscow. Now—how long ago was it?—he got the same vagueness from the law firm, and, this last call to the housekeeper at the Senator's Virginia residence grew annoyingly repetitious . . . "Miss Lansing is away on a sabbatical."

Uri reached for the manila folder, one the KGB Chieftain had given him before he left Moscow. He knew the content by rote, and disbelieved what he read. Valerie, a superior defense lawyer—a trial attorney—hadn't tried a law case in years? Her anonymity, her reclusiveness disturbed him. What was this *"sabbatical"*? How did it tie into her present dangerous mission? All the mystery made her exceedingly intriguing to Uri. It provoked him into concern and fear for her life and a desire to protect her from the perils to which she had subjected herself. *This is ridiculous . . . she probably has a lover*.

A recent memo on Valerie puzzled him. Contents: SUBJECT APPLIED FOR PASSPORT IN MARCH 1983. FRENCH, SWISS, ITALIAN VISAS. COPIES AND PHOTOSTATS ENROUTE.

The lover was at least a globe-trotting man!

He poured a refill, swirled the vodka around in the glass. Uri sipped the vodka, his free hand grasping the ornate gold watch looped on a thick gold chain through his vest. He finger-polished the timepiece with his thumb. Removing it, he flipped open the lid. The haunting refrains of Rimski-Korsakov's *Scheherezade* played.

Scheherezade . . . Scheherezade, indeed! His mother's favorite!

He could not hear the music without experiencing a flood of emotions and mental images of her. Pained, he snapped the lid shut. But memories of his beloved *Mamuska* afflicted Uri with sudden tenderness. He popped open the lid, placed the watch open-faced on his desk, listening to the refrains, staring at the image of a stunning ebony-haired, black-eyed beauty whose eyes stirred in him a haunting hunger for Mother Russia.

Oddly, from his beloved mother, Uri had learned of a most unusual odyssey—one of intrigue and curiously twisted by fate. It shook him to know that all he had prepared for in life hung by slim threads, threatening his existence. As menacing as the unseen forces propelling the world toward ultimate destruction, a similar unraveling—the blight of scandal—threatened Uri's hopes, dreams, ambitions . . . perhaps his life.

Oh, God! It happened so long ago—before my birth. . . .

He blinked the thoughts away. He had to or go mad.

He had known nothing about the past until late in 1978 following General Gregorevich's death when Zahara insisted upon secluding herself in the Gregorevich summer manor in Zhukova, an estate wooded with stately pines and birches at the outskirts of Moscow. Members of the Soviet elite lived in nearby mansions and grand old estates, ignoring the modern conveniences of luxury apartments in Moscow, where Uri resided. Away from home attending universities in those final years, Uri returned each summer to renew ties and walk leisurely about the estate with his unique and astonishingly beautiful mother.

How prodigious were the wounds produced in Uri since 1978? An assessment of the possible political damage was incalculable! Uri sighed heavily. And all of it over a damnable scrapbook of memorabilia concerning the life of a mysterious woman named Lomay St. Germaine, and an unknown Corsican! Uri's incessant questions and curiosity over his mother's preoccupation with the scrapbook merely increased her remoteness and her Mona Lisa smile.

A major contributor to the training of Uri's mind, Zahara,

fluent in five languages, also spoke several Arabic languages, including Farsi and Persian, with facility.

Uri, in awe of his mother, grew into manhood, reveling in her beauty and intelligence. He loved her beyond belief.

Her hobby! A mad passion for goats! Incredible!

Goats! Not lions! Tigers! Not even the Russian bear! *GOATS!* Anything was more honorable than the lowly goat! Zahara persisted in this passion, collecting them in priceless porcelain and handblown crystal. She wasn't satisfied with all species of goats! Only one, a goat unique to Corsica, the *moufflon*, a sable-coated beast resembling antelope with long, golden spiralled Capricornian horns. Uri's queries and remonstrations over this curious hobby merely reinforced her mysterious Mona Lisa smile.

Then in the winter of 1978, shattered by the death of his father in mid-year, December 1 marked Zahara's untimely demise. He floundered, unwilling to return to Zhukova for the reading of the last will and testament. Shortly before Christmas, Uri had mustered the strength to tidy up the legal necessities.

Uri broke into a cold sweat, his temples throbbed. Memories stirred inside him; perhaps disappointment over Valerie Lansing's absence fired his depression? He permitted the music and vodka vapors to transport him back in time. How could he forget that night five years ago? How? *God Almighty, help me!*

The falling of virgin snow in the Russian winter countryside was an enthralling scene from out of *Dr. Zhivago*. Uri piloted a horse-driven sleigh—a winter ritual in the Zhukova woods—grieving Zahara's death, loathing the moment of trespass upon her mementos.

Inside the stately halls Uri, greeted by an elderly servant and his wife, exchanged fountains of tears and fought to maintain the needed strength and decorum required by the new master of the house in these dark moments.

Struck at once by Zahara's lingering presence, the specters grew vivid. The air, scented with her floral sachets; her very presence abounded everywhere. Lace antimacassars lay on the sofas, even her silk-embroidered Chinese slippers lay at the foot of her favorite high-backed winged velvet chair in the large comforting room, a silken comforter tossed casually across it, just as she had left it.

317

Inside the enormous den—Zahara's favorite haunt in her later years—Uri touched his mother's favorite books, art objects, including the vast collection of utterly ridiculous porcelain goats over which Uri had relentlessly goaded her.

He picked up the slippers, clutched them caressingly to his breast, lamenting sorrowfully at the years spent away from Zahara at school. Tears rained down his cheeks, over the loss of his first true love, the woman he had adored. She was his Jocasta, and he her Oedipus who was destined to solve the riddle of the Sphinx—Zahara's legacy. He didn't know yet what lay in store for him.

Moving to the wall cases and glass shelves containing the unique moufflon, Uri despaired of ever again chiding her over the ugly creatures. If it would bring Zahara back to him, he would embrace the goats for all eternity!

He held them, eyed them endlessly. Goats! The one secret she had kept from him—gone to her grave never explaining their presence in her life. *Goats, for the love of God! What was their significance?*

He did not know! HE DID NOT KNOW! Would he lose his mind over these accursed, lowly goats? He strode defiantly across the room, opened the French doors and stood on the balcony in the softly falling snow. His face was hollowed with sadness, his mind lingering on a world of countless memories. The music from the stereo—his mother's favorite tunes from the World War II era—filled the room, reaching him on the terrace.

A sudden gust of wind, thickening snow flurries on his jacket, wet face and a drop in temperature returned him to the present. He went inside, closed the doors, brushed off the snow, suddenly chilled. He moved briskly to the hearth, warming himself from the bright fires, vigorously rubbing his hands together.

You're a realist, Uri. Face it! Death is inevitable for all. You were trained not to disintegrate in such moments!

He poured vodka from a crystal decanter, his eyes covering the room. The music—haunting and memory-evoking—was not Russian but *Lili Marlene*. He listened, raised his glass in a toast to the portraits over the mantel; his father in a beribboned uniform of a Soviet General, his mother adorned in simple black velvet and the family jewels. Uri braced himself, clicked his heels together.

"To you, beloved *mamuska,* and to you, Father. You are joined together in eternal love. You have left on earth in the body of your flesh and blood, your Uri, who loves you both with undying passion." He drained the glass and hurled it against the fireplace, shattered it to bits in true Russian custom.

Uri poured another vodka, strode to the far end of the high-domed room and stood before a door, hesitant, as if a dark cloud hovered over him. His hand trembled on the gold and crystal knob.

Steeling himself, he flipped the combination lock, swung open the large oaken door, and gazed about the pale wash of light inside the walk-in safe. He was trembling noticeably as he peered about the numerous shelves containing family art treasures and stacks of black velvet cases containing precious jewels. He set about opening the safe, removed the legal documents, and caught sight of Zahara's scrapbook behind a glass-enclosed case.

Then he saw the scrapbook! What special meaning did it hold for Uri? The leather-bound book with gold filigree ornamentation was not unfamiliar. He had asked Zahara out of boundless curiosity what it meant, but her response had not clarified it for him. "Uri, dear, it is my legacy to you at the right time."

Was this the *right* time? So great was the commotion in his heart, the emotion coursing through him, that he toted the book to the den, sat down at the desk, ignoring his vodka for a time.

Uri read voraciously, unprepared for the emotional cyclone unleashed upon him. He paled, but read on, not fully grasping the import of the contents. But the photos, a collection of mementos, slowly spelled it out. Realization brought a flush to his body, as if he'd been torched. Nausea descended; then, numbness.

In a state of semi-shock, Uri flung the scrapbook from him, covered his eyes, with his hands to obliterate all sight of the fiendish thing suddenly threatening his world. Uri understood none of the inner violence and hatred he endured in these moments. What he saw, what he read, was a twisted legacy reaching up to him from the bottomless pits of hell, threatening to disrupt his world, shatter it to pieces!

In a rage, he balled his fist before the portrait of his mother, bloodshot eyes pulsating with fury. Never in his wildest dreams did Uri suspect that Zahara, in recanting the spellbinding Scheherezade tales of high adventure, love and intrigue, had actually starred in them. Captivated in his youth by the tales' high drama, he now spat upon them, denounced them as aberrations, debaucheries, wholesale corruptions.

319

Uri's shock and disgust, his ruptured dreams, incited him to madness. For contained in the memorabilia were statements documenting his mother's birth as Lomay St. Germaine! Zahara was the heroine of those fanciful flights of imagination!

Now Uri drank straight from the decanter. When it emptied, he tore the hinges off the liquor cabinet, grabbed at anything, guzzled the contents determined to kill himself or lose all consciousness—whichever came first! The sum total of his torment read like a cheap novel.

The Third Reich had fallen. His mother, rescued by General Mikhail Gregorevich from a death squad in a Nazi prison camp, had been daringly smuggled into Moscow with forged papers bearing the name Zahara Gregorevich, to begin life anew as a Russian. Not once in his lifetime had Uri suspected. No hint of scandal had ever existed, until now.

Zahara, engaged in espionage for the Free French, had run a *House of Assignation!* in Sidi-bel Abbes—the cesspool of the world, home of the infamous Foreign Legion in Algeria! Daughter of the most infamous spy in World War I history, Zahara, herself, was born in illegitimacy, her son, Uri Mikhail, a *bastard!* He was *not* the son of the honored General Mikhail Gregorevich! Uri was a lie! His life had mirrored a foul, detestable lie! Uri ran his slender fingers nervously through his dark hair. General Gregorevich had lived a lie! His love for his whoring wife had transcended all bounds of Russian law. When he became party to the fraud, falsification of her papers, Mikhail Gregorevich had disregarded all he held dear in life by marrying the wench. Bringing her to Moscow as his wife, he had legitimized Zahara, her unborn son—him, Uri, protecting them with his honorable name.

Oh, Zahara! Beautiful mother! Love of my life! What do I do now that I know? Where will it all lead?

The ignoble truth of his heritage struck Uri a devilish blow. Threats of disgrace, dishonor, humiliation, shades of scandal if the truth should out, tormented him. In a fit of passion, he flung the scrapbook into the fireplace, praying for the flames to consume the diabolic truth. He hunkered down on his haunches, waiting, avidly watching the flames licking at the heavy leather binding.

Exorcise her, you fool! Exorcise her from mind! Destroy all memories of her!

Fired by these thoughts, Uri grabbed the fireplace poker firmly and thundered about the room in blind rage, striking at objects, knocking portraits off the walls, bringing the iron rod crashing down on lamps, furniture, chairs, statuary, *anything* in sight. Uri's bloodshot, distended eyes sighted on the goats. Now his fury increased. He whipped at them, lashing the poker back and forth, sending glass shards and ceramic pieces flying every which way. Spent, he lurched drunkenly to the fireplace, trying to catch his breath, his anguished eyes furtively watching the destruction of the book. He seethed in perverse delight. Now, he would expunge Zahara's existence, the threatening indictment of his bastardy, from mind.

Uri's breathing grew labored, copious sweat poured from his brow. He stared at the hungry flames chewing greedily into the thickly bound book. Suddenly gripped by panic, he raised an arm, guarding his face from the heat's intensity, reached into the fire, retrieved the burning mass, battling the flames to salvage it. He dropped it to the floor, yanked at a carpet, beat at the flames and black smoke in an attempt to stifle them.

What a stupid, irrational, totally insane act, Uri! Sever ties with your beloved mamuska? Never!

Assaulted by conscience, he reasoned. If General Gregorevich's magnanimous gesture had protected Zahara and her illegitimate son, could he do less?

Exhausted, he stared numbly at the smoking charred remains, dismayed at his unchained behavior.

When the charred memorabilia cooled he toted it gingerly to the desk, and turned on the bulb under a stained glass Tiffany lamp. Seated, he turned the pages slowly, rereading the inflammatory contents.

Uri was not an idealist. He believed that man was an imperfect being, flawed in some way or another. But he had never considered the unthinkable. Zahara—his mother, flawed? Impossible! These pages spoke different truths, shedding new light on the memory he held of her, and he bled internally. He needed to know the entire truth.

Who, if not General Gregorevich, had sired him? *Who* was his real father? He searched page after page. He must know! He needed to know that his entire life had not been a sham. Uri, at age thirty-four, read voraciously into the night.

The truth gripped him in panic! He was ruined politically! If his true identity was learned—all he'd prepared for in his lifetime was terminated.

Of his goal to be Premier of the Soviet Union—what a farce!

He wasn't even Russian! How could this be? It was and that ended that. For an instant Uri conspired all sorts of devilish thoughts. What harm could be done if he failed to speak of this to Uncle Nikolai Vladenchenko? But he could not.

Uri was not a deceitful man. Could he face the Soviet Premier? Continue the hoax?

For a week he clung to the delirium of demon vodka. But the more he drank, the less intoxicated he became, and obsessively he studied the scrapbook. *Scrapbook? Rather an indictment! His sentence to hell on earth!*

His mentality was Russian. His education steeped in Russian morals did not permit him to comprehend the boundless love of another era fusing Zahara and Mikhail Gregorevich. The General, a staunch Party man in the Soviet nation, had dared do the unthinkable—provide refuge to so infamous a woman! He contemplated his mother, fighting alternate forces of love and hate, vividly imagining the loving years of her devotion, loathing her for the deception foisted on him.

Uri bridled at the compulsion to destroy everything reminiscent of Zahara, especially the remains of those ridiculous goats. Was it a week ago he had wreaked havoc on them? His bleary eyes traveled across the room at the broken disarray, the remaining potpourri of offensive *moufflon*.

Several times he had tried to pick up the bits and pieces; unable to make them whole again, he had dropped them. Now he stared bleakly at the mess, hoping through some miracle of intuition to finally comprehend their mystical presence at Zhukova.

Once everything had been so enchanting. Now, nothing made sense.

Unable to think beyond the limits of his bastardy, Uri nearly destroyed himself. Days dragged depressingly into weeks, weeks into nightmares stretching to a month. In his self-inflicted isolation he refused food, drank vodka like an addict, refused all calls, drove the servants from his side and prayed for the oblivion that refused to break down his barriers.

Unshaven, unbathed, stinking of vomit, stale cigarettes, Uri hallucinated from malnutrition. He became disoriented, lightheaded, unable to think. When life itself became unbearable, he contemplated killing himself.

It was at this point that Uri's guardian angel appeared.

KGB Chief Andreevich Malenekov bore no resemblance to an angel, yet, unless his prognosis was wrong, he had arrived in time to ward off death's demons.

The foul stench reeking from Uri's body revolted the fastidious KGB Chieftain. He railed at the servants for not summoning him sooner. He picked Uri up bodily, undressed him, tossed the enfeebled culprit into a hot tub. He removed his tunic, rolled up his undershirt sleeves and scrubbed the gaunt, delirious Uri who by now, crazed out of his head, screamed impossible things about goats! Andreevich soaped Uri's face, shaved the scrubby beard, poured hot coffee into him, then dunked him into ice water packed with snow until the young Russian official screamed for mercy.

Malenekov's deep, husky words were not too kind. "Fool! No woman is worth suicide, Uri Mikhail Gregorevich, future Premier of Soviet Russia! It was a mistake to teach you Western ways. Be a Russian bear with women, comrade!" he ordered, misconstruing the reason behind Uri's suicide plans.

Uri did not correct Andreevich's misapprehension. Certain as he was of the KGB Chief's undying devotion to him, his fierce loyalty to Mother Russia was a more powerful reckoning force, one dictating discretion. Entrust Uri's unbearable secret to Malenekov? Never!

An hour later, Uri, wrapped in a warm blanket, sat in the study, aired and cleaned by harried servants. Propped up in Zahara's chair, hot soup was forced through his stubborn lips. Uri sighed despairingly, unable to ingest much nourishment. He cagily observed as Andreevich moved about picking up horns, goat legs overlooked by the servants in their rush to clean the ungodly mess he'd made.

Andreevich Malenekov, a barrel-chested, well-muscled man five years Uri's senior, moved with a strutting swagger and inborn Russian pride reminiscent of the vainglorious Cossacks of a bygone era. A master politician, adept at behind-the-scenes maneuvering, he had deservedly risen in the ranks of First Chief Directorate in charge of foreign espionage.

The two men had maintained childhood ties even after Uri went abroad to study. Andreevich matriculated at Patrice Lamumba

University, later joined the Soviet Army where he demonstrated unusual skills in Intelligence. He joined the various directorates until he found his niche in foreign espionage. "Foreigners are easily seduced if you bait them properly," he once confided to Uri. "Knowing their character inside out, their probable reaction in any given circumstance is of great assistance and when all else fails, cross their palms with silver."

Malenekov's personal alliance with Uri had contributed to his top position with the KGB. Despite his formidable ties he was a highly respected man of the Soviet fief, the KGB. Eventually he would have become Chief. Uri's clout had escalated his promotion by ten years.

Uri enjoyed his company. He frequently attended obligatory galas and dinners to honor Andreevch, knowing it was all part of the Soviet design. Uri needed solid friendships, loyal men to support him when it came time to assume the highest position in the nation.

For in Moscow, Uri Mikhail, too, was profoundly respected and held in high esteem by Soviet VIPs. *High esteem?* Lord God, if word leaked? He cringed.

Servants pushed carts laden with dinner before the fire. Uri forced himself to eat. To men of their stature food rationing was nonexistent, they got what they wanted when they wanted without difficulty. Coffee was served from a magnificent silver samovar. Zahara had mastered successfully. Andreevich sipped his demitasse and moving about the room, smoked an American cigarette through a gold holder, savoring each inhalation. Dark hawk-eyes missed nothing.

"I am stranger here too long, Comrade Uri," he said, approaching the wild disarray of goats. "I find it difficult to reconcile in mind that Uri Mikhail demonstrates a penchant for the lowly goat animal." They spoke English to perfect their fluency in the language.

"Yes, yes, it is a lowly animal. Do you never rest, Andreevich? Questions, questions! Always questions. But I forgive you. Memories are short. You forget. It was my beloved mother who indulged in so curious a fantasy." The edge to his voice did not escape the other. "It was you who gifted her with one such specimen, remember? Not one made of glass, or porcelain, Comrade, but a live one from the Steppes!" As he spoke, Uri worried why Andreevich spoke not a word asking why the collection was broken.

The KGB Chief roared with laughter. "Malenekov was sixteen years old! You would expect more from a love-stuck boy? Hahhh. . . . you, also, consider the fancy an incongruity—do you not, Comrade Uri?"

"You would have me tell this to my mother? A French woman?" Uri could have cut out his tongue for reminding Andreevich.

"Yes . . . Yes! For French such matters require delicacy. One does not scold a French woman. What a charming lady. She captured Malenekov's heart that summer. Malenekov would lay down life for her."

He returned, poured more coffee from the samovar. "For us, life was less complicated then, Comrade Uri. Yes, yes, what senseless rascals we were. But enough sentiments. I came to Zhukova especially to find you. When you could not be found in all Moscow. I was prepared to overturn the Kremlin to search you out. But your servant, fearing for your sanity, called me in confidence. Malenekov needs special dialogue with you. Now, tell me, Comrade Uri, what did you deduce in the matter concerning Moufflon?" He lighted another cigarette with the but of the last, placed it meticulously into the gold holder.

"Goats? You ask me about goats? You know everything and you will turn the Kremlin upside-down to ask me of goats? Comrade Andreevich, is it you or I who ails from demon vodka? The truth is I cannot tolerate the stinking beasts." Uri grimaced distastefully, studied the unyielding posture of inquiry in his guest and groaned balefully, "Surely, Comrade, you will not subject me to a dissertation on goats? I am not recovered from the night you expounded on the panda for hours on end! I beg, do not inflict passionate rhetoric on me this night—not while vodka pounds anvils inside my head."

"Not goats, you idiot Comrade! I am speaking of Moufflon with a capital M." He amused himself drawing lines on the tablecloth with the tip of his knife.

Uri made a disorganized gesture, touched his head lightly. "What the devil are you saying?"

"You received no briefing in Politburo? How long have you been here in Zhukova, Comrade?" The KGB Chief was visibly rankled. "Of what good is it to take time, effort, use valuable conduits to compile information for you young gods at the Kremlin who refuse to do their homework?''

That's how this *Moufflon* business began five years ago. Uri glanced through the file in his office at the Soviet Embassy reflecting on that encounter. The intriguing, highly controversial reports of Moufflon were incredible. An in-depth study of the enigmatic Moufflon followed. Uri knew as little if not less about him than he did when Andreevich spotlighted the man. He was indeed a mystery.

Less than a month ago, the KGB Chief brought an updated Moufflon file to Uri's flat in Moscow, accompanied by a detailed report on Major Brad Lincoln's recent insane travel itinerary. The itinerary, beginning with Lincoln's meeting with Commissaire Pierre Marnay, documented by *stuckachi* informers, astounded Uri.

That night, over dinner in the luxurious Moscow apartment, Andreevich spoke confidentially, once he ascertained the absence of listening devices, relating every detail about the assassination attempts on Brad Lincoln. He unveiled truths behind the deaths of Marnay, Kaltenbrunner, General Mark Samuels, recited names in the White House for Uri to be wary of in any political involvements.

"You, Comrade Uri, maintain valuable connections in Washington. I must stress the urgency of learning America's intentions concerning the Moufflon Apparatus. In January you disseminated facts at Pentagon hearings. So, immediately, Musaka Mubende was assassinated. The KGB believes the Nigerian's death to be warning to you. We know covert action is on the agenda. Whether it is with or without Moufflon's involvement is only conjecture at this point. Unfortunately, sources are clouded by rumors, originating in Zurich. Comrade Uri, you are a brother— part of me—surely as if we sprang from the same seed. When you are absent from Moscow in that infested, decadent, capitalistic America, I worry. I ordered agents, under diplomatic covers, naturally, to be with you constantly. In exchange, I expect a very special favor.''

Uri's dark probing eyes, distended like glittering solar balls, stared at the KGB Chief. "The KGB is unable to pursue the issue *without* my involvement? If it is discovered that I report to the KGB, my political credibility will suffer.'' Uri's voice broke off as he watched the swaggering official cross the room.

Malenekov flung open the French doors to the balcony, and leaning over the iron balustrade, inhaled the fragrant night air. A short distance below, bathed in white light, Moscow's Red Square, an impressive symbol of world strength, stretched out before him. The flat, stark lines of the Kremlin's forbidding, protective wall dominated Lenin's Tomb. The glorious onion-domed St. Basil's Cathedral, a fairy tale in its countless multicolored spires and facades, looked like a page out of history.

"It is worth to die for, is it not, Comrade Uri?'' he questioned as Uri joined him in the early spring evening. "I am a man who lothes ineptness. I cannot tolerate it, and more than ineptness, I am deliberately thwarted by impediments. Impediments to me are adominations, just as this Moufflon business is a worry to me.''

"Be more specific, Andreevich. What exactly itches at you?''

"What itches me? He asks *what* itches at me. You saw the file and you ask me such a question? Conjectures, rumors, errors, a few fairy tales here and there to make for fascination, yet to Andreevich it is merely a skeleton . . . no flesh . . . only bones. Intensified studies were done, Comrade, and what was produced? Skeletons! No real facts. You know what I would give for facts . . . not heresay?'' his voice raised in frustration.

"Judging from the size of the file, hearsay is not so much a rarity, eh?'' Uri said jokingly, hoping to diffuse his friend's obvious anxiety. Andreevich would not be appeased. He spoke, using his last name, as if he were speaking of someone separate from himself.

"Comrade, you are a diplomat; I am the Chief of First Directorate. We are friends but today, Malenekov is in serious trouble. The defeat he experiences now, this moment, has never before been felt in the career of any First Directorate of the KGB. Defeat is not a word in Malenekóv's head, not in his character. But why, tell me please, when KGB has access to dossiers of all men—all women—why does the KGB learn only the barest statistics on *Moufflon* since 1958, and nothing on those *invisibles*, those high-placed men who conduct this madness? *Da*? Good question, very good question. The most we establish is conjecture, incongruities exist, where none should exist. Well, Malenekov, I tell myself, there is only one man who understands complexities better than you. And so I come to you, Comrade

327

Uri. May we dialogue with ease, please?" Uri nodded. They retraced to the living room where Uri freshened their drinks. He handed one to the KGB Chief, and guzzled his own.

"I tell you, Malenekov stumbles where no rocks exist to stumble on, Comrade. You see, we begin in 1958 with the French de Gaulle. The traces begin and soon we find the Frenchman protects Moufflon. Yes, yes, such a man high in government gives this Corsican goat such privileges? Whew!" He grunted, sipped the vodka and growled like a Russian bear, feeling the ruts of cancer in his throat. You remember, Comrade Uri, we shared close ties with France, and deep political secrets in those days. De Gaulle, the iron man survived . . . ten . . . twelve . . . perhaps fifteen assassination attempts. Yes he was an iron man, steadfast in his silence concerning Moufflon. Ahh—you, too, share my suspicions concerning so unusual an alliance?"

"I am listening, Andreevich. Please continue."

The KGB Chief complied. As he spoke, Uri listened, a thoughtful frown creasing his brow. He strode to the fireplace, lifted his eyes staring at the enormous oil portrait of his mother.

Trigger words spoken by Malenekov opened locked drawers in Uri's mind. Drawers sealed shut in 1978, when he had resolved never to reveal their contents. An outpouring of names, dates, events:

World War II . . . de Gaulle . . . France . . . Operation Corsican Coral . . . Corsica . . . Sidi-bel Abes . . . code names . . . Lomay St. Germaine . . . Zahara . . . Moufflon . . . Mozarabe . . . Corsican goat . . . Corsican goat!

Uri wiped the sweat beads forming on his brow, denying the words screaming to him from the pages of the charred scrapbook.

He felt the burning penetration of Andreevich's inscrutable eyes upon him. Fearful that his friend knew the truth, guilt brought a flush to his cheeks. Quickly control returned, and he feigned detachment. "If the incomparable KGB butts its head against the stone wall—forgive the unintended pun—what can a simple diplomat like me do to help, Comrade? Intelligence is not my expertise—"

"You do yourself a disservice, Comrade. Gregorevich is not a simple diplomat! You are too important to us. More important than anyone in Soviet Union. I am a high official of State, yes, yes, and know you should not be involved. Yet, ironically, my good friend, Uri, only *you* can achieve the impossible."

328

Uri turned to him, astonished. "I can achieve the impossible? Uri Gregorevich? How? I know nothing—"

"You see? Even you can be fooled. Your ignorance, Comrade, increases your worth. Beloved Comrade, if the Premier should hear such ovations I make to you, realizing the dangers, Malenekov would be shot on sight. You see my dilemma. So, where does Andreevich turn if not to you?"

"Malenekov, for the sake of our enduring friendship, I resist telling you I consider you mad. If threats come and I die for no reason, my disappointment in you would be grave, indeed."

"If you die—reason or not—I shall put a bullet in my head."

"Is it so bad?" Uri was stunned.

"Much worse than imagined," he lamented. Yet with control, he continued, "Experiments take place in Switzerland, near Zurich—"

"*Experiments?* What sort of experiments?"

"Such a question, Comrade. . . . If I knew, if only I *knew*, do you think Andreevich would dare jeopordize your life? The secrets locked in my head could destroy nations, but I tell you, in truth, I am powerless in Zurich—"

"You? Powerless? Come, now, Comrade. . . ."

Up went a restraining hand. "True . . . a gross exaggeration to which I admit. . . ."

Uri smiled tightly. "What would the world do without spies?"

"There is one in Zurich, a spy . . . and one in the Persian Gulf. Both leak important information to the KGB. . . ."

"Two men. Only two men?"

Andreevich shook his head. "Women . . . *unique* women. The woman in Zurich plays the most essential role in the entire KGB. She gives her body to learn highly dangerous secrets, which our couriers intercept in letters picked up in Virginia—this Virginia so close to Washington and the CIA."

"Who is the woman? What does she know? Is she KGB?"

Andreevich finished off the vodka, poured another and made a disorganized gesture as he pranced about the room repeating Uri's questions. His next words stunned Uri completely. "If I say to you, Comrade, she is the daughter of an American Senator—a lawyer from the United States—not KGB at all, do you believe me?"

Uri blanched when he heard the name, "Valerie Lansing," from Malenekov's lips. *Valerie Lansing? His Valerie?*

"Comrade, I play no dangerous cloak-and-dagger games. You are speaking of Senator Hartford Lansing's daughter Valerie?"

"Yes, yes, he is the one. His daughter, brave woman, mixes with the most dangerous elements. Is true, she is ignorant that KGB intercepts messages, but we do what we must do."

At the disbelief registered in Uri's demeanor, Malenekov added information. "This same Senator is targeted by mysterious forces determined to undermine his political and personal standing in Washington."

Uri flashed on Lansing, a vain man, with a favorable constituency that kept him in office for a number of years.

But Uri wasn't interested in the trials and tribulations of Senator Lansing. Thoughts of Valerie prowling about in lion dens puzzled him. It explained her curious behavior to him, but didn't translate to answers he understood. "Why, Andreevich, does the American woman lay her life on the line for matters best left to the CIA or NSA?"

The KGB Chief did not disappoint Uri. He spoke and Uri listened. When the briefing, was complete, Uri promised his cooperation.

Uri Mikhail had listened enthralled at the identity of the second woman, a friend to Russia, playing spy in the Middle East. He could justify the Middle Eastern Princess' battle against Zurich. Her father, a reigning monarch in one of those many nations bordering the Persian Gulf, unseated recently was systematically murdered by subversives close to him. The royal family was exiled, that nation felled in chaos and bloody revolution, destroying all traces of her father's remarkable work. What was it called? *Blood vengeance.* Yes, yes, that was it. The princess sought blood vengeance.

But what drove Valerie Lansing to clank sabers with Zurich?

Andreevich coughed up countless motivations, insisted the file was comprehensive, containing far more data than he could impart in an hour or two. He insisted Uri's skill applied to the contents could uncover more complexities and supply a more provocative touch to what was surmised. Time would tell. He had other information to impart.

Uri poured more vodka. It was time to listen.

"Pay close attention, please. Here are the dossiers." He opened the impressive leather case by rolling a series of numbers, quickly turned off the alarm and removed the folders. As he did he spoke of the American Major Brad Lincoln, of the dangers tracking him. "The assassins, *Corsican Coral,* nearly finished him. It is true the Major lives an enchanted life, but he survives with a little help from KGB gremlins, yes, yes?" He tossed the briefs to Uri. "Here. International assassins. Study them. Avoid them as you avoid Agent Orange."

Uri beamed. "KGB agents saved the American, Lincoln? Excellent, Comrade. When I convey to my friend Miller such cooperation bestowed on behalf of the KGB the door to the Oval Office will swing open wider."

"Nyet, nyet, nyet!" the force of Andreevich's words startled him. "KGB participation in Major Lincoln's activities is *not* to be whispered. The matter is too sensitive for people in my own directorate. If I hear of such a leak, I will know Gregorevich alone is responsible."

"I would not appreciate such distinction. Explain, please," he probed.

"It will give rise to disturbing questions which I am not prepared to answer. You understand, Comrade Uri?"

"Too well. I am not cut out for anything but diplomacy," he backed off.

"Upon that I rely fully." Malenkov poured an ample jigger of brandy into his vodka.

Uri's brow shot up questioningly, grimacing. "Brandy in your vodka, *Commissaire?*"

"I drink a toast to the memory of the great Napoleon, Emperor. A smart man to abandon plans to conquer Russia. Otherwise, today we might be drinking this insanity called brandy, surrounded by French whores in gay, maddening bordellos!" He swilled down the brew, rolling his eyes in exaggerated amusement.

Could he know why Uri Mikhail found the toast unamusing?

Uri waited a half hour before placing the call to his young mistress, Sasha. The exotic white Russian with thick, wheat-colored hair and anthracite, almond-shaped eyes, a specialist in erotica, arrived fifteen minutes later. Sasha was young, desirable, sensuous, imparting a fiery passion; to look at her was enough to inspire men to fight over her.

This night, Uri, unable to function sexually, became frustrated at his impotence. Dark, unintelligible curses poured from his lips. Sasha listened; she didn't believe her ears, but she *had*

331

heard him clearly. *"Bloody damned goats!"* he repeated over and over again.

Uri willed himself to concentrate. He stroked her soft, supple body, trailing his fingers along the outer curves of her hips and breasts. No matter the sexual ovations, no matter where she touched him and with what, he felt no response from his intractable, betraying body. Desperately abandoning the effort, Uri made a few flimsy excuses—an overload of work, fatigue— what did it matter? He pressed a larger than usual sum of money in her hands, sent her home. "When I am less troubled, Sasha, I will call you. Perhaps we shall travel to Zhukova for a weekend?"

Long after Sasha left, Uri paced the confines of his apartment, chain smoking, his mind cluttered with Malenekov's words, and the reopening of deep wounds that had bled his heart for so long. Provocative statements uttered earlier by the KGB Chief, gaping holes in a puzzle, gave Uri cause for alarm. How much did Malenekov *know?* How much did he *guess?* The *Moufflon* business— how did it tie in with Zahara's past? His own? Was there no end to it?

Uri finished packing, prepared to leave for Washington the next day, unaware of the drama unfolding across the city.

Sasha entered her modest flat, her mind on the work ahead of her the next day. She undressed, flung off her clothing, and paused at the entrance to her bedroom to pour a glass of vodka. Suddenly, she stopped, her senses working overtime. Her eyes fixed on a slight movement behind a drapery. Cautiously she opened a drawer, removed a pair of long scissors, and easing over casually, she jerked at the drapery, yanked hard. Her eyes widened. She sobered instantly, lowering the scissors held firmly in her hand over her head, cursing in Russian.

"Andreevich Malenekov!" she spat in anger and relief. "If Uri Mikhail learns of your presence here, his disfavor would be difficult to contend with, Comrade!"

Malenekov remained calmly seated, observing the graceful girl move about the flat, her body voluptuous in the nude as it was in the silk robe she hurridly donned. "Then it would be wise for you to make certain Uri Mikhail learns nothing of my presence here."

"Why would I deceive him?"

"Because you love him." His lascivious eyes caressed her sensuous heaving breasts.

"One doesn't deceive the man she loves," she retorted, tugging hard on the sash.

"How righteous, forthright in concept, dear Comrade Sasha, but delusional. He will never marry you."

"Ah, Comrade, it is you who are deluded. I refuse to marry Uri."

"He has asked you, of course?" Rising, he crossed the room and felt the smooth texture on a bolt of silk fabric lying on one table.

"Many times," she lied, eyeing him cautiously, cursing her stupidity for not locking the contraband silk out of sight. "Unfortunately, like you, Uri is married to his politics. I refuse to become a widow to a live man. Russian men are notoriously poor lovers. Russian politicians are impossible."

"Your blackmarketing activities make you too independent, Comrade Sasha." He moved about, pulling back draperies, opening cupboards, eyeing the cache of contraband—record albums, perfumes, scented soaps, and, most profitable, stacks of pirated jeans. He sent periodic eye signals of his disapproval.

"Tread carefully, Andreevich. I am protected by Uri Mikhail."

"Yes, yes, of course. I wish you no harm. Uri is my friend. Will you cede to me, that I wish him no harm? I came to solicit your aid in a most sensitive matter."

It was true. How or why this strange alliance existed between such two unlike men baffled Sasha. It was not her place to question either man. She opened the windows to the balcony.

The sky was filled with glittering star points, few actually visible over Moscow since problems with air pollution increased.

"He may be in serious trouble. Tell me what happened tonight."

Sasha spun around, returned inside. "What makes you think anything *happened?*" Sasha flashed on Uri's remoteness, his strange impotence. She unlocked a liquor cabinet, removed a bottle of vodka and a can of Beluga caviar, brought two glasses and two spoons to the table, aware of Malenekov's denuding eyes on her, devouring her.

"You noticed no changes in him?"

"No. Quite, less animated. Nothing unusual, why?"

"You noticed *nothing* different in his behavior? His mood? Attitude? A brooding, perhaps?"

333

"Why do you repeat yourself? I tell you, no, nothing. Is it not forbidden to interrogate me while I am under Uri's protection?" She opened the caviar tin, placed a spoon in it and passed it to her uninvited guest. "Perhaps he wasn't up to his usual . . ."

"His *usual* what?"

She shrugged, spooned caviar into her mouth and washed it down with vodka. She poured his glass and nudged him to help himself. All this, while Sasha carefully sorted her words before this deadly adder. "He was tired."

"You stayed only a short while. Why?" He spooned the caviar.

"Ah, Comrade, the eternal spy, I tell you, he was tired. Tonight we made no love." She saw no harm in this revelation until he smiled, masking his cynicism. Sasha *knew* at once she had erred.

"Uri Mikhail Gregorevich abstained from rutting?" He burst into laughter. "Preposterous! Comrade, when that day comes, I shall turn into a fertile toadstool!"

She fixed tilted eyes sternly upon him. "Then, pray, begin the metamorphosis at once," she blurted, unaware he was goading her. "This night he felt incapable of making love. He blamed it on some stupid nonsense—some utterly ridiculous goats!"

Andreevich's dark eyes flashed a glowing triumph. Sasha knew at once she'd been had. Tears sprang to her eyes like liquid fire. She watched him drain his vodka glass, spoon an inordinate amount of caviar in his mouth, wiping the oozy black delicacy at the corners of his mouth with pudgy fingers. He bowed gallantly.

"Your enemies, Comrade Sasha, accuse me of protecting you for selfish reasons. Yes, yes, I would do it for you—and more—provided the interests of the government were not subordinated." He bowed, left her, still roaring with laughter.

Sasha, astute enough to *know* she'd unwittingly given him vital information, stewed and thundered about, filled with apprehension.

Tomorrow she'd make a discreet call to Uri's office to report this encounter with Malenekov.

Sasha slept uneasily that night. What had she unwittingly revealed to Malenekov that brought his personal triumph? She cursed her childhood, lack of sophistication. Like most Russian children living in isolated villages with shaggy, dirty dogs or pigs wallowing in the mud for playmates, she'd been transplanted in the great metropolis, taught a man's work and in time developed street-wise savvy. She became her own boss, and elevated from a hapless existence to one of firmly wielded independence, she felt fierce loyalty to Uri Mikhail for making all this possible. At times she felt sure she loved him with every breath in her, but Sasha loved her independence more.

Early the next morning Sasha, awakened by one of her employees, was confronted with an unexpected shipment of purloined jeans material delivered to her modest little factory. Forced to put aside other concerns, she set her staff working on designer jeans. Her pattern, prepared and cut from jeans Uri had bought her in Paris, was followed by eight women busily sewing copies and by nightfall three dozen pairs were being retailed to the highest bidders on a sidestreet near the Moscow Planetarium.

The black market tycoon had forgotten about Uri and Comrade Andreevich until two days later, *after* Uri's arrival in the United States.

Neither Uri nor Sasha knew the extent of Malenekov's sleuthing. Once he sniffed deception, his suspicions aroused, he was on the scent like hounds after a fox until he located the source of discomfort.

He had left Sasha's flat that night for Zhukova. He arrived in the darkest hours of night, a lifetime of expertise guiding him. Entering the mansion while the caretaker slept was child's play. He moved silently on the balls of his feet in the darkness to the den. He pulled up a chair before the remains of porcelain and glass goats, staring interminably at them. Long before dawn, using sensitive devices, Andreevich, who knew every inch of the Gregorevich mansion, located the walk-in safe. He broke into it expertly. He glanced at the jewels and precious artifacts, and focused on the glass shelves containing the badly burned scrapbook. The scent of burned paper and leather clung to the volume. He reached for it, carefully toted it back into the den.

Three hours later, Andreevich Malenekov, deeply enmeshed in the lives of those unusual people chronicled in the charred remains, was stunned, appalled, and curiously fascinated by its contents. His mind raced furiously, piecing together facts and events and dates. He glanced at his watch—the hour was late. He replaced everything, locked doors behind him, and slipped out the front door of the manor.

In the predawn gray mist arising over the horizon, a bright-colored sun popped into view, fanning light brilliantly through verdant treetops. Andreevich cleared his husky throat, quivering with exhilaration. He pulled up the collar of his coat. His expression as he boarded the car was hard, cold, his eyes troubled.

The sleepy-eyed driver came to life, started the car and drove off toward the city, wishing enviously he had partaken in the night's entertainment. Never had he seen Comrade Malenekov so bright-eyed.

Uri, of course, had no knowledge of the KGB Chief's sleuthing.

Now, Uri snapped the lid on the ornate gold pocket watch, cutting off the music and his reveries. He slipped it into his vest pocket. In less than an hour, he would meet with Bill Miller for dinner.

He glanced down into the courtyard. Mirror-polished limousines and liveried drivers parked bumper-to-bumper, awaiting the various departing Russian diplomats. He could easily grow accustomed to the opulence afforded by this capitalistic society, no?

Back at his desk he picked up the *Moufflon* file, slipped it into his alligator briefcase, locked it securely. He slipped into his jacket, moved out the door, briefcase in hand. So many loose ends dangled from the volatile information he carried. Loose ends could become a noose around his neck if the wrong parties stumbled on the information.

Chapter Twenty-One

May 5, 1983

> *But that I am forbid to tell the secrets of my prison house so that I could a tale unfold whose lightest word would harrow thy soul, freeze thy young blood. Make thy two eyes like stars start from their spheres.*
> —*Shakespeare*. Hamlet

These words, spoken by the ghost of Hamlet's father, came alive with meaning for Brad Lincoln on this night. The inactivity, the waiting, the implications of what lay ahead, created doubt in his mind.

The files were incendiaries; they contained information on Amadeo Zeller and his son Victor which were beyond credibility! Never before had he encountered a man the likes of Amedeo Zeller! The contents of the file were volatile enough, yet Brad wondered what *had not* been included in this in-depth dossier. Concern for those deeply hidden secrets added to his growing anxieties. And *Valentina Miles Varga Lansing!* Her life, curiously interwoven with the Zellers, posed frightening speculations.

My God! What have I stumbled on?

The information was deadly. He knew it, but so did someone else. Aaron—the young man had placed his life on the line for two lousy World Series tickets.

It was ten in the morning when this concern dawned on Brad. He picked up the phone, called the usual number. Brad slammed down the phone quickly. It was not Aaron's voice at the other end. He rechecked the number and dialed again. Where a stranger answered, Brad slammed down the phone hard. He rechecked the time, frowned, then on a hunch called Aaron's home. A woman answered, her voice tense, anguished.

"Aaron, please."

"Who is this?"

"I called at work. He's not there. I thought he might be home." Warnings flashed: Was she stalling for time, a trace?

"Aaron's *never* home at this time. *Why* would you think to call him here? *Who* is this?" she repeated, coldly efficient.

He took a chance. "Major Lincoln . . ."

"Oh, my God! Major! Aaron's dead! He was—"

The voice stopped and Brad heard muffled sounds before the line went dead.

Brad hung up the phone. He stared into space. Christ! His world was crumbling all around him. Innocent people were dead; his inability to set a fire under the motley White House advisors turned his stomach sour.

What the hell had he expected? A twenty-four-hour countdown to blast-off? He was no cherry to bureaucratic delays. But *now?* With so much at stake?

Sickened by the delays, watching the Oval Office trickle down to a near standstill, Brad tossed caution to the winds. He called the *Service*, the highest-classed whorehouse in all D.C. and vicinity. It was so high-classed it wasn't referred to as a bordello but a *Service!* He made an appointment for 9:00 P.M.

Frustrated by the knowledge contained in the volatile dossiers and now the death of Aaron, while the fuck-offs in the White House played with themselves, Brad needed physical and mental release.

He turned on the video monitors. The four o'clock news was on. He studied the screens. Nothing! Nothing about Aaron or his girl friend Cherry! *Dumb fuck!* The FBI would quash such news. And Cherry? Another Jane Doe unless someone stashed nearby made waves over the death. Brad was mad as hell, mad enough to throw caution to the winds, but he couldn't implicate himself, not yet.

It was four-thirty. Brad left his house and drove his new Datsun to an off-campus pub, Ole Hickory, halfway between his place and Johns Hopkins. The snow was gone. Spring scents filled the air, mingled with gasoline fumes off the causeway. Brad forced himself to focus on his scheduled meeting with White Bear—Doc Hadley. He parked two blocks away—half-heartedly glancing about for tails. What did it matter? They were closing in on him from all directions. He sensed the tightening lines and didn't give a *damn!* He slid from behind the wheel, locked the car and walked to the watering hole.

The pub was crowded, friendly, relaxed. The place reeked of stale beer, dope and warmed-over coffee. Hadley, at the bar, waved Brad to the last booth at the rear of the room. In his hospital greens and golf cap, Doc followed, toting two bottles of beer.

They sat opposite each other. Brad shoved two C-notes at the Doc. Hadley, eyes darting nervously about, scooped them up and shoved them in his jacket pocket.

"Last installment, White Bear. Shoot."

"You won't believe it. Remember how she struggled, resisted all attempts at my probing? The fear in her eyes? The way she recoiled?" Brad nodded. "No wonder! Embedded in the fatty tissues of the mammaries, under the coral tissue graft I lifted, was a pellet of poison. A forceful application in the proper place? Whammo! The pellet collapsed, spreading poison—enough to kill ten like her—through her system."

338

Brad listened, seized by gripping fear. *Berna! My God, the same scar tissue was on her!*

His throat burned. "Doc, bring that by me once more."

He did, adding, "The poison was impossible to isolate in preliminary tests. It attacks all body defenses at once. Unfortunately, she wasn't autopsied at once. The contributory anatomical and physiological imperatives that create chemical changes and characterize various reactions to certain poisons were absent. The residual traces had diminished through heavy perspiration and bodily elimination. Brad—what's this all about?" Doc guzzled beer from the bottle. "Was she some crazy religious fanatic? A member of a bizarre sect, ready to sacrifice herself for a cause? *Damned!* A suicide pellet planted surgically under the skin is sheer lunacy!" He lighted a joint, took a hit, passed it to Brad. Brad shook his head.

White Bear muttered self-condemnation. "I contributed to her death. I probed her boobs with enough application to disintegrate the damn pellet myself! How ingenious, those fatty mammary tissues offer more protection than most parts of the body. What a chance she took—selling herself as a whore! An animal with a boob fetish could have done her in a dozen times!"

Berna had favored her left breast during sex! All that libidinous maneuvering to avoid such pressure! Oh, God!

"Pathology was unable to isolate the stuff, but I guarantee the Chief Pathologist, a hard-nosed bastard and rotten loser, will move the firmament to isolate it. He hates not knowing."

"That's it, Doc? Nothing else?" Hadley shrugged, shook his head.

"Which leads me to the next point. I need your help."

Brad placed another hundred on the table. "Sell me your greens."

"*What?* Shit! You are insane. You know that—you're really nuts!"

"Can the flattery. I'm going to the john. Wait *five* minutes. Pay the tab. Are you paying attention? Make sure no one's got a bead on you, got it? Then come to the john, prepared to shed the greens and get into mine. White Bear, listen very carefully," he said urgently. "Your life *and* mine depend on your ability to follow orders. Once in your greens, I'll leave. You wait five more minutes, then come out the rear entrance . . . I'll be driving your van. Jump in, lay flat in the back and I'll take off, heading for

Hospital Emergency. By the time anyone figures what happened, you'll be safe. Me, too, I hope."

White Bear stared at him in disbelief. He handed Brad his car keys. "You're not the only crazy nut! You're making me paranoid!"

"Let's synchronize watches."

They did. The switch was made. Moments later, Brad exited the john, wearing the greens and Hadley's golfing cap. He waded through the smoke, waving his arm before him, clearing the air and ambled easily past the Needle. How could he have told White Bear an assassin was waiting to kill him?

Hadley waited for him crouched low behind two trash bins. Good boy. He sprinted to the van, leaped through the open door, lay flat on the floor as per Brad's instructions. Brad floored the accelerator, heading for the end of the alley. He slowed down, waiting to enter the stream of traffic. In the rearview mirror he saw two figures emerge from the pub, peer in both directions. Brad turned right onto a tree-lined boulevard. "You okay, White Bear?" He heard garbled sounds. "Talk louder! I can't hear you!"

"I'm sending prayers to the great sky god to protect us, White man. Someplace between here and the hospital, we gotta change places. I know exactly where to go to save your ass." Doc peered out the rear-door windows. "Follow my instructions."

"No. I'll drive to the hospital and grab a cab home."

"You won't get twenty feet! A brown panel truck is on our tail!"

Brad glanced in the rearview mirror. "*Shit!* Hang on, buddy!" He floored the accelerator. He couldn't get it past 50 mph. Brad cursed aloud. "I've gotta tell you, Doc, we may not make it! The van's a lookout! That means whoever is after me has a system of lookouts along the way. They've radioed ahead, sending signals to pick us up along the route, using unmarked vehicles. If we live through it, you'll get a new car outta this!"

"Yeah, yeah, I know. I saw *The French Connection*. I know how it works. Rest easy, pal," Hadley said brashly. "You just lost the brown panel job. They turned off the main street a half block back."

Brad glanced through the rearview mirror again. "Yeah? Well, keep those hopes high, we just picked up a new tail. The blue van with the moving dish on top."

The same fucking van parked on his street when he returned from Victoria Lansing's house! The same damned one!

Hadley's calm was shattered. "It's tailgating us! Christ! How many are there? Jesus, Brad, they've got assault rifles! Here? Fucking here in America? *Gun shooting in the streets?*" Hadley turned white. "I don't believe this! Dammit, go faster, faster! They're gaining on us!"

"How much gas you got in the tank? The indicator's busted. Enough to get us to D.C.?"

"*D.C.? I've gotta get back to the hospital!* It's right here at the next turn. . . ." His staring eyes trailed behind him as the hospital grounds whisked by and receded in the distance. "I'm on duty! What the hell are you doing? You just missed the turn—"

"*Shut up!* Answer my question!"

"I dunno! I can't think!"

"Hang on. Here goes nothing!" Brad cut the wheel sharply to the right, swerving off M Street. The tires screeching, the van fishtailing wildly. Hadley's bulging eyes peered apprehensively over the front seat through the front windows at the merging traffic up ahead. He turned to glimpse their pursuers, then back at Brad.

"Where the hell are you going? You're heading toward Washington Circle!"

"The safest place I know. How far away is the blue van?"

Hadley crept the length of the van, measuring distance. "On our fuckin' tail—that's where. Shit! They're trying to come alongside. Go faster! Faster—dammit! Those sons of whores have their guns aimed at us!" he wailed. "Holy shit!"

Brad's driving capabilities in this heap were limited to a few fancy gymnastics. Then, speeding toward them—the wrong way on a one-way street—was the ominous brown panel truck! Then he saw it!

A *gun!* A high-velocity, automatic weapon thrust out the open window! "Get down on the floor," he shouted. "*Now!*"

Splattering bullets chewed holes across the van broadside, shattering window glass. Brad ducked. The van careened, burning rubber, fishtailed wildly. He jerked the wheel sharply to the right and turned unexpectedly onto New Hampshire, heading for Constitution Avenue, leaving behind a trail of havoc!

Cars swerved, piled up, banged into each other, locking

341

bumpers. Screams from frightened motorists pierced the air, horns blasting eardrums echoed after them. D.C. would never be the same! The brown panel van was hopelessly enmeshed in traffic snarls. The blue parabolics-on-wheels tagged right along after them, dammit!

"Where are the fucking fuzz when a citizen needs them?" shouted White Bear.

Up ahead, the sight of the Capitol Mall reassured Brad. The Justice Department calmed him. The motor sputtered. "Oh, Christ! don't run dry on us right now. Give us a few hundred yards!"

The behemoth shuddered, sputtered, missed and lurched forward in dying spurts, about to give up the ghostly traces of gas in the drying tank. *Fucking heap!*

"Your worries are over, Mister Agent Man. The blue van turned off onto 4th Street." Hadley wiped the sweat pouring off his face, stared sullenly at the strafing of bullet holes along one side of the van. Breathing heavily, he moved forward as Brad heaved the wheel sharply toward the parking lot. The van died on them at last. *Goddamn!*

Brad turned off the engine, removed the keys, flung them to Hadley. "Follow me," he barked. "Just leave the van here. I'll have it picked up later." He leaped out the van and headed for the Justice Department, followed by a bug-eyed, terrified, yet fascinated medicine man.

Inside the building, Brad barked more orders. He motioned White Bear to the pay phones. "Call a friend at the hospital, someone you trust. Tell them your van was stolen. Ask him to sign you in at four-thirty—can it be done?"

"Not legally or on the up-and-up."

"Tell him to do it! Then call the police, report your van stolen. From Ole Hickory—that'll get you off the hook with insurance. You are insured—aren't you?"

Hadley, at the phone, did what he was told. Brad, at another phone, called a friendly Company mechanic, instructed him to pick up the van and house it until they heard from him.

In the men's room they exchanged clothing. "You all right, White Bear?" he asked the grim-faced, white-lipped intern.

"You must lose a lot of friends, pulling stunts like this."

"*What* friends? Look, you'll get a new car out of this. What-

342

ever you do, do *not* consider retrieving the old one. Don't go near it!''

"I've got a few personal things in it—''

"Goddammit! I said, don't go near it! No telling what they'll do. By now they have the license number. They'll track it to you. You stick to the story. It was stolen from Ole Hickory—got it? Now, take a cab to the hospital. Work as usual. If strangers show up asking questions—you know from nothing. You never heard of me! I'll handle things at my end. You ever mention me to your cronies?''

"Are you crazy? Don't answer—we've established that. No.''

"Your wife?''

"No way!''

"How do you explain the extra cash?''

"Extra hours. Doing *odd* jobs.''

"She buys that?''

"Why not? It's the truth. They are *odd* jobs.''

"Yeah, you're right. It's the truth. Look, take a cab at the rear of the building. Be careful, Doc. I mean *extra* careful. Don't try to learn anything more from Pathology. Later, when things cool off, you can always check the record. If you call me, do it on a pay phone. Use . . . uh, Sculptor Five . . . that's a good a cover as any.''

Brad watched Hadley hail a cab, board it, and drive off. He returned to the building and walked briskly to the front entrance. Hovering near the door, he peered outside, Doc's van in sight. He saw the blue and brown panel van cruise by several times. Glancing at his watch, he returned to the building's rear entrance, hailed a cab and went home.

Home by six, he poured himself a stiff drink. He was shaking like an alcoholic with DTs. Thinking of Berna living perilously with an implanted poison pellet made him ill. Where would he reach her if he could? What would he say? What right had he to interfere in her life? None at all—they had decided that when they separated.

He showered, shaved, steamed for a time, wondering at the recent developments. The fucking White House had stalled long enough! Everyone close to him was being killed off. Aaron! Goddamned! Aaron, a jewel—now dead! And his girl friend?

He turned on television, searched the channels for news—
nothing!

Brad turned off his thinking apparatus. Earlier, he'd taken a
chance when he made an appointment with the *Service*. No more
pussyfooting around. Tonight he wanted no gentle love; he
craved fierce, hard sex, anyway, every way possible—no holds
barred! Something bottled deep inside him needed venting; it
begged to be loosed and set free. No man living a secret life
twenty-four hours daily, weekly, monthly for nearly a lifetime
could exist without thwarting instincts, doing damage to himself
by frustrating his sexuality—in plain talk, fucking up his head.

At nine P.M. Brad drove through the heavily guarded gates of
the sprawling estate; he continued along the winding drive forested on both sides by enormous conifers lighted by a pale
silvery moon. A half mile ahead, glittering lights fanned the
night sky with brilliance.

The secluded mansion built behind foreboding walls originally
accommodated an eccentric billionaire. Situated on a thousand-
acre site, a clever enterpreneur with political clout had purchased
the real estate for peanuts, converted it into a unique, private,
highly touted whorehouse—America's finest, possibly the world's.

As he approached the manor, introspection fell on Brad. Violent rage alternated by depression lurked behind a frozen mask. To
parade boldly without control among those political higher-ups to
whom he was forced to posture a subordinate role was forbidden.
Brad had learned that a man must do in secret those things
necessary to preserve his sanity. Do a lobotomy on a Company
man and out would pop ghoulish perversions, two-headed reptiles,
crones, magpies, goblins, underworld demons and proud phallus
worshipers consumed in eternal fires of damnation. The torture
chambers of a Company man's mind conjured up sexual aberrations
not yet dreamed up in Freudian psychology.

He pulled up at the entrance, tipped the driver and alighted,
peering about at the glittering of limousines driven by attendants
to secluded niches under canopies providing them cover from
aerial detection by eager *paparazzi*.

Inside was a dazzling *mise en scène*.

The main room was immense, spherical, sunken, strewn with
low sofas and tables, draped by a cross-section of Washington
elite; sparkling men and women, foreign dignitaries, tawny—

344

skinned, turbaned Africans, Arab chieftains and shiekhs, ebony-skinned men wearing flowing caftans brocaded with gold threads, primly poised Japanese industrialists and numerous bored, liberated wives of notable public servants able to afford the high tariff imposed on the clientele. The *Service's* owners, their identities hidden behind corporate veils and protected by senators and congressmen, if exposed in name and deed, would send shock waves throughout the nation. Meanwhile, their own obscurity ensured privacy for a super-elite clientele of political wheeler-dealers. *And it was all legal!*

Brad ambled soundlessly through the thickly carpeted foyer on the raised level bordering the sunken room, heading for the bar located at the center of a rear wall. On his left, countless dramatically lit alcoves, filled to capacity, contained players engaged in various sexual positions under a flattering play of creative lighting designed to evoke emotional reactions and bring spectators to a frenzied pitch. On his right, Doric columns, two-stories high, circled the room. In between, diaphanous black scrims worked by an interplay of fans and lights stimulated the imagination. Its ethereal effects, perfect for the pot and hash heads and cocaine fiends. The snorters were everywhere, compotes of cocaine graced every table in the sunken lounge. The air, rife with easily inhaled dope fumes, was enough for him.

Brad paused at one alcove, craned his neck to observe an explicitly dramatized tableau. Couples strewn about on low sofas, observing with glazed-over eager eyes, engaged in their own foreplay and, in some instances, commanded more attention than the professionals on stage. Spotlights picked out three scenes. The first: two homosexual males with oiled bodies engaged in sodomy and fellatio. The second: two stunning lesbians, one a gorgeous black woman, the other an exceedingly pale white woman with long blond hair, both with oiled bodies, made love under soft pastel lights. The third: one male and two females, *menage à trois*, engaged in torrid sexual acrobatics; their antics choreographed so mechanically they turned Brad off. It was too studied for his taste.

What's wrong with me? No one—nothing looks appealing. Galvanize yourself, Brad ol' boy. Get back into the mainstream! How, God?

In the silent pandemonium of his mind, a desperate need surfaced, held back by his recent encounter with Cerulean. Fragments remained, of those escapades in Europe and North Africa, inhibiting him, lessons that screamed *survival* at him. Yet his soul trembled seismographically at the threatening earthquake in his loins. He needed release, the kind you don't get from hand jobs. He forced himself to view the tableau in the next alcove.

Two oiled black men with one white girl formed pretzel-like contortions on a raised, turning dais. Orchestrated like a Nureyev ballet, it stirred Brad. Not enough—but he was coming alive. He forced shut the spigot to his thoughts and concentrated on the sexual interplay, until like an infectious plague those thoughts returned. He moved to the next alcove.

The sheikh of his harem was being pleasured by a dozen stunning odalisques. They anointed him with oil, massaged him, rubbed him sensuously, performing any of a dozen erotic manipulations. Two nudes copulated him orally, others sucked his toes, a few flicked feathers on his naked body, heightening erogenous reactions. Another sat on his face, pouring champagne over her mound of Venus into his greedy lips. Others engaged in lesbian acts, throbbing bodies against bodies in whirlwind erotica. The pasha's life, highly appealing to Brad, exploded recent memories of physical sublimity afforded him at Prince Ben-Kassir's palace by Berna.

Berna! Once again thoughts flooded his senses. *That damnable scar! Oh, Christ! What should he do?*

Brad moved on, in desperate need of pleasuring on this night, if only to regain his sanity. He caught sight of an attendant nodding to him. Brad followed behind him to a private, sound-proof room.

The key words underscoring the scenario were: high-priced . . . sensual . . . stimulating . . . skilled craftswomen who *knew what* to do and *when* to do it.

The mirrored room, hot tub at its center, formed the proper setting. Two voluptuous nudes draped on the oversized bed smiled at him: So far, excellent. The third, an overblown brunette, sipped champagne, while squirming in the hot tub. Getting better.

Her black, moist curly hair, spiraling in tight ringlets, framed pale olive skin, her breasts, fully rounded and appealing, bobbed on the steamy water surface. Perfumed vapors escaping from the heated bath, colored lights fanned up from under water, kaleidoscopic reflections. It was better yet.

346

Rising, dripping wet and naked from the pool like the Greek sorceress Circe, she beckoned sensuously with animal-like movements. Dark, sultry eyes, a predator stance and sexual voluptuousness emanated from her like an intoxicating perfume. Her hands stretched out to him, breasts shimmering in a rosy glow of lights. She clapped her hands. The two women on the bed sprang forward and began undressing Brad.

"Come. I am Mara," the brunette said in a husky voice. "The blonde is Ursula, and the red-haired charmer is Zoey." Zoey was tall, curvaceous, with green eyes and a full bosom. They cooed, whispered soft innuendos, describing the treats in store for him. Ursula poured champagne, plied him with it and led him to the edge of the hot tub. Pouring oil from a silver and crystal falcon, she massaged his body until his flesh galvanized from head to toe. The girls rolled him over on his back. The massaging continued until every nerve in his body came alive and exploded in ripples of urgency. Ursula sprinkled cocaine on his glazed, swollen and erect penis. Mara moved in and with Ursula orchestrated the fellatio concerto. They sucked greedily, alternating with expert tongue butterfly licks, strokes, and manipulations, evoking low moans and erotic responses from Brad. His body twitched and jerked, engorged with blood of desire under their expertise; they flattered him, praised him, worshipped every inch of his body as if he were a young god. He hadn't felt such exquisite erotica in a long while.

In the background—pulsating music, the beat of savage jungle drums, the sounds of rain on a tin roof, aroused animal responses. Slender hands caressed his oiled body; they nibbled at his flesh, sucked his nipples with hot wet mouths until he gasped, moved beyond credibility to sensuous heights. Icy cold shocks of erection, stimulated by the cocaine, made him ramrod hard, inducing a series of ecstatic shudders, uncontrollable shocks raced through him.

When, at the height of his ecstacy, they rolled him into the hot tub, he could take no more. Shocked! The jarring contrast of cold and heat stunned him into a new heights of relaxation. The tightly coiled tension of the past several months assuaged at last, Brad began to feel reborn. The girls took turns plying him with more champagne. Oh, yes, it was sublime, beyond expectations.

Mara edged in closer, luminous eyes dilated to glittering onyx balls, red pouting lips open as she mounted him in the hot tub.

Brad lost no time demonstrating his own sexual skills. Ursula leaned over him, forcing one of her breasts into his greedy mouth, while she sniffed cocaine through a slender gold straw. She straddled Brad's shoulders, forcing her Venus mound into his mouth. Mara drove Brad's hardened cock like a filly in heat. Following a succession of wild, savage orgasms, Ursula dove into the water, caressed his scrotum, rubbing that tender area until Brad could no longer hold back. He shuddered, climaxing inside Mara. Mara, moved into trembling, shuddering orgasms, screamed like a banshee, scratched his shoulders, drawing blood. Zoey moved about, filling glasses, observing, masturbating, used wherever and whenever she fitted.

Two hours later, Brad sat at the bar, drinking Scotch, pondering the phenomena between euphoria and reality. More intriguing than the excellent servicing given him was the exceptional behind-the-scenes work done by invisibles handling clients expeditiously to the satisfaction of each. Cheap at five hundred bucks a pop. Insured against exposure, total confidentiality, no tricking hustlers—male or female—sauntered about to lure the client outside the bailiwick of the *Service*. Should anyone attempt blackmail or extortion, one call to the management and that foolish party forfeited fringe benefits for life.

Three discreet, courteous bartenders moved silently and swiftly behind the plank, filling orders. In the rosy dim glow, he caught sight of a stunningly handsome man actually flirting with him. Brad's all-seeing eyes picked up responses he neither needed nor wanted. He averted the gaze, sipped the second Scotch, a nightcap. *Christ! When the fucking faggots start to look good!* He shook his head, bemused at his thoughts. Hell! He'd just been serviced to contentment! De-energized by the girls, he was slowly recharging. He glanced at his watch—*nearly midnight*. Time had flown.

Something was happening.

His senses pricked, Brad craned his neck, squinted his eyes in the direction of up-tempo music drifting to the bar. Several people left the bar, drinks in hand, moving to the opposite side of the room, following the music. Brad turned back to the bartender, quizzically.

"Male strippers, sir. What a performance! What a draw!"

"Yeah, it figures," Brad muttered. A peculiar sense of *déjà vu* enveloped him. *Something was happening!* The short hairs on

348

his neck stretched, sending chills down his spine. The earlier sensual pleasures sated, his mind now worked sharply.

Damn! He stared into the mirror over the back-bar, a sudden terror creeping over him. Was it the blond assassin he saw staring brazenly at him? And the woman! Was it the brunette he'd seen at the Crazy Horse Saloon in Paris? *Oh, Christ! Was it—Berna?*

It was crazy! Bewildering! He felt sick to his stomach, just as he'd felt before he'd discovered Marnay's body. He stared at his hands. *Jesus! Not again!* Tunnel vision! As he glanced up the bartender, the mirror, lights—everything receded into the background.

Other faces framed that mirrored tunnel, loud, boisterous, sneering, clawing hands grasping at him. His expression reeking of danger Brad blinked hard, images pulsated, alien shapes creating a living nightmare. Things were happening! He felt the changes, was powerless to circumvent them.

The drinks! GODDAMMIT! The DRINKS! The insurance he'd banked on at the *Service* had been curtailed by unseen, unknown forces. He, like a *schmuck,* had played into their hands!

You've fucked up this time, Brad ol' boy!

He felt himself unwinding, each movement performed in slow motion. The glasses on the bar became animated, everything became surreal. Brad's eyes dilated, bulged, distended. He swept his hand across the bar, sending the glass flying. Hallucinations distorted his thinking. Where was he? Why was he here?

Chaos and confusion dictated the next few moments. There was a sudden loud commotion: several crashing sounds, screams, triggering other screams. Brad felt himself propelled off the barstool, held at either side by strong arms. He screamed internally! It was happening again.

Help me, someone, they're going to kill me!

When no sounds escaped his throat, panic came. His eyes blurred and dimmed, he felt himself going numb. A sickening thumping of his heart deafened him; he felt feverish, then icy. His chin, lips, tongue were swollen *and* numb! He could not swallow or breathe, his legs refused to support his weight. He felt his body swelling! He pondered the curious sensation of being blown up like a balloon! Then he made the connection.

That man eyeing him in the mirror was the Needle! And he'd done his job!

Loud voices followed by whirlwind action, all blurred to Brad, burst in all directions. *Gunshots* . . . one, two, three! *Oh, Christ, I'm a goner! And I couldn't save the world!* Brad sank into black oblivion.

Chapter Twenty-Two

WASHINGTON POST—OBITUARY NOTICE

MAY 7, 1983

LINCOLN, BRADFORD T., Major, U.S. ARMY, veteran of World War II, the Korean and Vietnam wars, suffered cardiac arrest on May 6, 1983. No funeral services are scheduled. The Neptune Society will place his remains in an urn at Arlington Memorial Cemetery. Major Lincoln has distinquished himself in the service of his nation. The Medal of Honor awarded to him posthumously will be placed with the urn on display in his crypt. Major Lincoln leaves no family.

Lou Hadley M.D. strode the hospital corridor toward the sequestered ICU ward, cordoned off, isolated and manned by armed security guards. Doctors and nurses assigned to the JOHN DOE occupancy were permitted no entry unless accompanied by a menacing guard. Approaching the area, Doc beckoned the guard, presented his credentials and entered with the watchdog.

He moved closer to the bed, stared hard at the prone, unmoving, ashen-faced patient. Nodding to the R.N. on duty, he asked for the work-up chart, studied it, peered critically at the life-support systems, the intravenous needle taped to the patient's arm, dripping glucose from bottle through tubes to the patient.

He studied the chart:

SEVERE TOXEMIA. SCOPOLOMINE COMBINED WITH LETHAL DOSES OF POISON OF UNKNOWN ETIOLOGY.

RESIDUAL EFFECTS? . . . EMERGENCY CARE ADMIN-
ISTERED ON PATIENT'S ARRIVAL RELIEVED CON-
SIDERABLE TOXIC SUBSTANCE. SHOULD HAVE RE-
SPONDED. LIFE-SUPPORT SYSTEMS PREVAIL. BRAIN
DAMAGE UNKNOWN. IF PATIENT FAILS TO RESPOND
IN TWENTY-FOUR HOURS, DIALYSIS RECOMMENDED.
PROGNOSIS . . . DIM. INDICATION OF PROBABLE
RECRUDESCENCE AGGRAVATES HIS CONDITION.
BLOOD SAMPLES IN LAB UNDER STUDY.

An expert eye gave a far better prognosis than a chart. White
Bear returned the chart to the prim, solemn-faced, middle-aged
R.N. She stared at him but said nothing, a hundred questions
forming on her tight lips. Setting the chart on the bedside table,
she pulled the sheet down revealing the patient's nude body. Dr.,
Hadley studied the massive blisters on the patient's legs, beginning at the feet, up to the groin. Ballooning blisters, ranging in
size from gumballs to a hefty softball, were dotted helter-skelter
on both legs and kneecaps. Dr. Hadley felt carefully around the
blisters.

"No one knows why blisters form," he told the nurse softly,
hoping to allay her fears. "Nature's way of working out the
poison, I suppose. Very interesting, to say the least," he added
in a voice carefully cultivated not to arouse fears in others.
"Keep me apprised, uh . . . Mrs. Waters," he said, reading her
ID, "of any change in his condition."

Doc Hadley, puzzled as hell, left ICU. It *was* Brad Lincoln!
Why had the *Washington Post* planted the obit on him? Would
they be interested in knowing Lincoln was alive—*for a fee?* Two
fucking years were left in his internship; if Lincoln died, he
could use the money. Could he leak the story for a substantial
sum and remain anonymous? Reporters were known to keep their
sources confidential. He had never talked *before—never!* Moving
along the corridor to Intern Quarters, he weighed the consequences.
What harm was there in leaking the truth?

As Doc Lou Hadley paced his quarters tempted by Satan,
Martha Waters, R.N., was doing what she could to make her
patient comfortable in ICU. She took his blood pressure, noted
it. She patiently checked the life-support systems; respirator,
D-5-W, cardiac monitor—all in place and working efficiently.
She replaced the nearly-empty D-5-W saline bottle with a fresh
one, removed the nostril tubes, aspirated her patient, sucking out

the foamy, collected saliva lodged at the back of his throat and nasal passages. Finished, she wiped his face with a cool damp cloth, applied glycerine pads to his cracked, dry lips.

Nurse Waters' movements and expression clearly reflected the patient's total helplessness. Something was wrong—he was not rallying. If she contributed anything, it was to ease his discomfort in these last, final hours. She performed her duties by rote.

Her thoughts, as she bathed the patient, centered on the argument raging at her house last night, a forced confrontation with her alcoholic husband. Protracted economic disasters, inflation, his sudden unemployment after twenty-five years on the job had wreaked havoc on him. Robbed of self-esteem, he was driven to heavier drinking.

Nurse Waters, preoccupied with her troubles, inadvertently crashed the aluminum washbasin into the patient's leg, spilling soapy water over him, accidentally bursting two of the blisters.

"Dammit!" she cursed aloud, reaching for the towels to sop up the soapy water. She folded towels under the patient's knees, observing the bloody puslike liquid ooze from the blisters. Catching it quickly with the basin propped into place, she peeled back the dead tissue, allowing for a better drainage. She stared at the open infection, then, giving a start, moved in closer, critically observing the area, suddenly forgetting her personal problems.

Startled, she yanked at the overhead light on a track, jerked it into place, lowering stark-intensity lighting over the open blisters. Hemostat in hand, she folded back more skin, blinked hard and drew back, gasping in revulsion. Her hand over her mouth to stifle a scream, she reached for the emergency buttons, pushing— banging on them. Her dark eyes widened in shock at the sight. *Oh, my God! Hurry, someone! Hurry like hell!*

Nurse Waters was a professional; she demonstrated courage. She picked up the hemostat, and, with the point of her scissors in one hand, popped a few of the larger blisters and folded the skin back with the hemostat in cross-sections. Ignoring bloodied pus squirting out and onto her uniform, her eyes riveted on the sores. She waited, watching. . . . In moments they emerged!

NEMATODES! . . . Jesus, Joseph, and Mary! Bloodsucking nematodes! Creepy, crawling, full-grown worms greedily sucking the patient's blood, multiplying rapidly, thriving on the intravenous dextrose were sucking the life from him. No wonder he hadn't rallied!

Now, two RNs and a security guard burst into the room.

"Look!" Nurse Waters pointed at the obscenity. *"Sweet sainted Jesus!"* She crossed herself. "Will you look at that?"

Nematodes emerged in battle formation, an army of them, peeking out at their executioners. Mary Waters pricked every blister open—warned by the others she should wait for a doctor to perform the excising. "If I did that, the poor chap will be dead. Those things have got to come out o' him!"

Staring at the appalling sight, nurses and the guard with queasy stomachs turned away, sickened.

"Go," shouted Mary Waters. "Summon the doctors on duty. Notify pathology. Something must be done for the patient before his blood is sucked dry!"

Chapter Twenty-Three

OVAL OFFICE
29 May 1983

"You stupid misbegotton son of ten jackasses!" President Macgregor was furious. "You'd be dead if Bill Miller hadn't ordered an intense covert surveillance on you!" John Macgregor shuddered. "What a God-awful thing—*nematodes!* It's bad enough when maggots invade skeletal remains *after* death, but when a man is alive? . . . Why in God's name did you go there—of all places? Brad, your timing was lousy!"

Brad balefully endured the presidential wrath. Obviously, the worst was yet to come. He saw it in the President's measured words, his suffused rage, the hesitant guarded manner—all telegraphing defeat. He shifted painfully in his chair—a cane at his side.

"I agree," said Brad weakly. "My timing was lousy. What excuse does the Oval Office have for the delays concerning the more vital problem, Mr. President? How do I convince you, sir, by delaying you are slowly closing the door to the only course of action open to us?''

An immutable shield of protection descended darkly over Macgregor's features, masking his irritation and dismay.

''You ask for everything and give nothing in return, Brad. You said the country appears as a braying jackass to the world. I agree. But what do you expect me to do? I refuse to submit my administration to further ridicule.''

Brad's silence triggered the President's rancor.

''What the devil did you expect?'' he fired smartly, indignation surfacing. ''You ask America to place its trust in a Corsican—a Corsican underworld czar! What the hell is he, exactly? Your reports—ambiguous to say the least—purposely diverted attention from his actual role. You stated, 'Moufflon is vaguely connected to a branch of international terrorism!' For Christ's sakes, Brad, how is a person *vaguely connected* to terrorism? That's like being a little syphilitic! Really, Major, you expect too much from our friendship!'' His masked rage was too contrived.

Silence, disquieting silence, prevailed as both men stared at one another.

''Mr. President,'' said Brad quietly. ''How exactly did you learn of Moufflon's involvements?'' A sinking sensation at the pit of his stomach prompted the inquiry.

''I'm not at liberty to say. But believe me,'' Macgregor said ruefully, ''it came as a shock!'' He avoided Brad's eyes.

''It's important I know. I doubt any but a dozen, perhaps two dozen, know Moufflon's true identity. It's been the best-kept secret since Coca-Cola. I was skeptical of bringing together antagonistic forces to form a relationship with Moufflon. I anticipated the flak demonstrated by your advisors—but not from you. Those nickel-and-dime advisors, *sir*, take orders from the *invisible* power cartel.''

Brad noted the flushed anger in the President, punctuated by a nervous shuffling of papers, a clearing of his throat.

Finally, ''You make serious charges, Brad.''

''You bet, sir. I know them for what they are now. Without substantive data, I was unwilling to unmask their treachery.'' Brad leaned over painfully to retrieve a few files from his briefcase. He glanced up into taciturn, presidential eyes, piercing with circumspection. He painstakingly placed the files on the President's desk, moaning slightly, each move, painful.

"I've duplicated these files, sir. Read them. A Justice Department employee, compiling the information covertly, was murdered. His girl friend was shot. She was about to tell me *who, how* and *why.* You read about it, sir. The media called it a drug overdose. *A self-inflicted drug overdose by a non-user?* Hah!"

"Murder? . . . You're sure? . . ."

Brad nodded, he spoke above a whisper. "Two people can vouch for Moufflon, in a way I cannot. In a way, your *advisors* must not learn. The first is Mrs. Lansing—"

"She knows him that well?" He stared speechless.

"*That* well, sir. She'll be candid with you. A remarkable woman, a *real* lady. An enigma. She faced live fire and death daily in World War II under ghastly desert conditions, trapped as Rommel's forces closed in on the allies in the Libyan desert."

"We're speaking of Mrs. Lansing? Valentina?"

He nodded and continued. "The second person is Prince Youseff Ben-Kassir."

The President's expression reflected his stupefaction. Not yet over the first shocker, his jaw fell slack, his earlier wariness gone. "The man travels in top company. A prince and a regal queen." He stared at the files before him. "What's this?" He opened the manila folder titled: AMADEO REDAK ZELLER, scanned the first several pages, eyes lifting periodically, probing Brad's, then falling again to searing words on the pages, his handsome features blanching. He turned pages, flushing at the inflammatory contents. He closed the file, forcing control. He reached for candy in a compote on his desk, chewed nervously, the changes taking place inside him obvious to Brad.

"Where-did-you-get-a-lead-on-this?" The words spilled slowly, evenly, his resistance collapsed, bit by bit.

"An intermediary kept under surveillance for months, innocuous fellow, a minor figure locked in a Mossad cell," Brad lied slickly.

The President jockeyed for position. Firmly, with a forced scowl, raised a protesting hand. "Just a minute, Brad. Your credibility has been severely damaged. The Joint Chiefs won't buy your story."

"Then check out the *goddamned* Joint Chiefs!"

"You *can't* mean what I think you *mean.*"

355

"I *goddamned* well do. Get dossiers on them! The real McCoy—those buried in GAMMA 10—not those held in security checks! Not the P.R. manure dispensed on campus *after* they became part and parcel of the destruction conspiracy!" Brad forced a calm, however difficult it was. "Whether you wish to believe it, sir, those men, those advisors—and I use the term loosely—navigate armadas of power for someone, not the United States!"

The President poured two fingers of brandy, gulped it down.

The needle on the gauge in Brad's hand moved furiously, he pressed.

"Sir, I want your undivided attention—off the record. Please turn off all recording devices—what I must say to you is only for your ears."

About to protest, with that bland look of innocence, the President acquiesced. He pushed several levers, picked up the phone, notified his communications officer he was going off the record. He nodded to Brad. "Done."

Brad placed the device on the presidential desk, waiting for the needle to fall to zero.

"You are insane—you know that? Out and out crazy! But not as mad as I for listening to your story."

"The truth, sir? Why should the truth bother you?"

"Truth? *TRUTH!* What in damnation is truth to *you* boys?"

"If I applied the same reasoning to *you* boys, higher on the totem, where would it lead?"

"I don't give a damn where it leads! He glowered, shuffled papers on his desk. "Look, this serves no purpose. It's counterproductive. Your strategy—however complicated—has produced two obvious results. One places my neck in a guillotine, the other makes me a target for international *hit-men*. I relish neither."

"And the third—*sir*? There is a third probable result, isn't there?"

The President's blue eyes sharply fixed on Brad, his shoulders heaved. "What *exactly* are you getting at?"

Brad tried to ease the pain for himself and Macgregor. He popped a pain pill to alleviate his, there was no way to erase the President's.

"I am gravely perturbed at your inflexible attitude concerning setting up a Summit Meeting with Moufflon—"

356

"*—Terrorists!* You expected the United States to powwow with *terrorists?*"

"The country should deal with the devil himself if it promoted peace! Don't you see, sir? Even *if* the balance of terror between the two super-powers is regulated—and they must be—third-world powers have the potential capabilities for starting thermo-nuclear war and thus involve the superpowers' own thermonuclear arsenals! Why do you think I've risked my life to find some way to bring the U.S.-U.S.S.R. together to regulate or abolish nuclear arsenals? We must find the means to destroy the H-bomb! If it means negotiating with terrorists or Satan himself, we must initiate the move!"

"Spare me the academics."

"Your *advisors* and you judge Moufflon morally without considering the social differences between our nations. I put it to you, Mr. President, that a morality abounds in Moufflon, one so unique it is difficult for your advisors to understand—perhaps, even you? If weighed on a scale, Moufflon's morality and humanity is purer than the sum total of the President's Secret Team of advisors—including the Joint Chiefs of Staff!" Looking at the President through narrowed eyes, Brad played his ace card. "I *know* them all, sir. Their innermost secrets—their Achilles heels!"

Brad studied the President's engorged features as he spoke.

"*All*, Brad? You *know* them all?"

"All, sir, including you."

John Macgregor's face sagged. The strong muscles, the lifts, the fatty tissue of his jowls seemed to disintegrate into a haunted look of confusion. No longer flamboyant, colorful, forceful, he was a crumbling figure, slowly dismantled piece by piece, a broken puppet incapable of functioning. Not totally crushed, life flickered briefly, then dimmed. The President wavered, his usual, velvet, rich pudding voice cracked.

"Then, you know about me—that I, too, was—"

"Yes, sir, from the beginning. Even before. I had only to know who financed your campaign, contributed to your support. The proof is in those files on your desk."

"You *still* trust me?" Bewilderment, glimmering hope crept into his voice.

"Yes, Mr. President."

"*Why? Why* in God's name—when I don't trust myself?"

"At the right time, you'll make the appropriate choice. The bottom line is, Mr. President, you must exercise *executive powers*. Don't let them intimidate you, scare you out of office. Think, Mr. President. You and I have been kept apart. How long? The numerous attempts on my life? God knows I should have been dead long before you planted the obit notice in the *Post*. Someone out there watches over me—like a guardian angel, keeping me alive to—"

"—become my conscience?"

"That's as good a reason as any. Look, Mr. President, you've been no better, no worse than any president with *limited* powers. I don't condone what you've done. Now you can make amends. Will you do it?"

John Macgregor leaned back in his leather chair, closed his eyes. A moment ago he was a heap of ashes, slowly life was returning, snapping the veins and arteries into place. Someone slapped on the silly-putty, molding him into human form again, the vital signs connected again.

"Mr. President, my eyes—these eyes—" said Brad, "have witnessed the best and seamiest side of life, both sides of the coin. Can you label a man who endows hospitals a humanitarian, if he covertly finances war, destruction, and the wholesale slaughter of people? It is hypocrisy at its worst!" Brad sighed, regarding the other with gravity as he shifted position in his chair to relieve the pain.

"You are locked into a disaster course if you persist in heeding your advisors. Plans are underway by our allies to curry favors with our enemies, weaken and strip America of every vestige of global pride and power. The undermining of your policy to render you ineffective began long ago. If you fail to see it in time—don't outlaw the possibility of a coup d'etat."

"Here? At the White House? *Never* in a million years!"

"Sir, you are dealing with a dangerous clique, men who consider you an outsider. All—madmen, sadists, so thoroughly perverted and jaded in mind and morals they are a viable threat to our existence."

"You believe it is *that* critical?" The President's jaw was slack.

Brad's upraised hand silenced the Chief Executive, his steely eyes intent on the electronic counter on the desk. The needle swung arcs, repeated sweeps across the dial. Brad held it up,

358

showed it to Macgregor, his fingertip over his lips. Rising from his chair with difficulty, he moved about the Oval Office, chattering inconsequentially, waving the counter wandlike in the air before him.

Brad, drawn to a place under the American flag behind the presidential desk, between two windows, noted the needle agitating with increased momentum. He scrutinized the flagpole from its base, his eyes sweeping up the pole higher . . . higher . . . higher. He pulled over a chair and, standing on it, trailed the counter up to the ball at the top, at the fierce-eyed American Eagle perched atop it. He inched closer, nodding with that all-knowing look.

"Yes, Mr. President, these reports seem in order," he said, signaling the President, pointing to the eye of the eagle. "I've been briefed on the capabilities of the laser anti-missiles. If you wish, I will study them with more exactitude than the expected cursory scanning." He mouthed the word—eye—to the President.

He stepped off the chair, scribbled on the desk pad.

The eye of the eagle! Bugged! End the meeting some way.

"Well, Sam, you've been most enlightening. I hope your vacation in the Caribbean relaxes you." Drawing wide-eyed curiosity from Brad, the President scribbled on the same pad: *You're a dead man, Brad, remember?*

Brad angled his head. *Touché.* He scribbled another message: *Be cautious. Will send a friend to trace the trap. Don't let on you know. And don't use the phones in this room. Find some excuse!*

The wire tap proved to be of alien origin; the source, outside the White House, was tied into telephone lines, traced to a non-existent address. A brilliant feat, well executed and untraceable. Brad suggested to the President tha tap should remain intact, not removed from the Oval Office. Knowledge of its existence permitted a perfect opportunity to disseminate misinformation.

"Conduct the bulk of your administrative duties in the West Wing for the next two weeks. Turn a painting crew loose inside to provide the necessary alibi to avoid the room. Meanwhile, I'll attempt to locate the source."

The President agreed. In the interim, whatever magic Valentina Lansing held for President John Macgregor, miracles were performed. Within twenty-four hours following Brad's departure from the Oval Office, a clandestine encounter was in the works between the President and Prince Youseff Ben-Kassir.

They were making headway. Weren't they?

Bill Miller, placed at the head of a Presidential Task Force of *Specialists* who knew their way around a bargaining table, selected six brilliant think-tank geniuses to formulate the plans. Under the tightest security measures, this coterie of negotiators, empowered to deal directly with Moufflon and his staff of advisors, chose a neutral nation in which to rendezvous—Algeria. The rigidly enforced guidelines preceding the summit meeting proscribed by Moufflon's advisors were adhered to the letter.

10 June 1983

Summoned to the White House for another clandestine conference with President Macgregor, Brad insisted that a TOP SECRET jacket be placed on all communiques with Prince Ben-Kassir. In addition, all data on Moufflon be locked in an underground vault in the White House, limiting scrutiny only to authorized personnel intimate with the *Moufflon* assignment.

"Still the Fort Knox security, Brad?" the President asked wanly, uncertain as to why Brad placed so much trust in him.

"Yes, sir. If word was leaked to the Zurich Cartel and those lying undetected behind international power thrones, Moufflon would become an instant target for assassination. I should dislike for the world to say, 'Pity—the only man who knew the truthful schematics of impending nuclear war in the Middle East was killed due to America's gross negligence in *fucking-up* security measures.' And I should dislike worse, hearing that the American President succumbed to cardiac arrest."

"My heart is perfect!—" The President stopped abruptly, his face flushed a deep crimson. "Tell me—what is this infinite trust you place in me, *General*?"

"I can't answer, yet. When I sort it out, I'll let you know." Brad stopped short. "General?"

"It's inconceivable to entrust this project to a mere major."

Brad frowned. He dotted the sweat pops on his brow. "I'd prefer, sir, you wait to hand out promotions until *after* we pull off the coup. Just pray, Mr. President. Pray damned hard we find no security leaks."

"*General*, these files on Zeller—how accurate are they? I mean, they *are* dynamite. I want Bill Miller and Tom Kagen to review them." Macgregor's voice was burdened. "So much has happened—so many innocent people slaughtered."

Brad shook his head painfully, dubious and deliberate. "I cannot dictate protocol or instruct you in the imperatives. You must be aware, sir, of the dangers. Your safety, Moufflon's, his entire network, mine, anyone involved in bringing our plans to fruition must dictate your strategy. This is the golden opportunity to bring peace to the world. Nothing—nothing must impede that initiative. Zeller sits at the tip of the global pyramid. Knock him off, and you still have the foundation and a very solid superstructure. Men at every level must be toppled simultaneously or the apparatus merely takes on a new figurehead, the son, Victor Zeller."

"What do you suggest, *General*?"

"Wait until *after* we liaison with the Algerian Prince."

"I understand the scope, the magnitude of their involvements—"

"No! No, you don't! If you'd seen what I've seen, experienced from every conceivable angle—you still couldn't grasp the complexity of the conspiracy! I don't mean to make mockery of the presidency, sir, but you *are* well buffeted."

"*General*, I am the *President!*"

Put that in a dime bottle and try to pawn it off as Coca-Cola!

Brad sighed, raised his arms in open-handed helplessness. "These men are committed to the death of *any* man who stands between them and their objective."

Brad stopped. He was tired, so *very* tired. His battle with nematodes had drained him immeasurably. Very little remained, but what there was of him would endure until Moufflon was given an audience.

He got to his feet, supported by a cane, turned to Macgregor. "You perused the files. You judge whether to expose them to Miller or Kagen. If you do—they, too, will know the truth, unless they already know. I suggest, sir, you secure the files until *after* the liaison with Moufflon." Wobbling slightly, he paused briefly, waiting to shake hands with the President before he exited.

Macgregor replaced the manila file on his desk, inadvertently uncovering the golden-globe paperweight. Brad froze and stared. Hesitantly, with reluctance, he lifted his eyes from it.

"Mr. President?—"

"General?"

"Uh—exactly what is that—that paperweight?"

"This?" Macgregor picked up the golden ball, bounced it up and down in his hand, scanned it, turning it slowly. "I don't really know. It was a gift. Peculiar, wouldn't you say? Half of Africa is absent, else it's a reasonable facsimile of the globe."

Brad, sweating copiously, left the White House, brooding prodigiously. *Why* hadn't he questioned Wolfgang Kaltenbrunner concerning MONDO XX? Berna had given him a reasonable explanation. Was it the truth?

His mind dwelled on John Macgregor. He knew the President had not told him the truth about MONDO XX. But Brad could not risk refuting him—not now. The President must believe him to be his staunch, dauntless supporter until after success came. Only in this posture could he rest, revitalize his energies, free from death threats.

Brad was driven from the White House in a black Mercedes with smoky glass windows, to another location, where he'd lived incognito since his release from Johns Hopkins Hospital. He missed his townhouse, his personal effects. The place was locked up, under tight security. The only way he could gain entrance was—he smiled. Dressed as an Arab, in clever disguise, he could pretend to purchase it—couldn't he?

Chapter Twenty-Four

ALGIERS, ALGERIA
NORTH AFRICA
28 July 1983

PRINCE YOUSEFF BEN-KASSIR, a tall, ascetic man in his early sixties, the mirror of British tailoring and impeccable barbering, wore his snowy white curly hair closely cropped to a well-shaped leonine head. His handsome features were set off by a black, silver-threaded beard framing black onyx eyes and skin of golden umber.

The epitome of continental class society, a worldly man, born to wealth and royalty, he had graduated St. Cyr Military Academy following his Oxford and Harvard years. In World War II he was Brigadier General in the Free French Army under de Gaulle. A man of enormous respect, a formidable power in his nation, the Prince used advantages in life as convenient tools to bring his people forward from the Middle Ages, out from under the fanatic rule of Abd-el-Krim, and into the twentieth century. Youseff's entire life became a warring testament against those religious zealots determined to subdue the people of Islam, keep them enslaved and ignorant under tyrannical rule. His father and his father's father had fought these deranged zealots at great personal risks, against enormous odds, suffering as they did incalculable losses of loved ones.

On this day, Youseff stood on the terrace of his palatial manor. A glaring fireball overhead reflected a rippling of crushed diamonds on the water's calm surface, one so intense, his eyes were shielded from the pulsating sight by dark-lensed glasses.

He glanced at his thin gold watch. The limousines had departed for Houahouari Boumediene Airport moments ago. Within the hour, formidable guests would arrive to begin what should have commenced long ago.

Three generations of Ben-Kassir's royal family had earned international prestige for supporting Algeria's emergence as a highly respected nation. Further global esteem came for their participation in negotiating the release of American hostages held illegally by Iran in the early 1980s. Accolades hurled upon the Algerian nation, personal compliments to the Prince, had brought him closer to his goal, when President John Macgregor invited him to a highly clandestine conference in Vienna, Virginia. The Prince had accepted, aware in advance of the costly courtship rites directed at him. What courtship rites they were! A month ago . . .

In the graceful mansion in the rolling green Virginia hills amid a clustering of VIPs and a phalanx of security guards, Secret Service men, both his own and America's, he had been wined, dined, complimented and provided with pleasurable diversions

363

until the arrival of President Macgregor aboard the Airforce One helicopter.

Following their introduction and a light luncheon, getting the diplomatic decorum and protocol out of the way, they secluded themselves in a den, already swept clean of any electronic equipment. They spoke, man to man, on a subject of extreme sensitivity—*Moufflon*.

The President's direct line of questioning lacked the subtlety of charging elephants. Momentarily taken aback by the gruff, brash treatment, Youseff grew quiet, contemplative, chalking up Macgregor's lack of grace and diplomacy to the tension and anxiety, increasing world crisis. The American was a heavily burdened man, thought Youseff.

"Will Your Highness assist my nation in a clandestine effort to bring together this highly controversial man, Moufflon, with a carefully selected Presidential Task Force, in a combined effort to better understand the threat posed to mankind?" the President asked.

Infinitely cautious, Youseff promised only to relay the message to Moufflon's advisors. He explained the complication of buffers at various levels, elaborating the fact that Moufflon was highly protected, giving no indication of his deep filial devotion to Moufflon.

"Where may I reach him? Is it possible to speak to him directly?"

To these queries, Prince Ben-Kassir pretended ignorance. His gaze was fixed upon the President with renewed intensity.

"I am willing to give my life to bring peace to the world," the President insisted. "I haven't many years left on earth," he added with strained tranquillity. "If I can leave the world any legacy in my name—let it be peace."

For an hour, the President alluded continuously to Moufflon. He had heard so much—was it all true? Was this man a miracle worker as his files indicated?

"He is an extraordinary man, Mr. President. In my lifetime, there has been none like him."

Upon the President's departure, Youseff observed the chopper lift off and head back to D.C. He had not made up his mind about John Macgregor.

Youseff spent an afternoon in the company of Valentina Lansing before boarding his jet back to Algiers—an extremely interesting and enlightening afternoon. From his palace, contact was made with Moufflon's advisors. He related personally to Darius Bonifacio his meeting with John Macgregor, his conclusions and caveats. The wheels, placed into mobility a month ago, proved fruitful.

Six sleek Mercedes limousines pulled inside the heavily guarded gate. The American Task Force and Moufflon's advisors, summoned from every corner of the globe, alighted, warmly greeted by Youseff Ben-Kassir. He escorted the entourage through the inner courtyard, where armed security men checked each man's credentials, and searched for arms or concealed weapons.

Moufflon's advisors entered the palace with a familiarity that startled the American Task Force. Escorted through the colorful, fragrant peacock court, stunned at the opulent marble halls, gilded columns, domed capitals inlaid with mother-of-pearl, the American Task Force was as awed by the decor as were their expectations of meeting both their host, Prince Ben-Kassir, and the elusive potentate, Moufflon.

General Brad Lincoln, supported by a cane, felt a soft ache in his heart as he ambled through familiar terrain. The sights, sounds, fragrant scents conjured thoughts of Berna. He looked for her behind every shadowy alcove, half-expecting her to leap out at him to relive their memories.

Beyond the spiral mosaic staircase was a long conference table. But first they were seated on the low sofas, to permit Prince Ben-Kassir to demonstrate the decorum of welcoming them to his abode. Each was served glasses of Chateau Lafite Rothschild.

Youseff raised his glass in toast. "Shall we drink to the success of your combined endeavors?" They all drank with him. Then he exploded the low-altitude bomb.

"I regret," he addressed himself to the American Task Force, "*Monsieur* Moufflon's presence at this encounter was not possible."

The American team led by Bill Miller eyed their opponents sullenly, expressing their chagrin and disappointment. Miller, distrustful and unyielding in the icy silence, exchanged disappointment with Uri Mikhail Gregorevich, each weighing the other's reaction to the unexpected news. General Brad Lincoln observed the exchange between them in silence.

"This is not satisfactory," Miller began. "You assured us in advance *Monsieur* Moufflon would be here to deal with us in specifics."

"I assure you, Mr. Miller," said Jean Louis Delon with the proper emphasis of authority, "we are empowered to speak for *Monsieur* Moufflon." The petite Frenchman, with marble features mirroring a sad, hard life, spoke of their intentions.

Listening to his cautiously worded text, the Task Force refused to warm to the occasion. Each team huddled, arguing pro and con over the wasted efforts of this quasi-summit meeting. Miller glared at General Lincoln. Effective results, he told the others, were not possible in lieu of the absence of the principal party.

They, none of them, knew or would be told that in another room secreted not far from them, sat the man most on their minds. In one of those countless ornately decorated rooms within the palace, Moufflon observed the goings-on as his advisors locked horns with the intractable American Task Force members.

Wearing shorts and sandals, his tanned skin deepened to honeyed tones, on his lower back on his left hip a tattooed bee—a bumblebee, sat Darius Bonifacio—the man they called Moufflon.

Seated in a comfortable upholstered chair, behind a polished ebony semi-circular desk in the Prince's study, Darius's eyes fixed intently on the oversized video screen, observing the unfolding of high drama. Youseff had entered moments ago, sat close by in silence, observing and listening to the disastrous conference.

"What do you say, Youseff?" Darius asked, speaking in fluent French. "Is it time to implement your expertise as host to this disgruntled lot? If let loose for too much longer, they will ravage one another."

The Prince smiled. "As usual, our thoughts coincide." He bowed. "I trust you will excuse me, *bon ami?*"

Darius, eyes riveted to the screen, observed as Youseff approached the hostile, verbally sparring group with outstretched arms.

"Gentlemen, please follow me. Luncheon is served."

The alcove was perfumed, one wall open to the azure Mediterranean, filled with low sofas, stunning mosaic inlaid tables, inches off the thick Persian carpeting. Stunning odalisques, eager to please, served the guests. Beyond them, at the center of a diamond-shaped pool, geysers spouted and fell in parasol sprays of liquid silver.

The guests sat where they desired. Youseff clapped his hands and instantly from behind tall columns came dancing girls in sheer silken skirts of gauze embroidered with golden threads and colored jewels, a tantalizing treat Westerners found irresistible. Sheer yasmasks covered the lower half of their faces as they entered the room, moving to sensuous, pulsating music played by the handful of musicians on drums, flutes, bells and African instruments with no names.

The *mise en scène* broke through the barriers of misunderstanding. For men were men, the world over. Appreciation of women, eternal.

The food, a work of art, seemed to materialize out of nowhere. Trays laden with native beverages, sweet, fresh and glazed fruits, were placed on the low tables. Beginning with fruit-based aperitif laced with wine and *gat*, the menu bill of fare progressed to mint-flavored Algerian tea, succulent *Becasse* smothered in lip-smacking sauces, artichoke hearts marinated in garlic, oil, and oregano, wines, a superb chocolate mousse, capped by espresso and Napoleon brandy.

Immediately following the ritual belly-dance, the Americans lost all inhibitions. They sat at the conference table, relaxed, willing to listen, negotiate and deal as best they could. Prince Ben-Kassir raised his arms for silence.

"Be assured, at this very moment, *Monsieur* Moufflon is viewing this meeting via satellite transmission. Unfortunately, time did not permit us to accommodate you by a two-way transmission."

The Prince bowed graciously and exited. The rest was up to them.

He reentered the salon, sat down next to Darius, his eyes locked on the screen. Bill Miller, in English, stressed the imperatives for reaching a swift understanding, in essence, reiterating Brad Lincoln's rhetoric.

"America believes this, uh, gentleman Moufflon can be instrumental in circumventing Armageddon." Miller paused briefly, his next query explicitly phrased. "Can Moufflon provide facts to the WPCC (World Powers Central Committee)? Not speculation, not flimsy circumstantial evidence, but solid, concrete indisputable facts?"

"*Oui, Monsieur* Moufflon is so prepared. First, for security purposes, we must agree upon certain guidelines." Dr. Delon, was as suave as a Rolls-Royce salesman. He studied Bill Miller inscrutably as the American scanned a sheaf of papers passed to each of the Task Force party. Delon shifted focus to Uri Mikhail Gregorevich, curious lights glimmering in his eyes. "Are the Soviets amenable to such a conference, *Monsieur* Gregorevich?"

Uri Mikhail nodded, glanced about at the faces of each man present. "My friends," he said somberly, "the world needs miracles. I believe, we must all believe, that *Moufflon*—whoever he is—can provide those miracles."

In the annex, Moufflon and Youseff observed the action at the conference table, listened to the words spoken, to the intonation behind each word, the body language and expressions of each speaker. The scene was being video recorded, including ocular and voice tapes for later analysis. Momentarily his attention was riveted on the handsome Russian on the screen. Then Jean Louis Delon parried back and forth with Miller, discussing the complications and possible delays if strict adherence to the blueprinted program were not enforced. Delon, wearing an undetectable hearing device, listened as Moufflon, from his room, made suggestions, revisions, and acquiescence.

A tangible aura of concentrated power permeated the room adjacent to them. The Prince's black sapphire eyes were locked on the Russian dignitary, misted with anticipation. Darius, observing Youseff, periodically grasped his friend's arm and pressed it in a gesture of deep affection.

"It goes well, Youseff? You burst with pride—no? The sight of him gives you new life—I see it. It is time for your love to be reflected closer up than at a distance." He spoke softly.

"How can I take from him what he has worked for all his life?"

"Better *you* tell him than the KGB."

"I cannot. Perhaps one day—but not now. Perhaps never."

Darius shifted his focus to Uri Mikhail on the screen. "What a handsome reminder he is of Zahara and your love. Four decades have passed, Youseff. We have remained steadfast, loyal friends—

the bond between us stronger than blood. The world changes, but our *friendship* endures."

Youseff, preoccupied, his eyes on Uri Mikhail, was transported back in time. "He is the image of his mother," he whispered tremorously.

"Yet, so much like his father," Moufflon said quietly.

"Before I forget," Youseff said, "General Lincoln gave me a letter for you. He said it was urgent."

Darius accepted the letter, his eyes on the screen.

Moments passed. The letter lay unopened on the desk. The Prince pressed. "He said it was important."

Nodding, the Corsician broke open the seal and unfolded the contents. Reluctantly tearing his eyes from the screen, he scanned the contents, then, sitting alert, reread the words slowly. He gazed somberly into the distance, staring at nothing, reread the message; then, using the gold butane cigarette lighter on the desk, ignited the paper. He dropped the burning embers into the ashtray, staring at it. Tears welled in his eyes, glazing the emerald orbs.

"What is it, Darius? What's wrong?"

"This is a day of atonement, Youseff. You look at a son you refuse to greet in loving reunion. And I—I have just learned that my own flesh and blood, a daughter I have never seen, consorts with the devil!"

"Explain, please."

"Her life is in great jeopardy. She plays the sleuth and knows not what she does." Darius's face contorted. He stared at the burning embers for a long time. "If I could roll the years back," he said at last. "I would—"

"—do exactly as you had to do," Youseff insisted gently. "Do not torture your soul, Darius. You've been too hard on yourself for too long. Look to the brighter side. It is coming full circle. The power and pulse of America is finally beginning to understand, to feel, the conspiracy of those anonymous men. We are winning. Winning, Darius. . . . We will gain international might and destroy those manipulators of currency who threaten world politics and the breakdown of governmental infrastructures."

Darius stared at his friend, unseeing. He moved as in a shadow to the balcony overlooking the vast sea. Colors of a sunset brilliantly lit the desolation of sand stippled in coral-lavender, white fire and brilliant orange. To Darius voices heard vaguely through the audio seemed planets away.

He experienced remorse. The dedication of his life to his nation, to mankind, had cost dearly, sent the love of his life into the arms of another man. He had known about Valerie, his daughter; prided over her numerous achievements. God, he wanted to see her, love her, hold her in his arms, make her understand him and the forces driving him.

Now, she was lost to him. He could not permit this!

Behind him, Youseff watched Darius struggle with his emotions. When Darius spoke, the voice was firm, his resolution strong.

"Zeller will be crushed. Once I doubted Vivaldi, doubted my involvement in a business in which I had taken no part. The doubts are gone. Valerie's foolish escapade *will* be countered!" Darius's voice turned deadly. "Pray to your Allah, Youseff, pray that Valerie comes to no harm. For if I find it to be so, I shall kill them both with my bare hands. I will not await a world court of justice to banish them to some faroff island exile."

The only solace Youseff could offer was his silence.

MEMO TO THE PRESIDENT OF THE UNITED STATES
SUBJECT: PROJECT MOONSCAPE

28 July 1983 . . . The Task Force members met with Moufflon's advisors. The following is our summation:

Maui, an island of the state of Hawaii in the South Pacific, was selected as the site of the WPCC Conference, February 1984—the date to be announced covertly only to WPCC members.

Seventy-eight delegates and their entourages shall be housed under the strictest security measures on the sugar plantation—named El Cid. Delegates must respond immediately and submit full dossiers on any and all members of their entourages—limit three per each delegate. Interpreters and all necessary secretarial pools shall be provided by the United States. Contracts with WPCC delegates shall be discreet and circumspect. Emphasis must be made upon the highly covert nature of this unprecedented historical summit conference and each faction sworn to secrecy. The site of the conference will be withheld from all delegates. They shall congregate in San Francisco and depart in a body for the final destination.

Herewith attached are listed the ramifications involved in collectively assembling WPCC delegates, and the security measures imposed by Moufflon, before he will address this distinguished body. He asks in advance that those nations attempting to advance self-serving purposes by taking advantage of the platform afforded them resist the impulse. It must be clearly understood at the outset that the only purpose of PROJECT: MOONSCAPE is to determine the reality of the existing global crisis, the threat of nuclear extinction. Upon that subject and only that subject, Moufflon will address himself, and enumerate the possible means by which this threat might be circumvented.

BOOK IV

Chapter Twenty-Five

PARIS, FRANCE
1 April 1983

PARIS, THE BRIDE OF THE SEINE was temperamental on this Saturday. Valerie Lansing pulled back the draperies in her apartment, scanned the skies. Intermittent sunrays splitting through glowering clouds attempted to relieve the three-day tedium of unexpected rain. She let the draperies fall back into place.

A perfect day to saunter leisurely through an art gallery.

Dripping wet, she had emerged from the shower a moment ago, wrapped in a towel.

She rubbed her firm, slim body briskly before a Cheval glass, pleased. The long, arduous hours spent designing her strategy was finally coming to fruition. A shudder of excitement, the elation of accomplishment boosted her morale.

Today—*aujourd' hui*—marked the culmination of a near-lifetime goal. Today—*aujourd' hui*—Victor Zeller was due in Paris to attend a special showing of the priceless Rothstein collection of art at the *Martinique les Blanque Galleria des Artes*. And today—*aujourd' hui*—Valerie would meet him to implement the next steps of her overall objective: the annihilation of the entire Zeller empire!

Valerie, for all her unique intelligence, instinctive, almost psychic powers of perception, had never learned her true heritage.

Valerie hadn't the remotest idea as to the true identity of her *real* father. She had no knowledge of Darius Bonifacio or the mystery man known as Moufflon. The only father she'd known was Senator Hartford Lansing. Satisfied and with no reason to probe the relationship, her bloodline—Scotch-Irish, Spanish, and a mixed Colonial potpourri—was an accepted fact. Valentina had tried, God knows how many times, but never found the *right* moment to tell Valerie. There was always tomorrow—and tomorrow was elusive.

During reflective moments Valerie sensed a wedge of mystery dividing her parents—they were not the *ideal* couple as seen through the eyes of Washington politics.

Dark shadows gripping Valentina had kept her secluded in the studio on the Virginia estate. Valerie had never trespassed in that locked Chinese Room of lost dreams and memories. But something deep within her mother had communicated the death of her soul long ago. On occasion, Valerie had attempted to probe Valentina's secret, draw her out. She received nothing but a loving embrace and reassurance that all was well.

During Valerie's formative years, traces of Darius were rooted in every move, gesture, especially in the ferocity of her compelling love. But by the time Valerie grew into adulthood, it was too late, for Destiny and her grandmamma Victoria Valdez de la Varga had taken a hand in the shaping of Valerie's future. Valentina's alarm was ignored. Her lamentations and attempts to dissuade Valerie from undertaking the volatile suicidal mission had failed. Such was Valerie's implacable resolve. Her determination to avenge Victoria became quenchless.

"You realize, Mother, in addition to the billions of dollars stolen from our families, that butcher massacred blood relatives!" Valeree had raged.

No argument assuaged Valerie. Not the fact that she was a millionairess ten times over or that the dirty business in question had taken place before Valerie's birth, before Valentina's. In Valerie's mind, time failed to minimize the extent of the wrongdoings or the injustice of a man's deliberate wrongdoings.

Valerie's overall objective was to annihilate the Zeller empire!

Valentina, up to the very last moment of Valerie's departure for Paris, had argued. "You are consumed by this monster. Look what it's doing to you. My dear God—you weren't born to vendetta!" Valentina had blanched and trembled as the words escaped her lips. To cover her frustration, she blurted nonsensically, "Do what you will, but you won't live to boast of success!"

Destroy Zeller! Destroy the Zeller empire!

With these words repeated in mantra fashion, Valerie rubbed her body with musk oil, perfumed every pulse point, and slipped into designer jeans. She had selected her clothing carefully, designed to lure her bait.

376

Now that the time for assault was upon her, she wondered where time had flown.

Veronique Lindley. Veronique Lindley was Valerie's cover name now. Two months ago on her arrival in Paris she had rented a flat on the Boulevard Montparnasse on the Left Bank, matriculated at the Sorbonne, enrolled in graduate studies. Known by friends and acquaintances as Veronique Lindley, her focus for all these weeks became the world of economics, international banking principles, languages, and the one subject at the apex of her purposely designed strategy: Victor Zeller. Weekends, spent incognito at the Lansing residence near the embassies, in a neat cul de sac, Veronique reviewed her files on Victor. Here, kept under lock and key in a walk-in safe, the work of nearly a lifetime was filed neatly away. Her flat in the Latin Quarter contained not a shred—not a newspaper clipping on Zeller.

Veronique Lindley, far from the typical student, stood out among the young men and women who came to study at the Sorbonne, *College de France*, and the *Bibliothéque Sainte Genevieve*. However often she congregated with fellow students in lecture halls and cafés along the indolent Left Bank, she just *didn't* fit in. She exuded a unique quality, an unmistakable touch of class and genteel breeding.

In the Latin Quarter, where the ghost of François Villon still prowled, where Verlaine drank absinthe and created poetry along the Rue Moffard and where once an unsightly, scrubby, nondescript Corsican had found solace in the arms of a half dozen whores, while dreaming of his Josephine and future mistress, France, the Left Bankers would always be suspicious of the *bourgeoisie*.

The distinct look of the *bourgeoisie* clung to Veronique Lindley, no matter how she toned down her apparel, relegating her wardrobe to simple, well-fitted jeans, sweaters, shirts, and elegant, costly boots. Nothing erased the *je ne sais quoi*, that indefinable something that turned heads wherever she went.

Veronique appraised her image an hour later. Sipping chilled white wine she viewed herself from every angle. She strove for perfection. Changes abounded in her. Her naturally curly hair, the color of fire, was now a tawny ash blond, streaked with pale silver highlights. Combed in that primitive look, wild and disheveled, she lifted portions of each shoulder-length strand with a rake for added abandon.

377

The existence and identity of Veronique Lindley was established with this sensuous look. She outlined her full lips into a pout with an ash brown pencil, filling in the thickness with pale pink lip gloss, struck a pose, affecting that sultry-eyed, langorous posture cloned by recent cover-girl models, and burst into amused laughter.

"Oh, Senator—if you could only see me now! Here stands the astute, brilliant lawyer you swore would one day be president of the United States." She trailed her well-manicured hands along her cleavage encased in the blue angora sweater, feeling the rush of excitement.

God! She had envisioned this day—this encounter—a thousand times in her mind!

As a child she'd demonstrated unique talents, an expedient way of managing things to her advantage. Her courage was formidable, her concern for others admirable. She grasped new concepts easily, with comprehension, displaying superb memory retention.

Valerie's formative years, spent at Grandmamma Victoria's side listening to tales of love, adventure, and intrigue fired her imagination. She grew into adolescence, fantasizing, out of touch with reality. Later, much later, *after* certain events took place, Valerie, no longer captivated by fantasies, was locked into destiny, guided by unalterable facts, knew her mission in life.

This vengeance—vendetta—against Zeller began in early childhood and bloomed one summer day. Summoned from Miss Porter's in Farmingham, Connecticut, to the deathbed of her Grandmamma Victoria Valdez de la Varga in her Chicago mansion, Valerie's finishing school days ended. The aging white-haired woman who still bore traces of a remarkable beauty inherited by both Valentina and Valerie, had exacted a deathbed promise from the child to avenge the terrible injustices done the Valdez family of Argentina and the Spanish de la Vargas from Seville, Spain.

"Anything, Grandmamma! I'll do anything, only please don't die!" Valerie had screamed, disconsolate with grief. But Victoria *did* die, and Valerie *had* promised. Later, Valentina had confirmed that the stories imparted by her grandmamma in Valerie's youth had chronicled Victoria's real life. The fortune left to Valerie included a legacy of diaries and legal documents.

And so began the meticulously planned vengeance.

What Valerie didn't know was embedded in her genes—the fire, spirit and determination and atavistic *know-how* to pull off blood vengeance with skill and expertise. She had but to dig down inside herself and activate those genes.

Over the years, observing the effects of the legacy, Valentina feared gravely for her daughter. What she had confided in Brad Lincoln was not the full extent of her fears.

The process began. Valerie grew up—attended law school at Georgetown University. In her spare time she mastered martial arts, became an expert marksman, and wielded a knife like any respected Harlem street fighter. She learned investigatory routines and procedures in the Justice Department, assisted by the Senator's clout. She graduated with honors, made *Law Review*, and joined the law firm headed by her father's uncle, William Jennings Lansing.

Actually, the tedious compilation and chronological filing of Victoria's papers began in her first year law school. By the time she passed the bar exam, the foundation of her case against the Zeller empire was laid, and it was a shocker!

Directing all her energies into the ambitious project, there were weeks, months, even years when she examined her sanity for pouring her life into a project fraught with complexities. But the surreptitious compiling of dossiers on the subjects—culled from highly classified corridors—revitalized her. Valerie knew instinctively she was getting closer . . . closer . . . closer to her quarry. It was like a drug high without valleys; it lasted for years. She never felt consumed with loneliness. She went on dates with men integral to her work; her associates viewed her as a curiosity, unable to make up their minds about her.

She'd accepted law cases, won them, but when the demand for her services infringed on her time, she took an indefinite sabbatical.

The sabbatical had lasted four years. By the time Valerie touched down in Paris, she knew Victor Zeller better than he knew himself. In theory, her plans were foolproof.

The dangerous game she played was lethal!

Lacking tangible knowledge of the man she was really after, knowing that it would be possible to penetrate those *verboten* corridors only *after* she succeeded in winning over Victor Zeller, and because she possessed enough ammunition to break through the outer barricades of the fort she had targeted, Valerie had dared do the impossible. Now, Veronique Lindley was ready. She had held herself in abeyance these many months for this moment of truth.

Veronique slipped into her trenchcoat, slung a Louis Vuitton bag over her shoulder, and swinging a combination walking stick-umbrella with one hand, locked her door, descended to the street. She lived only a short distance from the galleries.

Veronique moved through the swinging glass doors held open by a uniformed doorman. She slipped her trenchcoat through the strap of her bag and, moving into the large salon, kept to the edge of the crowds, her oversized dark-lensed glasses in place. Veronique flashed on the Impressionist art adorning the walls, eased herself through the different gallerias like a sensuous feline in search of prey.

There. . . . She found him! Victor Zeller!

Dapper, aristocrat, *Herr* Zeller, a very private man seldom caught unawares by a camera, stood at the center of art connoisseurs. Her first assessment: he was far more attractive than any photos in his dossier. At one point in her artfully designed stroll around the gallery she felt his dark eyes focus on her, glance away, then quickly do a double take, studying her in depth.

She moved from collection to collection, always aware of his observation of her. *Excellent*. Her studied, casual gestures produced a stunning effect. Veronique trailed her fingertips across her cleavage ever so casually, unbuttoned the last button of her sweater. The gesture, designed to produce an erotic effect, transmitted subtle suggestions of a feverish; sensual nature. She employed the dark glasses as an instrument of seduction, raising or lowering them, as desired, or flirting over the rims, whipping them off on occasion, tapping the stems against her lower lip contemplatively or brushing them slowly, caressingly. All of it worked for her—she knew it!

Victor Zeller caught bits and pieces of this stimulating young woman flashing past him. She stopped a short distance from him, seemingly preoccupied in a surreal painting. He eyed her obliquely, focusing definitively on the tips of her boots, up past the revealing, contoured jeans, enticing sweater, to her face.

She piqued Victor's curiosity. Unable or unwilling to avert his eyes, his glance lingered on her. The magnetism of his compelling eyes forced her to turn to him. She lowered the glasses, lifted unperturbed azure eyes to meet his gaze. She let it happen; a charge of galvanic energy sprang between them. Victor's expression intensified. Veronique pushed up slowly on the glasses, turned abruptly, blinked him from sight as she might dismiss a lackey and moved on.

She did it! She had snagged him!

Victor Zeller was caught. That smoldering look, the overall picture of her, an almost renegade abandon about her pulled him! He didn't know *why* he had to know this woman better than any other of a dozen or more who had openly flirted with him. The others paled in comparison to the wench. He observed her moving through the galleria, an enticing scent of perfume lingering behind.

Victor sniffed the air appreciatively, turned from the Curator, deaf to a dramatic oversell, "*Monsieur* Zeller—the collection is unlike any we've been privileged to show in our galleries. . . ." He desperately tried to make points with his affluent client, stared haughtily at Veronique, obviously irate: *he could strangle the little bitch!*

Victor ignored the man's outrage. Led by the pounding of his heart, the erratic throbbing of his temples and the stirring of his loins, he followed Veronique, slowly, so as not to overcome her.

What a wild creature! He envied her free spirit, the *joie de vivre* oozing from her. She was stunning! He noted with curiosity the subject of her scrutiny—a wall of Impressionist paintings: a collection of Monet, Degas, Manet, Reinor, Cezanne. She studied them with the appraising eye of a collector, a prospective buyer.

The little minx! Passing herself off as a connoisseur!

Tiring of the Impressionists, Veronique searched for the highly heralded Spanish Collection. Turning abruptly, she collided with Victor. The glasses, manipulated seductively, lowered. Eyes met eyes. Victor bowed slightly, his dark eyes telegraphed the proper desire. She gave him a wilting look, pushed her glasses into place and moved away, avoiding the drinking, chattering cluster of people who displayed more interest in contemplating bed partners for the night than in the art display. Homosexuals, obvious in their overt sexuality, found their own kind and attempted to further their careers. Too obvious, Veronique thought—more so than in Washington.

She moved on. Braless under the blue angora sweater, each calculated movement, sensuous, accentuating an animal-like intensity, combined provocatively into an unusual gait. Europeans marked her instantly as an outsider, a foreigner, *une Americaine*. Aware of more than Victor Zeller's eyes upon her, she turned at the end of a walkway, crossed a small wooden bridge constructed over a manmade stream. Rippling water over rocks, both sides banked with lush tropical foliage, ferns, fronds, and other flora.

Victor's attention went to her breasts, noticed how the movement against the angora stimulated the erection of her nipples. Her body screamed wantonly for seduction, yet her face, of noble aristocratic bearing, made for an interesting study. China blue eyes bordered by double fringed dark lashes flashed with sexuality in contradiction to an alternating cool appraisal in them. And that wild mass of silver-streaked hair! *Oh, God, not again!* thought Victor. *Not now!* Victor's emotions came to life from the deep recesses of his past.

He observed her from behind palm fronds as she appraisingly studied the Goyas, El Grecos, Murillos, Valasquezes, and Riberas. He saw her fish through her bag for a cigarette, moved in quickly, extending a ready flare from his gold cigarette lighter over her shoulder.

She accepted the light, inhaled deeply, and exhaling, turned to him. *"Merci bien, Monsieur."*

"Who *are* you?" he asked in a husky-voiced French.

"Who are *you*?" she countered, flirting outrageously to bolster her inner trepidation at the first verbal contact. She was flustered, disturbed. Her pulse raced. She had not counted on Victor Zeller's warmth or magnetic personality, nor his worldliness.

"I know who I would like to be," he said quietly, suggestively.

She gave him a questioning look. Nothing more—nothing less than bland expectancy. Behind the eyes her mind assessed, evaluated, formed conclusions.

"I am Victor Zeller, *Mademoiselle*. I refuse to wait for our host to properly introduce us and chance someone else getting you first."

"*Monsieur* Zeller, I assure you, I am not up for grabs—for sale, you understand. You have the *wrong* woman if that is your desire—"

"—I gave you mine, but you failed to tell me your name."

382

"Lindley, *Monsieur*. Miss Veronique Lindley."

"Lindley? Ah, the accent is American, but the look is French. Continental, at least. No matter. You belong here in Paris."

"Ah, *Monsieur* Zeller, you just made a friend." She smiled enchantingly. The game, thought Veronique, was not as easy a task as she had contemplated. It was difficult speaking like an empty-headed fluff when a well-developed vocabulary sat at the tip of her tongue, itching to be used.

"Good! Do you dabble in art?"

"Does it matter?"

"No. Will you come with me?"

"Where?"

"I'm not certain. Something about you draws me to you. I must learn why." He stopped. "Does that sound absurd?"

"Not in the least." *Damned! He was not what she expected at all!*

Taking her hand, he negotiated through the smoke-filled room to the foyer, where he picked up his beige trenchcoat from the attendant. He helped Veronique into hers then spoke in remote tones to the attendant.

"Convey my regrets to *Monsieur* le Blanc. Tell him *Herr* Zeller will call him in the morning, *merci bien*." He turned to Veronique, steered her out the glass doors.

"You like walking in the rain?" she asked.

"Only when I'm dressed for it. My car and driver are right here." He signaled the doorman, who, in turn summoned the Zeller chauffeur.

Veronique hesitated at the right moments; she appeared noticeably reluctant and was. She *knew* what lay in store for her. It was not easy.

Inside the sleek Silver Cloud Rolls, Victor turned on the stereo—and held her slender well-manicured hand, curiously studying the exquisite, unflawed diamonds in her ring. A platinum cage containing three four-carat, exceptionally fired stones.

"That's an extravagant ring to wear in these troubled times. The recent terrorist activities, the kidnapping of affluent people. . . . You shouldn't be walking alone—not even on a rainy day."

"I'm not. I am in your car, *Herr* Zeller."

He suppressed a smile. "Tell me about yourself. It is important to me." He took in every inch of her, from the tip of her boots to her hair.

"There's little to tell. I am a student at the Sorbonne, studying economics, international monetary systems, intergovernmental banking, comparative economic analysis. . . . Shall I go on?" she asked at his wide-eyed astonishment—more, disbelief. "What it really boils down to is I'm learning how to become a rich man's wife."

"Your candor is refreshing, but one statement contradicts the other. Why, to become the spouse of a wealthy man, do you study banking systems?"

"No, no, no, no," she insisted. "It's not what you think. Not just *anyone's* wife. Jake is a special man. Jake, my fiance, sent me here to learn and expand my horizons, develop taste, a blending of *savoire faire* and a smattering of banking *know-how*. There are problems, you see. Oh, dear, how do I explain? . . . Well, for openers, he's Jewish. I am . . . uh . . . what they call . . . uh . . . *goyim*."

"Wouldn't it be simpler if you converted to *Judaism*?"

Veronique burst into peals of infectious laughter. "That's funny. That's really funny! You know, Jake never asked me to do that. How ridiculous." She laughed again. "No, it's asinine! But then, what do the mere goyim know?"

"I don't understand. Do you love each other? This Jake—does he love you?"

Veronique's mood altered noticeably. "I'm sorry. I'm not in the habit of retailing my life to strangers."

"*Strangers?* . . . Yes, we are that. But after tonight, that will change."

Veronique felt a rush creeping under her skin. She was flustered, flushed, edgy. *Maintain objectivity!* she reminded herself, *this man is your enemy! This man is the son of the vilest creature on earth! The man who robbed Victoria Valdez of her life, inheritance and her loved one. Your plans for retribution preclude affection for this man!* She took herself firmly in hand.

She turned her attention out the window as the Rolls merged with other cars on the Rue de Faubourg St. Honoré. Here, the wealthiest women in the world shopped the fashion centers of Celine, Guerlaine, Hermès, Vuitton, Chanel and a dozen other glittering haute coutoure luminaries and their boutiques.

"Do you enjoy the Sorbonne?"

"It's different. Everyone expresses himself. They carry books, live on coffee, drugs, and *l'amour*. They rarely attend lectures, but *mon Dieu!* They frequent all the coffee houses in the Saint Germain des Pres to offer dissertations on every subject under the sun. It is sheer insanity!"

Victor snorted contemptuously. "Coffee house *cafards!* Beggars, the lot of them! They steal, cheat, traffic in drugs and other contraband. Pseudo-intellects—all of them! Most do not attend the Sorbonne—I promise," he said with visible viciousness. "Scratch behind the surface, you'll find an inner loathing for themselves and the world. I was there long ago and I am afraid for you, *ma chere.*"

Veronique studied him in profile against the moving traffic. She ignored the obvious vitriol. *Really, wasn't it the pot calling the kettle black?*

"So, tell me. What is your opinion of me?" he asked.

"What a strange question to ask. Does it matter what I think?"

"*Oui.* I am . . . what . . . twenty years older than you? Perhaps more."

"You haven't kissed me and you ask personal questions? Besides, I am older than I appear. I am nearly thirty. The freckles are deceptive."

Victor Zeller sighed. "I am still twenty years older."

"Are you married, Victor Zeller?"

"No. No woman in her right mind would put up with my lifestyle. There is no time in my life for marriage."

"That bad, eh? In America we have a saying. 'All work and no play makes Jack a dull boy.' "

"In Zurich we say, 'All work and no play makes Jacques very wealthy indeed.' "

"Wealth, is *that* important to you?"

"That's an ambiguous question." He opened the portable bar behind the chauffeur console, retrieved a bottle of chilled Dom Perignon. "Money, provides me a way of life I should loathe giving up." He changed the subject quickly. "Will you have dinner with me tonight, Veronique? Spend the night with me? I leave for Zurich in the morning." He poured two glasses of the amber liquid, handed her one, took the other, and clinked glasses. "To us," he whispered.

They passed the fifty-nine-story Tour Main-Montparnasse, an ugly modern-day creation of steel and glass visible from every corner of Paris. It jutted above the domes of the ancient city.

Veronique's eyes deliberately broke contact with Victor's. She stared at the monstrosity. "Pure sacrilege," she muttered. "Paris is Paris. It should be preserved, not bastardized with modern eyesores."

She sipped champagne, squirming under his smoldering scrutiny, aware he studied every gesture, weighed her words, observed her poise, the manner she sipped her champagne. He stared at the expensive leather boots she wore, eyeing every hand-stitched detail like a craftsman.

Incongruities struck Victor. She was not what she appeared!

An alarm sounded inside him. A warning. Something about this American woman did not compute. Her clothing! . . . Manner? . . . Poise? . . . Nothing computed with her flamboyant *joi de vivre!*

Victor hadn't come this far in life without developing a razor-honed instinct and a keen intelligence. Men of his caliber must exercise extreme caution these days. Kidnappings and assassinations by terrorists proliferated! Earlier at the galleries, four of his men mingled unobtrusively among the guests, sipping champagne, alert for stalking predators, radical elements, and God knew what else!

Now the woman, Veronique Lindley! An intriguing spellbinder . . . She *was* unique, he told himself, stripping suspicion from his eyes.

Discretion, Victor . . . Use discretion. She fits no ordinary run-of-the-mill classification. What do you know of her—her history? She must have a history, mais non? It can be verified—never fear.

"You are most desirable, *mon petite* Veronique." He patted her hand affectionately.

"I work at it," she said flippantly. "It is not easy being goyim."

The Zeller penthouse was superbly decorated. A breathtaking view of the *Ile de la Cité*, one of two islands at the heart of Paris, captured Veronique's attention. *Les Ile St. Louis*, farther to the north, barely visible, came to life as the lights of Paris blinked on. Behind her, Victor placed a match to the kindling, starting the fire on the hearth. He brought chilled champagne from the walk-in cooler off the kitchen. Valerie returned from the terrace, moved across the room, stepped down to the sunken conversational pit near the hearth. She admired the exquisite furnishings, a collection of Impressionist paintings, recognizing portions of the Rothstein collection and other rare objects of art.

Veronique faltered a moment—it was now or never! She pulled off the angora sweater, freeing her breasts; peeled off the customized boots; slid out of her jeans and sheer bikini panties and stood naked in the rosy glow of the fire.

Victor re-entered the room, stopped abruptly, sucked in his breath and moved toward her, champagne and glasses in hand. The stimulating fragrance of her perfume, Eau de Doblis, wafting to his nostrils, an aphrodisiac. He admired the lean, hard body, tanned to a string bikini line below the rounded hips. Her breasts, rounded, full with erect nipples in their areolas, trembled as a chill shuddered through her. She accepted the champagne from him, held it before her, her voice husky. *"Approviuvez-vous moi?"*

Victor placed his glass on the onyx table. He reached out, drawing her into his arms, the quivering flesh under his touch sending shock waves through him. He lifted her face to his, kissed her gently, then with increased ardor. His body, tense, hardening against hers, provoked an inner trembling, increasing his excitement. Abruptly, he pulled away from her, picked up his glass and the bottle in one hand, and pulling her toward him, searched her blue eyes dancing like green fire in the fireglow. He sighed ecstatically.

"To us, *liebling*. I have a feeling we may be right for each other. We will know soon enough, *n'est-ce pas?"* They clinked glasses, sipped the liquid and he led her into the next room.

Veronique stared about the dimly lit area, enchanted and curious. A glass cylinder from floor to ceiling stood at the center of the bedroom on a raised dais. Victor pressed a panel of buttons.

"Voilà! You see?" The wall behind them slid open, revealing a steamy hot tub banked by verdant ferns, palms and lacy greenery. A portion of the floor slid open, a console raised to full height startling her. Behind it a projection screen unfolded, locking into place. Another switch activated a video device. A Betamax system was activated, the screen lighted up with erotic films. Veronique tilted her head obliquely in a gesture of appreciation.

"Vive les electronics, *chere."* She reached into her bag,

removed a small black case containing six vials. "Do you use, Victor? Cocaine? Hash? . . . Colombian? . . . Amyl? . . ." She removed a joint, lighted it, inhaled deeply, retaining the toke and passed it to him. He studied her somberly, then took a hit before returning it to her.

"I need nothing to stimulate me," he told her. "You are more than enough. Perhaps *after* the fourth, fifth, sixth time? . . ."

She floated languidly toward him, and Victor drew her into the glass cylinder; he pressed a lever opening a floor drain, and from the ceiling a gilded shower apparatus lowered slowly into place, with four separate heads, each capable of producing erotic sensations as water sprayed their bodies. Another vial, a lather dispenser, sprayed perfumed soap. The lights dramatically subdued and controlled electronically by music glistened the iridescent droplets the rising color of a rainbow. They moved from cylinder to the hot tub, floating in weightlessness. Invigorating hot water from the whirling pool thrust against her body. She felt as if four men were making love to her at once. The sensations acute, erotic, driving her to incredible heights. Was it the Colombian? The Dom Perignon? The unquestionable talents of the shower, the hot tub or everything at once—including Victor.

Victor stroked her body tenderly, fed her tidbits from a tray piled high with canapes, skewered roasted meats and cheeses. He placed the tray at the edge of the hot tub and popping a canape, pushed a set of buttons on a panel. The picture on the large screen dissolved to a new picture. Veronique gulped hard.

There on the screen, larger than life, she and Victor became instant stars! From the moment she had entered the apartment a hidden camera had filmed her every move. She observed herself disrobe, a feeling of embarrassment flushing through her while Victor fed her a jumbo prawn dipped in hot sauce. She nibbled on it, feigning delightful surprise, giggled outwardly. Inwardly, she regrouped her forces. So! *She was under constant electronic surveillance—was she?* She hadn't counted on this, but was grateful she learned in this manner rather than be caught rifling through her possessions. She supposed it was his insurance should she prove to be an extortionist or a Mata Hari of sorts.

If he only knew. . . .

Her cover was secure. Let him photograph her all he wanted. Let him check her out—she had carefully implemented the cover apparatus a long time ago.

"You are *not* upset, Veronique?" he asked cagily.

"To see myself in the throes of ecstacy?" She laughed liltingly, her eyes on the action. "Mmmn," she cooed, "it is stimulating to watch the pleasure we shared." She sipped her champagne, then gave a start. Her face screwed into a frown.

"You won't—you *didn't*—you *couldn't*—show those films to Jake! Oh, my God! You're an investigator! And I fell for it!" She moaned balefully. "You're going to use it against me, aren't you?" She stared at him, feigning to be crushed, horrified.

Victor laughed aloud, heartily. He reached for her, held her in his arms, assuring her he had no such thought in mind. Tickled by the accusation, he repeatedly insisted such a thought was the farthest from his mind. "If anything, *liebling*, I would nurture the film, playing it over and over for my own pleasure."

He held her tightly, kissed her. The sexual overture began again. "Where have you been all my life?" he said wistfully, kissing her ears, neck, throat. "I've needed you for so long. See—we fit together perfectly. Veronique, oh, Veronique. . . . It's been so long since I've allowed myself to feel true emotion. Once we trust each other, I promise it will be exquisite together."

Listening to him, a part of her wanted to believe, but the better part warned her against the vulnerability of the moment.

Now the tocsin sounded shrilly in Veronique. *You know what he is . . . what his father represents. Hold to your purpose, Veronique.*

Victoria's voice, her image, the impressions of the vile contemptible truth came at her from all sides, galling her, increasing her determination. Yet, a part of her responded to the numerous changes, *spellbinding* changes occurring in her. Her body was betraying her. And it was *magic! Dammit! Dammit! Dammit!* Why must it feel so good with a man she was committed to destroy? *Why?*

"What's this?" she asked at the dark, almost undistinguishable tattoo on Victor's left shoulder.

He turned his head, hunched his shoulder forward and gazing at his reflection in the mirror, smiled tolerantly. "A tattoo. A bumblebee. Some silly thing my mother insisted upon to mark our lineage. Quite prestigious, I might add."

"A bumblebee? What's prestigious about a bumblebee?"

Victor rose from the bed, moved to a wall cabinet, pressed a lever, opening a partition concealing a wall safe. A few twists to the right, several to the left, and *voilà!* It opened.

Victor withdrew a black velvet case, returned to the bed and placed it before Veronique. "You must be very *special* to me, *ma chere*. You are the first woman to whom I have ever shown this."

He opened the lid; encased was a miniature jeweled bumblebee. A marquise-cut diamond comprised the body of the bee, gold filigree for the wings with emerald highpoints. "And this, long before lapidists ever cut a diamond in any but a brilliant cut."

"What does it mean? Is it a family symbol, a crest of sorts?"

"You won't laugh?"

"Why would I laugh?" An imperceptible smile tugged at her lips.

"It belonged to Josephine. A gift to her from my ancestor."

She laughed with good humor. "You mean *the* Josephine? *Napoleon's* Josephine? . . . Really!" *Well, well, well. Something she didn't know?*

"You see why I don't mention it?" His tone convinced her of his veracity. "The bee tattooed on my shoulder? My mother's ingenuity to insure I never forget my heritage."

She detected vulnerability in him. She played on that vulnerability, smiling ineffably, her glance smoldered.

The journey grew increasingly menacing in her risky role of an alluring seductress. Forced constantly to stand guard over her words and actions became the most difficult and exacting and exhausting role of her life. To relieve the torment—she succumbed to him sexually. The invigorating relaxation of the hot tub, champagne, and drugs facilitated the trying task. Oblivion came with orgasmic release.

At six in the morning, Victor, stirred to new heights, left Veronique asleep on the oversized bed. He felt terrific. The reason: Veronique. He carefully wrote down her name, address and telephone exchange and a few additional notes, bits and pieces of her conversation. He slipped the note into his jacket pocket, the video cassettes of their sexual interlude stashed in his briefcase. Pulling out a large wad of Swiss francs, he left the equivalent of five hundred dollars on the night stand and left the room.

He instructed his servants to let the woman rest, take her back to her flat in the limousine.

The Rolls wheeled along Parisian streets, headed for Orly. The rains had stopped. Spring had spread its magic overnight. Budding leaves took shape, flowers bloomed. Paris, bathed in a wash of sunshine, smelled fresh—new. Victor's inner ebullience, long absent, filled him with renewed vigor. The luxury of total surrender to a woman did not come easily to him and he marveled at the fates that brought them together. Was it love? Too well-schooled in the ways of man, his cynicism persisted. Such things just didn't happen. Not to Victor Zeller.

The Rolls swerved off the main road, headed toward a private airstrip adjacent to Orly. He thought of Veronique, smelled her presence and felt intoxicated by her. He chastized himself for leaving her. It was Sunday. Why hadn't he remained with her? The day could have been more rewarding than the previous night. The reason? His father had ordered him to return today. You just don't disobey an order from Amadeo Zeller.

The old man was plotting something sinister. He sensed it. Victor dismissed thoughts of his father; he refused to let anything destroy the pleasurable feeling of Veronique engulfing him.

Victor glanced up ahead. The Sikorsky jet was revving up for takeoff. He glanced at his gold watch. Seven on the button. Two burly bodyguards alighted the Rolls, peered cautiously around the area, opened the car door, and, moving into place at his flanks, escorted him to the waiting jet. Greeting him somberly at the hatch door, his pilot, Mosha Bauer, nodded perfunctorily. Victor handed him the note with Veronique's statistics and the briefcase.

Mosha Bauer knew what was expected of him. The former Israeli terrorist, part of the *Wolfgang Katz* conspiracy, who had posed a dilemma to Brad Lincoln, intrigued and baffled him. Bauer needed no instructions from his boss. The routine was simple. The requirements: a complete dossier on Veronique Lindley, including possible lovers, etc. His heavy jowled face expressionless, Mosha Bauer closed the hatch behind Victor.

Airborne, en route to Kloten Airport in Zurich, Victor's concentration waned. Images of Veronique flashed in his mind. Like a drug, she both stimulated and increased his need for her. He still felt her body, the scent of her perfume. The taste of her lips, kisses, body, clung to him, haunted like the bouquet of a rare elixir.

His mind flashed on her in critical analysis. She was bright, beautiful. Her intelligence deliberately understated and subordinate to his had bolstered his ego. It was an admirable quality in a woman in these days of the liberated female, who came off as hardened lesbians because they hadn't learned the art of blending both masculine and feminine qualities into an integrated whole of what was woman. A man's ego demanded that he be stronger, superior to woman in countless ways, although he knew inordinately it was a case of *nolo contenedre*. In her total submission to him in the sexual act—a plus in her favor—she had instantly made him her slave.

Then, what, Victor? What disturbs you about her?

A calculating quality that chalked everything in advance. A plotted scenario, carefully constructed, inciting action, exposition and climaxes. The staging clearly indicated unity, variety, and cleverly produced emotional highs and lows. The tempo—perfection. The emotional key—stupendous. The casting was pure heaven. The performance, an exquisite delight. The curtain calls, spellbinding. Then what, *Dumkoff! What?*

Motivation. He couldn't determine her motivation! Inescapably obvious to him was the one jarring fact: she had focused on no other man in the Art Galleria but him. He'd studied her long enough to know what he saw and he saw her look at no one but him.

Why concern yourself? he soothed himself. Mosha Bauer would investigate and ferret out the truth, so why make like a *shmegehgeh*? Victor smiled. The real *shmegehgeh* was that idiot Jake for turning Veronique loose in Paris! Of all places.

Passionate little minx, Veronique had worn him out.

Long ago Victor had promised *never* to fully uncap the turbulent pent-up passions inside him. Never demonstrate his love to another woman. Last night, for the first time in nearly thirty years, he had broken through the self-imposed barriers, made love with abandon.

Thirty years? . . . That long ago? . . . Was it time for him to bury the past, forget Sophia, his beloved Sophia, once and for all?

Sophia . . . The very name evoked a rush of painful memories. Apparently he hadn't cauterized the wounds, the live nerve

392

endings to stop the internal bleeding of his love for her. Why he continuously resurrected her memory, unable to keep her buried in his mind, disturbed Victor. His eyes darted to the console at his side just as the steward served his croissants and coffee. He opened it, removed a worn copy, yellowed with age, of Antoine de Saint Exupery's *Little Prince* in its original French text. Inside the flyleaf he read: *Pour mon petite, Sophia: May the beauty of the Little Prince's soul touch your heart forever. To see with the heart is the most important gift of life. With love and devotion, your servant, Antoine de Saint Exupery.*

Victor closed the cover. He sipped his coffee, without appetite, lay back in his thickly cushioned seat, closed his eyes, letting memory drift back to those years.

After the bloody battles, *after* the Free French Resistance fighters and the *Mozarabe* Desert Commandos began their special brand of bloodletting in Corsica and *before* the Axis troops in defeat had retreated from the island, Major Victor Zeller and a squad of Italian Intelligence officers had stormily fled the island in dispute with the Nazis. Less than a year after their triumphant Italian occupation, they had evacuated Corsica, leaving the determined Germans at the helm to steer the course.

By then, Victor had found his Sophia and taken her with him to Rome.

Sophia, the dark-eyed stunning Corsican, loathed Victor. He was the enemy to her. But it didn't matter. Victor loved her with all his heart. She meant the world to him. Victor had recognized the unleashed passion in Sophia's turbulent loins, the free spirit of her soul. Under his sexual expertise, the sultry-eyed, throbbing virginal body had come alive with sensuality. She had submitted to his sexual demands, but made it perfectly clear he would never possess her totally. *Never!* Still he didn't care. Believing he could win her love, he had expressed his genuine feelings in a thousand different ways. Life without Sophia was meaningless to Victor. To penetrate that solidified wedge she'd driven between them became, for Victor, an exercise in futility.

Victor, an enemy in war, would remain the enemy in peace to this Corsican. What a strange lot—Corsicans. Silent, brooding, noncommittal, with flashing dagger eyes capable of killing or loving. Victor, the resolute hero, was dauntless. He had conjured a thousand ways to tame this tigress, possess her in a way he *knew* she wanted to be possessed. Sophia had represented to Victor what the Golden Fleece had represented to Jason, the reason for his existence.

In Rome he had provided her with luxuries, a beautiful home, stunning clothing—anything she wanted. All this during the war! Still nothing pierced that icy remoteness. She didn't wear the clothing, ignored the jewels, moved about the house like a zombie. At his wit's end, he proposed marriage. She refused each and every time he broached the subject.

The war, nearing its end with mounting political unrest as thirteen political parties jockeyed about for power, complicated Victor's life. Mussolini, out of business, rescued by Hitler's men, remained in exile. The entire Italian Army under Il Duce's control was subjected to daily humiliations, yet the Allies kept them intact, subordinate to their rule to keep order.

By this time, Sophia's continued depression, her frozen, unresponsive attitude, had nearly destroyed Victor.

He knew how betrayal could descend into wariness, hatred, and a joyless existence—hadn't he seen enough of it for the past two years? If only Sophia would reject him, force him to hate her, do something that would make him understand her loathing for him. But she remained courteous, considerate, polite to the point of insufferable indifference.

One night, Victor could take no more. Following a heavy drinking bout, in his desire to awaken the feminine lust lying dormant inside his beloved Sophia's body, he took her to bed. She lay back against the silken coverlets. Victor slapped her, called her a whore, a bitch, a cockteaser! He heaped upon her all the vile curses hurled at the lowliest of street whores and ordered her to go. "Leave my house and my sight at once!"

Sophia had risen from the bed unflinchingly, and in silence dressed quietly in a trim woolen suit. She tossed her coal-black curly hair off her face, picked up her identification papers and walked toward the door. Victor, alarmed, screamed at her.

"What in God's name are you doing?"

"You ordered me to leave," she replied quietly.

Victor leaped from the bed, grabbed hold of her, held her tightly and, in a flagrant display of emotionalism, sobbed aloud.

"Don't you understand anything, Sophia? Don't you know how much I love you? You are tearing me apart. Does it mean nothing to you that I am dying inside? What must I do to make you come alive, respond to my love?''

She turned to him, dark almond eyes wide open, staring into his anguished features. "It is you who does not understand, Victor." She hung her head, studying the patterns in the Persian carpeting, trying to find the proper words. "How can I explain to you what has been and will always remain a mystery to me? I am Corsican. Without Corsica I am dead. What reason have I for living? I shall never come alive—never!"

"You deny your existence? You are a woman, Sophia! A woman with needs, desires, a life born to creation and you live a lie, a hoax. You are a fraud. You try to live a dream in your mind that does not exist. You exist! I exist! We are both creatures of God. Real flesh and blood! Nothing else matters except that we share together a life as best we can."

She shook her head. "You were the conqueror who must be resisted," she said simply, as if this explained away the two years of Victor's absolute frustration. Her iron will insured that this would never change. And this damnable Corsican thing inside her ate away at their happiness.

Victor blamed their ill-fated love affair on destiny. Had they met under different circumstances, his love for her would have melted this rebellious resolve. He told her so. But those dark eyes stared at him sadly. She shook her head at what she, herself, couldn't articulate. But then, there was so much more to Sophia than Victor would ever know.

Her home life, family, the profound mysteries surrounding her unusual love for her brother Darius—one that transcended the bounds of decency between brother and sister—could not be easily discussed. Destiny had intervened, making a shambles of what might have become an idyllic paradise for both.

In February 1944, Victor Zeller was summoned to Zurich. His father had sent a courier across the German-guarded border with an urgent request for Victor's immediate presence at his side. Victor, unwilling to leave Sophia alone, yet unable to take her with him due to the precariousness of travel, had no recourse but to leave her in the sanctuary of his mother's *palazzo*.

His mother, the Contessa de Bernadorf de Zeller, accommodated her beloved son. In his absence—Victor never learned the truth—something had happened. On his return, Sophia was gone. The Contessa gave no logical explanation of Sophia's sudden disappearance. Victor blamed his mother. He stormed, raged at her, his harsh criticism so scorching it brought tears to his mother's eyes. Something deep inside him suspected a collusion of sorts, a conspiracy against him. He returned to his luxurious apartment, searched every inch of the premises, looking for a clue—anything to indicate Sophia's whereabouts. She had taken nothing with her. No clothing or jewelry or household furnishings—nothing. Not even perfume—or precious nylons purchased on the black market—nothing! The drawers were filled, undisturbed in the elegant dressing room off the boudoir.

In a rage, he collected all her personal effects, packed them in trunks, and sent them to the Zeller *palazzo* to be stored until he found her.

Investigators, hired to find her, gave up in six months. They suspected foul play *after* the war, giving Victor little hope. When informed she had taken nothing of value, their curiosity waned. They no longer believed him. No woman in her right mind ever left everything behind! They had scoured Rome, Naples, Florence, Venice—lastly, Ajaccio, Corsica . . . nothing!

The contradictions in Sophia were too immense for Victor to sort; his concern piqued. Before he left for Zurich, her breasts had fleshed out, swollen in size, grown more sensitive to his touch; the darkening of the areola, and the mysterious eyes had taken on added luster. Had she been with child? He would never know.

Oh, how Victor mourned her; he cried out her name in dreams. Her image became so alive he would reach out for her only to awaken and find himself the victim in a vicious nightmare, left clutching specters.

To expunge Sophia's memory, Victor had subverted his sorrow in an endless parade of women, but none had succeeded in obliterating her or the hungry ache for Sophia. Victor fled Italy several months before V-E Day. To remain in Italy meant instant death at the hands of fanatics and crazy subversives. He joined his father, plunging himself wholeheartedly in the field of banking, compressed his life to fit into a rigid, unrealistic schedule of the workaholic. Was he mad for regarding his existence as valuable only as it related to Sophia?

God! He had loved Sophia! He no longer blamed himself that Sophia suffered mental aberrations, rendering her unable to reciprocate in normal human relations. His heart had hardened. He had erected stone barriers around his emotions and kept himself aloof to the fleshpot pleasures.

Victor had looked to his father for a perfect model for his future behavior. Amadeo Redak Zeller, prototype of a stone-cold, hard-hearted demagogue, ruled the earth with a tight fist. Zeller senior lived only for himself, caring nothing for others. "A man who lives for others annihilates his own consciousness and self-identity," Zeller senior preached to his son. "To obliterate the self by making others more important is a crime against one's self. Zeller's Law," he told his son. "You had better get used to Zeller's law."

And so, he taught himself survival techniques, to be dependent upon no one save himself. As for love—he no longer believed in the myth.

The demanding, fast-paced world of high finance and Victor Zeller experienced unique compatability. Victor was a driven man! Behind facades of obedience to Amadeo's dictates lurked blinding ambition to surpass his father's lofty accomplishments. Unfortunately, Victor retained neither knowledge nor scope of *those* accomplishments.

The trouble actually started early in 1983!

Never made privy to his father's private life and villainous deeds Victor had no idea what the future held in store for him when he agreed to participate in the scientific experiments underway at the Zeller Foundation by six researchers housed at the Zeller chateau. He became a willing pawn in the *gameplan*, believing he'd learn more comprehensive schematics to the entire banking world of Zeller.

The work, highly technical and covert, had begun in late January, extended through summer and early fall. He met Veronique in a state of emaciation; he had grown pale, pre-occupied, listless, introverted and brooding. Deep creases lined his brow; his handsome face, leaner, seemed harsher, taut; his eyes, vacant and shadowed by secrecy, sank further into their hollows, yet he still exuded a delicious Tyrone Power form of good looks. His weight loss, minimal, the definite signs of unmistakable exhaustion prevalent. How many nights had he spent pacing the floors of his Zurich townhouse, insomniac, unsure at the changes manifesting in him, wondering at the

397

profusion of data collected in his brain cells, sorting it, filing it in proper memory niches?

Then, suddenly, he flew to Paris and came alive for the first time in months. The priceless Rothstein art collection had baited him, but Veronique Lindley had galvanized him—made him human!

Victor arrived at Kloten Airport, and met by his bodyguards was whisked away in his Mercedes limousine into Zurich and the Zeller bank on the *Bahnhofstrasse*. In moments he was in the elevator zooming up to the penthouse, unable to decide the exact source of the exhilaration he felt. The images of Veronique, her perfume, lingering erotica wafting to his senses every moment.

The agenda was ponderous. Ignoring it, he showered, freshened up, drank a pot of chocolate-flavored coffee and reentered the busy, elegantly furnished office and sat at his desk. He glanced distastefully at the numerous messages. Inhaling and expelling sighs of vexation, he launched right into his tasks, but at every second, Veronique crept back into his mind like a gremlin to distract him from his work. He fought the irresistible compulsions to call her. When finally his will surrendered to the memory of her body enveloped in his, and he replayed the video cassette, in private, of their sexual sojourn, Victor could desist no longer. He made the call.

Veronique listened and hung up on him. Intrigued, he called again. She slammed down the phone harder. He placed another call, asking very swiftly, ''Tell me what's wrong? What did I do?''

''You bastard! I'll tell you what you did! You left money! I tore it to shreds and burned it! You presumed me to be a whore, bought for a price. Well, fuck you, *Monsieur* Victor Whoever-the hell you are! Who needs you?''

Victor, totally enchanted, laughed harder than he'd laughed in a year. He called her back. ''Did you really burn the money?''

''Yes!''

''Come spend the week with me in Zurich. My pilot will fly you to me, *liebling*,'' he said softly.

He was waiting for her at Kloten Airport, his arms outstretched to her, his resolve never to give of himself as he had to Sophia forgotten.

Chapter Twenty-Six

THEY SHARED VICTOR'S TOWNHOUSE overlooking Lake Zurich. It was an idyllic time for Victor. Every spare moment stolen from his work was spent introducing Veronique to the charm of Zurich and the canton. Together they prowled elegant shops, the enchanting boutiques and cafés on the *Bahnhofstrasse*, all the way to the Alstadt. They strolled hand in hand along cobbled streets, always shadowed by Victor's bodyguards.

Victor drove his Rolls-Royce Corniche through spectacular mountainous countryside and Swiss village hamlets surrounding the Zurichsee. They browsed in antique shops, cloistered cafés, confectionaries and *Konditorei*, from the Wohnmuseum to the Kronehalle Restaurant, where Miros, Chagalls and Picassos once hung on open walls without security measures and now were safeguarded under lock and key.

Time had no beginning, no ending. Veronique, no closer to meeting Amadeo Zeller than she was on her arrival, considered her options. She commuted back and forth to Paris. In summer, Victor asked her to remain with him in Zurich. Autumn disappeared, and suddenly winter worked in earnest to cover Zurich in a white velvet mantle. They drove about in a horsedrawn sleigh, listening to the tinkling bells, inhaling crisp country air, drawing their fox parkas closer to their bodies. Under a sable lap robe, Victor took liberties with her body and she, his. They kissed and sang songs with lusty bravado, most in Italian and French. They sipped Napoleon brandy from a silver flask when chilled and she listened fascinated as he repeatedly insisted he shared the Bonaparte bloodline, a fact she found amusing, but incredible. Victor insisted the brandy they drank was from the Emperor's private stock, and Veronique laughed. Whether she believed him or not, every word he spoke was committed to memory. He told her countless tales of his childhood, spoke of his mother whom he loved and very little of his father with whom he shared no common bond save for banking and finance.

399

"I doubt the Contessa and my father ever enjoyed the sexual highs we do, Veronique," he confided somberly. "They lived a different life, in a vastly different world than we."

Then, as quickly, as if he loathed memories, he'd become remote. "I prefer living in the moment. It's far more rewarding, darling."

Victor introduced her to his favorite vice, melted mint chocolate in hot coffee. Between chocolate mint and coffee-flavored kisses, soulful looks, ecstatic sighs, sexual interludes, he taught her art appreciation, introduced her to unheard-of musical classics and spoke of a future together.

Veronique withdrew in these moments. Sensing her remoteness, and vividly recalling Sophia, Victor did not press. That he entertained thoughts of a future with Veronique surprised him, for in the past, he hadn't abandoned fantasies of one day finding Sophia and recapturing her heart.

Meanwhile, Veronique calculated her steps. Time was becoming her worst enemy. Victor had not mentioned Amadeo to Veronique although she was sure the Zeller lion knew the little there was to discover about Veronique Lindley. How could she thrust herself gracefully upon the domicile of the man she intended to crush? Distressed by Victor's amorous ovations, she conceived a plan to cool his feelings without incurring his suspicions. She continuously injected references concerning her infidelity to the mythical Jacob—Jake—Bernstein.

"You can't be serious about *him*. After our affair? What we mean to each other?"

"That's just it, Victor. All I am to you is an *affair*. You haven't suggested in a remote way that I should meet your father. Are you ashamed of me? That we are lovers? We don't even socialize. In all this time, I've met none of your friends in Zurich."

He listened in silence. "You're right. We'll have to make the necessary changes."

They made love that night and the ecstasy for Victor became uncontrollable. "I must have you, Veronique. It will be difficult to arrange for a short while. I am involved in a matter of vital importance. The moment it ends. . . ."

It was November 30, a date Veronique burned vividly in her memory. It was the beginning of a ghastly series of nightmares, *unending* nightmares that Veronique had not included in her personal scenario. She couldn't have anticipated the diabolical horror waiting for her. If she had, she might have taken the first flight home, cancelling all strategies.

Victor loved skiing. Veronique had always held her own at Aspen and Vail. Gstaad was not Aspen or Vail and the Swiss Alps bore little resemblance to Colorado. The snowy slopes of Gstaad were star-studded with glittering international cinema stars and jet-setters on holiday. She and Victor took the ski lift to the highest station, prepared to descend the slopes.

Then a call came on Victor's beeper. He excused himself, entered the chalet, and made a call.

It seemed moments before the Bell 222 piloted by Mosha Bauer touched down on the nearby flatland, the tunneling icy wind blasting with blizzard proportions as he boarded. The chopper lifted off and flew back to Zurich.

Something urgent at the bank, Victor told her.

Later that night at the Zeller townhouse Veronique relaxed in a hot tub, sipped champagne and curled up before the fire awaiting Victor's return.

It was nearly 8:00 P.M. when they sat down to dinner, soft music playing in the background. Victor appeared preoccupied, moody. After dinner they rested on a sable robe before the fire sipping eggnog and Amaretto seared by a hot poker from the fire. Victor's dark eyes lingered over Veronique's body caressingly, conveying the depth of his love. The message in his eyes, with each caress, disturbing to Veronique, indicated the relationship had exceeded established boundaries in her mind. While she had no firm grasp of his desperate need for a relationship in which he could be himself, Victor refused to believe her participation in their romance was less consuming than his. Her actions, he insisted, proved otherwise, her erotic response was no act.

For Victor, Jake Bernstein did not exist. He refused to deal with any concern for the man. "You don't love him—never have! Forget him, Veronique!" His logic was impregnable.

In her need to orchestrate the scenario, Veronique secretly plotted to unearth some reason to return to Paris. Being Jake's fiancee, no longer a viable excuse, this night she searched desperately for another to extricate herself from Victor's complicated web. She needed time to regroup, to rethink strategy.

Oblivious to her discomfort, Victor lovingly stroked her silky, fragrantly scented hair, smoothed the wisps of her moist brow,

401

burying his face in the softness of her neck, nuzzling her playfully. Background music, his favorite Griffes, *The Pleasure Dome of Kubla Khan*. Suddenly, in an expansive mood, he pulled away slightly and with dramatic panache recited the Coleridge poem that had inspired Griffes to create the moving music. He spoke in a voice rife with love:

> "In Xanadu did Kubla Khan a stately pleasure dome decree;
> Where Alpha the sacred river ran through the caverns measureless to man
> Down to a sunless sea.
> So twice. . . . So twice five miles . . ."

Victor paused, repeated the last line, searching his memory for the words, a frown screwing his features.

Raising on one elbow, utterly absorbed, Veronique whispered, "Yes, Victor, please continue."

He could not and frustration set in. Futilely, he searched his memory for the familiar lines, but he could not recall the words. "Odd, I know the poem by rote."

Watching, Veronique lay before the rosy lights of fireglow. The relaxing effect of the hot Amaretto eggnogs and the fire's warmth mellowed her. She responded anew to Victor's hand on her body, writhing sensuously to his touch.

Victor delighted in pleasuring Veronique. And in return he got what Sophia could not give him. So much love abounded in this American beauty, it left Victor speechless. Why had the fates not brought them together sooner?

"I've seen the miracles of paradise, Veronique, *ma chere*," he cooed lovingly, his flesh tingling, coming alive at the touch of her soft, warm flesh. He held her closer, probed her body deeper, thrusting his in deep rhythmic movements synchronized to hers. He paused periodically, towering over her to stare at her, as if he couldn't be done with the wonder of her. The pink, rosy-gold glow from the fireplace transformed her; her skin took on a deep blush, her eyes, cerulean blue sapphires, glittered with glints of green fire points, and her hair shone brightly hued with burnished fire. Victor was lost in the allure of this Circean enchantress. Time and space took on different dimensions. The

402

world beyond their doors belonged to another era he had no desire to penetrate.

Veronique's superb controlled response to the love lavished on her, evoked in him a response in kind, as if she'd been the only love force in his life. They shuddered together, a tangle of arms, legs, erotica. To Victor, they were Adam and Eve, Apollo and Aphrodite, Paris and Helen of Troy, Anthony and Cleopatra, Samson and Delilah, the personification of universal lovers. But to Veronique—*Eve* and Adam, *Aphrodite* and Apollo, *Helen of Troy* and Paris, *Cleopatra* and Anthony, *Delilah* and Samson. She needed to keep the perspective of control.

And then all was shattered.

Briefly, for a moment suspended in time, destiny wreaked havoc on Victor. At the height of climaxing, Victor shouted as one possessed, "Victoria! . . . Victoria, my beloved! How long I've waited for you, needed you, loved you! Now, at long last you belong to me. You are mine. *MINE!* I shall never let you go."

Veronique froze. Her eyes snapped open. Her mind, suspended in the horror of the moment, chilled her emotions to a standstill while he exploded in heated urgency inside her body.

The repetition of his agony was almost a howl. "Victoria! Victoria! My God, Victoria!"

His features contained both his love and a sheer torment—and something else. A look she'd never seen before, the expression of a total stranger. His body arched rigidly before collapsing over her, convulsing until the ecstasy had spent itself.

Sensing her alienation, Victor cocked open one eye, pulled back slightly, opened the other and grinned sheepishly, as he usually did after pleasurable sex. Veronique, unyielding, assessed him coolly, struggling for control.

"Who is Victoria?" *As if she didn't know!*

Hazy, still euphoric, he leaned in, nuzzling her neck. She shoved him away, demanding, "*Who* is Victoria?" Resolve lay dully on her face like a mask of hardening clay.

"Hummmmmm?" He yawned lazily, pulling himself up. "I'll get the coffee if you get the chocolate mint." He grinned with amusement.

"*Victor! Goddammit! Who in the hell is Victoria?*" She spat the words venomously, shoved him aside, sprang to her feet, and, shrugging into her robe, tied the sash with short jerks. She reached for a cigarette, lighted it, clicked the butane lighter shut as Victor, on the floor, rolled over on his stomach. Crossing his arms under his neck, he lay there, his eyes on her, a curiously amused expression tugging at his lips. "I thought you gave up smoking, *liebchen*?"

"Don't you *liebchen* me. I'll do more than smoke, if you don't answer my question, you bastard!"

"What question?" he asked blandly, staring at her as she paced about working up a fury, her flesh winking flirtatiously at him with each movement. The thought excited him. So attuned was he to her body, he knew every pleasure point. Lust oozed from his dilated, pleasure-filled eyes teasingly. Aware of his growing tumescence, Veronique exasperated, with derision, speaking through clenched teeth.

"You've called me Sophia countless times in your sleep. You cried her name. I didn't mind. I neither expected or got a celibate, you bastard! But to call out *Victoria! Victoria! Victoria!* at the height of orgasm—not once, or twice, but more!—is purely insulting, Victor! Erotic ovations for some other woman is not my fulfillment of a fantasy, Victor! This time it is too real to be ignored." Controlled tears sprang to her eyes, their presence enhanced her position.

Victor sat up, the Cheshire-cat grin dissolved. He reached for his robe, slipped into it, pondering Veronique's burlesque of his apparent faux pas. "To Sophia, I admit, *liebchen*. I was in love with her once, a very long time ago." His words, as soft as pussy willow, he reached for her, drew her into his arms, lifting her chin, forcing her to look into his eyes. "But—*Victoria?*" He shook his head, shrugged, searched his memory. "I know no one by that name—I promise. Save the British Queen . . ." He shoved the silk shoulder of her robe down, baring her flesh, kissed her lightly, staring at the perky jutting of her ample breast. He kissed her again, tenderly, whispering, "You are delicious, *liebchen*."

Victor smiled irresistibly, hoping to dissolve her suspicions. Veronique would not be mollified. "Just tell me *who* she is, Victor. Don't lie about it." She shrugged the silk back on her shoulders as if this punished him in some remote way.

Victor flinched, a perplexed expression burrowing its way into his features. His bewilderment was genuine. "You are serious? I have, in some way unknown to me, offended you. I find your attitude and the accusation beneath you, Veronique. I am telling you the truth." Then, short of temper, he flared. "For God's sake, tell me what I said. What in hell was so offensive to you?"

Veronique gave him verbatim an accounting of the earlier drama. Victor stared at her, as if he thought her daft. He had no memory of the moment, tried desperately to recall it, but failed.

"Anything I say at this moment will worsen things, *liebchen*." To have mutilated your pleasure is unforgivable. I swear I have no conscious recollection—" Victor stopped abruptly, stared after her with a cold, hard expression. He was alone, talking to himself.

Veronique was slamming cupboards in the kitchen as she fixed coffee. Victor sat down on the sofa, stared into glowing embers of the fire, desperately sorting through Veronique's anger. Something inside him repeated, over and over like a broken record, *Hair the color of burnished fire. . . . Emerald eyes like jewels. . . . Victoria, my love. . . . Victoria, my eternal love. . . .*

Furrows creased Victor's brow. He clasped his head, shook it, trying to clear the confusion inside. It stopped briefly. He glanced up as Veronique returned, carrying a tray with coffee, cups, and mint chocolate. He smiled at her with a quick boyish pout.

"Do you intend persecuting me for an error over which I had no control, Veronique?" he asked softly. "I ruined your pleasure. That was unforgivable. If you'll let me, I will remedy the situation."

She avoided his reach. Still silent, she poured hot coffee over the mint chocolate in each demitasse. She handed him one, and, taking the other, sat on the sofa, curling her feet under her.

"Uuuuuuughh," he grimaced, tasting the coffee. "You know I loathe mint chocolate, *liebling*. Plain coffee is fine," he said easily, handing back the cup for proper reparations.

The shock on Veronique's face was total. Unknown to her, the beginning of the end was in sight.

"Veronique, I do wish you would not wear your thoughts on your face. It makes you readable, too predictable. Like a frightful cosmetic, it muddies your eyes. The trick is to be unpredictable."

Veronique, speechless, stared at the changes in this man, this total stranger, growing more distant with each passing second.

* * *

Victor slept soundly that night. Veronique warred with demons. She brooded the entire night, unable to understand the changes in Victor. She paced the floor, resolved to find some way to get back to Paris and regroup.

The next morning Victor awakened early. He showered, shaved, performed his customary calisthenics. He entered the kitchen, surprised to find fresh hot croissants and coffee awaiting him. He kissed Veronique, unaware of her deep anxiety following a sleepless night. He promised to call her a dozen time, fully apologetic if he had said or done anything to offend her. She accepted his kisses, pledges, and promises, smiling wanly, unaware that she would never again know the man she had met in Paris. The man she had known intimately these many months was lost to her.

Victor failed to call Veronique that day. He spent the entire day at the Zeller Chateau, conferring with an agitated Dr. Wilheim Zeiss. He demanded answers to countless questions. In session with Dr. Zeiss, Victor tried desperately to make himself understood.

"I'm panicked in trying to explain what I don't understand," Victor admitted to the red-haired, freckled doctor. "Images, emotions, feelings, foreign to my experiences compels me into unusual behavior. Explain what is happening, *Doktor?*"

Dr. Zeiss had turned on a tape recorder, in addition he jotted notes on a pad nearby. The maddening aura of clinical detachment surrounding the man in white irritated Victor.

"What's happening to me?" he raged. "I feel disoriented. Why do I feel like this? Do I know anyone named Victoria?"

"Given time," began Dr. Zeiss, measuring his words carefully, aware, as he spoke, of two cameras monitoring them. "A proper assimilation of the ingested material will reduce your anxieties. Accommodations must be made. Adjustments for your needs will occur in due time. We may have gone a bit too fast, Victor. The introduction of so much material too quickly has merely resulted in a few crossed wires. Your attitudes might vary, your tastes will confuse you for a time, but it will level off to where you shall exercise total control, merely drawing on the reserve within your brain cells, as you might a computer bank. The project is highly complex. We don't know all the answers. If we monitor you daily and you report the abnormalities, given time we shall uncross the wires. Keep objective, sir."

"Then, I *do know* someone named *Victoria?*"

"Your father does. Listen consciously to the tapes and you'll understand the subconscious inducement, I promise."

Victor nodded appeased. He settled back on the sofa, earphones intact. "It sure as hell plays havoc on my love life."

"You cannot afford to miss a day as you have in the past several weeks. Really, Victor, it's dangerous to the outcome of the experiment."

Dr. Zeiss, at once absorbed in his work, listened to the recording devices, feeling no compassion for Victor's anguish. He treated Victor like a guinea pig. The confusion caused by wrongful dissemination of data, regardless of the punishment inflicted on Victor, would be corrected. Dr. Zeiss fixed his thick-rimmed glasses into place. The experiment—intercranial micro-chip implantation—alien territory at this juncture, an unexplored scientific vista, would one day be heralded as a major breakthrough in the understanding of man's brain. The human element, Zeiss believed, was secondary to the success of the project.

Zeiss kept glancing at the camera as unobtrusively as was possible. Internal problems within the Zeller Foundation between Amadeo Zeller and his staff of six resident scientists was swiftly eroding the relationship. Something was drastically wrong, he knew it. The others knew it and recently began to evidence their fears.

Victor arrived home after ten P.M. and met with sullen estrangement. Veronique's questions concerning his whereabouts remained unanswered. He was the stranger she had encountered the previous night.

Something was drastically wrong with Victor Zeller!

Veronique observed him critically. His movements, attempts to force a conversation rang false, demonstrating the awkwardness of two total strangers at their first encounter. His actions were not typical, his words were measured, strained. His favorite foods, rejected at dinner, he settled for two glasses of milk. *Milk, for God's sake! He loathed the stuff!*

The strange alchemy occurring inside Victor's brain gathered momentum. Unfamiliar impulses reared their ugly heads. Images and memories—not his—strutted past his cranium in full-dress parade. Distinguishing between the real and unreal grew increas-

407

ingly difficult. His personal memory bank of thoughts, feelings, and images receded into the dim recesses of his mind, giving away to the newly implanted thoughts and ideas. Changes, Victor *did not, could not* comprehend, were occurring in him. He laughed when he felt like crying, cried at something humorous, experienced hatred when he should have experienced love. It was a life, not his, but one so much a part of him, that he was suddenly catapulted between the roles of observer and participant. His inability to articulate the changes manifesting in him created a rift in his relations with Veronique. They grew further apart.

On December 15 at nine P.M., Veronique dressed warmly in jeans, a fur parka and boots, and left Victor asleep on the sofa in the living room. She exited the townhouse, turned right at *Bahnhofstrasse* and ambled casually along the snow-banked Plaza toward the lake. Veronique grew increasingly aware of surveillance on her.

The dark streets were deserted, the weather unbearably cold. Edging closer to the public phone booth under the pale wash of light, Veronique peered about, then swiftly moved in, dropping coins in the slot. She dialed the overseas operator. "Please, operator, the United States. Virginia, area code 703. The number is 625-1000. Hurry, please."

She peered about at the shadows, stamping her fur-lined boots on the ground. Streetlights played oblique patterns of light and dark shadows on the snow. From somewhere along the frozen waterfront came sounds of a concertina. A loud stereo echoed from one of the apartments, blasting eardrums with punk rock.

"Hello, Mother? . . . This is Valerie. Can you hear me. I am speaking from a pay phone. Plans must be revised. Things are schizophrenic here. Mother—he called me *Victoria* the other night! Not once, but several times. No. . . . No, not the father—the son! Something I don't understand is happening.. I had better return to Paris."

"Come home, Val. Give it up. This insanity to keep faith with Grandmother's dying wishes is insane. I am worried to death over you," said Valentina Lansing.

Veronique tensed. She leaned against the phone booth, her eyes sweeping the area casually. Instantly her mood changed. She laughed gaily, saying, "I only called, Mother, to tell you I plan to stay in Zurich with Victor for the holidays. Mother, we're in love! Isn't that simply marvelous?"

"*Valerie!* What's wrong? Come home immediately! I'll send someone for you as soon as possible!"

"Very well, Mother. I'll get back to school, but as long as I am here, I intend to spend the holidays with Victor," she snapped. Veronique's hand inside her parka pocket gripped the .38 hair-triggered revolver. "Merry Christmas to both you and Father. I love you," she shouted loudly. "Merry Christmas!" Veronique hung up the receiver, turned, humming a tune, and stopped, feigning surprise. *The best defense is the offense, Veronique!*

"Oh, my dear, *Herr* Bauer! You gave me such a start! What on earth are you doing out so late at night?" She stared at the husky brute.

"It is dangerous to walk the streets of Zurich alone, *Fräulein*. If anything should happen to you, *Herr* Zeller would be upset."

Demonstrating the audacity of either the bravest or most fool-hardy woman on earth, she slithered her arm through his, pulled her parka close to her face to ward off a blast of icy wind. "Now you're here, *Herr* Bauer, I have no worries. Come, let us hurry back to the sanity of a warm hearth."

They walked along in the snow, Bauer uncomfortable at her overly friendly manner. Veronique, doing some fast thinking, gushed with countless questions. "Tell me, *Herr* Bauer, what is wrong with Victor? He looks so ill. He works long, exhaustive hours, comes home, totally spent. He refuses to eat properly. What shall I do for him? In the past two weeks he has lost so much weight. Shall I summon his physician? Or perhaps you will talk with him? Couldn't his father curtail a few of his most pressing duties? Perhaps if I called *Herr* Zeller, Senior, to explain Victor's debilitation? Have *you* noticed the changes in Victor?" They arrived at the townhouse entrance before Bauer had a chance to respond.

"*Gute Nacht, Fräulein*. If you wish to go walking at night, I suggest you advise me and an escort shall be provided as protection."

"Protection from *what?*" She peered about naively. "What dangers are there here in Zurich? Ahh, you mean the Movement—the crazy revolutionaries?"

"*Jawohl*. The Suisse malaise. Trash. *Gute Nacht, Fräulein*." The stony-faced butcher unlocked the door to the foyer, held it open until she was secure inside. He observed her enter the

409

elevator, close the gate behind her. Bauer entered the enclosed, heated cubicle where an elegantly uniformed doorman sat, reading the dailies under a dim yellow wash of a battery-operated flashlight. Bauer passed a few banknotes into the man's hand. The doorman tipped his hat.

Bauer yanked up the collar of his coat, shivered, retraced his steps back along the waterfront to the same telephone booth used earlier by Veronique. He inserted a coin, dialed a number, and spoke in German. "*Herr* Bauer here. Chief of Security at Zeller Bank. My clearance is AC-333. A long distance call was made from this telephone annex approximately ten minutes ago. Perhaps overseas. Locate and report destination."

Bauer waited. He peered about the dark, lighted a cigar, stomped on the frozen ground, conjuring up scenes of warm desert winds on the hot Negev, where he belonged—not here, where his balls turned to ice. His blood refused to circulate properly.

"*Ja, ja, Fräulein. . . . Gut.* The United States? . . . Groveton, Virginia. The residence of Professor E. J. Lindley . . . *Gut, Fräulein. Danke.*"

Bauer hung up, relieved. Good. The facts continued to check out. The dossier compiled on Veronique Lindley established that the American woman's father was a professor at Georgetown University. His wife, Vanessa, was a semi-invalid. Now, if the overdue dossier on Jacob—Jake—Bernstein arrived, he'd breathe easier.

Mosha Bauer, a cold, dangerous unpredictable savage, tugged up on the collar of his jacket, headed back along the *Bahnhofstrasse*, wondering why the American hadn't placed the call from the Zeller townhouse . . . As for Victor? It was true. He was acting very strange, but to antagonize the old man by questioning him concerning these changes in his son was a foolhardy task. Amadeo Zeller was growing more dangerous, especially now. The thought conjured a spate of bad memories.

The very life was being sucked from the octogenarian; his time on earth measured. He and Zeller had come a long way. If Mosha died today, this very moment, his awe and fear of Zeller was such it could reach across the grave to strangle him just as it reached across vast oceans to strike terror into the hearts of men to dance to Zeller's Law. Bauer reflected.

Gotterdammen! . . . Five days remained in which to perform

410

miracles! Bauer's obsession, a feat occupying each waking moment, was the meticulous preparation for the event on December 20. *Could he pull it off*? Could he?

An icy blast of wind nearly lifted him off the ground, chilling him, icing the sweat pouring off him. His hard, features reflected none of the turmoil churning inside him. Mosha Bauer feared no one and nothing, save Zeller. In his work he was a specialist. He approached each mission with the confidence of a multitalented professional killer, dissected impediments in the blueprint stages. He never failed. Yet, what was planned on December 20 could be his swan song. Was it possible Zeller intended killing *seven* birds at once? Including him?

Chapter Twenty-Seven

ZURICH, SWITZERLAND
December 20, 1982

SIX MEN, WARDING OFF ICY WINDS AND THE CHILLING effect of the rotors of a Bell 412 helicopter, left the French seventeenth-century Zeller chateau nestled high atop a snowy pinnacle tor overlooking the *Zurichsee*. They hastily boarded the gleaming white snowbird, taking respective seats in the executive cabin behind the pilot's cockpit. Dragna Kosevo stowed their bags in the rear compartment, closed the doors, stepped briskly off the vehicle, securing the hatch door and glanced up at the overcast, foreboding sky.

The pilot, Mosha Bauer, was cool, quiet, subliminally brutal. He was not a gentle man, yet he handled the two-million-dollar chopper the way most men handled women. He revved the engines, listening to the weather forecast from Zurich. The *bise,* a treacherous northwesterly, unpredictable as hell, produced a chill factor dropping the temperature to thirty degrees below zero. Bauer loathed it; he loathed anything that stripped him of control in the air.

411

Amadeo Redak Zeller, octogenarian, egocentric banking titan, observed the 412's departure. He wiped the steamy glass windows of the floral hothouse atrium. He tugged his sable collar closer to his neck. Zeller's opaque, nearly colorless eyes under the sable Cossack-styled hat peered at the outdoor scene through thick-lensed chartreuse glasses. The Bell 412 lifted off the helipad, and, turning ninety degrees, soared into bleak overcast skys southwesterly over the *Zurichsee*. He shrugged indifferently, turned from the window, economically retracing his steps over the bricked walkway to the open elevator, wicked triumph sparkling his eyes. He pushed a control button, got off at the second floor and moved noiselessly over Persian carpeting through a high-vaulted upper corridor.

Soaring, thunderous refrains of Wagner's *Götterdämmerung* filled the upper mansion from speakers positioned along the upper galleria hung with the works of Grand Masters, priceless statuary, oils, tapestries. Millions had been spent in the renovation and refurbishing of the Zeller chateau. In the art works, sculpture, and countless treasures—billions.

In Zeller's eyes, as he entered his sanctum sanctorum—a cavernous den, was the pronunciamento of death. It was finished—save for this last piece of business—the six scientists no longer existed for Zeller.

Mosha Bauer glanced at his silent, introverted, gloom-filled passengers in the overhead mirror. Each sat rigidly erect in his seat, exchanging uneasy glances. The six Zeller Foundation scientists dared not communicate their individual pangs of terror and helplessness. Periodically, they'd glance from Mosha Bauer, whom they loathed and didn't trust, to Dr. Wilheim Zeiss, their appointed spokesman, acting liaison between them and Amadeo Zeller.

Wilheim Zeiss, a genius at forty, bespectacled and earnest, supplied technical know-how behind each concept of brain study in Zeller Foundation experiments. Yet he lacked the one essential factor vital to discover perfidy at work—common sense. Zeiss, lettered in experimental psychiatry, parapsychology, highly advanced in computer technologies, had contributed vastly in making virgin discoveries in unconquered, unexplored horizons of brain study. Scientific marvels unfolding daily provided immeasurable gratification. Dreams solidified, shaped into comprehensible patterns. The exhilaration of discovery gripped him, blinded the others until too late the issue came into clear focus. *It was Zeller or them!*

Suddenly, a confused mixture of deceptions blew up before their eyes. The beast had turned on them.

The profuse sweat dripping from Mosha Bauer's face, underarms, and crotch under a uniquely constructed flight suit was measured by the pitch of his fear. He noted the rising tension in the others.

The scent of the kill! A stimulant to Bauer made him edgy as a prowling, hungry tiger. Two weeks of intensified briefing, uncovered dangers, *personal* dangers to himself on this mission. His only recourse was to follow the game plan and pray.

Amadeo Zeller sat on a throne chair in his cavernous den. Eyes inscrutable, he depressed a lever on the console at his side. The Wagnerian *Götterdämmerung* screeched to a climax, replaced by Chopin's *Funeral Dirge*. Zeller glanced at the video screens, at the diminishing airborne Bell 412, until it faded from sight. His arms on the velour rest of the throne, his fingers animatedly kept time to the depressing orchestral rendition. *Dumm, dumm, de dumm, dumm de dumm, de dumm, de dumm. . . .*

Mosha Bauer continued to sweat copiously. He checked, re-checked the numerous instrument panels, the vast orange, green, ultra-blue lights and meters. He studied the minicomputer strapped securely to his wrist, an instrument upon which his life or death depended. Compass readings: *On target*. Control panels: *Normal*. Bauer glanced out at graying skies, the icy terrain, shapes and outlines, indiscernible in the massive whiteness. He switched on anticollision lights. Snapped off dome and cockpit lights with jerky movements. His eyes nervously fixed on the magnetic compass and airspeed indicator. *Christ!* He loathed the unpredictable elements.

Wilheim Zeiss measured the degree of their danger by a recapitulation of the previous several months, the events that journeyed them into perilous waters. His freckled face relaxed into lines of fatigue. *What incredible fools they were!*

It began four years ago. He and his colleagues, hired initially

413

to keep Amadeo Zeller alive, free from degenerative diseases, had arrived at Zeller Chateau, seduced in time by luxurious lifestyles, the latest medical technology, modern laboratories, first class travel accommodations to medical seminars, financial compensation beyond their expectation. Could they have asked more from an employer?

Never! They jumped at the opportunity, reduced in time from a lofty plateau of thinkers and innovators to hedonists who profoundly exploited their baser instincts. Recently Zeiss and his colleagues had surrendered their souls to Zeller. In late October, when their uncertain position struck them full force, Zeiss had managed to secrete a diary in a box of purposely scuttled laboratory supplies to his cousin Johann who managed the pharmaceutical supply house. He had heard nothing, and this knowledge had compounded his fears.

Wilheim Zeiss lighted a Meerschaum pipe, drawing on it evenly. Glancing periodically at his companions, he condemned himself fiercely. To have fallen from Zeller's grace, betrayed by personal weakness and a cleverly utilized electronic surveillance done them, their conspiracy had been exposed, their position jeopardized.

He glanced out the chopper's window. What utter stupidity to think they could outsmart Zeller! He felt nauseous, his hands gripped the seat arms drained of blood.

Below lay Lucerne, nestled between icy lakes and ravenous snow-capped Swiss Alps. A blinding white winterland stretched to infinity amidst rugged, chaotic peaks. There—up ahead—Gstaad, a skier's haven, lay off the starboard bow. Skiers, brightly dressed, transported on ski lifts, got off at the pinnacle. Zeiss peered in the distance into rolling fog banks.

Zeiss relighted his pipe, glanced casually at his terrified companions. Each sat mute, frozen in their personal hells. He marveled at their audacious determination. *Match wits with Zeller?* What a fiasco! Hadn't Zeller laid open his Machiavellian mind to dissection? Christ! He had revealed more sides to his ubiquitous nature than had a trisoctrahedron. And they *dared* conspire against him? *Fools! Outrageous fools!* Himself included! The moment they committed efforts to the project their annihilation became a *fait accompli* in Zeller's mind.

Zeiss too clearly remembered Zeller's intractable law: *Any force of sabotage that threatens, undermines or interferes with the success of Zeller's project would be crushed. Anyone tarnishing or launching assaults against Zeller and associates is the enemy. Enemies must be destroyed.*

Zeiss had reconciled himself to doom when Zeller appeared on the catwalks overlooking the laboratory a week ago. He observed them at work through chilling, inscrutable colorless eyes and he smiled down on them! SMILED! Nothing was as revolting than to behold Zeller's cadaverous face and yellowed, clacking false teeth held in a fixed smile. Those *clacking* teeth broke the good news, not from the catwalk, but from the closed-circuit video camera. Zeller's deathhead face infected the entire laboratory with his evil presence.

"*Mes bons amis*," he spoke in French. "You are free to depart for your homes to spend the holidays with loved ones. Bonus checks distributed to you compensate for the satisfactory progress you've made. Your departure is scheduled for December 20. Plan accordingly."

Not a word alluding to their treachery! Nothing about the planned coup! He was the same Zeller of a year earlier!

AT THAT PRECISE MOMENT THEIR FEARS MAGNIFIED!

Yet they grasped for brass rings on the glimmering merry-go-round of hope, dispatched telexes to their families: *ETA Geneve, December 20, 1983 at sixteen hundred hours.*

Zeiss glanced at his watch. It was half past three. Another hour. His companions' numb, frozen faces were focused below them.

The luxurious Bell 412 plunged into the dismal swells of dense fog like a sightless animal attempting to crawl through a labyrinthian maze. The unpredictable northwesterly tunneling wind crashed into the underbelly of the fuselage, shaking the superstructure. A shudder of unexpected vibrations spread panic among the passengers, alarm at *flashing red lights* over the bulkhead. Belt buckles snapped into place. The men exchanged old fears, their faces blanching, whitening knuckles tensing in rigidity.

Mosha Bauer's flat monotoned voice attempting to calm them rasped through the intercom. "Not to worry. It is the *bise* asserting itself. It swept us a few kilometers off our course. Do not be alarmed, *Herr Doktors*. Bauer has everything in control."

Glancing from compass to clock, his right hand gripped tightly

415

around a knob on the console to his right, Mosha Bauer depressed a lever releasing a rigged mechanism, timed to detonate in three minutes. He switched on automatic pilot, checked his compass bearings. Approaching, off the port bow—*Les Diablerets*, a rugged snow banked, icicle peaked tor, few men had scaled. The countdown began. *Ten . . . Nine . . . Eight . . . Seven . . . Six . . . Five . . .* The detonator was activated soundlessly. In moments the treachery would commence.

Just a few more seconds. It was 3:40 by Bauer's watch.

Now!

A smoke alarm shrieked. The cabin congested thickly with blackening smoke, flames swelled and spread. The passengers coughed, sputtered, averted their heads, whipped out handkerchiefs to hold over their nose. The men beat at the flames with their coats, jackets, *anything!* As they fell to the floor, screaming like trapped animals, Zeiss' bright dark eyes, glittering with the knowledge of Zeller's triumph!

None of the doomed scientists saw Mosha Bauer bracing himself.

Four . . . three . . . two . . . one!

Bauer slid open the hatch door, flipped off the engine switches and leaning back, with a powerful thrust propelled himself out through the hatch opening just as the rotors sputtered to a stop. He was buffeted away from the fuselage, tunneled along the slipstream until a gusty wind crashed into his body with the force of a tidal wave forcing him into a free fall.

Spread-eagled, he tugged on the ripcord of the cleverly concealed minichute in his flightsuit.

Nothing! Jesus Christ!

Panicked by the longer-than-anticipated fall, the Swiss Alps rushing up at him, Bauer felt the impact of fierce winds assaulting his body. Loud snapping sounds, overhead, followed by powerful jolts of inertia, lurched him about, finally in an upright position. *Fucking chute finally opened!* Bauer, fighting the wind force, managed to press a remote switch on the wrist band, negotiating his body into a quarter turn in time to see the burning 412 corkscrewing to earth, explode in midair. The sky exploded. Screams from the bodies borne free of the disintegrating fuselage sailing into space amid broken debris, clearly discernible in the insulated vault of the mountains, sounded unhuman, echoed savagely through Mosha Bauer's ears and mind.

416

His enemy, the bitterly cold, freezing wind, iced his heart, rattled his teeth, chilled his blood, but those bloodcurdling screams, like those of ferocious eagles, reverberated off the icy spires, magnified in his mind.

Bauer, a veteran assassin, felt newborn panic. Snow and wind whipped at him, veering him obliquely off course. Futile attempts to navigate through his wrist device were met with frustration. *Nothing-fucking* worked in freezing iceland. Bauer peered below him, desperately searching—searching!

The point of rendezvous! Where in *fucking* hell was it? Thickly falling snow obscured his vision. The northwesterly swung him about in perilous arcs, drove him in updrafts, downdrafts, plummeted him crazily, whipping him through tunneling windshafts. For the first time in his life, Mosha Bauer experienced genuine terror!

Powerless against the formidable elements, steam fogging his goggles, visibility became nil. He cleared them. They iced again. He dabbed at the frosted compass dial, in renewed panic.

Christ! There—he saw it—*the signal!*

THREE WHITE FLARES! . . . followed by three yellow streaks of light! Mosha pressed a wrist panel button. A blinding flare shot above him, bursting to an umbrella of raining red flares.

CHRIST! They found him! The brothers, Milos and Dragna Kosevo, the Serbo-Croatians, had not failed him!

In his exhilaration Mosha failed to note the jagged, snow-capped peaks, like a thousand icy, upthrust knives rushing at him. Empty crevasses between lethal daggers, closer—closer—closer!

Holy shit! Bauer's eyes held on the formidable icy daggers. *If you fail to maneuver the chute properly?* He gazed around—there! a promontory of ice and snow, deceptive in size, yet, if he angled his fall correctly . . .?

A little more to the left, Mosha . . . C'mon, you must do it! Arms outstretched, prepared to grab hold, defying the wind, he struggled.

He made it! He clung to the razor-sharp icicle tor, fumbled blindly to pull a knife from his flight suit. He had a matter of moments to extricate himself before gusts of wind willowing the chute threatened to lurch him crashing off-course to his death.

Bauer made it—not a moment too soon. Wind tunneling at him snapped up the chute, sailed it along on air pockets out of sight. He breathed heavily, laboriously, in the thinning air, his shoulders aching from the strain of clinging to the icy promontory. He arched his body, jackknifed it several times before finally hoisting himself up, over the ledge, his chest heaving spasmodically. He gulped at the air, feeling a sudden giddiness. Peering below he caught sight of the chute spiraling downward toward the snow tombs where six *special* men were ground into skull and crossbones.

Bauer dismissed them from mind, considered the geological changes in this area, the sudden shifts of nature, recurring avalanches, possible quakes. Nature would eliminate any vestiges of the chopper and dead men.

ZURICH

The situation between Veronique and Victor had reached an impasse. Veronique, observing the disturbing changes in Victor, concluded she must leave him immediately. With no available barometer to measure the danger signs, she had jogged along with him, when crawling might have rendered the objectivity she needed. Their estrangement grew more pronounced, he withdrew physically. His remoteness, *maddening* indifference drove the wedge deeper between them.

"What's wrong?" she pressed in a valiant effort to promote a rapport. "Something I've done? I can't endure your silence. Shall I return to Paris?"

He didn't even pay her the compliment of a glance. He opened the newspaper, studied the headlines. Veronique knew at once something was wrong. His features blanched, his hands trembled as he placed reading glasses into place, absorbed in the contents.

"Victor—was is it?"

The vague effort he employed to appease her concern smacked of insincerity. Veronique's temper flared, salted with an element of fear. She had to know—not *knowing* was driving her up a wall.

"I'm a logical, patient woman, Victor. I need the truth. All right, all right, you no longer love me. Is that it? Is it your father who comes between us?"

A reaction flared for an instant, firing his eyes, then abated, his attention locked on the newspaper. Veronique, on a roll, goaded.

"I see. The same old story. Religious differences. You're another Jake Bernstein. Your family disowns you if you consort with a *shiksa*? It weighs so heavily in my disfavor you haven't guts to be straight with me. *Alors*, we end the relationship. *Bien*? Jews!" she spat. "Will I ever fathom Jews?"

Victor lifted dark luminous eyes to her briefly, only to dull again. Veronique trespassed. "I'm an expert, now! *Dammit!*" she railed at an obvious sore spot. Lighting a cigarette, she puffed, fumed, postured about, a la Bette Davis, flagrantly hurling acerbic remarks.

"What is it about Jews that attracts me? Why don't I fall for a gentile? I must be a masochist! Well, this tears everything. You are a Jew. I am gentile—a *goy*, and never the twain shall meet. *Voilà!* You are not old enough to *know* your mind? Or don't you have the guts to blow up a paper bag?" In a sudden burst of thespian elan she angrily tossed a book across the room. It crashed down on a lamp, toppling a vase, both falling to the floor loudly.

No reaction in Victor. She was talking to the four winds.

"Damn you! Look at me when I talk to you!" she shrieked. "Dammit, dammit! . . . Before my esteem of you is lowered, Victor, I am returning to Paris!" She challenged him, picking up momentum.

"Suit yourself," he muttered darkly. Rising, he slapped the newspaper down on the table next to him before he left the room.

Veronique strode across the room, picked up the book, lamp, and overturned jade vase. Her eyes fell to the newspaper headlines. She picked it up hesitantly, scanning the contents.

LES CLAIRON DU GENEVE
Geneve, Switzerland
ZELLER FOUNDATION SCIENTISTS DEAD

GENEVA, DECEMBER 21, 1983 . . . Ski and Police patrols are searching avalanche areas of Les Diableret to locate the Zeller helicopter that crashed in the area yesterday. Six Zeller Foundation research scientists en route to Geneva for the holidays are reported to have plunged to their deaths.

The Zeller pilot, Mosha Bauer, miraculously escaped death by landing on and clinging to an icy precipice known as

Lucifer's Tomb. His rescue took place in freezing temperatures, by two mountain climbers who witnessed the distressed aircraft and pilot's signals shot from a flare gun. Presently the pilot is in Les Diableret Hospital undergoing treatment for extreme frostbite, exposure and possible broken bones.

Herr Zeller, head of Zeller Foundation, respected financier and founder of *Suisse Banque Royale*, remains in seclusion at his chateau, unavailable for comment.

Names of deceased, presently withheld until families are notified and identification verified, will be published upon police investigation . . .

Veronique flung the paper from her, paced the floor, smoking incessantly, mulling the newspaper account. Victor's reaction to the tragedy exceeded his usual concern. Was it exaggerated or real? She must think, take action. Things were happening, in frightening ways over which she had no control. Her strategy was in a shambles, she must get out!

It was time for detours! For sheer survival!

She spent another sleepless night, her mind setting the stage for a final curtain call. It was time to make her pitch, now, while the sentinel-at-arms, Mosha Bauer, was absent.

But at breakfast the next morning Victor entered the dining room, drank his coffee, chain-smoked and paced in agitation, his strides, long, pantherish. He complained of violent headaches, a disorienting mental confusion. "So much material crammed into my head in so little time," he blurted unguardedly. He raved, ranted, rambled in a jumble of disjointed words, broken phrases that made no sense. His face, suffused in rage, contorted hideously. Blue veins at his temples wormed and throbbed noticeably. "It's an extension of my madness—you hear? I am my father's son! That makes me a madman!"

Veronique had turned from the window where she had been gazing at the newly fallen snow, listening with aroused interest. She moved toward him, her voice soft, conciliatory. "What do you expect? Awake all night, pacing floors, drowning in black coffee, popping pills. Christ, Victor, you're wired to an inhuman frenzy. Is it suicide you've got in mind?"

"But you are not concerned! You don't care!" He cursed abrasively, outraged at her unsolicited opinion. He unleashed a string of abusive curses at her, kicked at the furniture in uncontrolled rage, shoved chairs and tables viciously out of his path, exploded at the slightest provocation. If Veronique obliged with silence, it infuriated him. If she spoke, he hurled insults on her.

She was damned if she did, and damned if she didn't!

For no apparent reason, he strode across the room, flung open the doors to the snow-laden terrace. An instant assault of freezing wind howled through the room, billowing out the draperies. Victor stood at the threshold, inhaling deeply. Suddenly he clutched at his breast and left arm, complained of shooting pains. His hands shot to his head. He shouted, "My skull is cracking open! Oh God, I can't stand the pressure! I can't! Help me! Help me! Please!"

Quietly, Veronique approached him, shivering in her thin robe. She drew him inside the room, closing the doors behind her. She sat him down before the fireplace, pulled a Norwegian Blue Fox lap robe over his shivering body. She forced hot brandy through his chattering teeth.

"I am leaving you, Victor," she told him quietly.

"Try it! Try it again and you'll find the going tough! I can ruin you and I will!" He glared at her maliciously, his voice that of a stranger. She gave him a sharp, probing, silent look.

"Why are you doing this, Sophia? Why do you insist on leaving me? Haven't I been fair with you?"

"Victor . . . look into my eyes. Do I look like Sophia? Do I resemble Victoria? No. *I am Veronique!* Remember Paris? The Martinique Art Galleries? The Rothstein Collection? Don't you remember any of the months we've shared?"

"Play *La Tosca* for me, Sophia," he said, quietly staring into the flickering, brightly colored flames snapping loudly on the hearth.

Veronique moved to the stereo, and started the tapes.

Victor, lost in another world, pacific at first, metamorphosed as the music swelled in volume. "Corsicans! Damn you! Damn your hides! Damn you all!" he cursed darkly, his face contorted ferociously. It was not the face of Victor Zeller as she had known him. This man was a stranger!

Veronique left for Paris the next morning. She left a note behind for Victor, an open door for future negotiations.

Valerie Lansing wasn't finished with the Zellers—not yet!

It was only the beginning.

Chapter Twenty-Eight

> *"A wicked Prince, thinking he was acting in his personal interests, was not moved by the invisible hands which seemed to have created all the events in our revolution in order to lead us towards a goal we presently do not see, but which we shall before too long."*
>
> Montjoie,
> 1797,
> Writing of the Orleanist Conspiracy.

February 10, 1984

A RECORD SNOWSTORM SHUDDERED THROUGH THE northern cantons of Switzerland. By morning the wheels of Zurich commerce had jammed to a standstill. Snowdrifts piled eight feet high along the *Bahnhofstrasse* from the *Hauptbahnoff* to the lake, disguising the elegance and charm of its banks, cafés, expensive boutiques and *konditorei*.

The sun ruptured obliquely through overcast skies adding rare touches of purity and innocence to the cold, calculating epicenter of high finance.

Halfway up the *Bahnhofstrasse* from the lake, the stately graystone, *Suisse Banque Royale*, known intimately in banking circles as the Zeller Bank, stood imposing as a fortress—apart from the competition—undeniably austere.

Imposing. Austerity. The words perfectly described Victor Zeller these days.

Victor waited inside the glass-enclosed foyer adjoining the penthouse suite atop the Zeller Bank Building, peering at the overcast sky. Finally he heard the sound of rotors, then saw the Bell 222 hovering over the helipad about to land. He glanced at the gold Baum and Mercier on his wrist in annoyance. Damn Mosha! Ten minutes late. If he planned his schedules meticulously, why didn't others do likewise?

The world of Victor Zeller waited for no one. For several months during Veronique's intrusion on his life he had foregone a strict regimentation, now nothing interfered with his business regimen.

Slender, strikingly handsome, dark hair, a straight brow line, aqualine features and dark brooding eyes, he now resembled an El Greco painting. He had lost twenty pounds, and his face displayed a lean and hungry look.

Two security guards approached the glass cubicle, nodded to him. Victor glanced past them at the overhead chopper. *Why in hell doesn't Bauer land?* Victor thought of his father, once liaison Minister of Finance to Il Duce. Victor had inherited his father's deceptive cleverness, a glib-tongued facility to ease himself in and out of devilish situations. From Il Duce he had learned the art of marking time; how to parlay an imperious, intimidating manner into power. From his mother, Contessa Marie Clothilde, Napoleon's blood descendant, came his drawing room charm, finesse, a soft-spoken manner exuding immense magnetism. And what political duplicity he demonstrated came from observing international luminaries frequenting the galas and soirees hosted by his parents during Fascism's halcyon days, before the Axis alliance changed the course of history. The art of expedience mirrored his association with the German Wehrmacht soldiers in World War II. Despised for his Jewish blood, they dared not express their resentment in the face of Il Duce's protection of the Italian Intelligence Major.

Victor's thoughts broke off. At last, the Bell was landing; Victor reflected briefly how those impressionable days had shaped his destiny, but the irrevocable changes in him stemming from the past year's experiments had cancelled out his youth. He was no longer the same man.

Land, Mosha! Why the hell don't you set down?

Victor's stomach muscles contracted. Today he was disturbed by more than Bauer's tardiness. Earth-shattering news was about to burst the world wide open. He must get to his father! He must be there when the treachery descended. Business commitments dictated against Victor's absence from the bank today, yet, if *not* today, when his father needed moral support as he never needed it in his lifetime—then, when?

The crushing truth would explode via satellite transmission. Victor must prepare his father for the brutal truth. *He must!*

What irony! What *incredible irony*! Skillfully orchestrated treachery, launched on this day was a gross insult to Zeller. Treachery threatened even as his triumph proliferated in the Middle East. A devastating betrayal born halfway around the globe traveling at MOCK III was spiraling toward Zeller, about to shatter his empire.

Victor moved swiftly through the glass doors warding off the icy blast of the *bise*. The Bell 222 touched down long enough to board its passenger. Then, hatch doors secured, the chopper lifted, headed northwesterly past the snow-laden quays framing the cobalt *Zurichsee* toward the Zeller Chateau.

Mosha Bauer checked his instruments, glancing hesitantly at his passenger's reflection in the overhead mirror. Bauer was cracking up. The flight to the chateau seemed longer each time out. His physical recuperation since the December 20 tragedy had progressed without complication. Mentally? Christ, the trauma replayed incessantly. He developed neurotic loathing for flying in snowstorms, since the 412 crash they turned phobic. Excessive sweating set in, blinding headaches, churning guts, a fertile ground for breeding ulcers and unceasing nightmares which would not stop. He had but to blink and it came alive, like motion pictures.

Stop it! Concentrate on the flight! Other matters!

Victor Zeller! Concentrate on Victor, Mosha. Concentrate hard!

He studied the changes, peculiarities in Victor's recent habits. For ten years, Victor was the same, now he was a different man.

The American woman was right.

Something was drastically wrong with Victor Zeller. What?

He stared at the banking executive seated rigidly in his sable-lined overcoat, Russkie fur hat, viewing a three-inch hand-held mini-television set, earplugged into place. Mosha's thoughts stopped.

That's it! Victor was the image of his father!

The sudden lurching of the chopper snapped Bauer from his reverie. The brutalizing impact of the *bise* twisted the 222, then Mosha employed anti-torque devices, bringing the aircraft under control. A string of curses escaped his lips. The assault of headwinds meant a ten-minute delay. Victor had clearly expressed his chagrin at lateness, and a critical need to be at the chateau precisely at 9:30 A.M. *What in hell for?*

The sweats were on Mosha again. Tension. Airsickness. Fear.

Fear of what, Mosha? Death? Hah! You spit on death! You and death are old combatants, well seasoned in deadly confrontations!

Mosha blinked hard behind aviator's glasses. A dissembling fear hid behind a mask of bravado. Fears and memories of those fears haunted him relentlessly. *Stop it!*

He peered down his sharply defined hawk nose at the blinding white snow. Bauer knew every inch of the run between Zurich and the Zeller chateau as he knew the anatomy of women. Lately it grew alien to him. Mosha's home was the broiling hot sands of the Negev, not the freezing temperatures of the Swiss Alps. His arrival in the Zeller stronghold sanctuary had forced his imagination to convert snow to sand, icy peaks into sand dunes. His imagination had waned, self-deception worn off long ago.

But Mosha Bauer could not go home. Not to the land for whose existence he'd fought valiantly. A price on his head precluded his return. *A price on his head! Ten years ago!* Strangled by bitter injustice—would he never finish with these memories? *Never?*

Mosha's professional career as a terrorist began at age nine with the infamous Abraham Stern Gang, well before his *Bar Mitzvah*. The young sabra stole guns and ammunition from the British, acted as courier and lookout for the Stern gang, set up targets, infiltrated hostile military installations as a child, where no adult could penetrate.

At age sixteen Her Majesty's military offered a reward for Mosha and the sum of six hundred pounds over his head. Rounded up with other gang members, imprisoned, Mosha escaped, hid in caves dug under orange groves.

Fate intervened. Into their midst appeared an organizational genius without peer. Code name: Ben Ari, Hebrew meaning, Son of Lion. Ben Ari reorganized the old Stern gang. The first official act of his newly formed Lomay Heruth Israel (FFI), Israeli Freedom Fighters had helped the escape of professional Stern Gang terrorists, and with this nucleus Ben Ari patterned them after the bloodiest, most oppressive terrorist group known in modern times, the Serbian Black Hand. Their bylaws, and stringent recruiting patterns and extermination procedures, unilaterally adopted by Ben Ari, added ingenious touches of torture.

By April, 1948 Mosha had participated in the bloody massacres at Dir Yassine, fought against the *fedayeen* in Gaza, blown up the American Embassy in Cairo and survived the ticktacktoeing between *El Fateh* and the Mossad in a series of raids in the mini-wars following the establishment of the Jewish State of Israel in May 1948.

Ben Ari orchestrated the war under the guise of a rabbinical scholar, seemingly ineffectual, at times innocuous. But under that enigmatic mask worked a formidable, crafty strategist who earned Bauer's respect. The men's loyalty to Ben Ari was unimpeachable. Neither hanging or torture produced a hint of the Judean Lion's disguise or whereabouts. The young Jews serving Ben Ari and Israel, dedicated to bring the mighty British to heel, succeeded. They drove back one hundred thousand British troops into camps and fortresses holed up in a *state-of-seige*.

Mosha learned the truth about himself from the lips of Ben Ari.

Mosha's expertise was unmistakable, Ben Ari called the youth aside, complimented him for his valorous efforts. *"You are a born killer without conscience and should be commended for your honorable effort."*

Ben Ari left shortly after the founding of the Israel State, Mosha Bauer remained behind. In 1972, the Black September episode in Munich and the murders of the kidnapped Israeli Olympic Athletes so enraged the Israelis, Golda Meir called for a *gloves off* retaliation.

Mosha Bauer became a WOG. A *Wrath of God Terrorist,* a highly clandestine death squad. Teams of *hit* men, male and female assassins skillfully trained to pull off a series of global assassinations of their enemies.

The bloody terror began. Success followed success. The notches on Mosha's guns mounted in number.

Mosha Bauer glanced at the instrument panel, wiped the sweat from his brow, peered at Victor Zeller, as the wind, hidden in swells of clouds, caused the chopper to torque. Damned ice on the tail rotors! Engaging the defrosters, he worked the anti-torque devices into steadying the helicopter. He breathed easier. He thought of Israel, the hot desert, balmy winds and the nightmares

426

that became his legacy of torment. Forget it? *How?* How the devil could he obliterate the memories?

The WOGs, a traveling circus of the macabre—inventors of the diabolic envelope and telephone bombs—and their variable travel itineraries, kept them failsafe. It was virtually impossible for the enemy to locate them.

And then, one day in January 1973. Madrid, Spain. Mosha Bauer committed the unpardonable sin—*he became visible!* The mission: assassinate a special *kill* squad of the PLO for orchestrating a plot to kidnap Spanish Jews after extorting money from them. Mosha's team gunned down the *kill* squad, rescued the Sephardic Jews and escaped. Mission: *accomplished*.

A *special* PLO courier, a money carrier hidden in the slaughter room, concealed behind crates and potato sacks, had recognized Mosha. A half hour after the despicable deed was done, Mosha's photo, physical description and long list of his crimes made headlines in the capital cities of European nations. Labeled an international terrorist with a price on his head, Mosha was forced into hiding.

By spring of 1973, the WOGs had left a trail of bloodletting and destruction across Europe that deteriorated relations between Israel and Western nations. France repeatedly issued warnings: *Remove all terrorists from our borders or suffer consequences!* London harked brashly, *"Terrorism from Israel or any quarter of the world will not be condoned!"* In the end, it was Norway who stopped the WOG operation, broke up Israel's covers in Oslo. A half-dozen WOG specialists were arrested, imprisoned, and deported to Israel.

Mosha's positive identification proliferated, his face as familiar as any chief of state appeared daily in the newspapers.

It was the end of a bloody era that harmed their image abroad. Israel withdrew the WOG apparatus, confined their terrorism on the Fedayeen Headquarters in Beirut and training camps in South Lebanon. Internationally, Israel postured itself against terrorists. They openly denounced Mosha Bauer and any man like him!

Mosha Bauer, in hiding, learned later the betrayal, an inside job, had been master-minded by the WOGs to rid themselves of him. His coldblooded, calculating skill of murder was becoming a liability. They reasoned, such a man, a hair away from the threshold of insanity, if caught by the enemy, the *kill-crazy* Mosha Bauer stood no chance of bearing up under pressure.

Desperate days followed for Mosha Bauer. On the run, forced into hiding without sufficient funds, paying exhorbitant sums for forged passports and travel cards, Bauer resorted to stealing, killing and the commission of criminally immoral acts for mere survival. *Denied refuge by men whose lives he had saved?*

To end up in such shoddy circumstances after dedicating his life to the survival of his people—the Jews—was unacceptable!

Trapped in Trieste, he was ultimately betrayed by a drug-addicted prostitute, who for the price of a fix targeted him for the police. Arrested, transported to an air terminal by the *carabinieri,* Mosha capitulated; if his dismal future included internment in an Italian jail, so be it. It could have been worse—far worse; it could have been a Turkish jail!

Mosha never saw an Italian jail cell. The plane transporting him landed at Kloten Airport at Zurich. A waiting limousine whisked him away to a remote hostelry in a small Swiss village hamlet. Ordered to shave, delouse himself, bathe and dress in the clothing laid out on the bed, Mosha followed instructions meticulously, eagerly anticipating, while casting a wary eye for *whoever* waited at the end of the line.

Then from out of the shadows stepped the man whose face the former WOG had never forgotten. Older, less buoyant, perhaps, nevertheless, the face and those *colorless eyes* of his mentor, code name: Ben Ari, was unmistakable. The man who single-handedly became the most powerful force in the establishment of the Jewish state of Israel.

Ben Ari introduced himself as Amadeo Zeller, a banking impresario. He offered Mosha the fabled brass ring, and Mosha grasped it firmly. Security, a well-paying position as bodyguard, private pilot, with an occasional opportunity to hone his *special* talents. Bauer, as assassin without portfolio, shook with gratitude. He was saved.

There was more. Their eyes met. Bauer recognized the look, what was expected of him. By now, Mosha was numb, devoid of feelings. He could do worse than exchange sexual gratifications for protection and survival. *If all he need do on occasion was bend over . . .?*

The deal was set and Bauer was ensconced in the Zeller chateau. Then, miraculously the *Wanted files* on Mosha Bauer disappeared from INTERPOL's massive files! His infamous criminal history was deleted from police agency computers in Scotland Yard, the French SDECE, Intelligence offices in Italy, South America, West Germany, Norway! The former Israeli terrorist, Mosha Bauer, no longer existed!

How Zeller had performed the magic—and it was magic—was never revealed to him. When informed of the incredible feat, Bauer, stupefied, refrained from questioning Zeller, for by then he believed Zeller capable of performing *any* miracle.

The doors of Israel remained closed to Bauer, for within that province lived old enemies who'd know him on sight, enemies who might open a can of worms with the potential of jeopardizing both Bauer and Zeller.

Mosha was content. He swore he'd bend over for the old man a hundred times a day, if necessary, in repayment of his new lease on life. Peace—without turmoil—for the first time in his life.

Early in 1973, shortly after his arrival in the Zeller stronghold, they flew to Berlin to settle an old score. A Jewish collaborator, he was told, passing as a German in the Nazi Army, name of Wolfgang Katz, had secreted valuable records of the era. Records Zeller insatiably coveted, determined to obtain any way possible, including the killing of Katz. Mosha, given the contract, failed to come through for Zeller. Katz had escaped, fled back to East Berlin to the Soviets. The priceless Nazi records eluded Zeller once again. Recently, Zeller discovered the damaging records, secreted in Pentagon files of Gamma 10 in Virginia, remained under tight security. To date, every American government official on the pad to Zeller, had failed miserably in their attempts to confiscate those files. It was only a matter of time before Zeller accomplished the impossible.

Today, Mosha was making good money, more than he'd made in his entire lifetime. Older, wiser, he found himself, after dancing the hora of death all his life, at the beck and call of this egocentric monomaniacal billionaire who demanded twenty-four-hour-a-day dedication. Ten years ago, desperate to locate a sanctuary, Zeller's ovations sounded utopian. Moshe realized he could do little now to alter his circumstances. He owed his life to a man who stepped out of the shadows of a grim past to save him—Amadeo Zeller.

*   *   *

429

Mosha Bauer peered through orange-lensed goggles. There—up ahead—the seventeenth-century chateau. He glanced at his watch. Ten minutes late, all right, just as he'd predicted. *Merde!*

He glanced at his passenger, surprised that Victor Zeller had not reacted to the turbulence of the flight. A miracle! But the bewildering feeling persisted—the disquieting feeling that he was looking at the old man—not the son! Not completely understanding, part of his mind comprehended that he was witnessing an inexplicable metamorphosis. Was it a genetic twist of fate—or money and power that so changed men? Victor's frozen, impersonal voice, its cutting edge and absence of emotions, was a mirror of Zeller. His mannerisms, habits, moods were not the Victor he'd known intimately for ten years.

But there was a difference! Victor hadn't asked him to bend over yet.

Victor wasn't aware of Mosha's scrutiny. His concentration on the mini-video screen was rapt, for the Zeller family had enormous stakes at risk in the bloody military upheaval between the Middle Eastern warring factions. At greater risk to the Zeller empire was what transpired in Maui today!

Chapter Twenty-Nine

AMADEO ZELLER SAT STIFFLY POISED on a carved rosewood and carmine velvet chair in the baronial library in the east wing of the chateau, its walls spanning thirty feet in height. His expression was that of a vulture drooling over a banquet of human flesh before swooping down from its perch to devour it.

His opaque, nearly colorless eyes behind thick-lensed chartreuse glasses leaped from screen to screen on six of twelve video consoles recessed in an alcove a few yards from the Grand Baroque desk, a complicated panel control at his fingertips. He was caught up in elated reverie at the massive warring scenes.

Behind a facade of carved rosewood panels there was no hint of the complex communications systems and elaborate electronics installations or that their far-reaching capabilities were detectable. With their limitless resources, Zeller technicians had penetrated countless electromagnetic frequencies with the assistance of special converters, amassing highly classified data with no foreign nation the wiser.

Unknown to Zeller was Moufflon's wizardry in computer technology. The Corsican's staff of highly skilled technicians monitored all data, intercepted transmissions permitting Zeller to receive *only* what Moufflon wanted him to receive. Sophisticated tracking devices primed by intensified energy, banked in reserve at the chateau complex, facilitated by a switch could produce at any given moment the required energy to scramble Moufflon's devices. Added energy induced to overpower alien tracking devices could render Moufflon's apparatus useless. Covering himself on all flanks, Moufflon's personally recommended technologists were on Zeller's payroll, but *they took orders from Moufflon!*

It was the best-kept secret in the Zeller redoubt! The *only* secret!

But neither Moufflon nor transmission technologies raced Zeller's pulse as did the warring action on the screens, which fed him like human blood keeping Dracula alive before dawn. Each bullet expended, each SAM missile flaring into the sky, heightened Zeller's excitement. Every bomb dropped, exploding craters, sending bodies flying, rushed his senses like jolts of adrenalin. Watching the scenes of destruction, he clapped his bony hands with glee.

Zeller's thin, twisted lips parted in a rare, sardonic smile. Ill-fitting false teeth set into his cranium odiously resembled a grinning anaconda about to strike. The ghastly black hairpiece set on his bald pate, framing his cadaverous features, formed a perfect facsimile of a distorted abstract Picasso head.

Isolated from other men's scrutiny, Zeller maintained a chained grasp on enthusiasm. He rejoiced at the destruction of his enemies. His *enemies?* Anyone who failed to conform to Zeller's views. Today he was like a child viewing his first soccer game; the difference lay in Zeller's vested interests, his personal and financial stakes in the outcome.

Birth of the OPEC cartel, a shattering event to Zeller, had evoked in him a sworn oath to eradicate his natural enemies from the face of the earth. An ambitious plan, carefully orchestrated, took form. A Mephistophelian libretto of appalling war, bloodshed and massacre commenced in the Middle East, pitting enemies against enemies, brothers against brothers—using anything to incite and stoke the fires at inferno temperatures. Soon it would be ended in victory for Zeller!

Implementation of the Moufflon apparatus had escalated the Zeller scenario by a decade, providing the banking titan ample time to stitch together the final conspiracy.

Victory approached. Consummate victory was coming closer —CLOSER!

Zeller's waxy complexion flushed a pleasurable crimson as the warring destruction exploded video screens. Soon all his enemies would be decimated. The land—all of it—the oil, precious irrigation systems, hydro-electric plants, nuclear reactors hidden from the eyes of the world in underground locations, *and* all that white gold springing from nature, *the opium poppy*, would transform him to the most powerful monarch in history!

Zeller's ambition was obsessive: to be crowned King of Israel! Israel and the world would be made to bow and scrape to him for all eternity. Statues erected to his genius would chronicle his people as conquerors for all time!

Zeller entertained no illusions of himself, the world, nor his fellow man. His twisted psyche and ideology had parlayed guts and ideas into a billion-dollar empire, dominating every sphere of influence around him. From it had poured the *power* to forge a remarkably complex and devious future. Ruthless, cynical, merciless, hard-lining, cruel and bestial, his life was never free of miasmic intrigue. He had bluffed his way through catastrophes, torturous human events, negotiating every inch of the way with two despotic potentates, *life* and *death*, eventually developing his own set of values. *POWER* was life, *POWER* was his God. And *death*? . . . God Almighty, how he fought against it!

Death stood by the wings of his life, beckoning with sinewy, seductive fingers, enticingly. Kept at bay for the past ten years, gaining on him, *death* distressed Zeller, He was unwilling to deliver himself into death's hands. *Death*, taking root in his soul, gave an unearthly phosphorescence to his flesh as if he were already dead. He never looked into a mirror, avoided them like a plague. His mind, constantly embattled with his aging body, worked through and beyond its withering, decaying mass with grim and desperate defiance that shone incandescently through his opaque eyes. His skin, pulled taut over skeletal features, snipped and tucked by plastic surgeons, had contorted his lips into a thin, cruel line.

Zeller had triumphed over death!

A year ago he began the preservation of Amadeo Zeller's immortality. *Zeller would never die!*

Zeller *knew* at once the treacheries planned by his research scientists. Daily he had searched their faces for a dawning awareness of their predicament. The signs took shape in September, precisely on the day Zeller had circled on his calendar.

Zeller *knew* scientists absorbed in the abstract seldom kept touch with the mundane world. At some time or another, for no apparent reason, the smartest of men become fools, just as Zeiss, Schmidt, Anatole, and the others had succinctly demonstrated. Surveillance done every moment, day and night, produced the proof Zeller needed.

Zeller *knew* no man was immune to temptation over long periods of time. He also *knew* if these men were so inclined, the power to destroy Zeller, crush his financial empire and make themselves millionaires lay within their grasp.

Unfortunately for them, they were so inclined!

How could Zeller permit them to live? He could not.

They were *dead men*, now.

Zeller sipped lemon tea from Royal Doulton China. His attention shifted briefly from the screens to the white and pink jade clock on his desk. He frowned, engaged a lever on his control panel, activating a seventh video screen. Into focus appeared the Bell 222 hovering over the rear helipad. He grunted. Before it came down for a three-point landing he turned off the screen, his interest shifting back to the bloody war.

MAUI, ISLAND OF HAWAII
U.S.A.

Moufflon walked to the lectern in the large amphitheater built on the sugar plantation of El Cid. He wore a white silk suit, contrasting the sun-bronzed hue of his handsome features. A hush swept through the cavernous room; the seventy-eight WPCC delegates and their entourages sat forward like birds of prey anticipating a banquet of lurid revelations. Aides, secretaries, interpreters clustered about the delegates. All of them, including

433

imperturbable diplomats, had submitted to intensely rigid security measures.

But not without protest. Most delegates, surly at the denial of video consoles, bore expressions of insufferable arrogance and hauteur. Hostilities worn on their faces evidenced their inner anxieties.

Earphones were adjusted, secretaries with steno machines were poised to commence. Attenuated silence prevailed.

Moufflon, his arms on the lectern, began to speak. His English bore the slightest whisper of a French accent:

"Distinguished delegates—placed before you in evidence are briefs containing a twenty-year chronology of facts, events, including names, dates, accurate case histories and a personal involvement with the powers holding sway in the Middle East and infecting the lands with unparalleled bloody tyranny.

"You wonder, *who* is Moufflon? From where does he come? You wonder at his credentials. From where, you ask, comes the temerity to assert himself as a fount of knowledge about the forces of power who have dedicated their existence to the destruction of mankind. *N'est-ce pas*? Truly it matters not *who* is Moufflon, from *where* he comes or from where springs the audacity displayed before you on this day. What matters is, he stands before you prepared to make full disclosure of the dishonorable opprobrium permitted to proliferate in a planned destruction of mankind.

"And so, honorable delegates, I stand before you, alone, as the only bulwark able to remedy the sickness facing all our nations . . .

"So, to commence. Let me turn back a few pages in history . . ."

IN ZURICH . . .

Two burly Serbo-Croatians, the brothers Milos and Draga Koseva, wearing heavy winter garments, emerged from their quarters, a guest house forming a wing of the Zeller chateau. Two Dobermans leaped before them, prancing about in the snow, their spiked collars shining to mirror brilliance in the daylight.

Milos and Draga, opposite as night and day in both looks and temperament made for an interesting dichotomy. Milos, dark, swarthy-featured, was short, with the stature of a circus strong man; he employed intuitive onyx eyes as a doctor used instruments to test a man's heart, pulse and blood pressure. One glance and he knew the measure of a man's guts. Draga, tall, Nordic in appearance, blue-eyed, his brown hair worn touseled, possessed the face and expression of a dreamy-eyed poet and the soul of a monster.

Born innocent, victimized by World War, revolution, poverty and bloody war atrocities, both forced to witness the slaughter of their parents, the terrified youths fled to the sanctuary of a famous guerilla leader, Draza Mihajlovic. Born in Rijeka in the Croatian province of Yugoslavia, Milos and Draga, inspired by the guerilla, Mihajlovic, had engaged in countless battles until the leader's untimely betrayal and subsequent death by the puppet state and its foreign protectors. The Koseva brothers fled to Trieste, met covertly with Italian *partisani*, and joined to fight Axis oppressors. Few knew that the brothers Koseva, acting on Zeller's orders, were ringleaders for the ultimate demise of Il Duce and his mistress. In April 1945, that Zeller's retaliation against Il Duce and his mistress for treachery done to him was to be hung publicly in the nude, by their heels.

When Bauer and the Koseva brothers became Zeller's property, their criminal files, like Bauer's, disappeared from every European police file.

The Dobermans stopped barking, snipped the air, and leaped forward to reach it just as the chopper landed and the hatch doors slid open. They barked a greeting and vigorously pranced about.

Victor, flanked at either side by the Serbo-Croats, was propelled through icy winds toward the atrium. The brothers Koseva stopped at the archway, stomping snowy boots on the brick walkway.

Victor moved on through toward the elevator, followed by the dogs. He slipped the mini-television set into the pocket of his overcoat, removed his sable Cossack hat as the elevator door opened. He entered, pushed the proper button to the second floor galleria, glancing briefly at the illuminated, glass-enclosed bronze bust of his father recessed in a wall cubicle. Subconsciously he braced himself in an attempt to match the statue's erect posture.

The elevator opened onto an open second floor galleria displaying priceless art treasures by Old Masters. A sedate, liveried servant greeted Victor, relieved him of his greatcoat, cap and fur-lined boots. He moved soundlessly over the wide sweep of Persian carpeted flooring, under lustrous, thick-beamed wood ceilings. The Dobermans, panting excitedly, waited at the doors for him.

Victor paused before two enormous, fifteen-feet-high hand-carved rosewood doors, inhaled deeply, then flung them open. The Dobermans, named Eva and Adolf to satisfy Zeller's perverse quirk, loped across the room, up the steps to a second level where Zeller sat at his desk. They awaited a pat or two of acceptance, then retracing their steps, sidled past the approaching Victor and curled up before the brightly lighted fire on the hearth of the floor-to-ceiling stone fireplace.

Victor removed his snow goggles, rubbed his eyes, adjusting to the dim lighting. By now, he *knew* intimately the world of Zeller and all his father's atrocities. At times the complex had proved too hideous to contemplate. He was learning! Learning *what* he could lay open to scrutiny, *what* must be secreted, *what* could only be shown in half-lights and to *whom*. No longer could he be himself, for he was not one man, but two, and since he could not be what he was, he traveled a wary route and walked very softly past blind men.

"Greetings, Father," he called aloud. Amadeo lifted a withered hand in acknowledgment, the gesture signified his attention riveted on the video screen would remain there until he finished.

Victor stood before the stained-glass window, staring at the fascinating play of color and light on the biblical scene. Jacob's Ladder, depicting the encounter between Jacob and the angel of God, spanned thirty feet in height. The story of Jacob, synonymous to Israel in the Old Testament, fascinated Victor. In a rare moment of intimacy, Amadeo had confided a dream to perpetuate the Zeller name in twelve sons, as Jacob had done, if it meant employing a harem of educated, brilliant Israeli women to accomplish the feat, had tickled Victor's fancy.

But how in God's name was this possible, since the modern-day Jew had sired any number of non-Jews in their lifetimes? Zeller lamented woefully, lineages broken by impure bloodlines were lost. Zeller's attempts to simulate Jacob had failed. He was forced to exchange one dream for another, a more practical strategy, the eradication of every non-Jew in the Middle East!

Turning, Victor selected the rarest Napoleon brandy from a carved rosewood liquor cabinet, broke open the seal, poured the rich amber liquid into a thin crystal brandy snifter, disregarding the early hour, hoping to abate the rising anger fermenting in him.

He assembled his thoughts, searching for the *right* opening to unleash the rancorous information eroding his guts. Amadeo's preoccupation with the video screens afforded him time to prepare his litany—and today it would be *litany*.

Soundless in the luxurious thickness of Persian shalimor carpeting, Victor walked the length of the twenty-foot long burnished wood table bridging the stained glass window from end to end, until he fronted an enormous gold throne chair elevated on a three-step high dais. Next to the chair, a pedestal-base glass case contained an ancient, priceless Torah covered in gold filigree set with precious gemstones, woven into an intricate design.

Today, Victor overstepped his usual subordinate role, spanned the three steps and boldly occupied the *verboten* throne chair. He pressed a button on the control panel at his elbow; the throne rotated forty-five degrees, overlooking one-quarter of the west wall. Victor's gaze lingered on the recessed, fully lighted glass cases protected by intricate sets of alarm, so sensitive they tripped at the merest hint of breathing.

The first case contained the Zeller collection of spectacular gems. Diamonds as large as a fist, the most precious, a blood-red diamond displayed at the center of the collection, was reputedly worth in excess of fifty million dollars. Rubies, exquisitely faceted, varied in color hues from rose to ruby, from carmine to a deep purplish tone called pigeon's-blood red, dazzled under the play of lights. Cabochon cuts, many unfaceted, and others exhibiting asterism with six-pointed stars called star rubies fascinated Victor.

Star rubies, his father insisted, marked the sign of the Jew's greatness. Therein lay his adherence to the hexagram—the Star of David. If nature so produced the mark, was it not proof of the Jew's greatness?

The next case contained white, pink, and green jade objects from the Orient, their provenance dating to the emperors and empresses of Cathay. Shapes and designs seldom seen by collectors and connoisseurs the world over provided drama for the gold collection next to it. The largest, most extensive display of minted gold coins, circa 3200 B.C., to present-day Krugerands and Swiss francs, were protected in glass containers.

Victor pressed a button; the throne orbited another forty-five degrees. An unobstructed view of the remaining west wall, divided by a towering stone fireplace, enormous double-entry doors, came into focus. Two enormous brown sienna sofas in Spanish leather faced each other before the fireplace, separated by four long, low carved teak tables. Dark brown to beige throw pillows with carmine velvet and cerulean blue trim lay casually about on the sofas. Opulence personified.

Another forty-five degrees and he faced the north wall. A winding staircase to a loft wrapped three-quarters around the cavernous room that housed a formidable collection of rare books, art works, sculpture, and two sealed *mystery* rooms, off limits to him. Once curious about the contents of those *verboten* rooms, Victor's interest in them had abated during the recent cranial experiments. Today—*déjà vu*. For the first time he flashed intimately on the contents. Behind a flimsy curtain in his mind, the secrets contained in those rooms, no longer secrets, awaited his physical perusal. He was close—he felt it.

Or was he?

When Victor swung the throne chair another forty-five degrees, he fell into his father's line of vision. Amadeo's fury was barely containable. "You dare sit in my throne chair?"

"Guten Morgen, Vater," Victor tilted his head indulgently, the new-found knowledge made him brazen.

"Speak English!" Zeller's focus shifted back to the war. "Why do you come here on a business day? Fifteen minutes late! The twentieth century provides us ample communication devices, no? Use them!"

Undaunted, Victor stepped off the throne to floor level, crossed to his father's side, snifter in hand, and sat in the chair opposite Zeller, deliberately obstructing his view.

"How is the mighty Pharaoh of finance today?"

Zeller ignored the acerbic questions, his delusions controlled him. "They will erect a shrine to me, Victor. From such a shrine, the entire world will know the inexorable influence of Amadeo Zeller. And why not?"

"Oh, yes . . . why not? Zeller power tentacles reach into the heartbeats of all nations. Let's take inventory." Victor lounged in the chair. "Diamond mines, gold and oil empires, banking, stock manipulations, and digging further into your cesspool of existence you've added dope trafficking, the laundering of dirty money! Dealing dope for dollars to buy and supply arms to those nations you intend to control. What does this represent, Father? Eighty—ninety percent of your wealth?"

"Our wealth, Victor. *OUR WEALTH*, my son." His bony head jerked sharply, deadly eyes riveted on his son.

"What does it matter?" Victor shrugged. "More inventory—gold Krugerands, global properties, controlling interest in American banks, publishing houses, motion pictures, even television networks. God knows what else!"

Zeller removed a white tablet from a diamond-studded pillbox. He slipped it under his tongue, snapped the box shut with a click. Wary opaque eyes squinted behind those chartreuse lenses.

"Amadeo Zeller," Victor chanted. "Pharaoh of vast empires, yet you strive for more—more—more! What discontents you? Tell me, so I can understand!"

Icicles dripped on Zeller's early ebullience. He grew guarded as he might facing an enemy. "If you must vomit, do it and be done with it, Victor. You're drunk! At this hour!" His disgust was apparent.

"A billionaire ten times over, with assets in the trillions." Victor articulated ball park inventory figures. "The Zeller bank in Geneva, here in Zurich, branches in Europe, Israel, Lebanon! Let's not forget controlling interest in six of the twelve Federal Reserve Banks and ten of the twenty-four branches. Manipulate any of your thousands of obedient puppets and your slightest wish is filled."

Victor lighted a cigarette, smoked it through a gold holder. "How do you remain *invisible?* The extent of the empire I inherit is vague in my mind. Why is it necessary to traffic in power? Global politics? Narcotics? And this recent innovation—brain tampering! Here, dammit, at the cheateau—our own home!"

Before Zeller could reply, Victor quickly changed tack. "Do you know your reputation in certain circles? You are known as a *bastard*, a cabalistic son of a bitch!"

He would not be baited. "You think to incur my rancor at such words?" His head bobbed up and down. "They are correct on both counts. I was born a *bastard*, delivered into this world by a wanton bitch. So—where does that leave us, Victor? Do we continue this display of disrespect or do you explain what has diseased you against me?" Zeller swiveled back to the video screens.

"You don't understand! You just won't understand, will you, Father? *Father! Look at your son when he speaks to you!*" Victor drained the brandy snifter, smacked his lips loudly, and deliberately placed glass and decanter on Zeller's desk, knowing how he loathed anyone to violate his property.

"Suddenly you are some *meshuggah*!" Zeller retorted. "Today, of all days, eh?" He grimaced, clacking his dentures. "All your life you've known me to be no *normal* man, *nu?* From you now comes *schlocky schmaltz*?" He grunted. "Accept it, we are both cut from the same cloth. Our mistress is *power!* Gold is our life force, Victor, *gold!* Gold flows in our veins, *not* blood! Eighty-six years I've spent developing the empire I must soon turn over to you. I achieved every goal I set, save one or two minor upsets, and even they succumbed eventually. I permit no adversity to upset my goal. Nothing to deter me from ultimate success, you hear?" He interjected German, French, Italian, even Yiddish to punctuate his words, but turning from Victor, his eyes grew vacant. He stared past his son, swept up the Jacob's Ladder design on the stained glass window, out of touch with reality.

Victor synchronized his Baum and Mercier with the jade and gold clock on the desk. He cast a wary eye on the video screens, noticeably edgy. "Father, look about you. The fruit of your labors surround you. You are the wealthiest of men. Can't you leave it at that?" Then, his internal struggle visible in his expression, Victor continued, "After you die—*and you will die*—I will not live your life, with your monstrous hatred spreading cancerously in me."

"*Stop it! Stop it at once!* Never, *never* use that word in my presence! We are not compatible, death and I! *Understand?*" Zeller's blood pressure soared.

"Listen and hear me well, Victor. I *was* the wealthiest man once! *Was*, Victor! Now, my mortal enemies supersede me. After what I've done to acquire power, along comes the beggarly Arabs to parlay their oil lands into impossible fortunes! It is rightfully *ours! Our* oil! *Our* lands! *Ours* as decreed by the great God Abraham! Don't you forget that! No one dethrones Amadeo Redak Zeller! No one brings Zeller to his knees. We kneel to no man, Victor! We shall prevail!'' He paused long enough to take two pills, followed by a glass of milk.

"Now we talk. I am a Jew! An Italian Jew who fought for every dollar accumulated in the Zeller name. But you *know* this, don't you, my son?'' He eyed Victor cannily. "By now, what was buried in my brain cells has become your consciousness, *nu?''*

"You are neither Jew nor Italian! What are you Father? Victor's mottled face twisted torturously. "*Why did you do this to me?* You lived your life! How in God's name father do I live *two* lives? *Yours and mine*? Victor sank into a chair, his face ashen. *God* how he played for time.

Amadeo Zeller sat stiffly, a graven image of cold stone. He appeared lifeless, but the eyes glowed, burning incandescent coals.

Victor shuddered in revulsion. "I agreed to this experiment, thinking only to be endowed with your financial wizardry. Instead, your will, your depravities contaminated me. Are you satisfied knowing you created a monster? My God, *Father*, a monster without conscience!

"Shall I tell you the dilemma I faced a few days ago? A torturous dilemma. The Weiderhopf-Guggenheim-Whittzleboch, the Wurtmeir-Turrin-Munich mergers fell due. Four hundred eighty nine million dollars—American—in default! The cartel had inadvertently let the default slip by them. *Ten hours past due!* What perverse delight I took in exercising our right of default!''

"*Jawohl! Jawohl*, Victor! It was your right! *Gut, mein Knabe!''*

"In God's name, Father, Guggie is your friend! He, when others voted you out of the cartel, stood at your side, threatened to withdraw his financial support from the bank unless your seat with the banking fraternity remained intact!''

"*Nein! Nein*, Victor! You did the right thing! Once you permit contractual commitments to slip past you, you demonstrate weakness. Weaknesses are preyed upon by both friends and enemies!''

Victor studied the shriveled figure, then said coolly, "Sorry. Weiderhoph called when the news hit the wires. He begged me not to exercise the default. A delay occurred over which he had no control—''

"And? . . ."

"I extended the note six months—at reasonable interest," Victor admitted sardonically, then added, "Oh, I *didn't* want to comply. By God! How I fought the desire to do it *your* way! Next time—I might not resist. That *would* please you, wouldn't it, Father? It's what you've plotted for—an extension of your ego in my life and both of us in a son to perpetuate the Zeller lineage. What you failed to consider is that there is already a part of you in me. That diabolical might, heightened tenfold threatens to overwhelm me. Father, before you die, pray to your God Abraham for the salvation of my black soul!"

The octogenarian stared hard at Victor, impervious in manner.

"Try me! " Victor pressed passionately. "I am a living microchip phenomenon! A human robot. Where shall I begin? Ah-hhhh. In the early twenties you fraudulently acquired, after the wholesale butchery of a Spanish noble family—the de la Varga fortune. You manipulated men through numerous forgeries, naming yourself beneficiary of that family's holdings. You went on to orchestrate striking success by backing Il Duce and the Fascisti rise to fame and glory with the combined assistance of Swiss and British banking gnomes. How am I doing so far?"

Zeller's chest heaved, his pulse quickened and those terrible eyes fired sparks.

"Ah, let me continue . . . The betrayal came. Il Duce succumbed to Hitler's fanfare by electing to help *Der Führer's* Jewish problems, *nu*? But were they Jewish problems? Or merely an excuse. Low level conspiracies you orchestrated to promote future retributions. My God, father, you're not a Jew! But you used the Jews to further your own ends. You grew arrogant, demanding, with offensive temerity. You, special laison, Minister of Finance to Il Duce, respected manipulator of the *Quadrumviri*, fled Italy like a mad, diseased dog! You left my mother, Clarisse, and me, to face the music. You let them use us, intimidate us, until we were exhausted of all hope."

"I will never forget that humiliation," Zeller snarled. "Il Duce would not harm you, any of you. It was me he hated. He was your *Godfather*. He respected, adored the Contessa . . ."

"But you ran! Why would you run from a *friend* unless you . . . I know *why*, don't I, Father?"

Jarring telephone chimes sounded three times. Victor closed his eyes, inhaled deeply, waiting—waiting. Zeller placed a slen-

442

der gold cylinder upright before him on the desk. *"Jawohl!"* he rasped, inserting an ear disc into place. Listening, he shot scathing glances at Victor, then pounded impatiently on the video control buttons.

The dark six screens came to life, but scrambling, prevented transmission. Periodically the images cleared. They recognized Pierre Salinger from Paris and a panel of others engaged in some heated dialogue, rendered incomprehensible by transmission failure.

Something was happening! Everything Victor dreaded!

He approached his father slowly who pounded fiendishly on the control buttons, struggling to clear the transmission, cursing in German, French, Italian and Yiddish, his features contorting hideously.

Victor reached over, flipped off the phone connection. Startled, Zeller stopped short at his son's action.

"W-hat—w-what are you doing? Stop acting like a *Schutzstaffel!*"

"Schutzstaffel? . . . Why not? It's best you hear from me, my reason for coming here on this *business* day, to disrupt the world of Zeller." Victor's tone was frosty, disgusted.

He replaced the gold bar, turned off the video screens, removed the earphone from Zeller's ear neatly, unruffled, and to Amadeo Zeller his manner was terribly jarring. A flurry of hands warded off Victor's solicitous behavior. "Stop it! Stop it! I can do it myself! What the devil do you think you are doing?" His ugly face grew uglier, distorted by rage.

Then Victor committed the unpardonable. He sat on the edge of the great Pharaoh's desk. Zeller would have felled anyone else like a poisonous fly. Victor leaned in closer, his voice strained.

"Bad news, *Father*. I hope you don't assess it too crucially after so long and distinguished a relationship."

"Victor! *Gottverdammen!* Stop this slobbering over me! If you have something to say—do it!"

It was a matter of sound, the way the voice changes, became timorous or friendly, the way an apologetic note entered and the very soul of Victor added a frightened whisper to bold, unspeakable words. . . .

Victor winced at his father's imperturbability. "Very well, what do you call him—Moufflon? Yes, Moufflon. After a twenty-year relationship your Corsican co-conspirator stands before a lectern halfway around the world, spilling his guts, not to one, two or three people, not to an intelligence agency, but to a seventy-eight man delegation of the World Powers Central Committee." Victor glanced at his watch.

"By now the entire world knows the Zeller *modus operandi*, the secret plottings and schemings of the Swiss banking gnome, Amadeo Zeller."

In the silence Zellers teeth clacked noisily, disbelief spreading across his face, freezing into a deadly expression. His ghastly features jerked, settled finally into an unreadable mask.

"Why didn't you report this to me? You *kept* it from me?"

"Twenty-year alliances don't go up in smoke without reason. What motivates Moufflon's defection, Father?"

"I'll stop him! I'll stop him, my way!" With these words Zeller pulled his scrawny frame to full height, propelled himself across the room to the dais, climbed the steps and sat heavily in the throne chair. He negotiated the chair forty-five degrees, focused on Jacob's Ladder long enough to shrug off the sinking sensation and whiplash effect of betrayal.

"The game takes on new dimensions, *ja?* Uh—what exactly does Moufflon tell these, uh, delegates?"

"I suppose a full expose of your clandestine Middle East operations for the past twenty years . . .? Hummmn? We shall know soon enough. A prepared brief was *lifted*, copied and is en route to us via jet."

"Moufflon's attempt at a *coup de théâtre* is unacceptable. Zeller is not without strategy." Zeller lifted deadly eyes, his expression sinister. "A flaw exists, Victor. A blatant flaw." The words were difficult to articulate, but he spat them out. "We have *never* met—Moufflon and I."

Victor's jaw fell slack, his astonishment total. "Forgive me," he began, his head inclined obliquely. "For a moment I thought I heard you say—" Zeller nodded, suffused with minor mortification.

"You paid a man you've *never* met," Victor began, finding the words difficult, "an excess of fifty million dollars over the years—"

"—for jobs well done!" Zeller countered.

"*For jobs well done!*" Victor parroted, shaking his head scornfully. "Today he did the *job* on you, *old boy*." Inescapable zeal crept into his voice.

"The man wanted and needed anonymity. I, better than most,

444

understand anonymity. Recommendations came from the *highest* places, Victor. We began small—the job, well done, paved the way for the next, and the next. Five operations evolved to another five, the work kept on a piecemeal basis. Then I approached him, the implementation of my overall goal foremost in my mind. The proposal, as usual, was made by my intermediaries to his inner circle of advisors—not the nucleus, those advisors who protect his identity and influence his decisions, but the second ring of power, all formidible men positioned around the globe.'' Zeller finger-polished the gold ring on his left forefinger nervously.

"I received no immediate reply. Fifty million dollars—American, I offered! Two decades ago, before the spiraling inflation—the sum represented the moon. Nothing! I made the call. Me! It was not a simple task for me to make the first move. It denigrates the business principles I practiced in my lifetime. Refused outright, I persisted, increased the offer.'' Zeller shook his head negatively.

"I made a final offer—fifty million payable in advance, the remaining fifty payable at intervals after substantial victories. One hundred million for the total contract!''

"The final payment,'' Victor added ruefully, "was made two days ago. The cash picked up by courier in Geneva.''

Zeller set his glasses into place, angled his torso around and stared hard and questioningly at his son.

"I personally handled the cash transfer.'' Victor puffed thoughtfully on his long thin cigar. "The courier was a woman. Had you confided in me . . . Well, I can dazzle a few. A drink, perhaps, then dinner—''

"—and a stiletto through your aorta if you probed.''

"The courier—an assassin?'' Victor dug into his memory.

"Hah!'' Zeller snorted. "Interrogate one and you're dead. Attempts to penetrate Moufflon's organization at any level would instantly abort our relationship. He made this clear in advance. My objective was not to impair Moufflon's performance, but ensure my victory in the Middle East.''

"She was Italian,'' Victor murmured *sotto voce*. "Possibly French . . .'' He imaged the ageless, attractive woman dressed in a mulberry suit, dove-gray cashmere turtleneck sweater under a natural wild lynx greatcoat with matching fur hat, Cossack-style, covering her hair. She was the epitome of *moneyed* class. She

445

carried an expensive Burgandy English saddle leather briefcase. Victor had studied her via a closed-circuit video camera from the moment she entered the bank to secure the transaction. At one step, before money was placed into her hands, Victor, posing as a clerk, returned a card to her for verification of coded numbers.

The matter had taken a few moments. She initialed the numbers, handed both card and briefcase to Victor, followed him into a smaller alcove. She watched Victor count the money and place it into the briefcase in silence. Any attempts at conversation would have aborted the deal.

Victor had noticed dangling on a gold chain from her dove-gray suede Louis Vuitton handbag a set of keys for a Ferrari sports car. An Audemars Piguet platinum and diamond watch graced her wrist—an item too costly for an ordinary courier.

Later Victor had replayed the video cassette of the transaction, noting her subtle body movements. The feeling struck him. He knew her from her past. *Where* had they met? *How*? He confided none of this to his father, nor the fact that he'd used a photography specialist to blow up the video cassette. The courier had made an error. A serious error! The license number to her Ferrari was imprinted on a gold medallion. His man was busily at work attempting to reconstruct those numbers. And when he finished . . .

"Our immediate concern is Moufflon!" Amadeo cackled brittly. "His identity is a well-kept secret. He could be anyone. So, what are you thinking, Victor? Perhaps *our* conduits are corrupt? . . . Possible—but not likely. Milos and Draga are powerfully connected. Mosha Bauer is not without talent, yet . . ."

Zeller's expression, unreadable, he reached up, yanked off his hideous hairpiece. His skull shone wet with sweat. His features contorted like a death's head. "Our lives reach back to the roots of time and trail through history. If I didn't know better—"

"—know *what* better?" Victor poured more brandy, moved in closer to his father. He pressed the brandy into the older man's hand. "What is it, Father? Something buried in your subconscious? In mine, too?" he added ruefully. "One that ties us to Moufflon in ways not presently visible to us."

"*What?* What's that you said?"

"I'm not sure." Victor said slowly. "Think on it. A twenty-year silence. Then, suddenly, without visible provocation—

betrayal. Betrayal geared to explode Zeller's world. It makes no sense—''

''—yes! Yes, what?'' Colorless eyes focused on him like powerful lasers.

''I'm trying to say, Moufflon is *not* a man of betrayal, unless—'' He faced Zeller squarely. ''—unless something profound motivates a virulent hatred in him. Yes, Father, *hatred! Hatred* directed against you! Else *why* would he seek your ultimate destruction? Don't you see? A similarity exists in what Corsicans call an ancient blood feud and Sicilians call *vendetta*.''

Zeller was not listening. His focus had shifted to Jacob's Ladder. ''I believed I had discovered one man who understood me and could be trusted. I was wrong. So . . .? We pick up the pieces, go forward to victory. No one, Victor, not Moufflon or the Lord God Abraham deprives Zeller of victory!''

''You weren't listening—''

''Betrayal is unacceptable! You hear? *Unacceptable!*''

''What will you do when the media descend on us in Zurich? Or in Geneva to question our employees? Or in America? What of our banking reputation? How do we handle the glaring publicity, the notoriety of undesirable spotlights?''

''What we've always done. You worry? We control the media, *nu*? So, what's to worry?''

Victor broke open another bottle of Napoleon brandy, guzzled a glassful, his legal brain at work devising mental escape routes to circumvent possible adverse publicity. ''What you've orchestrated, Father—''

''—with genius, don't forget!''

Victor, exasperated, continued. ''*With genius*, Father.'' He frowned. ''I am trying to place facts into perspective. The finger of guilt will be pointed at Zeller. Nevertheless, Moufflon *executed* the plot.''

The shrill voice raged. ''As God is my witness, *Moufflon is a dead man*! You hear me, Victor? *A dead man*! A one hundred million dollar betrayal! No one fucks Zeller like this! No one tells the world what Zeller conspires—no one! Not even Moufflon! Set the wheels in motion! He shall be discredited worldwide! The media prints what Zeller dictates—nothing else. And the WPCC delegates will spit in Moufflon's face! Do you know why? Because Zeller owns them—all of them! Let them dare

447

speak out and we will put the screws to them, crush them financially and politically.

"Oh Victor, Victor," he chanted like a cantor. "There shall fall upon him such a name-calling! A slanderous profile done on Moufflon shall be disseminated by all our global allies . . . When we've finished . . . When we've finished. . . ."

Zeller, caught up in the task of counting the rungs on Jacob's Ladder was lost to his son.

At 2:00 P.M. Zurich time, a courier arrived at the Zeller chateau with the copies of Moufflon's Maui speech. Victor gave one to his father, and with the second copy ensconced himself in the east wing of the mansion. Here amidst a French Renaissance decor Victor's mother, the contessa spent lonely, desperate hours before her death. Victor didn't know all the details, yet, but since the MCI (micro-chip implantation) things were falling into place. He could wait until the time was ripe. He tossed a few scented fir cones into the blazing fires on the hearth. In moments the perfumed essence he remembered so vividly permeated the rooms, stirred his senses. Victor stepped back from the hearth, gazed up at the enormous oil painting of his mother. He studied her gown, smiling at the golden sheer silk, delicately embroidered with hundreds of tiny bugle beads, in the form of bees, silver-beaded bodies with gold-beaded wings. It was a facsimile of Josephine's coronation gown. Around her neck, on a golden chain, draped in the cleavage of her breasts, lay the priceless diamond and golden bee he had shown to Veronique in an impulsive moment.

Veronique . . . the thought of her sent a sigh of desperation shuddering through him, lasting less than fifteen seconds. He pulled a chair and ottoman before the warm fire, then quickly got down to business. He broke open the seal of the brief, flipped through the thickness.

A seventy-five page indictment against Zeller!

Two hours later Victor closed the brief. It was all there. *Enough to dismantle the financial infrastructure of the Zeller empire! Destroy Zeller for all time!*

Victor tossed more fir cones into the fires, staring at the brightly licking flames. Thoughts snaked through his mind, a wild set of flashing images, scenes of northern Italy . . . a monastery high in the mountains near Trento . . .

448

He let the scenes and conversations play themselves out. Then at precisely 4:30 P.M. he picked up the Moufflon brief, heading toward the west wing.

Midway across the downstairs foyer he stopped, his eyes focusing on the enormous solid gold mosaic inlay on the marble floor inside the entrance. He'd seen the symbol countless times before, but today it seemed doubly ironic. It was a solid gold hexagon surrounded by ancient Hebraic writings. At its center, within the six-pointed star was an utterly ridiculous replica of a fox! A bit gaudy, terribly gauche! The entire banking world considered Amadeo Zeller a sly fox, but to advertise it? In his own home? Victor smirked.

Victor lingered, his thoughts racing over the seventy-five page indictment, through the hurriedly compiled files he had collected since news of Moufflon's intended defection reached him through his American contacts.

Moufflon was very clever! Very clever, indeed!

Yet, not clever enough, Victor thought. Out of the masses of his recent studies one blatant fact had emerged, *Moufflon was Corsican!*

Victor's recollections of Corsica and its superstitious natives— Sophia!—vivid enough, he remembered the *moufflon* was considered a highly prized game for hunters. He also recalled how the Corsicans had rhapsodized at the moufflon's adroit cleverness in eluding its enemies. Victor was turning these facts over in his mind when he gave a start.

Victor's dark eyes widened in astonishment as it came together in his mind. He stood before the golden hexagon, eyes narrowing with interest. Hunkered down, he traced the outline of the animal at dead center with his fingertips.

"Well, I'll be damned!" he muttered, blinking hard. He rose to his feet, stood erect, planted his fists on his hips and roared with laughter.

Suddenly, the voice of Amadeo Zeller, amplified on the P.A. system, electrified the air. "Victor!"

Victor turned abruptly, eyes on the closed-circuit video screen a short distance from them, the raging image of Zeller reflected on it. Victor turned back to the gold inlaid mosaic. "A marten!" he said decisively. "Of course, it could only be a *marten*. The tail, rounded ears, no black mask! Crafted in gold, the differences are subtle. It's a *marten*, Father! Why didn't you tell me?''

"Victor! We have more important things on the agenda than foxes or martens! This *Gottverdammen* brief!"

Victor ascended the left stairs engulfed in thought. *Do we, Father? More important than martens?* He moved toward the library piecing together this enigmatic figurehead Moufflon who threatened the very core of Zeller network. Zeroing in on his personal bank of memories, Victor imaged vaguely the spectacular Corsican, who with his *Mozarabe* stuck thorns in Axis backsides in World War II. *Was it possible? Was it just possible . . .?*

Victor entered the library, ignoring the raving Zeller. He paused trancelike before the roaring fires on the hearth, his eyes coming alive at the hammering of his pulses, wild throbbing at his temples as a bonanza of knowledge exploded his brain.

Then a shadow moved before him, distorting the mental images and messages. It was Zeller. "Don't you hear me, Victor? What's wrong with you? The alternative plan, Victor! The *Alternative* Plan must be implemented at once! You hear?" He raged in almost comic caricature until one saw the power of his hatred oozing from every pore in his body. "Moufflon is doomed! *No* more discussions! *No* bargaining! *He* set the guidelines into place. Now we war with him! The gameplan will be played according to *our* guidelines! I accept nothing short of his total annihilation!"

Zeller's voice was pitched a level above hysteria.

Victor lifted *those* terrible eyes to his father. Zeller's madness ceased instantly; he saw himself mirrored there. He spoke more calmly. "The risks are monumental, exceedingly dangerous. If the plans go awry—" Zeller paused. "The target is Moufflon. Unlimited funds are at your disposal. Have you contemplated a base of operations?"

"No!" Victor towered over the shrunken old man. "The Zeller name must not be implicated in Moufflon's destruction. There are other ways."

"How? Tell me *how?*"

Silence . . . fifteen, twenty, thirty seconds seemed an eternity. *"I know Moufflon's identity*!" he said sotto voce.

"What? Tell me, Victor! I demand you tell me who he is!"

"No."

"What?" The old man cackled low in his throat. He sat,

nearly fell, into the throne chair, turned the pages of the brief as if he'd find the answer there.

"This time I'm running the show. I want it ended. When you die I want no more agony!"

The rumble began low in Zeller's throat, bursting into obscene, hideous laughter. Turning his back on the shrunken remains of his father, Victor crossed the room and began to climb the spiral steps.

"*Stop!* Where do you think you're going?"

"You know exactly where. The rooms denied me all my life."

"No! Not yet! I have spent a lifetime planning for that moment of victory. Now is not the time, Victor! Don't deny me now."

Victor faltered. "Upstairs in one of those rooms is a portrait of a woman—*not my mother*—with hair of fire and eyes like emerald jewels. Is she the reason I was named Victor?"

Zeller's head snapped so swiftly the brittle meshing of bones was audible. His eyes darted furtively from Victor to the loft, the crisis situation forgotten as wills crossed like sabers.

Victor taunted. "To *know* the contents of those rooms I need not physically cross their thresholds. Mementos of the past . . . relics of past accomplishments, *nein*, Papa? Private papers, foreign property holdings, records of stock manipulations, *embezzlements*, Father, of the original holdings before you fraudulently converted them to Zeller assets. And—"

"—yes, yes, and?"

"Valuable manuscripts. Priceless tomes. Your only failure, *Father*, was the secret Society of the Martens, *Compagnia Della Garduna!* You failed to locate the Seven Parchments, those laws and bylaws so highly coveted by you."

Unspeakable words descended upon Zeller like the stinging of a bullwhip cutting into flesh.

"The simple laws and bylaws of a defunct cabalistic society meant *that* much to you? Is that why the *marten* downstairs in the foyer stands at the center of the Star of David? Speak to me. I deserve at least an explanation!"

Zeller's terrible eyes locked on his son, his profile, rigid, unyielding as the design on the stained glass window. "Because I failed in that endeavor, and do not possess the Seven Garduna Parchments, I was forced to employ the Moufflon forces. They were my reason for existence. Now why do you vomit this defeat at my feet? What has the *Compagnia Della Garduna* to do with Moufflon?"

451

Victor leaned languidly against the staircase railing. He took pleasure in tormenting the old man. "You *really* don't know? . . . I don't believe it! You? The incomparable Amadeo Zeller is flawed."

Victor crossed the room to toss the Moufflon File and Maui text into Zeller's lap.

"The truth, under your nose for the past twenty years, and you *failed* to detect the *modus operandi*?" He laughed low in his throat. "Here, from your *own* files, I learned the truth." He tapped his head scar, site of his recent surgery. "Your twenty-year partner, the *incomparable, infallible* Moufflon, the man you trusted implicitly and paid one hundred million dollars, controls those precious parchments! The Seven Parchments of the Garduna, for God's sake, form the basis of his operations! That much for the *Society of the Martens!*"

As night fell silently the world of Zeller exploded.

"He isn't dead, is he, Father? The man you thought you destroyed?" Victor taunted as he stepped forward. "The rooms, the *verboten* rooms upstairs, contain memories of Victoria Valdez de la Varga, yes?"

Amadeo's hatred dripped like a hideous bloodstain. Pincer-shaped hands gripped the Moufflon files like sharp claws as if he were mentally siphoning off the man's life.

"*She* was the reason you refused to love Mother! *Don't deny it.* You have no secrets from me." Victor walked toward the glass cases containing the diamonds. He stared at them. "Recently control over things I say and do becomes difficult. Names spring from my mind. No! *Your* mind, *Father*. Images parade across my sight every waking moment. A part of me views with curiosity the strangers intruding upon my privacy, yet, they are *not* strangers. A part of me finds them familiar, as if I had actually known them. So *many* enemies, Father! You had no friends!"

Victor strutted before the throne chair, his stature, demeanor the image of Zeller in his youth. Zeller, both fascinated and offended, fired his opaque eyes to blue glints, watching his son.

Victor, without warning, slammed a balled fist into the glass case containing the diamond display. Shrieking, clangorous alarms pierced the air; the dogs jumped up, barked raucously, leaped to Zeller's feet on the dais. A hand signal subdued them. Zeller pressed numerous buttons on his control panel, reducing at once the shrilling alarms to a faint wailing echo, to nothing.

Blood spurted from Victor's hand, spilled onto the diamonds, his shirt and suit front. Whipping out a handkerchief, he picked at the embedded glass shards unflinchingly, bound the bleeding mass, then calmly removed a flawless, twenty-carat pear-shaped diamond from its mount. He held it to the light, satisfied.

"You don't mind if I take this, *Father*, to negotiate through the coming days?" Savage satisfaction fired his defiant eyes.

Zeller's face screwed into a pugnacious scowl.

Victor slipped the gem casually into his jacket pocket, poured more brandy and guzzled it. He postured flamboyantly before the octogenarian, his head tilted indulgently. "Why, suddenly, does the name, *Antonio Vasquez* seem familiar to me? . . . And *Don Francisco de la Varga? Seville*. Spain. The honeyed tones ceased, perplexity colored his features. *"Why do I feel revulsion at that name?"*

Zeller pressed. *"Who* isn't dead, Victor? You said he wasn't the dead—the man I thought I destroyed. I have destroyed so many . . ."

"Yes, yes, it slipped my mind. There were so many—no? Who else could I mean? The one man who controlled the Garduna Parchments."

"No! No!" he shrieked. "You don't know that! You don't!"

"Don Francisco de la Varga! If he isn't dead, someone close to him was given the Parchments and now Moufflon flourishes from their powers. Tell me, Father, why do I feel such loathing at the name de la Varga? Is it because you won a battle of wits over him? Why does the name disgust me?"

Amadeo glowed contentedly.

Victor scaled the dais, his unbloodied hand thrust under Zeller's nose. "Look! Look how I sweat and tremble at the name? Why don't I tremble and sweat copiously at the thought of Il Duce? He, too, was Zeller's enemy, no?" His voice dropped by decibels. "But, Victoria Valdez de la Varga produces overwhelming love in my heart, a curious, unrequited love. Such a passionate love, *Father*. Did no one explain that passionate love is quenchless thirst that cannot be satisfied?" He grinned diabolically, laughed contemptuously. "You didn't bargain for this, did you? That I would feel love for the woman you loved? Such an abomination, *Father* . . . What shall I do? . . . What *shall* I do? Have you any concept of the inner torture my soul endures since the MCI in my brain?" Victor shook his head at the imponderables swimming

453

about in his head. He caught sight of his father's reptilian eyes watching him like a python ready to strike, and laughed uproariously.

"You disapprove of the monster you created? Look again, *Father*. Satisfied? No? Too bad. A man with one life to live is penance enough, but two?" His lips twisted into a curious smile. "To learn you were a sentimentalist jars my image of you, old boy."

Zeller adjusted swiftly by instinct to a tone most likely to disarm his son. "This is no cat-and-mouse game, Victor. This is anaconda and mongoose. Mortal enemies fighting to the end—"

"Spare me the academics. I've adjusted my vocabulary, attitudes and manners to yours at the level which best strikes a responsive chord, *nu*? What is it you call it, *Father*? Ambassadorial aplomb?"

"Your timing is appalling, your sarcasm reprehensible. The MCI surgery was not designed to boomerang in my face!"

"What you're saying is you *goddamned* don't know the long-term effects of micro-chip implantation and care less what it does to me as long as Amadeo Zeller's influence is projected into the next generation. You don't give a diddling fuck about me!"

Victor swilled the brandy, bowed with mocking contempt. "I don't always know what will spill from these lips, *Father*. Away from you, I post sentries over my words and actions. Are you proud of your human guinea pig? Do I conform to your highest expectations?"

"*Victor!*"

"*Jawohl, Vater?*"

"I should have killed them! I should have killed them both! Even now, doubt exists, but not enough," he hissed above a whisper.

"Who? Killed both, *who?*" Victor prodded. He stopped abruptly, as if in that second he had endowed with vision into Amadeo's mind, Ironically, Victor was in perfect attunement. "Then, it's true? *It's really true?*"

Zeller glowered. "This discussion has ended."

Amaedo ignored his son as one would a mere bug. He spoke softly. "Those rooms upstairs contain the spoils of my victories. You shall be made privy to them, Victor, in this last, final triumph of Amadeo Zeller. You must promise to ensure proper homage paid to me. Will you do this? Grant my last wish?"

Victor fell victim to a long silence, his hand pained him. Then he crossed the room, placed the solid gold telephone cylinder at his father's desk. He sat down, pressed a series of numbers on an accompanying panel, observing as a small video screen lifted from its recessed position.

The screen came to life. The features, head and shoulders of a black man, wide, flat nose, flaring nostrils, thick lips and flabby jowls, stared through anthracite eyes at him.

Victor chanted, "Sagittarius III calling Cereberus I . . ."

"Cereberus I, here." The reply came in the King's English.

"Can we *parlez*? Are we safe?"

"Most assuredly. Make book on it, Sagittarius III."

"TARGET: MOUFFLON is about to be implemented. Contact top *specialists*. The figure—top dollars, Do you read me?"

The black man whistled low, amazement registered in his deeply set black eyes. "You ask the impossible, Sadge III."

"I pay to make the impossible a reality."

"What is *that* reality?"

"Four times the sum contained in the original dossier."

"Indeed?"

"Make book on it, Cereberus I."

"Affirmative. When do I disseminate the gospel of Cain?"

"I pick the time and place."

"You create complications. Is this a riddle? Sudden disaffection?"

"No riddle. Keep up with the times. Disaffection reads: *defection*. Estrangement with no remedy. Do you read me?"

"Precisely. Still you pose maddening complications."

"But think how exciting." Victor hung up. The astonished Cereberus faded as the screen went to black.

"How long will it take you to prepare the bank for your absence?" Zeller asked the moment Victor rang off the call.

"As long as it takes Bertrand to open the coded file and follow my instructions. In an emergency there is always Kreuzegg's assistant. A bright, capable chap, excellent, but he is Italian."

"You dare suggest it?"

"There was a certain Mademoiselle Veronique Lindley—"

"—a woman banker? We'd be laughed out of Zurich! *Mesuggah!*"

"She left Zurich long ago. Didn't your sleuths report to you?"

Zeller maneuvered the throne chair in a ninety-degree turn. He faced his son, poised at the double door ready to depart.

455

"Wish me good fortune, *Father*."

"You have inside your head a built-in mechanism ensuring success—me, my life! Future generations will remember Zeller's genius."

"*What future?* What generations? You overlooked something, *Father*. Those experiments, the surgery, exposure to the radium left me impotent. The Zeller strain ends with me."

"Impotent? *Never*! Zeiss assured me it would be ephemeral."

"Really? What else did Zeiss fail to confide in me?"

"There is always Clarisse!"

Victor bridled furiously. "Touch one hair on her head—dare explain this grotesque abomination to her, Father, and I swear I shall kill you, my sister and myself!"

Zeller's odious laughter assaulted the senses.

"I promise total destruction of all you've dreamed! Dare tamper with my sister Clarisse and I'll reduce Zeller to rubble!"

"So! It's come to this. And I say to you, Victor, move a single solitary straw in any way I find offensive and *your* life will terminate. The micro-chip containing the world of Zeller can be duplicated."

Victor stared at his father in reviled fascination. "I should bow before your Satanic Majesty," he said with sarcastic panache. "You'll pardon me if I do not."

Victor opened the door. The Dobermans loping to his side, rushed into the corridor.

Victor turned, a slight mocking evident.

"Father, all my life you've confronted me with *faits accomplis*. This time you shall be repaid in your own coin. My accomplishment will reach you via the newspapers. Only in this way can an equilibrium be maintained. *N'est-ce pas?*"

"Victor!" the voice rang out sharply. "Did you ever stop to think your fount of Zeller knowledge is *limited* to what was *incorporated* in the micro-chip?"

Victor's air intake was sharp. "You're not a bastard, *Father*. You were spawned from the sperm of Lucifer. You don't even frighten me any more," he said softly. "You forget, the genes of Lucifer are in me, also."

Victor turned away, sickened by the sight and sounds of his father, of the room, the Zeller chateau—*anything*—stamped with the name Zeller! What triggered the revulsion? He knew the answer. He despised men like Amadeo Zeller, men like himself.

456

Chapter Thirty

WASHINGTON D.C.
February 28, 1984

PRESIDENT JOHN MACGREGOR, scowling fiercely, left the VIP room of the Washington Hilton Hotel flanked by a cordon of Secret Service men. He stepped into a corridor filled with shrieking humans, forced a smile for reporters and camera crews, waved to hordes pressing in at all sides with the brisk, noncommittal manner he'd demonstrated for the past eighteen days since the Maui fiasco.

Hell had erupted and it refused to abate. A *TOP SECRET* jacket wrapped around the WPCC conference, affixed with *Highly Sensitive* labeling in no way deterred the journalistic vultures from sharpening talons and tongues and roosting in every available White House alcove, prepared to rip Macgregor to shreds. Insistent demands for interviews and news conferences aggravated the situation, rankling the Chief Executive.

John Macgregor was not talking! He would not talk until he was good and ready! Electronic exit doors swung open. Secret Service men moved in, shoulder-to-shoulder, inside carmine velvet ropes leading through the dismal, rainy day to a waiting Presidential limousine.

Macgregor fixed the Presidential smile into place, waved, nodded. Then for an instant, flickering hesitation crept into his expression. He sighted a face in the crowd. It disappeared. He immediately affixed that smile reserved for constituents. He approached the limousine amid cheers and jeers, as protest placards refuting U.S. foreign policy bobbed up and down around him. Support placards carried by a stalwart crowd of flag-waving, paid campaigners were shoved out of camera range, the more carrying the obvious stamp of an *invisible* hand orchestrating the scenario.

For days, the President had dug himself into a trench of silence, determined to persist in this posture until he received answers. Ten feet from the limousine John Macgregor, struck by premonitions, paused for a split second. Something nagged at him.

The well-oiled propaganda machine had been launched into action, even *before* the Maui Conference ended, clearly implying that a vicious campaign was under way, geared to discredit Moufflon *and* John Macgregor! Damaging propaganda, designed to smear the President's impressive record, circulated with rocket-fired swiftness into European capitals; deeply planted venom rushed through global bloodstreams.

Newspaper headlines screamed: *"Presidential Impeachment."* Strangely, damning rhetoric was not spouted by senators and congressmen until the thumbscrew applications forced them to condemn the administration.

Macgregor believed that the flames of propaganda, fanned by media hype only gave credence to Moufflon's *PROJECT: MOONSCAPE.*

The President reached the limousine. He turned for a final wave, forcing a bravado to cover the inner brooding. Suddenly the expression froze, metamorphosed into painful grimace. Shoved forward into the limousine by Bill Miller as a series of loud gunshots sputtered through the frenzied crowds, the President lay immobilized on the floor of the rear seat. The driver, fired by Miller's command to move, floored the accelerator. The limousine lurched forward, burning rubber, speeding furiously through traffic, guided by a Secret Service agent, radio in hand, calling, "CODE ALERT: *DRAKE is hit! Get us to a hospital!"*

The Secret Service swarmed like ants, crouching low, out of gunshot range. Total confusion overwhelmed them as they searched the area. Small circles of men in football huddles, frozen into immobility, would later swear they heard no gunshots.

Bill Miller flagged down the next limousine, piled in with several aides, shouting directives, *"Follow the President! He's been shot! Goddammit! Get cracking!"*

Panic-stricken, the driver came alive only to stall the engine. He restarted it, gunned the motor, apologetic, and finally screeched away from the curb, his horn blasting. Motorcycle cops converged from every direction, sped up beyond the presidential limousine, escorting it to the hospital, sirens screeching.

Outside the hotel, the overzealous Secret Service and officers on patrol had piled on top of the suspect in a pyramiding tower of bodies, discovering to their chagrin, after lifting themselves from the sweating wretched victim, that they had nabbed the wrong man. Two wounded agents, injured in the bloody salvoes fired earlier, lay on the sidewalks, oozing pools of crimson.

The milling crowds, unwilling to disperse, stared in stunned, bewildered silence, huddling closer, their furtive eyes searching, trying to locate the culprit. A burst of sniper fire sent them scurrying.

Police cars, sirens screaming, converged on the area from all directions. SWAT Squads deployed at once, surrounded the building where a suspected *sniper* had ensconsed himself. They found nothing except the expended shells of a *Dragunov* rifle.

The presidential limousine screeched to a halt at the emergency exit of the George Washington Medical Complex. A waiting staff of physicians, nurses with gurneys, navigated the Chief Executive into surgery as surgeons cursorily examined the massive bleeding from throat and upper shoulder wounds, exchanging dubious glances.

Voices clashed with unfamiliar sounds. The President, feeling little discomfort, saw only an endless corridor of interconnecting white ceilings and light fixtures with Bill Miller's anxious face hovering over him racing along the mobile gurney. The President's frame of focus narrowed to Bill Miller's face. The authoritative decree came in an angry, but subdued whisper.

"Get me General Brad Lincoln on the double!"

On the double evolved to ten days later, *after* the President's wounds healed, *after* the furor of the attempted assassination sobered the people, turning their mood docile. As an introverted nation of Americans examined the bodies of their consciences, General Lincoln arrived at the White House. For the past seven months, since the American Task Force had met with Moufflon representatives in the Algerian palace of Prince Youseff, Brad had continued to play his crucial behind-the-scene's role. He oversaw the Maui conference, hopeful that the man who brought the global dignitaries to one place, would bring them to peace. A few weeks later he prepared to unpin his star and lay it before the Chief.

The President, his left arm bound tightly in a sling, dismissed the battery of agents and aides from the room. The amenities over, two obviously strained men sat stiffly before the fireplace, a walnut drum table between them.

"All hell's broken loose, friend. Walking outside is out. The *gestapo* nixed it. The S.S. keeps me on a taut leash. Uh—tell me, do you have that, uh, gismo with you?"

Brad fished the mini-bug detector from his pocket, propped it on the table between them. The needle remained stationery.

Brad strolled to the fireplace, warmed his hands, then moving languidly about the room, searched all the nooks and crannies. His actions afforded a clearer insight into the highly specialized skills required in his profession.

Brad stood to one side of a white onyx and ormolu wall clock mounted in a gold frame behind the President's private desk. Perched atop the gilded frame was a fierce-eyed eagle, a replica of the bird perched atop the gold-ball flagstaff in the Oval Office.

Brad positioned himself beyond the periphery of the eagle's eye. "Sir, with your permission, I could use some coffee."

The President's upper torso turned stiffly at the waist, his expression puzzled. Brad whirled his finger in the air, gesturing the President to resume his original posture.

"Coffee? Of course. It's no trouble at all." He glanced at his watch.

"Thank you, Mr. President. I would appreciate that." Brad stepped back along the outer wall, hugging it, creeping in closer to the onyx clock and the enemy: *the eye of the eagle*. Brad sifted through an ashtray, selected a butt, and sneaking under the clock reached up and shoved the butt into the flaring eagle eye, fixing it firmly into place. Stepping back to appraise his handiwork, he returned to the President's side, picked up the detector, mosied back to the clock, fanning the device vertically, horizontally, in wide arcs before he was satisfied. Back in his chair, he answered the silent questions forming in presidential eyes. "Camera—yes. Sound—no. Lip readers . . . I'll explain later," he said softly.

"Are you always so cautious?"

"Always. My life depends on it, sir."

"Can we speak freely?"

Brad nodded. "So far."

"That man of yours . . . Moufflon?" Macgregor shook his

head. "An international vendetta rages against him. How the devil do they get the news before it explodes from the womb, dammit?"

"When you orchestrate events, you prepare for treachery from any side."

The President's paranoia leaked through his composure. His eyes darted to the eagle on the wall clock. "If someone reports the camera blackout? . . ."

"Pray they don't and if so, hope to God it's being done from *outside* the White House."

"In that case . . . if the device is rigged from external terminals—" the President paused, stunned. "You mean, it's possible the apparatus originates from *within* these halls?" His eyes widened, he dabbed at the moisture gathering on his upper lip with a tissue. Pouring water from a decanter, he took a pain pill, then launched his words of frustration. "We're in trouble. Brad, allegations leveled against Moufflon remained allegations until, by his own admission in the Maui speech, we were forced to confront the scope of his involvement in terrorism. *Jesus*, Brad—*terrorism*! Out-and-out terrorism?"

"We knew of his involvement, Mr. President. You find terrorism appalling when our own government has employed counterterrorism for decades?" Impatient, he wagged a reprimanding finger at his host. "We've washed this dirty laundry a dozen times. We are in crisis. Moufflon's accomplishments are overplayed by a bloodthirsty propaganda monster."

"Our advisors clearly indicate he is a viable threat—"

"To whom, Mr. President? To those who initiate the threat of nuclear war or those of us attempting to avert it?"

"Brad! Forces directed against me want me killed!"

"Then, let's sensibly examine the message they're sending you!" They locked eyes. The President, baffled, was struck by the cryptic words. "*If* they wanted you dead, sir, make no mistake, *you'd be dead!* I examined the sniper's nest, examined both the Dragunov rifle and empty shells, studied the trajectory angles. The sniper, either blind or incapacitated when he pulled the trigger, could have picked you off clean. He didn't. My guess? His orders were only to wing you."

"Your *guess?*" Macgregor's sparking blue eyes bore into Brad's.

"You've just had a glimpse of threatening dangers, first-hand.

461

The minute you overstep your role—'' Brad's logic irked the Chief.

"Is that so? *Is that so?*" The President uncharacteristically repeated the inane remark, Brad's words weighing heavily on him. He flashed on the electronic counter on the drum table, lowered his head, placed one hand on the bulging files alongside the detector and said tightly, "It's time to rid ourselves of the nightmares, General. I trusted your judgment, opposed my most violent antagonists. My reward: two empty bullet casings mounted on a bronze plaque for posterity. You suspect there'll be more?"

Brad hunched over in his chair, one elbow on his right knee, his left hand braced against his left thigh. "You ain't seen nothing yet, Mr. President."

Silence, underscored by the sudden intake of breath, and a groan as Macgregor shifted uncomfortably in his chair.

Outside, snow was falling. The windowpanes edged with lacy touches of glazed frost enhanced the homespun comfort surrounding them. The President spoke quietly "What Moufflon has said *would* happen, *has* happened. It makes a believer of me, Brad. But to have orchestrated the terrorism?—Why am I incapable of hurdling that fact? My God—*terrorism!*"

Brad postured as a professor to a recalcitrant student who persists in illogical pursuits. "I put it to you, sir, Moufflon is the power behind a significant resurgence in what today is labeled *modern-day terrorism,* and what was glorified in World War II as *Resistance* fighters, *Freedom* Fighters, the *Underground, Partisani, guerillas!* Any man forced to resist tyrannical rule by men who dictate their extinction have no recourse but to join the side of terrorism!" Brad stopped. He shook his head in annoyance. "The issue is not terrorism. The issue at stake is the constant pressures—the *indirect* terrorism afflicting *our* nation which Moufflon outlined. He detailed the pattern, sir. The *voices* are attempting to discredit America by demonstrating it cannot properly protect its people or property and cannot maintain law and order.''

"In setting up the Maui Summit we have only succeeded in arming our enemies with enough ammunition to blow us off the map!" The President exaggerated the issue in his attempt to explain his dilemma. "We've sparked bitter controversy among our fans and detractors. Enemies are having a field day. They call me inept, easily deluded, the worst advised primate in

462

captivity. You realize, Brad, that getting shot took the heat off the Oval Office these past several days.''

"What's that, Mr. President?" The scenario lit up, illuminating it clearly, erasing the worry lines from his brow.

The President repeated himself with proper indignation. ''I don't find the humor in my words . . .''

How could Brad tell John Macgregor he saw the fine work of Moufflon behind the recent assassination attempt. *How?* The act, done to evoke world sympathy, *had* succeeded in taking the heat off the Oval Office! Hot damn! No global propaganda machine could countermand such an exquisitely designed press! A *corsage of genius pinned on Moufflon for devising the brilliant tactic!*

''Sir, may I suggest the time might be appropriate for you and the First Lady to spend a weekend together at Camp David with Senator and Mrs. Lansing?''

The temerity of Brad's unexpected suggestion caused the President's jaw to fall slack in astonishment. ''The assassination attempt isn't enough, you want me boiled in oil?'' he whispered aghast. ''This messy Moufflon affair, the echo of impeachment hanging over me. . . ? You're crazy as hell! They warned me, General. All my advisors warned me! Do you know what would happen if I played host to Senator Lansing?'' He was outraged, and totally baffled.

''I had *Mrs. Lansing* in mind. You see, she knows—''

''After the Senator's scandalous affair? It would be political suicide for me . . .'' He stopped aghast at the suggestion.

Brad shrugged noncommittally. ''I suggest that Mrs. Lansing might explain Moufflon to you on a more confidential level.''

''She *knows* him that well?'' He bit his underlip. ''Why don't you tell me?''

''I don't know what she knows.''

''He's that good?''

''Yes, sir. *That* good. His organization is without peer.''

''You've already left me wide open to the ridicule of advisors after this Maui conference. I believe you know more than you're telling me.''

''Let me, if I may, encapsule it for you. Moufflon's services are in high demand. His interest lies in man's right to rebel against tyranny. Because he knows how one tyranny can easily be replaced with another, he is extremely prudent in weighing those nations of people who plead desperate causes before him.

463

Causes are scrutinized to ascertain if suffering from tyrannical rule is evident. *Invisible* scouts, dispatched at once to troubled areas, study the existent realities. If no escape is afforded the suffering except through revolt and insurgency, qualified men begin to train guerilla fighters. He adds troops from other areas to see them through a job well done. Compressed into one sentence, I'd say his life is dedicated to the furtherance of human rights *against* tyranny.''

"You dare deify a man who has trafficked in drugs? Involved himself in heinous crimes against humanity?"

Brad controlled himself admirably. Cliches came to mind, about *those who are free from sin casting the first stone*, but he desisted. Rather, Brad donned his glasses, removed a manila file from his briefcase, handed it to the Chief. Macgregor pulled his glasses from his jacket pocket and with one hand set them into place. He scanned the contents. "What's this—a list of Who's Who?" His eyes sped rapidly down the list of names.

"In a way, yes. You blasted Moufflon for trafficking in drugs. In post-World War II, who didn't?"

Transfixed by the list of names, the President glanced up startled. "General, you can't mean—"

"Precisely. American, European, Middle Eastern moguls, tycoons, financiers, corporate wizards, international industrialists—the list is endless—engaged in trafficking dope then, and are still engaged in a staggeringly high profit-making business."

"General! These names—some are our most respected families!"

"None are conscience-stricken amateurs. Don't you recall the *Dope-Diamond-Dollar* syndrome I reported last year on my return from the Moufflon mission? . . . ''

Macgregor repeatedly glanced from file to Brad, while Brad continued the briefing.

"The day the last official Nazi uniform was burned, buried or hidden by its last wearer, whoever he was, and the Allies put to death that phenomenon known as the Third Reich, tens of thousands of men vanished into the corridors of organized crime under various disguises and into docile-sounding organizations. They spread to protected sanctuaries, sprang up quietly, their lines of communication, finance and mother organization, intact.

"Those names you have difficulty in reconciling with organized crime, the power behind Hitler, power behind Mussolini, and every supreme egotist in power today, heads of numerous

464

international corporations and Trade Marts, have conduited billions of dollars to safety. Whether you like it or not, Mr. President, the drive for the almighty dollar is a measure of the times in which we live, the measure of greed permeating the globe. The devil has been a busy man these past forty years.''

"Brad! This man—this one!" He pounded the list in his hand. "By thunder, he was a former Secretary of State!"

"Does that make him less susceptible to crime than the average man, Mr. President? Study the path of the Golden Crescent and you'll find master manipulators industriously at work, winding up the *front* men. Those *respectable* honorable members of praiseworthy, righteous organizations, can't hide the bloodstains of their iniquity behind pastoral robes or that most sacred trust— public office.''

The President paled. His features were sharp and angular from his recent weight loss. The slimness of his frame as he dropped his glasses and rubbed his eyes accentuated his shocked reaction. "General! What have you set me loose upon? I shall never be able to look at these men again without seeing their names emblazoned on this list! What do you want from me? What more can I do?''

Brad padded to the window, staring out at the winter scene. Snow flurries thickened outside. "When I see snow, I am reminded that my journey began a year ago. Working against a timetable, I pushed, shoved, manipulated humans and dead men, death itself, to accumulate and lay the stats before you, Mr. President. A prodigious desire to give up attacked me frequently, but I did *my* duty as I've always done, even though at times I felt I was doing the devil's work.''

The passionate outburst shook John Macgregor. He stared at the General in a long, drawn-out silence. Brad lifted his chin defiantly with a stubborn lilt characteristic of him when pushed to the wall. The silence underscored the determination in each to either come to terms or terminate the discussion. The President dropped the file, making no effort to retrieve it. He glanced into the fire, staring at some internal scene of damnation, as if he were wrestling his soul.

"What would you have me do?" he finally asked.

"Consider the Camp David weekend with Mrs. Lansing. You must manage it, sir. Get her away by herself. I promise you'll know everything. Perhaps the First Lady might agree to entertain

465

the Senator, for propriety's sake. I understand they are both chess enthusiasts.''

"How long do you suggest I ask Mrs. Macgregor to entertain that scoundrel?''

"The entire weekend. More, if need be.''

Goddammit, Brad, you're paving the way for a divorce. I swear you're out to ruin me!'' The President's flair for showmanship had returned.

He was good! He had a way of rebounding in an often amusing fashion from the most precarious circumstances, thought Brad. Today, however, the usual twinkle accompanying humor was absent.

"No one knows Moufflon better than Valentina Lansing, Mr. President. Theirs was a long-lasting, passionate love affair—''

The President shot him a sharp, seething look, clenched jaws and jerking features. "You know everything, don't you?'' .

"If I did, I wouldn't be suggesting you meet with Mrs. Lansing. Oh, yes, remember,'' he added with exactitude in the recollection of long-past events, "Prince Youseff Ben Kassir, has known him for most of his life. Don't hold off on Mrs. Lansing for long, Mr. President.''

Chapter Thirty-One

MUNICH, GERMANY

MUNICH, AN OLD INDUSTRIAL CITY of many contrasts, bombed out during World War II and rebuilt with high-rise apartments and modern buildings, possessed its own special heartbeats; it was still the center of culture and of spies, intrigues and black deeds.

Herr Velden Zryden and his *Frau*, Marlena Zryden, were celebrating a successful ten-year marriage, three wonderful, robust children, and a long-sought prosperity in the growth of their business, the Zryden Toy Company. Velden's parents, both professors at the Bavarian Academy of Fine Arts in Munich, died when he was thirty-five. A prodigy, an *expected* prodigy from two such brilliant parents, Velden was not. Such dreams had long since faded into the reality that his mental capabilities would never mature beyond that of a sixteen-year-old. But for Velden, there was little of consequence to trouble him. God had endowed him with a special talent. He created dolls—not ordinary dolls, but figures of such exquisite perfection, his work was sought after by private collectors. He married Marlena in 1972, a talented accountant, a financial wizard smart enough to parlay Velden's God-given talents and *her* business acumen into a successful toy factory. Velden was hailed as the *Pied Piper of Munich*.

All of Munich recognized Marlena as the brains behind the business. "But, never mind, *liebchen*," she soothed Velden, when unthinking drinking companions flung unkind remarks at him. "Of what use would my brains be without the talent of your creation? Yours is the work of God, Velden—my work, merely a by-product."

So, on this blustery winter day, Velden, the toymaker, left the factory and went to the Mercedes showroom and bought for his wife, the financial genius, a sleek new automobile, a luxury car with every extra imaginable. *And why not?* Didn't she deserve such elegance after such hard work?

The day was cold, overcast, the weather indecisive, unable to decide if it should snow or rain. It compensated the deficiency by doing both. The children, bundled warmly in the new car with their parents, screamed with delight, for it must be driven, tested, appreciated, despite the ugly weather.

Marlena detested the soot-stained snow. "It's no longer virgin snow," she complained, settling in the front seat next to Velden, sniffing the new leather interior, examining all gadgets. "The snow resembles a dirty, used-up old whore!" she lamented, glancing at the slush forming on the windshield. Her husband admonished her for speaking so boldly before the children. In the rear seat, chattering gaily, writing their names on the quickly steaming windows, the children ignored grown-up talk.

Velden started up the motor, listening to the fine purring sounds, with a mysterious appreciation Marlena never could

467

understand. As he pulled out of the driveway, backed up and turned the wheel easing them along the crowded street, Marlena retreated into the overcrowded corridors of thoughts. Indeed, she had more to do on this day, birthday or not, than ride through the *Maximilianplatz Strasse* or view the *Englischer Garten* just to please her childlike spouse. The new doll collection due in two weeks was incomplete. The Handicraft Arts Festival, the only viable market for their goods, was *two week* away! And that incredible Velden! That genius had outdone himself with the new collection he named the *Marlena* Dolls. Dolls from every nation, so real and exquisitely formed, demanded authentic costumes. And this was the bottleneck! Working the women to sew these costumes to perfection had caused delays.

They rode in silence for several blocks. Velden winked at his wife, turned on the Telefunken stereo. "Imagine, *four* speakers, *liebchen*?" he marveled, bursting with pride. The rain fell like shell bursts of white fire in the gleam of headlights, alternating with mushy clumps of dirty snow splattering across the windshield, melting in ripples as the metronome-synched wipers swept them grandly to one side. Velden drove with such fierce pride, one hand on the wheel, the other uplifted like a virtuoso conducting the splendid symphony orchestra. Neither Velden or Marlena saw the traffic snarl up ahead as they drove along at dusk.

It struck like a thunderbolt. Screeching brakes, flashing, blinding lights—so many at once—caused Velden to avert his eyes. He slammed on the brakes. *Nothing!* He danced his foot on the brake pedal, harder—harder each time. Still nothing! Suddenly, there were screams, shouts, loud crashing sounds, metal crushing metal, human, blood-curdling screams of panic. Struck sideways by a large vehicle, the Mercedes spun into an uncontrollable skid.

The newspapers listed one survivor in the terrible crash that killed a mother and three children instantly. Velden Zryden, father and spouse, was in a coma in critical condition. Surgeons worked day and night to save the *Pied Piper of Munich*, for he had brought such happiness into the lives of small children. They stitched and sewed, carved and reshaped, trying to patch the poor man together. He remained on the critical list for a month— without visitors, in the ICU.

The family lawyer expedited funeral arrangements. Velden, unable to participate or view his family's remains, was dismissed from the hospital five weeks later, a changed man. Broken-hearted, heavy of spirit, he arrived dutifully each day at the toy factory. But he touched no toy, not even his precious *Marlena* Dolls. He sat for eight hours each day in his office, at his wife's desk—not his—hands clasped before him, staring straight ahead at nothing. His employees and friends mourned him.

They defended Velden's right to privacy. Most commiserated, "Why wouldn't he be a changed man? To suffer the loss of a beloved wife and children, catastrophic in itself, but to survive the ghastly accident and be hideously scarred as a living reminder of his folly? *Gott in Himmel!*"

Time to heal, time to cope, time to learn to live alone.

If his friends noted changes in his behavior and former habits, they refrained from speaking of them. Yet, wasn't it curious? . . . Velden, a former tea drinker, now sipped coffee with mint-flavored chocolate? Velden, a former beer guzzler, had lost his taste for lager and drank cognac instead. Sugar-glazed candy at his dish went ignored, and were replaced by Swiss chocolate mints.

On April 1, 1984, a buyer for the toy factory appeared on the scene. The sale of the business was consummated in a twinkling. Velden placed his house in the hands of real estate entrepreneurs and left Munich without bidding his friends so much as a fare thee well.

He arrived in West Berlin, rented an expensive townhouse in the American sector, and found a position in the office of the French Minister of Finance in the French Sector.

In the Ministry Office? Velden Zryden? If those closest to Velden had observed this miracle, how they would have marveled at this good fortune! For at some point between the tragic accident and his arrival in West Berlin, he had mastered an uncanny grasp for sums, mathematics and demonstrated a social flare.

The miracles continued to work. The angry red surgical scars on various sections of his face disappeared to produce a handsome countenance. His broken nose was reset. In time, a dental apparatus worn over his teeth was removed.

And such fine tailoring!

He resembled a British diplomat. The *old* Velden had to be prodded to buy a new suit at least once a year!

Within a month, Velden Zryden, a *cause célèbre* in West

Berlin circles, was introduced as a genius industrialist similar to those Washington dollar-a-year men who volunteer their expertise to resolve financial and economic problems in times of crisis. As financial institutions in various nations tottered precariously on the brink of disaster and government stability was shaken, Velden's expertise was in high demand.

Posturing about in this position of trust, Zryden gained access to *highly classified* files, *verboten* to outsiders. He grew increasingly involved in solving financial dilemmas, leaving little time to pursue personal interests.

Chapter Thirty-Two

"Woman creates the man, then devours him . . .
Corsican Proverb

BANDAR' ABBAS,
IRANIAN COASTLINE
PERSIAN GULF
April 1984

SEMIRAMIS, QUEEN OF ANCIENT ASSYRIA, architect of the world's Seventh Wonder, the Hanging Gardens of Babylon, had undergone a recent reincarnation, if in name only. Semiramis, a *cover* name given a real princess, was the daughter of a fallen Middle Eastern king whose vast wealth and sovereignty became so threatening to a covey of powerful financial entrepreneurs that he was toppled by them and died under mysterious circumstances.

"Death is the only insurance against a man who knows too much," Semiramis sighed. "*Mon Dieu*! How repetitious of late, *oui, cher*?"

They stood at the balcony of the deserted Royal Palace, a summer retreat, haunted by specters of the past. "Ah—the Island of Kish, at the mouth of the world's richest oil uterus—the

Persian Gulf. It brings back painful memories." Her dark, luminous eyes fanned over the intoxicating sweep of cerulean waters washing up on Iranian shores. Behind them, across the channel on the mainland, outlined against a hot sky, stood the ancient, bleached concrete fishing village of Bandar' Abbas, bathed in a glowing pink wash of sunset, to the west, the City of Lingeh. South of Kish, beyond the Strait of Hormuz, the Gulf of Oman spread farther into the ocean.

"How many are there? Eight—nine—ten nations bordering this womb of the earth? We are so close, we could reach out and touch the other." Semiramis sighed again, and turning to the lean, tanned Corsican, smiled wistfully. "Yet, the remaining animosities between Persians and Arabs seem irreconcilable."

Behind them, blinding lights of an orange-marmalade sun slipping below the western horizon fired the sea and sky above into a galaxy of glowing color. The hot sea breezes ruffled her long silky jet hair. A sheer golden caftan clung to her moist, sun-bronzed body, breasts bursting alive through wispy golden threads, her body deliciously outlined. She spoke animatedly, sweeping graceful, jeweled hands horizontally to punctuate her words and feelings.

"Look, Darius, how the island, shaped like a humpback whale, rises from the sea, a virtual paradise. Once a mecca for the super-rich, look, now—it's a ghost town of plundered hotels, casinos and shops infested by rats—both rodent and the human variety."

"The venom still infects you, Semiramis?" He spoke softly in French.

"Praise Allah! Let it be always so!" Anthracite eyes fired by an unbearably bright twilight rising from the ashes of a dying day. "They will pay for the atrocities done to my father, my family, to me! They shall pay in like coin—with their lives. For it is written, an eye for an eye—"

"It is also written to forgive is divine."

"*To forgive is divine!*" she parroted. "From *you*, Darius?" She laughed mockingly.

Darius' eyes glittered, but he didn't reply a few weeks ago, when Youseff came to him with the news of Berna's assassination, Darius had vowed a revenge that would show no mercy. But spiraling world events prevented him from launching a personal vendetta. He controlled himself and spoke quietly.

"Your deepest regret, Princess, is you weren't born a man."

471

"You *infer* I lack seduction?"

"*Au contraire, chere.* You possess enough for a dozen women. Simply put, you would prefer pursuing goals with less restriction, with opportunities more available to the male of the species."

"It is true. I fight to control dominating urges. Although silence and a seductive walk delivers private messages capable of mesmerizing most men. I use the tools of my trade well, Darius, thanks to your expertise in instruction."

Darius laughed good-naturedly. He laid her head on his bare shoulder, stroking her face, lifting wisps of hair clinging to her flushed, moist cheeks. "Your tongue is a beguiling tool. You flatter and praise a bit much, *chere*. You are perceptive beyond human explanation. I dare say, a bit spooky, as the Americans say. You read my mind like a human x-ray machine, a disturbing fact to me. It makes you vital to our work. Oh, Semiramis, you *are* overbearing, domineering, overly sarcastic and frigid. Yet you can turn hot as an oven at 500 degrees Fahrenheit! Inherited tendencies from your father?"

"Yes!" she snapped, moving away from him. "And proud of it. You know so much. Then you *know* I hate with bitter venom and love just as fiercely. I can claw like a tiger, scream and shriek like a banshee—or purr like a baby kitten."

He laughed at her drama. "What an incredible woman you are," he said, softly, pulling her back into his arms. "From the first time we met, you disconcerted me with your peculiar form of black magic—a witchcraft of sorts. It was startling to see it in work. Let me see, how do I describe it? You overwork a mystical sixth sense. You do! Then, instantly, you transfer that perception and I find I must submit to one of two reactions: fall hopelessly under your spell or run the hell the other way."

Semiramis' laughter filled the early twilight, then she changed tack. "Look, Darius, look around you. Kish is no longer the paradise envisioned by its former leader." Her voice softened. "He envisaged the island as an integration of Western and Middle Eastern cultures." She leaned over the balustrade, gazing dismally into the oppressive silence, her breasts bursting through gossamer threads. "English turf was flown in for the race track, French hostelries, even American television sets were imported for the hotels. Israeli factories, built for the desalinization of water, already under way . . . Oh, what plans he envisioned! Look, there—a casino. Nearby, down here, numerous Parisian boutiques constructed all along the ghostly mall.'' She straightened her body, pointing below.

''—and now this island paradise stands deserted, unattended. What has it all to do with you, Semiramis? Besides housing the guerillas?''

She continued, ignoring his impatience. ''Rats and soldiers invade the hotel rooms, stripped of furniture, all of it stolen or defiled. Bathrooms were torn apart, doors broken, master art works looted, along with the television sets. Why, Darius? Why does revolution leave such brutal scars? It is a place of the walking dead, housing for specters and filthy ragtag soldiers. It's true. We pay them to hide away here in the palace. We come and go at will until we overthrow the madman!'' She lit a hash cigarette and inhaled deeply, slowly exhaling.

A chained passion, rigidly controlled and poised with a surface smoothness suggesting black velvet, seeped from her. Her voice an extension of that velvet. ''May I put it to you, *mon cher*, that a worldwide conspiracy exists, determined to keep all the Middle East backwards. The future is up for grabs because generations of our people have failed to see the signs. Other nations covet us, wish to destroy us, remove our presence from our lands. Once we reigned supreme. Here, once, existed the cradle of civilization. Our progress diminishes daily because the Zeller network killed my father and wishes to wipe away all traces of our progress. They covet our oil, Darius, but I put it to you, they covet far more. A timetable is at work. The destabilization of the Middle East is the first step in controlling the Golden Crescent!''

Darius did not move. He neither objected by gesture or voice. He wanted her to continue, hesitated to urge her, concerned she might bolt. For Semiramis only blacks and whites existed—no planes of gray in between. It was love or hate. Either a firm yes, or an adamant no, *never* a perhaps. She was uncontestedly superior to any woman in the Moufflon network, save one, Berna.

Semiramis took Darius's hand in hers, led him inside the marbled walls of the King's bedchamber, toward the oversized bed fitted with gold satin bed sheets. She flipped on a battery-operated stereo. Instantly music—soft, mood music—filled the room. She passed him a plate of Iranian caviar, poured Dom Perignon in crystal glasses. Nearby a hot tub set into the floor of polished mosaic tile filled with swirling perfumed steamy waters arose in misty wisps of fog. She poured bath salts into the tub

473

and called to Darius softly. "For you I perform miracles, *mon cher*. Come, together we shall create momentary paradise. Let us harness these moments, take our pleasures, however brief, if only to forget the manmade terrors. Such moments are rare, *cher*."

The dim spectral glow of a purple-hued twilight thrust itself through latticed windows, casting arabesque shadows on the tile floor. She shrugged free of the caftan; it fell to the floor in a heap of shimmering gold silk. She stepped free of it, her satiny bronzed body curved softly in the flattering hues of lights. Everywhere around her, vases and urns overwhelmed with freshly cut roses, running the color spectrum from the palest ivory to a blood crimson. If she could, Semiramis would wallow in roses, her floral passion.

Darius's compelling viridian eyes held on her, his passions aroused by the subtle scent of musk and honey. He held out his hand to her. She moved slowly, swaying to the music. Long slender jewelled fingers reached out to him, fluttering like sensors, trembling at his projected magnetism. "Look at me, Semiramis. Don't turn from me. Look into my eyes." He stroked her cheek tenderly.

Darius stood naked before her. They had made love several times earlier. Both sensed this might be their last time together. "In you exists a delicate aura of tranquillity spiced with mystery," he whispered. Semiramis yielded at once. Suspended from a gold chain around her neck was a gold disc, at its center: Moufflon, the horns studded with diamonds. Presently the amulet was animated by the heaving of breasts, her furiously pounding heart.

Darius leaned over, nuzzled her neck, feeling the firm moist flesh under his skillful hands. Locked in embrace, they melted into one another, his arms tight, secure about her, comforting her, loving with increased passion, returning kiss for kiss. The throbbing of his erection against her body, the scintillating, exquisite feeling of skin against skin, aroused her sensuality. She trembled violently against him, unleashing inside her a desperate attempt at the impossible—a fusing together of two souls for all eternity.

Darius grasped her thick shock of black hair firmly, slowly tilting back her head. He kissed the curve of her neck, working up to her ears, lips, eyes. Hands touched hands, fingers explored, searching, probed, groped delicately, yet passionately.

The touch and feel of hot flesh against cool, cool against hot, irresistibly shocked the senses. Darius's lips sealed over hers. He swept her off the floor, laid her gently on the bed and lying beside her, caressed her body, smoothing the wispy black strands off her face. He stared interminably into those luminous eyes, black suns in the darkness, felt her shudder under the soul-stirring *Karezza*, peaking orgasmically until every nerve end was on fire. She begged, demanded, insisted on full seduction, reached hungrily for him, and pressing him back on the pillows, slithered down his firm, muscular body, manipulating him with articulate fingers, devoured him with hot moist lips.

Darius cupped her firm breasts, noting their swelling, the hard erection of the nipples quivering under his manipulations. Devouring them with tender ferocity, he relished in the outpouring of new heights and sensations.

Always in control, Darius deliberately held back objective reserve. A third eye constantly at work, he observed her in the candlelight of flickering shadows in the rose-scented room. Instinctively attuned, he listened for unnatural noises, sudden movements, anything to threaten their safety. He observed her performance, involvement, the effect jolting him, every movement, precise, smacked of professionalism. Darius frowned. *Why not?* Why wouldn't she react like a professional? Her involvement the past five years. . . .

All thoughts stopped. Responding fully to her erotic strokings, Darius took over. Together they soared, higher . . . higher . . . higher in the heavens, coming together like interconnecting psychic comets swirling to dizzying heights. Stars exploded! Thousands of stars. . . .

In the aftermath, sounds from a distance, coming closer, growing more audible, penetrated their senses: waves slapping on the shore, ship bells in the channel, foghorns in the gulf, the squawking, honking cries of flamingos in courtship rites along the water's edge, the incessant braying of pesty camels foraging for food.

Semiramis pulled herself into a sitting position, noting the time on the watch placed on the night table. She lighted a hashish cigarette, sucked on it, savoring it, poured the remaining Dom Perignon from the bottle near her. Her dark eyes held on Darius's muscular body, one hand stroked his head tenderly, until he stirred awake. She stared down at him, expelling a deep sigh. She had loved Darius the moment he stepped inside her hospital room five years ago, in Tripoli. Darius glanced at his watch. It was time to talk.

"Word is you're a dead man, Darius. Reassure me . . . tell me the rumors are wrong. Propaganda machines crank out manufactured misinformation about you. Every assassin worth his salt—including the best of the Red Brigades—aims to kill you. *Merde!* You know them—all of them. How will you stop what has already begun? They tighten screws to make them cough you up."

Darius accepted the champagne thrust at him, sipped it to wet his dry lips. "I care for you, Semiramis. I won't conceal my feelings. We both know the score—what we are fighting for. Global events fail to impress me. Each political chess move signifies increasing danger. What happens *here* in this infernal uterus of a never-ending oil supply concerns me gravely. *The Middle East is the key*. I need truth—not rumors, not heresay, not biblical legends, but pure truth unobstructed by fancy political rhetoric, hot air and smoke screens."

She sobered. "The eyes of justice are blind, *cher*!"

"Then we shall make her see!"

"Hah! Es *très dificile, bien âme*."

"The crisis here will not end until control is Zeller's. Beyond the oil is the Golden Crescent, capable of keeping *snow* over Beruit the year around."

Darius cut her a sharp glance, noting the curious illumination in her *knowing* eyes.

"You know what's at stake? Billions of dollars, *ma chere*. The bonanza is far richer than the controlled oil supply. The high costs of oil technology forces many nations to abandon it for higher profits and lower overhead—the fringe benefits of the opium poppies. The tentacles of the Golden Crescent spread from Pakistan and Afghanistan through Iran, Turkey, Lebanon, into Egypt, Europe and the West. It's the 3-D syndrome. *Dope-Diamonds-Dollars*. Dirty money laundered by the biggest names in the corporate world! Why do you think the contract on you doubled? Five million dollars American, *ma biene âme*."

"That's all?" His green eyes twinkled in amusement.

"You find it humorous? Even I might be tempted to kill you for such a sum. You realize what five million can buy?"

"If you live long enough to collect—yes. A helluva lot." Darius drew her close to him, an arm about her shoulders. She laid her cool face against his heart. "Why don't you, Semiramis? It would resolve both our problems."

She pulled away abruptly, tensing, eyes sparking dangerously.

"*Qu'est-ce que c'est?* And give *him* the satisfaction of victory? Never! Never!"

Now, Darius . . . now. This is the moment of truth!

"I came here to learn the truth. Is it true that the United States, Britain, and Israel are preparing to subdue by force, wipe out the entire Arab population? Alter the shape of the world and winnow its inhabitants?—via genocide?"

Her features blanched, lips parted, hung agape in astonishment. She reprogrammed her mind to accommodate herself to his words. "Then it's true? . . . So . . . That's it! . . . All these clandestine sessions, this summit meeting in Bandar' Abbas among camel dung and burro bums?" Semiramis gestured with sudden enlightenment. She walked the short distance to the hot tub, submerged herself, laving luxuriously, contemplatively. Darius followed her. He did not have to wait long for the information he wanted.

"Tonight you will hear the truth from Anthony Harding's vile lips. According to our intelligence sources—and for the purpose of understanding Harding's activities in relation to the countless murders and assassinations of world leaders—underscore the fact that Harding and his strategy are not to be identified with the United States and its policy. Harding, the Queen Bee, lords it over the drones and worker bees. *Comprenez?* He is Zeller's direct link. Harding implemented, at the outset of his power, a foreign policy aimed at bringing about the triumph of the strategic interests of *special* power groups within Zeller's network, including the British. Harding is known in certain circles for his capacity to turn the threats he proffers into action.

"He murdered my father, a man dedicated to his country, whose government was overturned by a coup d'etat in 1979. On Anthony Harding's orders my father was systematically injected over a period of four months—that's all it took the live cancer bacteria to breed inside him. Shuttled back and forth to foreign countries, he died in a strange land without the proper rites deserving a king. Not satisfied, Harding turned a madman loose in our lands, armed the army and destroyed every ounce of modernization brought to my nation. My five brothers were abducted, found in Europe in hiding, imprisoned, and summarily disposed of in torture. Anthony Harding killed my family as surely as if he personally wielded the *coup de grâce*. The orders came from Zeller. Naturally, all witnesses have disappeared!"

"*Naturally*. Zeller covers all flanks! Does Harding—has he an inkling of your true identity, Semiramis? The man is not without his spies."

"No. I've seen no hint."

Darius, disturbed by something nagging at him, asked, "Are you tempted—do you still feel affinity to the opium poppy?"

"To deny the insatiable craving would be a lie. I fight the temptation, praise Allah, every moment of every day."

Silent pandemonium ran amuck in Darius's mind. He re-opened the wound.

"Does Harding know your true identity?"

"No! No, how could he?"

"The same way I found out."

"No! . . . I tell you, no. In five years—no sign. I would know."

"Your remarkable nonchalance projects indomitable strength. If proven wrong, are you prepared to pay for the mistake in hard currency?"

"In five years have I instilled you with doubt?"

"Harding possesses *no* knowledge of the king's first marriage?" Warnings flashed in his mind. He probed. "Why do you protest so adamantly in this?"

"Because we discussed it." She slid languorously about the tub.

"You *what?*"

She smiled playfully, skimming the water's surface lazily with her hands. "Most men steeped in power are not of your genre, Darius. Harding is a pig. Drug-crazed . . . maniacal. A beast possessed with more sexual proclivities than any conspired by the Marquis de Sade. Harding boasts. I listen. At times, he frightens me, proves brutal beyond my comprehension. Yet, I willingly become a player in his sadistic game of political roulette, aware of the odds. The chances of coming out clean or alive are minimal." She slipped her champagne, glanced at the chronometer on the edge of the hot tub. "I do not evade your question, *cher*. Harding told me, when I asked, that the king's harem was liquidated in the schematics of westernizing our nation. The king, he insisted, gave the order. But he lied. *Agency* men finished them off so no pretender to the de facto throne could threaten it—save one, the future son of my father's new bride." She soaped herself. "When the *madman* completes the prescribed genocide in this bloody Holy War—they will move in against him, with Prince Persi fully programmed to move on their command. First, a *coup*, and *voilà*! My half-brother will be king *and* puppet.''

''Yet, your five brothers were gunned down and killed?'' Darius shook his head, unconvinced.

''Because they held positions of trust in the countless foreign business enterprises my father controlled and *neglected* to tell Harding.'' She stopped talking, appraised him insolently. ''You don't believe me.''

''In our business we disregard nothing. The facts don't add up. If your father's business interests were on a covert level, how did Harding find out?''

''How do I know? Harding's moles are everywhere—''

''Precisely. Everything has a purpose, even that which is hidden from the naked eye.''

In the lengthening silence, Semiramis stared at him, the glow of candles skipping ominously across the water's surface. ''Darius, my mother lacked royal blood, but she was my father's favorite. Long before those agency men inflicted the coup d'etat in my land, before the destruction of the king's harem, we were whisked away to Morocco. Later, the king remarried, named his firstborn of his bride legal heir to the throne. The king never abandoned us. Money was funneled to us to educate my brothers and me. In 1960 the king grew disturbingly aware of subversive machinations. He strengthened international relations with the Soviets. My father, no puppet, eventually was pressured by America to recognize the Zionist state of Israel. History has well-documented the rest. Chaos, bedlam, insurrection, as Arab nationalists marshalled forces against him. Despite the adversity, the king resisted, grew independently powerful, invested wisely in banking empires run by my brothers. And then . . . his world exploded. The rude, jarring awakening came. Our lives were irrevocably changed. From out of the stinking sewers of Paris, invisible power brokers resurrected a *madman* whom they armed, supplied with weapons and enormous power to overthrow my father's regime and created dissensions. Blood flowed in the streets. The loathing I once bore my father for keeping us hidden from world recognition took a different direction—it multiplied against his enemies. They destroyed my father's dream! His nation, his people, reduced to shambles by drug-crazed lunatics! A planned insurrection,

Darius, by Agency men, dreamed up by Anthony Harding acting under the directives of Zurich and his henchmen of international financiers." Semiramis spat with scorching contempt. "My father's time is over—mine is about to begin!"

"Your history is burned in my mind. Pray Harding is ignorant of it," Darius cautioned, not unreasonably.

The loud honking shrieks of mating flamingos below in the lagoon pierced the silence. Semiramis leaned over, retrieved a candle burning in a glass chimney, thrusting it at Darius. "Hold this," she ordered crisply, and turning her back on him, stepped up and leaned over. "The scars on my lower back . . . further down." She reached behind her, feeling the ugly keloidal scarring.

"What you see is the result of one *special* night of bestiality in the life of Anthony Harding. On his orders, fifteen men mounted me, ripped me open." She turned around, facing him. " 'Fuck the whore! . . . Fuck the whore! . . . Do what you will to her!' Not one of those perverse animals dared disobey their master. They took their pleasure in ways not yet invented." She shuddered, chills racing through her despite the warm water and the heat of the night. "Naturally, I survived. When was it?—a year ago? Yes, about then. I wrote a diary of *what* occurred, *who* was present and upon *whose* command the depraved debauchery was done to me. Twelve of the fifteen sexual deviates are well-known world luminaries, Darius. *Swine! . . . Whoremasters!* The diary and copies were placed in safety deposit vaults in France. Another is in Corsica, in the vault. If *something . . . anything* untoward happens to me, Harding knows the consequences. For strange and appalling reasons the contents of those diaries are far more damaging to Harding than an expose naming him as my father's murderer. So much for human values." She spat scathingly.

Darius controlled his rage, replaced the candle in its niche. He held Semiramis in his arms, comfortingly. Her tears spilled freely, then quickly she composed herself, seemingly embarrassed by her emotional display. This debauchery was not news to Darius. The craven incident had been reported within twenty-four hours. Then, as now, the cold, calculated hatred he felt for Anthony Harding and Zeller was incalculable.

Semiramis poured the last of the champagne. Darius shook his head, astonished at her recuperative powers.

"I dislike redundancy, Semiramis. But they *killed* five of your brothers and *fail* to know of *your* existence? I don't buy it."

"My mother, with the willing participation of a loyal servant, spirited me away to Paris, placed me in a covent, then killed the servant and herself. She left a note identifying them as wife and daughter of King Isfahan."

"I repeat, Semiramis, I *know* your history. Pray Harding does not."

"If he suspected it, in five years I would have learned, somehow. Just as I've learned Zeller owns Harding. One word from him and the United States crumbles. For years, Harding navigated it on a destabilization course. Americans don't seem to care—do they?"

"Does Zeller pay the rent on the Oval Office?"

Semiramis's black onyx eyes darted to his, wordlessly. Outside, the moonless night had converted to indigo. Gulls squawked, screeched rancorously. Distant sounds clashed—pelicans, flamingos, braying camels—thickened the night.

Darius asked again. "Your mind is no *tabula rosa*. Does Zeller own John Macgregor?"

"Isn't it obvious?" Her eyes reflected a primordial fear.

"I need cold, hard facts." Subtle ambiguities moving into danger areas irritated and transmitted treachery.

Semiramis, like a water nymph, lifted herself from the steamy tub, reached for a towel, and tossed one to Darius following closely behind. She toweled herself briskly, spoke economically.

"Macgregor is a marionette. He moves at the will and direction of another. Or do you prefer the simile of a wind-up toy who moves under battery power? Or a robot—".

She was dressing now, scoffing at the antics of the superpowers. "What a pair! The United States and the Soviet Union. They eye each other like heavyweights in the ring, testing each other after each punch. It's all a farce—a ridiculous farce! They bleed taxpayers to pay for war games."

She applied no cologne or scented emulsions. Lessons learned long ago taught her the dangers of an aroma. A perfume traceable to its owner at the wrong time in the wrong place spelled death. She pulled on a pair of faded blue jeans, a blue denim shirt stripped of all labels, and buttoned it halfway, her breasts temptingly visible.

"You are holding back, Semiramis. What is it you are not telling me?"

"It shows?"

"It shows."

"The Golden Crescent. I repeat, the *Golden Crescent!*"

Darius, in khaki trousers and shirt, tucking in the tails, paused, his gaze riveted on her. "Harding is implicated in dope dealing?" *So far, excellent.*

"You want my professional opinion or my womanly intuition?"

"Both. I trust one equally as I trust the other."

"Good old Darius. You never disappoint me." She reached up, brushing his lips with hers. Her manner at once brusque, efficient. "Professionally, he appears clean. He surrounds himself, *covertly,* of course, with the biggest dealers. No public or social contact with them. Intuitively, he's tainted. Dirty as hell! He orchestrates the laundering of dirty money behind the scenes. And to answer the next question forming behind those magnetic eyes, the laundering follows the same route you've known for the past two decades, with a few more stopovers in Beirut."

"*Touché.*" Darius smiled. She knew when to avoid using names. "You're certain of all you've imparted to me? It bears no hint of misinformation doled out to you?"

"Unless he is on to our network—and I doubt it. Unless he has a full make on me—and I doubt it. Harding tells me—in those brutal, sadistic, drug-crazed hours when I submit to his disgusting perversions and power-crazed megalomania—with whom he is connected and their intent to carve up the oil-rich regions in the Middle East. . . ." Semiramis stared off at something fomenting internally in her mind. She shook herself out of the mood, shuddering. "Oh, how my hate for that beast grows, cries out for vengeance!" She returned to the proper tack. "Due to his predilection for young men—oh, yes, that too, that above all—we planted a *special* agent in his midst who, given no insight into my testimony, verifies my assertions. He is a butcher, Darius. I have seen his artistry at work."

"Yes, he spares you? I've seen his debauchery and murder at work and I fear you may be falling prey to his sinister trappings."

"No. I have provided victims for Harding's sexual bestiality, low-lifes, men condemned to die in dungeons. Lately, though, Harding grows shaky. Rumors have it, Zeller is planning another coup—an internal coup—someone to replace him."

"*Victor . . . Victor Zeller.*" Darius offered up the name.

"My, my, you do amaze me. Far more, it disturbs Harding. A transferral of power to Victor Zeller means loss of revenue from the billions in drug trafficking networks set up from the Golden Crescent throughout the Middle East to Europe and America. . . ."

Come, Semiramis, tell it all. You know it as well as I.

The metamorphosis beguiled Darius. Gone was the ancient Assyrian queen, emerging was a modern potpourri of America, Paris and Rome—blue jeans, shirt, desert boots, jet hair piled atop her head, speared through with large hairpins, and dark wraparound glasses. The facade concealed the tragedy borne in her young lifetime, layered by a stout-hearted valor seldom found in women of her fabric. A bag, unmistakably Gucci, flung over her shoulder, housed a .9mm Browning automatic and shells. A sign of the times, Darius reflected.

She snuffed out the candles, took a last look around. "Come, *cher*, the boat awaits us. We are overdue in Bandar'Abbas."

Semiramis, daughter of a fallen Middle Eastern King murdered for his progressive Western alliances, remained an enigma to Darius. Defensive, guarded, rebellious to exasperation, a streak of fierce independence evident by the way she bridled indignantly at the slightest provocation. She had amateurishly grasped for grass straws plotting the revenge of her father's murderers. Joining the rebel forces of ragtag loyal remnants who had fought valiantly with her father against his enemies, her hopeless involvement with them had sufficiently demoralized her. Sweet forgetfulness and near-death came from the opium poppy—heroin. A four-year sentence, a crash course to death, nearly materialized via an overdose. Rehabilitation followed in an Algerian drug sanitorium, where her identity was revealed during intense detoxification deliriums. Her sub-conscious cries for help were relayed by courier to Prince Youseff Ben-Kassir and reached Moufflon in Corsica. Darius arrived, viewed her for a month before approaching her.

They dialogued. A protracted period of distrust ensued. Three months later, she acquiesced. Flown to Corsica, trained, reshaped, molded skillfully by Moufflon *specialists*, she had warmed to her new responsibilities. A display of superior intelligence, formidable objectivity, courage fired by desire, escalated her to a position of trusted confidante. Semiramis displayed unwavering patience—a requisite to anyone seeking vengeance against a sworn enemy—generated trust from her instructors, a trust conveyed to Moufflon. He bided his time until he *knew* she was ready.

*   *   *

The small craft approached the Iranian coastline. The sky was indigo, calm, midnight waters reflected no moon. Only the lights shining from shore danced on shimmering waters.

The skiff skimmed over the waters heading for the cover. At all sides of Kish high-powered spotlights from heavily armed patrol boats fanned the area as they knifed silently through the water. Menacing guns loomed in hulking silhouette, ready to fire on any trespassers. In the destabilized gulf, tempers were short, guns long and swift to seek a target.

"They prowl on patrol every quarter hour," Semiramis whispered to Darius. "It is imperative to reach the mainland in eleven—twelve hours at the most. If Kismet shines upon us . . ."

Kismet did. A dark sedan waiting on land at the cove's edge sped them through dark, dusty Bandar' Abbas streets so narrow the car's wheels rubbed against each broken curb. The dust-covered Mercedes sped circuitously, avoiding main streets to the outskirts, winding up corkscrewing roads past walls of squalid houses sweating with dampness, scorpion, fly and rat infestation.

"There—up on the hill!" Semiramis indicated.

The Moorish villa stood in silhouette, rambling at the crest of a hill barely visible from the road. The Mercedes swerved off the road, circled to the rear of the property, approaching stealthily. Heavily armed guards, indolently conversing with security police, smoked hash. A high electrically wired gate bordering the estate was manned by fierce-eyed sentries in lookout towers, carrying automatic carbines.

Shalamara, the driver, had switched off the headlights a quarter-mile earlier, and creeping through a grove of dwarf oaks took cover in a secluded brush of aromatic asefetida. She slipped out the car, flashed an infrared flashlight in signal. Two crouching guerillas crept forward from behind bushes, guns at the ready, employing matching semaphores. Heavily armed, alert as tigers on the prowl, they beckoned the newcomers forward.

Darius and Semiramis eased forward, cautiously alert to any unexpected sortie. They moved behind their guides along a narrow path to what appeared as a honeycombed grotto leading to underground conduits. Ten minutes later they began an exhaustive inclined ascent in a stifling, stench-filled dankness infested with rats and scorpions. The odious scents forced them to cover their noses with handkerchiefs and shirttails. A guide raised a halting hand before a heavy wooden and iron door, handtorches fanning the immediate area.

The guerillas eased up on a wooden crossbar, gently opened the door, admitting them to a dark, musty, spider-webbed wine cellar, and past cells that might have housed prisoners in the Dark Ages. Darius saw it instantly. His hand darted out, halting a guide. Semiramis nudged Darius, a finger held to her lips as one of the men, a skilled technician, dismantled the complex alarm system.

They crept up an iron spiral staircase to a minuscule landing, and crossed a treacherously narrow catwalk, forcing their bodies into twisting contortions between framework and wooden studs ending at a second-floor level. The interlopers were hidden from view to the gathering of celebrants below by lattice-worked panels.

From their positions they overlooked a gala in the grand mosaic-tiled salon with its golden archways and low sofas.

Sounds and scents of food, drink, hashish and opium vapors rose to their hideaway. Men talked, laughed, shouted above the oriental music accompanying the scantily clad, topless belly-dancing *houris* as they gyrated glistening oiled bodies to stimulating tempos of exotic drums. Clouds of potent hashish and cigar smoke clung cloyingly in the air. Dreamy-eyed men sucking *hookahs*, opium pipes, cocaine sniffers and other contrabrand, observed the dozen Messalinas peddle their wares.

A coterie of international, political luminaries relaxed on the low sofas, consuming caviar and champagne, ogling the quivering male and female flesh like children turned loose in a candy factory, while courtesans massaged and manipulated what erotic zones they wanted manipulated.

Darius snapped off the flashlight, felt for his Browning, his body flat against one wall, eyes peering obliquely through latticed openings. His expression was unreadable. He knew most of the partygoers. Financiers, industrial tycoons, highly placed politicians, military leaders, all men of international scope. From his safari jacket pocket he retrieved an infrared minicamera, took several photos, and shoved it back into his pocket.

Semiramis whispered: "There—you see? Anthony Harding in person. The Queen Bee and all his drones succoring to his needs. The man next to him is Sir *Alexander* York." Darius focused sharply on the younger man. "He's very handsome, *oui*? He is disturbingly connected with MI, but it is kept very hush-hush. Lord John York masterminded the Middle East scenario—under Zeller's clever and persuasive guidance, of course. The original plan is Zeller's. Somehow he permitted the plan to be born in Lord York's mind, thereby averting incrimination, should catastrophe follow."

"Then the rumors concerning experiments in Zurich are well founded?" Darius whispered. Semiramis hadn't heard him. Good. He understood far more than he confided in Semiramis. His eyes riveted on the slim man seated next to Harding. *Alexander* York, eh? *Very clever . . . What a clever coup if they pulled it off!*

"The one on Harding's right. Identify him, Semiramis."

"He is *not* what or who he appears to be."

"*Not who he appears to be?* Who, then?"

"You don't recognize the son of your enemy, *mon cher*? Wait until you peruse his manufactured dossier—it is a masterpiece."

Darius, primed by her words, stared, his eyes narrowing. He shook his head in disbelief. "You can't mean—"

"*Oui*! Victor Zeller in the flesh."

"The changes . . . *why* the disguise?" He committed the *new* Victor Zeller to memory.

"Wolf Spider followed him into the French Embassy in West Berlin. His contacts penetrated the cover. *How* and *why* the great lengths of the disguise are uncertain. But it is Victor Zeller. Fingerprints lifted from the Embassy sent to Wolf Spider confirmed it. You still harbor hatred and resentment for him over Sophia?"

"Hatred is a luxury I can ill afford. It clouds the thinking. French Embassy, eh? Cozy for him. Close to Clayallee 10 and the *Cat*."

Semiramis studied the shadowy play of arabasques on Darius's face, flushed with sudden astuteness. "Of course! To penetrate the Moufflon cover! *Oooohhhhlahlah!*" her eyes swam with mirth. "He does not *know* your real identity! Allah be praised. Then he does not know you are step—" Darius's hand flew over her lips, silencing her. He jerked his head, indicating the activity below in the salon.

Anthony Harding stood up, arms outstretched. The music stopped abruptly; dancing girls and musicians disappeared under a swirling perfumed cloud of sweat, bangles, beads and dope.

Doors closed behind them. Conspiratorial drones, drinks in hand, moved in closer to the Queen Bee, calculating eyes glinting unnaturally bright, held on Harding.

He spoke in French, acoustics in the cavernous room, poor at best, the words reaching Darius confirmed his worst suspicions.

"The string of prearranged coups, assassinations, including the continued destabilization of the Middle East began years ago. A year ago we moved in with renewed effort; escalation continues in earnest. Victory will be ours. Our goal—the eradication of Arab nations—and the Arabs!"

Deafening applause and boisterous shouts shook the rafters.

Darius glanced at his watch. He had what he needed. These were Harding's drones. Didn't they understand he would devour them as he had devoured others before him, the moment their servicing became obsolete. Darius touched Semiramis's arm, gesturing with his eyes that he was ready to depart.

"You've heard enough?"

"Enough to put the network in action." He held her arm. "You will return to Corsica with me. It's too dangerous for you to remain."

"No! She spun toward him, unbearably tense, eyes seething. "Not yet. See their faces. I, too, know them in all their ugliness. The furnace of my soul fires my loathing for them." she hissed.

"All the more reason for you to return . . ."

"No! There is a timetable! Violence escalates in various guises."

Darius led her through the narrow confines, Semiramis struggling against him. "Listen to me, Darius, you must listen," she insisted, controlling a rising hysteria. "Harding's covert meetings have set off subtle alarms in the highest circles. Once the overall timetable is known and can be synchonized to the plans, I promise I shall return to Corsica." Darius flashed the light into her face, and in the rays flashing on his she noted his stern disapproval. "I'll need time. A month, perhaps less. If my efforts prove futile, I shall withdraw at once." Compelling maniacal eyes pleading infectiously swelled his doubts. In a disturbed silence they traversed the few remaining steps out of the wine cellar to where the alert guards waited.

Darius responded to Semiramis inside the sedan as it sped downhill toward the waterfront. "Not a full month! Time may not permit such luxury. Two weeks, Semiramis. *Two weeks!* If you are not in Corsica at the designated time, Youseff's men will fetch you."

"And if I need three weeks?"

"*Two!* My word is final," he said sternly.

"I belong here with *my* people to fulfill my destiny!"

"So that's it! You fool! You silly, deluded fool! You've learned nothing. You'll end up dead—like your father. Do it my way—the right way. Topple the kingpin!"

"Hah!" she scoffed. "Your way brought the desert hyenas and jackals out of their holes! A pestilence of assassins on your scent are eager to hang your pelt to their trophy belts. I, too, could betray you. The sum offered is aphrodisia to my senses. You know how many arms it would buy?"

Again, Darius flashed the light on her face, studying the royal arrogant breeding oozing from her. "If you were to die needlessly—"

"—you would go on as usual. Would you really miss me, Darius?" She shrugged indifferently. She averted her head. "We are almost at the point of rendezvous."

Then she startled him. "Before you depart, I have a choice plum to deliver you. Lord John York's plan to carve up the Middle East."

Darius disguised his irritation. "You had them in your possession all the time. Why was it necessary to risk—"

"—so you heard with your own ears, saw with your eyes. Would you have believed me? Blueprints on papers often turn out to be forgeries."

Shalamara, a guerilla fighter dressed in fatigues, hair tucked under a commando beret, slim, and without cosmetics, easily passed for a young man. Curses burst from her lips. She braked the car, hitting the pedal hard, quickly tossed a pillow and *Haik* from the front seat to Semiramis. "You know what to do!" she shouted in Farsi. "Company ahead."

On the glow of headlights some fifty yards ahead two Iranian border guards obstructed traffic on the road. One waved his arm overhead, signaling her to stop, the other crouched, rifle ready. Darius gripped his Browning. Semiramis metamorphosed. She stuffed the pillow under her shirt, shrugged the *Haik*, a white tentlike garment worn by Moslem women, over her head, yanked, tugging it down under her body into place, smoothing it over the prominent pillow bulge over her belly.

488

"Speak Farsi, Darius. Play the irrational, prospective father," she urged as the Mercedes fishtailed to a skidding halt.

Shalamara quickly shoved two guns under the driver's seat out of sight. Semiramis screamed; her shrieks split the night air, startling the soldiers, taking them for an instant off guard. Jolted by her artful performance, the soldier shoved a high-beamed flashlight into her face.

The soldier's moves were cautious, professionally inquisitive. The second, gun poised, moved in closer. "Identification papers," snapped the first, one eye on the bulging belly, the other flashing on the auto's occupants.

Shalamara shoved the required items at him, shouting in Farsi, "Son of a ten-tailed scorpion! Are you blind not to see my mistress is in labor? Let us pass! Our destination . . . the clinic at Menab! By the black beard of Malik, may his curse be upon you!"

Banshee-like screams emanated from Semiramis.

"Be considerate, dog of the devil," Darius spoke in perfect Persian, drawing the officer's attention. "My wife is in torture. Minister Markarzi shall hear of this, infidel dog."

Shalamara let loose more colorful expletives. "You mother mated with a desert coyote! Have you no heart? No pity on a woman?"

Howling shrieks, groans, moans, curses, none affected the efficient soldier going about his duty, meticulously examining all identity papers. "My mother, may the Lord bless her memory, birthed ten children without a scream spilling from her lips. Bah! Woman of this generation are weak—without spine!" he prattled on in Farsi with a voice designed to penetrate the ears of the car's occupants.

"Permit Allah to change our roles, you son of a scorpion-tailed weasel," Semiramis spat out the window, scathing sarcasm spilling between curses, "and we shall witness the courage of the male specimen."

Darius drew her inside, held her tightly, stroking her hair, whispering tenderly to her. "Be still," he hissed. "There's danger in overdoing it. The soldier takes too much time. He seems to be waiting for something. Pretend to faint, pass out . . . that's it." Darius leaned out the window. "My spouse has passed out. The infant is not properly placed in her womb. Delays will endanger both mother and child."

"Move!" snapped the soldier returning the IDs. "Move swiftly!"

Shalamara moved! She floored the accelerator, shouting ahead in short, jerky leaps with each stuttering of the gears. "Keep alert, eyes open behind us. We can't chance an ambush." Semiramis shrugged out of the *Haik* and put herself in order.

Shalamara turned off the car's headlights, expertly eased the auto off the dusty road, crossed over the ocean road, made a sharp left turning southeast of Bandar' Abbas, past the complex of fisheries and docks. The car pulled to a halt, kicking up swirls of sand and dust. She switched off the engine, leaped out the car door, retrieved the guns from under the seat. Darius and Semiramis alighted quickly, peered about the area.

Darius reminded himself of his real mission: *why* he was here, *where* he was going, with *whom* he was dealing and the extent of the stakes involved as four armed guards bearing a rose insignia sprang cautiously from behind boulders. Sighting them, Shalamara, who stood with an M-16 rifle at ready, opened the car trunk, tossed them Kalishnikov assault rifles. Darius, checking the arms, recognized their source; his eyes signaled silent questions to Semiramis. She spat sarcastically, "Our Israeli friends provided them—who else? These are *our* men, Darius." Browning in hand, she sprang forward, conversed with them in Farsi. They handed her an oilskin pouch, which she quickly shoved under her shirt into her waistband.

Shalamara's task finished, she closed the car trunk, examined her automatic weapon, yanked out the cartridge and satisfied, snapped it back into place. "A few moments longer, *monsieur*." She used the receiver-transmitter held in her hand, conversed in code, and turning to Semiramis, whispered, "Everything is according to schedule."

Watching them, Darius's instinct warned him everything was *not* going according to schedule. Things were fitting too smoothly into place. Like a predatory animal in the night, geared for the unexpected, Darius shimmied to the top of a large boulder, peering out at the gulf through high-powered binoculars. The Iranian coastline from the Gulf of Oman, past the Strait of Hormuz, into the Persian Gulf, was not conducive to foreign infiltration. The entire area, including the Persian, Aden and Oman Gulfs, connected by the Arabian basin, diligently patrolled by a small flotilla of U.S. naval forces, made such a task as hairy as it was remote. Armed patrol boats from each nation bordering the Persian Gulf unflaggingly deployed their forces through the oil-rich uterus.

Here it was, thought Darius, all of it in diametric opposition: the exquisite beauty of nature itself and the ugliness of man's speed and his military hardware ensuring that greed.

Protection was needed and gotten. Rapid deployment forces (RDF) joined task forces drawn from U.S. Army, Navy and Marines sheltered on government-leased compounds at Bahrain, Hormuz, Muscat and Masirah Island—the jumping-off point for the ill-fated helicopters participating in the rescue attempt to free American hostages in Tehran in 1980. And if all this hardware and surveillance was not enough, Soviet Illyushin II-18 reconnaissance planes lumbered up frequently from South Yemen to peer inscrutably about the area.

Which was fine as far as Moufflon was concerned. Men trained in the Corsican network checked these patrols and reported heightened surveillance by all foreign covert agencies, including its laxity. The cohesive, tightly coordinated Moufflon apparatus had impeccably arranged the rendezvous with Semiramis. Murphy's law was unheard of in Moufflon's machinations where disasters rarely occurred. Pray God it remains so, thought Darius, peering through binoculars.

Darius saw the green lights. He wagged Semiramis forward. She shimmied up the boulder, laid flatly against it, eyes peering over the edge, awaiting the skiff's arrival. The stench of fish permeated, screeching flamingos continued to mate despite the interlopers.

"Listen, Darius, if you listen, you can actually hear it. They covetously eye our lands; they are carrion eaters." Cocking her head obliquely, Semiramis peered beyond the indigo waters surrounding Kish at the blinking lights of Hormuz. "The RDF ensures an unimpeded flow of oil and to deter aggression, so they say. I repeat, Zeller eyes us voraciously. He wants it all, Darius. Ultimately he plans to obliterate us from the face of the earth!" She fulminated, filled with enough vitriol to decimate an army. "Oh, how he plays God with such facility! My father's enemies, captive to him, foolishly make paper alliances with pigs like Harding and Zeller. But I swear to you he *will be* stopped! If my life has any meaning, it's to prevent those monsters from achieving their goals. If my life is sacrificed—I won't have died in vain. Corsican Jade and you have taught me the meaning of destiny.''

"You bloody, unrealistic fool! You've learned *nothing* from me! Who do you think finances this Holy War in your nation—Allah's magnificent army of specters? Christ! The surrounding nations, undermined daily by the overwhelming supplies of arms and ammunition available to them, encourages your nation to engage in warring skirmishes. *Why?* The dope your people harvest and convert in your laboratories serves Zeller's purpose. What better way to reduce your population and devour manpower? Your forces will weaken, most will be slain on battlefields, the rest succumbing to drugs, will be easily overcome. His key forces, held in abeyance, will mass in final triumph and ride herd over your lands without resistance. Is the truth so unclear?'' Darius with considerable patience masked an inner frustration. "Your emotions veil countless disguises, Semiramis. Think! Between the military and religious factions in your nation, dissent and rebellion escalate in a cleverly orchestrated design by Zeller's incendiaries, men like Harding. I repeat, Princess, your manpower is dying off in battlefields without purpose as brother fights brother in futility. What for? To prepare the way for Zeller's final victory? My God, look at the wholesale slaughter! The massacre! Defenseless thousands are uprooted, their homes bulldozed, and for what purpose if not to rid the land of people claiming title to it? Do the dead claim land? No! You say we taught you the meaning of destiny? Then, by God, turn the light on in your mind. Stop stumbling about in the darkness and see clearly what faces you!''

Semiramis stared at him speechless. She inhaled deeply from the hashish cigarette, retained it for several moments before exhaling.

"Stumbling about in the darkness is not a role I anticipate. There is more you aren't telling me, Darius. I can sense it.''

Camels brayed loudly as waves rolled on shore. Flamingos screeched. Land, sea and air blended and the night became electric between them.

"Please. If I am engaged in a comedy of gross errors rife with elaborately framed plots and counterplots designed by Machiavellian minds, I deserve to be enlightened.'' She placed her hand on Darius's arm. "Please, Darius. I must know.''

Darius turned from her, his eyes flashing on the chiaroscuro panorama of the gulf.

492

Darius quietly spoke out. "We discovered recently Zeller is not fully dependent on Moufflon to control the Middle East scenario. He prepares subversive tactics against and beyond Moufflon's ability to intervene. Do you grasp the implication of my words?"

Semiramis slid off the boulder, rolled over, drew her knees to her chest and sat hunched over, smoking hash, one eye on the radium dial of her chronometer.

After long minutes of silence she held up a monarchical hand, her eyes burning with fervor. "*Cher*, with you it's one set of values, with me, another. If you send me away, I shall move heaven and earth to return. Before Zeller's people materialize in my land, I will lead my people. We are organized, Darius, ready to move on your direction."

"You are insane! *Demence!*" he said desperately. He was cut off by a hissing gruff voice.

"*Monsieur!* Semiramus! The boat approaches!"

Darius shifted focus beyond the boulder. Four shadowy figures rowing a skiff toward shore approached, barely visible in the inky night.

Darius, with cruel dispatch grabbed Semiramis in a vicelike hold, shoved up the sleeve of her shirt, and flinging off the red cap on the flashlight flashed the light on livid track marks on her arm. She struggled furiously like a tigress against his hold and fell limp at his dismayed grunt.

"When in Christ did this begin again?" His voice trailed to a hush.

"*S'Arretez!*" Semiramis commanded. Instantly four commandos appeared, crouched, rifles aimed at Darius's heart. Darius released the girl, hands upraised, his body tense, on the alert for anything.

Semiramis regained composure. "Pray let no bitter wine flow between us, *mon cher*," she whispered, at once contrite. "If you hate me, it's a chance I must take, but I take it willingly. I cannot endure a contrecoup, now that I am *condottiere* to my men." She flashed the infrared flashlight on him. "My obligation to you is repaid with this." She handed him the oilskin pouch. "I am grateful you taught me so much. My duty is to my people, my loyalty is here in the land of my father. Anthony Harding will be handled *my* way. Something else, Darius, for old times' sake. I know Bernadette's killer's identity."

Darius stiffened, his pained eyes grew deadly.

"We play no games, *cher*. I know. Not the assassin, but the perpetrator."

Darius watched her, still as death as she took another toke, held it, ground the butt into the sand, and released the inhalation. She removed the red lid, flashed the light on his face. "It was Victor Zeller."

"Victor Zeller? . . . You're insane! It cannot be . . ."

"Was Berna not the courier who picked up a sizable sum from Zeller Bank—Geneva? He put a tail on her through the license on the Ferrari. Darius, this is my payment to you for all you've done. Your love for Sophia deserved the truth about Berna, *cher, my bon cher, adieu*."

Color had drained from Darius's face. Before he patched it together, before he could grab hold of Semiramis, a fusillade of fire butchered the night without warning. They fell to the ground, held in a cross fire by hidden enemy forces and Semiramis's men. Darius whipped out his Browning, returning gunfire. Semiramis slithered along the beach taking cover with her men.

Scrambling over the boulders, Iranian soldiers kept up the barrage of gunfire. Deadly trajectories lighted the area like bursts of spinning comets raining down on them. Grenade launchers from sheltered areas spit flaming pinwheels spinning over the beach, bursting in earsplitting explosions. Screams pierced the night. Men ran wildly, careening, lurching toward the sea, their clothing and bodies on fire. The inhuman shrieking screams were wracked with pain; others were blown to bits, their limbs torn from sockets, heads rolling off the bodies.

"Go, Darius! Go!" shouted Semiramis.

Darius flew toward her, tackled her to the ground. *"You are coming with me!"* But Darius was outnumbered, outgunned and outcommanded. Two guerillas pulled him off her body, dragged him to the sea. Less than ten yards away the men aboard the skiff had dropped their oars, picked up automatic rifles and spit fire at possible obstructors.

"I'm taking the woman!" Darius's words, muffled by gunfire, faded in the night. Semiramis was beyond his reach, the Soldier of the Rose had dragged her out of firing range. "Go, you fool! Go before the patrols return!"

Shouts, shrieks, clangorous honking horns from the approaching jeeps wheeled toward them, turning off the ocean road, headlights fanning the beach like a giant stage. Darius, lying near the waterline, saw the police forces and soldiers from Bandar' Abbas scramble out of the jeeps and run forward, taking positions ready to fire.

"Monsieur! Monsieur!" Shalimara, running toward Darius, pivoted on one foot, and expertly tossed a mini-grenade at the approaching squadron. Two jeeps and nearly a dozen soldiers exploded into the night. She tossed another and another mini-grenade in different directions—the effects, much like a mini-cluster bomb, were devastating. Yellow-white flames moved their deathly screams in competition with those of the honking flamingos, forced to seek repose elsewhere.

"Monsieur, go!" Shalimara shouted. "It is imperative!" She scooped up the oilskin pouch Darius had dropped in the skirmish and pressed it at him. "When I go—you go! *Allez!*" She tossed a diversionary grenade to the south, exploding the terrain for a quarter mile. A string of brilliant red explosions linked in chain fashion, and black smoke from the explosions dimmed the shoreline.

Darius, holding his gun overhead, backed into the water reluctantly. He saw Shalimara toss off her rifle, whip off her beret, unleashing a flurry of waist-length jet hair. She unzipped her fatigues, stood naked for a moment, then pulled the *Haik* used earlier by Semiramis over her head. She ran toward the ocean road, arms outstretched like a white avenging angel in flight, shouting incoherently in Farsi. "There—toward Minab!" She pointed southeast. A soldier braked a jeep to a stuttering halt, another soldier swept her up bodily in his arms onto the jeep, and with bleating horn honking loudly headed toward Minab, followed by what remained of the others.

Darius stashed the oilskin in his shirt, leaped into the waters, and swimming around, circled the skiff, gunfire exploding the water like a geyser. He swam to the bow, took hold of the line, and pulled it over his shoulder, swimming with the skiff toward the waiting trawler. A red light flashed on him from the skiff.

"Mozarabe" he kissed the password.

The trawler's engines were idling. Lowered pulleys elevated the skiff from the water onto the fishing vessel, already underway, heading through the Strait of Hormuz. Darius stepped from the skiff onto the slippery deck, overwhelmed by the stench of fish.

Fishing gear was thrust at him. He pulled on the ragged shirt, wincing at the pain in his arm. *Merde!* A flesh wound, creased by a bullet. Not dangerous, but bloody as hell. He pulled on rumpled baggy trousers over his own, donned hip-length rubber boots and covered his head with a black stocking cap pulled below his ears.

Standing amidships, he assessed his position as the trawler began a cautious route past Hormuz into the Gulf of Oman.

Darius had traveled from Djibouti to Kish under *cover* ID and papers. He shoved the Browning in his waist, studied the ID. *Hamul Tabas*, eh? The name didn't matter—the description, height and weight, were close enough. From Farsi Island? . . . Debatable. Light-skinned and green eyed? Why not? Did it matter? In a few hours he's be in Djibouti.

A hint of pale, mauve-pink light slivered over the horizon, mirroring the waters in a shimmering golden pink. Questions rushed at him. *Semiramis!* The nightmare of her addiction shook him. He regarded her frightening predicament; her terrorist activities and involvement with Harding presented grave consequences. If Anthony Harding had purposely set a trap to disseminate misinformation using Semiramis as his unsuspecting courier, the girl was as good as dead! Worse . . . the Moufflon apparatus was incapable of helping her.

The venomous lance thrust through his heart ate at him. Berna—killed at the hands of Victor Zeller! For an instant, standing at the rail, Darius felt like screaming—shouting at the injustice, at the appalling irony! Berna had gone to her death at the hands of her own flesh and blood. Victor Zeller was Bernadette's father, silenced by a deathbed wish by Sophia never to reveal! He felt sick! Outraged! His heart bled. Until now he had avoided the details, unwilling to deal with her death. Now, it was time! Had Youseff known? The others? And kept it from him? It was time Victor Zeller knew the truth!

Darius was startled from introspection by a thunderous roar of cannon, a barrage of gunfire bursting across the starboard bow.

B-A-H-R-O-O-M! Controlled explosions shuddered over the waters both fore and aft.

"Monsieur!" Captain Shadad, a burly, bearded man approached. "Look—three patrol boats fire warning shots! Do not be alarmed. Keep busy, observe the others, try to handle bait professionally."

Returning to the helm, the glowering captain idled the engines.

Patrol vessels approached; two from Masirah Island, one patrol boat off the port bow from Salah, a base in Oman. Their movements became synchronized on sighting the fishing trawler. Two hoisted U.S. colors, the third, Omani. Converging swiftly on the trawler, an American voice shouted over a bullhorn.

"Ahoy, Captain . . . Is that you, Shadad?"

Shadad nodded politely, his manner obsequious as three U.S. marines prepared to board his craft. The skipper, thirtyish, sporting a lobster-red sunburn, squinted in the glaring sunrise, averted his head, tugging down fiercely on his visor. He busied himself checking Shadad's permits and licenses, obliquely eyed by the fishermen.

Blood trickled from Darius's shoulder wound down his arm, spiraling around his wrist, spreading to his fingers. Darius swiftly leaned forward, submerged his hand into the live-bait sump, washing off the blood. The movement dislodged his gun; it fell to the deck with a dull thud. Before the American skipper discerned the movement, another fisherman swooped down, dropping a line over the gun, concealing it. Darius's benefactor hoisted another coiled line over one shoulder and moved aft, but not before Darius caught sight of a coral scar at the man's wrist.

Darius tensed. He stood alone, unprotected, unwilling to bring attention to himself. The contents of the pouch given him by Semiramis was incriminating. If they fell into the hands of *any* authority in the Middle East, it meant instant decapitation. The sensation of finding himself prisoner in a situation evolving so rapidly, playing like a practiced scenario, forced him to ponder the extent of Captain Shadad's knowledge.

Was this search part of a plan to seize bigger fish—Moufflon?

The other marines vigorously searched the vessel above and below deck. Captain Shadad, visibly disturbed, asked in broken English what was the trouble? Had he violated some absurd rule he knew nothing about? Were his papers not in order? "Why do you search me today and never before?" he demanded deferentially.

Darius's eyes narrowed at the ambiguous response. The American skipper blandly shuffled through permits, complex fishing licenses and papers vital to men fishing these troubled multinational waters, ignoring Captain Shadad's inquiries.

It took twenty minutes. Finished, the Americans reboarded their craft, thanking Shadad for the Iranian caviar, Captain's compliments. The Americans either ignored or failed to see the

497

hostility registered in the eyes of the crew, their ugly dispositions hidden under the implacable countenances of killers. Their thoughts as lethal as their capabilities, they conjectured cursingly at the search.

Never boarded and searched before! *Stopped*, yes! Questioned? Countless times on a weekly basis! But boarded and searched— never? Why now? The suspicious Americans had explored the oil-drenched relic of a vessel with an unusual diligence. They routinely made it a point of not intruding their presence upon the oil-rich Persian Gulf. *Today their presence was unmistakable!*

The untimely interruption spread rumors aboard the vessel. Was Shadad running dope? It had to be! *Raw opium? Morphine base?* Each knew of the illicit opium production, conversion laboratories and shipment routes. Why remain fishermen on the pittance they earned for backbreaking jobs? If they, too, ran dope, golden dinars would flow in their coffers.

Darius saw the envy pouring from them like punctured pus-filled cysts, their faces masked by greed. They stared at Shadad, hot-eyed, envisioning fortunes hidden aboard, gold dinars blinding them. Darius's concerned multiplied. One assassin aboard was enough. The thought of mutiny? . . . He busied himself with the image of a red scarred wrist.

Darius retrieved the Browning from the tangled netting and rising full height stared into Shadad's craggy sun-blackened face. Behind him the surly men doused and folded nets rigged for the lay. Obscenities abounded, no one conversed without assailing the other's ancestry in the vilest most contemptible terms.

"A fine, admirable crew you have. How well do you trust them?"

"Go below!" Shaded commanded, stormy eyes conveying a warning. "In the cabin is hot black coffee. Do not change your clothing. These are troubled waters." He insisted speaking fluent French.

Darius glanced sharply at him. Shadad's eyes fell to the bloodied wrist. "Tend the wound, at once." he said, irked by Darius's deliberate slowness. Darius spoke to him in Farsi, catching the man's widening interest. Shadad, a purported member of Prince Ben-Kassir's spy network, scowled fiercely again. He swiveled about, ordered his men to line up amidships at portside. They left their work reluctantly, glancing at brightening skies, cursing aloud.

"Might as well! The fish are safe from our nets on this accursed of unholy days! They are free to fornicate with mermaids!"

Shadad snapped orders. He moved past them, one after another pushing up their shirt sleeves, searching their wrists. *Nothing!* His cold eyes darted triumphantly to Darius. "We are seven in number, including you. All present and accounted for." To the men he ordered, "Get back to work! Prepare the nets! We've lost enough catch for today." The men scattered.

While Shadad started up the trawler's engines, anxious to get underway, Darius, disturbed at the unproductive line-up, descended the steep steps to a cramped, makeshift cabin below. Peeling down to his bloodstained khaki shirt, he dressed his wound with first-aid medication found in a box marked with a crude red X. The wound bled like hell, but the minimal injury would heal. He sprinkled it with sulfa, slapped a bandage on it, and slipping on his shirt glanced at his watch, wondering had his eyes played tricks on him?

Hardly. The lingering feeling of impending treachery long ingrained in his psyche refused to abate. He had seen the scar! He could not blink it away.

He warmed a pot of coffee over a kerosene stove, poured a mugful, grimaced at the strong chicory taste, and peering catlike about the ramshackle confines was unable to shake the feeling of surveillance. Standing at the porthole, gazing out at the pitching sea, he mentally measured the speed. Fifteen knots? Did it matter? He had left Paris seeking proof of the potboiling scenario in the Middle East and received for his trouble, Semiramis's defection and the name of Berna's murderer. He had never engaged in fantasies over Semiramis's loyalty; he dealt instead with the raw material she provided Moufflon—nurturing her for a limited role in the overall plan.

She was perfect for Anthony Harding! until he learned the full extent of the man's perverse criminality. Darius knew the limits to which he could push a hard-core addict. Rehabilitated for a time, she was destined and damned for all eternity to the fickle clutches of opium addiction. No addict could resist temptation forever. By her commitment to Moufflon, a lifetime contract in her case, Semiramis had come under the constant scrutiny of his circle of advisors, who, unbeknown to Semirami, had reported all her activities to Moufflon.

Defection to her own cause was suicidal!

Darius stood very still. He did not move, breathe. He listened acutely to the usual sounds, water slapping against the creaky hull, booted footsteps above deck, bits and pieces of conversations, curses . . .

There was something else . . . He sensed the presence of another!

He turned quickly, scanned the cabin interior. Had he overlooked a hidden cranny or niche? Semiramis's condemnation echoed in mind.

"Your way has brought the desert jackals and hyenas out of their holes!"

There—footsteps descending the ladder. Darius spun around, Browning in hand. When Captain Shadad appeared, Darius relaxed momentarily, arrested by the changes on the man's face. Then, suddenly, bedlam was upon them. Caught off-guard, Darius flinched.

He saw Shadad's arm dart out, flare gun in hand. The shot whipped past Darius, so close he felt scorching flame sear past his ear. Darius ducked, cursed aloud and spun around, gun at ready, stunned at the sight of a human flaming torch! Briefly, for an instant, Darius blinked back the image of a man, arm upraised, a sharp fish knife ready to plunge into him. The face was unrecognizable. The torch dropped the knife, his hair and clothing ignited, hoarse screams tore from the man's throat. Darius whipped a blanket off the bed, wrapped the burning wretch in it, rolled him on the floor, beating at the flames until only black smoke escaped and the charred remains lay inert.

Slowly he unwrapped the helpless mass covering his nose at the stench of human flesh charred beyond recognition. Before Darius determined if the man were dead or alive, Shadad grabbed a handgun from a holster on a wall peg, and fired three shots in the man's cranium.

Enraged, Darius sprang to his feet, broke Shadad's hold on the gun, shattering the man's wrist bone. Howling in pain, Shadad bleated, "I was doing my duty, protecting you at all costs, *Monsieur* Moufflon!" His face screwed up in excruciating pain. "And this is my thanks?"

Monsieur Moufflon! Shadad had called him *Moufflon!*

Darius stiffened, eyes narrowed to slits, his features unreadable. The body at his feet fell limp, air and life expunged from the wretched mass, his arms rolled over, the coral scar barely detectable.

"You see! You see!" Shadad bleated with exaggerated indignation. "He was a stowaway—aboard Shadad's vessel! A stranger to me."

Darius regarded the other in controlled silence. Would he *ever* know? Had the dead man aimed at him or Shadad? Had Shadad come below to waste Moufflon, to hang Moufflon's pelt to his trophy belt? Darius *knew* the answer. He *knew* the assassin. Cautious, wary-eyed, he stood away, gun aimed at Shadad. Before they reached Djibouti, Shadad would make another error . . .

He didn't. Ten kilometers out of Djibouti a helicopter's rotors sounded too close to the vessel. A voice over a P.A. system brought both Darius and Shadad above deck. Darius saw the familiar markings, smiled as a ladder lowered from its belly.

Prince Youseff Ben-Kassir!

Darius needed no invitation. Grasping the ladder, holding on tightly as it was raised hydraulically from above, Darius held the Browning on the pain-wracked, glowering Shadad, holding his broken wrist, grimly observing the surprising exodus.

The Sikorsky helicopter headed inland to a private airstrip in the French territory of the Afars and Issas, a few kilometers north of Djibouti on the North African coast.

A half hour later when the Prince's jet lifted off the runway heading in a northwesterly direction, Darius casually asked, "Tell me about Captain Farouk Shadad, Youseff. How does he fit into your network? How long has he been with you?"

"Farouk Shadad?" The glass in Youseff's hand paused in midair. "You speak of Captain Farouk Shadad in the present tense, Darius? He was killed a year ago."

"The devil you say?" He shook his head indulgently. "Then, dear Youseff, who do you suppose it was who piloted the trawler—the Killer Shark, eh?"

In the explication of the recent drama aboard the trawler, neither Darius nor the Prince solved the curious unraveling of events. "Perhaps both the dead man and Shadad—whoever he is—competed for my life?" Darius grinned in wicked amusement. Youseff failed to see the humor in the situation.

Darius opened the oilskin pouch, spread the maps before

them. Youseff scanned them curiously. He removed his glasses from his jacket pocket, set them over his nose, his interest drawn by the transformation of boundaries on the Middle East maps.

"Semiramis delivered these to you? From her hands to yours?" Darius nodded. "Am I suddenly obtuse?" asked the Prince. "I fail to understand. Are these or are they not duplicates of the maps you included in PROJECT: MOONSCAPE to the WPCC delegates last February?" Darius nodded in silence.

"Explain, in simple language, *s'il vous plaît*."

"In plain language—Semiramis was set up!"

"Praise Allah! Let it not be thus."

The attempts to suppress his anger and indignation evaporated. He raged. "I failed to exercise prudence. I should have pulled her off Kish a month ago! She needed time, she said, begged for a month. We settled for two weeks. Now I doubt she'll last twelve hours. I saw fresh tracks on her arms. Youseff, I blame myself. I should have dragged her with me. She has marshaled her own private army but I fear they are bought by Harding forces."

"In playing for enormous stakes, everyone is expendable."

"I should have protected her." His face turned deathly pale. "Never should have sent her to Geneva!"

"Darius, you are rambling—"

"—rambling?" Darius explained, watching the Prince pale.

"Victor Zeller ordered Berna killed?" Youseff was stupefied.

Darius shriveled the maps in a balled fist, eyes sparking. "I swear the taste of victory shall evade him. The unexpected is unacceptable to me. Berna's death, unforgivable. Now, I swear an oath before the Almighty that vengeance shall thunder down upon them!" Darius's voice, thorny as barbed wire and twice as devastating, grew subdued. It was the calm before the storm, Youseff feared, for it was always thus, in the past, before Darius thundered to successes.

"And the world will witness *miracle after miracle* as an army of vengeance shall sweep through those lands and recapture the lands of their forefathers." Youseff spoke in biblical tones.

"And if no lands remain? What then, Youseff?"

Prince Youseff Ben-Kassir stared at his lifelong friend in disbelief. "You can't mean—"

"Zeller's bag of tricks are endless."

*   *   *

Before they deplaned in Algiers, Youseff spoke solemnly. "You realize, when he learns his orders terminated his own flesh and blood, the only reminder he had of Sophia—it will destroy him?"

"If you think for a second that I care what happens to Victor Zeller—any Zeller . . ." Darius stopped abruptly, made a disorganized gesture. "First I must make certain my only child, my daughter, is safe."

Intermezzo

ON JULY 4, 1984, THE WORLD READ THE HEADLINES, poured over satellite photos of the Middle East holocaust. Miraculously, the two superpowers had exercised formidable restraints in detonating ICBMs and nuclear warheads from submarines in strategic locations.

The miracle—the *real* miracle—was they had *restrained!*

The question on all minds was *who* and *what* triggered the nuclear detonations. The Oval Office and the Kremlin both expostulated and categorically denied responsibility.

The Vatican's official statement struck at the heart of the problem: *"How pathetically disillusioning it is when civilized men, capable of making immense technical strides in electronic technologies, remain unable to promote human understanding. Wherein lies the fault? Would that such cleverness by men with such talented imaginations use such God-given talents not for the destruction of mankind but for the elevation above savages of the Dark Ages . . ."*

Chapter Thirty-Three

WORLDWIDE, THE STREETS OF THE CITIES became ghost towns. Usual street sounds dimmed, as if the entire mechanization of a people had been put on HOLD. The whole world was stunned, suddenly immobilized by the news of the holocaust as satellite photos inundated Maryland Space Agency. Was it true?

Had the unthinkable happened? Or was this a hoax perpetrated upon an unsuspecting public? The believers ran helter-skelter in search of foodstuffs and survival materials, appropriating everything in sight, preparing for a mole-like existence. The disbelievers got drunk, or tried to, and shook their heads. It couldn't happen! It wouldn't happen! Man was too civilized!

In West Berlin it was business as usual; people there were conditioned to war-ravaged lives.

Velden Zryden sat in his cushioned, swivel chair behind a directoire desk in his office at the French Embassy, jarred by the ringing of his phone and flashing red lights. His face screwed into a galaxy of frowns.

Of all the rotten luck! Berlin was in the middle of its film festival; lavish premieres, fancy balls and countless galas were on the agenda. International stars, elite repute from Hollywood, London, Paris and Rome had given West Berlin life. The nuclear fracas in the Middle East had exploded the scene. Producers, directors, stars and entourages had fled with a haste that would have reduced the biblical exodus to a farce!

He stared at the flashing red light bitterly. *What now?* He picked up the receiver, glancing at the listless clerks speaking in French. *"Bon jour. Monsieur Zryden here."*

"Victor—is that you?" The familiar voice brought swift action. He engaged both scrambler and voice-altering devices, his expression conveying his annoyance. *"Oui, Herr Schmidt. Herr* Zryden at your service. How may I assist you?" He spoke with decorum.

"Ach, gut. Ich verstehen. Can you talk freely?"

"Nein, nein, Herr Schmidt." He switched to German.

"Gut. Then listen. It's here, the opportunity of a lifetime. Your target is taking an eighteen-man task force into the Middle East. Nuclear scientists, hand-selected representatives of several governments. You will represent West Germany."

"What?" Velden Zryden, aghast at the pronunciamento, paled. "I—Is i-it, uh, safe?" The strong chiseled features sagged.

"From me you should ask such a question? Many satellite photos were destroyed, damaged by the intense radiation upon their reentry to the atmosphere—"

"—and you expect *me* to travel in that area?"

"If your target makes so noble and grand a gesture, believe

504

that he *knows* the risks involved, how to safeguard those who travel with him.''

"How exactly did *I* qualify for this mission?"

"You ask a foolish question. It is arranged. You will join other task force members in Paris for a briefing. Moufflon's personal Lodestar jet is undergoing modifications and retooling to accommodate the mission in a private hangar adjacent to de Gaulle Airport.''

"Is there anything else, *Herr* Schmidt?"

"Mosha will brief you in Paris. Bear in mind, Zeller banks hold all the papers on *those* lands.''

Velden felt a cold chill. "Please explain. I fail to comprehend," he muttered in a slow controlled voice.

"Let them all scramble for the land! America, the Soviets— even China intends to enter an acquisitional race for territorial rights.'' *Zeller owns the lands!* Those nations were in default. Who do you suppose masterminded billions in loans through the World Bank?''

Velden's throat felt the aridity of shock as a portent of doom crept through his body and soul. "You don't mean—I mean, uh—*you had nothing* to do with—uh—recent events in that area—did you?"

"The work of a lifetime, Vicor! If Zeller can finance wars—it can make government loans, *nu*?"

"And the collateral—?" He *knew* the answer, refused to utter the words. *You will have your pound of flesh, won't you, Father?*

"—the very land itself—all of it. Legal, bona fide, proper. Validated through the World Bank. What international court would dare contest my claim?''

Victor cleared his raspy throat; he was sweating. His eyes darting to the clerks, he lowered his voice, the stern repudiation remained. "*Herr* Schmidt!"

"Yes, *Herr* Zryden?" Zeller's voice pierced like a stiletto.

"An army, *any* army, can nullify paper," he said softly.

"I trust you will prevent such a likelihood."

"Good day, *Herr* Schmidt." Velden hung up the phone, flipped off scrambler devices, stared into space, his face, neck and arms dripping wet. Alternating currents of thought tottered precariously at the edge of his mind, creating a miasma of uncertainty.

His father was a raving lunatic! An out and out power-saturated madman who had succeeded in infecting him with the same saprogenic psychosis! Velden rose from his desk, walked to the water cooler, chills shooting through him. He helped himself to three cups of spring water. Alternating hot tremors evaporated the sweat. His eyes sparked in fierce appreciation of his father's genius. A secret smile twisted his lips. He swaggered across the office, out the door, along the corridor, feeling a swelling of power. He paused before a door containing security files, slipped his plastic card into a slot. He searched for the proper file drawer, inserted his plastic card into a slot titled U.S. Department of Defense. Metal file drawers sprang open. The terror and trembling shame he had experienced earlier vanished as he flipped through the drawer and located what he needed.

All the way back to his desk he thumbed through the file, preoccupied with the contents labeled: MOUFFLON. Attached thereto were three recently dated communiques. He nodded to the clerks and sat down, placing a *DO NOT DISTURB* sign on the enclosure around his desk.

Velden read the first communique from British Intelligence, a memo from Sir Alexander York's desk, signed by his adjutant, a Major St. Clair. He read:

HERR ZRYDEN: CONTAINED HEREIN IS THE CLASSIFIED INFORMATION YOU REQUESTED. THE DATA HAS NOT BEEN UPDATED IN TEN YEARS. SHADOWS EXIST IN THE SUBJECT'S LIFE PRIOR TO WORLD WAR II. TO THE BEST OF OUR KNOWLEDGE, FILES WERE DELETED UNDER HIGH PRIORITY REQUESTS UNCLEAR TO US. IF YOU REQUIRE MORE THAN SUBMITTED, I SUGGEST DIRECT COMMUNICATION WITH THE PENTA-GON. INFORMATION UNAVAILABLE TO US MIGHT BE READILY OBTAIN-ABLE THROUGH YOUR SOURCES. IF WE CAN BE OF FURTHER SERVICE, SIR ALEXANDER YORK SUGGESTS DIRECT CONTACT WITH HIM. SINCERELY, MAJOR J. ST. CLAIR.

Velden placed the communique back into the file and studied the impressive letterhead on the next. He read:

SUBJECT: *GENERAL BRADFORD LINCOLN*

Herr Zryden:
   Your recent inquiry concerning the above subject has been taken under advisement. We are sorry to inform you

506

we are unable to issue any information to you concerning this person.

A recent executive decree has labeled the matter highly sensitive. Perhaps if your Minister sends a confidential communique through the U.S. Ambassador, influence might be exerted in the *right* places.

A cursory search through our computers revealed the subject matter is deceased. However, another search through Concatenate-Alpha in our Clayallee division indicates this name present among those American VIPS on the security check who attended the WPCC Conference in Maui on February 10.

It could be coincidence. That would account for the deceased Lincoln, listed as Major. The man attending the WPCC Conference in Maui was a General. In any event, we couldn't supply you with a bio on either man for reasons listed heretofore in this letter.

We appreciate your inquiry, and would like nothing better than maintaining an open area of reciprocal traffic in State matters. An accommodation to you would mean an accommodation to us. However, nothing short of a Presidential decree would release information on this matter.

Sincerely,
J.H. DOLAN, Adjutant
Berlin Command HDQS.

Velden combed the thick file, studying everything from his school records to classified OSS duty rosters and CIA involvements. He studied the obituary notice without expression, replaced the items in the manila folder. He lighted a cigarette, smoked it through a gold holder as a nexus of energy pulsated cranial nodes. Scenes flashed past him like the frames of motion picture film rolling back in time to Corsica. He recalled the American OSS Captain Lincoln who in OPERATION WHITE CORAL was forced into an ancillary role when he fell under the protection of Major Darius Bonifacio, leader of the *Mozarabe* . . .

So much information floated into Zryden's mind. Dormant cells activated by power-light filaments swirled, twisted about, slithering through locked drawers of his past, another's past. Smoke swirled over his head from the cigarette. He closed his eyes, lay back in his chair, immobile until the mental incursions of images and scenes ceased. He had worked a tight caseload. Amadeo was right. It was time for Velden Zryden to absent himself from the French Embassy and get on to more vital matters.

The next morning a letter directed to the Minister of Finance arrived, advising him of a shift in personnel. Velden Zryden, transferred by executive order, the Minister was advised to discreetly hold Zelden's files and dossier in abeyance, prepared to make certain disclosures to the SDECE, U.S. Intelligence and BRITISH MI-6 in the very near future.

Chapter Thirty-Four

FROM THE MOMENT VERONIQUE HAD LEFT VICTOR AND ZURICH in December she had awakened night after night in a cold sweat. The nightmares had paved the way for a terror to take hold, the fear of the unknown. From the carefully orchestrated order of her life came disorder, chaos and bewilderment. Oh, she had sanely counseled herself in the light of day, aware of the folly of dwelling in shadowed areas of helplessness, and she knew to be terrorized by something unidentifiable in mind was sheer lunacy!

So much was ludicrous. The inexplicable changes in Victor creeping out of left field had intimidated her and when the critical break came she had fled Zurich, determined to use distance to examine the unorthodox personality disorder afflicting him. Her original mission, totally frustrated by the weird goings-on, demanded scrupulous re-evaluation. So she had returned to her Left Bank address, the place Victor knew, remained there for four months incommunicado. The nightly battle with ghostly visions had awakened her, sweat-drenched. Victor's face hovering over her like some obscenity became her nemesis, her nightly lamentation, *why can't I sleep?* The proliferating terror ceased only when she had faced herself squarely, admitting *You're afraid to sleep!*

It was true, afraid to nod off, fearing the truth, the psychological explanation to Victor's aberrations, she took pills to stay awake. She had lost weight, grew increasingly jittery, her nerves shattered. Suddenly finding herself at the edge of collapse, she determined to demolish the mystical alliance holding her captive to Victor Zeller.

That's when the calls began . . .

Morning . . . noon . . . night! Telephone calls, loud, jarring, unexpected calls in the deep of night jolted her from any momentary slumber she had wrung out of torturous nights. When she picked up the receiver, silence underscored by heavy breathing from the other end infuriated her at first. Annoyed, furious, a growing exasperation at her plight escalated heated wrath at her tormentor. *Ignore the calls! Wear earplugs!* she counseled herself for a time; then, when *after* she changed her phone number the calls persisted, she was shaken to the quick.

It was Victor! She knew it! "Victor, is that you?" she had demanded time after time. *Nothing!* Once or twice she heard the name *Veronique* whispered huskily before the caller hung up. That night and for a hundred nights after it was the same—heavy breathing, silence and her name whispered, "*Veronique . . . Veronique . . .*"

The bastard! The cruel, perverted bastard!

Enough! She had to take steps to avert a total breakdown.

And so, on a rainy day in April, *after* the note arrived from West Berlin, she knew action was mandatory. The note, a simple one-line command written in Victor Zeller's hand, read: "Tint your hair red."

Tint your hair red! Why, for the love of God? *As if she didn't know!*

Veronique Lindley's imagination soared. Valerie Lansing's did not. Veronique had experienced more than Valerie's sheltered environment had produced in her lifetime. The note, plus the surreal influence Victor still exerted on her, despite the distance of separation, dictated prudence. *Sever the influence, Val! You must!*

The curious personality twists injected into Victor Zeller's psyche had given rise to a strange journey into a realm for which Valerie Lansing was not prepared,

By mid-April she relinquished the memories, escaped the nightmares and took refuge in the Lansing Paris townhouse located on a quiet cul de sac far from the Left Bank. Her hair, tinted back to its natural brush-fire red, she kept herself busy from morning to night leaving her little time to think about Victor. She went shopping in those expensive boutiques on the Rue Faubourg St. Honoré, returned home each night completely spent. Under the care of the French couple who tended the Lansing house she regained some weight, and enjoyed an equilibrium of mind where recently only turmoil dwelled.

She had relaxed in the upstairs den, watching television, reading books. But no matter how many times she vowed her indifference, she knew she was not finished with Victor Zeller.

For Valerie it was a quantum leap forward. Her thoughts became constructive and on them she built a solid foundation to springboard action.

She burned the midnight oil, writing as swiftly as her hand could fly, filling page after page with facts. And she knew the truth!

It was following the tragic death of the Zeller Foundation scientists that the personality changes in Victor escalated!

She typed this fact, tacked it above her desk, stared at it until the magic began. Methodically, painstakingly, she collected data from newspaper morgues on the accident. She recreated skeletons of the six men, adding bits and pieces until she formed a composite and bio on each, stopping at a point short of her goal. She realized she needed positive reinforcements from family members.

Valerie began her work with dedicated fervor, employing an investigative expertise capable of turning a private eye green with envy. She used wigs, unusual makeup, and clothing to disguise herself. She presented herself as several different personalities with business cards to match each and introduced herself to the deceased scientists' families as a reporter from various newspapers interested in a hot story.

Her progress was slow. She had uncovered no stunning revelations, no deep dark, lurid secrets or violent hatred of the Zeller family, not even a skeletal hint of scandal seeped from locked closets. The scientists, habituated to secrecy, had engaged in clandestine research without imparting a clue of their involvement to their widows. Checks had arrived monthly from the Zeller Foundation, Zurich, while they were alive. Now, generous insurance proceeds provided handsome annuities. *Why complain? L'homme propose et Dieu dispose, oui?*

Mutatis mutandis, Valerie thought. Changes, alterations were always made to fit a new set of circumstances.

Eventually it seemed that unless a miracle could be conjured, the end of a dry run was in sight for Valerie. Only one interview remained. Nothing had worked the way she'd planned. What essential ingredient had she overlooked? Five total bust-outs . . . could the sixth prove magical? Discouraged, tempted to forsake the trek to Mont Blanc to meet with the Widow Zeiss, she changed her mind at the last minute. She'd come this far. . . .

Valerie geared her sleek white Maserati sports car up the quaint, winding roads into the village of Chamonix, mecca for exuberant mountain climbers daring to scale the dangerous, austerely majestic Mont Blanc. It was early in May, springtime in France was totally breathtaking.

Valerie geared down in her approach to the village, drove under a tangle of cablecar wires, for here was the starting point for spectacular cablecar rides across glaciers to Courmayeur in Italy. The sight of Mont Blanc shooting upward of fifteen thousand feet was both awe inspiring and uplifting. Valerie's spirits soared; perhaps this day would provide the miracle she needed.

Valerie found the Zeiss house and Wilheim's widow charming and gracious. The frail, petite, wispy-haired brunette with sad setter eyes fully adjusted to the opulence of her new home, cooperative and disarming, poured tea and served French croissants filled with zesty cheese and marmalade. Under this fuss and ado, Madame Zeiss studied the drably dressed, brown-haired reporter, efficient behind tortoise shelled glasses. She confided surprise that anyone showed interest in the tragedy after so many months.

"My husband had yet to reach his full potential in the field of brain study and research, *mademoiselle*. Admittedly he was very talented and adept in computer technologies. Unfortunately, he did not speak of his work at Zeller Foundation, *mam'selle* uh—" she glanced at the card, "uh, Barnes, *oui?* And at the end, communication was censored. Telephone calls monitored. If Wilheim made the slightest mention of his involvement—*mon Dieu!* Disconnection. The phone call would end. Always his letters came with regularity. By fall—mid-August—or was it September? *Alors,* they made little sense. He wrote briefly, it was the usual scribbling, hello, how are you? I miss you, hope to see you soon. Nothing more, getting to be less each time. No longer did he sign his letter with affection, merely yours, Wilheim.''

Valerie let her ramble, she seemed willing enough, and it sprang from a stream of consciousness needing venting. In previous interviews she had asked direct questions. In any event, Madame Zeiss's recollections were concise. Her hostess paused in reflection for a moment.

''Yes, the letters, too, suffered from censorship. I am certain Wilheim knew this, so why bother to write what wouldn't be read, *oui*? And then, *mam'selle*, something most *eccentrique* happened.'' She pondered a moment, noticeably shaken, undecided whether or not to confide in this dowdy reporter sipping tea in her house. Appraising eyes went to work, she glanced again at the business card as if to reinforce her strength and determination. Then, almost as if in afterthought, she continued. ''*Oui*, most peculiar.'' She sipped her tea thoughtfully. ''As chief of research, Wilheim requisitioned supplies from a pharmaceutical firm in Geneva where works his cousin, Johann Verner. One day Johann received a curious requisition written in Latin, coupled with strange unfamiliar scribblings, mathematical equations. Confused, unable to make them out, Johann was certain Wilheim had gone mad! The shame of Johann's inadequacy in deciphering the notes, disturbing to him, for he is a man of pride, prevented him from taking the order to the managerial staff, for fear of being ridiculed. Instead he transported the cryptic vouchers to a friend, a physicist. The older man pondered the writings. The equation, he insisted, made little sense. On first perusal he discerned the scribblings to be some sort of distress signal, a call for help. But before alarming Johann he desired additional confirmation.

''*Alors, Mam'selle* Barnes, it took four colleagues two days to patch together the meaning of the equations. Whoever sent the requisition, they told Johann, had ordered *no* supplies. What was requisitioned was help—assistance to extricate the scientists from a most untenable position. It was unmistakably an SOS! Six lives were in danger. *'He is a monster who will stop at nothing!'*

512

Those words burn in my brain for all eternity. No names were mentioned.''

"Was nothing done to learn the nature of the dangers?"

Ester Zeiss turned sad mournful eyes out the window, at the verdant countryside. She sighed wistfully. "The order dated November 30, 1983, reached Johann in February, 1984—"

"—but they died in December—" Valerie stopped abruptly.

"*Oui, Mam'selle,* precisely. The order, lost in the holiday mail or delayed by the intervention of fate, came too late."

Shafts of sunlight piercing the shutters cast oblique light on the cozy, chintz-covered sofa and chairs. It shone on a low oval table littered with framed photographs and porcelain collectors boxes and bric-a-brac. One photograph, momentarily spotlighted by the sun's rays, caught Valerie's attention. Madame Zeiss's focus shifted to Valerie's intense gaze. Precisely, as if on cue, the ornate cuckoo clock on the wall struck two o'clock. The widow Zeiss smiled.

"Every day at this time the sun shines on Wilheim's photograph. It is a good sign. Please ask what you will. I am doing the right thing in speaking up." She sighed, blew the photo a soulful kiss.

Valerie's spirits soared. "Does this, uh, Johann, uh—did he retain the original requisition? The cry for help?"

Ester Zeiss shook her head. "*Mais non,*" she continued in her regional French. "*Je l'ai.* I have everything here." She drew herself up, crossed the room, opened a glass-panelled étagère, rummaged through a quilted box, returned with the frayed, crumpled original. "Johann delivered it to me after it was decoded. Take it." She pressed it into Valerie's hand. "It provides me little solace. If my husband feared for his life, he would have found some way to tell me. We were close—very much in love. *Herr* Zeller was good to us, kind and considerate. It is not my desire to make upon him *une discorde chinoiserie* in his few remaining years."

Oh, Ester Zeiss, how deluded you really are. Good? Kind? Considerate? Amadeo Zeller? Hah! Better you should consort with Satan!

Valerie kept her thoughts to herself as she read three letters Wilheim sent his wife before August 1983 and a few scant lines after that date. The contrast, significant in the stilted words, implied a man working under severe strain. If the desperate plea for help couched in the body of the requisition had alerted

513

Johann, it screamed at Valerie. The accident itself, proof of the prevailing sinister plot, had been made to look accidental. Madame Zeiss summed up the *tête-à-tête* two hours later. The tagline addendum to her story reflected her apprehension. "If it was *not* an accident, but rather a planned homicide, who would dare contest the Zeller Foundation?"

Who, indeed?

Pensive Valerie leaned down to stuff the data into her briefcase when a loud crash shattered her eardrums. Bullets strafed the room, shattered windows. She swiftly leaped to the floor, lay flat until the barrage stopped. Turning, she saw Ester Zeiss—what was left of her—sprawled back on the sofa bleeding from multiple bullet holes, eyes staring upright in shock.

Christ! oh, Jesus Christ! Valerie heard the sound of footsteps approaching. She was done for! She fished for her pearl-handled .38 from inside her briefcase, a few feet from her. *What to do? What to do?* She crept toward Ester's body, bloodied her hands with Ester's blood, smeared her face and blouse and crept under the coffee table, inert.

Out there someone was trying to kill her—would kill her unless . . .

The door opened. One eye opened to a slit, she saw a pair of legs enter cautiously. Her hand gripped tighter around the gun under her. She watched the feet approach, stop first at Ester's body, shove it to one side; it fell heavily off the sofa onto part of Valerie's legs, immobilizing her. The legs moved to the briefcase, yanked out the contents, and leaning down shoved his face closer to Valerie to make certain she was dead. As she had been trained, Valerie moved swiftly. She pulled on the trigger, and shot five bullets into the man's face, emptying the chambers. Crawling from under the table, she was unable to recognize the bloodied, faceless dead man. How could she have known she had killed Draga Koseva? One of Zeller's precious watchdogs, a precious commodity to the Zurich banking titan.

Shoving the papers into the briefcase, she fled the house just as the cuckoo bird chirped four times. She had to reach Grenoble, from there hire a chopper to Monaco, then a plane to Paris! *Run, girl, run!*

She gunned the Maserati, spun out the wheel and careened through narrow winding streets, tires screeching. She couldn't leave Megev soon enough. Shaking internally, fighting the blinding glare of the late afternoon sun as it bounced off the crystalline white slopes of Mont Blanc, she felt an inner suffocation, torn at the thoughts of Ester Zeiss's fate. Guilt seared her insides. Had she unwittingly blazed a trail, announcing her perfidy against Zeller? Had the other scientists' families she had interviewed compared notes? Informed Zeller? The Zeiss house was wired, it had to be! Sudden thoughts of Mosha Bauer placed a spur of fear to her ribs; she floored the accelerator.

One of the year's most celebrated races scheduled for high-altitude slopes above Chamonix on the *Course des Amethystes,* caused a severe density of traffic along the dangerous *corniche.* Forced to slow down interminably, especially around dangerous curves, Valerie was lost in thought, reviewing over and again what might have tipped her hand.

It was dusk. The bright headlights of oncoming cars in the increased traffic was worse than the deceptive glares of a setting sun. Forced to concentrate on driving, she geared down, shifting with the expertise of a Le Mans driver, unable to shoot out and beat the traffic.

At last, on the other side of *Chambéry,* enveloped by a moonless night, she entered the Province of Isère and began the descent to Grenoble. Her eyes, accustomed to the dark, she glanced out the rearview mirror and blinked hard. *CHRIST! . . .*

Something was wrong! Headlights, tailgating her for the past several miles, had suddenly disappeared. Before she made sense of this in her mind she felt the tumultuous impact as a car, its lights off, came at her from her blind side, forcing her dangerously close to the precipice. Valerie jerked her head around trying desperately to make out her attacker. She saw in silhouette a dark figure hunched over the steering wheel, closing in against the side of her car.

She floored the accelerator, shot out ahead; her assailant stuck to her, sideswiping her repeatedly, with resounding crashes and crunches as fenders and doors crumbled under each impact. Unable to measure the depth of the ravines in the darkness she knew her only chance of survival was to clear the second car, take her chances on the corkscrewing *corniche.* Lacking that ability? . . .

She remembered the terrifying fear lodged in her throat choking her as the last crashing impact forced the Maserati to snap the guard rail and sail into a womb of blackness.

515

"You are a very fortunate woman." The doctor's words as Valerie regained consciousness filtered through her consciousness. Her swollen eyes, barely able to focus, turned everything hazy, distorted perception. Wafting from unconsciousness, she approached consciousness trying desperately to understand what the man in white was saying.

"It's a miracle. Not a broken bone in your body. The car . . . totally demolished, but you escape with severe bruises, a few sprains, but no concussions and spinal injuries. Truly, *mademoiselle*, it is a miracle. A few days' rest and you'll be able to walk out of here."

Valerie understood at last. Her mind tied ends together and something buried inside her screamed, *"Go home, Valerie!"*

Go home? After all she'd endured?

By God, she had trespassed! Gone too far. The *briefcase!* Her *papers!* She asked the nurses, had her personal effects been recovered? She was told that the police found what remained of a tattered briefcase, the contents apparently scattered to the winds. *Fine.* Just *great!* The evidence was gone! Had her attempted assassin combed the ravine and stolen them with her *cover* ID? Who was she? What name had she given Ester Zeiss? Could she continue the fiasco? When the police asked questions, she replied simply, "I am Valerie Lansing, American, daughter of U.S. Senator Lansing. Please contact my family." She would say nothing, *absolutely* nothing about Ester Zeiss or her presence in Megev.

Valerie was home, at Fox Run, shaken, churning with ambivalance, wearing a neck brace, knee elastic as valor badges earned from her recent brush with death. She was greeted ecstatically by Valentina and the Senator who eyed her scratches, deep abrasions, cuts, weals and visible bruises with sympathy and gratitude for her survival. Loaded with painkillers, Valiums and numerous drugs to keep her mobile, she actually felt little physical pain. Her agony was mental.

On the plane back she had reviewed minutely every detail leading up to Ester Zeiss's death, the internal guilt surging. She had read all the papers, tried to get a handle on her assassin, the man she left behind, and found nothing. What remained was unpalpable depression.

Valentina panicked at the noticeable changes in her daughter, whom she had not seen in over a year. She didn't press for a week, then finally urged, "A catharsis might help, Valerie." They sat in the cool patio overlooking the rolling green Virginia hills, the sun overhead brightly lighting up the occasional horseback rider cantering in the meadows below. Sipping tea quietly, letting the cool air invigorate her, Valerie finally unloaded the heavy burden.

She began bit by bit, confiding the tactics employed to meet Victor at the Paris Galleria, how they spent what appeared idyllic days in Zurich. She lamented at her inability to meet Zeller senior, and continued the odyssey with the changes occurring in Victor, causing her exodus to Paris, and the subsequent journey through nightmarish worlds. She recanted her research of the scientists, vividly explicating her doubts, theories and fears and how they all fitted in with the adversities afflicting Victor Zeller. She capped off the story with the information gleaned from Ester Zeiss. "I had the evidence in my briefcase. It went over the ravine with me. The police found it—empty. If only I had learned the identity of my assailant, the man I killed at the Zeiss house."

Pale, Valentina listened, sensing an overwhelming dread for her daughter's safety. "Finish this evil thing! You must desist! What's the sense of it! I curse my mother for wishing this blood vengeance on you! Don't you see—who dares defy Zeller?"

As Valerie listened to her mother's pleas, burgeoning thoughts assaulted her. She had unwittingly tapped the subconscious, opening locked drawers and her mind linked together the pieces of information she had gathered.

Valerie sipped her iced tea, inhaling the fresh Virginia air, feeling a surge of strength and determination. An hour later she kissed Valentina and amid a storm of protests drove to her own townhouse in Georgetown, recoiling as she entered the foyer at the pyramiding mail stacked on a marbled-topped credenza. She fanned through a stack, stopping at several marked with the prestigious emblem of the Russian Embassy. Uri Mikhail Gregorevich? . . . Hummnnn. She picked out six letters from the Russian diplomat, strode into the classic antique-decorated den, placed the letters on the rolltop walnut desk with its lion's claw feet. It felt good to be home, free of pretense and duplicity, just to be herself.

An hour later Valerie had bathed, shampooed her hair, and dressed casually in jeans and sweatshirt. She shook out her damp curly hair, toweled it, and tossed it off her face, carefully favoring her stiff aching neck. She snapped on her neck brace and set a pot of coffee to brewing. She padded around barefooted, and in moments phoned an order into the market, ordering a stock of groceries.

Back in the den she unlocked built-in file cabinets, pulled out thick tomes of collected data and began the long tedious hours of reading and rereading the Zeller files before she commenced to fill sheets of yellow foolscap, jotting a chronology of collected thoughts. She studied the notes, reflecting.

When the groceries arrived, Valerie signed for them, locked the door and returned to the kitchen, searching for chocolate mints for her coffee. She was addicted to coffee this way, thanks to Victor. Sipping the steamy brew, she returned to the den. Victor's image persisted in intruding on her thoughts.

Valerie angrily snapped a pencil in two and tossed the pieces on the desk, fiercely determined to find the answers she needed. She reached for the phone just as it rang. Her hand jerked back as if she'd touched fire. Who could it be? Who knew she was here? She picked up the receiver hesitantly. Before she opened her mouth, Valentina's voice came on line. "Valerie, engage your scrambler." She complied.

"A friend checked out the death in Megev," she began. "The man, your assailant and Ester's killer, *does not* exist."

"What?"

"Just listen. French SDECE identification vis-à-vis dental charts and partial skeletal reconstruction produced a remarkable likeness to a man who *does not* exist."

"You're not making *any* sense, Mother."

"When I say he doesn't exist I mean his records were removed a long time ago from INTERPOL, the SDECE, British MI-6 and I doubt they exist in the CIA or NSA."

"How do you know this?"

"Please, dear, take my word for it. I can't take time to explain. The facsimile and dental charts obtained from Zurich prove beyond any doubt the man who you left behind in Megev was Draga Koseva, a valuable property of Amadeo Zeller."

Valerie whistled low. "I made the big time—did I? Then who was it shoved my car over the corniche?"

"Draga's brother, Milos Koseva, who worked in tandem with him. He, too, does not exist, in the same way."

"How will I know for certain?"

"My source is unimpeachable."

"What's the point in all this? No one knew my identity."

"Darling, you're not that naive. The point is be exceedingly careful. The ferrets can dig up your identity if you moved under a dozen aliases. They can trace you through the auto."

"It was a rental. I used the cover ID."

"Valerie, don't take this lightly. I am sending bodyguards to watch over you."

"Here?" Valerie laughed. "I'm safe here."

"General Brad Lincoln believes otherwise. Incidentally, it's time you both compare notes. His involvement in the Zeller affair will astonish you."

"Ah—I see. That's how you got the information on Megev."

"Not quite. I cannot discuss it, presently. Take care, love, and be expecting a call from General Lincoln. Brad's an old friend."

Valerie understood, said her farewells and replaced the receiver. Thinking quickly, she picked up the cordless phone, switched it to *talk*, and got a dial tone. She placed a few calls of her own, old former CIA cronies, now in private investigations. She gave them the name of the Koseva brothers, asked them to come up with something on the double. She hung up, placed another call. If she could arrange it, her every waking moment for the next two weeks would be occupied.

She did. She met with two formidable Georgetown professors, distinguished men lettered in the field of psychiatric research, presently involved in revolutionary brain research and computer technologies. She got them for three hours a day, at luncheon at her house, and proceeded to pick their brains. Valerie posed hypothetical questions, demanded explicits. What she got was long-winded, ambiguous dissertations, more hypothesis and a rash of speculation. When she complained bitterly at their evasiveness, they replied:

"Counselor, you, more than any, must realize it is easier to manufacture a half dozen facts than one truth or single emotion."

When the ridiculous turned absurd Valerie escaped to the university library, pored voraciously over the latest computer

519

technologies in the field of brain study. The fascinating all-engrossing subject lured her until she lost track of time.

Her CIA experts called her. Sorry, they couldn't get a handle on anyone called Milos or Draga Koseva. Could she be more explicit? She could not and thanked them.

She walked the floor all night. The intense heat wave broiling D.C. was staggering. Wouldn't you know the air conditioner went on strike? She cooled herself off by rubbing ice cubes on her pulse points, and walking about in a nude lace string bikini.

Early the next morning, she laid on a recliner, around six A.M. staring at the stacks of books, and manila files scattered on the polished oak table at room center under a large Tiffany lamp. She closed her eyes.

The facts paraded across her mind, yet something was missing. Something infinitesimal was out of synch or completely missing or escaped her scrutiny. She yanked off the murderous neck brace—it was suffocating—she was sweating unmercifully. The clock chimed seven times. The sun was up and drove up the temperature to broiling. She prowled about the room, trying to find a cigarette, and found a gold case of hashish instead. She lighted one, inhaled deeply, holding the toke, as she puttered about the kitchen setting a pot of coffee to brew.

She took another toke, held it, and felt a relaxation surge through her. Why had Zeiss sent an S.O.S. to Johann? Why? What could they possibly have known that drove Zeller to murder? Why were they held against their will, then shipped home at the last minute in so grand a style? *To make it look less like murder, you dimwit!* Would Zeller sacrifice a new two-million-dollar aircraft? *If it saved two billion dollars, why not?*

When it dovetailed, she shook her head in denial. *It couldn't be! Valerie, don't get schizophrenic now!* It was too ridiculous! Then she pushed back her memory and recalled the changes in Victor that December 20, when he read the lethal headlines. Suddenly it seemed less ridiculous, less like the folly of an overworked imagination.

Valerie leaped from the recliner like a fanged tigress moving in for the kill. She knew! By God, she *knew!* Perhaps the facts were still hazy, the blueprints unclear, but she had strung together enough facts to suspicion the ignominious truth and that suspicion was based entirely on facts. Her imagination, or was it intuition, had filled in the gaps, but by God, if it was the last thing she ever did, she intended to uncover all the facts!

It was eleven A.M. when she called her mother. She only needed to tie a few loose ends to ascertain if the theory running helter-skelter in her brain was a viable one. She dialed, got a busy signal and hung up. In the kitchen she toasted a bagel, heaped it with cream cheese and returned to the den. She tried dialing again. Waited for the dial tone, munching on the bagel.

C'mon, Mother, answer the phone.

"Mother—is that you? You sound so far away. I wanted you to know I'm leaving for Paris tomorrow . . ."

Valentina's voice sounded dull, as if she were in an echo chamber. "Thank God it's you! I've been trying to reach you all morning. D.C. lines are jammed. Haven't you heard?"

"Heard what?"

"Turn on the television. You'd think D.C. was in a state of siege instead of panic. The White House has been cordoned off by the military! Nuclear warheads exploded in the Middle East this morning!"

"*What?* Oh, Christ! Look, I'll drive there right away—"

"No! You can't. All roads leading in and out of D.C. have been sealed up tight by the National Guard and the military. The Senator's been called to the White House. All hell's breaking loose."

"You're there alone? Mother, come in to Georgetown or I'll come to fetch you!"

"You aren't listening. Look, turn on the television, catch up and I'll get through to you somehow. If I don't, you try reaching me."

It was July 4, 1984. The entire world reeled under the tragic, frightful news. Nuclear warheads had destroyed one quarter of the globe while she was buried in Zeller litter! Once she got over the initial impact and learned the entire world was only on hold and had not gone mad, her determination to return to Paris heightened.

Nothing short of death itself would prevent her from destroying the world of Amadeo Zeller—*nothing!* Not her mother's pleading or cajoling, no amount of pressure brought to bear would deter her from her singular purpose. She would meet Amadeo Zeller someway, somehow, to settle the long-awaited score. She announced her decision the next day to two despairing parents.

Senator Lansing threatened cancellation of her passport and travel visas if she didn't listen to reason. He failed to understand her obsessive rebellion. *And* this madness to get to Europe while everyone there was trying to get to the United States during this unpredictable holocaust! Why it was insanity!

Valentina's efforts to dissuade Valerie failed. Forced to use a trump card, she demonstrated a mother's chagrin. "You promised to meet with General Lincoln!" she said with maternal petulance. She hoped Brad could convince her daughter he might prove more valuable in quarterbacking a few plays against Zeller . . . Else—*GOD HELP HER*!

And *HE* did with Valentina's nudging.

The next twenty-four hours produced a bagful of miracles.

Out of the void came the opportunity for Valerie to join the prestigious WPCC Taskforce in PROJECT: MOONSCAPE. She learned the enigmatic *Moufflon*, who had turned the world on its backside in February by predicting the nuclear ravagement five months in advance was presently in Paris retooling his Lodestar jet, preparing to embark with an expeditionary force of hand-selected nuclear physicists and scientists over the desecrated Middle Eastern pyres as observers capable of measuring and estimating the extent of the damage. Those on the periphery of power believed him insane. Those in the *know* felt otherwise.

General Lincoln's reluctance at the outset to permit Valerie's presence on the mission for reasons he refused to discuss faded to oblivion. And when he was persuaded to accept her, for additional reasons he refused to discuss with Valerie, it was her turn to express bafflement. In any event, the times spent with Brad had fattened her Zeller files.

No matter how she pried and did so with a surgeon's skill, her attempts to probe Brad's brain further than he permitted failed. He knew plenty and held back, Valerie felt. *Why?* It didn't occur to her until much later, since she'd been so forthright in sharing Zeller secrets, that he might be holding back *highly classified* data.

Valerie packed, taking inventory of the gear required by Taskforce members, the rest would be doled in Paris. She was intrigued by the sudden reversals, the new dimensions shaping her world. What boggled her mind beyond all belief were the implied hints that super powers intended to scramble for rights to the nuclear-ravaged lands.

Listening to the accumulation of alarming facts, Valerie observed the frightening thinking of a society she'd never really seen in the past. Wrapped in her insulative cocoon, however dangerous, were the branches of trees in which her cocoon nestled. She made a mental note, when she returned, to involve herself in the political arena of this nation. She owed the Senator that much. One thing was certain, the gathering of politicians at Fox Run she'd encountered these last few days were a different breed of men than she'd rubbed elbows with in the past—or had she failed to view them in the proper perspective?

What was it Brad Lincoln expressed so succinctly? The *fucking* world has gone mad!

On a personal level, most perplexing to Valerie was her mother's display of support. It was a sudden change, an unexpected reversal of tactics. Valentina's compliance to this venture, her retreat to a neutral corner, actually encouraging Valerie to join the near-suicidal mission after she herself had vociferously declined several times, boggled her mind.

Dammit, it was all so peculiar to her. Something proundly mysterious was happening, and not all of it was revealed to her.

But it got her back to Paris—didn't it?

Halfway over the North Pole on a Condor flight she remembered Uri Mikhail Gregorevich's unopened letters. She felt a strange pang over her heart and didn't know why.

Chapter Thirty-Five

PARIS, FRANCE
10 July 1984

A SWELTERING HEATWAVE HUNG IN A QUENCHLESS PALL over Paris the day Velden Zryden checked into his suite at the Bristol on the Rue Faubourg St. Honoré opposite the British Embassy. Briefing for WPCC TASKFORCE members commenced Monday, July 13, A.M. Meanwhile, the Zeller townhouse was off-limits, he could neither occupy it or go near it. Possible covert surveillance on him dictated his moves.

So, Velden did what any newcomer to Paris might do out in the open for anyone to see. He spent Thursday and most of Friday making like a gawking tourist in the stifling humidity, searching through the Left Bank for art works and out-of-print novels. Hopefully he'd drive the Secret Service detail assigned to him, stark raving mad.

It left the entire weekend to kill . . .

Paris . . . Veronique Lindley. One without the other was unthinkable to him since they had lived and loved together. Suddenly he wanted Veronique and every aching memory of her passionately. Nightmares of those last days spent in Zurich had evaporated into layered mists and foggy recollections. Not a splinter of unpleasantry remained.

Somehow, someway, if only to assuage the profound longing ache he felt since their separation, he determined to glimpse her.

There was little time for Velden to debate the issue. Once he checked into the Embassy and orientation began, departure from the confines was not possible. Forced to make swift decisions, he opted for a weekend with Veronique. Passionate recollections of their love affair spurred Velden. What a fool he'd been to let her go. How to approach her now, after all that had happened? How would he explain the Velden Zryden cover?

He couldn't. To confide in Veronique matters held sacrosanct between father and son would place her in dire jeopardy. Control had returned to Victor just as Dr. Zeiss had promised, alleviating his fears. Recurring obstacles reared ugly heads periodically, but he had managed inordinately well with the exception of one— Amadeo. Amadeo's personality rankled him, hounded him beyond endurance. The moment aggressiveness was detected in an adversary, Amadeo's personality surfaced. Internal competition between the warring personalities caused Victor unendurable frustration. His vigorous attempts to control the situation invariably resulted in subordinating his role to Amadeo's forcefulness. It left him agitated, depressed, self-destructive.

Victor preferred the soft approach with business opponents. Reinforced by advance preparation, invariably better informed than an adversary, Victor skillfully executed strategy and concise tactics on the heels of tiger-shark aggressiveness. He came in for the kill brilliantly, his opponents seldom realizing how skillfully they had been had.

Amadeo's temerity, domineering abrasiveness and what amounted to out and out intimidation placed his opponent on guard. Endless haggling to the point of exhaustion when all else failed, he employed dirty tactics, attacking the other on a personal level. Subtle extortion always forced his opponent's hand. A recitation of their infidelities or illegal manipulations forced capitulation. Victor loathed this method. Victor believed that a man attacked personally became one's enemy for life. To him, business was business, wins and losses part of the daily peril that kept you alive and on your toes. You pay your money and take your chances. Zeller's Law equivocated to: *Never take chances! You pay money to ensure victory!*

Zryden turned off these thoughts. He gazed out the windows across the street at the Paris skyline, the British Embassy in the forefront busy with clandestine comings and goings. Catching his reflection in the shiny windowpane, he studied his tousled bleached-blonde hair, turned in profile, examining the reshaped nose, protruding frontal teeth created by a dental device snapped over his own teeth. Pale blue-eyed contact lenses over his dark eyes changed their hue. A few light scars wandering lines on his forehead added irascible charm to Velden Zryden; he spoke often of his scars as he might valor badges for surviving a vicariously experienced near-fatality. He shook his head in a helpless gesture. *Nothing is as it ever was for you, Victor . . . Nothing, not even Veronique, can be the same!*

But wait . . . would Veronique recognize him as Victor Zeller? His own father—not even Mosha Bauer, had known him! Until Zryden's business terminated, he dared *not* chance discovery!

Veronique was a complication he could ill afford. Velden didn't, only God knew how much Victor longed for and needed her.

What would be the harm if he presented himself as Velden Zryden? Dare he chance it? Just to see her once before embarking on this suicidal mission . . . The thought infected his senses, stirring desire for her. Turning, he stared at his image in the full-length mirror on the bathroom door. He didn't know himself. No hint of Victor Zeller bounced off that image. She'd never know him—never! He'd make certain of it. He could do it. He knew it.

A half hour later, Velden went into a movie theater and exited quickly out a side entrance, hailed a cab and swiftly sped out of the area. He ordered the driver to pull up along a curve of the *Bois de Boulogne* and ambled along under the broiling humidity of a sweltering sun. Radiating heat waves actually lifted off the sidewalks, temperatures soared to unbearable degress. Had the nuclear explosion caused unendurable heat?

Seemingly impervious to the brutal temperature, he swaggered along the crowded *Bois* wearing light blue seersucker trousers and shirt, his jacket flung casually over a shoulder. Glancing at the address on a card, bribed from Veronique's former *concierge*, he matched it with a street sign. *Voilà!* He turned the corner onto a quiet, sedate cul de sac, at once impressed by the opulence.

The area reeked money and tradition. Immaculate, artistically landscaped gardens, perfectly trimmed, they looked unreal. Bushes resembling French poodles lined the arc of the cul de sac. Nineteenth-century façades of regal, imposing apartments and townhouses set on their own plots were guarded by black iron-spiked palisades. Rolls-Royces, Mercedes, Bentleys and other limousines prowled the area like lions guarding their lairs.

The opulence created distortions in his earlier assessments. It was a far cry from her flat on the Left Bank! Hesitant, guarded, his eyes in all directions at once, searching for untoward movements, especially the Secret Service who by now must have realized he'd given them the slip, he slowed down, stretched his gait to ambling toward an austere graystone. He glanced casually at the shiny brass name plate on the black iron gate. He read: *Honorable H. B. Lansing.* Momentarily the name meant nothing except that it signified what Veronique might be doing at such a residence. Crestfallen, it struck him.

She had found herself another man! And why not? She could have any man!

Or, perhaps she was leasing the manor? Yes, yes, that was it! Her dossier indicated substantial patrimony. Frowning, he continued on past the manor, followed the arc to the opposite side of the dead end street lined with red Japanese maples.

Velden paused, leaned against a trunk of a shady, colorful tree, providing him momentary relief from the bake-oven temperature. He had rehearsed the scenario a dozen times. He would speak German to her, introduce himself as Velden Zryden, a friend and colleague of Victor Zeller who had sent felicitations.

Victor was ill, he'd say, a breakdown. Too much work, not enough play, and all that rot. Perhaps she'd offer him a drink. He might accept; then again, might not. If her reaction when he mentioned Victor's name was favorable? . . . His heartbeats accelerated. He could not bring himself to cross the street, ring the Lansing doorbell. Twice he walked away, returned, then furious with himself, hailed a cab back to the Bristol.

The next day, shortly before lunch, drawn back to the Lansing manor, he bought a bouquet of yellow roses and retraced yesterday's steps to the elite cul de sac and positioned himself under the red maple, perspiring copiously. He inserted the stems of the bouquet through the wire fencing, leaving his hands free to agitate the stifling air.

Infuriated at himself, his studied campaign of pompous detachment, Velden stood there a full hour before abandoning the plan as foolhardy. He shoved his jacket over one shoulder, dabbed at the sweat on his face, glanced at his watch, and turned to leave.

He stopped in his tracks, gasped aloud, retreating partially around the tree trunk so he could see and not be seen.

Approaching him on the same side of the street was . . . ?

Was it Veronique? The gait was Veronique, but something distorted the image. Something about her? He clung to the tree, sidled around it, concealed from her sight. She was less than fifteen feet away, coming closer . . . closer . . . Now ten feet away . . .

The stunning redhaired wench was *not* Veronique Lindley! Her skin was lighter, creamier, the eyes the color of jade, not entirely green but hued a pale blue—almost viridian in the sunlight. He stared dumbstruck, unable to chain the driving compulsion. He felt strange, curiously overwhelmed. Memories surfaced, images formed. She was five feet away, ready to step off the curb and cross the street.

"Victoria . . . ?" He called the name softly, but loud enough for Valerie to hear. She spun around, startled, then searching his face, paused questioningly. He repeated the name in a hoarse voice.

"Victoria. It *is* you, is it not?"

Valerie failed to recognize the slim blond man, but she *knew* him at once. "Why, yes, I am Victoria," she replied alluringly. "I'm afraid you have me at a disadvantage." She smiled, her temples throbbing like giant kettle drums.

Victor! Victor Zeller! This stranger was Victor Zeller!

"Don't you remember me? Madrid—1922? *Antonio Vasquez?*"

If Valerie had *not* known the entire scenario, she might have apologized, insisted he had the wrong party and left him standing in the street. It *was* Victor *pretending* to be Amadeo Zeller— Valerie knew his father had used the alias of Antonio Vasquez when he met her grandmother Victoria Valdez in Madrid! *Christ! What madness!*

Why the disguise? The eyes, nose, hair was different! Why?

Valerie incautiously pressed on, side-stepping the precautions she had assembled in her research of mental aberrations.

"But of course! *Antonio Vasquez!* It's been so very long!"

"Yes, it has." He spoke to her in Spanish, thrusting the floral bouquet at her. "A great deal has happened, *querida*. You see, I have a confession—I am *not* Antonio Vasquez—never was. I am Amadeo Zeller." He spoke with a certain panache, as if he expected homage to be paid the name.

Calmly, deliberately feigning no reaction, she thanked him for the flowers. "What brings you to Paris?" she asked inanely.

He sighed deeply joyous, slickly sidestepping her query. "Oh, my dear Victoria, now that I've found you I shall never let you go. My love, my very precious love, tell me what happened that night I left you with the sisters at the cloister. On my return from Cordoba you were gone. I thought surely—dead. You look exactly as you did then." A schoolboy ebullience flowed.

The pent-up bravado drained from Valerie. Her expression remained serene and controlled despite the tremors shuddering through her.

God help her! The conversation was madness—the encounter insane!

Sweat rippled across her forehead, dripped at her temples, her curly hair coiled in damp ringlets. Swallowing was impossible, her throat felt parched. She poised herself very cautiously. "I live across the street in the graystone. Do come to tea. Tell me about all those years in between."

Inside the library, with the air conditioning turned on, they felt less exhausted. She noticed the disdain in his appraising glances, a comparison to some design in his mind. Valerie regretted giving the servants the weekend off. How could she have foreseen the events of the next twenty-four hours? *How?*

528

She excused herself, prepared a pitcher of iced tea, returned from the kitchen to find him pouring cognac from a crystal decanter at the bar. He sipped it, scrupulously examining the Chagall on the wall.

"You must exercise prudence in purchaing art, Victoria. So many are copies, incredibly well done. Even the artist copied seldom can make the comparisons with facility."

"Especially the dead ones," she said airily. The joke fell flat. "Well, is that a copy or the *real* thing?" she pursued it solemnly.

"The real Chagall," he retorted with the firmness of an expert.

"I'm glad. What a travesty if it were proven a fake. My uncle, curator of a museum, would develop apoplexy."

She poured the iced tea for herself, sat opposite him in the Regency decor admitting to her total bafflement. She saw a desperate internal battle ravaging this man's psyche. "Would you care to dine with me this evening?"

"Truly I have no appetite, Victoria. You afford enough joy to nourish me these few remaining years."

Valerie's eyes darted sharply to his genuinely desperate eyes. She saw reflected there an awesome resistance to death, the encroaching infirmities of old age, the agonizing shackles of an aging corpse—yet he was young.

Remember you are confronted by Amadeo, not Victor Zeller!

Scoffing at his conveyed diffidence, she intimated, "Surely you can point with pride to your vast accomplishments, *oui?* You've lived a full life, enough for ten men. Are you not yet powerful enough to suit yourself?"

"You *know?*" Genuinely surprised and elated, he repeated, "You *really* know of Zeller's accomplishments? . . . Ah, Victoria, dear Victoria. In failing to become my wife you relinquished a throne of glory. I would have made of you a queen, an empress, whatever you desired. It was all for you—all of it."

"All of what, Amadeo?" Her eyes widened naively.

"*Everything!* The banks, lands, diamonds, oil, gold. Such a collection I have in Zurich—you wouldn't believe," he said, eyes rolling. "They alone could transform you to a Nerfertiti, for certain. I have accomplished enough to satisfy any mortal longings." He lifted his head obliquely and peered at her secretively "Recently my immortal longings, as well."

She stared at him, quietly, eyes probing. *"Immortal* longings? I don't understand . . ." *But she did. The man was mad!*

"Then come with me, live in my chateau in Zurich. Share my last remaining days and I shall tell you all about it." He lifted his eyes to an invisible plateau, beyond her sights and understanding. "Soon there shall be global transformations. You will see tributes to my greatness. Politically, economically . . ."

"Global transformations? Political? Economic? Tell me so I can understand these changes."

Amadeo eyed her cannily, teasing, provocative eyes undressing her, drinking in her beauty. "I shall live through my son, and his son, for all eternity," he said softly, in a hushed voice.

"Your son? You have a son? Tell me about him." she urged, gently patting the empty space alongside her on the sofa. "Seeing you today, Amadeo, is like handing me a book with half the pages missing. I seem unable to make sense of anything you say. It has been so many years."

"Yes, yes, of course. Even I fail to comprehend the extent of my ambitions when we first met," he replied sitting at the far end of the sofa, ill at ease. "A man my age prattling on about ambition sounds peculiar, doesn't it. Well, why should we concern ourselves with *my* accomplishments?"

"Truly I wish to hear of your successes. The world sees too few exceptional men."

"Not always successes. I failed twice. Once with you and again on a matter which is unrelated to our relationship."

Valerie rose from the sofa, crossed the high-walled, pastel room, and returned with a decanter and two brandy snifters. She poured two, handed him one. He twirled it, warming the glass with expertise. Valerie sipped a bit to coat her palate, then settled back to twirl the snifter with equal expertise. All the fuss and ado acted as subterfuge to cover her growing wariness.

Despite the creeping disquiet pervading her senses, she ached to hear more to verify her own image of this craven, depraved ghoul. Whatever was taking place, Valerie laid no claims to understanding the phenomenon. Yet, she listened with honed perception, trying desperately to make sense, not to the words as much as to the transformation, the embodiment of Amadeo in the physical body of his son, Victor, who pretended to be someone else. She had yet to learn who was disguised inside this German shell seated nearby.

Valerie listened, asked subtle questions, unable to make sense of his rantings. An hour later, after listening patiently to sentences and phrases spoken with the temerity of a dispicable tyrant, her assessment was as it was before—the man was insane. But which was which? Which was the most dangerous? *Amadeo? Victor, or the blond man? What was his name?* So far, she didn't know.

"I have brought the world to its knees with the thrust of a million thunderbolts!" he raved. "And I promise there shall be more even if I am not present in the flesh to bring further destruction upon my enemies."

Valerie blinked hard. Yes, she *had* heard correctly. Momentarily Valerie made no connection between Amadeo's words and global events. Frustrated by what she did not understand, she excused herself. Lifting her hair off her shoulders with one hand, she fanned herself, complaining of the heat and the need to change into something comfortable.

She returned moments later wearing a sheer jonquil yellow tailored silk robe. Her hair piled atop her head was wrapped in a matching silk turban. She dabbed at the prickly sweat with cotton balls drenched in cologne. She found him seated, staring at the bouquet of yellow roses he'd gifted her with earlier. He neck-craned around at the sound of her footsteps, and then shocked Valerie by bolting up from the sofa, staring at her, and in a stiff military brace clicked his heels together. He bowed, kissed her hand, waiting until she was seated before dropping the incendiary.

"So kind of you, *Fräulein* Lindley, to offer me the hospitality of your house. Please, may I express *Herr* Victor Zeller's profound regrets at not being here in person to see you. His business keeps him traveling all the time. He is seldom in Paris."

If Valerie had registered shock at the earlier encounter with *Amadeo,* she had postured remarkably well. But this new twist reached deep inside her for every drop of bravado stored. "Ah, yes, the world is too much with us all, uh—*Herr* uh . . . ?"

"Zryden. *Herr* Velden Zryden. Do call me Velden."

"And you may call me Veronique," she said testily.

"Yes, Victor has raved over his Veronique. Too bad spats have a way of dissipating. . . ."

His words washed over her while Valerie struggled to tame her thoughts and emotions. Who was this curious composite, first Amadeo, the self-effacing, egomaniacal, homicidal, twisted brute and now Velden Zryden, an imperious, dignified, self-conscious, many-shadowed reflection of Victor. And she questioned her sense. Why allow any part of the composite inside her doors? If Valerie possessed a shred of precognition or talent to read a crystal ball, the forces already arrayed against the Zeller bastions might have imprinted upon her mind and the terror of the next twenty-four-hour period eliminated.

Twenty-four hours later! Valerie left her guest—whoever he was—fast asleep in her bedroom on *her* bed! Exhausted, shocked by the excruciating pain wracking her body, alarmed at the disorder of thoughts riding collision courses in her mind, she retreated from the bedroom, padded quietly along the second floor landing to the study, locking the door, bolting it behind her. She had popped painkillers and finally slipped Nembutols in her guest's last drink to rescue her from the protracted revulsion of her shocking predicament.

Now, sort through this chicanery of madness!

Halfway through the nightmare, it had occurred to her to flee the mansion, check into a hotel, *anything* until her Monday A.M. rendezvous at the Embassy. Several facts in the bizarre, bloodcurdling excursion into the past were unclear to her, and she forced herself to resist the impulse to flee and damned near got herself killed. Now she had to dissect the debacle in her mind. Much of what Amadeo had imparted to her had coincided with Victoria's diaries. She simply needed to know more to bridge the gaps.

But so much had happened! So very much!

Weak from the copious loss of blood, pale, her features drawn tightly by both pain and medications, she brought coffee pot and cup out on the upper balcony, and leaned against the wrought-iron balustrade, peering at the descending twilight in what remained of the heat-wilted day. She needed respite to think . . . think . . . think!

Twilight in Paris was magnificent; it arose from a hot summer's-day ashes, transfigured into sultry wisps of gold and frosty orange, clustered around a waning sun as the fireball plunged beyond the western horizon. As she watched the setting sun, Valerie's cumulative fears gathered momentum. Never had she believed herself capable of experiencing paralytic fear so intense it rendered her incapable of movement. Yet, last night, too numb to recall *how*, *why* and *when*, she submitted herself sexually and to whom of the three she unwittingly became victim, she prepared herself to receive Amadeo's sexual advance. She only vaguely remembered the transition from Velden back to Amadeo.

She had prepared cold lobster salad, chilled champagne, and wheeling it on a serving cart back to the library where the air conditioning worked best, she'd stopped to remove the hair scarf, shake out her fiery curls and applied lip gloss before reentering the room, unaware she had unwittingly triggered a mechanism in her guest causing Amadeo to surface.

She *knew* it was Amadeo watching her every move with a predatory smile. A prelude of squeamishness swept through her, a beginning fear at the silent messages registered in Amadeo's ravaging eyes. The intensity of his expression immobilized her will. The thought of relinquishing that will to this sinister man who had peopled graveyards and made funeral pyres of her ancestors shook her. Struck by this overwhelming susceptibility to him and a growing conviction of her impotence against him, she reasoned her only recourse depended upon her skill to resist antagonizing him.

Why should she fear him? Hadn't she mastered the art of self-defense?

How they ended in her upstairs bedroom in the Lansing mansion wasn't clear to Valerie. It happened with lightning speed. She was on the bed, naked. He had stripped off his clothing, kicked off his shoes savagely, drained half the brandy glass, braced himself, and yanked back the silk sheet, devouring Valerie's nakedness with those *unbearable* eyes. Her loathing of *Amadeo*, compounded by her knowledge of him, was neutralized by her utter fascination in the psychological mystery of what transpired as one personality faded into the next. Had she known the enticing picture she presented to *Amadeo* was the culmination of a sixty-year-old dream . . . ?

To *Amadeo* she was a glowing pearl on an iridescent shell, a highly faceted, precious gem on a silk drapery. The muted softness of rose-colored lights fanning from a translucent Conchalamp on a nearby table flattering the rounded contours of her full breasts, the erect nipples of her areola, fed him like tasty appetiz-

533

ers before a feast. He trailed his hand lightly along the rounded hipline, to the patch of red hair where her slim thighs met the most secret places of worship. Amadeo stroked his throbbing organ, it thrust out before him, engorged, demanding.

The edifice of Valerie's feigned complacency crumbling, she recoiled slightly. It was too late. Without preamble Amadeo fell on her forcing the air from her lungs. Simultaneously he clamped fierce, cold lips on hers, siphoning off all air. Valerie, tried to resist, shoved, pushed, struggled to wrest herself free of his grasp. *She couldn't breathe!*

Suddenly the folly of her inquisitive—vindictive—nature loomed before her. Vivid awareness of her predicament forced her to resort to desperate means for mere survival. She pulled her arms from under him, reached overhead, groping for his neck, eager to connect with a pressure point. Marshaling all her strength, she pressed at a point between his neck and collar bone—hard—until he buckled from the unexpected thrusts, groaning at the incursion of pain.

Rolling to one side of him, Valerie desperately gasped for breath, sucked in long gusts of air, holding him at bay, trying to explain. ". . . Couldn't breathe . . . cut off air supply . . ." her voice attenuated.

Brutally Amadeo mounted her again, commanding harshly, "Stroke it! Suck it! Damn you!" he snarled. The *rutting ram* in heat—organ erect—violently ramrodded her unlubricated vagina, jackknifed her knees for deeper penetration. The first thrust was unbearably savage. More demoralizing than the pain was the lightning stroke of shock done her. No rhythm accompanied the assault. He adjusted himself, unhurriedly taking aim, taking as long as necessary between the strokes to be certain, then throwing his entire weight and force into and against her. Valerie screamed at the vile, unmitigated rape! He could no more hear her than he could hear a dream figure calling from another skull. Deaf to her pleas, he bunched his muscles, pinned her flat, tinkered for aim, then struck!

He was going to maim her—kill her if he chose. Valerie tried to clutch at his thick shock of blond hair, and he retaliated by placing the point of his elbow on her throat, leaning on it, immobilizing her.

If she should thrash from side to side . . . ? Dreamer! You're dead!

He lumbered like an elephant on spidery legs toward the destruction it created, his eyes rolling, pinpoints in the shadows. Violent flames seared her insides, the penetration, thrust with such force, had torn through delicate vaginal membranous linings of her uterus. Engulfed at once with turbulent spasms, a molten-white heat so unbearable, she clawed at his face with long, sharp fingernails, pounded his head, temples. The strength drained from her. By then, it was over. He shuddered in exaggerated protracted spasms, and spending himself in a lengthy ejaculation, fell hard on her.

That she managed to push him off her was a miracle! She had laced the last bottle of brandy with Nembutol, a precaution against such predicament.

Valerie struggled upright, her labored, agonized breathing cutting the silence. She remained immobile, feeling the hot rush of blood and semen from between her legs. Valerie touched herself, felt the warm sticky coagulation of fluids, drew her hand to the light, appalled. Her entire hand was covered by blood. She drew the sheet between her legs, pressing against the swollen orifice, hoping to slow the hemorrhaging. Forcing her legs over the side of the bed, she pulled herself up, unsteadily, legs buckling under her. She cast a backward glance at the loathsome creature—*whoever he was*—and trembled.

Valerie held on to table, chair, anything, blood droplets mingling with oriental arabesques on the Persian carpeting. In a final lunge through the dressing room door, she locked it and groped along a wardrobe wall. She slid back a mirrored panel, reached into a drawer for a pearl-handled automatic. Something stuck between her toes. Wincing, she ignored it, pushing forward to the next room.

She dragged herself into the bathroom, locked that door, and checked the gun clip. It *was* loaded. The gun, suddenly irrelevant, she would have laughed had it not pained her to do so. The gun in hand was like locking the barn door after the felony. Valerie placed the gun on a fur-covered bathstool, opened the hot water tap, forcing water into the tub. She grabbed a towel, placed it between her legs to halt the flow of blood, reached into the medicine chest, popped two Demerols. Her body shook convulsively, the pain, intensely acute; she grew furious.

The bastard! The perverted sadistic beast! Damn him!

She lay in the hot tub attempting to calm her chaotic thoughts.

She felt as if she'd been flung into a swirling miasma of black terror, swimming for her life through a cesspool of decadence. The violation done her, abominable! She tried to piece together the continuity of events. One fact was irrefutable.

That bestial thing asleep on her bed was not Victor Zeller! The brutal primate deserved to be castrated! For the next hour, until relief came from both medication and hot water, she remained a mental basket case. Her eyes trailed to the .38. *Let him come at me again . . .*

A bit late for safeguards, Valerie, isn't it? You were warned about involving yourself in this bizarre and risky business! Valerie argued defensively. *A savage rape was not on the agenda!*

Before her defensive armor cracked irreparably, she dragged herself from tub to shower, shampooed her hair. Finished, she wrapped it in a towel, and wrapping a larger one around her body, shoved a few items into a small cosmetic case.

Something had caught her eye, glistening on the carpet. She painfully lowered her body, picked up the fragment, held it in her hand, suddenly aware—a blue contact lens stared at her, sightless. That's why Victor's eyes seemed different. Christ! How to put it back into Velden/ Victor/ Amadeo's eyes before he discovered it missing. How?

Unlocking the door, she padded through the dressing room to the second door, hoping to ease past the sleeping figure, grab some clothing and retire elsewhere in the house. She stopped in her tracks.

Velden sat up in bed, smoking a cigarette in the dim light.

"*Fräulein* Lindley . . . If I've done anything to cause you undue alarm . . ." He indicated the blood-stained sheets. "When I sighted the blood . . . Are you all right? I would leave, but suddenly I am so exhausted. Will you permit me to sleep a little longer?"

Before Valerie's anxiety intensified and communicated to him he rolled over, curled up fetally and fell into sound slumber. His total lack of recall, sudden shift in personalities iced Valerie's veins. Grabbing a silk robe from the chair, she slipped the gun in her pocket and moved closer to the bed, placing the contact lens next to his empty champagne glass.

Moments later she was locked in behind the upstairs study door. Reluctant to take a Demerol for fear she'd fall asleep, her hand gripped the gun. If *Amadeo* dared intrude again—she stared at her shaking hand. In her condition she'd miss elephant hide at five paces!

Now she waited for a pot of coffee to brew, standing at the balcony. It was night. A breeze rose off the Seine. Thank God! A break in the dreaded heat wave. Unwinding the toweling from her head, she shook loose her hair, toweling it briskly for a few moments, evading as she did the barrage of questions stampeding across her mind.

The pivotal question? Why was Victor Zeller masquerading as the innocuous Velden Zryden? It *was* Victor under that utterly ridiculous bleached-blond hair, misshapen nose and contact lenses! How Amadeo got into the act was mind boggling, but for Victor to subordinate himself to the role of a dandy like Zryden . . . ? The scenario read like pages from a Freudian primer.

Valerie, as a member of that elite organization, the American Bar Association, had learned the imperatives of taping conversations for later review. Unfortunately, out of the twenty-four hours she had recorded only four. She had hoped to capture the nuances in his voice, the tempo of speech. To review the tapes now was to court disaster should he awaken. Why hadn't she had the foresight to use videotape?

Wish for the impossible, girl. You're lucky to be alive!

Forced to review this Amadeo/ Victor/ Velden phenomenon, Valerie examined every wisp of evidence as if she were on trial for her life. She asked herself endless questions, reviewed her talks with Wilheim Zeiss's widow. A connection existed between the dead scientists and Victor and Amadeo. She'd stake her life on it. But what was that connection? She had thought she knew the answers after conferring with the Georgetown shrinks—but she knew nothing! *NOTHING!*

A captive of both the heat and humidity of Paris, she went inside to escape the cloying discomfort of both. She turned off the ineffective air conditioner—the noise was grating on her nerves. She popped another pain pill, curled up on a deeply cushioned recliner, nearly dozing off, when suddenly she sat up alert. Spikes of fertility fired her thoughts. She had it! The answer lay truant in her brain waiting to be caught. Slippery as an eel it eluded her; a scattering of puzzle parts floated about in her brain.

Stop thinking about it! It'll fall into place at the right time—
you know it will!

Pencil and pad in hand, she began listing the articles packed in her flight bag preparatory to flight time on the morrow. *Good. Change your thoughts consciously to something else.* Unconsciously, she twirled a long strand of silky red hair around her finger. Her *red* hair.

Her concentration drifted back to Victor/Velden/Amadeo.

She opened the music box on the table beside her, removed a cigarette, and puffing thoughtfully, the mirror-lined lid of the box in her hand, reflecting her image held her captive as the growing enigma concerning Victor Zeller became increasingly complex. The mental sorting and sifting of facts gave her no rest.

Victor Zeller *knew* her as Veronique Lindley. Amadeo knew her as Victoria Valdez of Argentina. Velden Zryden called her Veronique. Victor had not appeared at all. Velden explained he had come in search of Veronique Lindley to convey Victor's felicitations. How had he found her here at the Lansing address? Veronique's name was not listed. She stopped. Recalling Mosha Bauer and his talents, she scratched that theory off her mental notepad.

Then Valerie caught sight of her image in the music box lid. Still wrapped around her finger was a strand of red hair.

RED HAIR! . . . RED HAIR was the trigger to Amadeo's personality!

That night in Zurich, making love before the fire, Victor had called her *Victoria*! The firelight had transformed her hair to a pink golden glow! Oh, God! She had it!

And that note from Berlin! A simple command to tint her hair red!

A subliminal desire, one so forceful it compelled Amadeo to surface? *Why? Why? WHY?* What in damnation was transpiring? Was it some mystical, subliminal psychological imperative buried deep inside Victor to be like his father? What caused the flights into multidimensional personalities? *Velden Zryden* appeared functional. In his presence she had noted no outbursts, no excitement or anger in which she sensed danger. *Victor Zeller* had never intimidated her until the night the six scientists made lethal headlines. She had no gauge to measure Velden Zryden, but *Amadeo*—ugh! She grimaced.

538

Amadeo was aggressive, overbearing, and cunning. His sexuality, brutal, his first thrust inside her body more demoralizing than her stupidity in subjecting herself to the assault. Amadeo's assault contained no rhythm; he was a bloody, rutting beast. The sexual act to him was release and conquest—nothing else! At least Victor had cultivated the *art* of loving.

Thank God Victoria had resisted the virulent beast, Amadeo. If his genes flowed in her blood? . . . The revolting thought shuddered through her burning, aching body. She felt as if she'd been cut up and dissected by a battalion of sadistic butchers. Duped by her over-eagerness to indict!

Prior to the seduction Amadeo had boasted of his exploits, his adroitness in finance and business, politics and how he manipulated the less talented men of the world. He aired contempts, hatreds, pent-up humiliations done him by those he intended to pay tenfold.

Valerie had resisted interrogating him with barrister adroitness, certain he would have spotted duplicity at once. However ill-equipped she'd been to handle the personality shifts, she had demonstrated indomitable strength. That she had encountered, in some unfathomable manner a facsimile of the man responsible for the atrocities done her ancestor, had both awed and appalled her. She had flirted outrageously with him, determined to learn the truth from his lips and unwittingly became a pawn in sexual debauchery that nearly killed her.

Time worked against Valerie. Questions plagued her. Why did Victor persist in the Velden Zryden deception? For Valerie it was no longer a question of setting a trap for Victor. She was compelled to and would have followed through but couldn't achieve these ends until the complexities of the special taskforce mission had ended.

For a moment Valerie battled against the idea of postponing her pursuit of the truth. Yet the excitement of joining the Moufflon Taskforce was beyond the realm of anything previously experienced.

So, here she was in Paris, about to risk her life for something incomprehensible. She considered her mother's changed role before she agreed to the mission. "Your role as *special* envoy to the President can be arranged." The statement had stupefied Valerie; she had refused outright, not once but several times.

Valentina had baited her enticingly. "The leader of the

Taskforce, Moufflon will impart information to wrap up your case against Amadeo Zeller." *Just like that!*

So, Valerie had hooked into and psyched herself in Taskforce madness.

Now to exorcise the Victor/ Velden/ Amadeo triumvirate from mind. At least for a time.

She finished her coffee, retraced her steps to the bedroom, easing cautiously past the sleeping figure on the bed, into the bathroom, locking the door behind her. When she emerged, her red hair was buried under bleach and tawny blond toner. Whoever awakened from her bed must deal with that fact. And blond hair seemed safer all around. Or was it?

Dressed in flight fatigues, bush jacket, flight bag in hand, she slipped out the door, descended the stairwell and placing the USA/WPCC flight bag in the entry hall, glanced at the grandfather clock. She had plenty of time. She entered the kitchen, prepared breakfast.

"*Fräulein,* accept my apologies. Usually I do not sleep so long." He spoke in a German accented French, and mixed the two on occasion. "I am exhausted. Endless preparations for my journey, I suppose."

"Come, let me fix you a light breakfast."

"Coffee, *s'il vous plait.* Perhaps a croissant?" He entered the cheery kitchen of bricks and copper hoods and chef styled ovens glancing appreciatively at the homey surroundings.

"Was I—did I d-drink too much? If I abused your hospitality, in any way, I beg humble apologies. I would not have come if *Herr* Victor Zeller had not insisted—"

He remembered nothing of the previous night? Not of Amadeo nor the brutal assault upon her? What madness is this? No reaction to her new hair color?

How skillfully he portrayed the German, Velden Zryden. A quick look at him confirmed he had found the contact lens. Thank God!

"May I share your chocolate?" Victor yearned to caress her with love eyes. He got feigned indifference in return. She passed him the chocolate. "You seem in pain, *Fräulein.*"

"Yes. Menstrual cramps," she said with overt frankness.

Velden blushed, flustered. "May I use your privacies?"

Valerie led him to the guest bathroom. "Soap, towels, shower if you wish. My uncle's shaving things are in the drawers. Accommodate yourself."

Velden nodded, disappeared behind the door. She had cleared one mystery—it was her uncle's house. Next learn the identity of the Honorable Hartford B. Lansing, he told himself.

While he tended his toilet, Valerie sped up the stairs gathering all traces of dye bottles, bundled them in a plastic bag and tossed them down a trash chute to the basement. Next, the soiled linens from the bed went down the laundry shoot.

Downstairs she readied herself for departure. She set alarms into place, locked the rear doors, checked the French windows.

Finished, Velden Zryden reentered the corridor headed for the foyer. His eyes fell to the flight bag, arrested by the sight of the USA/WPCC insignia. He heard her footsteps, watched her enter the corridor. Dare he ask her what was becoming apparent to him?

"Are you leaving on holiday, *Fräulein*?"

"The trip I take is no holiday. It's a scientific expedition—nothing to interest you."

He was at once polite, accommodating, trying like the devil to keep calm. "May I take your bag?" *It couldn't be. It simply cannot be!*

"I have already called a taxi. May I drop you off someplace?"

They were out the door, Valerie secured the townhouse. Across the street the slouched figure of a man in a blue beret was leaning against the same tree Velden used on Saturday. Velden stared momentarily at him, trying to sort out this new development.

"*Herr* Zryden?" Following his line of vision she frowned, repeated herself.

"Yes, yes, of course, *Fräulein*. What is your destination?"

"The American Embassy. And yours—?"

Velden turned to her, eyes boring into hers, unparalleled confusion setting in.

"Is something wrong?" She glanced from Velden to the blue beret.

"Uh—no. I uh, too, go to the Embassy. But first I must go to the Bristol." He averted his head, felt sick to his stomach.

"*Merci bien*. I shall get off first and you continue to your destination." She fumbled with her handbag, suddenly disquieted.

They boarded the waiting cab, settled in the back seat.

541

Valerie forced light laughter. "Wouldn't it be hilarious we were to embark upon the same trip?"

"I should think not. The mission upon which I go is highly risky, dangerous, and classified. What is your destination? Something more frivolous than mine." He injected a superficial tone to his voice.

"Sorry, I am unable to discuss my travel itinerary. My trip is classified. Give my felicitations to *Herr* Zeller," she quipped. "Do tell him I miss him immensely and hope he is well."

"*Ja, ja*, I understand. I shall tell him." But Victor did not understand. The flight bag identical to his! Nuclear physicists, scientists, any number of people before Veronique qualified for this mission. *Why her?* He didn't like this new twist.

She alighted from the cab before the impressive American Embassy. "*Auf Wiedersehen, Herr* Zryden," she exclaimed breezily. "Good luck to you." She turned abruptly to an accommodating Embassy aide who had stepped forward taking her flight bag, requesting clearance papers.

"*Auf wiedersehen, liebchen*," he muttered softly. To the driver he snapped, "The Bristol, *s'il vous plait!*"

"*Oui, Monsieur Alleman*." The driver shot into the merging traffic. Velden, peering behind him, through the rear window noted two men boarded another cab tailgating them. *The man in the blue beret*. Good. His man . . . Velden's thoughts turned to Veronique. Her presence on the voyage presented complications. If by some curious oddity she identified him as Victor Zeller? . . .

Suddenly more complications loomed to disturb Velden. He could not remember anything from Saturday to this morning. Awakening, blinking at the distortion of sight, he had found the contact lens on the nightstand. The bloodied sheets confusing and distasteful enough, he dove into his memory to probe its contents. Apparently they had slept together.

But wait—she mentioned menstrual cramps. Then, *nothing* had happened. Touch a woman in ovulation? *Never!* He vaguely recalled the maple tree, the yellow roses . . . Nothing after that.

"The Bristol, *monsieur*! We are here!" The driver shouted to be heard over the raucous traffic sounds, tooting horns, drivers whizzing by on mopeds, Citroëns, Renaults and their frenzied, nerve-wracking driving breaking every traffic law.

Velden alighted the cab, paid him, skirted through the pedestrian traffic toward the hotel entrance. He paused slightly, the *blue beret* was coming toward him. He quickened his pace.

"*Herr* Zryden! *Herr* Zryden! Please, a moment . . ." The *blue beret* called to him.

Velden stopped cold. Behind dark glasses he took in the area peripherally. What could happen in broad daylight with so many people?

Obstructing him was a small, bony-faced man with a sharp beaked nose, the ruddy complexion of a drinker, pockmarked face and a mustache. He spoke in a regional French, and grasped Velden's arm clawlike.

"We must speak someplace in private, *Herr* Zryden."

"This is as good a place as any."

"We have a *mutual* friend."

"I doubt any friend of yours could be a friend of mine."

"*Herr* Bauer wishes you to call him before embarking on your voyage. Listen—"

"*Herr* Bauer? Has he given you a number to call?"

"—you must call Milos and Draga," the *blue beret* added nervously. "You will know where." He opened his jacket, a packette outthrust.

"Koseva? But, how would I know—*Oooooof!*" Before Velden sensed the trap, the *blue beret*'s hand, wielding a sharp blade, made a forward thrust and plunged the knife into Velden's rib cage. Velden, grabbing the man's hand, twisted it inward and downward, his right knee jammed into the assassin's groin. He disarmed him in a moment, but in the next the man pulled out a gun. Velden grabbed it, turned it inward toward the man's stomach and down. The gun exploded. The man leaped up into the air, back and down on his knees. Velden turned abruptly, not waiting to see the results and walking swiftly through the Bristol doors, headed through the crowded lobby to the elevator, holding his seersucker jacket over the spreading pool of crimson.

With every beat of his heart he felt the spurting of blood. He dared not look to see if he left a trail of crimson behind him.

In moments he was inside his suite. He tore off his jacket and bloodied shirt, turned on the overhead lights, examined the two-inch open gash. Quickly he ran to the closet, removed his flight bag, and from it, his shaving kit. Back in the bathroom he dumped the contents on the marble dressing table, and removed a false bottom. He removed one foil packet, serrated in half, tore both sides open with his teeth. He retrieved a purple capsule, opened it and poured the white powder on the open wound. Short of a laser to cauterize it and stop the bleeding, his miracle drug was incredible. He held the wound together, the sweat pouring off his face, down his neck. He counted to twenty. Before his eyes he witnessed the healing miracle, the flow of blood slowed; the wound began to repair itself.

Marvels of medical science! There were obvious benefits to retaining research scientists in a medical complex on the Zeller premises. The drug promoted healing with a velocity spanning a month's time. He tore open the second half of the packet, removed a pink capsule, popped it internally. He sipped a half glass of water. The drugs, as yet unnamed, generically were marked by numbers: respectively, EWH1000 and IAS1000, meant external wound healing and internal anti-shock. Identical numbers indicated symbiotic usage.

Last Friday on Velden's arrival at the Embassy he had undergone a physical examination, received clearance to briefing sessions. Today, a second physical was compulsory. He brooded over his stupidity, he could not risk disqualification now, after his impeccable planning—pray no other complication arose.

Velden Zryden had committed serious errors! Victor Zeller would not have acknowledged Mosha Bauer or the Koseva brothers! The capper was, Draga was dead and he forgot!

He slapped on a Band-Aid. By the time he arrived at the Embassy, the wound, reduced to a hairline scar, would be barely visible. He'd have no problem convincing a nosy medic the scar was six months old.

Velden opened a pack of chewing gum, chomped on a piece noisily. Dressed in beige fatigues, bush jacket and boots, he glanced about the room, flight bag in hand. Mosha Bauer would transport the remaining clothing to the Zeller townhouse. He left the room, locked the door and stepping briskly along the hall to the elevator descended, his thoughts roiling. *Who* suspected him? *Why?* What had he done wrong? Mental flagellation ensued. *Damn!* Velden cursed. Victor should have interceded, found a way to warn him.

Velden alighted the lift, elbowed his way through the crowded lobby to the men's room. *Victor Zeller*—not *Velden Zryden*—should be joining the Taskforce! Only *Victor* could salvage that idiot toymaker's stupidity!

544

Chapter Thirty-Six

*"We move about exploring . . . And at the end of our
exploring will be to arrive where we started and know
the place for the first time. . . .*

T.S. ELIOT

IN MAY, WHILE VALERIE WAS FIGHTING FOR HER LIFE
in the French Alps, a shift in the balance of domestic powers
within the East Wing factions of the White House tottered
precariously. The President and his First Lady were talking
calmly over a rare, quiet dinner when the conversation escalated
into heated diatribe, probing questions and finally stubborn
acquiescence. "You'll understand in due time, Geralee," the
President insisted firmly.

"Host the Senator and Mrs. Lansing, John? You must be
insane!"

"Very well, I'm insane. But attend to the details at once!" He
exasperated in a sabre-sharp voice, causing her to wince.

The abrasiveness of his tone brought immediate reaction from
his wife. Geralee Macgregor set aside her brandy, play-acted the
obedient wooden soldier: saluted him, walked stiff-legged to the
phone with tight-lipped submissiveness, and dialed a number.

The President, watching her, found no humor in the antics.

Valentina Lansing at the other end of the line listened to the
forced, politely phrased invitation mouthed with the warmth of a
robot and declined at once. "The Senator is away, Geralee.
Perhaps on his return a schedule can be arranged—"

"—do come despite his absence, Val." Geralee's mellifluent
tones patronized. "The President conveys the imperative of talk-
ing with you concerning matters of vital, mutual interest. The
Senator and I would only be decoys, dahling, to divert the press.
Oh, dear, you know the mechanics of subterfuge better than I.
You're so accustomed to Washington politics."

Oh, am I, thought Valentina, finding the moment irresistible

545

as images of Geralee and Anthony Harding flickered explosively in her mind. She controlled herself admirably as Geralee pressed the President's request, appending her words with a firm, "A helicopter will pick you up at your farm and fly you directly to Camp David. Dress casually, my dear. It's breathtakingly lovely and so *Americana*."

Geralee replaced the phone, and with a smug, satisfied smirk announced to the President, "All done, sir." She returned to her chair, polished off the brandy and with a tone of condescension nudged him a bit. "I just broke protocol for you. I hope it's appreciated. The First Lady never makes direct calls of this sort . . ."

John Macgregor, cutting her a sharp look, bit back the impulse to extend the private sortie between them. He thanked her, carried his coffee to an adjoining study, engaged six video monitors and stretched out comfortably on the sofa, this relaxation a rarity for him since the February Maui fiasco. Frowning, he fixed on the various news anchormen, thinking it uncharacteristic of him to cut Geralee off in mid-sentence. For nearly a year their relationship had deteriorated from bad to worse. He simply was unable to assimilate emptyheaded chatter of late—tonight was no exception.

Geralee, a svelt, highly photogenic woman in her fifties, looked thirtyish. Her figure, slim-hipped, was one over which designers drooled. Her studied, unruffled composure, every seam in place as if she'd been sketched, was idyllic for them and they plied their wares with the brashness of street hucksters brandishing gifts upon her, if only she would honor them with her endorsement.

She floated gracefully about social circles, grandly dressed, the epitome of charm, with a measured warmth, depending on the social over which she reigned. Unquestionably the motivational force behind her husband's political career, her displayed uncanny talent of *using* the *right* people in the *right* places for the *right* positions had catapulted John Macgregor through gubernatorial and White House residences with skillful dégagé. Her icy sagacity in social functions, was as vital to the President as were his constituents.

Geralee, Bar Harbor's most eligible coed, fell for John *Savage* Macgregor for his mow-'em-down, steamrolling gridiron magic at a time when "You Gotta Be a Football Hero," swept through

American lore. John's concentrated brooding, charming boyish rascality surfaced lazily through a ruthless masculinity and dashing quarterbacking heroism, capturing her heart. They fell in love, married and remained together for decades as idyllic partners, totally seduced by politics, sharing a climate of mutual self-respect in a rare, one-in-a-million marriage.

On the eve of their wedding John asked his bride, "Do you think I'll turn out to be what you want me to be?" Her reply had been a firm, "No doubt exists in my mind at all."

Ferocious, fang-baring columnists conspiring against the marriage had failed miserably in their efforts to find a shaky closet skeleton.

Confidence, faith, mutual trust and respect, essential ingredients to a successful marriage, had been held inviolate. It had worked.

But make no mistake, the President's unwavering devotion and open graciousness to his wife was not to be interpreted as weakness or a knuckling-under female dominance; his was always the final word.

Geralee's practiced fixed expression of devotion in the President's presence; attacked by rivals and reporters as posed, theatrical and superficial, was all that and more. Geralee was the first to admit it. Exposed brutally in her neophyte politicking days to the catastrophic results of a probing camera lens, she determined to thwart the neurotics who thrived on and got their kicks in concocting renditions of anything rapturous between husband and wife. Geralee's scrupulous resolve induced her to laboriously study professional camera techniques and favorable angles. If any vulturous camera lens intended to fix the President and First Lady on film for posterity, she'd be prepared.

Before the Oval Office crackled on the horizon of John's hopes and ambitions, Geralee persisted in posturing about as First Lady. Politics had seduced Geralee. She possessed no qualms about anything save those tormenting all-aging women held in public view.

The agony of age lines, skin deterioration, false teeth, glasses, sagging skin where uplifting was preferred. All this signaled disaster to her, and she attended to the nuances before they evolved to serious problems. Such pretentious vanities had presented the only disaster to Geralee Macgregor's world as she knew it.

Until recently.

Of late she grew bored with her own perfection. Actually it began a year ago. She fell madly, insatiably in love with Anthony Harding, the Secretary of State.

Geralee took her coffee into the study to be with the President. She poured a jigger of brandy into the Royal Doulton china cup, unaware that the President observed her through lidded, hypercritical eyes. An imperceptible frown flickered across his face before settling into masked indifference. Internally he was deeply concerned. She had taken to drinking again—a bad sign. She seemed edgy, unnatural, too studied, the eyes glazed over at times, and less coherent or interested in their lives.

Geralee sat down in a high-backed, winged chair, arranging the folds of her flame-red lamé hostess gown in perfect drape, stopping abruptly, realizing she had no audience to please, no photographic session on the agenda. She sipped the spiked coffee, actually amazed at the abandonment of past virtues. How had it happened? How had she permitted it to happen? She stirred the coffee with trembling fingers, sipped more, then rose quickly to her feet and walked to the window, thinking of the stock requisitions she must sign for the coming State dinner. Let's see . . . filet mignon, baby lobsters, pâté de foie gras, shallots, mushrooms, strawberries, ice cream, Dom Perignon White Chablis, Red Burgandy . . . mmmn, so may other things.

It was dusk, she stared out at the Jacqueline Bouvier Kennedy Garden. Mockingbirds rested on heavily laden maple leaf boughs. Cardinals chittered away, mourning doves foraging about called plaintively and low, echoed inside the study.

Geralee flicked her long manicured fingernails, her increasing nervousness a cover-up for a *cause sans honneur*, was getting to her. She lived in daily fear of discovery. For the past three months she had barely got through the turmoil of rescheduled dinners and social functions. The President's every waking moment had been consumed by vital State matters, and it fell upon her to administer iron-fisted instructions to insure proper coordination for each social function. Sometimes she felt like chucking the entire mess down the toilet.

Fortunately she had qualified, experienced staff experts who meticulously followed her instructions. If she became truant, they could fill in without damage to First Lady prestige. It wasn't easy to do what was expected while a legacy of turmoil bombarded the Oval Office.

Geralee glanced over at the dozing President. A dark wedge of desperation had driven them apart. Once as close as peas in a pod, they seemed unable to communicate. How many times she had wanted to unburden her soul! Tell him everything!

It would crush him! Crumble his entire world! And hers!

She tiptoed out of the room, along the carpeted corridor to her private quarters, a recently redecorated, ultra-feminine room where she could wrap herself in total privacy. The scent of fresh bouquets scented the room, giving it allure.

She sat at the ivory and pumice escritoire, shuffled listlessly through the neatly stacked *Thank You* notes requiring her personal signature. She lighted a cigarette, her eyes trailing to the ivory and gold French phone inches from her.

Prompted to pick it up, she resisted admirably, puffed instead on the cigarette with visible tremors. Her eyes on the phone again, she marshaled all her resistance against making the call. Geralee had endured this nightly ritual for months. Here, in her pastel sanctuary, hand on the phone, tempted time and again, resisting bravely, she asked herself how much longer she dared play this lethal game with herself. God *knew* she had resisted! One night she might not be able to, then what?

Any little thing ticked her off. Last month their vacation was cancelled; a long-anticipated vacation at their home in the Florida Keys. She actually intended to confess everything to John. There in the tropical setting, amid familiar surroundings, she could have unburdened her soul. Instead they had contented themselves with retreats to Camp David. *Retreat!* Hah! Camp David was fiasco! Presidential aides, advisors, clustered thickly around John like bats in daylight caves; they hovered over him without apology to her.

Constant competition for the President's time against burly Secret Service men, aides, foreign dignitaries and diplomats rankled her. She felt inept, useless, in the way.

The personal cost to become First Lady was enormous; the fringe benefits had far exceeded the price paid—for a time. The heady elixir of sovereignty, ephemeral at best, she wondered how she'd fare without the recognition and respect she got once the power sceptre was removed from her bejeweled, manicured hands?

Periods of such introspection and value judgments held her in line recently, but for how much longer? Geralee was now caught up in booze and pills to diffuse the rooting anger and feelings of inadequacy.

When was it—a year ago?

She had danced with Anthony Harding at a State dinner. He had flirted outrageously with her, whispering sweet nothings, flattering her in ways she desperately needed from John and despaired because he didn't fill her needs nor was he inclined to.

The music was grand, a waltz of the forties played as Harding swept her about the crowded floor. "You're a flirt, Geralee Macgregor. Deep down you are an untouched passion flower oozing with seduction. Without you John would not be President. You are his armor, strength, the iron will that moves him. Oh, God, so few of your kind exist! What I could achieve with you behind me!" He spoke brazenly, unabashed, with a strong vigor, and stared into her shocked, mildly amused, slowly melting eyes. At first offended by him, she relegated it to humor, but looking into his eyes, she saw cold, lusting sobriety.

She felt him harden against her, pulled back, only to be grasped firmly in his strong arms. "See what you do to me? No woman has done that to Anthony Harding in God knows how long. No, no, don't pull away from me. Let me savor every blissful moment. Besides," he chided, "if you do, I shall stand naked before this auspicious gathering where all can see the hard-on you've given me," he cooed, bringing crimson flush to her cheeks.

And Geralee, *damned* if she did, and *damned* if she didn't, hung steadfast to his pirouetting body as he whirled her out to the terrace in the fresh air. "Don't leave me. Stay, have a cigarette with me. You know," he said after inhaling a few drags, "you are a damned, hard, cold, ravishing beauty, all svelte, voguish on the outside, tied with *Woman's Wear Daily* bows, primly wrapped and labeled: *DO NOT TOUCH*! But inside, churning your insides, is a sweltering furnace of sensuality begging seduction."

"Anthony! Mr. Secretary, stop this!" She giggled, thinking the farce had gone too far. He was drunk, that was it—he was loaded!

He grabbed her hand, placed it over his hard crotch. "See what you've done? You've give me a hard-on and believe me, First Lady, that hasn't happened to old A.H. in decades."

She wouldn't know the extent of this truth until much later.

"Really," she tried pulling away. "If the Secret Service or White House aides see this abominable behavior—"

"Promise you'll meet me! Promise! Anywhere—the Carlisle, Hilton, Watergate—"

"—you're mad! Never any of those places!" She stopped, aware of the double-edged meaning her words produced.

Geralee pulled herself together. "Mr. Secretary, I am going back inside. I'll forget all you've said and suggest you do the same. I am the President's wife. You, a member of his cabinet—a trusted member, I might add. You wouldn't want me to relate this outrageous behavior to him, would you?"

"You won't. You want me more than ever, now. I can feel the juices churning inside you. Your eyes are sparkling like jewels. You never really entered the giddy world of romantic adventure before you married and it's time you did. You passed it up, opting instead for an exceptional marriage to a man you shaped and molded skillfully into the Presidency. You did, Geralee, you deserve a gold star, but in so doing you passed up being a woman. Right at this moment, your heart is aquiver, your pulses are racing, temples throbbing. Don't deny it. Moments like this come once in a lifetime. I'll call you, make the necessary arrangements. You just bring yourself. Give the watchdogs and feisty Dobermans the slip and I shall promise you paradise."

Geralee had spun on her heels, furious, and entering the ballroom, took a moment to put herself in order, to mask the glowering wrath she felt. The President was dancing with Senator Lansing's wife. Immediately a White House aide stepped forward, offered his arm and staring at her flushed face asked if she was feeling unwell. She nodded and mumbled something about the lobster. "Will you escort me to my suite? Tell the President I am lying down for a few minutes."

That's how it began and continued for nearly a year. Harding treated her like a lusty red-blooded woman with needs, desires and fantasies needing venting, not a stone statue or an institution.

She fought further liaisons with him; each time she retreated from some hidden countryside rendezvous, like a fugitive sneaking around disguised, she swore it would be the last time. But with a drug-crazed addict's weak resolve, lured by wild and unleashed sexual excitement, she went back for more, driven by animal lust.

It was not a simple feat for the First Lady to engage in illicit love trysts undetected by the dozen or more curious eyes watching her every move, protectingly. Geralee found she was not without a unique cleverness in conjuring a thousand discreet ways to liaison with A.H. God, how many lies had she manufactured? How many deceptions she had foisted upon the Secret Service? How many designers in New York had she ferreted out? How many hairdressers? She had looked into spas and retreats, conjuring a sudden illness. How many deviations in plans had she managed? Enough to nearly span an entire year.

Geralee paced the bedroom floor. If the President had learned of the affair? Oh, Jesus! The thought panicked her. But if he had known, she would have noted a sign in him, wouldn't she? His interest in the Oval Office and coterie of hangers-on, all too consuming, left him no time to contemplate her. Good old Geralee was always there in the clinches, when things got tough.

She lighted another cigarette, glancing at the locked liquor cabinet at the end of the boudoir. God, she needed a drink! A real drink, not an after-dinner liqueur. How long ago was it? January.

By January confusion had disrupted her thinking. In the past Anthony had provided her aphrodisiacs, he said, to unleash a deep-seated passion, a sexual sensuality needing expression. By then she'd become insatiable, unable to concentrate on anything except the uncontrolable nymphomaniacal drive for urgent sex and its fulfillment.

Morning, noon and night, she marked time from one sex orgy to the next, unable to dismiss Anthony Harding from mind. And when he flew abroad on matters of state, he left her a box of pills to calm her, he said, "To assuage the hunger in you for me." In his absence she grew listless, depending more on her social secretaries and housekeepers to arrange her social engagements. No longer did the affairs bear her special touch. It all was a bore, and she didn't care!

Didn't care! Later she turned green with envy thinking the White House could get along without her. Was it this that brought the change in her? No. Truly she felt lost, overwhelmed by frightening remoteness, the feeling she had lost her soul, and the next day would find her with less courage, less patience, totally sapped of strength.

But then Harding returned, and she came alive again, if one can be dead and alive at the same time. She began to sense something was terribly wrong.

Actually it began when Harding began to ask her intimate questions about the President. Geralee consciously declined to reply, and Harding, the prick, had turned aloof, cold, pulled away from her like a petulant schoolboy and she had yielded, at times uncontrollably discussing personal, political and other matters. She had divulged vital information she wouldn't have done of her own volition.

She would have killed to keep Harding as her sexual partner! She could not deny, even now, that her wish was longing to surrender—to have that immense body and personality overwhelm her. Such was the pandemonium of her troubled mind.

Geralee advanced toward the phone. Her trembling, wavering hand reached out and snapped back instantly as if she'd touched live wires. *Don't do it! Don't! You've been through hell! You want more of the same?*

In January, something jarred her, shaking her to the core. She knew things weren't right, but under Harding's hypnotic mystique—whatever the hold he had over her—she seemed unable to acquiesce to anything save Harding's demands. Those fiery dark eyes ignited her soul. She was deteriorating internally without knowing why and resisted going to her personal physicians at Walter Reed. But the feeling persisted, and Geralee, intelligent as *any* woman attuned to her mate, sensed alienation in her last encounter with Harding and got the shock of her life.

Rejection occupied no place in her mental landscape. Before anyone did it to her, she opted to get to bat first and cut him off.

She sought help.

What was his name? The gentle, country doctor in the unlikely town of Triangle, Virginia had suggested her ailment was symptomatic of drug withdrawal. Controlled substance, he called it. She must give up all alcohol and drugs. She had urinated blood; tests indicated severe liver damage. Astounded, she had chirped the familiar aria thousands before her had vocalized, "But, doctor, I don't drink *that* much!" And she didn't, but couldn't prove it by the tests. He requested she leave a sampling of all ingested medication. "In a week, after complete analysis, I shall confide the results," he told her.

Geralee, wigged, dressed sedately, using an alias and dark-lensed glasses, returned to Triangle a week later, emerged at the rustic cottage shaken, her face ashen, disbelief flooding her senses. She hadn't eaten in days, and felt like regurgitating, a case of dry heaves. The ride back to D.C. took forever, and finally, returned to her sanctuary, she moved zombie-like in her boudoir in the East Wing. She refused all calls, including Harding's, *especially* Harding's. She wandered through crowded corridors nodding mutely, forcing a placid smile, avoiding gawking tourists, and locked herself in the library reading all she could find on the subject of cocaine and heroin addiction.

Fear blitzkrieged her mind. The whole thing was crazy! *Impossible!* Addicted to popping fifty pills within forty-eight hours? She should have suspected and didn't. Aghast at the progression of facts piling up in her mind, she refused to believe Harding had *dared* compromise her in a bold act determined to destroy her and John. But as the facts assembled, they massed into a tower of premeditated strategy. Geralee, infuriated at her naivete, marshaled hidden forces and set about putting her house in order. Drowned in memories, bludgeoned into clear perspective by *those* memories, she quietly, without fanfare, entered the battlefield in full armor, guided by a preponderance of New England grit and stamina, guts and determination.

A spa in Florida, specializing in drying out boozers, withdrawing pill freaks and separating drug addicts from their habits, became her home for a month. The timing—perfect. The approaching Maui Conference occupied every waking moment of the President's time; he barely missed her.

Geralee moved doggedly to the liquor cabinet. Clean for three months, one Scotch wouldn't hurt—would it? It was either drink or reach out and call that ghoul, Harding. She chose the lesser of two evils—Scotch. She belted half a glass, then refilled it, tossed it down her throat, letting the burning sensation worm through to her intestines. Soon would come a glow, a welcome, relaxing glow.

She had made it through another day!

She padded out the door to the study reflecting briefly on that month at the spa. She'd taken the treatment cold-turkey! Two solid weeks of torturous nightmares had reduced her to animal behavior. Wallowing in her own excrement and vomitings, she had begged for death a thousand times. Instead she encountered the vilest of lower world demons borne of hallucinations and malnutrition. The third week found her afflicted by an over-whelming weakness, assuaged only by rest, food and psychiatric counseling. She had fought the battle and won, only to be cautioned how many more battles loomed on the horizon of each day and must be fought as they came. That it was not over, not wrapped neatly and tidily in a package with a giant red satin bow, came as a blow to her. Warned never to drink or take pills again, she was summarily briefed on the irrevocable physical and brain damage she courted. Her system was not immune to the continued abuse of drugs.

Geralee paused a moment in the kitchen area, reached for a diet drink from the refrigerator in the quiet restaurant-like galley. She continued back toward the study, brooding, in a sense petrified at her foolishness. More ate away at her, and it grew worse every day since her return.

She was still stunned by the progression of events, but no longer afraid, for the implications, as clear as they were, were still shadowed by doubt until that day—that last day they had spent together, when Harding had harshly enlightened her on the role she played in his life.

He had shown her photographs. Large 8 × 10 glossies. With brutal clarity there was no mistaking her; she recognized the obscene animal in herself, the passion and lust-filled greed. The most sordid humiliation of all was she pretended indifference to the pornographic shots of them together. Whatever coercion or extortion he intended didn't matter, but the all-consuming, ani-mal disease that made her *want* him, crave him, and felt that he might not need her or want her anymore, sickened her. The seduction, she reasoned, had been successful enough, but shaky, weak from the impact of his revelation, and the disgust etched into his face for her, pushed her off the edge into the depths of personal degradation of which she'd never believed herself capable. "You don't need the photographs. I'll do anything you want. All I want," she told him with ferocious crudeness, "is to be fucked by you, morning, noon and night!"

Geralee shuddered at the recollection, at his wicked triumph that day, and only later when the image of that look returned time and again to haunt her, did she mobilize against him. Knowing him for what he was, even now as she walked softly past the security guard at the end of the corridor, Geralee wanted to warn her husband against that sidewinding, slithering slime, to suggest he not take Harding into his confidence, that he must rid himself of the contagion before it became epidemic. But she was unable to garner the cunning needed to slaughter Harding politically. Worse, her loathing for Harding and his vile, contemptible ploys to wreck her life was powerful, but when she learned of his proclivities for young men and little boys, her loathing reached explosive porportions.

What shook Geralee to the core was the inner humilation and knowledge she still craved this human depravity and this craving was driving her up the wall. She fought the craving as an addict fought his craving for drugs, never knowing for sure when she'd lose.

Was it to be a never-ending battle? If so, she promised herself she'd face it and ultimately she'd win or lose. She couldn't have it both ways. She nurtured the insidious thoughts daily, knowing that when the time came, she wouldn't hesitate a moment to kill if she must. In three months the photographs hadn't surfaced—or had they?

Geralee's hand trembled on the gold doorknob. She entered the study.

John Macgregor had cat-napped, awakened at nine P.M. to find Geralee asleep in the chair. He covered her with a satin coverlet, turned the light low, snapped off the video monitor and left the room, heading for the Oval Office. He understood Geralee's discontent. His own sexual urges and loving moods had suffered from an over-burgeoning of insoluble problems.

He walked along the corridor, taking the back stairs to the first level, needing the exercise, thinking of Geralee and her remoteness, her untouchable attitude. In bed, it was pure release for him, little sexual excitement, and he didn't know why. Unable to strike up the rapport they both enjoyed nearly a year ago, he was unable to take her into his confidence. He blamed it on age, but that was deception. Something hidden, invisible to the naked eye, formed an impenetrable barrier, driving the wedge between them deeper.

Too much had happened. Too much!

In the darkness, seated in his chair behind the desk in the Oval Office, faint illumination filtered through the colored windows from the spotlights outside on the White House grounds, playing weird patterns of lights and shadows inside. He swiveled his chair about, eyes trailing up the flagpole, riveting on the glaring-eyed golden eagle perched atop a ball at the pinnacle.

A thousand scenes played across his mind for several moments, then placing them on hold, he picked up the phone, dialed an unlisted number, waiting as it rang at the other end. "Valentina . . . I had to call. Geralee didn't give you the opportunity to refuse. Is this weekend suitable?"

"Thank you for acknowledging my position. This weekend is simply not feasible, John. My daughter was injured in an accident in France. I expect her home momentarily. You will forgive me? Is it as urgent as Geralee intimated?"

"Yes. It can wait. Yours is a higher priority. I pray the injuries are not serious."

"Thank you. I'll get back to you as soon as I know . . ."

The President rang off. He felt isolated, mentally wearied and more alone than ever. He seemed unable to sit tall in the saddle. muster enough energy to propel him to action. He reflected disconsolately on his mounting political woes.

Inexorably the gargantuan, slickly oiled political machine of the *invisible* cartel pressed tighter and tighter on John Macgregor. Ultimately it would isolate, engulf and strangle him. He believed this and this belief was suffocating him.

Dammit! He touch-opened a cabinet under his desk, produced a flagon of brandy, poured a tumbler full and gulped it defiantly. Far-reaching Presidential powers provided no answers to his dilemma. How would he extricate himself from the greedy bastards. who demanded *control—Control—CONTROL!* of the executive branch of American government? *How?*

Christ! They owned him lock, stock and barrel! He was worse, far worse than any of them. He had permitted the seduction!

They were the arch destroyers! Determined to annihilate everything in the world that failed to suit their purposes. Whole populations uprooted, exterminated because *they* took a dislike to them! *They* studiously put into practice theoretical genocide—right under America's nose! Their nihilism, if followed to its logical conclusion, would convert the planet into a universal graveyard! Their covetous ways perpetuated greed to own and *control*!

The President poured another brandy, unable to shake the clear emergence of an ugly pattern from which he was unable to extricate himself. Could he escape that shadowy niche at the

557

pinnacle of power, urged on by men of *control* to commit the ultimate crime, the perfect atrocity, annihilation of mankind? *All* mankind, save a power elite of supermen who by their own humble admission deserved to rule and control the world?

How many before him had listened to their seduction? How many *greedy* politicians on-the-take had taken? Christ! He felt sick!

Macgregor unlocked his safe, removed the *HIGHLY CLASSI-FIED* dossiers submitted by General Brad Lincoln, those including the Zeller files. He had reviewed them time and again. On this night he reviewed them meticulously.

By early morning the President, numbed by the explosive contents, felt the earth crumble and slip away from him. His own perfidy, embodied in the diabolical machinations of Amadeo Zeller, cleverly mirrored in mind. Was he, John Macgregor, America's president, a disgrace to the office? A betrayer of his people? A puppet? An expertly manipulated marionette doing the bidding of the most wretched, contemptible man to walk the earth—a raving psychopath?

The covertly compiled files, if aired publicly, shaped into the worst political nightmare in U.S. history! Zeller and his *control* army had infiltrated every branch of U.S. government, held the nation by the proverbial balls, squeezing them into impotence.

The pressure began following the Maui Conference. The Oval Office fell prey to a venomous slander and media assault. That the highest echelon in government was unable to halt the abuse against him brought a fulminating Macgregor out of the Presidential dugout to play ball—his kind of ball. But the slander aimed at demolishing Macgregor's administration picked up momentum. Moufflon, rallying swiftly to the rescue, had offered his services once again, despite the Maui betrayal.

John Macgregor's life was expendable, no one more cognizant of this fact than he. He also knew how Zeller's robots, busily at work, could feed the nation a vicious manufacturing of his treachery, embellishing the deeds far beyond their actual bounds. One way out of the mess was unacceptable—*assassination*!

Assassination—their most effective tool, huddled at the edge of the President's thinking. If they *got* him—who would become the next puppet to adorn the Oval Office.

Brad Lincoln's caveats replayed in the President's mind. *"Talk with Valentina Lansing. She'll fill in the missing pieces!"*

CAMP DAVID MARYLAND
A FEW WEEKS LATER

Rustic cottages, a stunning landscape scattered along one side of a small mountain was sheltered by thickly clustered oaks and the honeyed scents of wildflowers. All the natural wonders were defiled by a high-wire security fencing winding along its perimeter. The scene was conducive to great silence and meditation.

"It was called Shangri-La by Franklin Roosevelt," the President pontificated as they walked the woodsy path early in the morning. "Later Dwight Eisenhower renamed it to honor his son David. Since then the site has become a monument to limited peace. Here on these very grounds, President Jimmy Carter brought together two mortal enemies for a brief, historical moment."

"The Camp David Accords." Valentina interjected, inhaling the saturated scents of dogwoods, redbuds, sassafras.

Standing mute at the paned windows of the Presidential cottage, beleaguered by livid jealousy, Geralee Macgregor observed the couple anbling along the winding path. Despite their lack of privacy and the constant presence of the Secret Service men deployed at respectable distances from them, Geralee couldn't rid herself of the surfacing envy.

A half hour ago, shortly after breakfast, she had abdicated her role as wife to that of an *understanding* First Lady. She regretted the move. Thoughts running wild in her mind wreaked havoc on her senses.

What secrets did Valentina Lansing cover that could possibly interest the President?

Now, she thought about it, even Harding had asked her questions regarding Valentina Lansing.

Valentina to Geralee was a functional machine of absolute perfection; a stunning arrangement of eyes, nose, lips, hair, spectacular bone structure and statuesque body. She commanded enviable poise, elegance, wit, courage. She's ageless, *dammit!* Geralee thought with a twinge of self-consciousness. *Dammit! Dammit! Dammit!* Did she have to look so perfect? Avocado designer jeans, silk shirt, cable knit sweater tossed over her shoulders in the brisk morning air. Even the wind worked for Valentina, tossing her red hair about, enhancing her allure!

Geralee withdrew from the window, furiously. *You're in your dotage, ceding your husband to this woman for three entire days!*

John Macgregor and Valentina scuffled along the path, skirting the dining areas and conference rooms on the property, the sounds of their boots crunching dry twigs and pebbles amid shadowy lanes.

The cloying, unmistakable essence of skunk permeated the air. They both grimaced tolerantly. Oblique starbursts splintered overhead treetops, glistening the lower reaches like varnished leaves. Dotted along the path between boulders, pebbles and a mossy embankment, tiny pink flowers sprouted in a fragrant mist.

In the distance the magnificent Blue Ridge Mountains reigned majestically over the valley misted by floating fog banks, giving pigeonholed views of stately creations. The dew on the hills and leaves sparkled like faceted gems. Wildflowers on clumps of red, white and yellow foliage abounded.

The President articulated a glowing historical retrospective, pointing out landmarks, quoting names like Catoctin Furnace, Frizzleburg, Funkstown, Freeland. . . . Valentina, at home in this setting, listened politely with avid interest, wondering what it really was he wanted from her.

Ever constant, numerous footsteps, behind, at all sides of them, formed an invisible cordon of protection. They were swarms of unflaggingly persistent men in their devotion to protect the President—the Secret Service. Overhead a Huey Cobra, an unmarked Army helicopter, dipped, soared, banked and rose horizontally with its noisy putt-putt-putting rotors, policing the area, constantly communicating with deployed ground forces.

As long as the President kept mobile, relatively hidden from possible overhead attack, their jobs were easy. Should he sprint out into open spaces—*pandemonium*! A speeding-up protective effort would be put into motion. Despite the constant surveillance and distractions on all sides, the couple maneuvered as best they could, speaking in quiet tones.

The President asked Valentina carefully posed questions, at all times aware of the close proximity of the agents. "Tell me what you know of this man, Moufflon," The President began, picking up a stick and snapping off the tiny twig protrusions, bit by bit.

Valerie gazed at him, then, past him up at the throbbing blue sky as if she needed an uplifting energy to speak. She began slowly. "Bear with me, Mr. President, if my story sounds illogical, a figment of a wild, vivid imgination." She paused. "Don't expect it to fit into a tidy package, neatly labeled and wrapped in brightly colored ribbons. Five centuries before Moufflon's physical appearance on earth, Destiny was moving people into proper places preparing for him."

"We are speaking of the man, Darius Bonifacio, a Corsican, are we not? Don't add the burden of supernatural to an already incredible human being. Turn him into a young god and I'll bolt faster than wild cheetah!"

"Yes, of course, Darius Bonifacio. Not *exactly* a Corsican, yet a truer Corsican than any man born on the island save one. He is a truly remarkable man."

Together they stepped into a shadowed lane, drenched with crispy coolness. Valentina shrugged into her sweater. Macgregor placed a hand on her arm, staying her. "I consider you a most remarkable woman. I don't know how to deal with you—never have."

"Ah—you see, it's because I've belonged to him all my life. He is the light of my heaven. He holds my heart within his heart, but is unaffected by it. He loved me for a while and it lasted forever."

"And you have been *my* unrequited love. Do you know the hell it is wanting to make love to you, yearning to take you into my arms?"

Valentina paused, stared at him, eyes searching his. "*You* make love to *me?*"

"In a moment, if the orchestra and balcony seats weren't sold out." He gestured to the entourage flanking them nearby. "And right over *there*, on the grassy knoll, under God, for the whole world to see."

Valentina laughed. "You say that because you know you're safe."

He sighed with mock desperation. "If *I* were not *me* and *you* were not *you*, we could run off together, make new memories and kiss off this crazy world. It's getting to be a wretched place."

Valentina scanned the periphery. Noticeably impatient agents studying the couple were eager for them to move on. The

561

President grinned wickedly, aware he made a perfect assassination target, he often bedeviled the agents by pulling the unexpected.

"We're outnumbered, outdistanced, and outgunned. If I decided we must fornicate this moment, what do you suppose they'd do?"

"We'll never know, will we, Mr. President?"

"No," he sighed, "we won't. I don't regret trekking the back roads of memory lanes. I promise not to interrupt." He gestured over his heart, delivered a parenthetical sermon on the merits of being a good listener. Beads of sweat broke out on his forehead, yet his blood seemed iced. For reasons buried deeply within his psyche he seemed disinclined to listen. From what he'd read in those accursed files, soon to be sewn together by threads of truth, he wondered where it would lead.

He shook his head. The time for delay was over; it was time to listen to what General Brad Lincoln suspected Valentina alone knew. He was blunt. "We are here conversing because of what is happening in the Middle East. I've whipped myself mentally a hundred times since I let him down—this Moufflon of yours."

Valentina did not reply. She scuffed up pebbles with her boots.

"You don't agree with my politics, do you? Yet your financial backing was always there."

"I did once, Mr. President. Not recently. But I do understand."

"God! Spare me that understanding. No one understands!"

"Not all men can bulwark such obvious pressures."

"I am not *any* man. I am President of the United States. That places me in a *special* category. The nature of the facts you present crystalizes my doubts. I am consumed with curiosity and deeply aggrieved."

"With your permission, suppose I continue in an effort to assuage those doubts?" She sat down alongside him on a split rail fence. She indicated a rising frustration. "You make it difficult, Mr. President. Let me get on with it or you'll never hear the truth. My courage is waning." She smiled grimly and lit a cigarette.

He made an apologetic gesture. "Please carry on."

"If there is a contemporary beginning, this is how it began. Believing what I tell you, you must accept the truth of my story, for it is the way my mother Victoria Miles Valdez de la Varga of Argentina lived it. Darius was born a bastard. Adopted by a

562

madman, he was programmed to kill. But destiny overruled the tampering of this special child and determined he emerge unscathed and victorious from a savage, bloody vendetta in which he was merely a pawn, moved men into positions benefiting him. The man who would be Moufflon was molded by Destiny into the man she decreed.

"An in-depth investigation conducted in the 1920's that continued until the day Victoria died, produced a verification of facts, all certified by a prestigious law firm in the U.K. and QIS (Queens Investigative Service) founded by the late Sir Arthur Duns Scotis."

Macgregor acknowledged the highly accredited, distinguished investigative firm with a perceptible tilt of his head. His attention captured, it was held morning, noon and night for the entire three-day weekend. The story continued at her retreat at Fox Run, Virginia, on her own turf. Following the narration of her own life, one nearly as incredible as Moufflon's, the President retired to the White House where he somberly reviewed Valentina's story and patched together the disturbing hiatus in Zeller's life.

He reassessed the accumulated data on the redoubtable Amadeo Zeller, his loathing for the man incalculable. He managed for the next several weeks to avoid the phobic carping of all *special* interest groups. A press release indicated the President was suffering from a virus, but rallying steadily. Actually he was stalling for time, waiting.

What would Zeller's tentacles latch onto next?

Chapter Thirty-Seven

July 7, 1984

President Macgregor's *hotline* call to the Soviet Premier precluded a stampede at the Oval Office. Special interest groups demanded audience. *Demanded the President's time!* Bold, hardliner spokesmen had made themselves perfectly clear.

"Miracles are needed, Mr. President. Miracles only we can provide. Crisis upon crisis will continue to befall America, ravage the economy beyond repair, destroy your credibility, force your recall from office—anything short of a White House coup—"

"This is blackmail! Downright blackmail!" The President exploded, flushed with purple rage.

"That's a harsh word, Mr. President." The spokesman flouted his clout. "Two years ago, America on the verge of internal collapse, a soaring inflation, rising unemployment and numerous other factors created adversities in your administration. You needed a respite. We provided it. You boldly ascribed to our principles in the wind of international dissension. Our people goosed Wall Street. Stocks soared. The Dow Jones peaked at record numbers, higher than any in Wall Street history. We lowered interest rates, gave people hope until *after* the election. We came through for you—now the favor must be returned. *PROJECT: MOONSCAPE* must not succeed! Take measures to scuttle it!"

Wearied, overburdened, he stared at the covey of men positioned high in government, men he and his predecessors had personally elevated to *control* status. An elite group with *special* duties answerable to no one. Sickened by them, he dismissed them all. "I need time to plan the necessary strategy," he said icily.

"Don't bother, Mr. President. The strategy has been worked out and approved." The spokesman, a powerful brokerage tycoon on Wall Street and London, shot smug electric glances at his equally audacious companions. "You have until July 31 to abort the mission, else our people will take over. The Moufflon Taskforce is scheduled to depart at 1600 hours Paris time."

Even John Macgregor wasn't privy to the schedule, yet!

Collectively their presence defiled the Oval Office. Long after their departure the stench of their perfidy endured. Macgregor *knew* them for exactly what they were and loathed himself for permitting the ongoing seduction.

July 31, 1984

AT 1600 HOURS, PARIS TIME, Moufflon's silver Lodestar jet, a reconverted 747, taxied under heavy military escort to the end of a private runway in a sector adjacent to Charles de Gaulle International Airport. The pilot revved the engines with open throttles. Like an impressive, shuddering behemoth, the Lodestar bellied forward, slowly gaining momentum and lifted off the runway, airborne.

Outside the texture of darkness changed, shifting in smears and patches as the Lodestar zoomed eastward. Inside the forward cabin, separated from navigator and pilot's cockpit by a narrow, dimly lit alcove, a somber-faced taskforce, wearing silver, radiation-proof flightsuits with sturdy calf-high protective boots, sat buckled in assigned seats. Each displayed apprehension, uncertain of what lay ahead. Most were engrossed in their phenomenal electronic wrist chronometers, devices capable of measuring and controlling blood pressure, heartbeats, pulse rates and the stabilization of multiple threats to the human anatomy. In addition, each operated on variable radio frequencies, enabling communication between Taskforce members eliminating the need to shout above the engine drone.

Left sleeve armbands bore dual insignias, the USA/WPCC above the flag emblems identifying each member's national origin. Nameplates over the heart area denoted military or professional rank.

Valerie Lansing gazed cursorily about the cabin and fell to numbed introspection. She peered broodingly out the porthole at the black dome of night.

So much had happened to Valerie in a short time. A brutal two-week briefing had left angry scars on her. An overwhelming redundancy of *kill-power* drummed daily into her had drained her. Tottering on an emotional razor's edge, only grim determination and her intractable perseverance to see this thing through held her glued together. She had psyched herself into detachment, prepared to view the Middle Eastern nuclear disaster objectively and absorb, *without* bias, the revolutionary technologies advanced at the seminar.

Steeped in unparalleled fascination of computer science and the imperative technical data to be utilized aboard the Lodestar to their destination, Valerie had momentarily blocked from mind—in the interest of science—the loss of millions of lives in the wholesale nuclear destruction.

How those scientists rhapsodized! "What remains for nuclear survivors poses marvels beyond space frontier barriers! For two weeks, you of the Taskforce will ponder pulsars, quasars, black holes! high-intensity cannon . . . particle-beam bazookas! . . . magnetic fusion reactors! . . .'' On and on it went.

The words generated thoughts, giving Valerie no peace.

Kill-power! . . . Kill-Power! . . . KILL-POWER!

Valerie's cool, analytical absorption at the outset was jarred. Facts, purposely distorted, twisted subtly to conform to an alien design had forced her to lose perspective for a time. Millions of agonized humans had died—and *no one mourned them!* It was incredible to observe Taskforce members praise and glorify the electronic wizardry of thermonuclear war by-products and give no notice to the millions of dead humans! When the cloying suffocation came upon her, she felt she had been cleverly manipulated.

By God, Valerie resented it!

She had left the briefing, a changed woman!

Emotions, she learned, were illogical to scientists and failed to compute. Human bloodied carnage strewn about battlefields failed to move them. When had they in their insulated lives heard the screaming torture of agonized souls, maimed and broken human torches ignited by phosphorus bombs running wildly amid other grisly, desecrated bodies seeking refuge where none could be had? Had any scientist actually *heard* the horrifying shrieks of ravaged, hideously deformed bodies broken to bits by the explosive charges of their ingeniously contrived cluster bombs? Had any witnessed faces blown away, hanging by bloody, sinewy strands of fibrous nerve endings, mangled shreds of an arm torn from its socket? Or shock-crazed men, women and children stumbling about, staring vacant-eyed at arms with no hands, dripping puddles of blood from spigot-like limbs. *Hell, no!*

Still, they advanced kill-power!

The Lodestar soared higher above the clouds. The imprint of Valerie's outrage was so fresh in her mind she was unable to blink away the thousands of *classified* photos of human slaughter spinning around in her head. Manmade death raining down on those poor wretched souls was tearing out her guts. *Global genocide!*

Damn them!

Valerie laid her head back, closed her eyes, but no rest. She knew there was something else behind her anger and frustration. While the scientists' stark objectivity in the face of the nuclear holocaust disgusted her, she realized that other more vicious men manipulated their performances. The men in *control*. Men like Amadeo Zeller and in every nation his puppets, the up-front political marionettes in power and in the military.

Reviewing the inequities, Valerie's stormy blue eyes grew lidded as the Lodestar broke the sound barrier. Wide awake, she sat up alerted, then fell back into her seat.

So alienated by the events of the past two weeks, Valerie had ignored her companions as if they didn't exist. She was digging in her flight bag when a sudden lurching jolted her. She glanced about. The other passengers swiveled around, necks craned, eyes darting furtively toward the tail section, furrows deepening worried brows.

The pilot's soothing voice purred through the intercom. Some flimsy excuse about airpockets brought the others into repose.

You could have fooled me! Goddamn turbulence felt like after-shocks in the wake of comets or some catastrophic event. She glanced cursorily at the others, shrugged back in her seat, counting the internal scars meticulously, chafing impatiently. Where could she begin to list the grievances? She had navigated a minefield of cool, calculating, terminally egomaniacal, technological giants during briefing, abraded at their condescension and smug smiles if she demonstrated feminine frailty. Her agility, resourcefulness and thick elephant skin got her through rough waters.

If she had postured about as the local *enfant-terrible,* she might have understood their disdain. *But why the animosity toward her?* And it *was* there, every moment of every day, a growing insoluble puzzle.

Signaling no demands for special favors from the specialists she had expected, but never got equal treatment. Rather, her questions had reaped snide remarks, looks of long suffering. But something else fed her agitation.

Velden Zryden's constant stares unnerved her. Sir Alexander York disturbed her more. His boundless leering curiosity constantly irritated her beyond her own comprehension. Uri Mikhail Gregorevich was easier to read; he was smitten with her. Damn! Why hadn't she read the letters! Eye contact between them sparked hidden messages. In Paris he had slipped her a note. She knew it by rote: "I desire fervently to reach out, envelop your heart with mine and cannot. But I will send you silent messages with my eyes for you to know precisely what I mean. Be truthful, you adore me as I adore you and have from the moment we met. You resist me, feign indifference, but deep inside you know."

Please, Uri, don't squeeze me into an emotional corner, not while I'm climbing a Matterhorn of doubt!

Both General Lincoln and Uri had voiced their obvious displeasure at the change of her hair color, chastized her for it. She purposely avoided them as often as she could without appearing obvious. None could understand the pressure and isolation from which she operated.

Valerie swallowed, popped her ears as the Lodestar soared higher into the gray sky. There was no sign of the sun. There appeared to be no stratosphere above the clouds, only gray density, not a spar of light as they climbed higher. She glanced at her chronometer. Hell, only ten minutes out of Paris and it felt an hour. She fell to introspection again.

Beyond the human elements contributing to Valerie's distress was her incomprehension of something called *Systems Dynamic Models*! Imagine, a *summa cum laude* graduate defeated by a systems dynamic model! Fundamentally, the model and DYNAMO computer language presented to Taskforce members represented a piecemeal bureaucratic analysis that tended to understate difficult but highly critical questions *designed* to hide stark truths behind mountains of ambiguities!

"My dear Miss Lansing, you should not permit those eggheads to riddle away at your foundation," Uri Mikhail said pleasantly, taking the seat next to Valerie.

She glanced at him, seemingly impervious to his words and continuing on her mental tack, abraded him. "The grotesque thermonuclear damage done in the Middle East needs no damnable DYNAMO computer jargon to disguise its full horrors!" she retorted. "Why didn't *you* question the purported scientific findings? Christ! They couldn't explain anything without a buffering of a thousand suppositions."

Recoiling playfully from her verbal assault, Uri attempted to keep a straight face. "Perhaps their answers might have confounded me more than your questions," he smiled tolerantly.

"Don't patronize me, Russian."

"Far be it from me, Yankee. . . . Look," he said quietly, adjusting his communications device to discourage eavesdroppers. "We both know semantics played a strong role in the Paris

568

seminars. Those briefing scientists deliberately held back lucid translations.''

''Then you agree? We were being manipulated?'' She lowered her voice, glanced around them. Uri also glanced about.

''Yes, assuredly yes. You merely chose the wrong arena to ventilate your thoughts. Why clank sabers with robots programmed to a task?''

Valerie stared at him, then fell back slackly in her seat, expelling air in exasperation. ''I suppose you're right. My four meticulously composed letters of resignation fell fate to a shredder, Uri. I chickened out.''

''Oh? . . .'' he smiled. ''Doesn't everyone understand systems dynamic models?'' He chirped good-naturedly.

She glared scathingly. *''Everyone doesn't!''*

''So, in demonstrating the guts to ask, your rewards fell short of ridicule. You received censure from the others, yes? You play-acted your way through a brutalizing two weeks determined not to emulate their deficiencies and handled yourself splendidly.''

Valerie peered at him, picking at a hangnail, searching his eyes, uncertain how to take his compliment. ''Scientists laboring night and day for decades unraveling the mystery of the Black Hole and we were expected to absorb the SDM in two weeks?''

Uri laughed warmly. ''I admit the jargon *was* confusing . . .''

''I suppose you understood those models?''

''A year's indoctrination prior to the Paris briefing helped.''

Aghast, she burst out into laughter. ''You mean . . . Dammit! . . . I wasn't a total bust-out?!'' Valerie shook her head at the self-flagellation. ''Well, I did grasp the mechanics behind space colonies manned by computer-guided robots and androids. And those mock-ups of high-energy laser beam cannon posed in orbit capable of delivering ultrawatt bursts precisely on target astounded me. What did you make of *Gideon*. Isn't he incredible?''

''Gideon . . . Ah, the electronic robot aboard the Lodestar? Yes, yes, truly incredible. Capable of repairing the superstructure while in flight. To think we owe it all to the Russian Sputnik, the beeping ball that started the dash into outer space in 1957.''

His patriotic words depressed her. ''Yes, between the two superpowers, rocket research was electrified, and for what? We, none of us seem capable of ending man's inhumanity toward man.''

"Long ago Sun Tsu wrote: *When the thunderclap comes, there is no time to cover the ears.*"

"But the thunderclap has come. The ears were uncovered to hear, but you politicians will not listen. Your ears have become deaf, seduced by the electronic marvels of the future."

"We are not all deaf. Why do you persist in alienating me?"

Valerie buttressed the emotional appeal he transmitted. "I don't, really I don't. I'm like this always. Until answers are settled in my mind, I'm unresponsive to all else."

"Ask on, my American beauty, I shall gladly be your sounding board."

"Very well . . . man has skyrocketed from a defensive position largely subordinate to nature's alternatives in the past to a new and dominant one of *near* control. So tell me, oh god of wisdom, why?"

"The nature of man ever inclines himself toward war, my dear. I doubt its capacity to change after a six-thousand-year similar history."

The past two weeks told the story. The scientists, the *Doomsday* machines constantly reiterated *kill-power*! Deadly arsenals! Ingenious laser cannon capable of vaporizing marauding enemy missiles! Particle beams weapons capable of pulverizing an army of tanks at five miles! Geostationary laser battle stations! Advanced tanks with composite armor! Binary gas, so lethal, a quart of the poison would wipe out the population of Chicago! And anti-missiles systems! The weaponization of outer space!

Valerie raged. "My God, Uri! Space technologies to launch nuclear warheads in space! Can you men think of nothing but war games to annihilate mankind? Why not prevent ruthless men from deploying death to the masses whenever they see fit?"

"Global leaders attempt to implement controls!" Uri countered. "A superpower took umbrage, spread a protective umbrella over all those responsible—" Uri broke off, irked by what he perceived to be political naivete by Valerie.

Before Valerie could react, a terrifying flash and thunderous roar shuddered through the Lodestar. Shock waves followed, spending its strength some twenty miles away. Startled, Valerie gripped the seat arms firmly, rechecked her seat buckle. The jet jolted, lurched, bounced bumpily for several turbulent moments, like the pitching and yawning of a ship. "We're getting closer," she whispered, fully alert.

570

Uri nodded mutely, his focus, followed by Valerie's, shifted over the bulkhead to the half-dozen video screens. Outside a perpendicular screen of impenetrable black smoke clung almost stationary. The video monitors transmitted this black density, nothing else. Uri turned to Valerie. "Sleep, you look exhausted."

"Sleep?" She shrugged. "Sleep is where we confront what is better left unexamined."

The Junior Soviet Politburo VIP studied Valerie in profile. Dense blue eyes dancing with diamond flashes and white flecks of excitement reflecting animated video screens held on her. "Is there no depth of surprises in you, Valerie Lansing?" He reached to hold her hand. "You must have received my calls, my flowers—yet not a note of acknowledgment except from a secretary."

"Surprises?" She forced a wan smile. "What you see, Russian, is an intersection of influences from cradle to womanhood. Prim, proper, refined in manners, brilliantly educated with a staff of well paid, know-it-all secretaries who tell me very little."

"You speak nothing of the unconscious, stirring you to passions?"

"A mystery that is not there," Valerie smiled, slipping her hand from his. *"What you see is what you gets,* my friend. My life is an open book."

Uri chuckled. "On that point we are in violent disagreement. You, a woman veiled in mystery, obtained—however way you managed it—a formidable position with the WPCC Taskforce, to the exclusion of countless, more qualified specialists. Uh-uh, you cannot fool Uri Mikhail. You must be in the service of the CIA"

Valerie's hearty laughter sobered instantly. Not at the ridiculous implication of Uri's words, but at Velden Zryden's glowering hate-filled stares stabbing across the aisle at them. What she saw chilled her. She had deliberately avoided him, and turned now to peer out the porthole. She felt Uri's hand over hers on the arm of the seat. Quickly drawing it back, disengaging it, she clutched both her hands together in her lap. Changing tack, she rode herd over their earlier conversation.

"Where is the breathtaking adventure in the science of destruction, Uri? You *men-in-control* are bent upon preparing for a world of androids—not humans. You saw the by-products of space technology—do you buy it? Artificial hearts, kidneys, limbs, prostheses to fit every broken, maimed, diseased portion of the anatomy? A future of bionic men and women loom ahead. Why not a prosthesis to replace the diseased portions of the human brain that further man's inclination to hate and persecute his fellow man? *Dammit!* The illustrious Dr. Carronton implied all this was the next earth-shattering development!''

''Are you some evangelical crusader? A specialist on the subject? I declare you are inclined to tread dangerous waters.''

Valerie, masking her fury, nervously glanced at Velden Zryden, then sought a subject to divert Uri from the subject matter which so accurately described Velden Zryden.

Uri detected the subtle unease, peripherally noted the object of Valerie's sudden distress. Uri thought of the things Andreevich spoke of Valerie Lansing and his beguilement with her increased. Yet, by God, something was frightening her, above and beyond this superficial gibberish. Their eyes met and held, each trying to read the other with Uri holding the distinct advantage.

Uri finally broke the silence. ''Yes, yes, I was offended by the scientific double talk and I applaud you refusing to be lampooned by their derision. You did not knuckle under their impressive *literati* degrees. You, Valerie Lansing, deserve to be knighted, if woman were privy to such honor.''

Valerie flushed self-consciously. ''I didn't know my feelings were displayed under glass. Second-class roles are alien to me, subservience never a learned habit.''

''Don't apologize! Ask yourself, Madame Lawyer, how in hell they'd fare in explaining the intricacies of a *tort? Res Ipsa Loquitor? Res Judicata* or the *voir dire* of a jury?'' Valerie laughed vigorously.

''Uri—what really galled me is, here I am at age twenty-nine. Despite two academic degrees, a consummate understanding of American jurisprudence, I suddenly discover I am an illiterate to those scientists. *Illiterate!*''

''You care that much what the men you despise think?''

The words shook her, made her feel ridiculous in a sense.

''I know how you feel, and hope you only discuss the matter with me. Ventilate your frustration on me only and remember, science to those emotional cripples in Paris is a brotherhood, a total commitment in life. Any trespasser infringing upon their bailiwick . . . Valerie—they don't deserve your emotional outrage.''

572

"Infringing on their bailiwick?" She spat indignantly. "Tell me, my Russian friend, that this is not possible when an *invisible* army of global potentates call the shots? One man, *ONE* man at the top of the totem decides the destiny of all nations—their survival or obliteration. Under his directives, marching to his drumbeats is an army of homicidal, genocidal maniacs—"

Uri moved swiftly. His lips over hers sealed off her words. Shaken, she backed away protestingly, trying between the frantic kisses to search his intent eyes. He held her, back to the others whispered, "Don't utter those words to another soul! Do you read me? Now, be a good actress. Kiss me back as if you meant it, then slap me indignantly! Do as I say!"

Observing the tête-à-tête via closed-circuit video monitors and headsets, using the only open frequency of communication able to tap into the receiver-transmitters of the Taskforce, Prince Youseff Ben-Kassir and the Moor, Matteus Montenegro, listened to every word spoken between the young couple. They sat in Moufflon's private cabin in the *empennage* section, mesmerized by the action on screen. They witnessed Valerie react to the urgency in Uri's voice, observed her strike Uri's face resoundingly, noting her heart wasn't in the gesture. Uri stroked his cheek lightly, whispering, "You do wonders for my ego, my American beauty. Keep in mind, should you need me I am only across the aisle from you." He bowed politely.

Youseff smiled as Uri retreated to his assigned seat; he nudged the Moor to note the dour expression on Zryden's face. The jaw fell loose, shapeless, the face, wooden and pale. The Moor studied Valerie's features. "Highness, she knows more than she reveals."

"Is it not as it should be? After all, she is the blood and flesh of the man we both know and love to a fault. *And my son fancies her! If I had astutely planned it, I couldn't have worked such miracles. Kismet indeed works in strange, marvelous ways, my friend.*"

As a steward moved forward serving snack trays and hot coffee to the Taskforce, Matteus witnessed the stark hatred for Uri in Velden Zryden's features. *"He is an interesting study in contrasts, Youseff. I wonder if he measures to the old man's viciousness."*

* * *

573

Used to chocolate in her coffee, Valerie tore open a packet, poured the contents in her thermos. The steward moved on. Valerie's eyes met Velden's penetrating, unnerving fixed stare. Nodding imperceptibly, she casually broke eye contact, wondering what black thoughts he conjured over Uri Mikhail's audacious behavior. Catching Uri's image peripherally, and suddenly afraid for him, she failed to return his smile, not while Velden's fixed on her like adhesive. A hundred flaring thoughts assailed her; at the bottom of each she felt hot, smoldering coals of excitement ignite and fire brightly at the thought of Uri. His kiss had tingled her toes. She felt ridiculously breathless at the telegraphed messages to her she refused to decode—not here and now where Velden's damnable scrutiny intimidated the hell out of her. She recalled Uri's words to her in briefing:

"I desire fervently to reach out and envelop your heart with mine You adore me. You haven't told me, but you do, I see it in your eyes!"

Valerie turned her head toward the porthole, a wicked, pleasured smile tickling her fancy. Something else he said . . . "I feel like a butterfly pierced by a pin, captive to your heart." Well, one thing about Russians, they were poetic. She sipped her chocolate, suddenly struck by another icy chill.

Why hadn't security pierced Velden Zryden's *cover*? Security wasn't *that* lax! Dossiers on every Taskforce member had been scrutinized by four Intelligence groups, each highly skilled.

A half hour later Valerie was still battling demons of thoughts. She poured the remains of her chocolate coffee, rang the steward for another thermos and fell to introspection once again. She needed emotional insulation or she'd become dysfunctional. How was this possible? The afterglow of Uri's kisses still curled her toes! One kiss! And Valerie Lansing melted? Impossible! Or was it?

Instantly besieged by busy scenes and countless voices, she glanced about the cabin interior. She hadn't really absorbed the unique surroundings. Uncharacteristic of her, when normally she examined every nook and cranny of her environment before she fell at ease. Her eyes caught sight of Sir Alexander York. *Dammit!* Would he never desist? Clearly she was the object of his attention—not to be confused with usual male attentiveness—she felt like a germ on a slide. Unnerved by his persistent scrutiny—it bordered on perversity—she averted her gaze, checkreined her rancor. Her eyes trailed to the cabin ahead of her, through the thick glass hatch door leading to the navigator and pilot's cockpit. For a time she studied the man, Moufflon, in profile, wondering at his absence during briefing. His presence aboard the Lodestar long before the Taskforce boarded was announced when they settled in assigned seats. Nearly everyone's neck craned to catch a glimpse of this specter.

Uri's words, his actions, intruded upon her thoughts. He *was* a friend. A sudden furnace intensity in her loins urged her to reach out to him. She held herself in check. She dare not place him in jeopardy, not now. *Oh, God, was it love she felt for him?*

Velden Zryden seethed with rage. He stared at Valerie Lansing with hatred and loathing. When Velden Zryden had questioned her in a brief moment of contact, she had blithely replied that Veronique Lindley was a name she had assumed when she entered the affair with *Herr* Victor Zeller. Jealousy could be dangerous, *non*? She had wanted to avoid detection by an emotional boyfriend—her charade had been an entertaining game, *non*? He watched her eyes grow guarded as she spoke.

He was wary of her for many reasons, consumed with worry at what she knew or may have surmised concerning *his* cover. Velden's disquiet began in the early days of briefing when Mosha Bauer had managed to smuggle in volatile information. Decoded, the message named Valerie Lansing as Draga Koseva's assassin. Draga and Milos, assigned the task of eliminating the nosy investigative journalist scrounging around for information from the families of the deceased scientists, had trailed a certain Velma Lane, American, credentialed by *Time* Magazine to Megev. Draga entered the Zeiss house certain he had wasted the occupants. Outside, Milos saw someone running from the house, fleeing in the Maserati, but it wasn't until the reporter got to the outskirts of Grenoble before he sent her reeling off the edge of the *corniche*. Milos tracked down the ravine, found the papers, collected them, and certain she lay dead, sprawled below on a rocky shelf in a treacherous, inaccessible, vertical drop, he abandoned her. Milos left, traced the automobile rental. The credentials matched: *Velma Lane, American*. Time *Magazine*. Mosha Bauer checked both Paris and New York personnel offices. No Velma Lane was employed by them. By the time they returned to the site, the Maserati was gone and the girl had vanished. Police records indicated such an accident had occurred at the site described. A patient taken to the Grenoble hospital turned out to be the daughter of U.S. Senator Hartford Lansing! Name of Valerie Lansing! V.L.! *Veronique Lindley* V.L. *Velma Lane*! and V.L. *VALERIE LANSING!*

He had kept his eye on her during the last weeks. Nothing untoward had occurred until the final days back in one of those rooms at the Embassy corraled for briefing seminars. He would never forget what happened three days before briefing ended!

It was the ten A.M. session. The briefing scientist, Dr. Lanyard Carronton from Cambridge University in England stood at the center of a dismal, large lecture hall surrounded by models, graphs, enlarged photographs, charts and screens. He cleared his coarse throat, caused by addiction to chain smoking, addressed the Taskforce with a compelling air of an uncompromising tyrant, a self-styled technological genius. "Comprehension of the elaborate technology to be employed, the *robot* programming and *Mind Control* is mandatory, but I doubt will be comprehended by your briefcase laymen. Nevertheless, my presence here is to introduce you to the elaborate technology to be encountered on the Lodestar, and hint at what you will encounter in PROJECT: MOONSCAPE."

The opening statement made, Valerie entered the lecture hall a moment late wearing beige flight fatigues. She lit up the room and men's psyches with galvanic bursts of energy. Her body, voluptuous with each movement, exuded a compelling aura, distracting to Taskforce members and instructors. Valerie, absorbed in the electronically programmed robot *Gideon* standing to one side of Dr. Carronton, was oblivious to the effect she had created.

"Now that the human distraction is over, I pray you of the Taskforce will find the energy to concentrate on the subject at hand." Carronton, a man of sixty, spoke and moved with the lethargy of a wearied man burdened by overwork. Glaring at the imperturbable woman, he concentrated on the urgent business, speaking without interruption for an hour.

As Valerie listened, grasping with facility the highly technical language, one less intimidating than the systems dynamic models, she listened with growing trepidation to Carronton's lectures.

Panic flickered across her face; periodically Velden caught glimmerings of these unguarded emotions.

Velden had no way of *knowing* the alarms sounding in her, or that periodically she stole sidelong glances at him, noting his ghostly pallor and voracious interest in Dr. Carronton's lecture clarifying matters buried in Victor Zeller's subconscious.

Simultaneously Carronton's words unveiled mysteries tucked in the recesses of Valerie's brain, spotlighting them. *Voilà!* Connections were made! What she had not understood and thought she had, in her research at Georgetown, was coming together and, her eyes darted bravely toward Velden, noting his reaction, as if this in and of itself was the proof she needed to validate her theory.

At times, Velden was so absorbed with Carronton's explication he had dropped his guard. The scientist articulated the principles of Wilheim Zeiss's cranial work on Victor Zeller so that his true predicament was fathomed at long last. Christ! Victor/Amadeo/Velden was walking proof that the theories Carronton advanced in the seminar actually worked! Oh, the questions he had wanted to ask! He *needed* answers to frightening compulsions, kaleidoscopic mood changes and emotions tearing him apart.

Valerie's intense scrutiny of him forced his attention on her. He noted her startled, yet controlled reaction, her pointed shift of attention between Carronton and himself.

Jolted by the silent message he read in her eyes, doubt surged through him. Up to that moment she'd given no indication she held the most minute inkling of the trilateral personalities of Victor/Amadeo/Velden. Profound concern over *what* she *knew* or *guessed* shook him.

That night he paced the floor, chain-smoked, fearing the worst. Adding to what Mosha Bauer imparted concerning the Widow Zeiss and Draga's death, coupled with her true identity, he reviewed all options to terminate Valerie Lansing.

The next day, her demeanor was no different from that of previous days, and Velden had chalked off his phobic dread to imagination. He fell into the mood created by Dr. Carronton at the unveiling of the robot, *Gideon*, and its stupendous capabilities.

A half hour into Carronton's lecture, Velden, captured by visuals barely heard Valerie's dialogue with the swarthy-skinned, dark-haired scientist. Carronton shoved his bifocals down his nose, annoyed at the interruption, yet sparked by the inquiry. "Please, madam, repeat the question."

Valerie complied. Velden, listening, acutely paled, his features immobile, hostility burning in his laserlike eyes.

"Well, Dr. Carronton?" Valerie persisted. "*Is it* possible to stimulate dormant brain cells by external means? Induce them with energy capable of transferring thoughts and images from one brain to another?"

"Mental telepathy," muttered the crusty Carronton, "is a proven science."

"No! Not telepathy." Valerie insisted. "I suggest a reprogramming of the human mind vis-à-vis those—uh, say supercomputers you've described at great length. We've seen how micro-chip implantation can make the blind see, the deaf hear. What of mind programming? The ability to reprogram a deficient mind—or let us say, increase the ability of a normal mind to function at genius level? Something beyond suggestion or hypnosis, something technical, mechanically perfect, incapable of human error—say like *Gideon*, here."

A hush swept the room, the others turned to stare from Valerie to Carronton. Velden's skin crawled, his heartbeats accelerated and he felt Amadeo's personality surfacing. Threatened by Valerie's queries, unable to sort the dangers, he broke out in a cold sweat, endured a coiled internal terror tightening inside him. He felt Amadeo emerging. He must suppress him, he *must*.

"Well—uh—" Carronton squinted, peered at her nameplate.

"Lansing," she curtly supplied the name.

"Yes, well, Miss—uh, Lansing. The principles of vibration as applied to mental phenomena may polarize brain waves at any level the *projector* desires, thus gaining perfect control over his mental states and emotional moods. Simultaneously he is able to affect the minds of others, producing in them desired mental states. We've come a long way in recent decades. Now computers handle the transference—"

"—similarly to the programming of robots?" Valerie trembled inwardly. An incipient vestige of terror shuddered through her. The power behind Velden's eyes riveted on Dr. Carronton and on Valerie caused her to falter.

Tilting her head obliquely, pondering the question, Carronton nodded. "Yes, it is possible."

The others gasped as the import of the words sunk in.

Increasingly distressed at the questioning, Velden clenched and unclenched his hands nervously, long a habit of Amadeo Zeller's.

The glasses worn by the scholarly Dr. Carronton softened his features. When he removed them to wipe his sweaty eyes, the face became blunt, powerful, the eyelids, fleshy, the gray eyes, hooded. "Ah, then you do, I take it, comprehend the marvels poised at the portals of science?" He fronted expressionless eyes on Valerie in a disconcerting look designed to disconcert.

"I do not suggest a cranial micro-chip implantation—"

"Why not?" countered Carronton. "Implanted pacemakers stabilize and control arrhythmia and other cardiac disturbances. Devices at work for diabetics controlling insulin doses superior to human ability have saved numerous lives. You've already witnessed rudimentary sight and hearing restored by chip implantation . . .? Swiss scientists working on *Mind Control* report admirable results."

Velden was sweating abnormally. Valerie, undaunted, skated on thin ice. "But the mind itself . . .? What of hereditary factors? Can emotional states and memory also be manipulated electronically?"

"Preferable terminology, uh, Miss Lansing, is: the remolding of the brain into positive states. Perhaps, if I may reassure you, this technology is indescribably more accurate than the frightening lobotomies of the past which reduced man to a vegetable when criminal tendencies and otherwise abnormal personality traits were excised by the process. However, may I suggest we do not stray beyond our initial premise. At mission's end, visit me at Cambridge—" He cut her off, launching at once into the talents of a computer they would encounter aboard the Lodestar.

"Dr. Carronton," Uri Mikhail spoke up, "I do not wish to belabor the points well taken by Miss Lansing, but please explain. You said earlier, by neutralizing body rhythms, man can master his moods, feelings and thoughts?"

"Precisely. No longer will the masses of people be swayed by mental giants. Computers and micro-chip technology will control him. Man's future will depend on his ability to astutely reprogram his mind, eliminating weakening emotional factors, thereby permitting him use of his own potential to the fullest."

Swell! Hitler, use your potential to the fullest!

The Taskforce shuddered at the implication of his words.

"How will you preserve the brilliant minds of men who purportedly form the superior side to men's mentalities? Or is this possible?" Valerie asked.

Velden's suspicions ballooned! A sinking sensation gripped him. Valerie Lansing *knew*! . . . There were thousands of ways to kill a person. You could poison her, watch the smile turn into a rictus. You could hold her throat until it grew hard, and the flesh quivered under your hands. You could . . . Oh, Christ! Valerie knew he was *Victor Zeller*.

Now, aboard the Lodestar, Velden directed hostile eyes on Valerie with the controlled gaze of a psychopath compelling eye contact with him. The galvanically charged message transmitted from his dark eyes to her iced her blood. She looked right through him, blandly, as if he didn't exist.

Valerie had explored dozens of motivational possibilities, causing the changes in Victor, and after the briefing, *knew* the six dead scientists had programmed him in some hideous fashion. How or why it was done remained an enigma.

Micro-chip implantation! Micro-chip implantation. The thought hadn't entered her mind, much less the necessity of the surgery.

Now as she grasped the nuances in this trilateral demon, and following their encounter at the townhouse in Paris, her suspicions had coalesced with fear. The manifest changes in Victor as *Amadeo* and this supercilious *Velden* and later his presence at the WPCC briefing had freaked her out, shriveled her guts. *God*! She must confide in General Brad Lincoln!

But, how? Until she *knew* the malediction Velden planned, what could she say that would be believed? Who would believe so preposterous a tale? Before she did anything, she must defuse the lead wires firing Velden. Did she dare appeal to Victor?

Sweat rippled across her forehead, her concentration, fierce.

In her own way she was forceful and determined. Her habitual expression under pressure became unreadable impassivity. Once profiled in a newspaper article following a victorious court battle, Valerie was described as cool, quiet, subliminally brutal, a strange amalgam of contradictions, testy at times, frequently euphoric, at times self-effacing, but *always*, "Valerie Lansing is a woman in control."

Always in control? What a crockful!

Valerie unbuckled her seatbelt, and moved languidly toward

the restroom facilities, adjusting the temperature controls on her flight suit. Sweating, wringing wet, her body heat had risen several degrees. She entered the cubicle, locked the door behind her, promptly dashing cold water on her face. Staring at her reflection in the mirror, she dotted her pale features dry. She caught sight of her fingernails. *Christ! Picked to the quick!* Never, *never* had she desecrated her body like this!

Moments later, wrapped in a cocoon of solemnity, she returned to her seat determined to eject that trilateral persona, Victor/Amadeo/Velden from mind. She must not create suspicion in Velden's mind! *Detachment, Valerie! Detachment is your only ally!*

Her gaze traveled back to Moufflon through the thick glass hatch door. Jolted internally by an overwhelming flood of emotions, Valerie stopped short, tried to sort the outpouring, and forced to changed her focus, wondered at her sanity in making this trip.

She could have refused outright. She *had not*. She could have abandoned Victoria's vendetta. She *had not*. She could have relinquished ancestral ties, turned her back on bloodlines, lived her own life, her reality. She had done none of these things. *Why not?* Valerie knew in her heart had she been chained, locked up, she would have found the means of extricating herself to fulfill the promise made to her grandmother. *Why?* She possessed no exceptional bravery! The vicissitudes of a rough, ready life had never pierced her insulated existence. No one questioned the power and prerogatives of a Senator's daughter *except* the Senator's daughter, herself. Now, under severe self-scrutiny, the discoveries jolted her.

Strongly inclined toward her Argentine, Scotch-Irish antecedants, she possessed no Lansing, Colonial-American characteristics. None of that upper-class, Harvard-Cambridge brouhaha so prevalent in the Senator's lineage. At times she felt a stranger to him, as if she belonged to someone else. Overwhelming Valerie all her life had been visions of other worlds, instinctive feelings of a tribal ancestry unfamiliar to her, yet, known intimately. Always a champion of the underdog, outspoken against issues offending her egalitarian sense of justice, Valerie had fought a compulsion to join freedom marchers, fight tyranny, because she knew such power came from high places—not commoners. Steeped in mute sobriety, Valerie came into full view of Senator Lansing's dream for his daughter—for her:

The first woman President of the United States!

President of the United States? Not until this moment had she truly kindled the dream. *President?* A platform to articulate truth! Hah!

The complexity of her emotions was ripping her apart. *First, Valerie, Come to terms with this hideous, shapeless form emerging from deep inside you, plotting a vendetta of destruction against Amadeo Zeller and his son.*

Valerie rang the steward for a coffee refill. She glanced at her watch. *Only forty minutes out of Paris?* It seemed hours ago. She sighted General Lincoln, thought of her recent cool treatment of him. After his dramatically stated disappointment in the change of hair color, a bone of contention between them at the first briefing seminar, she pointedly avoided him. How could she explain she dared not appear with red hair? That it might trigger danger? Who would believe in the trilateral persona of Victor/ Amadeo/Velden? She must make amends. Now, as never before, she needed a friend!

Uri Mikhail Gregorevich was in love! One kiss and he bloomed richly in the emotion of love! Thirty-nine, going on forty, years and love, nourished, had burst into full bloom! Incredible! Uri had experienced few of Valerie's emotional upheavals these past two weeks. Keenly observant of her mood fluctuations, he had sensed her mental battles. Ready at the slightest provocation to hurl lethal salvos at anyone, Valerie epitomized all that was exciting and daring to him. Drawn to her by the contagious lust of drama oozing from her, despite the defense mechanisms she had erected to keep others at bay, he had broken the ice! He kissed her and she *loved* it! She did!

Uri, never a reckless dreamer, dealt in realities. Drinking, dining, talking shop, politics was reserved for his dignified uniformed colleagues at the Kremlin or Soviet Embassy in D.C. —seldom with women. To Uri, Valerie posed more the enigma to him than PROJECT: MOONSCAPE. This wholly desirable woman had captured his heart. But curiously, she had kept him in abeyance like a frozen vegetable until she was prepared to thaw him.

No more. The kiss had thawed him. He needed more from her. Uri made his move. He stood over her. "May I join you again?"

Valerie shook her head vigorously.

"Still angry? I thought we'd made a truce. Why are you angry—"

"Not now!" she snapped caustically. Swiveling about, eyes flaring, she added, "Who's angry?"

Uri, perched on the seat's arm, frowned. Something had occurred in the past ten minutes to metamorphose her into a tigress. *What?* A steward placed fresh coffee before Valerie. Uri, despite her abrasive manner, slipped into the seat, watching her tear open a fresh packet of chocolate. He flipped on his communications device. "Marvelous invention this. I prefer the others do not eavesdrop on our conversation."

"Good. Don't talk. Just leave me alone!" Beyond Uri's head she noted Velden's frozen loathing directed at her. Or was it Amadeo's hatred she detected? "Uri, do yourself a kindness. Do not talk with me. Give me no attention. Pretend I am a stranger. Else I cannot be responsible for what might happen to you."

The enigmatic statement brought Valerie under Uri's total scrutiny. He studied her pale, worried face, the erratic breathing heaving her breasts under the flightsuit, her futile attempts to control visible agitation. "What is it, Valerie? What's wrong? What can happen to me aboard the Lodestar?"

"Please, don't ask. I know only if you indicate any interest in me, something terrible will happen." Her eyes flickered past him to Velden. "Earlier—earlier the kiss . . . it meant nothing. *Nothing!*"

Uri refused to believe her. The taskforce had been required to distribute a complete dossier to every other member of the group. He flashed on the dossier in her lap, read the printed name in the upper right-hand corner: VELDEN ZRYDEN. Shifting his focus to Valerie, he saw she was terrified. "I had hoped to discuss our host with you. Why do you suppose Moufflon keeps himself aloof to the taskforce?"

Listening to their conversation via closed-circuit video apparatus, Prince Ben-Kassir and the Moor tensed, exchanged glances, their eyes tight on Valerie and Uri.

"Please go, Uri," Valerie implored. "I know less about Moufflon than you or anyone else aboard the Lodestar."

"About your *own* father? That, my dear, is hardly credible."

Stunned, Valerie stared at Uri, eyes widening, probing his. Her lips formed words, but the stupefaction was so intense the words locked in her throat. Victor/Amadeo/Velden, was forgotten.

The shock communicated at once to Uri brought his unintended faux pas into focus. He flushed crimson, the suppressed smile frozen, unable to spread. He tried desperately to swallow his words, couldn't. "You did not—what I mean is—" He faltered painfully, recollecting his own personal trauma when forced to come to grips with his bastardy. Apologies, inappropriate as they were inadequate, he blurted. "Will you forgive a prize fool? How could I *know* you *didn't* know? What I mean is, your presence among the taskforce is indicative of a *special* relationship—"

"—to the American President, yes."

"*Not* to Moufflon?" Uri, tilting his head obliquely, smiled delicately at what he construed to be a deliberate lie. "Dear Valerie, I have it on excellent authority—"

"KGB authority?" she snapped icily.

"The *best* authority," Uri muttered sotto voce, with concern. "If you need a friend, truly, I am nearby." Standing, towering over her, he gazed at the tousled streaked blond hair, shattered. Pictures of her fell through his mind like a dropped sheaf of snapshots—Valerie as he met her at the Lansing estate in Virginia; Valerie in coveted newspaper photos attending social events; Valerie standing valiantly up to the briefing scientists giving them go for go; Valerie in her revealing flight suit reeking of womanhood that needed devouring—and he, destroyed by a sentence that had taken a year to nurture.

Uri retreated to enemy ground wordlessly, catching, in passing, the satisfied gleam in Velden Zryden's insolent gaze. *Bastard!*

Uri, bedeviled to distraction by the man who had ogled Valerie unceasingly for the past two weeks mentally flashed on the Velden Zryden dossier. delivered to him, thanks to Andreevich Malenekov's foresight, before the taskforce briefing ended. Valerie was lost to him; he had stupidly alienated her, shoved her back into full retreat, into that damnable shell she occupied like a tenant.

Silently he patched together the real chain of events as he knew them, that had coerced the Swiss financier Victor Zeller into jeopardizing life and fortune by assuming the Velden Zryden *cover*. Uri's distinct advantage over the others was the utilization of Russia's human fact-finding warehouse, Malenekov and the formidable KGB. Uri *knew* intimately the most elusive of facts concerning everyone aboard the Loadstar. The possible exception:

Moufflon. He *knew* that Valerie, posing as Veronique Lindley, had lived with Victor Zeller for a time as his mistress. *Why?* He had yet to learn. Before PROJECT: MOONSCAPE concluded, Uri intended to learn more than Valerie's deception and the terror she fought valiantly to obscure.

Meanwhile Valerie felt totally impotent. Every nerve ending in her body sizzled, fired and spent like a dud was now numbed without feeling.

Moufflon—her *father?* . . . *Her father?* Why would Uri advance so outrageous a remark if it were counterfeit? Her eyes traveled to the glass hatch door. Peering at him, at Darius Bonifacio, a.k.a. Moufflon, indefinable emotions sparked. Uri's words rushed at her interminably.

"*About your own father? Hardly credible. Hardly credible!*" Facts, conjectures, recollections, memories stirred in her mind, creating sensations of inexplicable curiosity. Studying Moufflon, she flushed, her temples throbbed.

Valerie's expression darkened, alien emotions shuddered through her. She felt the need to run, flee, sort things in her mind. She hadn't professed to understand the savagery of her soul, nor the impatience of her spirit as she grew. But *why* had Valentina kept the truth from her? The Senator—for goodness' sakes—had devoted himself to her. She had never guessed—*never*! Yet . . .

Her eyes held on Moufflon; her imagination soared. Was Moufflon the answer to the deep, mysterious longings, inexplicable yearnings that tore at the core of her being? Impatience kept her on a taut leash; an inner policing force riveted her to her seat, held her from approaching Moufflon.

Conspicuous by his absence throughout briefing, Moufflon stood at the fulcrum of controversy, unruffled at the epicenter of stormy seas.

Earlier, as Moufflon boarded the Lodestar flanked on all sides by six armed security guards, Valerie's eyes met his. Briefly he searched her face, studied her hair coloring, and whipped past her as if she didn't exist. Valerie had continued to stare after him, unable to resist drinking him in. After reading the body of the Maui text, she *knew* or thought she *knew* the connection between Moufflon and the insanity of the recent nuclear holocaust.

Now, in a ponderous silence, she reexamined Uri's words. If Uri spoke the truth, she understood Valentina's insistence in affirming that Moufflon *knew* Amadeo Zeller better than any man on earth! She closed her eyes, bent her head forward, shoulders sagging slightly under the ponderous weight pressing down on her. She tried to think. She must . . . think!

Victor Zeller's fraud as Zryden had caused her countless sleepless nights. She *knew* a *deadly* vengeance aimed at Moufflon incubated in his mind—or was it Amadeo's mind? Valerie didn't know how she *knew*, only that she knew Moufflon's life was in jeopardy. She couldn't betray Velden Zryden until she knew what was conjured up in his diabolical mind, until she *knew* exactly *who* on this precarious journey could be trusted.

Valerie in an inexplicable moment of jaundiced mirth burst out laughing, a humorous image forming in mind. She saw herself drowning in a swirling miasma of inky waters calling for help. From the shore she heard the briefing scientists' voices rising in roaring cadence. "If you couldn't swim, you should have learned computer jargon! No one can understand you!" Then, surrounded by a sea of blood-red roses, she floated farther out from shore to infinity.

Chapter Thirty-Eight

STARK TERROR NUMBED THE PASSENGERS. At the beginning of turbulence, warning *RED LIGHTS* flashed over the bulkhead: *FASTEN SEATBELTS!* The Lodestar's occupants complied at once.

Outside, an abrupt, murky fog obscured visibility. The jet's lights lanced through the thickness. Oblique shafts of dawn lights, creeping somewhere, somehow over an eastern horizon, instantly curtained by darkness, fought to shine through the solid density of the ceiling to little avail. Overhead cabin lights illuminated the Lodestar's interior. Taskforce members focused their attention on the six video monitors over the bulkhead.

High resolution, wide-angled color cameras equipped with infrared sensing devices mounted into the superstructure's wings swung into action, transmitting at once. A computer voice described in analytical drone the photographed areas. Awed by the incredible sights, the taskforce stared in frozen silence at the disappearing civilization receding on one screen and the approaching congestion of a murky sunless mass coming into camera view off the port bow.

Indigo smoke spirals hovered over the remains of a conflagration. Nearly four weeks ago and the land still smoked?

Approaching Eastern Turkey, they gaped, appalled at the converging landscape entering their sights. Instantly transmitted to them was the extent of inaccuracy conveyed by satellite photos, the low definition of mass devastation.

Dominating the naked eye in endless profusion, open craters staggered over the earth's surface. Thousands upon thousands of symmetrical pockmarks saturated every square mile as far as the eye could see. Earth, sky and water, converged as a barren wasteland, a frightening, alien moonscape on earth. Only engine sounds punctuated the silence, droning, purring, powerful engines transporting them to hell!

General Brad Lincoln exchanged disturbed glances with Colonel Jim Greer, recently reinstated and promoted in rank through the Defense and Tactical Reconnaissance Forces of the U.S. Army Air Force—a cover for intelligence activities. These two had seen everything! Hiroshima! Nagasaki! Bikini! None compared to this. Greer unsnapped his seat buckle, lurched aft to the observation window with the others. He snapped his safety buckle into an overhead track. Nikon camera fitted with telescopic lenses in hand, he focused and held the electronic shutter in place, taking photo after photo.

Chains of craters resembling those left by meteors sprawled below with raised rims and surrounding aprons of ejected materials, hummocky, strewn with boulders, hills created by the rebound of subterranean rock. There were no signs of humans, animals, buildings, landmarks, as these men had previously known the area.

General Brad Lincoln, frozen in his seat, felt outrage, indignation at the fiendish destruction. *It shouldn't have happened!* None of it! Who had heeded Moufflon's warnings? No one! Bastards! Their shameful political bungling, a blight on the history of mankind, *could not* be written off as error in judgment!

Dr. David Sen Yen Lu, a micro-oriental with a giant's brain, speaking via the inter-com, commanded Brad's attention. He listened:

"Instantaneous bursts of neutrons and gamma rays from blasts close to the earth's surface intensified the heat rising in temperatures in the tens of millions of degrees centigrade. The secondary effect of the explosions commenced with hurricane winds, gusts of incalculable velocity fanned and spread the flames destroying every inflammable object in its path. Oil refineries, stockpiled crude, acting as highly combustible incendiaries added to the intensity of the fires. The result: the ensuing holocaust, what you are witness to.

"Judging from the absence of life and vegetation, we can roughly estimate that the warhead contained an aggregate amount of energy equivalent to the fifty megatons of TNT mentioned in briefing."

Brad Lincoln made swift calculations. The Hiroshima bomb dropped from the *Enola Gay* in August, 1945, a thirteen-thousand kiloton payload, declared Hiroshima a brush fire by comparison. He turned in his chair, stared glumly at his colleagues. Most, intimately acquainted with the area below, searched frantically— and futilely—for familiar landmarks.

A few passengers evidenced nervous tics. Here, an uncooperative blinking eye, there, a fierce tugging at torn, abused cuticles. Some bit at raw, swollen underlips, others licked at arid lips, swallowing nonexistent saliva. The signs were present; the taskforce was as chicken-shit scared as he!

Valerie's earlier trauma, cancelled by what rushed past them on the video screens, had left her seat, slipped into the empty one next to Brad Lincoln, aware of Velden's orbiting eyes observing her movements. "What alarming *stats*, General. More people killed in the first two hours of nuclear explosion than were killed in all the modern wars of history?" She listened critically to Dr. Sen Yen Lu's oratory, eyes riveted to the video screens.

"A proud testimonial to mankind," Brad muttered darkly.

"Judging from the Maui test, our host predicted it on the button. Why did no one listen, General?"

"We're here to learn *why* they didn't." Brad studied her pale, wan features. "So, you've emerged your cocoon, Miss Lansing? Have you—?"

"Don't ask. I'm not prepared to spill my guts," she snapped in good form, "You don't radiate the best of spirits, General."

"With good reason. My displeasure lies in the laxity of security. What's your excuse for ill temper and a bad disposition?"

Valerie ignored his remark. "Laxity?" she noted the knuckles on his hands whitening as he gripped the seat arms. "Personally I feel like a confined microscopic specimen—"

"He multiplied my work tenfold by accepting questionable characters I wouldn't trust to dump garbage." Brad's head jerked toward the area behind the glass hatch door. Obviously he directed his wrath at Moufflon.

"You know him well, don't you, General? Why does he hold himself aloof to us? We are anxious to know him better."

"More determined than you, Miss Lansing?" Brad unbuckled his seat belt. He eased himself to his feet noting her anxious look. Catching herself, Valerie averted her gaze but not before Brad Lincoln traced her reaction to the German, Zryden. Falling back into his seat, he quickly activated the communication device on his chronometer.

"What has Zryden to do with you?"

Valerie donned her barrister mask. "I haven't the vaguest idea what you mean." She lied. He *knew* she lied. And she *knew* he *knew* she lied. *Swell!* "Trust me. When I can, I will explain."

"Don't force me to hypothesize, Miss Lansing. I tend to intricate hypothesis. I get lost in thickets. It can prove dangerous if I am wrong." He hissed impatiently, the implication startling.

"I lack the proper answers. That's the straight of it," she insisted. "Conjecture at this point is insane. You'd declare me certifiable!" She held his hand, placed it along her cheek bone, a fixed smile forming on her face. Speaking through her teeth, she suggested he laugh as if she'd told him a humorous anecdote.

Brad complied, adding, "You have an extraordinary capacity to endure." On his feet he nodded curtly, and turned to walk aft in the cabin, caught the lethal, hard look on Velden's face.

Damn! I need more intrigue like the Roman Christians needed lions!

The enmity scrawled across Zryden's face exuded more than deep-seated hostility; it was violent hatred. *For Valerie or for Lincoln?*

Nodding perfunctorily to Velden in passing, Brad noted the subtle tilt to the German's head, the hint of military gesture, one stopping short of saluting. Instinct forced distortions in Brad's thinking as he moved amidships. Zryden, one of the men aboard

589

transmitting danger signals to Brad, Valerie's reaction to the man compounded the dangers. Brad had sniffed a *manufactured* cover in Zryden's dossier at first sight. Fingerprinted in Paris along with all the taskforce members, Zryden's were the only set that failed to arrive from INTERPOL and Clayallee 10 in West Berlin before the Paris departure. Brad loathed depending on inept operatives for any aspect of his own security. In this instance, numbing frustration had set in by Moufflon's absolute power in clearing three dossiers Lincoln had adamantly rejected as poor security risks. Velden Zryden headed the list. The Nigerian Kasavubu Katanga ran a close second and third—oh, yes, third was the very British Sir Alexander York of London.

Damn! Valerie Lansing would have to take care of herself; she had managed admirably in the past, hadn't she? Yet, thought Brad as he entered the restroom, locking the door behind him, the terror in her eyes—unmistakable terror had alarmed him. *Hummmnnnn . . .*

Brad relieved himself. Finished, he laved his hands with perfumed *sapone* from a gilded wall dispenser. Plush, customized fixtures—wasn't everything the finest? One could grow accustomed to this. . . .

Suddenly Brad lurched forward, thrown off-balance as the Lodestar hit an airpocket. He grabbed hold of a gilded side rail, steadying himself. In the increased turbulence Brad's hip struck the tiled counter top. Wincing at the impact, the movement clumsy at best, he heard a discordant clicking sound, a sound that didn't belong. He cocked his head, listened intently. There . . . he heard it again! A springlike click—the snap of a lock opening. He peered about the confines puzzled. The door was secure. Good. He lifted the commode cover, listened for some sign of the previous distraction. Nothing. He dropped it into place, sat down, and heaving his torso forward peered squinty-eyed under the mosaic tiled counter; fingers feeling under the counter lip, slowly, inching his way from one end to the other. There . . .! Something! . . . The counter top was loose!

How in the bloody blue blazes . . .?

Brad fumbled, pushed, yanked, shoved, pulled, pounded on it—nothing! The *damned* thing *had* to lift like a car hood! The latch! Where was the latch? He glanced at his watch. Four minutes had passed. To remain much longer might bring undue attention to himself. Alert at once, he peered about for a camera lens—a hidden imperceptible device. Brad, excellent at ferreting covert surveillance, found nothing, not a damned thing.

Two minutes sped by. Brad, sweating in the restrictive confines despite the air conditioning, lowered the temperature control on his flight suit and got back to work. *Dammit!* Still nothing! The counter top was either solid or unbudgable. He'd return later and try to solve the mystery. On his feet, he pounded an impatient fist on the tiled surface. *Voilà! Open Sesame!*

The lid, whooshing swiftly to an upright position, startled him. The entire tiled lid—holes where it fitted precisely over basin and taps—stood upright on a tightly coiled spring. Brad's eyes, shifting focus, widened. Arrested momentarily, astonishment evolving to grim sobriety, Brad's mental processes stuttered as he sorted the disturbing, unanticipated sight! What he saw . . . what he couldn't believe was . . .

A *goddamned arsenal*! Neatly arrayed firearms, ammunition, knives and vials filled with numbered drugs—no *names*—just numbers printed on the jackets! *Fucking weapons! Perfect for a skyjacking!*

The *bête noir* to this mission, a *fucking* hijacking, spelled disaster. He sat heavily on the commode cover, brooding. He was certain this was not Moufflon's precautionary measures—not with lasers at his disposal. He scanned the contents critically, filing mental pictures in his mind, and brought the lid down into place over the gilded tap fittings and ceramic pastel basin. Once secure, he tried to open it; it was unbudgable. Brad fell against it, heavily, pounded on it, simulating his earlier movement. Nothing! So, it was an unexpected freak accident, a one-in-a-thousand chance, culminating in a lucky moment of discovery!

He glanced nervously at his watch. Seven minutes had elapsed. He must talk with Moufflon! He needed black coffee, something in his stomach. Scotch, more palatable to him, was forbidden. Moufflon had banned alcohol, cigarettes, drugs, even aspirin for reasons he failed to elucidate. Brad had six Percodans stashed on him. He popped one, five remained.

His exit from the head was dignified. He closed the door behind him and headed aft to the galley. Inside he listened to a disenchanted French chef grumble over the passenger's disinclination to eat. Brad placated him. "It's not your cuisine, Phillipe. If you saw what the camera communicates, you, also, would be affected."

591

Brad left the galley, balancing a tray in one hand. He negotiated his way forward, easing past the observation window. A steward coming toward him placed a sealed telex on his tray. Brad nodded, and once in his assigned seat, placed the tray on the secured pullout shelf before him, and peered out the porthole window.

Stretched across the sky was a mourning cloth of dismal ashes. Attempts made by an inexorable sun to pierce it failed dismally. Brad buckled his seatbelt into place, not a moment too soon.

The Lodestar struck repeated turbulence. Waves of rising nausea gripped the passengers. The rolling, yawing, banking movements of the *empennage* jolted the occupants, turned them squeamish. The pilot's voice on the intercom suggested that the remains of a disabled communications satellite had burst through the upper stratosphere whizzing past the Lodestar like a meteor and had caused the turbulence. The Lodestar shuddered in the tunnel-like gusts of forceful winds for several frightening moments, then stabilized smoothly.

While the others wiped the sweat from their faces, Brad decoded the message and read:

TAKE PRECAUTIONS. THREE ASSASSINS ABOARD LODESTAR. INTENSIFY ALERT. ADDITIONAL INFORMATION TO COME. Signed: BERNARDO (code name for Bill Miller)

Committing the message to memory, he burned the message and crumbled the ashy remains, depositing them in the air chute. Wrapped in a shroud of cynicism, Brad sipped coffee. *Two assassins not enough? Now there are three? The whole fucking world wanted part of the action!*

Brad's appetite waned. His eyes behind dark lensed aviator's glasses trailed to the starboard side of the plane, fixing on the tail, muscularly built, vigorous Sir Alexander York. He studied the Britisher; the man was perusing the contents of his mahogany saddle leather briefcase.

Something about Sir Alexander York failed to compute in Brad's mind. Three men aboard the Lodestar, each presenting grave security risks, offended him. Colonel Kasavubu Katanga, Velden Zryden and Sir Alexander York, Brad felt, should have been rejected on the face of their dossiers, despite Moufflon's objection to the contrary.

York's dossier, a composite of perfection, his accreditation impeccable, listed him as one of Her Majesty's finest in the Secret Service. York's bore a more credible content than the slickly manufactured dossiers of the Angolan and German's, yet something nagged at Brad Lincoln. For two long weeks Brad had observed the son of Lord John York, his brilliant mentor at Bletchley Park in 1940. Prompted at the outset to pass the forty-five-year-old distinguished barrister through security when he recognized the name, Brad, an old *pro* from way back when, desisted. He did not believe the biblical parable: *Like father, like son.*

Lord John York was not at issue. Sir Alexander York was the subject of Lincoln's discontent and abounding curiosity. The Britisher occupied more of Brad's attention and thoughts than he desired.

York, Jr. bore a striking resemblence to the young starry-eyed Laurence Olivier who was thrust upon the world as the rebellious, dashing, brooding, tormented, albeit romantic Heathcliff in the film, *Wuthering Heights*. Brad sensed the studied expression in him; every move, gesture, manner carefully premeditated. Avid self-awareness of the aura projected, done extemporaneously becomes magnetic; if borne with a trace of affection sizzles flatly.

Yes, that was it! York moved like a stage actor in total command of his instrument—body—choreographed for the occasion!

Brad closed his eyes momentarily. If only he sat in judgment of Lord John York. He knew the man's background by rote, even now some four decades later, when he served in York Sr.'s command at Bletchley Park in 1940.

John York, at age seventeen had joined the RAF as a scout pilot. Shot down in a dogfight over Belgium, captured, held as a POW, he mastered the German language. Having learned French as a teenager, he traveled the world as a soldier of fortune, lumberjacked in Canada, turned jockeroo in the Australian Outback, spent time as a mercenary in the Pancho Villa Revolution, safaried in the Sudan, Kenya and Rhodesia, journeying to countless British ruled territories. Sometime between World Wars I and II John earned a law degree at Oxford, joined British Intelligence in 1930, a branch of the RAF. He traveled to Germany, struck up personal acquaintances with Adolf Hitler, Alfred Rosenberg, Rudolph Hess, Erich Koch and several high-ranking senior officers in the Third Reich nucleus. As constant companions who shared common interests, the Germans encouraged York to keep Britain out of the fracas stewing between Germany and the Russian Bolshevists. However, John managed secret liaisons with Adolf Hitler, worming his way into Third Reich echelons he managed a formidable *coup d'eclat* by extracting from *Der Führer* his plans to destroy the entire Russian Communists regime!

Brad mused over these intricate liaisons more vigorously than in the past. Viewed by historians and politicians of the era, *after-the-fact* these curious liaisons undeniably substantiated the facts that Britain had actually financed Hitler's rise to power in the early days to keep the Russian bear away from the west. Now, as Brad examined the facts with brilliant 20-20 hindsight and a forty-year expertise, he concluded, how else could John York have learned from Hitler's top generals the strategy of Blitzkrieg?

How was this possible? History has proven the Nazis to be no dunderheads. How had John York accomplished this superhuman feat? Or—was his action part and package of a more cunning scenario?

Forty years ago Lincoln had gazed upon John York as a role model. Now? Brad reexamined Lord York's real character. To do the job correctly, he lacked the linkage to York's formative years, those years that mold the child into manhood. Brad did the next best thing. He conjured up a forty-year recollection of the tall, slim, cold, hard-faced giant of a man who with his silences, unusual moods, merciless detachment and genius was looked upon as a model of perfection for the work in Ultra. Those silences and cold detachment, it was whispered at Bletchley, had stemmed from his POW days when survival had taken on beastly proportions. Brad recalled when York entered the room dark clouds descended. Back-room whisperings negating his manhood ran rampant in those days, his dwarfed penis constantly ridiculed. Yet the snotty twits stood to attention when York entered the study chambers.

John York wore his past achievements like valor badges. He created an aura of invincibility around the space he occupied. York's flinty gray, ice-chip eyes had struck terror in Brad's young heart in those days. Dare to drop a pen or shuffle papers when York lectured and his flaring eyes would sprint across the students' obedient faces, see into their souls and reflect no emotion, nothing but a bland countenance; what a chilling effect!

York, Sr. was unreadable. York, Jr. was equally as unreadable. Brad sipped his coffee grimacing distastefully at the cold dregs, his thoughts locked about John York. What was obscured forty years ago by that aura of impenetrable genius became clearer to Brad. The revelation—it could be defined as nothing else—stunned Brad. Now, he saw Lord York stripped of heroic glitter, he recognized the extent of the man's canny, criminal mind. *Criminal mind*?

A criminal, thought Brad, in society's eyes works beyond legal boundaries. The criminal working both sides of the law with impunity is reverently called an *intelligence officer!* Who, better than Brad Lincoln could define the perfect classification for the criminal mentality? Enabled to indulge in every perversion and crime known to man, including murder, none were as perfectly equipped as the flaming faggots masterminding British Intelligence in its highest reaches.

S-H-I-T! . . . Forty years of adulation crumbled in a split second!

Judging from John York's close, extended confinement with top-ranking Nazis, *especially* Alfred Rosenberg, he had elicited every plan, hope and aspiration of the Nazi Four Thousand Year Reich! *How*? *Why*? What were the extent of the stakes involved, the rewards of so risky and dirty a business? Brad rolled back his thoughts to the numerous plottings swept under the rug at World War II's end. Facts uncovered at Nuremburg, apart from the war crimes, loomed before him and he knew John York's involvement. From Erich Koch, another Nazi warlord, York had gained insight into the character and mentalities, the attitudes, thought patterns, figures of speech and *how* the Nazi High Command responded to stress. York had learned how far they'd bend in a stiff wind, for the *right* person!

Christ! York had learned privileged information not even a psychiatrist could unless permitted access to the chambers of a man's mind held sacrosanct. Unless . . .

Only in certain intimacies did men drop their guard for such revelations! Men talked to their wives, their mistresses, lovers—in unguarded moments. *Lover to lover! Man to man!*

In 1940 rumors of John York's sexual proclivities proliferated, a word dropped here and there in special circles concerning his sexual aberrations failed to interest Brad in those days. He vividly recalled York's frustration, the indignation suffered when on his return from Germany the fruits of his labor, ignored by those who walked power corridors, had withstood jaundiced scrutiny. Throughout the 1930's York's numerous jaunts to Berlin to visit with his Nazi friends abruptly terminated in 1939, vis-à-vis expulsion from that city, ordered by his lovers never again to set foot on German soil. *Nor killed! Not incarcerated or tried for espionage!* Merely *ordered* out of Germany! What a ton of kindling that left open for conjecture. One little match could blow open the entire British Military Intelligence mission.

Brad sipped his coffee. What he'd give for a cigarette! He wondered how many top secrets had been bandied about in those early days before the Third Reich moved forward into posterity? How many covert movements were aired while lovers rutted between legs and buttocks during those Sodom and Gomorrah days in the exchange of sadistic debaucheries and uncomplicated delights shared between men? No one knew for sure. Propaganda machines cranked up by the Allies had hung a hundred shrouds on all truths, including the extent of Nazi warring strength. Shadowed by guilts of their own blunders and stupidities, the Allies had pointedly refused to exhibit Nazi warring superiority in its utter perfection, even if expounded upon by their own super-British Intelligence agent, John York. It took the fall of France in 1940, abnormal pressure from the Air Staff and finally John York himself with his cronies to stumble upon the most startling discovery—breaking the German War code—the UL-TRA secret—before Winston Churchill warmed up to York's reports and the scientific marvels already grasped by the Germans to pay credence to York's invaluable dedication. All that was so long ago. But there was more. Chilled by the thoughts he harbored, Brad refocused on the matter, time and again.

Lord John York, according to certain *infallible* files, had purportedly died in 1976. *So, let the dead stay dead, Brad!* But had he died? Maps sketched in Lord York's inimitable, distinctive style, coded and dated 1983, had surfaced through the

Moufflon network and were contained in the presentation brief, PROJECT: MOONSCAPE, disseminated in Maui this February last.

Chew on that nut for a while, General!

Brad shifted focus to Sir Alexander York. A month ago York's dossier arrived at the U.S. Embassy in Paris, his elation at the name, immeasurable. If the son measured an iota to the fabric of Lord York? . . .

"Don't hang yourself on the comparison between them," Greer had suggested to Brad when he discussed his high hopes. "The son must be assessed strictly on his own merits. But it does seem crazy," Greer added with an ominous note, "why a man with York's background . . . well, dammit, Brad, why the fuck Sir Alexander York, K.C. (King's Counsel) a senior barrister, a man whose name was recently placed in nomination in the British High Court by the Lord Chancellor, would toss away all he'd worked for to embark on a near-suicidal mission? Why become an adventurer in the tea-and-scones times of his life? Gamble it away in PROJECT: MOONSCAPE? Uh-uh, man, I don't buy it."

Brad didn't either, but he needed fresh input. Greer had shuffled through the glowing letters by prestigious Britishers alluding to Alexander's honesty, integrity, devotion to duty and all that rot, trying to find more lurid, shadowed revelations and finding not the wispiest hint of libertine behavior, held his nostrils tightly, rolling his eyes. "You can believe this shit, General, but I can smell a manufactured dossier a mile away."

And now, reflecting on the conversation, Brad concurred with that observation as he had before Greer initiated the thought. Britishers in the realm of knighthood frowned on breaking educational lineage in the family. It simply was not done. So—why had Alexander received his law degree at Cambridge—not at Oxford, Lord John's alma mater? It failed to compute; the data appeared to be contrived.

Brad sipped coffee dregs, ordered more from a steward, glanced at the overhead video screens. No changes. Dr. Lu's voice pierced his consciousness briefly, something about atmospheric changes, rises in temperatures outside the Lodestar. Brad tuned him out, concentrating on the man described in the dossier on his lap.

Under the glitter of Lord John York's stellar achievements and

597

devotion to the Crown, nothing in Alexander's history hinted at the stouthearted, adventurous inclinations reminiscent of his remarkable father. Actually, Greer was correct in his assessment. The bulky dossier bore the distinct odium of a meticulously manufactured lie!

That was it! It was manufactured and that meant . . . Just to be certain, he perused it again, fine-combing the fact, wondering at the time it had taken to compile and list impeccably so many facts. More time than had been alloted to taskforce members prior to flight time and that meant . . . *the dossier was born long ago!*

For what purpose?

Fresh coffee arrived. Brad sipped it, munched on a cheese croissant, mulling facts over in his mind. Spilling crumbs on the folder Brad brushed them away, nearly upsetting it. He moved swiftly to catch it as it slid off his knees. About to slam the damn file shut, Brad riveted on two unopened letters tucked into the back pocket of the manila folder. *Hello? . . . What have we . . .* he remembered. The letters had arrived prior to departure and he had hurriedly shoved them into the folder pocket.

The first contained a birth certificate, a note attached to it read: *Birth certificate to only infant born in Woodridge England December 17, 1930 to John and Melissa York.* Brad impatiently scanned the certificate. So . . . Why the *tzimmes*? The second letter contained a copy of Alexander York's law degree, dated 1967. Brad's eyes behind dark glasses danced over the fancy Latin script, puzzled, shifting his focus from one certificate to the next, hardly noting the subtleties. *Was he suddenly obtuse*? Then he saw the discrepancy!

Tempering passion with reality, the truth congealed, turning Brad crimson with discomfort. He backtracked, painstakingly rereading each word, noting commas, periods, ellipses—he must be absolutely correct. It was all there, staring up at him. The truth struck him with the impact of a head-on collision. Then just as quickly, he bit back a sharp rejoinder to his previous reaction.

Very little shocked Brad Lincoln. In his long, varied career he'd seen the seamy side of every society from the Australian aborigines to the decadent Crown heads of Europe, but this was his *first!*

His first reaction was to stare across the aisle at Sir Alexander York, the handsome, well contained man, but deliberately avoiding doing so, he chose instead to flip back through the dossier in a desperate hope an error had occurred. He found the physical report. Scanning the four page, single spaced, neatly typed report he learned nothing. *Nothing!*

What shook Brad Lincoln? . . . *The birth certificate and law degree both stipulated the name, Alexandria—not Alexander!* That's what created the internal chaos! He cleared his throat, inhaled deeply, never before finding the confines of a plane as restrictive.

The dossier stated between the years 1967 to 1974, before *Alexander*, a junior barrister was counseled by an eminent Queen's Counsel, Q.C. and later traversed the usual period of waiting to become Q.C., and later reached the pinnacle of his career to become King's Counsel, K.C. he had taken a seven-year sabbatical abroad in the Foreign Services. The nature of Sir Alexander's pursuits—*naturally classified*!

Classified my ass! In the seven-year interim Alexandria had become *Alexander!* Was that it? A sex change? An actual sex change? So what? What was the significance of such a metamorphosis? How was it all wrapped up in PROJECT: MOONSCAPE? Was the man really Alexander York or was it a *cover*? Not a sex change but a *cover*? *Think*, Brad, *THINK!* Perhaps a member of British MI, infiltrating, taking over a role similar to that of Lord John York: Had he been so taken by the name York he had overlooked important details? Evidently, *schmuck!*

Brad slapped the dossier shut, slapped the file against his thighs, contemplating every step involved in York's final clearance for this project. If the dossier *was* manufactured, it was done by the slickest, most efficient apparatus in the business—British MI, the agency that graduated from their ranks, the most proficient global assassins!

S-H-I-T! Brad reached for his single-shot pen gun Berna had given him at the Prince's palace. He had yet to use it, but kept it with him, now, as he rolled the smooth metal between his fingers he relaxed, the energetic façade of the past several months and fatigue etched into his features. Had he grown careless? How many more surprises lay in store for Moufflon and PROJECT: MOONSCAPE? He regarded the complexities surrounding Valerie Lansing, questioned her presence aboard, and his sanity in permitting it. The dangers posed by her presence were unclear, but threatening. Christ! What was her reason for converting that heavenly hair of fire into a blond? Why the need for the disguise? Why would the color of her hair matter to anyone? And if all this wasn't enough to strafe him out, what of the cache of weapons in the *john*? And the telex: *Three assassins aboard*! Now, this enigma over York! Did Moufflon know? Did he?

Brad replaced the pen gun carefully in his flight suit pocket and glanced up toward the cockpit. He must convey this last twist to the York scenario to Moufflon.

An alarm rang on his chronometer, stirring him from reverie. It was time to prepare and disperse the *diplomatic pouch*. He placed the York dossier and certificates in a manila file, sealed it and scribbled the name Moufflon on it. He removed another manila envelope from his flight bag, studied the designee's name and rang for a steward. Vaguely Dr. Lu's voice infringed on his thoughts.

For *Christsakes*! The scientist was *damned* near eulogizing the holocaust!

Velden Zryden lowered his binoculars, unhooked his safety belt from the overhead track, edging his way beyond the periphery of men huddled around the observation window, unobserved, under the echo of Dr. Lu's narration. Weaving his way aft toward Moufflon's private quarters, he stopped abruptly. *Damn!* Two shadowy sentinels seated menacingly in the dimly lit alcove obstructed him. Beyond them, Velden noted two additional men, Prince Youseff Ben-Kassir and a tawny-skinned Moor he failed to recognize.

Approaching Velden, affording him a perfect segue, a steward wheeled a tray brimming with hot coffee and snacks. He quickly reached for a tray, as if this was his purpose in approaching the forbidden area, drawing no untoward glances from the guards. Balancing the snack tray, he retraced his steps past the observation window to his assigned seat in the forward cabin. Once buckled in firmly, he sipped his coffee, noting with mounting irritation the smoldering looks Uri Mikhail transmitted to Valerie Lansing.

Actually Velden loathed the Russian. He'd asked himself a dozen times why he felt antagonism toward the man. Was it because he'd found no flaw in the diplomat? No tinge of mediocrity, nothing hinting at possible corruption? No skeletons in the closet. After perusing taskforce dossiers Velden *knew* intimately his allies from his enemies. *Uri Mikhail Gregorevich was no ally!* When it came time to differentiate between each, he'd be prepared. Velden considered Valerie Lansing his most viable enemy.

Observing her, an erection made him hot, desirous of her. He struggled mentally against Victor Zeller's flesh and internal images of a hot, passionate love affair, and forced Amadeo to assess the liabilities she posed aboard this mission. How much of Valerie's introversion, detachment was natural? How much was studied, deliberately posed to deceive? He did not know, but if he guessed? . . . The questions fired at Dr. Carronton? . . . If push came to shove, if Amadeo perceived any sudden change in her demeanor? . . . He would silence her!

Cool off, Victor! Velden, back in form policing Victor's passions forced him to reflect astutely. Poisoning his mind were flagrant lies she had promoted while posturing about as Veronique Lindley. Influenced by the object lessons taught him by Sophia, Veronique's deception, a sham at the outset, was unforgivable. Her betrayal began, for God's sake, *before* they met at the Martinique Galleria, *before* they traversed the Swiss Alps and she desecrated their love nest in Zurich. Yes, yes! He saw it clearly in retrospect! A planned deception, plotted long before to advance some sinister evil against Zeller. Why must the pain be *damnably* acute?

Betrayed by Sophia, abandoned by her, aided and abetted by his beloved mother, *la contessa*, now Veronique! *No!* Not *Veronique!* Valerie Lansing! An American attorney. Daughter of a U.S. Senator!

A snide leer wormed over Velden's lips, his darkly veiled eyes masking inner satisfaction at the irony contained in the clever scenario. In Paris, the Lansing name on a shiny brass plate on the portal post had sounded no warnings. But as he studied Valerie's dossier, stimulated by the micro-chip implantation of Amadeo's memory bank, there resulted a most enthralling cranial readout: *Senator Hartford B. Lansing, a political pawn, belonged lock, stock and barrel to Amadeo Zeller!* Velden grinned with exquisite evil.

He glanced at his chronometer. An hour out of Paris? It seemed ages. Few changes were occurring outside. He reconsidered Valerie Lansing. *Why* had she deceived Victor? *Why?* Her motivation escaped him. Certainly *not* on behalf of her father,

601

the Senator? Her presence aboard the Lodestar both intrigued and offended him. What qualified her incursion into matters of State? Of the highest priority, in sensitive areas and among distinguished scientific and political scholars? Inquisitive spools of thought threading judiciously through Velden's mind clashed constantly with Victor's feelings. In the Paris briefing she had avoided him to the point of downright discourtesy!

But wasn't that as it should be? She knew Victor, not Velden!

Velden doggedly attacked Mosha Bauer's failed efforts. In essence the Zellers had been had. So skillfully created was the in-depth probe on Veronique it bore no earmarks of a *cover*. He marveled at her adroitness in pulling off the coup, marveled more at the network designing her cover. The mechanics of compiling Velden Zryden's dossier clearly indicated how manufactured facts could be tailored to any purpose for the *right* price. Palms greased in the highest echelons of government amounted to small fortunes. To Zeller such costs were negligible, but to Lansing? . . . From where came enough Lansing money to buy the power to corrupt, verify and falsify dossiers?

Perhaps, Amadeo, you do not know Hartford B. Lansing as well as you should, eh?

Victor took perverse pleasure in playing against the cranial implant, as if he entered into combat with his father.

Velden, munching a croissant, sighed imperceptibly. Victor had loved Veronique! What had driven her to penetrate the Zeller family? What brand was the unique hatred aimed against them, and it must be *hatred* that triggered so dedicated a resolve. Embattled by raging internal conflicts, verification of Valerie's treachery eluded him. Actually, what had she done to vilify the Zeller family? Hadn't she supported Victor in Zurich by her strength, against the horrendous internal warfare splitting him in two, changing him into a demon?

Velden's eyes grew vacant, then Amadeo's image formed behind those orbs:

Ten of the eighteen-man taskforce recruited for PROJECT: MOONSCAPE belong to Zeller! Concentrate on the others. Be especially concerned with the Moor! Remember Corsica, Victor? Remember the Moor? Are they one and the same? And think seriously on General Brad Lincoln. Did you not receive his official obituary from the U.S. State Department?

Velden, squirming uneasily, shifted about in his chair. Instinctively he felt surveillance on him. Glancing about, he saw nothing overt, but he *knew* it was coming from those *verboten* quarters in the *empennage*, the area he earlier had failed to penetrate. Blinking Amadeo to the unconscious level to elude his inner tormentor, he flashed on the tawny-skinned Moor. He eased forward, searched his flightbag, flipped through the dossiers in near desperation. Before he lost control of his faculties and became a babbling idiot he must learn more about the Moor. There was none—no dossier on the Moor. Why not?

He sat up again to ponder this and as he did he gazed at the formidable figure of Moufflon huddled with the navigator behind the glass hatch door. Velden's features varnished a pale, haunting ache and when suddenly those verdant eyes lifted, and penetrated the glass hatch door to bore into Velden's, he was shaken to the quick. The reactions coming from his inner depths both mystified and beguiled him.

What was it he felt for Moufflon in that instant? Unidentifiable emotions were running the spectrum from contempt to absolute respect elevating his curiosity beyond bounds. More profound and bedeviling were the complex stirrings, difficult to ignore or isolate as if he were bound inexplicably to this man, the brother of Sophia!

Come to your senses, Victor! This is no superman, this Moufflon! He's a mere mortal, Darius Bonifacio, the Corsican you should have captured on that infernal Blood Island in 1943 before the Axis retreated.

What Victor felt in that moment bespoke something cryptic, more disconcerting than met the naked eye. A poignant connection, albeit it invisible, created pandemonium in his mind. Had viewing Moufflon at long last in the flesh removed the glitter of legend—reduced him to a mere mortal? Two decades spent listening to his father sing the praises of so *singular* a human had evoked Victor's envy, a curious, twisted impulsive envy resembling an ephemeral sibling rivalry. Now he engaged in a circumspect observation of Darius Bonifacio searching his uncannily familiar features, sensing something occult, exceedingly profound. He experienced a kinship, a bewildering force linking them in a web of design he failed to understand.

Was it umbilical in a sense because of Sophia?

Darius glanced up from his charts, and locked eyes with Velden/Victor/Amadeo, through the hatch door. Victor casually broke eye contact for in that moment he felt he lay bare, as if Moufflon had seen through the trilateral deception and the Velden Zryden *cover*! Christ! What he'd give for a stiff brandy!

Enforced self-restraint, constant fear of discovery, endless distrust of his own shadow and the growing complexities of his mission left brutal scars on him, traces of a haunted-eyed expression concealed behind tinted dark glasses.

"*Monsieur* Zryden? . . . ." He glanced up at the manila envelope thrust at him. "*Pour vous, monsieur*, from the diplomatic pouch. My instructions are to deliver this to you at precisely twelve noon, Paris time. Please sign here." The steward spoke French.

Velden initialled the receipt, observed the steward with interest as he moved about doling envelopes to various passengers.

Velden shifted his focus to the manila envelope, at his name and time of delivery stamped on it. He hesitated breaking the seal, recollecting vividly Mosha Bauer's intimate descriptions of those cleverly contrived envelope bombs devised by the WOGS. Surely not aboard the Lodestar? . . . He sighed in relief when nothing happened when he broke the seal and tensed at the outpouring of five 8 X 10 glossy photos.

Everything in Velden/Victor/Amadeo iced, and for an interminable period of time hung suspended in frozen immobility. *Don't react! Don't give any outward show of the volcanic eruption inside you!*

When he could, he glanced up casually to ascertain if any eyes were fixed on him to observe his reactions. He saw nothing overt. Slowly his attention fell to the photos. He shuffled through the first four, each graphically depicted the body of a brutally assaulted, battered, dead woman. The longer he stared the more familiar she appeared, yet nothing definitive emerged. The fifth photo was a full-faced reflection of a beautiful, alive woman, wheat-colored naturally curly hair, hazel brown eyes—as stunning a beauty as he'd ever seen. He turned the photo over, scanned the statistics.

Velden Zryden's mask fell away. Victor deflated like a punctured balloon, his face turning a mottled gray sagged. His heart broke into bits. He read the attached note as panic and desperation fired a slow sizzle in his belly, rapidly turning into a hard lump of ice. He swallowed hard, reread the note: *Monsieur* Zryden: "Enclosed are photographs, proof of death of the cou-

604

rier for which you engaged my services to terminate. Enclosed is her identity card for your perusal. The card, as you can see, reads, Bernadette Bonifacio. I probed and learned she is the daughter of the Zurich banker, Victor Zeller, by Sophia Bonifacio.''

Velden felt suspended in some godawful time warp, the wildest of improbabilities bearing down on him. Drenched in an icy sweat chilling him, alternated by hot flushes, he experienced a curious breathlessness, as if he were having a coronary. Was this some cruel joke? Someone, beginning with the *blue beret* at the Bristol in Paris, was on to him. *Who? WHO?* His heart thundered like an anvil as he marshaled his composure, collected photos and shoved them into the envelope. He placed them in his flight bag. He could not breathe nor catch his breath and suddenly concerned he'd hyperventilate and need assistance, he checked his chronometer, took a blood pressure reading. Christ! 190/110! His pulse read: ninety beats per minute! Velden forced his attention out the porthole at the black nothingness, experiencing the agony of inner terror, as if hands around his neck were squeezing the very life from him. Blood throbbed at his temples, roared in his ears. He must not let anything happen to him. He fumbled with the chronometer, turned a lever to coronary, and let the flight suit do its job.

His face, hard as beaten iron, pondered ominously. *Concentrate! Concentrate, as Dr. Zeiss instructed you.* He must not permit anyone to view his private inner hell and damnation. He must not!

His own daughter! His and Sophia's. Bernadette Bonifacio Zeller!

Moufflon had sent his own blood and flesh to her death! He had inculpated the girl in his business with Zeller! A chilling, inscrutable look hardened his features, while internally he was crumbling. Had he seen the familiarity in Bernadette at the Geneva bank, unable then, to label it? God, had she known?

His face white to the leaden lips, he turned his loathing on Darius Bonifacio, staring mutely at him, thinking how little resemblance he bore to the dark eyed, sultry beauty of Sophia who had turned his world inside out. Try as he did to hold that loathing, it disintegrated as something frighteningly familiar in Darius, provoking his imagination. If he didn't know better . . . *Stop it! Stop letting your imagination run wild!* But was he?

Velden shook his head as Amadeo surfaced, the image forming behind his eyes. The internal laughter was Amadeo's, the harsh, whining voice, unmistakable. *"It isn't your imagination, Victor! Take another look! Go ahead. The resemblance is there. Think! THINK!"*

Victor's piercing eyes searched Darius's features, cowering inwardly as the ghostly trail of Bernadette's death haunted him. Sweat trickled until he was drenched under his flight suit. Images of his past collided in his mind, one superimposed over the other. Thoughts coagulated until recognition became undeniable.

What connection was there between Darius Bonifacio and himself. What?

It was Bernadette, his daughter!

Victor shut his eyes at the galvanizing truth. He would never be the same. *Never!* The inner loathing was detouring, taking a different course.

Through a secreted closed-circuit television, the Moor and Prince Youseff Ben-Kassir studied Velden's reactions from Moufflon's private quarters. They noted on the various gauges the changes in his blood pressure, and pulse, the various readings he took on his chronometer. Slowly they exchanged glances. The Moor's face was deadly. "There can be no mistaking him. It is Victor Zeller."

"Let us presume he is the first prospect, *oui, mon ami?*" Youseff said quietly. "*A coup sûr*—without fail, Katanga is number two. Who then is the third?"

"Perhaps you? Or me? Or the girl? Perhaps there is a Manchurian candidate aboard the Lodestar. Does it really matter?"

Youseff tilted his head obliquely. "You are quite right. Why would it matter?"

Lieutenant Colonel Kasavubu Katanga, an ex-guerilla fighter from Angola, black, powerfully built with the furtive black eyes of an underworld demon, had fought in civil war in the 1960's alongside a madman who rose to power to become the nation's Chief of Intelligence, General Zolo Bengali. Guerilla warfare and all its dehumanizing aspects had taken its toll of Katanga, including one eye, now covered by a black patch. The protracted crisis of civil war extended for too long a period had devastated the black man. One night, as he neared his village, Katanga with a hundred men raided the outpost. He loathed his first cousin, lusted after his wife. That night he slashed his cousin to death, and in flights of insanity hacked off limb after limb, mutilating the face beyond recognition. Tearing off his clothing, comingling sweat with his cousin's blood, he pursued the screaming wife, raped her, killing any of the children who interfered. It was not enough to have emptied his bags of hot semen into her, he indulged in bestialities and when satisfaction came he slaughtered her, too, but not before she had plucked out one of his eyes. Screaming in bloody torment only for that moment, the eyeball hung from its empty bleeding socket by a few nerve endings. Then he returned to the politics of his work, ordered the village burned to cover the vile deed. The stench of flaming flesh and blood clung cohesively over the trees in the scorching sun luring the earth's predators. Vultures wheeled ecstatic arcs overhead at the banquet of death spread below them, desert jackals and hyenas sniffed the scent miles away.

Katanga fell with exhaustion a week later, and was hospitalized. With General Bengali's assistance, Katanga had adjusted, risen in the ranks to become the General's Cyclopean eye, ears and gun. The Angolan was, at best, certifiably insane. Rational on occasion, overwhelmed periodically by an unchained brute force, the General was the only man capable of controlling and rendering him rational.

Alternate states of megalomania, precipitating the paranoia, found release in erratic outbursts of irrespressible hatred and uncontrollable violence. Katanga was a terrifying instrument of death. Controlled by drugs to disguise the psychosis, Katanga, under the Svengali domination of General Zolo Bengali often demonstrated keen intelligence, a cunning and loyalty Bengali got from no other man. To withhold the miracle drug, Bengali knew precisely the end product of his manipulation, a powerful lethal weapon programmed to kill.

Katanga, a hulking, brooding man, lumbered back to his seat from the observation window. His only interest, the target of his concentration, the only reason for his presence with the taskforce, was a clandestine assignment to kill Moufflon. Katanga had departed Luanda, capital of Angola, having been handed a slim manila file stamped in code: TARGET: MOUFFLON.

He had endured the Paris briefing, boarded the Lodestar under a glowing dossier manufactured with political expediency. Before journey's end, before the Lodestar's reconnaissance mission ended, Moufflon would be a dead man—General Zolo Bengali richer by five million dollars.

The clean-shaven black man with oversized elephant tusk teeth sat heavily in his assigned seat, a short distance from General Brad Lincoln. His Cyclopean eye trailed up to the overhead video screens, holding briefly, then slowly, in a vertical drop held on the profile of Moufflon through the glass hatch door.

Katanga would give up the other eye to know what transpired in the cockpit.

The cockpit and navigator's niche was an area of intensified activity. Moufflon, the object of Katanga's concentrated attention, wrapped up the intensified briefing with his navigator, in the preparation of another journey. Unfurling a chart, Darius rewound it tightly, his eyes intent on the steady blips on the radar screen, darted to the computer readout screen centered amid highly sophisticated scanning systems, laser reflectors, seismatic devices and sensitive warning systems with capabilities beyond man's comprehension.

Engine sounds diffused verbal quips between the pilot, Frenchman Geoffre Honore and the voice of the *Grim Reaper*, Moufflon's affectionate name for the incredible computer aboard.

Honore, a former fighter pilot, veteran ace of the Indo-China Campaign, and now Moufflon's private pilot, was a craggy-faced, ruddy-complexioned, brown-haired man with blue hawk eyes and a nose to match. Built like a weightlifter, with broad, muscular upper torso, narrow-waisted and slim-hipped, his legs stood a bit short of Atlas perfection. The face was battle-scarred and hardened. A marvelous sense of wit and humor had steered him over the rough courses. Honore drank heavily, spouted Byron with a passion, fully converted to the politics of cynicism by life, war and the strutting majordomos who postured about, running the world. His familiarity with jets, international airports and a hundred private fields where a plane could sit down in an emergency qualified him to fly Moufflon and he did so with the dégagé and grace of a soaring eagle. A loyal Frenchman to the core, he tailored that loyalty to the specifications of his profession. His confidence, absolute knowledge of aircraft, his profound respect for the elements, made him a natural flyer. Flying was his life, living an avocation. It was precisely what Honore wanted and got. The salary far beyond his needs, his loyalty all-consuming to Moufflon, what else could he want for? The question bothered Honore more than it did Moufflon.

Moufflon listened to the rhetoric between Honore and the *Grim Reaper*. In French the conversation centered on chartings, atmospheric conditions, alien trackings, radiatiōn testing, intricate electronic equipment that prevented aerial and ground forces from penetrating their frequencies. Concern over the ECM and HUD systems (Head Up Display) projected on the pilot's windshield in phosphorescent electric green and hot orange, comparable if not more refined than the capabilities and essential massive data input of United States F-15's and F-16s fighter planes. Intrinsic to survival were the jamming and anti-jamming systems capable of aborting an enemy missile determined to obliterate the mission, crew and passengers.

This crew believed with conviction many clandestine apparatus operating close to the areas to be traversed would delight in destroying this mission.

The *Grim Reaper* amazingly ran on a micro-chip smaller than a human fingernail. A flip of a switch converted readouts and articulation to five separate languages.

For the past six months, Moufflon working night and day with gifted scientists, technologists, incredibly knowledgeable men and women oriented to aerospace and computer technology, fully absorbed in the miraculous strides made by dedicated specialists, had converted the Lodestar, preparing the aircraft and taskforce for a journey into uncharted waters.

At this moment, Moufflon reflected on little else save the computer screen readout. He listened to the *Grim Reaper*'s robot-like voice, synchronizing the gadget on his left wrist, much like those worn by the taskforce. Moufflon's played his favorite tune, *La Tosca*.

Shortly, an altogether different journey would commence.

Chapter Thirty-Nine

AMIDSHIPS TWO SECURITY GUARDS UNLOCKED A CHAINED GATE to a spiral staircase leading below into the belly of the Lodestar. In the nose of the Jet, Darius Bonifacio, carrying charts and briefcase, wearing identical radiation-proof attire as the taskforce members, emerged from the cockpit, and moving aft stopped abruptly at the staccato sounds of a telex embedded in a wall niche. He picked up a wall phone and dialed a coded set of numbers. A glass shield sprang open revealing a mini-telex and its printed readout. Tearing it from the instrument, Darius decoded it, and scrutinizing the contents read:

> EMPLOY PRECAUTION . . . BE LIKE MONKEYS AND CATS, SILENT AND TRICKY . . . ONCE THERE WAS ONE, THEN TWO, ALONG CAME A THIRD BUT NOW THERE ARE FOUR . . . WOLF SPIDER . . .

Darius, without expression fed the readout to the greedy, razor-sharp steel claws of a paper shredder built into the wall niche. The glass shield fell into place, locking it securely.

So, what else is new—it was a lucrative assignment. Three assassins, now four? Does it really matter? Darius smiled, inscrutably. He moved aft into the Lodestar, nodding to some, making eye contact with General Lincoln and Jim Greer.

He descended the spiral, clankety iron stairs as special taskforce members scheduled for the next phase fell into step behind him. Security guards positioned at either side of the stairs examined their credentials, checking ID, adding, "You'll be prepped below. Step carefully. please."

The taskforce members descended, flightbags in hand, their features blanched, uncertainty in their eyes. Confidence was essential. Their programming in Paris fell a bit short, but they refused to reveal their innermost fears. Each converted into functional machines for the next leg of the journey as they were greeted below by a staff of attendants.

They gazed about the futuramic, spaceship atmosphere, awestruck, and assembled in a line before a pressurized cabin. Bubble-shaped helmets equipped with air purifiers, temperature controls, oxygen preserves and communication devices were placed over their heads, secured into the ringed tufts of steel around the necks of their flight suits. A convex section of shatterproof, see-through plastic afforded each peripheral vision. Once sealed, the flight suits provided ample protection against substances of a deadly nature comingling dangerously in any atmosphere they traversed. Their attire, equally as efficient as those worn by astronauts with few modifications, permitted incursion to the danger zones with minimal exposure to radiation.

Each was escorted through a second hatch door leading to the interior of a uniquely constructed helicopter cradled within the belly of the Lodestar, named the *Scorpion*.

Moufflon, buckled in behind the pilot controls, engaged at once in data logging, following strict aeronautical proceedures. He spoke French, citing passenger names, approximate location before takeoff, giving latitudinal and longitudinal readings into the flight recorder—the instrument imperative in the event of disaster.

Prince Ben-Kassir, next to Moufflon in the copilot's seat, busied himself synchronizing clocks, checking the magnetic compass fire detection and warning alert systems. Careful inspections conducted prior to flight by crew and computer to verify peak performance, the copilot was bound by law to recheck navigational systems.

General Lincoln sat behind Moufflon at portside. Valerie Lansing, seated next to him, and at her right, Uri Mikhail Gregorevich, and alongside him at extreme starboard, Velden Zryden. The third row commencing with Dr. Sen Yen Lu at portside behind Brad Lincoln and Jim Greer at starboard sandwiched between them, Sir Alexander York and Colonel Katanga. The two solitary seats in the *empennage* were occupied by the Moor, Matteus Montenegro and one security guard, a musky-skinned, heavy-set, thirtyish, black curly-haired silhouette of a prizefighter, named Gabriel Gadi, translated to Hebrew, meaning *God is my strength, God is my fortune*.

The claustrophobic atmosphere inside the *Scorpion*'s dimly

lighted interior turned cloying, creating mounting apprehension in each of the rigidly immobile passengers. Reflected on their faces were last-minute attempts to conceal second thoughts.

Matteus Montenegro, an octogenarian, didn't look a day over sixty. Flashing onyx eyes, his white curly-hair framed a craggy face upon which was etched the history of mankind. In a strange, enduring symbiosis spanning five decades the Moor, the only man completely in Moufflon's confidence, was admitted to the mission without formal dossier and security clearance. In stature and appearance he exuded so formidable a menace his presence aboard the *Scorpion* preyed heavily on four of the occupants' minds.

Four men, including Zryden and Katanga, recognized the strategic position occupied by the Moor in the chopper's tail. From this vantage point any attempts at foul play could be aborted. All passengers aboard, increasingly aware of the Moor's presence and protection, sensed instinctively his inclination: he would waste anyone planning deadly action against Moufflon. None of the *four* predators aboard chose to further speculate on the relationship between Corsican and Moor.

Other priorities held sway.

Seat belts clicked into place. Hatch doors slid shut, locked electronically. A radar screen blipped alive on an overhead console, the readout screen visible to all occupants. The audible French exchanged between Geoffre Honore the Lodestar's pilot and Moufflon pierced their headgear earphones, commanding their attention as Moufflon complied with Honore's directives. Instruments checked, Moufflon flipped on numerous switches, engaged the motor revving the engines.

The *Scorpion*, Moufflon's special brainchild, possessed totally redundant systems, a pair of turboshaft engines, each rated at 620-shaft horsepower for takeoff and 598-shaft horsepower for continuous operation. Each with separate drive input into the main transmission, separate fuel and oil systems and separate controls. A torque limiting system and load sharing power management system controlled both engines. In essence, the *Scorpion* was fail-safe. Should the unexpected happen, the chopper, under electronic control of the Lodestar pilot, would work on automatic pilot.

The taskforce, taught in briefing how to read pertinent instruments, fixed apprehensive eyes on the gauge registering the degrees of radiation outside the massive 747. A steady glowing yellow light indicated safety; any change in color progressing toward coal-red increased the risk factors. At the slightest hint of danger a slick warning system consisting of flashing ultraviolet lights and beeping sounds would lock into place until a manual change of course was activated. If manual change was blocked, the automatic pilot takeover took effect immediately, powered by the incredible electrical wizard and computer, the *Grim Reaper*, until they navigated safer areas.

Damned bloody computer was nearly human, Valerie reflected, feeling her teeth chatter at the engines' high-velocity vibration. Up ahead, as hangar doors in the Lodestar's belly opened, the sudden impact of turbulence violently shook the *Scorpion* superstructure.

Moufflon propelled the *Scorpion* forward. Lurched free of its moorings, ejected from the jet's belly like a fetus from its womb, the *Scorpion*, held in midair momentarily, then glided, soared, dipped, swayed in what seemed an eternal sea of blackness. Moufflon, like a skilled automoton, operated switches, levers and buttons, engaging a hydraulic system. A steel cylindrical girder shot up through the superstructure negotiating four bladed rotors, locking them securely into place. The tail rotor engaged whirred smoothly. With the overhead rotors in full swing, the craft held in a hovering position. From the underbelly of the fuselage, two sleek winglike struts jutted out, extending six feet at either side. Rectangular hatches slid open, a half dozen high-velocity infrared color cameras mounted on rotating bases, elevated into position, their lenses orbiting in 360° swings. Electronic shutters activated, they transmitted photographic results instantly on interior cabin video screens.

The *Scorpion* moved! Flying in low, the chopper hovered over stark areas of devastation. Years of well-practiced detachment and objectivity deserted the passengers. Horrible lacerations in the monotonous landscape, reminiscent of a vile, advanced case of syphilis, imprinted endlessly on the earth's surface, jarred them.

Deathlike stillness prevailed. The rotors, too, sounded aborted and vague. Devastated areas where once roads, buildings, lakes and forested hills teemed with human and animal life, left the taskforce cold, their blood iced. Not a specter of humanity existed for as far as the cameras probed.

Streets, once teeming with gay, beautifully dressed people, in architecturally stunning buildings in a magnificent landscape of swirling, white, sandy shores, azure and crystal waters and verdant greenery, swaying palms dating to Biblical days had converted to a frightening landscape of desolation. An endless mass of scorched earth created a crazy-quilt pattern of intransigent cracks ten feet wide on parched desert floors. In the distance, sand dunes appeared as cresting waves about to engulf the land from east to west. It was insanity—total insanity.

The *Scorpion* banked, circled and headed in a southeasterly direction.

Inscrutably the Moor's focus held on the occupants; he missed nothing, noting the terrified silence, the rising tensions in each as the *Scorpion* tossed fitfully in the surrounding turbulence. Thousands of feet overhead, massive cloud formations darkened sunless skies to an unbearable chiarascuro twilight.

A blue light flashed on Valerie's communication device. She pressed the button. Uri Mikhail's voice came through. "Are you all right?" She turned slightly, encumbered by the space helmet. Their eyes met. She nodded slightly, blinked her eyes, whispered "Yes." He whispered back, "I think I'm in love with you."

Before Valerie reacted, their attention was taken by the droning voice of the *Grim Reaper*. A computer readout appeared in tandem on the screen:

ATTENTION SCORPION . . . DO YOU READ ME? . . . YOU ARE ENTERING NUCLEAR CONGESTION AREA CONTAINING LETHAL FALLOUT, RADIATION, TOXIC FUMES . . . SOCKED IN BY LOW PRESSURE AREAS. MOUNTAINS, DUE NORTH ARE CAUCASUS . . . THOSE SCANNED TO THE FAR EAST, POSSIBLY HIMALAYAS . . . SCIENTIFIC DETERMINATION INCOMPLETE. REPEAT . . . SCIENTIFIC DETERMINATION INCOMPLETE. STEER CLEAR . . . DIRECTLY BELOW YOU ARE REMAINS OF LAKE VAN . . . NOTE . . . NO VISIBLE REMAINS EXIST . . . YOU ARE CHARTED IN SOUTHEASTERLY DIRECTION, SCORPION . . . CHECK HEADINGS . . . YOU ARE TRAVERSING DISTANT SHORES OF LAKE URMIA . . . USE SAME APPROACH PATTERN TO WHAT WAS ONCE TEHRAN . . . HOLD STEADY TO COURSE, SCORPION . . . PREPARE YOURSELF . . . NO LANDMARKS IDENTIFY IRAN . . . THE PERSIAN GULF EVAPORATED TO DESERT . . . CHART SOUTHWESTERLY, SCORPION . . . REPEAT . . . SOUTHWESTERLY . . . THIS IS X-N-O . . . GRIM REAPER . . .

Listening numbly to the voice of the *Grim Reaper* before it signed off, the chopper's occupants came to grips with inner frustration, displaying marked antagonism toward the forces of devastation below.

Colonel Kusuvubu Katanga, the avenging butcher of death, an animal normally unaffected by what he saw, stared with his one black bulging eye at the nuclear aftermath. Visibly shaken by the images projected on the camera screens, he momentarily shoved TARGET:MOUFFLON from his mind. Only two months ago he had traveled to Cairo, Tehran, Tel Aviv . . . Now, there was nothing left. Nothing left of the dark-skinned, black-eyed, young Arab lad who had pleasured his sadistic bent. Nothing but a black, unvarying void . . .

Velden Zryden, restricted by cumbersome headgear, feeling claustrophobic and the dizzying effects of vertigo, confined his observation to video screens. He sucked in his breath to a muffled gasp. He took no pleasure in viewing the funeral pyres of Syria, Jordan and now in the approach to what was once Jerusalem. Something in Velden's mind struggled as he studied the dramatic changes. Sweating abnormally, he lowered the temperature controls of his flightsuit. Amadeo was surfacing, outraged at what remained of Israel. He shivered in the cooler temperatures, his lungs heaved, he trembled noticeably, slumped over, sagging in his seat.

Uri Mikhail caught the expression in Velden Zryden's face. He flipped on all channels, muttering in a filtered voice. "Something is happening to Velden Zryden!"

"Increase the oxygen flow to him!" Moufflon ordered instantly. Uri followed the command. In moments Velden's heavy-lidded eyes fluttered open at the increased flow of oxygen. He perked up, glanced at his watch. "What happened?" Uri explained. "Was I out long?" he asked. "A minute, perhaps less," Uri replied, staring intently at Velden.

"*Danke,*" Velden muttered fully. "I am freezing cold." He raised the temperature gauge, much to Uri's silent astonishment. The cabin temperature had been climbing steadily as they flew over the smoking pyres, radiation intense outside the chopper.

Until his body temperature shot up under the protective gear Velden experienced disorientation, a peculiar dizziness. With the warming of his blood, he regrouped his thinking processes concentrating on his focus prior to unconsciousness. *Israel!* It was

615

Israel! He stiffened perceptibly, stared out the starboard bow, at the mass of fogbanks rolling in from the Mediterranean, obscuring the landscape below. The sudden loathing and alienation he felt was Amadeo's, not Victor! Estrangement born in Victor's mind in opposition to Amadeo contorted his features hideously.

Uri's puzzlement magnified as Zryden's features twisted. He swore to himself a stranger had peered out from under the bubble helmet, certainly not the man the dossiers listed as the German, Velden Zryden. Uri forced himself back to the moment, staring at the video screens and the formation of gale force winds sweeping up sands, debris, everything in its path.

Another civilization buried under sand and sea and for what?

Valerie's rising nausea, and reaction to the maddening infamy sobered her as never sobered before. The devastation was far worse than satellite photo facsimiles indicated—what lay below was a mesa of the dead! Nothing existed!—not even flesh-eating vultures! Briefing communicated the inability of any living creatures to survive unbearable rising temperatures in the hydrogen black wake. Terrifying lightning flashes, thunderous explosions, rumbling shock waves and searing fires spreading, spreading in all directions had ultimately metamorphosed into smoking pyres of a death wake.

Once the land of fabled Arabian Nights, Scheherezade and romanticized Biblical figures conquering empires, where political disputes between Pharisees and Saducees had created a myth they called Jesus with an ideology to instill hope in a world of hopeless men—it was now reduced to a land of doom. A feeling of stupidity tied to slim figments of hope in her mind, Valerie retreated again into her isolated shell, staring at the lifeless outline against the sky until patches lay on her eyeballs refusing to let them open.

Prince Ben-Kassir's violent displeasure, matched by General Lincoln's wrath, both held fast to the belief: *this shouldn't have happened!* Not one match should have been struck to dry timber! Why hadn't they arrested the sickness before it spread virulently? Both men failed to comprehend the horror: Hadn't nations had their fill of wars with conventional weapons? Enough to desist in the proliferation of nuclear arms? Apparently not!

The Prince heard Moufflon's signal, saw his hand gesture to peer below as the *Scorpion* swooped closer to the ground area. He sickened at the sight. What was once one of his homes in

Alexandria, where one of the North African peace treaties was signed by the Allies and their Axis enemies, was a total wasteland.

Youseff muttered an Arabic prayer: *Allah, God, My Lord Muhammed, Yes, even you, Jesus. If any of you miracle workers exist in another dimension, pray explain for what diabolical purpose you permitted Moloch to take human form to destroy mankind? You have given the beast a special gift! You have made him relentless! And now, too, we shall be relentless!*

Peering down at what was once Israel, Brad considered his own personal destiny. He had read a great deal in recent months about the people considered to be his ancestors. No connection fired or inspired him. He was Bradford Lincoln, by choice, American by birth and nothing else had mattered. But he'd been curious on his recent trip to Egypt and had taken time to book passage to Tel Aviv.

He had found Israel to be like navigating a minefield. His sanity, his life, depended on agility, resourcefulness and a sense of direction. For three days, his nerve endings were perpetually frayed, his temper a few degrees below boiling. He felt eyes on him, sinister probing, curious eyes riveted to him wherever he went. He felt a stranger in a land of strangers. No biblical atavisim coursed through his veins at the sight of the Wailing Wall. He felt no pulse beat, nor a throbbing of his heart at the sight of biblical Jerusalem. He found the people, as a whole, constrained, irritable. The food, most wholly Arab, didn't measure up to his expectations. He had expected the New York Deli and got the offerings of Omar the tentmaker. He had left wondering what all the hulabaloo was about. Or was he spoiled by America itself?

Now, there was nothing! . . .

Colonel Jim Greer held himself remote to his surroundings. Nerves of steel, a calloused approach, the inevititable by-product of his life in clandestine operations performed for his country had weathered him to expect the very worst in mankind. Frankly, he didn't give a shit for mankind! When did they *ever* learn? Was it Santayana who said, *Those who fail to learn the lessons of history shall be forced to relive them?* Who the fuck cared any more? Not the genre of mankind he'd rubbed up against for the past forty years! The U.S. government should have and didn't isolate the infectious atomic virus back in 1945 when American was King of the Atomic Mountain. Instead they fell prey to almighty megabucks, and strong financial influences governing American thinking, erasing all conscience with megabuck power! Americans didn't think enough of themselves to elect *proper* men to office—killed off those inclined to decency and hadn't the guts to protest the *cover-ups!* Fucking Anthony Harding! Zeller's arm deserved to have his nuts drilled into concrete! Along with Zeller! Oh, *fuck* it! *Fuck 'em* all! They *fuckin'* deserved what was happening!

Dr. Sen Yen Lu's scientific perception of the devastated lands was affected by shapes, depths, consistencies of crater formations, the absence of animal or vegetable life. Engulfed by massive accumulations of barometric pressures, gravity-held path of the target, mathematical equations, and mechanical actuations of controlled mechanisms and the incalculable behavior of the warhead itself, he kept busily dictating his computations to a computer back in Paris. He prayed the full destructive capabilities, dependent on the numerable variables, would be retransmitted to him shortly. He paused momentarily studying with inscrutable clinical eyes the onset of billowing hurricane winds rising off the starboard bow as the *Scorpion* headed out of the headwinds traversing a southwesterly direction.

"What do you make of it, Sen Yen?" Moufflon's calming voice piped into Dr. Lu's frequency directed the scientist to observe the erratic compass readings, and make a few metal calculations.

"Changing topography by the winds create electrical disturbances. Once you slip through the electromagnetic fields held together by gravitational forces, it should pass. Respectfully, Darius, I am concerned about a reaction to the rising temperatures outside the *Scorpion*. What are the limits of planning board calculations before the outer perimeter alert is activated?"

"The *Grim Reaper* is programmed against such an eventuality."

"No chance of a systems breakdown?"

"Now, you ask?" Moufflon chided. "To ease your mind I shall covertly check all systems. Meanwhile, will you in your best travelogue voice describe the manmade madness. Hammer it home, let them feel the strangleholds to the jugular. Read me?"

"Ah, a perfect diversion. They all resemble the dead ashes of a cadaver's remains." He tuned in all their frequencies at once, transmitted oriental objectivity and calm among the *Scorpion's* occupants.

"My friends, below us and all around for as far as you can see is a violently arranged landscape created by the fury of the bomb's aftermath. Desert floors will be steadily carpeted by materials and odd debris windblown from mountains, crushed and shattered by the hydrogen explosion. Notice, below us the River Jordan runs dry. The closer we get—it appears the *Scorpion* is butting extraordinary head winds—to the Mediterranean—" His voice broke off abruptly.

The *Scorpion*, caught in shocking turbulence, Moufflon engaged all anti-torque devices in a fierce attempt to counteract the severity of the torque. The occupants tensed, held the seat arms tightly. The phenomenon produced was the solidifying of their thoughts.

Death! Death *in* the skies, *from* the skies, *mystifying black death* held them fast in its grips. They saw no sunlight! No life force! No animation! No living thing outside the *Scorpion* existed! Observing the phenomenon in mute silence, jarred into a stark reality for which—briefing or not—none was prepared, belief or disbelief notwithstanding, it struck them at once.

Because it became difficult for each to compress the extent of their personal trauma, because their attention was rapt, feelings bottled inside them, because they were unable to feed off their companions the reassurance needed to stabilize their emotions, their faces grew hard, closed and afraid. Drained of needed dramatic responses that *normally* enabled them to navigate through life's crises, they sat immobilized, impotent of reason.

Colonel Jim Greer cued into Brad Lincoln's frequency as he peered outside the *Scorpion*. "Hiroshima and Nagasaki were merely petards by comparison, General. It's out there, somewhere, someplace in this colossus of popped boils. There's gotta be a goddamned horizon!"

His contagion was heard at master controls by Moufflon. He cued into Lincoln's frequency. "Calm, Greer, General. Hysteria at this point is inappropriate. Prepare yourself. We have passed the halfway point to our destination."

"Swell," Brad muttered, trying to abate the mounting queasiness.

Moufflon studied his instruments and chartings, speaking in French to the computer. Listening intently, sighting the readings blipping across his screen, he beamed into Youseff's frequency.

"Prepare yourself, Youseff. We shall be touching down at the predestined site shortly."

No travel itineraries issued to the taskforce in advance, two men *knew* the touchdown point. Moufflon *and* Velden Zryden!

The *Scorpion*, capable of vertical lift and descent, and able to approach jet speeds in horizontal flight, soared higher, gaining airspeed.

The *Grim Reaper* came alive to announce they had traversed the area of what was once Saudi Arabia, beyond Oman and Yemen. Moufflon took a moment, then lowering the *Reaper's* volume, turned off all audio.

General Brad Lincoln spoke into his recorder, unheard by the others. "Mr. President, half the continent of Africa was destroyed! Split in half as if some Herculean surgeon wielding a giant scalpel had lopped off half of Libya, Egypt, Ethiopia, the Sudan, then slicing through Kenya, scooped out the island of Madagascar. Proceeding northerly, processing in its bloody wake, the nations of Saudi Arabia, Israel, Jordan, Syria, Iran and Iraq, the nuclear surgeon had steamed shoveled his way through Afghanistan and Pakistan, stopping a hair's breath from the Russian border . . . ." Brad stopped recording abruptly, flashing on the golden globe paperweight seen first in Wolfgang Katz's office, later in the Oval Office, and what Berna had described as the Global 2000 Conspiracy! Christ! The topography of the land nearly matched the golden globe! A few years too early—yes?

Valerie Lansing, too, recorded her observations. Very little differed from Brad Lincoln's myopic observations. Then she snapped off her recorder, aware that Uri Mikhail was studying her lips intently. That awareness dissolved instantly, as isolation fell on her.

The sky blackened. Uri reached over, touched Valerie's gloved hand reassuringly. Their eyes met briefly in the semi-darkness as massive cloud formations densified. Valerie tuned into his frequency. "Where are we? Do you know, Uri? We're forty minutes past rendezvous with the Lodestar." She fought to keep emotion from her voice.

"Wherever we are, we are in good hands. It's best you waste no emotions on hypothesis."

"I loathe being kept in the dark!" She muttered apprehensively.

"I was hoping you'd reassure me. Surely your father confided—"

Valerie pulled back her thickly gloved hand, annoyed at him, and aware of Velden Zryden's attention locked on them. Tuning him out, she dialed to Brad Lincoln's frequency. "General— what's our destination? I need air! When do we connect with the Lodestar?"

"We don't! I suggest increasing your oxygen input . . ."

"Dammit! I don't need oxygen! I want air—FRESH air!"

Chapter Forty

HEADLINES:

WASHINGTON POST
August 10, 1984

USA/ WPCC TASKFORCE LOST, RADIO CONTACT BROKEN!

Washington, D.C. (AP) The White House refuses comment on the missing Lodestar jet carrying USA/WPCC TASKFORCE members. As previously reported in earlier communiques, the *Scorpion* helicopter maintained contact with the mother ship for six hours. Contact severed by computer malfunctioning. Reports verify that transmitted aerial photographs and communiques received in the Paris terminal.

Bill Miller, Senior White House aide, conveys President Macgregor's deepest regrets at recent developments. European Allies, the United Kingdom, Italy, France, West Germany and new member U.S.S.R. have joined a coalition to man massive search flights to locate the whereabouts of the Lodestar and its taskforce. Taskforce members, a prestigious group, rigorously trained for this mission are listed on page two . . .

It was two hours past twelve, the midnight oil burned brightly in governmental offices scattered across D.C. At the White

House men and women huddled in the Press Room, bent over telex machines and telephones awaiting developments.

In the Oval Office the President dismissed the entourage. They left grateful for the respite hot black coffee luring them like a wailing Circe.

"Bill . . . Tom . . . wait up a moment," the President called.

The aides lingered, wearied from the strain, silent and brooding at the bombardment of unexpected, unwanted news.

"Bill—what the hell's happening? It was a stupid thing to do, giving Moufflon total control of the TASKFORCE! The blunder of my career. What do we do? Where do we go for information?"

"I don't see you had any choice, Mr. President. After Maui—"

"There's no one? No one to communicate with—?"

"The pilot, crew and remaining taskforce members aboard the Lodestar returned to Paris under the tightest security wraps, sir. The pilot, Honore, insists he awaits contact from Moufflon."

"*Moufflon?* They're alive?" Macgregor stared from Miller to Kagen.

"Sir, I don't know. Can't even hazard a guess. If you want, we'll fly the pilot to D.C. under wraps, for your personal interrogation. Honore told our people at the Embassy, the *Scorpion* broke its moorings and took off from the Lodestar's womb without a hitch."

"What about the Corsican stronghold? What do they know? Anything we don't?"

Tom Kagen insisted, "We'd be better off communicating with BRITISH M-I. I'm told their tracking is elaborate—"

"Better than the Kremlin's?" Bill Miller tensed.

"Why would BRITISH M-I engage in elaborate tracking?" asked Macgregor.

"One of their top men is aboard the final phase—"

"*Top men?*"

"Sir Alexander York, sir. The best they have."

"The best they have, eh? Very well, we'll sit on it." He dismissed them with a nod. "Go ahead, you both need rest."

The President's tetchy capacity for patience evolved into downright orneriness. He was cantankerous as a bear. He tossed the late edition of the *Post* into a wastepaper basket, turned off the lights, sat in the darkness, stunned by the unexpected blow.

Nothing was as silent, lonely and isolated as the Oval Office when the staff shut down for the night. Soon, news of the

Lodestar's disappearance, disseminated to the public at large, would be read about at breakfast or heard on early morning television news along with altered, obfuscated facts. Given a review of the *Post's* morning edition, he had read the contents, observed the news beamed via satellite, without reaction, his personal fears for the safety of the taskforce and Valentina's daughter absent.

Why did he get the feeling the whole thing was a sham—that it hadn't happened? How could it? The planning had been impeccable. Dammit! You never could get truth from the military or politicians! The very nature of their professions demanded maximum convolution of truth—didn't it? He loathed political expedience; lies headed the list. Yet, each time he lied to his constituents it became easier. Attempts to offset the lies by speaking truth was a thankless job. No one believed the truth. The danger lay in believing his own lies.

He reached into his liquor cabinet for the Remy-Martin, poured an ample amount, sipping it slowly, and facing out the windows at the spotlighted Rose Garden grounds, he gave in to a barrage of inner thoughts unleashed like torrents in his mind.

No man, he believed, could be trusted with absolute power. Adhering to this belief, he had relegated authority to the best, shared presidential powers with them in the broadest sense possible. In recent years, he had experienced subtle changes in himself. When the Chief Executive becomes powerful enough to overwhelm both the Congress and the Senate . . . when he is ruled by executive order and attempts to exercise rights that belong to the community, he places himself in tyrannical posture. What man, once he comes to full power, can remain completely sane? Inevitibly he must surrender to self-indulgent fantasies, rejoice in his own majestic utterances and lose the most precious of possessions—his humanity. To enjoy power was an affliction of the *damned!* To enjoy hurling war and destruction upon other nations was an affliction of Satanic damnation.

Why hadn't he seen this in himself sooner? "Caesar's laurel wreath," wrote the poet William Blake, "is the greatest poison known to man. To exert power over your fellow man is tantamount to an act of treason." And, Macgregor thought, if he utilizes the resources of modern technology to maintain himself in power, he is doubly guilty for stealing from the people what is rightfully theirs.

John Macgregor on his feet paced the Oval Office floor. In the beginning he had tormented the people with promises, rejoiced in their weaknesses, demanded their trust, their votes, their lives while he remained indifferent to anything save his thirst for power. To ask him to rule for the benefit of the people was to ask more than he was prepared to grant. Yet, he was forced to give that appearance at all times.

Ultimately the people were to blame for putting such men into power. They permitted the seduction—joyously! Never taking time to learn enough about politics, they are too willing to let someone else think for them. Servile accomplices, they became willing victims for anyone promising the moon!

He paced for hours, brooding, pondering the phenomenon . . . angry, sour-stomached and loaded with self-pity.

Dawn broke over the eastern horizon. John Macgregor took his seat behind the desk. He sensed something rotten stank in the District of Columbia, the intolerable stench of political corruption. The *special* interest groups had disappeared like rats in a sinking ship, since he'd bucked them early in July. Recently the more stalwart of those men, unable to function unless they *controlled* and *manipulated*, had displayed the unmitigated gall to *name* his successor before he personally tossed his hat into the ring for a second term!

Name his successor—would they?

What was it Dr. Robert Martine told a gathering of colleagues recently?

"Personally aggressive leaders are mostly sexually inadequate men possessed with delusions of empirical grandeur, obsessed with military glories, need statues erected to their memories!" The ballsy shrink added pointedly, "Better we erect statues to them, retire them to rest homes, keep them docile with drugs and let the world live!" Dr. Martine pontificated this theme on national television, flagrantly naming global impresarios with whom the world should thusly deal. Three days later, after his erstwhile pronunciamento made newspaper headlines and talk-show hosts pandered after him, speculating on his daring, the forty-three-year-old lettered man was found dead in his Paris townhouse, victim of a *heart attack*. An *artifically induced* heart attack, the intelligence reports insisted.

His deep concern was Geralee. No matter how often she pressed, he had refused to confide in his wife. He told her nothing. *Why would he confide in a woman so possessed with history? She'd be destroyed!* The sexual urge stirred him, but he resisted it.

The President watched the sun rise. He reached for the house phone, ordered a light breakfast and large pot of coffee from the kitchen. Soon the place would be buzzing with activity.

The Chief of State who once possessed mesmerizing richness of articulation, able to convince his constituents of anything he wanted them to believe, had become a preposterous absurdity to himself and a nation no longer able to believe in a politics written so casually with the blood of innocent victims.

Why? Why? WHY?

Because you, John Macgregor, Esquire, placed other interests before American interests! An internal soliloquy burst inside him.

You sold out, John! Sold out to the advisors who mucked up America in previous administrations! You blamed them for everything from spiraling inflation to the bottoming out of the economy. You used political rhetoric of the thirties, forties, fifties—obsolete in the eighties—and you shoved it down American throats. No self-respecting American knew who or what to believe any more.

Certainly not their government!

The President's breakfast cart arrived. He was ravenous, gulped down the coffee, ate his ham and eggs as if he hadn't eaten in days. He felt better, sipping fresh coffee in the rare solitude of the impressive Oval Office, he swiveled about in his chair, peered out through the tinted windows at the lazy beginnings of a sweltering day. The noisy rotors of a D.C. police chopper putt-putt-putted noisily. It circled, banked, came in lower and lifting vertically moved out of sight. Shadows of light paled the room's interior and the President found himself studying the wide wing-spread of the brass bald eagle perched atop the flagstaff, recalling the sophisticated surveillance and wire-tapping equipment General Lincoln had detected.

Noises, soft, muffled, familiar sounds reached him. Nearly eight A.M. The White House secretarial personnel was arriving to begin a new day. If he intended doing something, it must be done immediately, without delay.

He swiveled about, the golden eagle in his focus, the golden globe paperweight placed on some personal papers taunted him. "For too long the eye of the eagle has been upon me," he said, sighing, his voice laced with desperation. Reaching behind him, without turning, he opened the top right hand drawer of his desk, withdrew a .45 automatic. A light prism catching the silver metal flashed brightly for a split second. He drew it closer . . . closer . . .

The buzzer on his desk sounded. Blue Presidential eyes flared in annoyance. Swiveling around, he pressed the intercom lever. "Yes, Marybeth . . . what is it?"

"Good morning, Mr. President. I wasn't sure you were in. There's a package . . . from the First Lady. The usual, a single yellow rose affixed to it."

John Macgregor put away the gun. "Bring it in, please." He shut the drawer, reset the gold paperweight on his desk so the inscription: MONDO XX faced him, and glanced up as the secretary entered carrying a long florist box.

"I'm not certain who delivered it, sir. It seems it has been here all night. Should I take it to the S.S. first?"

He noted the yellow rose, smiled. "No. It's fine."

Marybeth, a winsome middle-aged well-preserved woman, paused at the threshold. "Bill Miller and Tom Kagen want to speak with you, sir."

"Give me a half hour." The President picked up the yellow bud, inhaled its bouquet, and removing an older bloom from a cloisonne bud vase, he inserted the fresh, smiling wanly at Geralee's gesture. Normally packages destined for the Oval Office passed the scrutiny of a dozen vigorous agents before the President ever saw them, if at all. The yellow rose, a secret between the First Lady and himself, indicated a *no trespass* by employees. He untied the elaborate yellow satin bow, and slid off the lid, shoving aside the yellow tissue impatiently, grinning ineffably at the facsimile of himself made up as a doll. He reached to lift it from the box, his smile dissolved to frozen fury. He examined the accompanying paraphernalia, glowering blackly. Fired by wrath, he grew resentful and indignant. He hammered the intercom button. "Marybeth! Get Mrs. Macgregor on the phone!"

Having already anticipated the command, Marybeth had the First Lady waiting on the line. The tone of the President's voice caused her momentary alarm. She made the connection, hung up her end, and quickly poured a cup of coffee from a nearby machine. *What the devil was wrong?*

"Geralee . . . if this is your idea of a joke—"

626